RIKA ACTIVATED

RIKA'S MARAUDERS – BOOKS 1-3

OMNIBUS EDITION

BY M. D. COOPER

LAYING LOW 274
RETROSPECT 297
ORIENT SPACE AND AIR 302
PERSEPHONE JONES 319
MOON LANDING 327
RECOVERY 348
HOME 360
MURDERER 365
DUCKING OUT 369
A NEW TEAMMATE 376
STAVROS 384
DINNER WITH A DICTATOR 392
CRACKING THE CODE 401
CATCHING SOME TAIL 405
AMY 408
LITTLE THIEF 411
APPROACHING FATE 416
HANDOFF 420
THE CLUB 423
THE NEW ACT 429
AFTERMATH 438
CONVICTION 443
THE STORM BEFORE 449
ASSASSINATION 458
RIKA'S MARAUDERS 469

RIKA TRIUMPHANT 475
FOREWORD 477
PREVIOUSLY... 479
UNVEILED 481
SPACE IN SPACE 492
COLLABORATION 509
A TRIP DOWNWORLD 519
DROPSHIP DOWN 532
A DEEPER GAME 547
LAYERED CONCERNS 551
RECONCILIATION 562
DROPPING 567
RECONNECTING 578
THE MEET 583

RIKA'S MARAUDERS – RIKA ACTIVATED

VISIT FROM THE GENERAL 609
SETTING THE TRAP 619
DEFENSE OF HAMMERFALL 625
ATTACK ON ATLANTIS 640
REVELATIONS 649
DEPARTURE 663
BRIEFING 666
GOODBYE BASILISK 672
INSERTION 675
THE FURY LANCE 683
STEALING STARSHIPS 694
CAPTAIN RIKA 707
TANIS RICHARDS 711

MECH TYPES AND ARMAMENTS 713
3rd MARAUDER FLEET 4th DIVISION 720
9th MARAUDER BATTALION 'M' COMPANY 721

THE BOOKS OF AEON 14 727
ABOUT THE AUTHOR 733

THE AGE OF THE ORION WAR

Humanity has not had an easy time expanding into the stars.

Though no intelligent extra-terrestrials have ever been found, we struggle enough against our selves and our creations. War has forever marred our history, and it continues to do so.

Though conflicts such as the Sentience Wars and the wars of the Sol Dissolution took billions of lives, these wars were contained within a single stellar system, and did not spread across the stars. Without faster-than-light travel, it simply would have taken too long and been too costly to make war on neighboring star systems.

The advent of faster-than-light travel removed that constraint. When the FTL Wars broke out in the late fifth millennia, they devastated humanity.

Wave after wave of dark ages washed over human space, and much of the great knowledge of the past was lost.

In the late ninth millennia, a tentative peace has finally emerged. Accords and Alliances have built up a fragile stability that has allowed humanity to crawl back from the brink of complete self-destruction.

Then a ship from the past is found—a ship containing technology long thought lost: the *Intrepid*.

This one event is the match that lights the powder keg, throwing humanity into the greatest war it has ever seen—a war that spans tens of thousands of star systems across the Orion Arm of the galaxy.

The Orion War

Such a war has many fronts. A conflict spanning hundreds of systems with trillions of deaths is but a skirmish. But to the people fighting those battles, it is not a small event on the edge of space; it is their lives, their families, their very civilizations that are on the line.

The long-running war between the Genevians and the Nietzscheans is one such skirmish. It is here that we find Rika. Her government, desperate to hold back the Nietzscheans, has resorted to barbaric means to achieve victory.

Mechanized humans.

RIKA OUTCAST

RIKA'S MARAUDERS – BOOK 1

FOREWORD

Rika has a special place in my heart. I don't know why, but she does.

I think that a part of it comes from her original inspiration, which is the character 'Clara' in the TV series *Killjoys.* Clara was a woman who had her right arm replaced by the bad guys at 'The Factory'. It wasn't a voluntary mod, and she's not happy about it, but ultimately she learns how to live with it, and it makes her stronger.

The woman who played Clara in the TV show was very convincing, and I thought, "What would it really be like for someone who has undergone that sort of modification?"

Obviously, for the purposes of a TV series, they can't afford convincing, full-body cyborg alterations—but my (and your) imagination can.

This brings us to Rika. She was born in the Genevian Commonwealth, an interstellar alliance of star systems that fought a desperate war with the Nietzscheans. Her government did not have enough AIs to continue to create combat mechs, and NSAIs were not effective enough...

So they used humans. Unwilling humans.

Rika was one of those humans.

CITIZEN A71F

STELLAR DATE: 09.22.8939 (Adjusted Years)
LOCATION: Tanner City, Kellas
REGION: Caulter System, Genevian Federation

Rika sat behind the grey plas of the defendant's table and looked around the courtroom. Its walls and ceiling were a colorless off-white, with over-bright lighting, and hard concrete floors. She hadn't expected it to be welcoming, but she had thought courtrooms were supposed to look more upscale—another thing the vids lied about.

The tan, one-piece jumpsuit she wore was loose, but still managed to bind in the armpits and groin; Rika shifted on her hard chair in an attempt to get more comfortable. The movement made the chains that connected her wrists to the table jingle, and she felt herself flush. The whole situation was a mistake, just a horrible mistake.

The judge would see that, and in an hour she'd be free and clear.

Rika glanced at the public defender sitting beside her. He was flipping through a virtual stack of pages only visible to him. She had no way of knowing if they pertained to her case, or to one of the many others he was likely tasked with.

He looked sharp in his black court-suit, and the grey wig complimented his heavy brow—beneath which were sharp, blue eyes. His lips were full, just the way she liked them, and Rika imagined what it would feel like to brush hers against them. To press her nose into his cheek and—

Her daydream was interrupted by a voice calling out, "All rise for the Notable Judge Pliskin."

Rika leapt to her feet, eager to show her respect for the judge, and completely forgot about the chains holding her wrists to the table. The cuffs jerked her arms to a stop and she slipped, slamming her face against the table.

"Stupid girl," she heard her defender mutter as he bent over to help her to her feet.

Rika's eyes filled with tears, and she felt a trickle of blood run down her face as she stood and stared at the table, too embarrassed to look up at the judge as he took his seat.

Behind her, a few snickers could be heard from the gallery, and Rika did her best to ignore them, chanting *'back on the street in an hour'* over and over in her head.

Once the judge settled in his seat, the rest of the court followed suit, and Rika carefully lowered herself back to her hard plas chair. Her defender hadn't even acknowledged the blood on her face. Rika bent down and tried to wipe it off, but was certain she'd only smeared it around.

"Case number 823.3234.A433," the court clerk read out. "The commonwealth versus citizen 4C399EB2-76AB-4CB1-AD9D-9F01B69EA71F, who also goes by the name 'Rika'. The charge is theft of a valuable worth over fifty thousand credits."

"What?" Rika tried to rise, but her defender placed a hand on her shoulder, keeping her seated.

"Quiet," he whispered, and glanced at the judge who was giving them a disapproving glare.

<*But all I stole was a crate of food,*> Rika pleaded with her defender privately over the Link. <*It wasn't even worth five-hundred credits.*>

<*That's not what the report says. Says here it was a valuable military-grade scan suite for a patrol ship,*> the defender replied. <*I'm going to see what I can do, but you're certainly not getting off for this.*>

Rika was stunned by his response. She had opened the crate; it had been filled with food. There had to be some sort of mistake.

"Seems open and shut," the judge was saying. "You were caught on surveillance stealing the crate, and it was found in your possession. How do you plead, citizen Rika?"

"Plead?" Rika asked, bewildered by the speed at which her fate was being sealed. "I plead innocent of what you're accusing me of. I stole a crate of food, there was no scan suite inside."

"Innocent?" the judge leaned over his high desk. "This is a capital crime, citizen Rika. We are at war with the Nietzscheans, and you have committed a crime against the war effort. The maximum punishment is death. If you plead innocent, this will go to trial and it will be swift—that I can promise you."

"But…but…" Rika stuttered.

This is impossible! I'm only nineteen; there's no way my life—miserable though it's been—can end like this.

"May I have a moment?" her defender asked the judge.

"Very well," the judge replied.

<*Look,*> her defender said. <*The judge is right. They have you dead to rights on this. Look at the prosecutors; they're not even paying attention to the case. It's a zero-effort win for them. Your only hope is to plead guilty. I'll get the judge to give you a military sentence. You'll do a few years behind a rifle, and then you'll be out.*>

Rika slumped in her seat. She couldn't believe what she was hearing. It was a nightmare. All she had tried to do was get some food, and now she faced death or military service? Which, given how the war was going, was probably also a death sentence.

<*Well?*> her defender asked.

Rika didn't respond, and after a moment he spoke up. "My client pleads guilty, and begs the court's mercy. She will gladly accept a military sentence."

"Will she, now?" the judge asked. "I need your affirmation, citizen Rika."

The judge's words sounded to her like they were coming from underwater, all garbled and warbly—but she understood their meaning, and nodded slowly.

"Very well," the judge replied. "A military sentence of five years is issued. You are to be remanded at once to the Genevian Military Police for processing."

Rika lowered her face into her hands. She wouldn't even get a chance to say goodbye to anyone. Not that many people cared what happened to her. None of her so-called friends had shown up to court today.

She didn't even see the defender approach the judge's high desk and receive an envelope, as rough hands seized her wrists and disconnected her shackles from the table, and reconnected her wrists behind her back.

"This way," a gruff voice said, and she felt a shove on her shoulder.

Rika barely paid attention as she was marched down a long corridor lined with holding cells. She was pushed into one, and the door slammed behind her. Barring a mat on the floor, the cell was completely empty. Rika fell to the mat, curled up in a fetal position, and cried herself to sleep.

Some time later—she was uncertain how long, as her Link access had been severed upon her guilty sentence—her cell door opened, and a stern voice ordered, "Get up, girl. Time to go to processing."

Rika assumed 'processing' was some sort of procedure where the police handed her over to the military, but when her eyes focused on the speaker, she saw that the woman who spoke to her was in a military uniform. Clearly that form of processing had already occurred.

The woman led her through the long hall of holding cells, all empty now. Had they been filled when she came? Rika couldn't remember. Once beyond the cells, they passed through a cold, dark corridor that led to a solitary door.

Her escort grunted softly as she opened the door to reveal dim evening light; as Rika's eyes adjusted, she saw an unadorned bus waiting in an empty parking lot.

The bus was half-full of men and women, and the military woman led Rika to its door. A man with a sheet of plas stood beside the yawning portal and looked up at her, his eyes narrowing with distaste.

"Conscript A71F," her escort said, using just the last four digits of Rika's identity.

"So it seems," the man said with a nod. "Good haul today, eh,

Jenna?"

"Decent enough," the woman, who Rika now had a name for, replied. "This one's a bit scrawny, though. Wonder what they'll do with her."

"Who knows," the man grunted. "Can always use meat for the grinder, no matter what it looks like when it starts."

Rika didn't like the sound of that, and she looked at the man, who gave a smile that did not reach his eyes.

"Your new life awaits you A71F, get on the bus."

Rika walked carefully up the stairs. She didn't want to slip again—one smear of dried blood on her face was enough. At the top of the bus's steps she saw an empty row, and slid into the seat by the window. Rain started to fall outside, and she closed her eyes, desperately wishing that someone would walk onto the bus, call out her name, and announce that there had been a mistake and that she was free to go.

Nothing even remotely close occurred.

A moment later, the man who had been outside the bus climbed the stairs and took a seat at the operator's controls. The door slammed shut, and the vehicle began to move.

Rika fell asleep again and when she woke, it was still night. The bus had stopped at a gate, and the operator was talking with a guard outside his window. The door opened, and two soldiers stepped onto the bus. One stayed at the front, rifle held up, stock against his shoulder, while the other walked down the aisle, examining the human cargo.

"All clear," he announced when he got to the back.

The soldier with the rifle nodded, but his weapon remained trained on the conscripts. Only when the first solider passed him did he lower his weapon and walk off the bus.

The door closed, and the operator set the bus in motion once more. It only drove for five minutes before stopping at a large, nondescript building. A group of soldiers stood out front. When the operator opened the doors, another pair of soldiers walked onto the bus.

These two didn't carry rifles—rather, they swung stun batons, slapping them in their hands. One soldier stayed up front, while the other began walking down the aisle.

"Get up, you lazy scum. Your glorious future in the Genevian Armed Forces awaits you. First row, out!" the soldier walking the aisle hollered.

One of the men in the first row didn't rise fast enough, and the woman hit him across the shoulders with her baton, causing him to cry out in pain.

"I said, *Get! Up!*" She screamed right in his face, then grabbed his jumpsuit, lifting him bodily from his seat, and tossed him into the aisle. "Now mooove!"

The man scrambled to his feet and promptly fell down the stairs. Rika stood, ready to get off the bus the moment the woman passed her row. She noted that the stairs would be slippery from the rain-soaked boots of the guards.

"Fucking moron," the soldier grunted. "Not that it matters; you scum will make a proper contribution to the commonwealth soon enough."

Given the other man's reference to 'meat for the grinder', and this soldier's choice of words, Rika's level of concern about what lay in her future intensified.

Once out of the bus, she joined the other conscripts in a long double-row. The rain had lessened, but it was still enough of a drizzle to make them miserable. She saw the first man who had fallen down the stairs standing at the head of the line next to hers. His nose was broken, and blood poured down his face; no one made a move to help him as he sniffled and wiped the blood from around his mouth.

As the bus emptied out, Rika looked over the others. They all wore the bulky jumpsuits, and the least disheveled of them still looked as bad as she felt. She was surprised to see that only half looked like street-rats; the rest of the men and women appeared to have seen baths and good food in recent days. The clean hair and trimmed fingernails were also dead giveaways of a better life.

She did a quick sum as the last woman stepped from the bus, followed by the soldier and her swinging baton. There were thirty-two of them. Thirty-two miserable souls unwillingly added to the Genevian war machine.

The other soldiers formed up around the conscripts, and the baton-wielding woman yelled into the rain-soaked gloom, "Move it, you fucking filth! We don't have all night!"

They marched into the building, and were led down a long corridor to a wide foyer. At the end of the foyer stood a man at a small podium. Behind him were three numbered doors. The man looked the shivering conscripts over for a moment before turning his gaze to a sheet of plas on the podium.

"Conscript B43E, door 1," he announced, and one of the cleaner, though no less miserable, men shambled forward, and stepped through the door as a guard opened it.

The man at the podium carried on, announcing the conscripts' codes and a corresponding door. Rika noticed that there was a clear class preference. The most fit were sent to door one, and the street rats, like her, all ended up going through door three.

It came as no surprise to her when her name was called.

"Conscript A71F, door 3!"

She walked on unsteady feet toward the door, doing her best to hold back the tears that threatened to spill down her face. If she started crying now, she knew stopping would be impossible. Once through the door, she found herself in another long hall, and slowly walked until she came to a bright white room.

Eleven other unwashed scum like her were waiting there, all shivering with cold. After she entered, one more girl joined their number, and there they stood: an unlucky thirteen.

Rika noted that the room was tiled, and drains were set in the floor. Above, there were sprinklers, and along one wall were several large wire baskets on wheels.

A pair of guards entered the room—one with a rifle trained on the conscripts, and the other with a decoupler for their shackles. As he freed each person, the guard with the decoupler gestured for them to stand along the wall near the baskets. Once the last unfortunate soul stood in a ragged line in front of the baskets, he barked one word.

"Strip!"

No one moved for a moment, and he eyed them with an unpleasant stare. "If you sorry assholes aren't butt-fuck naked in one minute, I'm going to have Lars here shoot you all in the kneecaps. Fuck knows you won't need them anyway."

The possible meaning behind his words terrified Rika, but she followed the instructions. Something in his voice made her think he was very serious about shooting them in the knees.

She pulled off her shoes and the jumpsuit, tossing them in the tub behind her. She hesitated at removing her underwear, but despite the guard's hungry gaze, she thought that any ogling from his eyes would be better than bullets from his rifle. As she pulled off her bra, she glanced at the others, who were pulling off their undergarments as well.

Somehow, they all looked better naked than in the ill-fitting jumpsuits. Not that any of them looked great. Most bore the look of hard living on the streets, or in low-rent government housing. Rika had to admit that she looked better than most, though she was shorter and thinner than all but one other girl.

"Get under the nozzles, close your eyes, and clench your dicks, assholes, and pussies. This is gonna sting," the not-Lars guard said with a coarse laugh.

Rika stepped gingerly across the cold tile to the center of the room. She clenched her fists and closed her eyes, prepared for the worst.

When the spray came, it was warmer than she had expected—but it hit hard, scouring every part of her body. Then it began to sting; then burn. She felt like her skin was on fire, but didn't dare to open her eyes. Nearby, a man screamed in pain, and the guard laughed.

"I told you not to open your eyes, fucker. Don't worry, little bitch; you'll get rinsed off in a minute. It'll stop burning, then—

mostly."

Rika felt something sliding down her head and shoulders, and she tentatively reached up—her hand encountering a strange, lumpy mass. She recoiled in horror before she realized it was her hair. She touched her face, and found that her eyebrows were gone; she ran her hand higher, and felt her smooth scalp.

"That's it," the guard advised as the warm spray continued. "Brush all that shit off yourselves. The sooner you do, the sooner we can give you the final rinse."

A minute later, the spray changed in pressure and the burning feeling on her skin eased. The man who had opened his eyes a moment before was reduced to a mere whimper, and Rika hoped his vision hadn't been permanently damaged.

"Open your eyes," the guard called out, and Rika tentatively followed his instruction. All around her were the glistening forms of her fellow conscripts. Hairless, with red, irritated skin. "Look at you all," the guard chuckled. "Like shiny little dolls."

"A lot better than the shit-stains that came in here," the guard with the rifle, Lars, spoke for the first time.

"OK, meat," the first guard yelled. "Move!"

At his words, a door opened up on the far side of the room, and the naked, hairless, shivering conscripts filed out.

This time, the corridor was short and well-lit. It opened up into a large room with three long boxy structures running down its center. They looked almost like train cars, though conduits connected to them at regular intervals.

At the near side of each of the long boxes were wide, dark openings, with a pair of technicians standing before them. Rika noticed that no additional guards were present, but she doubted even the two who followed them in were needed. Each member of the thirteen conscripts was utterly cowed, their spirits broken. They would not put up any resistance.

Rika also spotted automated turrets mounted on the ceiling, and knew that any attempts to escape would be met with more force than she cared to encounter.

The technicians on the far right called a citizen number, and one of the men walked over to them.

"Right, then," she heard one of the technicians say to the man. "You're a good size. We'll fit you for the K1R. Good thing, too; we have a quota to fill on those, and you lot rarely live up to the reqs."

The other technician pulled a metal harness along an overhead rail until it slapped the man in the back. Clamps wrapped around his thighs, torso, biceps, neck, and forehead. Without further preamble, it lifted him into the air as he cried out in alarm, and then it pulled him into the dark opening of the long structure.

One by one, the other conscripts were called forward. Each was racked just like the first man as the technicians made cryptic remarks about what they were suited for.

Eventually it was just Rika and the girl who was a hair shorter than her. They stood close to one another; not touching, but taking whatever comfort they could from another human's presence in the hell they found themselves in.

"A71F," one of the technicians at the far-left structure called out.

Rika approached, and the man sized her up. "Hey, Rick, she'll probably work for one of the new scouts, won't she?"

The other man eyed her up and down, likely measuring her with his augmented eyes. "Yeah, she's great for it. Looks like a hundred sixty seven centimeters and just under fifty kilos."

"Has good Link-tech, too," the first technician said. "Won't have to spend too much to make her brain worth using."

"Using for what?" Rika asked quietly. It was the first time she had spoken since the courtroom, and she surprised herself—it was almost as though she had forgotten how.

"You'll find out soon enough," the technician replied as Rika felt the rack slap her on the back.

This one was different than the others she had observed; it clamped tight around the top of her thighs, and again just above the knee. It did the same around her arms—one just above her elbow, and the other uncomfortably jammed up in her armpit. Another clamp wrapped around her head, followed by one around her neck, and two around her torso.

"No!" she cried out, struggling against the clamps. "What are you doing to me? Where am I going? Please, I have to know!"

The technician named Rick slapped her ass.

"Somewhere where *that* will never happen again," he leered.

The rack lifted her up and pulled her toward the dark opening of the long structure, and Rika began to writhe with fear, bucking and straining against the bonds.

"Hey! Stop that!" the first technician called out. "You're gonna miss the—aw, shit."

Rika felt something hit the clamp on her neck and slip to the side. She wasn't certain what she had just avoided, but she was glad—until she heard the technician named Rick laugh behind her.

"Well, I guess you don't want the anesthetic, then! Don't worry, the pain will make you pass out soon enough."

"What?" Rika cried out, and then she felt something hot against her elbow. She strained her neck, trying to get a good view, and shrieked in terror and pain as she watched a laser slice her arm off at the elbow. The light from the opening was fading, but she could still make out her forearm, falling free from her body and landing in a pile of limbs below her.

The scream that tore from Rika's throat was cut short by her collapse into blessed unconsciousness.

"See?" Rick told the other technician. "I told you she wouldn't make it past the first limb."

"Good for her; would have sucked if she was still awake when it started cutting her skin off."

A thud came from behind the pair, and they turned to see the thirteenth conscript unconscious on the ground.

"Well," Rick laughed. "At least we don't have to worry about her struggling."

MECHANIZED

STELLAR DATE: 09.23.8939 (Adjusted Years)
LOCATION: GAF Base 99A1, Kellas
REGION: Caulter System, Genevian Federation

Rika woke with a strangely muffled scream, and began thrashing.

It took a moment for her to realize that she could move her limbs; then a moment more to realize that everything felt wrong. Her eyes were open, but she couldn't make out anything around her. She blinked rapidly, the motion of her eyelids coming down strange, like her eyes were too slick.

Around her, a room slowly resolved into view. Coupled with the feeling of something cold and hard against her skin—which felt coarse and almost numb—she inferred she was on a table. She looked around and the vague shapes slowly solidified into stacks of equipment. Not medical equipment; more like what would be found in some sort of workshop.

She tried to sit up, and was served with the brutal reminder that she was missing her arms from the elbow down. She lifted a leg and saw that it too had been severed, now ending at the knee.

Rika closed her eyes tight, and a whimper escaped her. She laid her head back and shook it.

No no no no!

After a minute, she opened her eyes again and looked at her arm. That was when she realized why her skin felt coarse and numb—where there should have been pink flesh, there was only a matte grey covering.

She rubbed her stubby arms against her torso as tears began to streak down her face. As she did, there was a moment of incongruous relief as she realized that her breasts were still present; though they were little more than nondescript lumps under her artificial epidermis.

The end of her arm stumps were cold against the 'skin' of her torso, and Rika realized that her limbs were capped with steel, from which protruded small, ridged cylinders, roughly four centimeters long and three across. When she attempted to bend her elbow, or gave what she assumed was the mental equivalent of moving her elbow, the small cylinder moved. She realized it must be mounted to a ball-joint of some sort inside her arm.

It took her a few minutes to grasp what this all meant. She had been prepped for cybernetic limbs. Rika had seen soldiers in combat vids with cybernetic limbs, but never all four—and she had always assumed it had been a voluntary modification.

Apparently she had been naïve.

Rika lifted her head as much as possible, and pushed her pelvis up. She took a moment to realize that putting pressure on the ends of her limbs didn't cause any pain—there were some small miracles, at least.

A glint of light caught her attention, and she noticed a metal port in her stomach where her belly button used to be. She took more care to examine what was left of her body, and saw another pair of ports at the bottom of her rib cage, two more in her thighs, and another pair on her biceps.

Careful examination with her arm-stub led her to discover that there was one at the base of her neck, as well. Her movements on the table also revealed that there were several more ports running down her spine and, she noted with a grimace, another between her ass cheeks.

"Oh, shit, you're awake!" a voice nearby said, and Rika turned her head to see a man approaching. "Must have screwed up the sedation. I hate it when they do that."

The man was young, not too much older than Rika. He held part of a sandwich, of which he took a final bite, chewing rapidly.

"I wish they'd at least tag you when that happens. Then I'd know you were gonna wake up," he said around the mouthful of food.

Rika attempted to speak, but found that she couldn't part her lips, or move her tongue—or her jaw. She had another minor freakout, and the man placed a hand on her stomach. The sensation of human contact was calming and welcome, though it felt oddly muted through the matte grey material that covered her.

"Easy now, you can't talk anymore. I'll get your Link back up in a bit. You're probably hungry, too; let me give you something—not too much, mind you, I don't want you to get queasy."

He grabbed a tube from beyond her field of vision, and attached it to the port on her stomach. A strange sensation of her stomach filling came over her, though she had not swallowed anything.

"I'm really excited," the man carried on as he detached the tube. "You're the first of the SMI-2 scout models I've had the opportunity to build. They're new and super-advanced. You're going to love it, I bet."

Rika desperately wished that she could tell this 'assembler' that she would love to have her limbs back, but that wasn't possible. She made *hmmmm*ing noises out of her nose as loud as she could—which also felt weird, for reasons she couldn't identify—but the man just patted her on the stomach again.

"Don't worry, you're in good hands. I've put a thousand of you guys into mechs. You'll be up and ready to fight in no time. I have to admit," he said with a hungry smile as his gaze swept up and down her body. "It's gonna be handy to have you conscious, being my first scout mech and all. We can make sure the fit is good."

The assembler touched her stomach again, running his hand across it. "This new carbon-polymer is really great, too. No more of you mech-meats having stinking skin that needs to be cleaned all the time. Pretty sexy, if you ask me. Too bad they sealed up all your useful bits down here."

As he spoke, the man reached down and patted her crotch.

She jerked away, recoiling from his touch, though she could

instantly feel that there was nothing there; she was smooth as a child's doll between her legs. Rika lifted her pelvis up, trying to get a better look at this new indignity that had been bestowed upon her, while the man walked toward a rack and lifted up a long item, carefully unwrapping its plas covering.

Rage and shame mingled together. She was just a thing to him; an object that deserved neither respect, nor remorse.

If I had my limbs, I would—

"Oh," he said while looking over his shoulder. "Once you're built, don't even think about hitting me or anything. You'll regret it if you do."

Rika couldn't help it; she was already thinking of beating him senseless. Searing pain tore through her mind. She would have screamed if it had been possible, but she only managed to make loud, breathy grunts as her chest heaved from the shock.

The assembler chuckled. "Gets 'em every time. You have a compliance chip in your head now, Mech A71F. You'll never have an unsavory thought about anyone in charge of you again."

He held up the object he had unwrapped. It was a leg, a long one. It looked strange, and Rika realized that was because it was shaped like a horse's hind leg: double-kneed, with the first one bending backwards. The foot, if it could be called that, was more like a three-taloned claw, with two on the front, and one at the back for the heel. The limb appeared to be made of some sort of dark carbon-fiber material, and had overlapping ridges where the joints were located.

"Lay still," the man said, and Rika felt her muscles stiffen and was suddenly unable to move. The assembler lifted the limb in the air and spoke again. "Raise your right leg."

Rika found that she could move her leg now, and lifted it into the air.

"Think like you're pointing your toes," her assembler said, and then nodded with satisfaction when the cylindrical nub on the end of her thigh pointed straight out. He then slid her new leg into place. It covered her whole thigh and seated into the cylindrical protuberance with a satisfying *ssshhhhuck* sound.

"Looks pretty good," the man said with a nod, and he lined up a pair of rods, each with two holes, across the thigh-section of the attachment. He shoved them into the holes, and Rika felt them slide through her leg. They must have passed right through her femur and out the other side. She realized that's what the ports she had seen were for. He ran another pair of rods through the back of her leg using a set of ports she hadn't spotted, and then turned toward a console.

"OK, I'm going to connect the leg to your nervous system, then we're going to put it through some tests."

The next hour was filled with Jack—which was the assembler's name, as she finally learned—slowly adding limbs, and testing out every possible piece of functionality.

When he was done, she stood on the floor in front of the table, flexing the joints on the double-kneed legs that were attached to her thighs—which still felt awkward to walk on, but Jack said she'd get used to them before long.

Her left arm, thank the stars, was relatively normal, with a three-fingered hand at the end of a nondescript limb. Jack had explained that it was useful for a mech to have a hand so that it could do things like operate doors, or manage its own feed and waste tubes.

During the fitting, he had continually referred to her in the third person as 'the mech', and she slowly had begun to think of herself as nothing more than a piece of hardware. A part of her mind screamed that this was mental conditioning—likely enhanced by the compliance chip in her brain—but there was really nothing she could do about it.

Her right arm ended in what Jack referred to as a 'multi-function weapons mount'. Currently a long sniper rifle was attached to it, and she practiced aiming while Jack lifted another object off the rack and set it on the table.

"This is a bit different. Since you don't have skin to clean anymore, it's going to fit a lot tighter—but it's more flexible, too."

He lifted up two pieces of a shell that would wrap around her torso and between her legs. It had an almost chitinous look to it, with the overlapping plating. Jack pressed the front piece against her torso, and studs protruding from the armor—for that's what it was—sunk into the ports there. He repeated the process with the back, and then fiddled with an overlapping plate between her legs, finally driving a long shaft into her pelvic bone to pin the armor in place.

Next he placed chest armor over her upper torso, front and back, and anchored it into place as well. The chest armor was less flexible; only a small bulge revealed that under all the steel and carbon fiber, she was still a woman made of flesh and blood.

"Can the mech bend over?" Jack asked. "I want to test full range of motion. Touch your toes…or your claw-feet things…"

Rika did as instructed and bent over, touching the front claw on her right foot with her right hand, and then tapping the muzzle of the rifle against the other.

"OK, good," Jack said. "Now twist side-to-side…OK…then arch your back."

Rika followed the directions without pause. She had received two additional mental shocks from the compliance chip for responding too slowly, and she wasn't about to let that happen again.

"Hmmm," Jack muttered. "A bit of slippage when you arch backwards; but I suppose you won't do that much, and your skin underneath can still stop a bullet."

He turned to grab one more thing from the rack.

"And now for the mech's grand finale!" He turned and showed Rika a featureless black oval, which he deftly split in two. "Your helmet."

Rika twitched backward. The helmet looked like it belonged on a robot. It would take away the last appearance of her humanity, and make her nothing more than a machine.

"Don't move," Jack said sternly, and Rika found herself paralyzed once more. She blinked rapidly, the only movement she could make, as Jack placed the back and then the front of the oval around her head. It was dark inside, and her breathing was loud in her ears—until something snaked into her ear canals and all sound ceased. She felt something wrap around her neck, and knew she was now completely entombed in her matte grey shell.

<OK, Mech.> Jack's voice came over the Link; the first time she had received any mental communication since the courtroom.

Rika realized that with the Link, she had access to basic information like the date and time. She saw that her sentence had only been commuted three days prior.

Three days…

It felt like a lifetime had passed; like the Rika then was another person.

All that remained now was Mech A71F.

<I'm going to activate your helmet's visuals and swap out your natural optics. They'll still work as a fallback, but you'll default to external sensors now.>

The black interior of the helmet was replaced with a full three-hundred-and-sixty-degree view of the room. If Mech A71F hadn't been locked stock-still by Jack's order, she would have fallen to the ground as waves of dizziness came over her.

<Wha…I can't tell which way is forward,> she said in a near panic.

<Easy now, Mech. There are indicators on your HUD, and it will feel perfectly natural in no time. Give me a moment while I put on your external power pack and remove these hookups. You have SC Batts inside, too, but this external one has a lot more juice.>

She watched with startling clarity in the dimly lit room as Jack disconnected the power cables that had been attached to her limbs, and placed a small, oval battery pack on her back. A readout appeared on her HUD showing that the external battery was 98% charged, and would last fourteen days at its current drain. Estimates appeared beneath that data showing that under strenuous activity, the battery would only last five days.

There was a brief snapping sound in her ears, and Mech A71F

realized she could hear sounds in the room again, but not with her ears. The sounds were fed directly from the helmet's sensor array into her brain.

"Can you hear me?" Jack asked.

<*Yes,*> Mech A71F replied. <*Loud and clear.*>

"Good," Jack replied. "Run full diagnostics."

She wasn't sure how to, at first; then suddenly she knew exactly what to do, and she ran the diagnostic routine on her armor. It showed green across the board, and she reported that to Jack.

"Good. Mech A71F, you are ready for combat. You will receive final subliminal training en route to the front. Exit this room and follow the route highlighted on your HUD. It will take you to your transport."

<*Understood,*> Mech A71F replied, and took her first faltering step toward the door—and the rest of her life.

*****

Author's Note:

If you haven't read the Rika prequel, *Rika Mechanized,* you may want to do so at this point. It tells a story of Rika's time in the Genevian military, and paints a picture of what she had to go through to survive the war that her people ultimately lost.

However, it is not necessary, and you may read on to see what is in store for Rika next…

DEKAR'S DREGS

STELLAR DATE: 07.02.8948 (Adjusted Years)
LOCATION: Dekar Station, Merchant Docking Ring
REGION: Outer Rim of Parsons System, Nietzschean Empire

Nine years later…

"Hey, Rika, you have a ship to load! Get your tinhead out of the stars and get that shit loaded, or I'll dock your pay!" Bay Chief Hal yelled at Rika from two berths over.

"Not a tinhead anymore," she muttered in response.

"You'll always be a tinhead to me," he called back.

"Damn, Chief Hal has good hearing," Chase said from across the stack of pallets. "Guy can hear a mouse across the bay."

<*Yes, I can.*> Chief Hal spoke into their minds over the Link. <*Now get that damn ship loaded. You have ten minutes. After that you eat into their departure window, which means they might get fined, and if they get fined, they sue me, and if they sue me, I take it out of your pay; so* ***move!***>

Rika let out a long, silent breath, resisting the urge to walk over to Chief Hal and slap him clear across the bay.

<*Not worth it,*> Chase said privately, apparently reading her expression all too easily.

<*But, damn, it would be satisfying,*> Rika said with a mental sigh.

<*No argument there.*>

Rika stepped up to the cargo stack and slid the rods protruding from her forearms into the slots on the top of the crate, hefting its three hundred kilos with ease.

She noted that the crate was stamped with a Nietzschean logo, indicating that it was confiscated material, seized as the spoils of war.

The war her people had lost.

'My people'.

Rika no longer considered the Genevians 'her people' any

more than she did their Nietzschean conquerors. The Genevians had taken her body from her, thrown her into desperate battle after desperate battle, and made her kill thousands of enemy troops.

All for an unwinnable war, where the high command squandered the lives of the mechs—and the soldiers fighting alongside them—until there was nothing left.

When the Genevians finally surrendered, the peace turned out to be no better than the fighting.

That the Nietzscheans despised the Genevians was no secret; their actions during the war did not belie their hatred in any way. Rika had believed that the only thing they hated more than Genevians were their mechanized warriors. As one such warrior, Rika had expected to be executed when the change of masters had occurred.

Some of the mechs *had* been killed, but only the ones who had gone insane with rage and hatred and could never be integrated into any society again.

The rest—Rika included—had spent some time in internment camps, but eventually had their compliance chips and military hardware removed, and were set free.

'Free'.

Whatever freedom was, Rika was certain it was not present where she had ended up.

What Rika had learned in the five years since the end of the war was that, though the Nietzscheans hated the Genevian mechs because of the destruction they wreaked during the war, they respected them as warriors for rising above their circumstances. That respect had translated into their release back into society.

However, the Genevians felt great shame for what they had done to their own citizens. Unfortunately, that shame did not include any form of respect, acceptance, or financial aid to help rebuild the mechanized warriors' organic bodies.

Those conditions made for scarce work. Rika had moved from one manual labor job to another, until she finally ended up at

Dekar station on the outskirts of the Parsons System.

It was surreal to be here, slinging cargo in a system where she had fought so many battles—many of them victorious.

But every hard-won ground battle was balanced by a loss in space; Rika still remembered boarding one of the last ships that had evacuated the Parsons System, when the Genevian fleet retreated and abandoned it altogether.

An abandonment that had not hurt Dekar Station in any way.

Though the Genevians had lost the fight in the Parsons System, Dekar had prospered. The station was on the fringes of the system, and when the Nietzscheans had attacked seven years ago—just over two years before the end of the war—Dekar had surrendered without a fight.

There was no profit in fighting against a superior enemy—especially when your own space force ran from almost any conflict—and the owners of the station were far more interested in profiting from war than actually fighting a war.

Fleecing refugees had also become a substantial business on Dekar as the years passed.

It sickened Rika to be here in their company. But where the denizens of Dekar were cowardly, they were also pragmatic. It hadn't taken long for Bay Chief Hal to realize that, with her mechanized body, Rika was stronger than ten fully organic humans and far more versatile than a bot.

The icing on the cake was that, unlike with a bot, he didn't have to pay for repairs when her robotic components suffered damage. *She* was responsible for that.

Which was the reason Rika was so deep in debt.

Well, part of the reason.

Rika had spent most of her initial earnings on getting her face reconstructed after what the Genevians had done to it. It was no small expense, but well worth it.

From the neck down she was still covered in her matte-grey skin—no longer sheathed in armor—but her head looked as it had before that fateful night when she'd been sentenced and ended up in the Genevian military's human chop shop.

She allowed her thoughts to continue to wander, and it helped pass the time as she and Chase loaded the freighter. He worked the loader, pulling the crates off the bay's grav conveyers, and Rika carried them into the ship's main cargo bay, stacking them according to the Supercargo's directions.

Even with her slow start, Rika finished the job just under the ten-minute deadline set by Bay Chief Hal. Without a word of thanks, he assigned her three more ships to load; when that work was complete, another two.

The workload wasn't unexpected; they didn't call Bay 1217 'Hal's Hell' for nothing. He ran it with a ruthless efficiency, and many discerning captains requested berths in Bay 1217, keeping it busy at all hours—much to the dismay of his dockworkers.

Chase wrapped up his shift seven hours later and passed Rika a message as he left, *<Gonna be at Krueger's tonight. Stop by when Hal finally cuts you loose.>*

<Thanks,> she replied. *<Maybe I'll do that.>*

<Maybe I'll see you, then.>

They both knew she wouldn't show up.

Chase had always been kind to her, but he had grown even friendlier since her facial reconstruction surgery, asking her to join him for drinks nearly every night.

Rika didn't fault him for not finding her attractive when her head was just a faceless orb with two eyes and not even a nose; but the fact that he had only asked her out after her surgery hurt more than she cared to admit.

"Pining after a real boy?" Hal's voice sounded nearby, and Rika looked back, staring down at him from her 2.3-meter height—towering over him.

"Haven't seen one," Rika replied. "Just talking assholes around here."

Hal snorted. "Have it your way, Rika. Another ship just came in. Needs to be cleared out and loaded back up in two hours. You just bought yourself that job."

Rika bit her tongue and nodded as she walked to the ship that Hal pointed at, examining the work order he passed her over the Link.

Getting it done in two hours by herself was going to take a miracle.

A DANCE WITH DENNY

STELLAR DATE: 07.02.8948 (Adjusted Years)
LOCATION: Merchant Docking Ring, Dekar Station
REGION: Outer Rim of Parsons System, Nietzschean Empire

Rika walked slowly through the warrens of Deck 741, one hundred levels down from Hal's Hell, and just three away from her quarters. The wide corridor was crowded with other workers heading home or up to the docks to begin their shifts. Refugees, long-since turned to beggars, huddled along the bulkheads; the poor and unfortunate who had fled the fall of the Parsons System, only to make it to Dekar and no further.

She felt pity for them, but not so much that she could afford to share any of her spare credits—were she to have such a thing. The war had taken everything from her, too. These beggars may think they lived in a hellish afterlife, but Rika knew that even their blighted existence was far more desirable than hers.

An indicator flashed on her visual overlay reminding Rika that her internal batteries were down to ten percent. Back when they were new, the batteries could hold a charge for far longer, under a lot more strain—but now they were showing their age. Just a few hours of overtime, and she was running on her last joules.

Maybe it would go better if I didn't antagonize Hal so much, Rika thought, shaking her head with a rueful smile on her lips.

A dozen meters down the corridor stood her favorite food stall—well, her favorite stall that served any food she could afford. Jessie, the owner, would also let her plug in for a quick charge while she ate.

As Rika approached the stall, she saw a few members of Pinky's gang further down the wide passageway, alternately mocking and extorting refugees and passersby.

Rika did her best to ignore them, hoping they wouldn't spot

her. No small number of local gang leaders were constantly pressuring her to join their ranks. They promised parts and power, but little respect.

"Long shift," Jessie commented as Rika approached and leaned an elbow on the counter.

Rika smiled at the pink-haired proprietor. The fact that Jessie never mentioned Rika's mechanized body, and always looked her in the eyes—even before her surgery—was the other reason why Rika frequented her stand.

"You too," Rika replied. "You were here when I left for my shift this morning."

Jessie shrugged. "Yeah, Annie ditched me again today; said that she had some sort of ache or pain. I kinda don't mind, though. She's a shit worker, and if I don't have to pay her ass, it's a win for me."

"Yeah, she can't flip a burger for the life of her," Rika replied. "And now that I can eat burgers again, I hate having to settle for what she can produce."

"Never fear, Rika—your favorite mystery meat delight is coming right up. Maybe someday, both you and I can get off this shit station, and I'll cook you up a real burger."

"I'd like that very much," Rika said as she spooled out her charge cable and handed it to Jessie, who plugged it in behind the stand's counter.

Rika felt a sense of relief as her charge meter showed the power trickling back in. Running out of power in the warrens was one of her worst fears. She harbored no illusions about what would become of her should that happen down here.

With power, she was one of the most formidable people on the station. Without it, she was scrap metal waiting to be picked clean.

A memory of being racked for transport came back to her; how the military removed her limbs and left her helpless, little more than a piece of equipment stored on a shelf.

She would never let that happen to her again.

If there was one thing she was thankful to the Nietzscheans for, it was the removal of her compliance chip. Her future was grim, but at least she was in control of herself again.

Jessie poured Rika a cup of black coffee, and she inhaled the aroma, savoring the eight ounces of joy that was waiting for her.

"I still don't know how you get coffee here," Rika said after she took her first sip.

"Everything comes through Dekar," Jessie shrugged. "Just have to know the right people."

"Those have to be some people," Rika chuckled. "Even Hal bitches that he can hardly get coffee."

"Well, I wasn't always running a food stand down in the warrens," Jessie replied with a sardonic laugh.

"You've mentioned that before," Rika said. "What was it that you used to do?"

Jessie gave Rika a sad smile as she slid a plate holding a burger and fries onto the counter. "Maybe I'll tell you sometime, Rika. Not today, but sometime."

Rika picked up the burger and took a bite, enjoying the savory flavor as it hit her tongue.

"Mmmm…tastes better every day," Rika said.

"You're crazy," Jessie laughed. "But I'll take the compliment."

Rika swallowed her bite and picked up a fry. "Best oatmeal fries this side of Parsons, too," she said before popping it into her mouth.

As she ate, a loud bang sounded down the corridor, and she turned her head to see one of Pinky's gang members holding a gun on a refugee. No one appeared to be harmed, so Rika surmised that the first shot must have been fired as a warning.

"Fuckers," Jessie swore. "Can't rise to your feet around here without someone trying to push you back down."

"They bother you at all lately?" Rika asked.

Jessie smiled broadly and shook her head. "Nope, not since you caved Begee's face in last month. They give me hella dirty looks, but everyone knows that if they mess with me, they're gonna get a visit from you.

"Good," Rika said around a mouthful of burger.

"Not that I need it," Jessie said with worried eyes. "I have enough connections that Pinky may mess with me, but she's not going to do anything too stupid. You, on the other hand…your bleeding heart shows too often. One of these days, someone's going to take advantage of that and cut it out."

Rika sighed. She did her best not to give a damn, but it didn't always work. Jessie was right, though. One of these days, it was going to bite her in the ass.

"I'll have one of your fine cups of coffee, Jessie," a voice said to Rika's right, and she turned to see the sneering face of Denny, one of Pinky's lieutenants.

"Oh, hey, Rika. Thought you were just some dirty parts someone had dumped in front of Jessie's stall…well, I guess I wasn't really that wrong."

"Fuck off, Denny," Rika growled.

"Rika! I'm here to spend my hard-earned credit on some of Jessie's fine brew. Best on the station, if you didn't know."

Jessie gave Rika an imploring look, and then gave Denny a long-suffering one. "Payment up front, and you can have all the coffee you want," Jessie bargained.

Denny's face adopted a wounded expression and he touched a hand to his chest. "Jessie! Are you calling me unscrupulous? You cut me deep, cut me to the quick!"

"Yeah, I am," Jessie said. "Credit."

Denny muttered something incomprehensible as he fished in his pocket for a hard chit. He finally pulled one out and slapped it on the counter.

"Man of my word," he said. "I'll take a large."

Jessie turned to grab a cup, and Denny stared longingly at her ass.

"See that, Rika? Jessie's built all nice and proper. Not like your hard, carbon-fiber rear end. I bet she gives a good fuck, too—though I suppose you'd be good for something, now that you have lips again."

Rika took a bite of her burger and did her best to ignore Denny. She knew he was just trying to egg her on; he had checked her out on more than one occasion. Though there were augmented bones and muscles underneath her matte-grey skin, her ass didn't look that far off from its original appearance. It wasn't covered in skin, but that wasn't so unusual.

"No comment, Rika?" Denny smirked as Jessie wordlessly handed the gang member his coffee with one hand, and took the credit chit with her other.

"You hear something, Jessie?" Rika asked with a wink.

"Yeah, some sort of dripping," Jessie replied. "Like a leaky faucet, or something."

"A snot faucet, maybe," Rika said with a laugh.

"Watch yourself," Denny cautioned, his voice dropping, and even managing to sound a bit menacing. "Pinky wants to play a long game with you; get you over to her side through slow persuasion. Me? I don't see the appeal so much. Maybe I'll just take you out of play right now."

Rika looked down at Denny, and slowly raised the remainder of her burger to her mouth, popping it in and chewing slowly.

"Maybe you should try," she said around a mouthful of food. "Then I can punch your mouth off the shit lump you call a face, and no one will have to listen to you anymore."

As she spoke, a small voice was wailing in her mind, reminding her that she only had fifteen percent charge, and that a fight in the warrens was not what she needed right now; but another part of her just wanted to do the universe a favor, and wipe the stain that was Denny from existence.

"Fuck you, Rika!" Denny shouted as he took a step back and pointed a ballistic pistol at her. "I'm sick of your superior attitude. You're shit, just like the rest of us, and you can still bleed and die."

While Denny pontificated, Rika reached down and unplugged the charge cord from her side, then took a step away from Jessie's stand.

Denny kept the weapon trained on her head, while Rika kept one eye on his trigger finger and the other on his feet as he twisted to track her.

After a minute, Denny seemed to reach a decision. His brow furrowed an instant before he pulled the trigger. It was all the tell Rika needed—she jerked to the side, and the projectile flew through the air where her head had been.

Her arm shot out, and her steel fist slammed down on Denny's right wrist, shattering the bones within.

The gangster screamed and dropped his gun, but his look was not one of defeat; more like pained joy.

Rika turned to see seven more members of Pinky's gang approaching—each one of them armed, and all appearing to be spoiling for a fight.

"Gonna get it now, bitch," Denny hissed as he dove to the side of the corridor.

Rika dropped as well, reaching for Denny's discarded pistol as a hail of bullets and pulse rifle blasts flew overhead. She scampered behind a pillar and double-checked her body's readout.

She had been hit in the side and the leg by three ballistic projectiles, but none had done any damage. The low caliber weapons the gang employed wouldn't be able to penetrate the artificial skin covering her body. But without the plating on her cyborg limbs—taken by the Nietzscheans at the end of the war—a lucky shot could wreck a knee or an elbow joint.

"You sure you want to do this?" she called. "It's gonna get messy."

"Fucking kill her!" Denny shouted before anyone had a chance to respond—not that Rika expected any of the gang members to argue for clemency.

Rika knew that the pillar would only protect her for another minute before the attackers surrounded her. The corridor offered little cover, which meant that her best defense was a strong offense. One that involved taking a better weapon than the pistol she now held.

She peered around the pillar and quickly scanned the corridor with her eyes, wishing that she had just *one* of the drones she used to carry back in the war.

Three goons on the right, which meant the other four were on the left. She jerked her head back as a round struck the pillar, just three centimeters from her eye.

She responded by reaching her arm around the pillar and firing back at the approaching attackers, her visual overlay providing targets based on the gang members' most recent positions.

Two separate screams let her know that her predictive algorithms were working just as well as ever. She estimated that her enemies were within two meters on the left side. Rika took a steadying breath, dropped to a crouch, and then leapt out around the left side of the pillar, kicking at the legs of the closest attacker while firing into the torso of another.

The pistol got off two shots before it jammed, and Rika threw it aside as several shots struck her chest. She saw that the shooter was one of the gangsters on the right side of the pillar.

She leapt to her feet, grabbed the man she had shot, and flung his body at two of the attackers, then delivered a roundhouse kick to another guy, shattering his ribs and probably his spine with her three-clawed foot.

A spray of bullets hit the bulkhead nearby, and Rika threw herself at the shooter, breaking the woman's neck with a well-aimed blow.

The rest of the fight passed in a blur, and less than a minute later, Denny's accomplices were either dead or drawing their final breaths.

Rika cast her eyes about, searching for Denny—the piece of shit who had started this, who had brought out the killer in her.

As she looked for him, Rika realized that the corridor was nearly empty. The refugees and other passersby had cleared out to avoid getting caught in the crossfire.

A wave of sorrow hit her with the realization that her months of careful control—when she had thought that she was improving, becoming human again—had really just been a thin veneer over the vicious machine that still lay underneath.

The sound of shuffling feet reached her ears, and she turned to see Denny sliding out from behind a pillar several meters away, still cradling his shattered wrist. His wide eyes stared at her with fear, and she saw tear streaks down his dirty cheeks.

"Get out of here," Rika said wearily. "Tell Pinky I don't want to see her dicks down here anymore."

Denny nodded manically and then turned and ran.

Rika let out a long breath and took a step; that's when she realized that the fight had not been entirely one-sided. An actuator in her left knee had been hit by a bullet at some point, and she had limited motion in the limb.

She would have to pick up a new one from a nearby mod-shop. They wouldn't have one with the right specs for her, but she should be able to retrofit one of their civilian models.

Rika hobbled back to Jessie's booth and leaned heavily on the counter.

"I think I'll need another coffee," she said.

No response came, and she realized that Jessie was nowhere to be seen. The stall was small, so Rika leaned over the counter and peered into the corners around the stove, table, and chill-unit.

Her breath caught, and a choked gasp escaped her throat when she finally caught sight of Jessie.

The stall owner had hidden underneath the front counter, and a stray shot had passed through the thin walls of her stall. The wound on her forehead was small, but the back of Jessie's skull was a tangled mass of blood, pink hair, and grey matter.

Rika turned aside and threw up; spewing out her burger and coffee, followed by whatever else was left from her lunch earlier in the day.

She tried to hold back the tears, but it was impossible. She collapsed to the ground, sobbing uncontrollably.

Which is where the station security found her eleven long minutes later.

P-COG

STELLAR DATE: 07.09.8948 (Adjusted Years)
LOCATION: Combat Information Center, MSS *Foe Hammer*
REGION: Interstellar Space, near the Praesepe Cluster

David eased back into his seat in the *Foe Hammer's* CIC and set his coffee pouch in the pocket on the side of his chair. If there was one thing that the Marauders had over the military, it was that the Old Man let people drink coffee at their posts.

Not that coffee was the *only* thing better than the Genevian Armed Forces—but it certainly ranked high on the list, as far as David was concerned.

He pulled up the logs he was reviewing and gave them a visual scan, looking for patterns that may not be apparent to others. He spotted a few interesting alignments in timing, data size, and destinations.

Probably nothing nefarious, but still worth checking, he thought before pushing them into one of his analysis matrices.

As a P-Cog, or Pattern Recognition Specialist, David's job was to look for things others missed. Even though a dozen other humans and AIs had been over these logs, there was always a gem nestled in them for a P-Cog to pick up.

It was his special gift from the Genevian Armed Forces during the war with the Nietzscheans. Some draftees— conscripts, if he was being honest—got the real shit mods, like the mechs; especially the K1 models. But other poor saps, like himself, got their heads jammed full of upgrades that served other purposes.

David's upgrades were dedicated to spotting patterns and ferreting out connections between seemingly unrelated things.

Massive NSAI grids usually performed tasks like that, but some wiz in the GAF's R&D division decided to capitalize on the one thing that humans had in spades over NSAI: intuition.

David had known all his life that he had good intuition. He

could talk his way out of almost anything, and spot good and bad deals a mile away. It had made him a great contract negotiator before the war, and his services were always in high demand.

When he was drafted, the aptitude tests had picked up on his abilities, and he was shipped off to a lab filled with a lot of unfriendly-looking folks in gleaming white coats.

That was when the poking and prodding inside his brain had begun. Thankfully he remembered little of it; though there had been lucid moments. Moments punctuated by fear, terror, and agony.

In the end, he had come out packing a lot of extra hardware between his ears. Enough that his skull needed passive cooling—which accounted for his lack of hair and the addition of cooling fins on his head.

The adaptation had earned him the nickname 'Sharkie' in the military—even though he'd never seen a shark with seven fins.

After the war, David had attempted to return to his prior work, but because of the mech-conscript program, most Genevians assumed that any GAF-modded person was a criminal conscript, not a draftee.

Few people would hire him, and those who did wanted to use him to hide criminal activity—not seek out wrongdoing.

That was when a friend from his division had told him about the Marauders, and how the group was almost entirely filled with Genevian Armed Forces vets who were trying to find a place after the fall of Genevia.

David had enlisted as soon as he could travel to a recruitment center, and look where he was now: working in the CIC of the Old Man's flagship.

A yawn escaped his lips, and David picked up his coffee pouch and took a long draw of the bitter drink. At least here in the Marauders when he found something wrong, he could do something about it. Most often, the wrongdoers were unsavory types that would see the business end of a Marauder rifle before long.

Until this operation—the goal of which was the overthrow of the Theban leadership, and facilitate the forcible annexation of Thebes by Septhia.

As far as David could tell, both the Septhians and Thebans were good people. Sure, they had their issues; but on the whole, their governments represented the people, elections were as fair as any, and the populace was content and prosperous.

He understood that the Septhians were worried about Nietzschean expansion—everyone spinward of the Pleiades was. It seemed like nowhere was safe from the specter of war anymore. All of the major empires and federations in the Orion Arm were gobbling up their smaller neighbors at an alarming rate.

Though the Praesepe Cluster was small—less than one hundred light years in diameter—it contained well over a thousand stars; the nations within its bounds were tightly-knit, possessing great strength in numbers.

That is what made David wonder about the Septhian desire to attack Thebes. Septhia was a much larger alliance, with over fifty member systems compared to the Thebans' five; but there was no reason he could see why the alliances couldn't work out mutually beneficial treaties.

Over the years, the Septhians had made frequent overtures to the Thebans, offering them a place in the alliance—but the Thebans had declined each time. David could see why. Thebes was on the edge of the cluster, facilitating trade with systems deeper within Praesepe.

They also controlled one of the few areas in the cluster with less dark matter, making Thebes a gateway into the star cluster.

David pulled up a map of the cluster on his console, overlaying the stars with the latest dark matter dispersion maps. Dark matter was the Praesepe Cluster's greatest strength, and its most vexing problem.

Outside of star clusters and stellar nurseries, dark matter was only found tightly packed around stars. But in clusters like Praesepe, it was everywhere—making FTL all but impossible.

Without entering the cluster through a region of space like the one Thebes controlled, it could take decades, even up to a century, to travel to the cluster's inner reaches.

While there were two other alliances in the cluster that controlled regions of space with sparse dark matter, they were on the far side. Thebes controlled the clearest dark matter region near the Nietzschean border—a border that was only thirty light years away after the Niets' conquest of Genevia.

David ran a hand across his head, tracing the grooves between the cooling fins—a pensive habit he had picked up after getting the mods, and constantly worrying that his brain was somehow going to hemorrhage from all the alterations.

He was not the first person to see this obvious connection. If the Nietzscheans were planning to annex the Praesepe Cluster—an act that would expand their empire tremendously—then Thebes was the obvious place to start.

But rather than attack, a far better plan for the Septhians would be to convince the Thebans of this possibility, and aid in bolstering their defenses.

Scuttlebutt amongst the Marauders maintained that the Thebans must have received such an overture, and viewed it as the first step in a slow takeover after all the other diplomatic attempts had been rebuffed.

David could see that possibility, but all his intel on the Theban President, a woman named Ariana who was just now entering her seventh term, showed her to be a competent and reasonable person.

Would the Septhians really resort to toppling the Theban government just to secure the rimward edge of the Praesepe Cluster against the Nietzscheans? They must have made a very convincing argument to the Old Man for him to engage in this sort of subversive action—an action that had Marauder teams operating as assassins within Thebes.

One thing was for certain: if the Nietzscheans got wind of this before the Septhians had secured Thebes, the Niets would undoubtedly strike, and strike hard.

Which was one of the many things David was keeping a keen eye out for. There could be no leaks from the Marauders that the operation was underway.

Thus far, there had been no leaks that he could see. Not that David was surprised; if there was one thing the Marauders had in common, it was a deep hatred of the Nietzscheans.

But something was tickling in the back of David's mind. There was a thread that he couldn't quite see, waiting to be found and pulled. Something didn't feel right about the arrangement with the Septhians, with the whole plan in general.

There was a piece missing, or out of place, or both.

David brought up a new set of logs. The details and content of the Old Man's arrangement with the Septhians was not accessible to him, but the logs of the communications themselves were.

He spread out a holographic matrix and began filtering the logs into the framework, looking for patterns that only a P-Cog would spot, searching for that clue that would explain to him what was really going on.

KRUEGER'S

STELLAR DATE: 07.02.8948 (Adjusted Years)
LOCATION: Rika's Quarters, Dekar Station
REGION: Outer Rim of Parsons System, Nietzschean Empire

Rika lay on her hard bed, trying not to think about the last few weeks. She had seen a lot of death over the years—a lot of it caused by her. She had watched teammates die in her arms, and witnessed the enemy cradle their dead comrades.

Somehow Jessie's death was worse.

Jessie was just a woman trying to make the best of a shitty situation in a shitty world.

She had died because of Rika. Because Rika had let Denny—one of the most pathetic examples of humanity ever to breathe air—get the better of her.

Rika felt as though darkness was pressing at the edges of her vision, and she knew she was slipping into a deep depression.

While the Nietzscheans had pulled her compliance chip, they had left the other mental augmentations the GAF had inserted into her head.

Those augmentations had dosed her with drugs, and given all of the counseling that a non-sentient AI could provide; but it still wasn't enough. Rika knew that she needed human companionship to help pull her out—but that was just the sort of thing that got her in this mess.

She remembered what Silva—scout team Hammerfall's leader, and her dear friend—had told her when the war had ended: *"Rika, things are going to be hard for us, maybe harder than the war. There's no place for us out there, back with...people. But we have to try. If we shun humans...that's when we stop being human."*

Rika and Silva had been separated by the Nietzscheans when the Genevian military had surrendered. Rika had searched long for her former team leader, but it was as though the woman had disappeared.

Rika feared that the Nietzscheans had found Silva unfit for a return to normal society, and had killed her.

She sincerely hoped that had not occurred. Silva had always struck Rika as the most well adjusted member of Hammerfall. If the Nietzscheans had found Silva unfit for reintegration, Rika couldn't imagine how they'd given her a pass.

"Enough!" Rika said aloud, and sat up, grabbing a cloth to rub her eyes. The action sent a new wave of sadness through her.

It was the little things she missed the most. No one ever thought about how a mech, with cold steel hands—which Rika's angular steel appendages barely counted as—couldn't even *rub their own fucking eyes!*

Not unless they wanted to accidentally gouge them out.

Maybe getting my face back was a mistake, Rika thought; not for the first time, either. The debt she was under was crushing, and the repairs from the fight with Denny and his thugs a few weeks back had pushed her under even further.

Rika had been forced to reach out to Pierce, a loan shark—no, a loan megalodon—to get the money to repair herself so that she could get to work at the docks, and slowly wear herself out for the next pending repair.

Pierce had demanded a consolidation, saying that there was no point in her being last in line to pick Rika's sorry ass clean when she reneged on her obligations.

She had paid off all Rika's other debtors, which had an upside: none of the small fish were going to ask for a little something extra when Pierce came around to settle up.

Of course, the downside was that Pierce pretty much owned Rika now. For all intents and purposes, Rika worked for her.

As if her existence couldn't be any shittier.

"No!" Rika shouted. She wasn't going to fall into this trap and cry herself to sleep *again*. A walk around the station—the parts of the station worth walking around—was just what she needed.

She looked at her jacket, torn from where her arm had caught on it earlier that day, and decided not to bother donning it. It had been her last piece of clothing; the loss of which contributed to her current spate of melancholy self-loathing.

Rika rose and walked the two meters from her bed to the san unit, and picked up her brush, running it through her hair, and then wiping her face clean. She reset her makeup—another expenditure she had wasted money on after getting her face back—to be a touch darker than she wore at the docks.

Satisfied with her appearance from the neck up, she examined her body, ensuring that no bits of mattress or dirt were stuck in it.

Rika allowed a small smile to grace her lips. It wasn't all bad, if one ignored the fact that her arms and legs were hard steel, and glossed over the armor mount points on her hips, shoulders, and elsewhere; the organic portions of her body were rather attractive, the matte grey 'skin' the military had given her was smooth and perfect, bulging slightly where her augmented muscles rippled beneath.

"OK, Rika. Let's go have a nice walk, look at the stars, and take our mind off what a shitbucket our life is."

She barked a laugh. *Talking aloud in the third person is probably not a good sign.*

Rika left her small room and walked through the narrow passageways toward one of the larger thoroughfares with walkways along the side, and room for groundcars in the center.

When she reached the broad corridor, the station was alive with light and life as people went about their business. It had reached the end of the second shift, and everyone was enjoying as much revelry as possible before the next day's drudgery was upon them.

Rika passed a couple wrapped in a passionate embrace. Their lips were locked together, bodies ignoring the world around them, and Rika's thoughts flashed to Chase; he was probably still at Krueger's, where he had invited her once again.

A maglev train screamed by, hanging from the overhead, far above the street traffic flowing around Rika, and she decided it was time. She had enough credit for one drink, and having that in the company of friends was just what she needed.

She strode down the walkway, threading her way between the other pedestrians. Most made way for her—bumping into a mech was not usually an enjoyable experience—but she had to skirt around some groups who gave her steely looks and refused to move.

Before long, Rika reached a maglev station and boarded the train that would take her to the outer docking ring where Krueger's was located. It was close to Hal's Hell, but not too close—which suited her just fine.

She doubted sleep would come to her tonight. Maybe after having a drink with Chase, she could start her shift early and put in some extra hours to catch up on her already-late payments to Pierce.

The maglev station where she disembarked was only one hundred meters from Krueger's, and as she stepped out onto the docking ring, Rika could hear the boisterous revelry spilling out of the establishment.

Krueger's was frequented by an equal number of merchant crews and locals, and it was always full of happy, and some not-so-happy, drunks. Tables surrounded the bar's main entrance, with umbrellas over each—a silly affectation within the station, but it did serve to add a more welcoming feel.

Rika looked for Chase around the tables outside, her augmented vision scanning the patrons, and highlighting those who gave off excess heat or heavy EM fields as heavily-modded. Most had a yellow glow surrounding them, but a few were outlined in red, and Rika subconsciously cataloged their threat levels and potential responses.

Chase wasn't outside, so Rika strode past the tables toward the entrance, catching a few catcalls.

It was nothing new. Though her nethers were still sealed under the more durable skin the military had given her—and unseen by even *her* in years—it didn't change the fact that, without the jacket she'd left back in her quarters, she was essentially naked.

"Look at that!" a man called out from a nearby table. "Now that's what I call a cargo loader!"

Rika winced, but kept walking.

Her enhanced hearing picked out the man's voice as he turned to his friends. "Saw her working in Hal's Hell earlier today. Imagine having her on board? Work all day, and still have enough charge for play!"

The taste of blood entered her mouth, and Rika realized she was biting her cheek. Maybe her torn jacket would have been a good idea—it didn't typically affect the number of comments she heard, but it did cleanse the content a little.

They'd say stuff like that to anyone. It's not because you're a mech, she thought to herself. *Don't let it get to you, Rika.*

Once inside the bar, the crush of bodies shielded her from most eyes, and she relaxed in the anonymity. She scanned the crowd and saw Chase down at the end of the bar with two of his friends—a man named Terry, and Terry's sometimes-girlfriend, Trina.

As Rika approached, Chase caught sight of her and his face lit up with a brilliant smile—the sight of which washed away the filth she felt from the man's comments outside the bar.

Chase rose from his stool and held out a hand to welcome her. "Rika! I was starting to think that you were allergic to something in here! Really glad you could make it."

Terry gave her a kind smile, but Trina's eyes narrowed and her lips formed something closer to a smirk than a smile.

"Great to see you again," Terry said. "Chase is always talking about you, you know—all good things, of course."

Rika saw Chase flush, and noted that his pulse had quickened.

"Well, she *is* amazing," Chase said with a genuine smile, apparently going for broke. "I wouldn't be able to survive Hal's Hell without her around. Rika's like my guardian angel."

It was Rika's turn to flush. Chase's acceptance of her was one thing, but she didn't think anyone had ever called her an angel.

"Thanks, Chase. I wouldn't have made it through my first day in there without you," she said with a small smile.

"What do you drink?" Chase asked.

"Or do you drink at all?" Trina asked with a smirk. "Other than oil, of course."

Terry elbowed Trina, and Rika ignored the woman, determined not to lose the little high that Chase's statements had given her.

"I've got enough credit for an amber ale, if they have any," she replied.

"Rika, seriously, your money is no good here," Chase said as he leaned over the bar and shouted for something called a Rikers Amber. "You'll like it," he said with a smile.

"Thanks, Chase. I really appreciate that."

"Nonsense, Rika. I've been saving some credit to buy you a drink for months. These chits have been so sad, trapped in the depths of my accounts, I have to set them free."

Rika laughed, the sound almost foreign to her ears.

"You don't do that enough," Chase echoed her thoughts. "Maybe if you start coming out with me, I'll get to hear it more. It's certainly worth the price of a few beers."

Rika felt her flush deepen, and a strange feeling crept into her heart. Just a sliver, but she knew what it was: happiness.

Chase bought her more drinks that night, and though her enhanced metabolism kept her from becoming drunk, she enjoyed the buzz. Terry was pleasant company as well, and even Trina kept her snarky comments to a minimum.

As the time slipped well into the third shift, Terry and Trina left, and Chase began to look tired.

"I can't tell you how great it's been having you here tonight, Rika," Chase said, his words slightly slurred. "Being with you is like a dream come true."

"Chase," Rika said with a smile. Though her heart soared to hear his words, she demurred, "I'm nobody's dream."

"Are you kidding?" Chase asked, as his eyes slid down her body and up again—something that they had done a few times during the evening. It wasn't leering; it was appreciation—something she was all too eager for him to feel.

"Rika, you're a goddess. You're the epitome of perfection. And I'm not just talking about your smoking hot bod..." he flushed at that, and Rika was glad that the alcohol had elicited that unfiltered comment from him.

Rika smiled. "Do go on."

"Uh, yeah, what I mean is that there's so much strength in you. You got dealt one of the shittiest hands ever—and I don't even know the half of it—but you're so *strong* in there." As he spoke, Chase touched a finger to her head. Then he lowered his hand to rest above her breasts.

"And here."

Rika leaned forward and closed her eyes, silently begging whatever stars may still care about her to show Chase what to do.

Either they were listening, or Chase didn't need any prodding; his lips met hers, and he leaned forward, wrapping his arms around her. She slowly embraced him, taking care to keep any pointy or sharp edges facing outward.

They moved into a back corner of the bar, Chase pushing Rika against the wall as they continued to press against one another. Chase explored her body, commenting with a laugh that her armor mount points made for useful handles.

Rika wished that she had managed to save enough money to reconstruct her nethers. If she had been able to have sex, she would have taken Chase right then and there in the back of the bar.

Though that was not possible, it didn't seem to diminish Chase's hunger for her, and they pleasured one another as much as they could. Eventually Rika felt a tap on her shoulder, and she turned to see one of the bar's staff.

"We're closing up now," the woman said, her smile not unkind. "You two lovebirds are going to have to take that somewhere else."

"Ah, shit," Chase sighed. "I was hoping we were stuck in some sort of temporal disturbance, and this could last forever."

"Well," Rika said as she gently ran a steel finger down Chase's chest. "There's always tomorrow night."

"C'mon, guys, I gotta clean up," the woman said.

"OK, OK," Chase said as Rika stood and helped him to his feet. "Damn, girl, you're not even tipsy."

"Takes a bit more than a dozen beers to set me back," Rika said with a giggle. *A giggle!*

She helped Chase walk out of the bar and onto the docking ring. They both took a long breath, soaking in the myriad scents of Dekar's ring, and Rika smiled.

Maybe things weren't so bad after all.

Chase took her hand—growing steadier as they walked—and led her toward the maglev station.

"Why don't you come back to my place?" he asked as they reached the platform.

"Oh, stars, Chase," Rika whispered. "I can't think of a damn thing I'd rather do right now. But your shift starts in six hours, and I need to put in some extra time to get caught up with Pierce."

"Fucking work. I'd rather work at fucking," Chase grinned.

Rika's face fell; the sorrow she thought was gone crept up on her once more.

Chase stepped forward, a look of concern on his face. "Oh, shit, sorry, Rika. I know you can't, and I'm perfectly OK with that. I'm into *you*. All of you, the total package." He stroked her cheek. "Don't you worry about that at all."

They kissed again.

"I'll see you in a few hours," Chase said, and boarded the next maglev car as it pulled up. She watched him take a seat, still a bit wobbly, and then the train whisked him away.

A smile tugged at Rika's lips, and she let it spread across her face. *Have I found love? Is it just the alcohol, or does Chase really feel so strongly about me?*

Though he didn't start asking her to Krueger's till she had a face, he had always been nice to her. But she had thought maybe he just had a fetish for mech girls.

She chuckled. Maybe he did, but his affection for her seemed genuine; if he got turned on by her machine parts, maybe that was just fine. They weren't going anywhere soon, anyway.

A thought occurred to her about Chase's invitations to the bar. *Maybe he didn't invite me before I had a face because I wasn't able to drink! Was his change in behavior more to do with compassion than an appreciation that was only skin-deep?*

How did I stumble across someone so amazing in a place like Dekar?

Rika turned and walked back onto the docking ring's main sweep, whistling a tune—so happy that even the thought of sixteen hours in Hal's Hell couldn't put a dent in her joy.

"Rika!" a voice called out from behind her, and she turned to see a dozen men and women approaching. The joy that had filled her so fully evaporated in an instant, replaced by dread.

These were Pierce's enforcers.

"Pierce wants to see you," one of the men said. "You're late, and it's time to pay up."

"What? No!" Rika cried out, taking a step back. "I'm just a week late, and I get paid after my shift today! I'll be square!"

"Too late," one of the women said with a cruel grimace. "Come quietly. You may be tough, but we're ready for you. Won't be like when you fought Denny and his asswipes."

Rika could see that. Every member of the group was armored and held serious weapons—not to mention net-casters.

She lowered her head and nodded. "OK, lead the way."

"Good call," The first man said, and the group formed a box around her, marching her back to the maglev station.

They took a train halfway around the docking ring and then led Rika through a maze of corridors until they came to a manufacturing district.

Rika was led into a warehouse, past stacks of crates, to a small office along one wall. Standing in the entrance to the office was Pierce.

"Rika, Rika, Rika; what am I to do with you?" Pierce asked, her ruby-red lips pressed into a thin, disapproving line.

"Pierce!" Rika said. "I tried to tell your people I'm getting paid today. I was going to work a double to get enough money. You'll get it today, I promise!"

"Oh, don't worry," Pierce said with a chuckle. "I know I will. Hal will turn over what pay is owed you, but your time slinging cargo is over. You see, you misread our contract."

Rika frowned. The contract had been simple—just one screen. It had outlined the amount of debt, the transference from other lenders, and the payment schedule. What could she have missed?

"I can see that you're confused," Pierce chuckled. "I'll admit I did it deliberately. You see, there was a clause in there—a particular form of legalese used here on Dekar—that means if you fall more than a week behind…well…I own you."

Pierce finished the statement with a broad smile and spread her arms wide.

Rika felt like she'd been hit by a tank. "Own?" she asked.

"Oh, yes, 'own'. I gotta say, I love the Nietzscheans. They don't endorse slavery, but they figure if you're dumb enough to get made a slave, then that's all you're good for," Pierce replied, and let out another throaty laugh before continuing. "Now, I normally don't care for owning people. Messy business. People have all these needs, and you have to care for them; the ones dumb enough to get made slaves usually aren't worth it."

Pierce stepped forward, her eyes walking down Rika's body and then back up, boring into Rika's eyes.

"But you…you are a prize worth having. An SMI-2 scout mech. Top of the line. Sure, you don't have a lot of your military hardware anymore, but you have the internal mods and augmentations. I know; I saw the recordings of the fight with Denny and his pack of morons. You're not a woman, honey; you're a weapons platform. One that people are willing to spend top dollar to get their hands on."

"What?!" Rika shrieked as Pierce's words sunk in. "You're going to *sell* me?"

"Yup! Auction's tomorrow. I could have nabbed you sooner, but I figured I'd let you work your last few days with Hal so I could collect your pay." Pierce tapped her head. "Always thinking, always taking opportunities. Not like you, Rika. You may have been great at war, but you suck at life. There were opportunities all around you; you could have been a queen on Dekar, but you allowed yourself to be chattel. Being a slave is your lot, little Rika. You're just a killing machine, and there's a lot of killing that needs to be done out there."

Rika's vision swam as rage filled her. She would not be sold; she would not kill on another's orders ever again.

Of her own volition, though—now that was another story entirely.

She took a swing at Pierce, but the woman had been ready for it, and danced back as a series of pulse blasts hammered into Rika from behind. Then one of the net-casters fired, and Rika was wrapped in carbon-fiber strands.

"You fucking *bitch!*" Rika screamed. "I'll kill you for this! Kill you! You hear me? I'm going to tear you limb from limb!"

"Rika!" Pierce said with mock concern. "You always seemed so calm, so levelheaded." Then Pierce's brow lowered, and a wicked smile spread across her lips. "I'm glad there's still a killer in there, though. That'll bring top dollar for sure."

Rika struggled against the net, feeling it begin to give against the power that surged through her limbs. "Better run, Pierce," she grunted as a part of the net tore open. "I—"

Her words were cut short as she felt a stinging sensation in her neck. She reached up and pulled out a tranq-dart, then yanked more of the net apart and climbed to her feet, fighting the waves of dizziness that threatened to topple her.

"I—" she began to speak, but two more darts hit her, and then a fourth.

She took a step, but the ground was in the wrong place; she realized that the darts contained nano, not drugs. Her foot seemed to be floating above the ground, and then her face smashed into the deck.

Pierce approached and leaned over, her face close to Rika's.

"Should never have got your face back, Mech A71F. It made you weak, and exploiting weakness is what I do best."

Rika tried to reach out and grab Pierce, but her limbs wouldn't respond. As her vision went black, she heard Pierce issue an order to someone nearby.

"Get a compliance chip back in her. I want her under control for the auction."

AUCTION

STELLAR DATE: 07.02.8948 (Adjusted Years)
LOCATION: Pierce's Warehouse, Dekar Station
REGION: Outer Rim of Parsons System, Nietzschean Empire

Rika woke with a start, as though the nanotech suppressing her conscious mind had shut off at a pre-programed time—which was probably the case.

The room she was in was small and spare, with a few crates stacked along the walls, and a door to her right.

She tried to move and realized that she was mounted on a rack; its hooks set into the hardpoints on her back. Rika considered attempting to tear herself off it when she felt a familiar tingle in her mind.

A compliance chip.

The vague memory of Pierce ordering someone to install a new one came to her, and Rika let loose a string of curses that would have impressed even her most foulmouthed teammates back in the military.

<*Ah, you're awake,*> Pierce's voice entered her mind over the Link. <*And right on time, too. Gotta love it when tech works. You'll be happy to know that the auction is underway, and more than a few people have shown up to bid on your lot. I have to admit, even I didn't expect a payday this big off your sale—if I had, I might have put you up for auction sooner.*>

Rika didn't have anything to say to the woman speaking in her mind. Nothing that wouldn't make her sound like a raving lunatic, at least.

<*No rejoinder? No threats to kill me?*>

<*No,*> Rika replied. <*I hope you have a big celebration tonight, basking in the joy of selling off a fellow human being—and then choke and die on your favorite dish.*>

<*Oh ho! There we are; love that spunk, Rika. Don't worry, though.*

I'm not getting joy from selling a human being—you're just mech-meat. Surplus military hardware that I picked up for a song. Pull yourself together, now. Your lot number is up soon. Or throw a tantrum and give me an excuse to show off how well the discipline system works—I'm OK with either.>

Rika seethed but she didn't respond, and she felt Pierce leave her mind a moment later.

Her thoughts drifted to the previous night, to her time in Chase's arms. *Why did I wait so long?* To just have one night of happiness, and now to descend back into hell was too much, far too much.

Rika forced herself to calm down, taking deep breaths, remembering how she used to make her mind go still—how she would focus on a point of light within herself, and push away all her fears.

It was working, sort of, when the door opened, and two of Pierce's guards entered wearing powered armor. She suspected that they weren't taking any chances.

One stood in front of her and smiled. "You're a serious piece of gear, Rika. I was half-hoping that Pierce would keep you around. I bet folks wouldn't miss a payment if they knew you were coming by."

"Yeah, but you saw all the people interested in her lot. Boss said she'd give everyone on the takedown team half a percent. That's gonna be some serious coin."

"Hey," the first guard said as he released the locks on the rack and pushed it toward the door. "I said 'half-hoping'."

The other guard chuckled as he held the door open, and Rika considered reaching out and slamming his head against the door frame, but thought better of it as the tingle of discipline rose up in the back of her head once more.

The guards wheeled her down a short hall and then through a doorway and onto a raised platform.

Rika realized that she was still in the same warehouse as the night before, but the stacks of crates had been moved to create room for the nearly one hundred people who were gathered in front of the platform.

Some sat in rows of chairs, while others stood behind the seats and along the sides of the room. Each held a sheet of plas with a number on it, and Rika could see that many were adjusting their posture, readying to raise their plas in the air.

Humiliation flooded through Rika; to be wheeled out on the platform like she was a *thing*—which is exactly how they viewed her—was almost too much to bear.

Only the memory of the previous night kept her from breaking down. Chase saw her as human, as a person. That meant she was, no matter what these people thought.

"You can see here that we have a fine specimen of Genevian mech technology, manufactured at the height of the war, with all the latest enhancements government money can buy," the auctioneer began, smiling as he walked in front of Rika and gestured to her body.

"It has augmented muscles, an upgraded skeletal system, military neural mods, and," the auctioneer gave a soft chuckle, "a compliance chip."

The sound of soft laughter came back from the crowd, and Rika grimaced, turning her head to the side.

"Don't let her demure attitude fool you," the auctioneer cautioned. "You have all seen her combat record, and the footage of the recent fight on Dekar. Mech A71F is top-notch and ready to roll."

The pair of guards walked back onto the stage, carrying a crate between them. They set it down next to Rika, out of her field of vision, and began to open it.

"But that's not all!" the auctioneer cried out. "The seller has managed to secure an OEM multi-function weapons mount for our little mech, here.

One of the guards stood holding the tool necessary to remove Rika's limbs. He slotted it into her left arm and released the locking bolts, sliding them out and slipping them into a pocket.

He gave a twist, and pulled.

Her days in the military flooded back—the numerous techs who had repaired and rebuilt her time and again. She chuckled. "Gotta twist it a bit harder than that, you fucking squishie."

There were a few chuckles from the crowd, and the man flushed, giving her a dirty look. He twisted again, harder this time, and her arm came free. Rika stared down at the stub of a limb that remained.

The man lifted up a weapons mount attachment, complete with a GNR-41C sniper rifle, and slid it onto her arm, twisting hard in the other direction.

The new appendage clicked into place, and Rika saw the weapons specs and loadout appear on her HUD as the guard slid the locking rods through.

"Look at that!" the auctioneer cried out. "Is that a war machine, or what?"

Rika saw nods of approval and shook her head. "Except that I'm a fucking lefty. I need this hand for a handheld weapon. You got a gun mount for the wrong arm."

"I imagine you'll adapt," the auctioneer said, and shrugged before turning back to the crowd. "Let's start the bidding at fifty-thousand Nietzschean credits!"

Rika knew he'd start there. It was the amount she owed Pierce and, by law on Dekar, bidding had to start at the amount owed. Sadly, she would not get to keep any excess.

Plas placards flew up around the room, and the auctioneer continued to raise the bid until it was close to a million credits. Around that point, Rika saw Pierce step out from behind a stack of crates wearing a cheek-splitting grin, and she wished she could get off the rack and tear that smile right off Pierce's smarmy face.

As the bid amount closed in on one and a half million credits, many of the bidders fell out of the race. Only two remained.

One was a slender woman with a glowing red tattoo over her right eye, and the other was a cloaked figure in the back of the room, his face shrouded by a hood—though Rika's enhanced vision could make out a bearded chin and sharp nose beneath the cowl.

The woman bid up to one and a half million, and the auctioneer scanned the room.

"We have one and a half million Nietzschean credits for the SMI-2 mech. Do I hear one point five-five million? Going once..."

"Two million!" the shrouded figure in the back called out.

"Two million Nietzschean credits!" the auctioneer cried out with glee, looking to the woman with the red tattoo. She shook her head and lowered her placard. "Sold to the man with placard number forty seven!" the auctioneer shouted.

The two guards had carried off the crate that held her arm, and now returned to wheel her off the stage.

"Nice haul, Rika!" one of the guards whispered. "Gonna buy a new rifle with my take. Thanks a mil!"

"Or two mil," the other guard laughed.

They returned her to the small room where she had first awoken. The man who fitted her before pulled out the limb removal tool, and slotted it into her left arm, removing the bolts, and then the multi-function weapons mount and GNR-41C sniper rifle.

Rika hoped against hope that he would put her regular arm back on, but her worst fears were realized when he instead slotted the removal tool into her right arm.

"Hey, you don't need to do this," Rika said. "I have the chip; I can't hurt my...owner."

"Pierce's orders," the man said with a shrug. "I think it's because she got a really small cryopod for transport. Cheaper that way."

He pulled off her other arm and then moved to her legs. A few minutes later they were both laying on the floor, and Rika's HUD switched off the overlays that monitored those systems. It felt empty, seeing the world without all of her peripherals data framing it. Now all that remained was her charge readings and standard bio-data.

One of the guards flipped open a crate, and Rika saw a small cryopod within. He keyed in a code, and the pod's lid split open and slid aside. Then the guards lifted her off the rack and carefully carried her to the pod.

"Shit, Rika, you're heavy. What did you eat last night?" one of the guards asked.

"Don't be such a pussy," the other said as they lowered her into the pod.

"Speaking of pussy…I sure wish she had one," the first guard said as they stood back. "Look at her. Without limbs, she looks like a little grey puppy. Stars, I'd fuck her sideways all day."

"Shut up and—" the first guard's words were cut short by a scuffle in the hall, and Rika peered up to see Chase burst into the room.

"Rika!" he cried out. "No, Rika—when you weren't at the docks today…shit, Rika, they sold you!"

"Chase, please," Rika whimpered, humiliated that Chase had seen her like this—just the shell of what was once a person.

"Hey, dickhead, get out of here," the second guard yelled, turning to Chase and shoving him backward. "Deal's done. She ain't your girlfriend no more.

"Get off me!" Chase yelled and shoved back, only to get a fist in his mouth, followed by another in his solar plexus. He fell to the ground, gasping for air, his eyes locked on Rika's.

"Go," she mouthed the words, not trusting her voice. *"Please go."*

Chase's eyes were filled with pain, and tears formed in their corners.

"I'll find you, Rika. I don't care where they take you; I'll find you and I'll set you free. I promise!"

"Yeah, right, loverboy," one of the guards said as he kicked Chase in the stomach. The other guard reached down and grabbed Chase by the hair, dragging him bodily into the hall.

The first guard turned back to Rika and pushed a button on the cryopod. As the lid closed, she caught one last glimpse of

Chase—he had been thrown against a wall and was getting punched in the stomach.

Then Rika's view of the first man who had ever treated her like a person was cut off, and everything went black.

THEBES

STELLAR DATE: 12.15.8948 (Adjusted Years)
LOCATION: Warehouse on the northeast edge of Berlin
REGION: Pyra, Albany System, Theban Alliance

Rika felt the slow return of consciousness that followed cryostasis. She had been through it before, and it was just as unpleasant as she recalled. The process was akin to becoming un-drunk over the course of thirty seconds.

As her brain began to accept stimuli from her eyes, she saw that she was in a room with a wooden ceiling. Wood. Dust. She was planetside somewhere.

Sounds reached her ears: scuffling, something being dragged around, low voices.

"This isn't right. Does she get paid, at least? How can she be on the team if she doesn't get paid?" one voice said. Female. Soft, but with a rasp.

"She's not really a person, she just needs parts and power. She belongs to us now."

The second voice was male. It was low, and even though the words were spoken softly, they still carried a deep resonance.

"Shut up, you two, she's waking up," said a third voice. Also male, but a touch nasal—like the owner had a sinus issue of some sort.

Rika closed her eyes and rotated her neck around, getting a feel for moving again, before opening her eyes again to see yellow eyes peering down at her from a dark-skinned face, framed by long black hair and a warm smile.

"Good morning, Rika. I'm glad you made the trip without any trouble. Sorry about the mode of transport; it gets a bit tricky to bring military hardware like you into the Theban Alliance."

"Thebes?" Rika asked, trying to remember the Alliance's systems and worlds.

"Yeah. We're on Pyra, their capital world. In the Albany System."

Rika closed her eyes and nodded, finally recalling the interstellar cartography of the Theban Alliance.

"Jerry, give me a hand here," the woman said before looking down at Rika. "Oh, by the way, I'm Leslie. We're glad to have you on the team."

"Stop talking to her like she's a person," the deep voice said. "She's 'on the team' like my rifle is 'on the team'."

Leslie grimaced. "You're going to have to ignore Barne. He's not really good at anything but shooting."

Another face appeared over Rika, and she saw a mess of blond hair atop a grizzled face.

"Lieutenant Jerry," he said with a nod.

"Lift your…arms, and we'll pull you out, and get you on the rack," Leslie added.

Rika nodded and allowed herself to be lifted out of the cryopod; though it was not as if she had much say in the matter. Not unless scurrying around on the floor and biting ankles could be considered a viable escape plan.

As they carried her to the rack, Rika confirmed that her location was indeed a warehouse; one filled with old wooden crates, amidst which appeared to be a small staging area filled with surveillance equipment and no small number of weapons.

Leslie and Jerry grunted as they lifted her high and set the rack's hooks into her hardpoints.

Leslie gave a long exhale and leaned against the rack. "Stars, you're heavy."

"I've heard that," Rika said. "Who are you, if you don't mind my asking? You don't look like the guy that bought me."

She saw Leslie wince and give a meaningful glance at Jerry, who looked away.

From behind her, Barne, who she still hadn't seen, gave a throaty laugh. "That was probably Gregor, our outfit's quartermaster. He always gets us the best toys."

She could tell that Leslie and Jerry weren't fully comfortable with the idea of having a slave on their team—though Barne was coping with the idea easily enough by treating her as an object to be bought and used.

Rika found it ironic that of the three, his reaction was the easiest to deal with. The way Jerry and Leslie were behaving made her feel ashamed. Barne just made her angry. Anger was something she could use.

Her anger at Barne and the situation she was now in could mask the sorrow she still felt from her final moments on Dekar Station; final moments that were, for her, just minutes past. She could still hear Chase's grunts as Pierce's guards beat him, and the painful lump was still in her throat, threatening to unleash the type of emotional outburst that would not serve her well in her current situation.

Rika knew that she was in the midst of a professional crew. If they had any reason to believe that she would be a hindrance to their mission, they would put her right back in the cryopod. Rika would do just about anything to keep that from happening.

Strength and surety were her best allies now.

With a conscious effort, Rika pushed down her emotions and drew upon the pre-battle calm she had worked so hard to develop during the war.

She took a deep breath. "You're a mercenary crew," she said, peering around at the crates of weapons, munitions, and intelligence gathering equipment.

"Yes," Leslie replied. "We're with the Marauders. This is Team Basilisk—we're a spec-ops group."

Rika had learned of the Marauders not long ago. One of their recruiters had passed through Dekar looking for Genevian veterans to join the mercenary outfit. He had called Rika more than once over the Link, but she had ignored him.

For whatever good that had done.

"So, Rika," Leslie said. "Let's put you back together."

"You sure that's wise?" Barne asked. "Mechs are psychos,

every one of them. We put her together, what's to stop her from killing us?"

"Relax, Sergeant. I have the tokens for her compliance chip," Jerry said, stepping around Rika to look her in the eyes. "But I won't need to use them, will I, Corporal Rika?"

Rika took a deep breath, the words flowing from her mouth by rote. "No, sir. You won't need to."

"See?" Jerry said with a smile. "Been out awhile, but you still remember your place."

"If only our space force had the guts you mechs had," Leslie said, more sympathy than admiration in her voice.

Rika snorted. "Mechs get in the fight while the spacers take flight."

Barne barked a laugh, finally walking around to eye her from the front. "Is that what you little mechs all told yourselves?"

Rika noted that Barne looked like he sounded: a large man, dark-skinned and barrel-chested. His right arm was robotic, but skinned with a smooth metal that flowed and rippled in the light.

"Like it?" he asked, holding it up. "Lost this to a K1R that the Nietzscheans captured and turned. Fucking mechs; no real soldier would turn on his own."

Rika wanted to tell the man that a slave has no loyalty to its owner, but knew that making such an utterance here and now would not bode well for her future.

"Seriously, Sergeant," Leslie said, casting a caustic scowl in Barne's direction. "Stop waving around that bullet magnet you call an arm. Give me a hand with the crates."

"Fuck no. I still say that we do this without her. You put the tin soldier together if you think she's so special," Barne said as he skulked out of sight.

"Orders say we use her, so we use her," Jerry said. "The Old Man didn't dump millions of credits on all her hardware just to leave it—and her—in crates."

Barne only grunted, and Jerry shook his head. Leslie opened a case, and Rika saw her legs. Leslie and Jerry carefully lifted her right leg out of the case and aligned it with the socket on the end of her thigh.

"Turn it right," Rika said. "Yeah, like that; then push and twist."

The pair followed her directions, and before long, both her legs were in place.

"OK," Leslie said as she kicked open another case. "Now for your gun-arm...or, I guess it's called a 'multi-function weapons mount'."

Rika chuckled. "I rather like 'gun-arm'. But is there any chance you can give me both my regular arms right now? I can swap over to my gun arm when we need it."

Leslie looked up at Rika. "You don't want it?"

"I'm left-handed," Rika replied. "That gun-arm is a left-side one...makes life miserable for me. Back in the war, I had a right-mount GNR."

Leslie glanced at Jerry, who shrugged. "Makes sense to give her regular arms—especially if we need to go out on any more recon. A meter-long rifle barrel kinda gives you away."

"OK," Leslie replied. "Two regular arms coming right up."

After a few false starts, they got both her arms on, and Leslie lowered the rack, allowing Rika to settle on her own feet.

"Thanks," Rika said. "Feels good not to be hooked up on that thing.

"I'll bet," Leslie said. "We have something else for you."

Jerry walked over to where Barne was preparing a meal, while Leslie led Rika over to another case, and flipped it open. There, with its various components set in shipping foam, was a set of SMI-2A9 armor in what appeared to be pristine condition.

The emotions that Rika felt flow within her were far different than she expected. Rather than revulsion, she suddenly wanted to be wrapped in the armor—to feel its protective shell around her, keeping her safe, making her invincible.

"You look pleased," Leslie said quietly, her yellow eyes serious. "I wasn't sure you would be. I—I knew a few mechs back in the war. They weren't really happy people."

"Not a lot of happy people in the war, if I recall," Rika said. "Still…I know this is crazy, but I'm looking forward to putting it on."

Leslie reached up and touched Rika's shoulder. "We understand how…how it is to miss the war. Things were simpler then. We had our orders, we had our missions; we did what we had to. Afterward…the rules didn't make sense anymore. It's why we signed up for the Marauders."

Rika nodded. She knew that all too well. As she stared down at the armor, she wondered if perhaps finding herself with this mercenary team was a good thing. Even so, a few questions burned in her mind.

"Do the Marauders often employ slaves?" she asked without equivocation.

Leslie shook her head. "No. You're the only one…in your situation that I know of—but you're not the only mech. There are a few others."

Rika's head snapped up. "Silva?"

Leslie frowned. "No. No one by that name. The ones I know the names of are Herman, Grace, Liv, and Freddie. Herman is a K1R, and the others are AM-2s and 3s. Know them?"

Rika shook her head. "No, the names don't ring any bells."

Leslie shrugged. "Didn't think so. Want any help with the armor?"

"No, I got it."

"Alright, then. We're going to go over the mission brief with you after we eat. Based on the speed at which Jerry is burning the food, that'll be in about fifteen minutes.

"Hey!" Jerry called out from the hot plate he was standing over.

Leslie met Rika's eyes and smiled. "It's going to be OK. The Old Man is a good guy. I bet that if you do a few missions, he'll sort you out properly."

Rika wasn't so sure. The sort of person that bought other

people wasn't usually the type to 'sort things out properly'."

Leslie walked away, and Rika looked down at the armor. It was a newer model than what she had been equipped with back in the war; though the helmet was an older model.

First, she set the two pieces of armor that wrapped around her waist in place—what the women of Team Hammerfall had always referred to as the 'corset'—and sucked in.

She had gained a bit of weight since the war, and the armor was made for someone a size or two smaller than her—but once the two sides met, they hooked onto her mount points and ratcheted into place.

Rika pulled out the chest plate and set it into place, carefully ensuring that each of her breasts was seated properly before pushing the armor down into the mounts set in her sternum and shoulders.

That was one advantage of being an SMI-2 mech; every meat the GAF had put into her model was a thin, lithe woman. It was the whole point: small women with lots of hardware, who could still function as highly mobile scouts.

The rest of the armor only took five minutes to put in place, and Rika smiled as she examined her arms—no longer seeing the raw understructure, but something that looked a bit more like a real arm, with layered plating giving it form.

She stretched up, and then side to side, lifting one knee to her chest, then the other, ensuring the fit was good. She reached down and touched her toes, and then pivoted, pushing one leg straight up into the air while grasping both her calves.

"Nice view," Barne said, and Rika glanced over at the mercenaries, realizing that they were all staring at her.

"Fuck you," Rika replied as she lowered her leg and stood up straight.

Just as she was now cocooned in physical armor, Rika wrapped herself in the mental armor of quick comebacks and coarse language. She was in a pack of wolves, and there was no way she was going to reveal weakness and be torn apart.

"Food's ready," Leslie said, gesturing to a plate of reheated MRE's sided with a few slices of buttered bread that sat on a crate.

"You eat food?" Barne asked, as he pulled himself onto another crate and rested his plate on his lap. "I thought you mechs all took that nutricrap."

"Yeah, I eat food," Rika replied. "NutriPaste tastes a lot like I imagine your balls do, except it actually has substance. But I spent a decent amount of credit to get a face again, and I didn't go through that so I can pump crap into my stomach—not like the hookers that suck you off."

"Whatever," Barne grunted, flushing as Jerry and Leslie laughed.

"Oh, you're in for it," Leslie said. "She seemed meek at first, but it looks like our Rika's got some teeth after all."

"We'll see about that when we hit the shit," Barne said. "Anyone can talk a good game. How many kills you have, Rika?"

"Beats me," Rika said. "I never counted."

"You may not have, but the GAF did," Jerry said around a mouthful of the meat-substance from the MRE. "What was your confirmed count?"

"Just over seventy thousand," Rika shrugged. "But there were a lot more unconfirmed. Like I said, I never really kept track."

Leslie made a choking sound, and Rika glanced at her to see a look of awe on the woman's face.

"How…how did you…"

"Kill so many people?" Rika asked. "Simple. We never got days off, never got any leave. I was in for four and a half years; most days, I killed thirty Nietzscheans. You do the math."

"Thirty a day…" Even Barne sounded impressed.

"Doesn't work out to seventy thousand," Jerry said. "You're still short twenty thousand."

Rika nodded as she took a bite of bread and chewed it slowly, savoring the fresh taste. She swallowed and said, "There were a few above average days in there. I nuked a regiment, once. That upped the count a lot."

"Shit," Barne whispered.

"Think she can do the job, now?" Jerry asked.

"Now I think she's too much for the job," Barne laughed, his deep bass voice resonating in the crates around them.

"So, what is the job?" Rika asked Jerry. "And does it get me my freedom at some point?"

"The orders didn't say anything about your freedom, but there was a note about some sort of packet with your enlistment details. The packet wasn't in the crates, though—could have something about working off your debt. After this job, we'll hook back up with the regiment where you'll get to meet the Old Man, and we'll see."

Rika nodded slowly. That would have to do for now. So long as Jerry had the codes to her compliance chip, it was in her best interests to take him at his word and be agreeable.

"The mission," Jerry said, "is simple. We're here to kill the Theban President, and as many Theban top brass and politicians as we can.

Rika almost spat out her mouthful of bread. "What?!" she asked.

"Septhians hired us—or so we think. They want to shake things up, and this job will give them their in," Barne said.

"The four of us are effectively going to topple a government?" Rika asked.

"No," Jerry smiled. "There are thirty Marauder teams in the city now. We all have specific targets, and we're to strike simultaneously four days from now."

"And who's *our* target?" Rika asked, dreading the answer.

Barne gave her a predatory smile and leaned in close. "Like he said; the Theban president."

THE CHASE

STELLAR DATE: 10.25.8948 (Adjusted Years)
LOCATION: Starview Lounge, *Noon's Glory*
REGION: Approaching Maui, Ontario System, Septhian Alliance

It hadn't been easy, but Chase eventually learned the name of the hooded figure that had purchased Rika at Pierce's auction—Gregor. He worked for the Marauders, a mercenary outfit comprised mostly of Genevian veterans from the war with the Nietzschean Empire.

By the time Chase had been able to track him down, the man was long gone from Dekar. Not that Chase had any idea what he would have done had he caught up with Gregor.

The more he looked into the Marauders, the more dead ends he found. With the Genevian systems now a part of the Nietzschean Empire, the Marauders didn't operate openly within their borders. From what Chase could tell, their headquarters was somewhere in Septhia; at least that's where most of their public recruitment centers were.

Septhia—one of the many interstellar nations within the Praesepe Cluster. Once an ally of Genevia, they had not gone so far as to openly join the war with the Nietzscheans, or offer them any real assistance.

Nevertheless, Chase knew that's where his best chance of finding Rika lay.

The memory of that night with Rika was still crystal clear in his mind. The soft skin of her face, and where it met the coarse grey skin at her neck; the soft hints of her breasts. She was a beautiful woman, but he found her striking blue eyes to be her most captivating feature; they could convey so much, and held so much strength.

Chase knew that those eyes had seen things he could only imagine—yet they were still kind, and had shown him that there was a gentleness inside Rika. One she kept buried deep below the hard shell that she presented to the outside world.

He let out a long breath and signaled the bartender for another round, then turned on his stool to gaze out the window on the far side of the bar. It wasn't a real window. The bar was somewhere in the middle of the *Noon's Glory*, but the holodisplay perfectly rendered the external view with a three-dimensional effect that made it appear as though open space began just after the last table.

Ahead, slowly resolving into more than just an indistinct blob was Maui—a massive orbital habitat on the outskirts of the Ontario System. Ontario was one of the systems near the rimward edge of the Septhian Alliance, close to its border with Thebes.

"What's your business on Maui?" a woman asked as she settled onto the stool next to him. Chase glanced at her out of the corner of his eye, seeing enough to note that she had dark hair, and wore a loose grey suit.

"Looking for someone," he replied, not really interested in having a conversation—though still glad for a little human contact at the end of the three-month journey. Septhia wasn't far from the Parsons System as the photon flew, but the *Noon's Glory* had made several stops along the way. Enough that Chase was starting to feel like he should have tried to book private passage—though that would have completely depleted his savings.

"Aren't we all?" the woman said with a laugh. "Anyone in particular?"

"A friend," Chase replied. "We got separated by… unfortunate circumstances."

"A lot of that going around lately," The woman responded. "I hear that the Parisians just attacked the Roman Republic."

Chase shook his head in dismay. "Galaxy is going to shit lately. It's like the FTL wars all over again."

The woman nodded. "All thanks to that stupid old colony ship showing up—no one's even seen it since it left Bollam's World, yet they're all still fighting out of fear and distrust."

"I think people just needed an excuse. Mind you, not everywhere is a mess," Chase said. "Praesepe still seems unscathed; no wars to speak of in the cluster."

The woman nodded. "Yeah, we need places like this. Have to have somewhere safe to build new ships and weapons. Good business in that."

"That's not what I meant," Chase replied.

"I know, but that's my business, so it's how I look at it."

"Oh?" Chase asked. "I didn't get your name, by the way. I'm Chase."

The woman offered her hand. "I'm Sally. Nice to meet someone willing to chat; been a long, dull trip."

Chase chuckled. "Yeah, I've caught up on all the sims, vids, and even did some reading on the trip."

"I have to ask, this person you're trying to find…is he or she a romantic interest?"

"She," Chase confirmed.

"How do you know she's on Maui?" Sally asked.

Chase gave a long sigh and reached for his drink. He took a sip before answering.

"She's probably not, but I'm just chasing leads right now. I might have to take work for a bit on Maui. I can't afford to go chasing her all across the stars on my savings."

"What's the lead that brought you here?" Sally asked.

"Well, she got pi—she joined the Marauders; they're a merc outfit. They have a recruitment place on Maui. I have no idea what I'll do once I get there—I'm not sure if I can convince them to tell me where she is."

Sally laughed, and then took a sip of her drink, her eyes twinkling above the glass. "You're probably right. You could enlist, though."

"That crossed my mind—which is nuts. I've had my fill of fighting."

"Have you?" Sally asked. "Chase, formerly of Hal's Hell on Dekar Station in the Parsons System. Before that, squad sergeant in the second platoon of Charlie Company, 4326th Regiment, 23rd Battalion, 19th Division, Genevian Armed Forces. Have you had your fill?"

"What the hell is this?" Chase scowled. "That information isn't in any shipboard database."

"You're right about that. But I knew it before I boarded back at Hintin. Gregor sent me; he was curious who was looking into him. From what I can tell, there's nothing to worry about, though—just a lovesick boy, chasing after a girl."

Chase slammed his drink down on the bar, spilling its contents as he stood, and took a step back. "You're a Marauder? You fucking slaver! Where's Rika?"

"Hey, easy now," Sally raised her hands defensively. "I don't know where she is, but she's listed as active duty on the roster."

"Active duty...so she's fighting in a war somewhere," Chase said, his tone accusatory.

"To my knowledge, the Marauders are not currently fighting in any wars. But she's probably fighting somewhere."

"You know she's a slave, right?" Chase asked. "She was sold at auction."

"I saw that in her record. The way we see it, the Marauders saved a Genevian war hero from a horrible future somewhere. She'll have to work off the money we paid for her, but she's no slave."

Chase gave a cynical laugh. "Most people don't make a huge distinction between slavery and indenture, you know."

"Yeah, well, we're not a charity," Sally shrugged, and took another sip of her drink.

"It'll take her *years* to pay that off!"

Sally nodded. "But it's a small price to pay for freedom."

"If she survives," Chase spat. "I know how you mercs operate. Chew people up and spit them out."

"Hey! Check your attitude, Sergeant. I was enlisted in the GAF, too. Staff sergeant. Did my share of time in the shit. I'll tell you one thing for certain: we treat our own a lot fucking better than we got in the war. If Rika survived that, then she'll do fine with the Marauders."

Several of the bar's other patrons had turned to stare. Sally pointed at Chase's stool. "Now sit the fuck back down and finish your drink. What you didn't spill all over the bar, at least."

Chase was at a loss for words, but followed Sally's instruction and retook his seat on the stool. He picked up his glass, took a long look at it, and then downed the remains in one swallow.

"Another one for my friend, here," Sally said to the bartender before giving Chase a conspiratorial smile. "It's on the company dime, anyway."

Chase felt like an ass for losing his temper. It wasn't going to get him any further with Sally, and he was glad that she didn't just tell him to shove off and leave. Still, it took him a few sips of his next drink to ask the question burning a hole in his tongue.

"So, can I see her?"

Sally smiled. "You really have it bad, don't you?'

Chase chuckled softly. "Rika's an amazing woman; you'd understand if you knew her. She's...she's so strong inside, like a diamond."

"Forged in the war's crucible," Sally said.

"Breaks the metaphor, but yeah. She thinks that what they did to her broke her...ruined her. But she's wrong; they made her better."

"You into mod girls?" Sally asked with a raised eyebrow.

"No...well, yeah, a bit. But that's not what's special about her. Shit, I can't believe I'm telling all this to you."

Sally winked. "It's one of my specialties."

"Huh...I can tell."

"Look, Chase, you're a good guy. Your heart is in the right place, and you're not afraid to call a broom a broom. I was serious about you enlisting—the Marauders could use a man like you."

Chase had been mid-drink, and he coughed, getting more than a little on Sally.

"Sorry," he said, and handed her a napkin.

"Don't worry, I get that a lot," Sally said with a grim smile. "So, should I pass you a contract?"

Chase knew that if he said no, his chances of seeing Rika again in the next decade were slim to none. He wiped his mouth, took a deep breath, and nodded.

"Yeah, send me the contract."

NIGHT

STELLAR DATE: 12.15.8948 (Adjusted Years)
LOCATION: Warehouse on the northeast edge of Berlin
REGION: Pyra, Albany System, Theban Alliance

The rest of the team had gone to sleep; though not before Barne gave Rika a stern admonishment not to 'try any sneaky shit' during the night.

She had to admit that she'd considered it. Jerry had not given her any specific orders to remain in the warehouse, and so long as she could maintain a mental belief that leaving the warehouse was in the best interests of the team, she could fool the compliance chip and not be disciplined.

But she had nowhere to go, and she suspected that somewhere in the armor she now wore was a tracking system that would bring the Marauders right to her.

There was also a part of her that liked being part of a team again. No one here was responsible for buying her, and Leslie and Jerry didn't seem to have any issue with her being a mech. Barne wasn't happy about her, but she suspected that was because he was used to being the biggest muscle; but he hadn't called her 'meat', so that was a plus.

For now, she'd play along and see where things went.

Well, you do ***know*** *where this is going; you're going to assassinate a president.*

Rika knew that a younger version of herself would have been horrified, or perhaps morbidly curious about doing something so crazy. But she'd spent a lot of time on the streets. 'Kill or be killed' was something she had embraced long before the military had carved her up and made death her full-time job.

As a scout mech, she had relied on her GNR-41B sniper rifle to take out more than a few thousand enemies. She didn't feel any special remorse at the thought of actual assassination—a realization that worried her more than a little.

All her work to become a normal person since the war had ended—as much as was possible—seemed to have been nothing more than a veneer over what still lay beneath.

The killer.

She pushed those thoughts down and brought Team Basilisk's intel on Pyra and their target location up on her HUD.

Pyra was the second planet from Howe, which was the name of the primary star in the Albany System. It was strange that the system's star and the system itself didn't share the same name; it was also odd that no planet or star in the five-system Theban Alliance bore the name 'Thebes'.

Not that any of that mattered.

Pyra was a well-settled world, boasting a population of five billion. Most of that number was concentrated in mega-cities, leaving the majority of the planet's seven hundred million square kilometers of land open for farming and recreation.

The world had continents at both its north and south poles, making for a colder climate in the temperate zones than was common on terraformed planets. However, from what Rika could see, the locals had a real affinity for winter sports. She wondered if that was cause or effect.

She focused in on the location of the capital city, on the outskirts of which lay the warehouse the Marauder team was occupying.

The city, named Berlin, was nestled in a wide bay on the east coast of one of the world's continents; just a few degrees below the northern tropic line. Unlike the mega-cities elsewhere on Pyra, Berlin had an older more cultured feel. Local laws restricted building heights so that none could come close to the height of the capitol buildings. Rika noted that long-range urban shots would likely be out of the question.

She brought up the dossier on her target. President Ariana appeared to be popular with her people, having been recently voted in for a seventh consecutive ten-year term.

That was too long for anyone to hold power, by Rika's estimation. Maybe the Marauders were doing Thebes a favor by ushering in a change of the guard.

As Rika reviewed the president's daily schedule, as well as the briefs and dossiers of her guards and staff, the local time slipped past midnight. She noted that it was now the twelfth day of the third month on the local calendar. Strangely, a month named Julius.

She set a countdown: eight hundred hours on the morning of the fifteenth. That gave her just over one hundred and eight local hours until she pulled the trigger.

It was going to be a long wait.

She straightened and stretched her arms overhead. The feeling of being armored was still comforting, though the change in balance was taking some getting used to.

Rika turned and looked behind her at the sleeping forms of the other three members of Team Basilisk. *'Other'? Does that imply that I am one of them?*

She walked quietly to the crate containing civilian clothing and grabbed a long robe. At first, she had wondered why the team had equipped her with full armor—it wasn't ideal for blending into an urban population—but when she saw that the local fashion tended toward long flowing robes, it made more sense.

The robe they had supplied her with was more than simple cloth. It contained impressive EM-masking technology, and would even flow around her body in a fashion that masked her double-kneed legs.

She carefully pulled it over her head. The robe was made of tan cloth, with intricate white whorls across its surface. She left the cowl down and crept to a staircase that led to the warehouse's roof.

Her augmented vision revealed the steps least likely to creak and groan under her considerable weight, and she made it to the top without waking anyone below—she hoped.

The door on the roof was unlocked, but she saw a sensor on it and punched in the code to deactivate it—that much the team had trusted her with; then she pushed open the door.

Rika drew in a deep breath, relishing the scent of the clear night air as she leaned her head back and gazed at the stars above.

"Wow," she whispered, taking in the stellar beauty above her. The Theban Alliance lay on the rimward edge of the Praesepe Cluster, which consisted of a thousand stars, all within one hundred light years. Pyra was in the stage of its local year where the night sky was dominated by the display, illuminating the city and forests surrounding it with far more light than even most moons reflected.

Rika walked by the light of that brilliant display to the edge of the warehouse's roof, taking care to follow a route that would not pass over the team below, and leaned against the decorative cornice lining the top of the building.

Genevia—now a part of the Nietzschean stars—was not visible in the night sky at this time of year. She wished it were; Parsons would be visible from Pyra. She could have gazed at its light and wondered about Chase: where he was, what he was doing.

For her, it had been less than a day since they had been in each other's arms; for him, it had been well over a hundred. Did he think of her? Was he even still on Dekar? Rika doubted that she'd ever know.

She pushed the melancholy thoughts from her mind and gazed around her.

The warehouse was situated on the northeast side of the city, near a long string of wharfs mostly filled with recreational craft—though a few commercial fishing vessels were visible.

Rika wondered about a planet with so many inhabitants using human fishing fleets. Perhaps it was some sort of recreational activity.

To the southwest, seventeen kilometers distant, rose the capitol buildings. Rika gauged the building's spires to be no more than five hundred meters tall, but no other building in the city crested one hundred. Five kilometers north of the capitol and sixteen kilometers from the warehouse, lay the presidential estate.

The intel the Marauders had gathered showed that the presidential palace's grounds bordered a national forest, and that the president often went for a run in the morning on its twisting paths.

That would be their primary strike point, close to the palace grounds—Rika didn't want to be too deep in the woods if the president's schedule changed that day.

The sound of footsteps on the stairs and the soft swish of the door opening a moment later reached her ears, and Rika turned to see Jerry approaching.

"Quite the view up here, isn't it?" he asked as he carefully walked across the rooftop toward her.

"Checking on me?" Rika asked.

Jerry shrugged as he reached he side. "Maybe a little bit."

Rika gave a soft laugh. "I would have, too. Sorry I woke you; I just wanted to take a look at the city with my own eyes. There's always something missing from the intel. Everyone sees things differently."

"It's OK," Jerry said as he ran a hand through his messy tangle of hair. "I wasn't really sleeping well, anyway. I'm surprised you're not, though; I always find that cryo takes a lot out of me."

"I soaked up a lot of calories today. Took in some NutriPaste after the meal," Rika said. "I can make it a few days without sleep if I'm well fed."

"Yeah, that's fine for the body, but what about the mind?"

Rika turned to Jerry, meeting his dark eyes. "Seriously? You care about my mental state?"

Jerry gave a self-deprecating laugh. "Well, it's not entirely altruistic. I'm not excited about the thought of an overstressed, exhausted mech within arm's reach."

"And here I thought you cared," Rika said, turning back to the view of Berlin and the distant lights of intermittent air and ground traffic, flitting about under the starlight.

"Hey, I'm not exactly excited about having you here against your will," Jerry said. "But orders are orders."

"By 'against my will', you mean as a slave," Rika said.

"Hey, you're not a—" Jerry began, but stopped when Rika shot him a quelling glare.

"Am I getting paid for this job? Can I leave?"

"Uhh…well…"

"Slave," Rika said in a tone that brooked no further discussion on the subject.

Jerry didn't speak for a minute, and then he let out a long breath.

"Look, I admit that I didn't want you here—and before you go and get all pissed off at me, I don't mean *you* specifically. I mean anyone who's not Jenny—she was our last sniper. Got killed a few months ago on another op. We knew they'd send someone to fill her shoes, but we weren't expecting…"

"A slave," Rika finished for him.

"You think you're the only one that knows what that's like?" Jerry asked, anger seeping into his voice. "I was drafted, just like you. I didn't want to be in the GAF, but I couldn't leave, either."

A sour laugh escaped Rika's throat as she turned to face him. "Are you serious? You got *drafted*? I was *coerced*. Hell, I don't even know if there is a word that combines 'entrapment', 'coercion', and 'blackmail' into one. I stole food. *Food!* And for that, I was given the option of enlistment or execution!"

Jerry's face fell, and he swallowed. "Shit, Rika. I had no idea. They always told us you mechs were mostly volunteers; that the compliance chips were just to keep any that went nuts from killing the rest of us."

"Yeah, well now you know. So maybe what happened to me was a *bit* worse than when you were drafted."

"Our government was really just a bunch of fucking shitheads, wasn't it?" Jerry asked quietly. "Ever wonder if we're better off since the Nietzscheans won?"

"Fucked if I know," Rika said. "Now instead of our government flushing us all down the drain, we're doing it to ourselves—all while the Nietzscheans watch and make a profit off our backs."

Jerry nodded. "Yeah, it's pretty rough in some places. But you see that a lot after a war. I've been around a bit since then, and some of the other Marauders even longer. Things are shit almost everywhere. Everyone is attacking everyone."

"Seems nice enough here," Rika said as she looked over the city. "Well, 'til we kill off their leaders, at least."

"Kill or be killed, Rika. That's the way of it. Twelve thousand years of civilization, and that's what we humans do best. I'd rather be one of the killers."

Rika had no response for that. She agreed, but she didn't want him to think that she was OK with what they were going to make her do.

"Well, now that I know you're not going to jump off the roof and leave the premises, I'm going to go see if sleep will visit me tonight," Jerry said as he straightened.

"'Night," Rika replied.

Jerry tentatively laid a hand on Rika's shoulder, and she did her best not to flinch. Human contact was not something she'd had much of, other than the evening with Chase, which was beginning to feel like it was in her distant past—or like a dream.

"I meant what I said before," Jerry said. "The Old Man's a good guy. He'll reward you for a job well done. I know it."

Rika turned her head and met Jerry's eyes. He appeared sincere; his heart rate was slow and his blood pressure low.

"Thanks. I hope so."

Jerry turned and left, and Rika resumed gazing out over the city.

Berlin.

Where she would assassinate a president.

THE GENERAL

STELLAR DATE: 12.14.8948 (Adjusted Years)
LOCATION: Combat Information Center, MSS *Foe Hammer*
REGION: Interstellar Space, near the Praesepe Cluster

General Mill closed the report from Gregor on the situation with the mech girl, Rika. She had been successfully delivered to the team on Pyra assigned with the assassination of President Ariana. However, there had been no time to brief her or Basilisk before her arrival.

Even worse, the packet explaining that she only had to work off half her debt to the Marauders didn't make it into the shipment; just the information for Lieutenant Jerry on how to use her compliance chip to control her if there was an issue.

Still, the coordination officer on Pyra hadn't picked up any distress signals from Basilisk, so General Mill had to assume that all was as it should be—difficult as that was.

Operation Phoenix was still a go.

Mill rose from his desk and walked to the window in his ready room. It didn't look out over the stars, but instead down into the main shuttle bay of his flagship, the *Foe Hammer*.

He watched as two B'Muths were loaded under a drop ship, ready to hit the dirt. The massive, four legged walkers were well suited to different types of ground combat, both urban and rural. They were one of his favorite weapons platforms.

The Septhian Government hadn't contracted the Marauders to launch a ground assault on Pyra, but he suspected they would. The Thebans may look like a soft target, but Mill knew it would take more than a series of assassinations to take them down.

When Septhia came calling for troops, the Marauders would be ready.

Near the assault craft, a dozen fast exfiltration ships were loading supplies, getting ready for departure within the hour.

<*General?*> the voice of the regimental administration AI entered his mind.

<*What is it, Laura?*>

<*The* Romany *and the* Djinn *have just jumped in. They're maneuvering into position now.*>

<*Very good. Thank you, Laura. Have they brought any updates from Pyra?*>

<*Just that the coordination officer on the ground still has a green light on all missions,*> Laura replied.

<*Excellent,*> Mill replied.

Mill returned to his chair and sat down, spreading the mission briefs out once more. He had never planned a covert operation this large before, though it was not his first regime-toppling action—just his first as a mercenary.

There were forty teams on Pyra; thirty in the capital city alone. Another three-dozen teams were spread out in the Albany System, ready to take out targets on the other worlds, and key stations.

His contact in the Septhian government had assured him that different outfits had the four other Theban star systems well in hand. He suspected that the Septhians meant the news to comfort him—but it didn't. Instead, it kept him up at night. If any one of those other mercenary companies messed up and got caught, it would put his people in jeopardy.

Which was another reason why fast exfiltration teams were preparing their crafts for departure in the bay below.

Mill pulled up the holodisplay of his fleet relative to the Albany system. He was taking a risk, assembling his ships within the Theban alliance; but with his vessels seven light-months away from the Albany System's primary—a main sequence G-spectrum star named Howe—there was little chance that they would be spotted.

It also made a jump into the Albany System a nine-hour trip, which was far better than jumping all the way from Septhia; it was unfortunately still far enough out that any rescue ops could take a day or more with the final insystem flights.

General Mill rose and paced across his office, the myriad things that could go wrong flooding his mind. A small voice was telling him that Phoenix was a crazy op; that there had to be a better way to secure the Praesepe Cluster against the Nietzscheans.

There probably was, but he couldn't think of it at the moment.

TRUST

STELLAR DATE: 12.16.8948 (Adjusted Years)
LOCATION: Warehouse on the northeast edge of Berlin
REGION: Pyra, Albany System, Theban Alliance

"Well that's just great," Barne said. "They send us a tin soldier and all her toys, but they forget the fucking ammo for her rifle!"

"I can use the electron beam," Rika suggested.

"Maybe," Jerry said. "But if they have magnetic deflectors, it won't work. The kinetic power behind your rifle's uranium rods is a lot more reliable for this sort of kill shot."

"Any chances we can get some rounds?" Leslie asked. "Maybe from some of the other teams?"

"We don't even know where the other teams are," Barne said. "Fat chance of getting ammo from them—though it wouldn't fit anyway. No one else has anything close to that caliber of weapon."

Jerry stroked his chin as his eyes flicked up—his Link tell. "I know a gal; she operates a site from Pyra these days."

Leslie raised her hands. "Whoa, Jerry. I know who you're thinking of. We're not going through Cheri—that bitch is nuts. Didn't she try to kill you during the war?"

Jerry shrugged. "Yeah, but she tried to kill everyone at least once. It was a sort of rite of passage for our 'toon."

"No wonder we lost." Rika shook her head. "What are the chances she has the right ammo for my girl?"

Barne laughed. "*Your* girl already, is it?"

Rika shrugged. "When your weapon is a part of you, you tend to get attached to it."

"No pun intended," Leslie chuckled.

"Focus, people," Jerry said. "And yeah, she has some. Five rounds."

"What?!" Leslie yelled, then lowered her voice. "You reached out to her already?"

"Yeah. I routed it carefully. Look, she's a long way from here; it's going to be off the locals' radar. We jet up there, get the ammo, and then come back. One day. We have plenty of time."

"I didn't mean that," Leslie replied. "I mean that we can't trust her. Rika's gun doesn't shoot marshmallows. The reasons you need those rods are few, and there aren't any legal ones on Pyra."

"She has a point," Rika said. "I read the orders. We're to have no contact with anyone outside of the mission parameters. Risk of exposure is too high."

"*Corporal* Rika, it's my call. We're going to meet with Cheri, get your ammo, and be back by morning." Jerry said with finality.

The reprimand stung, but Rika was pleased that he used her rank to keep her in line, rather than Discipline.

"Who's 'we'?" Barne asked.

"Leslie and I," Jerry replied.

"I should come, too," Rika added. "I can make sure they're the right spec."

"No," Jerry said with a slow shake of his head. "You're our ace in the hole. Besides, it's a bit hard to get you on a cloud hopper or a maglev across the world. Your cloak is good, but I don't want to test it against a hundred scanners and keen-eyed security guards."

Rika nodded silently. She knew he was right, but the thought of getting out and about was too enticing to not have tried.

"Just going to leave me here with her all day?" Barne asked. "What if she goes nuts and kills me?"

"She won't; right, Rika?" Jerry asked. "Rika won't harm any one of us. Correct?"

Discipline tingled in the back of her mind. The compliance chip recognizing a direct order that required confirmation. *It's like he's read the manual or something since last night,* she thought.

"No, Jerry, I won't harm you three, or any other Marauder." She hadn't needed to add the last part, but she wanted them to be at ease.

"See?" Jerry smiled. "Safe as houses."

"However, I'd like to scout the primary location," Rika said.

"Oh, yeah?" Barne asked. "Something wrong with our recon?"

"There's always something wrong with someone else's recon," Rika replied. "Plus, my eyes are better than any of yours. I see things you can't."

Jerry gave her a long look before nodding. Barne snorted, and even Leslie looked surprised.

"You'll scout the site, and be back by night, right?" Jerry asked.

"Understood," Rika replied. "And 'night' is…?" The last thing she needed was an ambiguous order with a compliance chip in her head.

"Uhhh, twenty-two hundred, local time," Jerry replied.

"Plenty of time," Rika said. "Thanks."

Jerry and Leslie wasted no time dressing in their long, flowing robes, and they left the warehouse while Rika was still trying on different gloves, looking for ones with a good fit.

"Think that gloves are gonna hide the fact that you only have three fingers on each hand?" Barne asked with a smirk.

"They may cover themselves head to toe here, but they still have mods," Rika replied. "Three fingers shouldn't raise too many eyebrows."

"Just make sure you keep your neck covered," Barne said, pointing out that Rika's armor encased her neck right up to her chin.

Rika grabbed a shawl, wrapping it around her neck and over her head. "There, look good?" she asked.

Barne walked around her and nodded. "Yeah. If I didn't know better, I'd be fooled into thinking you're human."

Asshole, Rika thought, though she only nodded in response.

"Better get going. Long walk," Barne commented.

"Thirty five klicks round trip," Rika replied as she slipped pads over the toes on her feet to cover her metallic footfalls. "I walk at just under four an hour; won't even take nine hours to get there and back. I'll still have time to smell the roses."

"You do that," Barne said with a grunt. After a pause, he said, "Well, fuck off already. I could use some time alone."

Yeah, like forever, Rika wanted to say.

She turned and walked to the warehouse's north entrance; a different one than Jerry and Leslie had used. She reached up and set the alarm on the door to pause for thirty seconds, and then stepped through, out into the bright morning sun.

She pulled her robe's cowl up to shade her eyes, not wanting to use their filters to dim her vision. After spending months on Dekar station—which wasn't brightly lit *anywhere*—feeling the warmth of Howe's bright yellow light on her face was pure joy.

It occurred to Rika that this was the first time the light of a yellow star had struck her skin since the day she was caught stealing food.

Nine years between exposures to real sunlight. *Nine years.*

She walked across the loading dock, then hopped down and crossed a stretch of dull grey pavement to reach the back road. According to the map she had pulled down, the road connected the warehouse to a larger street half a kilometer away, and saw little traffic.

She had to admit she was impressed by the location Basilisk had chosen. The warehouse was one amongst several in a small cluster. None appeared to be in heavy use, but there was some traffic in and out that would serve to mask their arrivals and departures.

It was also far enough away from the city center to avoid any heavy surveillance, but still close enough for an efficient strike.

As Rika walked, she took in the local foliage, which was thick and lush—though she didn't recognize most of it as anything other than types of ferns and palm trees. Maybe there would be coconuts; she had enjoyed climbing coconut trees in her youth, and getting a drink of that sweet milk within.

Before long, the road she was walking alongside of reached the larger thoroughfare, and she turned left, heading west into the city.

Ground cars flitted by, most hovering above the road on magnetic systems. Some a-grav cars moved through the air further above, though still staying above the roads. Rika took a deep breath, savoring the light scent of ozone and charged electrons.

"Gotta love planets," she said to herself with a smile.

She strolled down the sidewalk at a leisurely pace, enjoying being outside in the sunlight with no one around who wanted to hurt or kill her. She had a full charge—on new batts, too, thanks to the Marauders—and was in no hurry to return early and spend the evening with Barne.

I think I'll wait outside till twenty-two hundred on the nose.

The feeling was exhilarating. She had food, charge, and nowhere to be for the better part of a day. The feeling was so foreign she barely recognized it.

She wondered if it was possible to be relaxed and excited at the same time.

Rika passed through the commercial area around the docks, and into a residential district. She smiled at other pedestrians as they passed—some walking alone, like her, and others in groups or with children.

They all wore robes like her, though many had their heads exposed. From her research, Rika hadn't seen any religious reason why everyone on Pyra wore robes out in the hot sun; it just seemed to be the fashion.

Strange as it was, the custom suited her fine. If everyone on the street was wearying skin-tight polymers, she doubted that Jerry would have let her roam about for the day—unless it had been a world of heavy modders. Then she'd fit in perfectly.

The residential district gave way to rows of small shops along the street, and Rika laid eyes on a coffee shop that had a holosign displaying a rotating array of drinks that made her mouth water.

Each of the Marauders had fake idents, and was masquerading as a Theban visiting Pyra. Rika's used her real name, though it cited her birthplace as Lils—an orbital habitat further out in the Albany System. She had credit, too; physical, and online in a planetary bank.

When she'd checked the balance, it had blown her away. She may not be getting 'paid' for the job, but she had more disposable credit available than she had seen in years.

She decided there was no reason not to treat herself to the local delights—a perfectly reasonable thing to do for a tourist. Rika approached the shop, and as she pushed the door open, the scent of freshly ground coffee beans hit her nostrils. She drew in a deep breath with a broad smile on her lips.

"Has that effect, doesn't it?" a man said with a grin as he walked past, holding a steaming cup of coffee with an intricate pattern in the frothed milk floating on top.

"Sure seems to," Rika replied.

She looked over the menu and opted for a caramel latte. She had never tasted caramel before—not outside of a sim, at least—and wasn't about to pass up on this chance.

As she ordered the drink from a woman with a kind smile behind the counter, she felt a pang of guilt for the turmoil the Marauders would cause on Pyra in just a few day's time.

Unbidden, the memory of Chase being beaten once again dominated her thoughts. *Is he still there? Still slaving away in Hal's Hell while I go for sunny morning strolls, and drink my latte while planning the death of a president?*

That was months ago for him, she reminded herself. *He's recovered; he's forgotten about you, for now. Probably chasing some other girl.*

She wasn't so sure, though. He had asked her out for drinks every day for months. Chase didn't seem like the sort to give up so easily.

But where would he go to find me if he had the means to do so, which he doesn't? Even if he found out I've been bought by the Marauders, what would he do? Visit their HQ?

She didn't even know where that was. For all she knew, it was on a ship, or on some rock, floating in the interstellar void. That's the sort of place she'd always heard that mercenary outfits operated out of.

"Rika," a sweet voice said, and she turned to see the woman behind the counter holding out her drink.

"Thanks," Rika answered, and took the cup, touching it to her lips and savoring the scent before taking a taste. "Stars!" she exclaimed. "Oh, wow, that's so good."

The woman giggled. "Glad to make your day. Next, please?"

Rika realized she was holding up the line and stepped aside, taking another sip of the coffee as she walked out of the shop and back into the late morning light; all her worries about past and future already forgotten.

"Oh, stars," she whispered. "Can't this just last forever?"

* * * * *

Rika strolled down the paths in the forest to the north of the presidential palace, taking in the sights with an innocent joy that was barely an act.

Even though she was surveilling the protections the president's security had placed along President Ariana's running path, the high volume of cameras, automated turrets, and sensor systems didn't diminish the joy she felt.

Shit, if this is slavery, I'll take more of it, she thought; but then a frown creased her brow.

No, a gilded cage is still a cage.

She knew agony awaited her if she didn't get back to the warehouse by the proscribed time. That was not freedom.

The chain may be long, but it was still present.

She refocused on the task at hand. Rika knew from the intel that Team Basilisk had gathered already that the president took only one of three routes through the forest for her early morning run. However, all the routes converged at a specific point; a dozen meters beyond that point, the trail passed into a wide glen.

Rika walked through the glen, looking at the large trees that bordered it, eyeing each in turn, looking for one with the right branches in the right place.

As she reached the far side of the clearing, she spotted the perfect tree. It had a cluster of trunks that stayed close together for almost twenty meters before branching out. She could hug one of the trunks, and rest her rifle along a branch. The cloak she wore could double as camouflage, and there was mesh back in the warehouse with which to cover her GNR-41C.

She would be invisible.

Rika kept walking further down the trail, noting fallback positions and places where Jerry and Leslie could hide.

Their job would be to keep on the lookout for anyone who may compromise Rika's position—but also to finish the job, should Rika's shots not prove fatal.

That wasn't an outcome that worried Rika. She would kill President Ariana; it was a foregone conclusion.

Barne's job was the getaway. He would park a truck holding several hoverbikes nearby, and would also pay off a local bike gang to drive by the palace and throw rotten fruit at it.

Two kilometers away, there would be other transportation for them to switch to, and access to three possible safe fallbacks. She hadn't been given the location of the fallbacks yet, but Jerry had assured her that she would know about them in due time.

Rika nodded to a young couple as she walked past, giving them a warm smile. The gesture wasn't entirely disingenuous, but enough to make her feel guilty for enjoying this peaceful place, knowing that she would forever mark it as a place of mourning.

Instead of admiring the beauty of the glade, passersby would remember their beloved leader and revile her killer.

Better her than me, she thought, pushing the concern from her mind once more.

Eventually Rika left the park and took a different route back toward the warehouse, walking at the slowest pace she could manage while still giving herself a buffer, in case she ran into any trouble.

Rika hadn't bothered to mention to Jerry that receiving discipline while out in public would most certainly reveal her—and their operation. If he'd known, he probably wouldn't have let her go on her own; now that she had spent this day in paradise, she was all the more glad that she had omitted the information.

Or maybe he knew; maybe he was trusting her, allowing her to prove that she was part of the team.

Quite the risk to take.

Dusk was beginning to fall as she neared the warehouse. Everything appeared to be as it was when she left, save the positions of transport vehicles around some of the other buildings.

As Rika walked down the road, something caught her eye: a light was on in one of the warehouse's windows. Not an overhead light, but a small one, close to the glass. Rika focused on it, picking up slight pulses in its intensity.

They contained a message, which she decoded: *Intruders. Seven.*

Rika slowed her approach and casually stepped into the ferns lining the road, activating her robe's camouflage. Once hidden from sight, she ducked down behind the greenery and switched her vision to IR, followed by UV, as she scanned the perimeter for sentries.

She picked up two—one rounding a corner on the far side of the building, and another one closer, walking past the road she had been strolling down a minute earlier.

Rika remained still, praying that her robe's camouflage would fool whatever sensors the closest sentry possessed. He paused a moment and then resumed his route, heading south around the warehouse.

The robe that had hidden her form would now be a hindrance. Rika pulled it off and bundled it up before stuffing it beneath a fallen branch. The scarf and pads on her feet followed.

Thirty meters of open space lay between the warehouse and

the trees. Rika considered her options. She could run across, hoping that no one spotted her—but if whoever these people were had half a brain between them, there would be motion sensors that would pick up her movements.

She eyed the roofline, looking for a good landing spot—something that wouldn't make too much noise, or transfer vibration into the building's wooden structure.

Walking east, keeping well within the tree line, she saw a loading crane that sat ten meters from the building. That put it only twenty from cover; an easy jump even without much of a start.

Rika checked the ground and moved a few branches out of the way. Then she backed up several meters and took off at full speed. As she left the trees, she pushed off, soaring through the air and catching the crane with her still-gloved hands before swinging underneath and arcing through the air to the cornice around the roof of the warehouse.

She caught it with her clawed feet and crouched low, scanning the rooftop. No sentries were visible; though several air conditioning units blocked her vision. Rika carefully crept across the crushed rock on the roof to a staircase, which led down into the warehouse below.

It wasn't the one she'd used the night before—that one let off almost on top of where Team Basilisk had set up their base. This one would bring her down on the far side of the warehouse, a few dozen meters away.

As her hand stretched toward the door, she prayed that whoever had taken the warehouse had disabled the alarms, or her element of surprise would be gone in the next few seconds.

The door was unlocked, and as she eased it open, Rika saw that the sensors were indeed off. Analyzing the stairs leading down to the warehouse's wooden floor, she took slow, careful steps—the wooden stairs only giving two soft creaks as she went.

Given how much the old building moved and sighed as the sun set and the air cooled, she hoped it wouldn't be noticeable.

Once down the stairs, Rika ducked behind several dusty old crates and looked for movement and heat sources. Though she had spotted two sentries outside, Rika had to assume that there were at least seven within. Maybe more. Barne may not have seen the whole team when he set up the light.

An IR bloom appeared to her right, and Rika saw a woman prowling past, her eyes on the doors and windows, not looking within the warehouse. She walked within four meters of Rika and then kept going.

Rika considered taking the woman down and seizing her weapon, but she didn't want to alert the other intruders without getting a better grasp on what was happening.

Carefully moving from cover to cover, Rika crept through the warehouse, spotting two more sentries before reaching a stack of crates with a small gap between them. She peered through and saw Barne with five other figures.

Two of the intruders held Barne against a stack of crates while one of the others paced in front of him.

"You said she'd be back by now! Where is she?" the pacing one asked—a woman, though rather husky sounding. Rika wondered if she had always been a woman, or if she was in the midst of a gender change.

Barne gave his deep chuckle. "How would I know? She's just the meat. I don't talk to meat."

So much for no one calling me 'meat' yet, Rika thought.

"Well, ping her again," the woman said.

"Just did," Barne said with a shrug. "She's not answering. Maybe she ran off."

A smile formed on Rika's lips. She had received no message; maybe Barne wasn't a complete ass after all.

"Cheri got it out of Jerry that your mech girl has a compliance chip. She's not running off, and she wouldn't miss her return deadline."

Barne laughed again, leaning back against a crate. "Back in the war, I saw a mech lose its shit. AM model. It killed seventeen men and women in my regiment. The LT was hitting it with more Discipline than he ever had before, and it just kept coming. That shit is a rope, not a chain."

Rika wondered about that. She had never heard of any mechs successfully resisting Discipline; granted, she had only met a few hundred, and there had been over a hundred thousand of her kind in the war. It was probably safe to assume that tales of mechs resisting Discipline were kept hushed.

The woman continued to press Barne, and Rika took the time to examine the intruders.

Like the sentries she saw before, they wore robes—though theirs were not as advanced as the one Rika had spent her day in. Her enhanced vision traced the outlines of light armor as they moved, but the speaker's was heavier and powered to some extent.

Their weapons were multifunction rifles, capable of firing pulse rounds and projectiles. None of the intruders appeared to be carrying beam or plasma guns.

She turned and looked behind her, catching sight of one of the sentries twenty meters away. That would be her first target.

Rika crept back through the warehouse, angling toward where that sentry would be in a minute's time. She waited behind a crate, and when the sentry's boot came into view, she rose to her full height, clamped her hands around the person's head—a man, younger by the looks of him—and broke his neck in one swift twist.

She grabbed his rifle as it slipped from his lifeless fingers and looked it over. It was the same model as the ones the others carried. Rika also saw that it was biolocked.

Without an unlock kit, it would be death to grab the weapon's grip—for a human. Even so, Rika wasn't keen on the idea of shorting out her hand. Looking around, she saw some metal strapping nearby and quietly wrapped it around the weapon's grip. Holding the gun by the stock in her left hand, she took a deep breath and slipped her right hand onto the grip.

Nothing happened. She wondered if the weapon's biolock was enabled. Then sparks flew from the metal strapping wrapped around the grip, and it grew hot in her hand—not that Rika cared. Then the sparks ceased, and she carefully pulled off the strapping.

It was easier said than done, as some of the pieces had been welded together by the electrical current. Once she had them free, Rika checked the weapon's readout and realized that the pulse functionality had been fried.

No matter, she thought. *I wasn't planning on using that, anyway.*

The weapon had a mechanical firing system for the projectiles, and she checked its action, making sure that it was still functional—which it was.

Time to kick some ass.

Rika circled around to come in behind Basilisk's staging area, where the intruders were holding Barne. During her first kill and the time it had taken to make the weapon usable, the woman yelling at Barne had moved on to hitting him.

That was good news for Rika. It meant that three of them would be distracted. The remaining two—a man and a woman—were standing near the cases that her armor and weapons had been in. Rika crouched low, getting right behind them before leaping up onto the cases and stooping down.

She gave a wild scream as she grabbed the intruder on her right by the hair and pulled him off the ground, while firing three rounds into the back of the female intruder's head.

The woman fell to the ground, dead, while the man writhed in Rika's grip, his hands wrapped around her wrist.

Rika flung him straight up into the ceiling, but by some miracle he managed to hold onto her wrist. She swung her arm back down, slamming him into the ground as she jumped off the cases and landed on his chest, smashing his ribs like they were twigs.

The two guards holding Barne had seen the whole thing, and for the five seconds it had taken for two of their comrades to die, had simply stared with mouths open.

"Oh, there she is," Barne said with a laugh, as he pulled his right arm free and grabbed one of the men by the neck. Barne grunted and swung his arms together, and his two former captors slammed into one another; then one of them—Rika wasn't sure which—got a boot to the chest.

Rika had only been watching Barne with half an eye because she was busy emptying her weapon's magazine into the large woman who had been driving her fists into Barne's gut a moment before.

The rounds ricocheted off the woman's armor, and she gave a grim smile. "Gonna take a lot more than that to kill me, meat."

Rika threw the weapon aside and charged at the woman, driving both fists into her torso, and the satisfying crack of shattering armor plates reverberated up her arms.

The woman, for her part, staggered back, but didn't go down. She set her teeth, grabbed Rika's forearms, and delivered a powered kick to Rika's gut.

The blow pushed Rika back, but she was on the woman a moment later, grabbing both of her arms. Rika rotated her wrists, twisting them nearly all the way around—one of the benefits of being less than human—until she heard two loud cracks, and the woman began screaming.

The sounds were like music to Rika as she planted a foot on the woman's chest—her three claws digging into the cracks that her initial blows had caused. Her heel claw drove through the cracked plate and the under-layer, sinking into the woman's gut.

Rika took a deep breath, straightened her leg, and pulled the woman's arms off. Her enemy fell to the ground, and Rika planted her other foot on the woman's chest, tearing her chest plate off.

"I. Am. Not. Fucking. *MEAT!*" Rika screamed, and slammed her foot into the woman's chest while tearing the other free, pulling a string of intestines out into the air.

"Holy shit," Barne whispered from behind her.

Rika turned to see Barne standing over the two men who had

been holding him back, his eyes locked on the pair of arms she still held.

"What?" Rika asked, her voice still filled with rage. "Don't like your rescue?"

"Uh…no…" Barne stammered. "I just haven't seen anything like that since…"

"The war," Rika said with a nod. "Guess the war's not over yet, is it?"

"I don't know what that means, but could you put those arms down? They're creeping me out."

Shots rang out and ricocheted off Rika's armor. Barne ducked down behind a crate, but Rika turned, catching sight of three more enemies closing in. Her IR and UV blend also picked up the two sentries from outside entering through the north and south doors.

The closest attacker was twenty meters away, and Rika rushed toward him brandishing the arms she still held, as the assailant fired before ducking behind a crate for cover.

It didn't help.

Rika slammed into the crate at full speed and pushed it back against another stack, crushing the man in between. She strode around to see him struggling to get up, his right arm hanging limp at his side.

Wordlessly, she swung one of the severed arms, striking him in the head, before grabbing him by the throat with her foot and tearing him free from the crates. At the apex of her swing, she let go, and he flew headfirst into a nearby support pole.

She wasn't certain if he died before or after he hit the pole, but as his twitching body landed on the floor, she knew it didn't matter.

Gunfire sounded from Barne's position, and responses came from two locations.

<Thanks for the rifle,> Barne said.

<You're welcome. Let me know if you need me to come and rescue you again.>

<Fuck off.>

<That's more like it,> Rika replied.

Rika selected her next target—the sentry entering through the south door—and ran toward her. The woman didn't fare any better than the rest had.

Rika circled around the enemies in the warehouse, getting behind the one furthest from Barne, who was trying to move into a flanking position.

She smashed the farthest sentry's head. Barne opened fire once more, and then stopped and called out that he was clear.

Rika returned to Barne's position. "You got two?" she asked.

"Yeah," Barne said with a nod, as he dropped the rifle and walked over to one of their supply crates.

"So Cheri sent them, did she?" Rika asked.

"Yup," Barne said with a grunt, and pulled out a tank of light brown liquid. "Bring all the bodies over here; we have to clean up."

"'Clean up'?" Rika asked.

"Yeah, we have to get out of here, and we can't leave it like this."

<Get out of here to go rescue Jerry and Leslie, right?> Rika asked as she stalked off to grab bodies.

<Yeah, but first we dissolve these dickheads. Then we load up all our gear onto a truck, and burn this place to the ground.>

<Won't that look suspicious?>

She grabbed two of the closest bodies and carried them back to where Barne had pulled all the equipment out of a case and was pouring the liquid into it.

"Nope, the crates on the far side of this warehouse are fireworks. We'll just set something up so it looks like a spark from a truck started it, and then we'll watch, well, the fireworks."

"What are fireworks?" Rika asked, walking away once more.

<What…seriously? The things people shoot up into the sky that go boom and then rain sparks down everywhere.>

<Sounds like you're describing AA guns or something.>

<Kinda. They're old school, but these Thebans seem to like old-school.>

<I've noticed.>

Rika gathered all the bodies and then walked to the east side of the warehouse where she had spotted a cleaning closet. Inside, there was a hose and some cleaning supplies. Rika spent the next twenty minutes getting the bits of bone, blood, and hair out of her armor.

<Be back in a minute. Just need to go get my robe,> she informed Barne.

<Get a truck while you're at it,> he replied.

<Do you have the codes for it?> Rika asked.

<No, I said get ***a*** *truck, not get* ***the*** *truck; Jerry and Leslie took ours. Steal another one.>*

Rika sighed. *Have a nice stroll through the city, enjoy a latte and a walk through the woods…check. Kill a bunch of people, dissolve their bodies, and steal a truck…double check.*

She grabbed a hack unit from the staging area before walking outside, and carefully surveyed their surroundings. By some miracle, the commotion within the warehouse didn't appear to have drawn any attention. Rika didn't see another person as she retrieved her robe and pulled it on, wrapping the shawl around her head once more.

The cluster of warehouses had no shortage of trucks, though most were too big for their needs. Something with a box only eight meters long was preferable.

Rika was walking around the fourth building when she spotted the perfect candidate: a white box truck with no markings on it whatsoever. She pulled the lock off the back and lifted the rear roller door. A bench ran along each side of the interior, and duffels filled the space in between.

<I think I found our visitors' truck. It'll do perfectly.>

<Great. Bring it around to the dock and start loading our stuff up. I'm about half done, but we'll have to take their armor with us. Stuff won't melt down.>

Rika walked around the truck and opened the driver's door. She pulled out the hack unit and then slapped it on the truck's control panel. The Marauders' tech was good. Thirty seconds later, the truck started, and Rika climbed in and drove the truck to their warehouse's loading docks.

It occurred to Rika, as she pulled the truck up to the building, that this was the first time she'd ever driven anything with wheels.

It was strange to feel it bounce and jostle over the uneven pavement, but it also gave her a sense of power. It took her two tries to back it up to the dock, and then just fifteen minutes to load all of Basilisk's gear.

"You're pretty damn fast at that," Barne said as she approached where he was carefully pushing the last body into his makeshift vat of acid.

"I have a lot of experience," Rika replied. "Why do you use acid for that? Can't you get nano to do it better?"

Barne nodded. "Yeah, but it's hard enough getting what we need planetside for missions like this—like your rifle's rounds. Acid, we can source locally and make out of stuff that no one will wonder about."

Rika nodded silently, watching one of the attacker's faces dissolve. She knew that she should feel something—be sad, angry, something.

Mostly she just felt disappointed. Disappointed that she had killed so viciously, disappointed that her perfect day had ended like this.

She had noticed, however, that Barne hadn't said a single insulting thing to her since the fight. It seemed like he couldn't decide to be wary of her, or grateful that she had saved him.

"Can you help me with this?" he asked as he closed the case. "There's a drain over where you cleaned off. We can pour this down, and rinse it out."

"Sure," Rika said, and lifted the case, carrying it over to where Barne had directed.

"I gotta ask," Barne said from behind her. "Why did you save me? I didn't order you to."

Rika set the case down next to the drain and shrugged. "I don't know…it never occurred to me to do anything but help you. I know you don't really want me here, but I'm on the team." She gave him a slight smile. "Even if it's like how your rifle's on the team."

Barne's face reddened as he opened the crate and carefully drained its contents.

"I'm sorry about that. I can be a bit of an ass sometimes."

"A bit?" Rika asked with an arched eyebrow.

Barne laughed, "OK, a lot. And probably more often than 'sometimes'."

"How bad do you think they're hurt?" Rika asked, changing the subject. No point in making Barne feel like she was going to forgive him just yet.

Barne grabbed the hose and began spraying out the case. "Hopefully not too bad. Jerry's sweet on Leslie, and if Cheri's worth her salt, she probably picked up on it. A few good bruises and cuts on Leslie, and Jerry probably spilled it."

"Shit, I thought he'd let her take a bit more punishment before he ratted us out."

It was Barne's turn to give her a raised brow. "He wanted to make sure they hit me here before you came back. That way *you* would have the element of surprise, not them. He knew I could take whatever that woman had to dish out."

"So you don't think he ratted us out?"

"No," Barne replied. "He wanted us to live so we could come save them. Which is why I'm so glad you decided not to make a run for it. Looks like his trust in you wasn't misplaced."

"I guess I have a trustworthy face," Rika said with a smile.

"Or something. Just don't shriek again, like you did when you tore that woman's arms off. Scared the shit out of me."

Rika laughed and clapped Barne on the shoulder. "Good, I think you could use a little less shit in you."

THE ROMANY

STELLAR DATE: 12.16.8948 (Adjusted Years)
LOCATION: Enlisted Commissary, MSS *Romany*
REGION: Interstellar Space, near the Praesepe Cluster

Chase settled into his seat in the *Romany*'s commissary and eyed what the cooks were trying to trick him into eating. It looked like steak and eggs, but he doubted that the Marauder ship had enough steak to feed their entire crew such a meal.

"Wondering what the mystery is with the meat?" a voice said from across the table, and Chase looked up to see Ralph—one of the squad sergeants from Chase's new platoon—settle into the seat across from him.

"Aren't you?" Chase asked.

"Nah, we're just out of port; it'll be the real thing. Once we're a week in, then you can start to worry about what the protein really came from."

Chase stabbed a fork into one of the steak tips and gave it a tentative bite. "Damn! This *is* real meat…or such a good fake that I don't care."

"Oh, you'll know when they start faking it," Sergeant Casey said as she sat next to Ralph. "We've got good cooks, but they're not that good."

Chase took another bite and shook his head. He'd never expected to be sitting on a warship, talking about how shitty—or how good, in this case—the chow was with his 'toon-mates again, but here he was.

For a woman, he thought to himself.

But he knew that was oversimplifying things. Rika wasn't just any woman; she was *the* woman. He was going to find her, and then…and then they'd figure something out.

"What do you know about where we jumped to?" Chase asked.

Ralph shrugged, but Casey gave a conspiratorial smile. "Command's not talking, but I can recognize the stars out there, easy. We're still in the Praesepe Cluster."

"That's not saying much," Chase replied.

"Well, what if I said that we're on the rimward edge of the cluster…and that we jumped very close to a system?"

"Still not following," Chase said with a shake of his head, but Ralph exclaimed, "Thebes!"

"Got it in one!" Casey grinned at Ralph. "Thebes is key. Powerful, small; some might say it's ripe."

"We're attacking a sovereign nation?" Chase asked, his eyes wide. From what he knew of mercenary outfits, they disrupted trade routes, harassed settlements, or operated as hired security. But he had never really thought about them being part of an invasion force.

He wasn't sure that it sat well with him. Still, he supposed it was better than oppressing civilians on some backwater world. An invasion force would at least be fighting a military.

"What's wrong, Chase?" Ralph asked. "You look like you just ate something that didn't agree with you."

"Just thinking about what the action might involve."

Casey shrugged. "Hard to say. For all intents and purposes, the Marauders are pretty new—even though we have a large force. The Old Man has been selective in what jobs he's taken, but it's usually stuff that will piss off the Niets in some way or another."

"Plus a few jobs for the Septhians here and there," Ralph added.

"Yeah," Chase said with a nod. "They covered some of that in orientation. "But they didn't say anything about taking on something like the Theban Alliance. I kinda thought we'd be going after bad guys."

Casey shook her head. "Seriously, Chase. You were in the Genevian Armed Forces. Can you really say that there were 'bad guys' in that last war? Sure, the Nietzscheans were—and are—

raging assholes, but our government wasn't exactly sunshine and roses, either."

Chase didn't reply—his thoughts were on Rika and what his own government had done to her. She had never told him any stories from the war, but he knew what the mechs were made to do. Any mech that made it to the end of the war had a lot of blood on their souls.

"Not to mention that our fleet admirals were built from buckets full of stupid," Ralph added.

"I'm curious," Chase said, pulling his thoughts away from what Rika might be doing at that moment. "How did the Old Man get so many ships, anyway? He wasn't in Fleet Command. He was ground assault, right?"

"Right-o," Ralph said. "I was in his division back in the war. We kicked a lot of Nietzschean ass, but we kept losing because we had no space-support. Slowly, as dumbass fleet commanders got blown into space-dust, the General drew more and more ships under his direct control. Even though he wasn't fleet command, he was the senior officer after a lot of losses.

"He was good; could do more with twenty ships than some admirals could manage with a thousand. So, the top brass let him keep them. Gotta say, it was nice knowing that if you needed to call down starfire, it would hit."

"There were a lot more than twenty ships outside when we jumped here," Chase said.

"A lot of people didn't just lay down arms when the government surrendered," Casey said. "Some joined the Marauders. Plus, there are two other outfits I know of that are made up of Genevian ships and soldiers."

"I heard a lot went pirate, too," Chase said. "Mind you, I was inside the Nietzschean Empire. They're not subtle with the propaganda, and I didn't buy most of it, but I still didn't expect so much organization. I just figured that most defectors were solo operations, hitting soft targets for supplies and credit."

Ralph nodded. "Yeah, there are a lot of solo ships out there;

people who think that they can make a difference on their own. Every few months, a handful come to the Marauders with their tails between their legs. Old Man takes 'em in, but he breaks their crews up to integrate them. At the beginning, a few took advantage of his refit and resupply and then took off again."

"Bastards," Chase said. "I may be new here, but I can appreciate what the Old Man is building. Maybe if he'd been in charge of the Genevian Space Force, we'd still have a nation."

Ralph raised his glass of milk. "I'll drink to that. Maybe someday we'll kick the shit out of the Niets and get it back, too."

The three touched their plastic cups, though Casey shook her head. "I don't want Genevia back, but if the Old Man were to set up a little corner of space under himself, I would settle down there."

"So," Ralph said after he downed his milk. "What is it that got you to enlist? Got tired of living in Niet-land?"

"You could say that," Chase said. "I wasn't like you two; when the orders came down to surrender, we just had our asses handed to us. The ship's captain turned off the shields, and allowed us to be boarded. I was pissed—more than pissed. I'd just watched half my platoon die, and he was just giving up. Some of the crew fought when the Niets boarded us; I would have, if I could have gotten to a weapon in time…."

"Heard a lot of stories like that," Casey said. "What happened?"

"They tossed the whole lot of us onto Mortlach. Took me half a year to get off that shithole."

"Damn! You got off Mortlach?" Ralph asked, his eyes wide. "Half our freaking people are still down there."

"Yeah, how'd you swing that?" Casey asked.

Chase shrugged. He knew, but he wasn't ready to share it yet, so he related his customary story.

"They were letting people off for a while. Since I didn't fight the boarding, I was on the 'good' list. I'll be honest…it made me sick to leave. So many left behind."

Ralph and Casey nodded in agreement.

"Maybe someday..." Ralph said again.

Casey snorted. "Don't get your hopes up, Ralph. It would take the overthrow of the Nietzschean Empire to get our people off Mortlach."

"A guy can dream, can't he?" Ralph asked.

From the faraway look in his eyes, Chase wondered if there was someone down on Mortlach that Ralph was holding onto hope for. Not that there was much hope to be had, with a place like that.

"So, Chase...nice little bit of evasion there, but you were dicking around out there for years. Coulda joined the Marauders long ago. Why now?"

Chase figured it would slip out some time. "Looking for someone."

"Oh, yeah?" Ralph's eyes lit up, and the eagerness in his voice solidified Chase's earlier suspicion. "Who's the lucky girl?"

"What makes you think it's a girl...or even romantic?" Chase asked, not entirely comfortable discussing his search for Rika with people he had just met a day prior.

Casey chuckled. "It's a girl because you've glanced at a couple of the prettier Marauders to pass us by, and may have let your eyes linger on my tits; though I'll give you a pass since I spilled gravy on them when you did it—"

"You got nice tits," Ralph interjected with a grin. "I glance at 'em all the time."

"Yeah, Ralph, you have the subtlety of a supernova; I kinda notice. Plus, I have to keep a napkin handy for the drool."

Ralph took on a wounded look while Casey leveled a stare at Chase.

"It's good to know your teammate's motivations. Helps them bond," Casey said. "OK, we know it's a girl, and suspect your interest is romantic. Where is this girl, that you'd join up with the Marauders to find her?"

As Casey spoke, a look of understanding dawned on Ralph.

"Casey! Chase's girl is *in* the Marauders!"

Casey snapped her fingers. "By the Old Man's wrinkly ass, I think you're right! Look at Chase, red as a tomato!"

"Don't talk about tomatoes," Ralph said with a shudder. "I fought on Boston where they have those freakish tomato forests. Fucking juice off the stems could peel the camo layer off your armor. And house-sized tomatoes? Are you fucking kidding me? Some things just can't be unseen."

"Seriously, Ralph? They were just plants. I fought on Boston, too," Chase said.

"Don't change the subject again," Ralph shot back. "The girl. Who is she? Is she on the *Romany*?"

Chase sighed and shook his head. "Not that I've seen. She's not on the roster, and no one knows anything about her; before I enlisted, though…well, let's just say that I have it on very good authority that she's in the Marauders."

"Name," Ralph said.

"Yeah, tell him," Casey said around a mouthful of eggs. "Ralph knows everyone, and if he doesn't know 'em, he knows someone who does."

"Rika," Chase said. "Her name's Rika."

"What's her specialization—if she has one?" Ralph asked.

"She's a mech," Chase replied, his tone guarded.

"Really?" Casey sat up.

"What model?" Ralph asked with a look of concentration on his face as he reached out across the Link.

Chase hated that people thought of mechs—well, Rika mostly—as models. Even if it was a good way to identify them.

"She's an SMI-2," Chase replied.

"Ohhh yeah," Ralph grinned. "SMI-2s were all chicks; they were some hot meat."

Chase felt the blood rise in his face once more. "Ralph, you seem like a good guy, but if you call Rika 'meat' one more time, I'll cave your teeth in, got it?"

"Dude—" Ralph began to say, but Casey put a hand on his

shoulder.

"Cool it. Both of you. Ralph, apologize. Chase, ease up on the macho reactions, 'kay?" Casey said.

Ralph sank back in his chair and stared at Chase—who returned the expression. Suddenly Ralph smiled and nodded.

"Sorry, man. You're right. I picked up a lot of bad habits in the war. We were all meat to the brass. Mechs saved my life more than once, too. You'll never hear that word pass my lips again, unless I'm talking about our delicious victuals, here."

Chase was surprised by Ralph's words—the man's recognition of his misstep shaming Chase for having such a visceral reaction.

"Me too. I just really want to find her. I'm worried we're going to get into some crazy action here and one of us won't make it out."

"No chance," Casey said. "Marauders do the fucking-up of shit, not the other way around."

Ralph let out a sound that was half snort, half laugh. "Casey, that has to be the worst metaphor I've ever heard."

"We turn the enemy into shit fuckers?" Casey asked.

"I vote that we abandon all analogies combining fucking and shit," Chase said. "How's about 'we rub their faces in shit'?"

"For fuck's sake!" a woman said from a few seats down. "People are trying to eat, here!"

"Sorry," Chase muttered.

"Either way," Casey said. "Now that Ralph's on the case, he'll ferret her out. Not a lot of mechs in the Marauders. People will have seen her."

Ralph grinned and nodded. "Sergeant Ralph is on the case. I'll find your smecksy mech girl in no time! I might have to extract payment with some leering, and maybe a bit of drooling, mind you."

"Way to own your misogyny, Ralph," Casey said.

Chase couldn't help but smile at Ralph's enthusiastic grin. "You're a class act, Ralph. Seriously, though, I appreciate it. Finding Rika is...well...I just have to do it."

RESCUE

STELLAR DATE: 12.16.8948 (Adjusted Years)
LOCATION: Northeast Berlin
REGION: Pyra, Albany System, Theban Alliance

The fireworks had been amazing. Rika had stared out the truck's window at them for a full five minutes before fire drones finally arrived and began putting them out.

She imagined that they must be even more impressive in the sky than on the ground.

News feeds on the local nets had been abuzz about the fire, but there was no mention of anything suspicious about it—though it was far too soon to tell. Rika doubted that inspectors would be able to start crawling through the mess until the next day.

Barne drove the truck several kilometers and then parked it in a garage next to another, equally nondescript truck—though this one was black. Together, he and Rika swapped all their cargo over and swept the truck clean. Barne had informed her that it was long-term storage parking, and that he'd rented the space till the end of the month.

They would be long gone by then.

The drive to the next location was short, just ten minutes, and they pulled into another warehouse area before reaching a self-storage lot.

"We going to set up shop here?" Rika asked.

"No," Barne replied as he opened the storage unit's door, revealing a smaller car.

By the time he had driven the car out, and she had parked the truck in the storage unit—which it just barely fit into—Howe was beginning to rise in the eastern sky.

"I haven't asked, because I assumed you had a plan, but how are we going to get to wherever Cheri is?" Rika asked. "Jerry said it was halfway around the world."

"He was exaggerating," Barne replied as he leaned against the car. "It's near Jersey City—about seventeen hundred klicks up the coast. They have high-speed highways here, and this baby can do four hundred an hour. We'll be there by lunchtime."

Rika nodded and opened the back of the truck, and then she jumped up and opened a crate. She tossed two rifles down to Barne, followed by a duffel bag full of ammunition. She turned to another case and opened it up, pulling out her gun-arm and helmet.

"You think you'll need that?" Barne asked as she jumped out and pulled down the truck's overhead door.

"Maybe. I'd like to keep them close."

"Sounds reasonable," Barne replied with a shrug.

Five minutes later, they were pulling onto the highway, the car sliding onto a high-speed maglev ridge and accelerating to top speed.

Rika opened up a panel on her leg and pulled out her charge cord, sliding it into one of the power sockets in the car.

"Glad it has that," she said. "Wouldn't want to go into our big rescue with only half a charge."

Barne gave a soft laugh. "I know what you mean…I don't have to plug in—not modded enough for that—but I do need to eat a ton to keep going."

"Speaking of which," Rika reached into the back and grabbed a fistful of protein bars, dumping half in Barne's lap.

"Thanks…" he said, a pregnant pause hanging between them.

Rika didn't want to spend the next four hours in an uncomfortable silence, so she asked, "What is it?"

"Well," Barne began. "What's it like? I mean, I'll be honest—you were kinda sour and mopey at first. But in a fight…I've never seen anything like it. You just charged them like their guns were shooting spitwads."

"Well, in my defense, I woke up in that warehouse only minutes after being sold at auction—by my reckoning," Rika replied. "I was feeling just a bit down. Shit...that was still just over two days ago for me."

"At auction?" Barne shook his head. "I had no idea..."

"Is one form of selling a slave somehow more dignified than another?" Rika asked, her tone acidic.

"I guess not," Barne said. "But I hadn't really thought about how the regiment got you. I figured they had you in a warehouse at HQ or something."

"Yeah, back to miniscule differentiations of humiliation."

"Sorry...you don't have to be such a bitch to me about it. *I* didn't chop you up and sell you off after the war." Barne's face took on a pouty frown, and Rika realized that she was punishing Barne for what others had done to her.

"Gah. I'm not good at this, Barne. Personal interaction and I are not close friends."

"You too, eh?" Barne said, and then laughed. "Look at the two of us—both shithead messes after the war, barely able to talk to anyone, and stuck together in here."

Barne continued laughing, and Rika joined in, letting the cathartic release calm her down. Eventually, when they were silent once more, Barne glanced over at her.

"You didn't really answer the question."

"Which question?" Rika asked, knowing full well what he was referring to.

"About what it's like. What they did to you."

Rika looked down at herself, at her steel limbs, at her three-fingered hands.

"I won't lie," she said. "There are times when it's wonderful. The power, the speed—they're intoxicating."

"You like killing," Barne said quietly. "I saw it in your eyes. Don't try to bullshit me. I know the look; it stares back at me in the mirror every day."

Rika didn't respond for a minute. Then two. Then five. She wondered if Barne was going to let it drop, but knew he wouldn't. She knew she shouldn't.

"There are two Rikas," she said at last. "There's a Rika who just *stopped* that night when they took me, when they made me into this...machine. That Rika would give anything to go back to how things were—hell, she's still just a nineteen-year-old girl. I can't stop her from wanting to go back to before—she craves it constantly. But there's this other Rika. The one that came out on the battlefield, the one that survived the war, when so many others didn't..."

Rika closed her eyes, and the vision of Kelly—her friend laying before her on the deck of the shuttle with a hole blown clear through her torso—came back to her.

"I know that guilt," Barne said.

"Yeah, all the psych programs go on about survivor's guilt," Rika said. "But they don't tell you what to do with the other feeling..."

"The joy you get from killing," Barne said.

"Is it joy?" Rika asked. "For me it's just rage; I want to make them all pay for what they did to me—for what they took. But maybe...maybe you're right, Barne." Rika let out a long sigh. "Maybe there is joy mixed with that rage."

Barne nodded, silent for a minute. "I don't know if it's wrong or not, Rika. But it's what we are now. We're killers, you and me. Why don't you rest a bit? We'll be killing again soon enough."

Rika closed her eyes and leaned her head back. A killer. That's all Barne saw when he looked at her; it was all he had ever seen. The only difference was that now, she had killed to save him.

Maybe he was right. She was on Pyra to kill. Though she had spent her day enjoying a lovely walk, its purpose had been to help her kill more effectively. Even the rescue they were about to undertake—even if it was bloodless—was just so they could kill once more.

Killer....

*****

The sun was beginning to set as she and Barne settled behind a rock to survey Cheri's 'hideout'. Though it only took a few hours to reach Jersey City, it had taken several more to get deep into the nearby mountains and make their way up the steep valley without being seen.

"How come this Cheri person gets a nice villa at the foot of a mountain, and we had to hang out in a dusty warehouse?" Rika asked.

"Covert mission," Barne said. "Cheri doesn't seem to be doing the 'covert' thing, here."

"Barne, I was kidding," Rika said.

"Huh, musta been your robot voice."

Rika opened her mouth to give Barne a tongue-lashing he would never forget, when she saw the twinkle in his eye.

"Asshole," she said, and gave him a mock punch on the arm.

"Ow! Shit, Rika, even your pretend punches hurt like balls. Ease up, OK?"

"Sorry-not-sorry," Rika replied in a robotic voice.

Barne chuckled. "Now who's the asshole?"

Rika shook her head and allowed a small smile to grace her lips. If someone had told her that two days after being sold at auction she would be smiling—with the people who had bought her, no less—she would have slapped them upside the head. And not in a nice way.

Is this Stockholm Syndrome? she wondered. *I never felt this way about the GAF…I hated them. Well, most of them.*

She made a note to have her internal psych-eval program check for Stockholm the next time she ran it. For now, getting Jerry and Leslie out of that rather nice-looking villa was all that mattered.

The question Barne had asked echoed in her mind once more. Why *had* she saved him? Sure, there were all the issues with getting offworld, and where she would go without the help of Basilisk. That was all logical and fine; but Rika knew she hadn't thought of any of that when she saw his warning in the window.

She'd had a teammate in trouble, and she had to rescue that teammate. Was that some sort of leftover conditioning from the military, or was she just so desperate to belong somewhere that she'd side with her owners?

"Hey, Rika, you with me?" Barne asked.

"Yeah, sorry."

"Enough dicking around. Time to get frosty. I can see seven sentries, what's your count?"

"I see eleven—make that twelve."

Barne and Rika had parked the car further down the valley, and hiked the last few kilometers to the villa. Since it was rather secluded, they decided to go in packing. Rika had spent the last two hours of the car ride adjusting the socket and mount on her gun-arm, so that she was able to place it on her right arm. It felt good to have it there. Even better, since it was the GNR-41C, and not the old B she used to have.

A JE78 multifunction rifle was on her back, and two pistols were slid into the clips on her thighs.

But the icing on the cake was her helmet. It was an older model, the one used by SMI-1 mechs. It only had two-seventy vision; not the three-sixty of her SMI-2 helmet from the war, but it fit. That helmet had only fit so long as the wearer didn't possess a nose or ears.

Given the fact that she had spent a lot of credit getting those features back, she was glad not to have to sacrifice them again.

Her hair, however, had been a different matter. It had taken several tries to get the helmet on and sealed without blonde strands sticking out around her neck, causing the seal-leak warning to flash.

In the end, she had lain down on a log with her head hanging off, while Barne carefully placed her hair in the helmet, and then raised it up to her head.

That was, of course, after joking that they should just shave it all off. He had almost called her 'mech-meat' at the time, but stopped himself, a look of apology on his face.

She hadn't made a big deal about it. He wasn't swearing at her, and calling her military hardware anymore, so she'd take what progress she could get.

Now as she watched the sentries through her helmet's enhanced sensors, she remembered how good it felt to have the extra senses it provided. She could hear animals in the brush two hundred paces away, see through haze and fog clear to the edge of the horizon, and even see through some of the walls in the villa.

"What's our plan, then?" Rika asked.

"Not sure," Barne replied. "I estimate we could take out five or six of those sentries before they figured out what was going on. But then they'll be on high alert. I bet there are at least forty or fifty of them in there, and they probably have no small number of automated defense systems, as well."

"Want to do something crazy?" Rika asked with a sly grin.

"How crazy?' Barne asked.

* * * * *

An hour later, Rika stood with Barne on the mountain slope, a kilometer above the villa.

"Let me get this straight, you want me to get on your back?" Barne asked.

"Yeah. You get on, and I'll run down the mountain. There's an escarpment sixty meters from the villa. Running downhill, I can probably hit one-fifty before we get there. Then I jump, we sail over everything, and—if I aim well—we smash right through that glass ceiling in the back."

"So your plan is to run down the mountain and jump into the villa," Barne said. "That's crazy."

Rika nodded. "Yes, I said that before we climbed up here. What did you think we were going to do?"

"I don't know, I figured you saw a secret door with your fancy helmet."

"Wouldn't that be nice," Rika laughed. "OK, climb on."

"This is the dumbest thing I've ever done," Barne complained, as he clambered up onto her back and wrapped his arms around her neck.

"I *really* doubt that this is the dumbest thing *you've* done," Rika said.

"At least you're sexy," he said morosely. "If you were a guy mech, I'd never live this down."

Rika wanted to tell Barne to shove his backhanded compliments up his asshole, but he might like that too much, so she let it drop.

"Hold on tight!" Rika said instead, and began her run down the mountain. She wove around rocks and trees, careful not to jostle Barne overmuch. Her speed crossed over a hundred, and then a hundred and fifty kilometers per hour. The edge of the escarpment rushed toward her, and Rika leapt off it at nearly one hundred and seventy kilometers per hour.

She gauged her trajectory and saw that her aim was true. The glass ceiling on a rear room of the villa's main structure rushed up to meet them, and they smashed through it and slammed into the room's floor.

Barne leapt off her the instant they broke through the glass and landed nearby, rolling to his feet, the medium armor he wore helping to absorb the shock.

The sensors in Rika's helmet, coupled with her neural augments, gave her a full layout of the room by the time she landed—and smashed a rather expensive-looking table.

Two men were standing near one of the doors, both looking surprised, though still raising their rifles.

Rika shot one with a ballistic round from her GNR-41C, while Barne took out the other.

<*Which way?*> Barne asked over the tightband they had established. So long as they were close or in line of sight, the signal would be very difficult to pick up, and they would run little risk of detection.

Rika swept her active scan across the room and saw a cluster of people sixty meters to their right.

<*A big group that way,*> she said, gesturing to a door that led in the general direction they needed to go.

Barne ran to the door, flattened himself against the wall, and then reached out and turned the knob. Rika leapt through into the hall beyond, her GNR pointed right, and her JE78 covering the left.

<*Clear,*> she announced and turned to her left, walking quietly down the hall toward an intersection. She reached it and scanned the area again, picking up movement in the corridor to their right—the direction they needed to go.

She nodded to Barne and he moved to the other side of the hall, holding his rifle ready.

He had visual before she did and opened fire, taking out two enemies in seconds.

<*They're not armored. She must really trust her perimeter security,*> Rika said.

<*Or she's just cheap. Why give your goons good armor when you can sell it?*>

<*The more you tighten your grip, the more slips through your fingers.*>

<*Sounds about right,*> Barne replied as he peered down the left hall.

Rika moved down the right, and Barne followed after, covering their six. Behind them, the sound of raised voices came from the room they had crashed into, and Rika picked up the pace, not wanting to be caught in a crossfire.

Ahead, a door opened and three guards rushed out. None had their weapons ready, and Rika made short work of them.

At two more intersections, Rika paused to listen and scan, each time leading them further into the south wing of the villa.

<*Just ahead,*> Rika said, gesturing to a set of double doors at the end of the hall.

<*Behind us!*> Barne replied, and fired a trio of rounds at a pair

of guards that had darted across the hall behind them. <*Looks like reinforcements are catching up.*>

Rika flipped her GNR to its electron beam mode. The next time one of the guards leaned out to take a shot, she fired.

A straight line of blue lightning streaked down the hall—a nimbus glow of blue cherenkov radiation further emblazoning its passage. It hit the guard square in the chest and burned a hole right through him. Lightning arced all around his body, blowing out the overhead lighting and setting a wall on fire.

<*Showoff,*> Barne said as he kept an eye out for more pursuers.

Rika turned back to the doors at the end of the hall. She could pick up five figures on the other side of them. Two seemed to be seated, with another one nearby. Another pair was on either side of the doors.

She took aim at the figure on the left side of the door and fired her electron beam again. The force of the electrons travelling a hair under the speed of light blew a hole right through the wall and the person beyond. Rika smiled as the wall splintered, and the left-side door groaned before the top hinge came free and fell to the ground. Rika peered around the door to see Leslie and Jerry strapped to a pair of steel chairs in the center of the room.

Behind them stood a tall woman with mousy brown hair. She wore a cozy-looking red sweater, navy leggings, and fuzzy white slippers. If she was the nefarious Cheri, her wardrobe did not mirror the reputation.

The guard on the right side of the door moved into view, and Rika fired a ballistic round from her GNR, taking the top of his head off.

"Rika! No!" Leslie cried out as Rika stepped into the room. Barne was close behind, taking up position behind the remaining door, watching the hall to their rear.

The woman punched Leslie in the back of the head—a blow that was well delivered, and Leslie's eyes grew unfocused.

"So, you're the great Rika," the woman said. "These two have told me a lot about you."

Rika looked at Leslie and Jerry. Jerry's mouth was covered by a gag, but other than that, he looked OK. Leslie had a few bruises and a chunk of her hair was missing, but she didn't appear to have any broken bones that Rika's quick scan could see.

"And you must be Cheri," Rika said cautiously. "I have to admit, I'm a bit underwhelmed here."

The woman didn't even have a weapon. Rika raised her GNR but Leslie pulled her head up straight and cried out. "Rika, run! She has the Discipline codes."

Cold dread washed over her. The moment the GNR pointed at Cheri, a spike of Discipline hit Rika, and she lowered the weapon.

"That's better," Cheri said. "Getting your location was easy; too easy, if I know Jerry, here—which I do. Still, I sent Gamine in with a team to see if they could pull it off. I suspected that Gamine couldn't manage, but then I'd still get what I wanted: you. Except you'd deliver yourself, all nice and tidy. Gamine was getting a bit too big for her britches, so it was really a win-win for me."

Rika took a step back. "How?"

"How did I get the Discipline codes from Jerry?" Cheri asked as she stroked Jerry's head. "Oh, I just used a nifty little tool I got a while ago. It breached his neural security and extracted the code from his mind. It was easy to find; people always try not to think about the thing they want to hide the most, but in reality, it's all they think about."

Rika shook her head in denial. "No, there's just no way…"

Cheri's eyes narrowed. "Rika. Kill Barne."

The words flowed into her mind like ice water, and the tingle of Discipline grew stronger. She turned to Barne and saw true fear on his face as he stepped away from her.

"Rika, no, please," he said, raising his rifle.

She darted forward, swatted the gun out of his hand, and reached for his throat. But she couldn't bring herself to hurt this ass of a man. He was her friend—she hoped he was, at least.

Rika pulled her hand back, gritted her teeth, and lowered her head. She remembered what Barne had said, about mechs that somehow fought Discipline.

She turned to Cheri.

"No."

This time it was Cheri who looked concerned. Though it was just for a moment; then a wicked smile crossed her lips. "Rika, Kill Barne now. That's an order."

Even before Cheri had spoken, the Discipline sent searing pain into her mind. But not just her mind—it made her entire body feel like it was on fire. Like her skin was melting off, and the only way to put it out was with Barne's blood.

Blood she would not spill.

The pain brought her to her knees and she gasped for air, fighting against the searing agony. Still, she managed to raise her head, and she stared into Cheri's grey eyes.

"No!"

The Discipline hit her harder this time, tearing at her mind, bringing unimaginable agony. It was as though white-hot knives were in her brain, slicing away every part her, cutting her to pieces.

The pain subsided for a moment and she gasped for air, realizing that she was now sprawled on the ground with her JE78 a meter away. She wondered when she had dropped it.

"Rika!" Cheri yelled. "Kill Barne *now!*"

Rika glanced to her right. Barne still stood weaponless, and she wondered why he hadn't made a move to grab his rifle and kill Cheri. She was unarmed; it would only take a second.

Maybe he wanted to see if she had the strength. Or maybe he worried that killing Cheri wouldn't erase her last standing order—which it probably wouldn't.

Crippling waves of pain wracked Rika's body, but somehow she managed to get back up to her knees.

She whispered, "No."

Then she got her feet under her, and managed a crouch.

"No!"

Cheri kept screaming at Rika to kill Barne, to kill Leslie, Jerry, all three; but Rika barely heard it at all. What she did hear was Barne give a soft laugh behind her.

"I knew you had it in you, girl. Go get her."

Something snapped in Rika's mind. The compliance chip was still functioning, still delivering its debilitating waves of pain, but somehow it didn't hurt anymore. Instead, the pain had become power; a rage that had been building ever since that dickhead technician named Jack had gleefully assembled her, and used the compliance chip and its Discipline to control her.

Years of *real* pain and anger gave her strength to fight against the artificial agony.

Rika sprang forward, flying over Jerry and Leslie to land behind the woman who was now the focus of all her rage. Rika stretched out her arm, the motion feeling slow in her pain-fueled rage, and snapped Cheri's neck.

She expected the pain to stop, but it didn't. It seemed to get worse—something she had not thought possible. Rika realized that her heart rate and blood pressure were both dangerously high. She fell to her knees, looking up to see Barne rushing forward to tear the gag from Jerry's mouth.

"Compliance systems off!" Jerry shouted.

The pain was gone in an instant. All that remained was the pounding of her heart in her ears. Rika pulled herself to her feet and scanned the room. The guards that had been closing in behind them were almost at the door.

Rika raised her GNR and fired three bolts of lightning, blowing a hole in the door with the first, and then tearing holes in four guards with the next two.

She saw three other guards run down the hall, two of them tossing aside their weapons as they went.

Barne had already cut the straps holding Jerry, and the LT stood on shaky legs, giving Rika a grateful smile.

"Holy shit, Rika. You are one hardcore woman."

Rika smiled and rapped her fist on her chest. "No way, LT. In here, I'm a squishie, just like you."

FLIGHT

STELLAR DATE: 12.16.8948 (Adjusted Years)
LOCATION: Northeast Berlin
REGION: Pyra, Albany System, Theban Alliance

Jerry and Leslie were embracing and taking deep breaths, while Barne checked the corridor to ensure that no more of Cheri's guards were interested in becoming statistics.

"Did you get eyes on the ammo?" Rika asked, remembering their need to find ammunition for her GNR-41C.

Jerry pulled himself away from Leslie and nodded. "She showed the rounds to us." He turned and led them through a door in the back of the room to a well-appointed office.

"I'm really sorry about this, everyone," Leslie said. "This is all my fault. Cheri asked what we needed the rounds for, if we'd retrofitted a GNR onto a mount of some sort—stars knows none of us could fire that thing without it tearing our arms off."

"No, it's not your fault," Jerry replied as he approached a cabinet on the wall. "You just slipped up."

"Slipped up in the den of the lion, and let her know that we had an SMI-2 with us," Leslie replied. "Sorry, Rika; looks like you're a hot commodity."

Rika nodded absently. She was still processing the fact that she had beaten Discipline—that she had weathered the torture and come through the other side. Even so, the rage she had tapped into scared her. It was worse than what she had felt during the war, worse than what she felt when she killed the woman who attacked Barne at the warehouse.

It was raw, and primal, and not something she thought she could control.

"Hey, mission control to Rika," Barne said, snapping his fingers in front of her face. "You OK? I gotta say, I think that counts as the second time you saved my ass in as many days."

Rika focused her eyes and smiled. "You got a big ass, Barne; it needs a lot of saving."

Rika looked to Leslie, realizing what the woman had been saying, and gently placed a hand on her shoulder. "It's OK, Leslie. For all we know, Cheri would have done this out of suspicion alone. Never trust someone who combines fuzzy slippers and sweaters."

"Uh…I frequently wear fuzzy slippers and sweaters," Leslie replied with a grin.

"Well…maybe you should stop," Rika replied, her voice dead serious.

Leslie's face fell and she took a half step back.

"Leslie, seriously! Who doesn't like comfy sweaters and slippers? I was kidding."

"Rika! Don't do that! I just watched you snap a woman's neck like you were twisting the cap off a bottle. You're a bit scary, you know that?"

I've noticed, she thought, her eyes turning downward.

"Hey! Leslie, be nice to Rika," Barne said as he gave Rika's arm a light punch.

Leslie's eyebrows were nearly at her hairline. "What happened with you two, anyway? I thought you hated her, Barne."

"Rika?" Barne asked. "I'd never hate her. She's a Marauder. She's Basilisk."

Rika gave Barne a smile, and as her gaze swept across the room, she noticed Jerry was sagging against the cabinet he had been trying to open.

"LT, you OK?" she asked.

"Yeah. Cheri wasn't gentle when she pulled the compliance codes out of my mind. I thought I was doing better, but…I seem to have developed one clusterfuck of a headache."

Leslie rushed to his side and half carried him to a chair.

"I think…she might have the ammo in there," Jerry said, pointing to the cabinet.

Barne looked it over. "Locked."

Rika approached the cabinet, placed a hand on the left door, and prised her fingers into the small gap between the top of the cabinet and its right-side door.

It was solid, but Rika gave a quick jerk and the door tore off its hinges. She pulled the left one open and spotted a slim black case. Her rad counter crept up, and she flipped the latch, opening it.

Inside lay the dull grey forms of five depleted uranium sabot rounds in mint condition. Just what her GNR-41C wanted to fire.

"Stars, you're handy to have around," Leslie said. "Who needs bolt cutters when we have Rika?"

"That's me, your one-stop utility tool," Rika chuckled, surprised that Leslie's statement didn't sting—and that her own response wasn't caustic.

"Can we keep her, LT?" Barne asked.

Jerry pulled himself up straight in the chair. "Of course we can, Sergeant. Like you said—Rika's Basilisk."

Rika felt a lump form in her throat, and redirected the conversation before she had to find a cloth to wipe tears from her eyes.

"We have a car a ways down the valley," Rika said. "But I don't think you can make it that far, Lieutenant. We can steal one here, or I can carry you."

"I don't think my head would appreciate being slung over your shoulder for a run through the forest," Jerry replied. "Let's steal one of Cheri's cars. Bitch won't be using them anymore, anyway."

"Want me to carry you through the villa, at least?" Rika asked.

"No. We need you ready for a fight," Jerry said as he rose. "I might use Leslie as a crutch for a bit, though."

Barne had been watching the entrance to the office and now moved out into the foyer beyond, which was still clear of any hostiles. Careful not to get too far ahead, he led the way down the corridor to the intersection.

"This way," he said, and turned right.

Rika posted herself at the intersection until Jerry and Leslie were past; then she moved in behind them, walking sideways so that her two-seventy vision could see both ends of the hall.

They were nearing the end when someone stepped out from an intersection behind them. Rika fired and then caught sight of a telltale insignia on the figure's chest.

<*Shit, I just shot a cop,*> she said to the team, zooming in her vision to see if the person—a woman—was still alive. Rika let out a long breath as she watched the officer touch her armor and then scurry out of sight.

<*It's OK, she's alive,*> Rika relayed.

<*Yeah, but what are they doing here?*> Leslie asked. <*It's not like Cheri was the sort to be on good terms with the local constabulary.*>

<*On the take?*> Barne asked, as he reached another intersection and checked down the halls. <*Clear.*>

<*Who knows,*> Jerry replied. <*Good or bad, dead cops can put a serious wrinkle in our mission.*>

Rika ran an active scan, looking through the walls as far as she could.

<*Yeah, we have company for sure. There are two groundcars out front, and an air-cav overhead. No, make that four cars out front.*>

<*So probably eight cops…and after Rika just fired on one of them, they'll come in ready for bear. They don't run around without armor, like the shitheads Cheri had,*> Jerry said.

<*Whoops,*> Rika replied, a sheepish tone to her voice.

<*This is a bit bigger than 'whoops', girl. Garage is down here to the right,*> Barne said.

<*Cops' cruisers are all pulled up out front. From where we are, they're about forty meters to our left,*> Rika added.

Jerry peered back over his shoulder. <*Rika, we need a diversion—but don't kill any of them. We don't need a cop-killer manhunt before the operation goes down.*>

<*On it, LT,*> Rika said, and tossed the ammunition case to Barne. <*Hold these for me, will you?*>

<*Oh, yay, I get to hold the radioactive ammo,*> Barne groused.

<*It's not **that** radioactive...anymore,*> Rika said as she turned down the left corridor. She checked her magazines and saw that her GNR still had twenty-two ballistic rounds and enough charge for six more electron beam shots before she would start tapping into her reserves.

All Rika had to do was disable the cruisers and take down the air-cav—which may be human-piloted—without killing anyone.

She considered her options. *Not* killing anyone wasn't really her specialty. Perhaps there was a side-window she could get to that would give her a good angle on the four cruisers.

Rika spotted a staircase and took it up to the second level. At the top of the stairs, she rounded one corner, then another, and almost collided with two of Cheri's guards.

Terror filled their eyes and Rika grinned. These two, she could kill. She punched one in the face, caving in his nose and cheekbone, while the other fired his rifle into her side from only two meters away. The rounds ricocheted off and one struck him in the chest. Rika felt a twinge of pain and realized that a bullet had slipped through a point in her armor where two of the plates overlapped. She fished it out and noted that it was clean. No blood. Score one for her carbon-poly skin.

"Stop!" A male voice called out, and she turned to see a cop down the hall, leveling a rifle at her.

"Uh...no?" Rika responded, and dove into a room to her left as the policeman fired.

Are they supposed to do that? she wondered. Details of police procedure—when they could fire on suspects and all that—was not something she had ever needed to know in the past.

She stood inside the entrance to the room, waiting for the cop to step through. Five seconds ticked past, then ten, then twenty.

Shit, he must be waiting for backup. Smart man.

A moment later, weapons fire sounded and a barrage of projectiles tore through the wall where she was standing.

I guess they have IR, Rika thought. She considered her options and then did the exact opposite of what the police expected: She broke through the wall and rushed them.

There were two of them, and neither even had time to register surprise before Rika tore the rifle from the first cop's hands and smashed it into the head of the second—as gently as she could manage.

Then she hit the first cop on the side of the head with the barrel of her GNR and watched him fall.

"Damn squishies," she muttered, examining their vitals. "You'll live."

She returned to the room she had just burst out of, which had an excellent view of the four cruisers parked below—pulled up right in front of the broad stairs leading into the villa. Rika scanned them for occupants. Her luck, such as it was, had held; they were empty.

Rika took aim and fired an electron beam at the first cruiser, blowing a hole through it and shattering its battery. She fired on the second, and was lining up on the third when an all too familiar sound met her ears.

Gatling guns always take an instant to spin up before they fire, and that telltale whine was all it took for Rika to dive out of the window as the room above and behind her was cut to shreds from the high-velocity rounds.

If those dumbasses kill their own people back in the hall, I'll kill 'em, Rika thought angrily.

She looked up and saw the air-cav only twenty meters above the cruisers. It had stopped firing, but was repositioning to shoot at her new location.

Rika didn't give it time to take aim. She ran across the open space in front of the villa's main doors and leapt off the ruins of one cruiser onto the villa's wall, her feet grasping a windowsill. She crouched, and a second jump propelled her to the villa's roof.

The air-cav was turning, and its gatling gun was winding up once more when Rika leapt from the roof, sailed through the air, and landed on the air-cav.

She looked inside and saw that there was indeed a human

pilot in the cockpit. Rika leveled her rifle at him and screamed "*Land*", loud enough that they probably could have heard her halfway down the valley.

<*Nice distraction,*> Barne said as he raced by in a car, down the twisting road leading into the valley.

<*Took you guys long enough,*> Rika replied as the air-cav touched down, and she gestured for the pilot to get out. He jumped out and ran into the villa. Rika saw that the air-cav's controls were still initialized and hopped into the cockpit. She brought the craft a few meters off the ground and unloaded its gatling gun into the other two cruisers.

Once they were suitably disabled, she brought the air-cav up over the villa and pushed the manual control stick forward. The air-cav pitched, and Rika jumped out, landing again on the villa's roof.

The air-cav sped forward and slammed into the escarpment behind the villa before falling to the ground in a twisted heap of metal.

Rika turned and scanned the road, easily spotting the car her team had stolen from Cheri's garage. She leapt off the villa's roof and chased after. A few shots came from the villa as Rika disappeared into the night. Most missed, and those that didn't were unable to penetrate her armor.

She rolled her head back and laughed as she ran down the mountainside, not bothering with following the road. She reviewed her sensory capture of the battle. As far as she could tell, she hadn't killed any of the police. Maybe she wasn't *just* a killer after all.

Rika neared the location where the other car was hidden and scanned the area to make sure it was clear. As she looked up, a flash of light appeared in the skies, and a scan showed that there was another air-cav closing in. IR indicated another human pilot—this time approaching at a much higher altitude.

Rika raced to the road, reaching it just as the air-cav opened fire on Basilisk's escape vehicle. Her electron beam wouldn't be effective against the air-cav at its current range, so Rika sped up, racing toward it. Ahead she could see Leslie leaning out of the car, firing on the air-cav. Her shots were hitting the craft, but appeared to make no impact.

Barne swerved the car wildly, avoiding the air-cav's spray of bullets. It pulled around, coming in for a strafing run behind the car. Rika knew it wouldn't miss this time, and scanned the trees for a good candidate to climb. They were all young and spindly; then her eyes locked on a thirty-meter pine close by.

Without a moment's hesitation, Rika leapt into the tree's branches and clambered up its trunk. When she reached the top, Rika leapt toward the air-cav, closing the distance enough—she hoped—and fired her electron beam.

The straight line of lightning streaked out and hit the air-cav on its left side, taking out one of its a-grav units and sending the craft into a tailspin.

The pilot, either purposefully or by accident, opened up with the gatling gun, and fifty-caliber rounds filled the air in a broad circle around the falling air-cav.

Rika saw that the car with Team Basilisk in it was past the falling air-cav, but she was not. In fact, her trajectory still had her approaching it.

A round struck her thigh, then another hit her in the chest, and two more slammed into her left arm.

Rika hit the ground hard and rolled to her feet, her HUD registering severe damage to her left arm. She looked down and saw that an armor plate had been shattered below her elbow. She tried to flex her fingers, but they didn't move.

She glanced over the rest of herself and saw that her chest plate had a microfracture; she was otherwise all right. Ahead, the air-cav's damaged a-grav unit burst into flames, and Rika rushed forward to save the cop inside.

Within, she saw a woman slumped over the controls. Rika reached down to tear off the craft's canopy, when she remembered that her hand wasn't working.

Thank the stars for clawed feet, she thought with a smile, and smashed her foot through the canopy's clear plas, and then pushed the eject button next to the woman's chair.

An instant later, the chair flew from the downed craft, and deployed a parachute. It settled down to the ground one hundred meters up the road.

"You'll thank me later," Rika said, running from the burning air-cav and ducking into the trees a second before it exploded.

Four minutes later she arrived at the cars. Leslie was helping Jerry into the backseat of the vehicle she and Barne had brought. He looked a bit better but was still holding his head with one hand.

Barne had the trunk open and pulled out a small package. "Hopefully we didn't leave too much DNA in the villa, but we'd best scrub what we can."

He held up the package and then tossed it into the car they had stolen from Cheri. Small silver filaments spread from the kit, sweeping over every surface in the vehicle in a matter of seconds before retracting into the box.

"Like we were never here," Barne said with a smile.

He closed the trunk and got in the driver's seat while Rika collapsed in the passenger's side.

"You OK?" Leslie asked. "Your arm looks funny."

"Yeah, mostly," Rika replied. "Took some shots to my left arm—not the organic part. Not sure how messed up it is yet, but my hand's offline."

Barne backed the car out of the copse of trees it was hidden in and gave Rika a smile. "You know, being a mech must not be so bad sometimes. No pain, and you can swap that arm out in minutes."

Rika closed her eyes and sighed. *Maybe it isn't so bad. Maybe not* always, *at least.*

DELIBERATION

STELLAR DATE: 12.17.8948 (Adjusted Years)
LOCATION: Enlisted Commissary, MSS *Foe Hammer*
REGION: Interstellar Space, near the Praesepe Cluster

David sat in the *Foe Hammer's* enlisted commissary taking a meal at a table with Aaron and Genevieve, two other specialists who worked in the fleet's CIC on the ship.

"Something's not right," David said, and he reached into his pocket, pulled out a dampener, and set it on the table. It wasn't uncommon for the CIC teams to discuss their work at lunch, and because it got more work from them at the same pay, their superiors allowed it—so long as they took precautions not to be overheard.

<*What's that?*> Aaron asked as he plugged a packet of nutri-paste into the socket in his stomach. <*Seeing things out of the corner of your eye again?*>

David smiled at Aaron's pet term for his abilities. Aaron wasn't a P-Cog. His augmentations had been focused on heavy mathematics for close-quarters fleet engagements; the alterations he had undergone at the hands of the GAF were even more extreme than what the mechs had undergone.

Where David's alterations had been focused on enhancing the interconnectivity in his brain, Aaron's had been centered on adding raw computational power. In the war, the official term for people like him was 'Non-AI Sentient Computer'. Just like the mechs and the others who were heavily modded, the military had both treated and labeled NAISCs as objects.

Unlike with David, they hadn't bothered with saving any visual aspect of Aaron's humanity. His head was a half-meter-tall grey ovoid with two bulbous lenses where his eyes should be—though no organic eyes lay beneath. His face was also devoid of nose or mouth; his air coming through two breathing ports on his upper torso, and his food through the NutriPaste socket on the surface of his stomach.

David admitted that 'torso' wasn't quite the right word for Aaron's body. Because the Genevian Space Force had treated NAISCs like mobile organic AIs, they had removed all of Aaron's limbs and set what remained of his body inside a hard shell.

Though David had never said it aloud, Aaron looked much like a snowman that just needed the bottom ball.

Luckily for Aaron, the Old Man had taken him in right at the end of the war, and had a mobile stand of sorts constructed for him. It had a cup that his body sat in and six legs—any of which could also double as hands, as needed—stemming from the stand upon which the cup sat.

The level of technology to undo what had been done to Aaron was outside of what the Marauders possessed, and David had been impressed with the level of self-acceptance Aaron managed. David was sure that he'd lose his mind if he were in his friend's place.

One thing was for certain; it made Aaron one mean Snark player. He could simultaneously play six games against separate opponents, and typically win five out of the six.

Teams on the *Foe Hammer* continually tried to beat him—many of their players were heavily augmented as well—but the best contenders had still only managed two wins to his four.

<Hey-O. Mission control to David,> Aaron said. *<You were saying something about something not being right?>*

David shook his head. "Sorry, not enough coffee today."

"A P-Cog's favorite stabilizer," Genevieve said as she held hers out to David. "Need my packet?"

"No, I'm OK, just had one—it'll kick in shortly," David replied.

"Suit yourself," Genevieve replied.

David nodded his thanks. Genevieve was the most normal-looking of their little group. After the war she was able to access her savings, and she'd had enough money to get her shark fins replaced. She now sported a head covered in thick hairs that served the same purpose as his steel ridges.

Not that anyone would mistake the gleaming, white, one-centimeter-thick strands for real hair, but it certainly beat metal fins.

Genevieve was the backbone of their unit. Nothing fazed her; she never became upset, worried, or even agitated. She was an endless sea of calm. David had relied on her more than once to help him through hard times.

She always held herself perfectly erect, and her high, sloped forehead spoke of an origin in New Sweden—though her family had lived for generations in Genevia, on one of the terraformed planets close to a G-spectrum star.

As a result, Genevieve had naturally dark skin that contrasted with her white 'hair', giving her an otherworldly look.

<*You're staring,*> Aaron said privately to David.

<*Damn…glad she doesn't mind. I think I stare at her a lot.*>

<*Pretty sure she likes it,*> Aaron replied.

David coughed and tried to get his mind back on track, pushing down the excess stimuli around him to focus on what he had discovered. Patterns, analyzing connections—that's where he found his peace.

"It's with Operation Phoenix, of course," he began. "I'm worried about its effects."

"You mean the change of hands for the Theban stars?" Genevieve asked.

"That's one way to put it, but yeah," David replied. "See, I don't think that this benefits the Septhians as much as everyone would like to think it does."

<*Everyone wonders about that,*> Aaron replied in a tone that let them know there was a detailed analysis coming. <*The upheaval provides little advantage over a strong Thebes, should the Nietzscheans, or anyone else, attack. But the Old Man believes it's for the best; while I can see a lot of ways things can go wrong, properly handled it can work in the Septhians' favor. It's not as though there is no support in Thebes*

for a merger with Septhia. Portions of their congress have been arguing in favor of it for decades. It's been their president, Ariana, who has quashed it. Makes sense that the Septhians would want her out of the way—>

"David does have a point, though," Genevieve said, interrupting Aaron's spiel. "By that logic, there should just be one team hitting the president and nothing more—well, maybe her VP, too."

"OK, I know it's all just suspicion and conjecture and I can't go anywhere with that," David replied. "But it did start me digging. I began to look at all the logs for the Old Man's talks with his Septhian contacts who arranged Phoenix in the first place."

<*Hey, whoa, what?*> Aaron asked. <*Dude, that is not OK. You can't spy on the Old Man.*>

"I didn't look at the messages themselves, just the logs in the comm systems."

Genevieve frowned. "Marauders, the Old Man especially, talk to Septhians all the time. Septhia is where our main facilities are. How could you pick out the communication with the contact for this operation amidst all the noise?"

"Because it was different," David said. "It had a unique pattern."

<*In what way?*> Aaron asked, his curiosity apparently piqued.

"It was in the packet segmentation on the comms," David said. "Septhians don't use octal code in their comm systems."

"Yeah, they use that weird-ass base-9 setup. They folded their parity bit right into the data structure. It's always a pain in the ass to translate."

David nodded. "Yeah, and you can see the pattern it creates in the headers alone—you don't even need to look at the message content. But there was a subset of messages where the pattern was different, and they were all communications sent to the Old Man."

<*So?*> Aaron asked. <*This is obviously being run by their black-ops folks, with no link to their prime minister—all the better to have*

plausible deniability if we fuck up. It's why they hired us in the first place, rather than doing the job themselves.>

"I thought about that, too," David said. "But I really wanted to know how to achieve that pattern. I got kinda obsessed with it. I converted messages from a hundred different source systems into base-9, and then back to base-8; everything from raw-binary to SAI analog code systems. A lot were close, real close, and within the margin of error. But there were three that were dead matches."

"Here goes," Genevieve said.

"The Tarurae high command's exalted network, the Trisilieds space force comms, and…the Nietzscheans."

<That's ridiculous,> Aaron said. *<The comm NSAI would have spotted messages of Nietzschean origin, even if it had been passed through Septhian relays and converted to base-9 and back.>*

"I don't think so," David said. "See, it wasn't that the whole message was a red flag—just the parity bits. And not all of them, either—it was a weird pattern that looked almost random. Well, it still does, but I know something's in there. It's a pattern I can almost make out, like a detail that, if I just squint at right, I'll see."

<I still don't like that you've been poking around in the Old Man's messages,> Aaron said.

David raised his hands and nodded. "Hey, Aaron. I appreciate what the Old Man's built for us here as much as anyone. But if I have a Nietzschean connection to Phoenix, I have to pursue it. Do you think you could take a look at what I have?"

Aaron didn't respond for a moment, and then his long head nodded. *<Send it over.>*

David passed his analysis over the Link to his friend.

<Well, you're right about an anomaly, but it seems too random; not caused by specific comm hardware. Maybe…>

"Maybe what?" Genevieve asked.

<Well…older Nietzschean comm systems used a processor that had a rounding error. It never really caused issues for them; in fact, they leveraged it as a part of their encryption…>

"Simulate it," David said.

<What do you think I'm—shit! It's a dead match now. I can create the pattern by running the base-9 translation through a processor with the rounding error.>

"That's it, then. There's a Nietzschean somewhere in the Septhian government!" David exclaimed.

Genevieve sat back and let out a long whistle while Aaron's ovoid head pivoted. *<That's far from a smoking gun. Hardware ends up all over the place, especially old stuff. Gets sold as surplus in every system.>*

"I think your findings are sound enough to take it to Commander Siemens," Genevieve said. "I would, at least. Let her decide if the intel should get pushed up the chain or not."

<Let's hope not,> Aaron said. *<We're only twenty-eight Pyran hours from launching Operation Phoenix. Barely enough time to call the thing off, if it's true.>*

RESITUATE

STELLAR DATE: 12.17.8948 (Adjusted Years)
LOCATION: Northern Berlin
REGION: Pyra, Albany System, Theban Alliance

It had taken the team five hours to return to Berlin, and then another three to get the truck and drive it to one of their fallback locations.

It was another warehouse, but this one was smaller and newer—and decidedly cleaner. Leslie laid Jerry down on a cot in a nearby storage room and walked out rubbing her eyes.

Barne was away, taking the car to another storage location. That left just the two women to finish setting up.

"Jerry gonna be OK?" Rika asked as she attempted another reroute to get her arm working.

"Yeah," Leslie nodded. "I gave him a brainfix. The kit should deal with the swelling Cheri's methods caused; that appears to be the worst of it. The kit didn't report any neural damage—thank the stars."

"What about you?" Leslie asked Rika as she approached. "You took some hits, there."

Rika shrugged from where she sat on a crate. "I've seen a lot worse. Except for the gatling guns on those air-cavs, nothing out there was high enough caliber to really hurt me."

Leslie gave Rika a smile. "Well, I guess we should unload the truck."

Rika grinned and held up her left hand. "I'm going to need a hand. Literally."

Leslie covered her mouth and laughed. "Oh, shit. I totally forgot—you can't get your gun-arm off to put on a good arm, because your other arm is shot."

At first Rika wasn't sure if Leslie was making light of her plight, but she decided to believe that Leslie was just laughing at the irony of it, and chuckled. "Yeah, like I said; I literally need a hand."

"Where is your other one?" Leslie asked.

"In the cab of the truck," Rika replied. "Tools are in the back."

"I'll have to pull your armor off first, won't I?" Leslie said as she examined Rika's arm.

"Yeah, a bit tricky otherwise," Rika replied.

Leslie met Rika's eyes, her own showing a look of worry. "Do you mind if I get the rack, Rika?" she asked. "I don't think I can manage this without it."

Rika nodded. "No, I don't mind. I'll help you get it out…I can at least shove things around, if you need me to."

Thirty minutes later Leslie had the rack set up, and Rika stepped back, settling her armor's hardpoints into the hooks.

Leslie slid a tool into Rika's armpit and gave a twist, loosening the armor on the shoulder.

"Is that weird for you, Rika?" she asked as she slotted in another tool and opened up the armor around Rika's bicep.

"What, having someone else take my armor off?" Rika asked. "Not really; happened a lot in the war, especially when I took damage."

"Well, I was referring specifically to me slotting a tool up into your armpit…"

"Oh, that? No, not really. It does kinda tickle, though."

Leslie looked up at Rika, their eyes meeting before Leslie snorted. "Rika, the unstoppable killing machine, is ticklish?"

Rika had begun to smile, but the expression faded. "Please don't call me that."

"Shit, sorry," Leslie shook her head. "I spend too much time around these guys. Lovable bundles of testosterone that they are, they get me acting like everything is up for being a joke…"

"It's OK," Rika said. "Some mechs like being killing machines. I…I don't really know what I like."

"Well," Leslie grunted as she unfastened the armor from Rika's forearm, pulling it free where the damaged plate had wedged into her arm. "I can tell you this: you're a sight to behold when you're at it. The way you leapt from the building and landed on that air-cav? That was one of the most badass things I've ever seen. And I've seen a lot of badass shit in my day."

Rika shook her head as Leslie pulled the last of her arm's armor off. "Last night was nothing. Shoulda seen the time that my team and I took out a nuke-flinging K1R. That thing was a nightmare."

"How big was the team?" Leslie asked absently as she looked over the damage in Rika's arm.

"Three," Rika replied. "Though just two of us were on the K1R. I pulled a move like the one with that air-cav."

"Just two of you took out a K1R?" Leslie shook her head in wonder. "You sure you need the rest of us on this mission?"

"Well," Rika said with a laugh. "Looks like I need a mechanic to keep me running."

"That you do," Leslie said. "Let me get your gun arm off, and give you your right hand back. I'm not sure what we should do about that left one. It's beyond my skill to fix, and we don't have a replacement."

"Maybe we could find you a big hook. Arrrrr," Barne said with a lopsided grin as he walked through a nearby door. "I bet that would scare the shit out of the enemy."

"Give me a hook, and I'll use it to give you those friendly punches on the arm," Rika replied.

"Huh," Barne said. "Maybe a pillow attachment would be better. Think of it; you could lay that pretty head of yours down whenever you wanted and take a nice snooze."

Pretty?

Leslie snorted. "Shut up, Barne. Go make yourself useful and unload the truck."

Barne shrugged and walked away. "I'll take a look at that arm you got shot up when I'm done unpacking. I might be able to get it working again."

As Leslie removed the armor on Rika's right arm, she chatted with Rika about the Marauders—describing some of the missions they'd been on lately, and what it was like to work in a mercenary company after being in the Genevian Armed Forces.

"It's a bit different, for sure," she said. "Everyone keeps their military rank—for the most part, anyway—but the structure is weird. I mean, Jerry's a lieutenant. LTs aren't usually in charge of four-person fireteams."

"How does it work when you do platoon or company-sized ops?" Rika asked.

"Well," Leslie smiled. "We're spec-ops, attached to Alpha Company in the second Battalion. There are forty battalions now in the Marauders—which the Old Man has split up into four regiments."

"So, about twenty-five thousand soldiers altogether?"

"Closer to twenty-eight," Leslie replied. "There are a lot of spec-op teams like ours that aren't part of the regular structure. We report right to Alpha Company's CO, Captain Ayer. She's a good woman; sometimes a bit soft on the guys when they need a sterner hand, but I like her."

"And who's the Old Man?" Rika asked.

"Oh, I guess we never call him by name, do we?" Leslie said with a grunt as she twisted off Rika's gun-arm and stumbled backward, nearly dropping it.

"Shit, this thing weighs a ton! How do you just wave your arm around like it's nothing?"

Rika shrugged as much as she could, hanging on the rack. "Seems light to me. I do have to adjust my balance when it's on, though. It's why I preferred it on my right arm…felt more natural there."

"Well," Leslie groaned as she set the arm and the attached GNR-41C down on a crate. "You may have to adjust it back and get used to its weight on your left."

Rika nodded. That was her expectation, as well—unless Barne could work a miracle with her left arm.

Leslie picked up Rika's right arm and slid it into place, giving it the required twist.

"Right, the Old Man. He's General Mill. Was in the Genevian army for almost seventy years. Hates the fact that the war is over; some of the Marauders think that he's building us up to eventually strike out at the Nietzscheans."

"That's nuts!" Rika exclaimed. "Even with a million soldiers, he wouldn't stand a chance. "He'd need a fleet, for starters."

"Hey," Leslie raised her hands defensively. "I said some. Not all; certainly not me." She slid the bolts into place and locked them down. "OK, you're good to go. Hold on while I reattach your right arm's armor."

Rika waited silently while Leslie finished the work. "OK, Rika. Right as rain on the right, right?"

"Wow," Rika laughed. "You're a regular comedian, Leslie."

Leslie grinned. "Yeah, I get that a lot."

"No, you don't," Barne said as he walked past.

"Shut up, Barne," Leslie said good-naturedly.

"How's the LT, by the way?" Barne asked as he stopped beside the two women.

"I think he'll be alright," Leslie replied.

"I hope so. Tomorrow's the big day."

Rika held her left arm up for Barne to see. "I doubt you'll be able to fix this. Looks like the control mechanism and one of the actuators are shot."

Barne grunted. "Yeah, you're right. I could probably source the parts, but it may arise suspicion—especially this close to the job."

"S'OK," Rika grinned. "I'll just get to relax here and watch you do the heavy lifting for once."

"Need me to swap out your left arm?" Leslie asked.

"That'd be nice. I don't think I could flip the mount back around on the gun-arm with one hand."

"Hey," Leslie said with a smile. "What are friends for?"

Rika and Leslie continued to chat as they reset Rika's gun-arm to mount on her left. They talked about the Marauders, Basilisk's past missions, and what the future might hold.

It felt nice—like maybe Rika had finally found a place in the universe, after all.

REPORT

STELLAR DATE: 12.17.8948 (Adjusted Years)
LOCATION: MSS *Foe Hammer*
REGION: Interstellar Space, near the Praesepe Cluster

Commander Siemens was off duty. By the time David had passed his findings through the CIC's Officer of the Watch, who wanted to crosscheck everything he and Aaron had uncovered—with a particular focus on the amount of unauthorized time spent on the task—before finally getting the Commander's attention, several hours had passed.

Siemens had entered the CIC with a furrowed brow and tousled hair, but paid close attention as David laid out the information, and grew more rapt as the P-Cog went on. When David showed the simulation Aaron had constructed, her eyebrows shifted from hanging low over her eyes to nearly disappearing into her hairline.

"Holy shit, specialist! If this is true, we have to call off the whole op!" Siemens exclaimed.

"That's the point I've been trying to make," David said, casting a hard look at the OOTW.

"Come with me," Commander Siemens said as she rose and left the CIC. "I'm calling Colonel Niels; the operation command team is assembled. When they see this…."

David followed Commander Siemens through the corridors surrounding the CIC, and then up a lift to the *Foe Hammer*'s mission management deck. The deck was a beehive of activity; people were rushing about, checking and crosschecking the status of drop ships and assault teams, and reviewing status updates from ground coordinators.

Siemens led David into a meeting room filled with officers being addressed by Colonel Niels.

"Sir!" Commander Siemens said as she rushed in. "I know you

said to wait when I pinged you, but this can't wait. We have critical intel on Phoenix."

"What are you talking about?" Niels frowned. "We're running the intel on this op. What does fleet CIC have that could be relevant?"

"My specialist here, a P-Cog, has ferreted out a Nietzschean connection to Phoenix."

One of the officers sitting at the table, a major named Sarah, nearly spit out the water she was drinking. "Are you serious?"

"Unlikely," another said.

"Please!" Commander Siemens raised her voice. "This is serious! We believe that General Mill's contact in the Septhian government is actually a Nietzschean operative!"

"Show me what you have," a calm voice said from behind David, and he turned to see the Old Man himself standing at the entrance to the room.

"Yes, sir!" David said. He took control of the room's main holo projector, and nervously began to outline his findings. As he spoke, the General's face grew more and more red. David started to wonder if he would find himself on the wrong side of an airlock before he was done, but Siemens nodded whenever he faltered, so David pressed on.

When he was done and Aaron's simulation results were floating over the table, the General blew out a long breath.

"Laura," he said. "What do you think?"

<I can see no fault in the findings,> she said. *<Specialist David's logic is sound. I believe we have been played.>*

"Colonel Niels, Phoenix is shut down. Initiate Operation Ashes. We jump for Pyra in t-minus fifteen minutes."

"Sir! Yes, sir!" Colonel Niels said, and a moment later every person in the room was pulling up new displays, and the halls outside exploded with increased activity.

General Mill placed a hand on David's shoulder, and he was surprised to feel the Old Man's grip shaking slightly.

"P-Cog Specialist David, you may have just saved the

Praesepe Cluster from the Nietzscheans…and my folly."

THE HIT

STELLAR DATE: 12.18.8948 (Adjusted Years)
LOCATION: National Forest, North of Presidential Palace, Berlin
REGION: Pyra, Albany System, Theban Alliance

Rika walked through the forest drawing in deep lungfuls of the moist, predawn air. Her robe—a new one, since her old one was somewhere in the valley below Cheri's villa—rustled quietly around her as she enjoyed what she knew to be the last few minutes of peace she would experience for some time.

She held her coffee lightly in her right hand and took another sip. Using that hand with fine control was taking a little work, but Rika was more concerned with using her GNR on her left.

In yesterday's combat, when her gun-arm had been in place, it had felt like her proper right hand. A gun—a multi-function weapons mount with a GNR-41C—felt more natural than a hand.

She took another sip of coffee, raising her third finger off the cup as she did. This appendage, with fingers and the ability to grip and hold, just felt strange. Maybe that had been one of the things that had bothered her so much after the war, and she hadn't been able to name it—or to admit it to herself.

She took a final long drink of the coffee, tossed the cup toward a trash bin, missed, and picked it up to deposit it more carefully. Even if she found herself with a gun-arm on her right side more often than not, she still needed to work on her fine motor skills. There was no telling when she'd need them, now that she was in the Marauders.

I'm in the Marauders.

Rika still wasn't certain what she thought of that. Basilisk was one thing. She had bonded deeply with the team over just a few short days—something that life-or-death situations seemed to facilitate. However, the Marauders were a different story. Somewhere within their structure were people who thought it was OK to buy and sell humans. Her, specifically, and that wasn't the sort of group she wanted to call family.

Rika was nearing the large glen with the tree that she had scouted out three days prior, and she turned off onto a smaller path that eventually faded away but took her close to the tree. She crouched behind a bush and activated her robe's camouflage systems and then crossed the final few meters to the tree, carefully scaling it.

Once in position, Rika stretched her left arm out and reached under her robe with her right, drawing out the GNR-41C that had been strapped to her back. She carefully wedged it between herself and the tree while pulling out the shroud that would cover it.

Rika slid a loop from the end of the shroud over the weapon's barrel, and then grasped the weapon and brought it up to her mount.

It took two tries to get it on, and at one point she almost dropped it; then the GNR-41C slotted into place, and her HUD updated with its readings and loadout.

Rika nodded with satisfaction as she saw the five uranium sabot rounds show up on the weapons loadout.

For the first time in years, Rika was fully functional.

With the weapon in place, Rika pulled her helmet from a pouch under her robe and wrapped it in the shawl before carefully placing it on her head. This time Leslie had helped her prepare by pinning her hair up, and Barne hadn't made any jokes about shaving her head.

The helmet registered a positive seal, and Rika pulled the cloak's cowl up over her head.

It was time to wait.

She knew that somewhere nearby, Leslie and Jerry were getting ready to take their positions. Not too soon, though; their hiding spots were closer to the presidential palace and not as well hidden. The pair would take their positions at the last minute, ready to finish the job and give Rika covering fire if she needed it.

Rika hoped that Jerry would be all right. He seemed better today—though he said his head still felt like he'd gone a few rounds with a starship. Rika had kept a close eye on him, and the LT had only wobbled once while the team got ready.

If it were up to her, he would sit out the mission—but there was nothing she could do to stop him. He *was* the LT, after all.

Rika checked the local time: just a few minutes after 06:00 hours. The Theban president wouldn't be passing by until the end of her run at about 08:05. Rika couldn't use the Link or anything else that could give away her position, so she started practicing her breathing while touching her thumb to each of her fingers.

It was something to take her mind off what she was about to do. Killing Cheri and her goons had been one thing, but she was now lying in wait to assassinate a head of state.

To topple a government.

Rika had researched the Theban president in greater depth the night before. From what she could tell, Ariana was a good woman. She had several grown children, and they seemed to love and respect their mother.

There was no husband in her life, but that was normal in Thebes. Long-term spousal relationships were rare.

Rika swallowed, forcing down her uncertainty. She had just found a place where she fit in. Failing to complete this mission would put that in jeopardy.

It was distasteful, but it was her job. It was what she was.

*****

The time slipped past 8:00, and Rika re-checked her GNR-41C, making sure the uranium sabot rounds were ready to fire and crosschecking her targeting reticules.

Several presidential guards had passed by fifteen minutes before without giving the tree she was in so much as a second glance—after that, no one else operating in an official capacity came by.

This surprised Rika. She had expected to see several more guards keeping ahead of the president; so far, she had only seen a woman and two kids run past.

Another minute slipped by, and then Jerry reached out to her.

<Rika, we have a problem.>

<How so?>

<Barne just got an update: the president's schedule has changed. She got pulled into some meeting at the capitol building,> Jerry replied.

<Crap, really? What's our fallback?> Rika asked.

<The president is the most important target. The other teams will already be in motion; that means we need to get to the capitol and take her out fast.>

<What, just waltz into the capitol and kill the president? Sorry LT, but that sounds a bit nuts.>

<Just wait till you see Barne's plan. Then you'll ***really*** *think we're nuts. Meet us back at the rally point. Quickly.>*

<Got it,> Rika said as she carefully descended the tree.

She wondered if Jerry remembered that he hadn't reactivated her compliance chip. Either way, it was nice to get an order and not feel the warning from Discipline in the back of her mind.

If he *had* remembered and left it off, she owed him one hell of a thank you.

Once on the ground, Rika pulled off the GNR-41C and slipped it back under her robe. She started moving through the brush, but then remembered her helmet. After quickly removing it, she rewrapped her head in her scarf before replacing her cowl.

She reached the path a minute later and jogged to the meet-up point where the rest of Basilisk was waiting.

The hoverbikes were out, set up beside the truck, and Jerry and Leslie were sitting on the back, chests heaving from their run.

"You guys out of shape or something?" Rika asked with a grin.

"Har har," Leslie replied between breaths.

<OK, so Barne's intel has the president in the east wing of the capitol building. She'll be in a room with windows, but we don't think that even

your rifle can shoot through them,> Jerry began while Leslie spoke out loud about her run, bending over to stretch her calves.

Rika laughed aloud and said something in response to Leslie, while replying to Jerry over the Link.

<*Stands to reason,*> Rika said. <*I imagine a couple of shots would make it through, but they'd have moved her by then.*>

<*Right,*> Jerry replied. <*Which means we need to get you into the capitol, and fast. The other hits are about to go down, and once they do, you can bet they'll get the president to a bunker as soon as they can.*>

<*So what's the big plan for getting me into the capitol?*> Rika asked. <*I seem to recall you saying it was 'nuts'.*>

<*Oh, it is,*> Barne laughed as he stepped around a stack of cases in the truck holding several explosives. He jumped off the deck and walked to one of the hoverbikes, and then lifted the seat. <*This one's yours, Rika. It's got a little something extra.*>

*****

Rika sped down the streets of Berlin at over three hundred kilometers per hour, with four police bikes and two air-cavs hot on her tail. Ahead, she periodically caught sight of Jerry and Leslie on their bikes, weaving in and out of the slower street traffic.

A car pulled out from the side of the road, and Rika boosted her hoverbike, jumping it into the air and over the car. She nearly hit another vehicle, and swerved sharply to avoid it. Behind her, a car also swerved, and slammed into another, obstructing the road.

Now that was more like it. *The harder the pursuit, the better.*

A map of the city streets floated over her vision, and she saw that after a right in three blocks, they would be just two blocks from the government parking garage.

She slowed the bike and dropped her foot, dragging it along the street to swing the bike around the corner, and then she jammed on the throttle again. Ahead, Jerry approached the parking garage and fired into the guard booth.

Instantaneously, stop posts jumped up and turrets dropped down, firing on Jerry as he sped off. Leslie was just a second behind him, and she tossed a detpack at the entrance to the garage. Barne was monitoring feeds, and blew the pack at just the right moment for maximum damage.

At least Rika hoped it was maximum damage. She scanned the entrance, trying to see if any of the stop posts had been taken out. Her vision cycled through several modes and picked up a gap wide enough for her bike.

Rika passed through it a second later. One of the turrets sputtered a few shots at her, but none did any noticeable damage.

She slammed on the bike's rear brakes and turned left up the ramp. Guns fired on her the whole way, but their tracking wasn't fast enough to deal with an overpowered hoverbike ridden by a mech who felt no fear—at least, no fear about this.

Six levels later, she was on the roof of the parking garage. Rika got her bearings and pushed the bike's throttle wide open. It bucked, rising up as it raced across the rooftop, and Rika hit the edge at exactly the three hundred and twenty-two kilometers per hour Barnes said she needed.

Except she didn't hit the *edge*. She ramped off a car and sailed through the air, waiting for the prescribed ten-count to pass.

Time seemed to slow, and she looked around, her view augmented by her two-seventy vision.

Ahead loomed the capitol building and the east wing where the president was having her meeting. Below her laid a few smaller buildings and a park. As Rika passed over the park, she pushed off the hoverbike, sending it down and her up.

Four missiles streaked out from hidden defense points, targeting the bike. Rika watched, soaring higher, as the four missiles reached the bike at almost the same moment.

Right before impact, the bike exploded.

The blast gave Rika the extra push she needed to make it up to the building's roof. Unfortunately, the force also sent her cartwheeling through the air, so when she landed, it was on a skylight.

A thousand kilograms of mech, steel, and high-density glass fell into the room below just as the remains of the bike smashed into one of the room's windows and fell to the ground.

Huh…the window did hold up. They should put that glass on their skylights.

Rika looked around, her locator systems finding her on the building layout she had saved that first night when she had reviewed Basilisk's intel on the operation.

This was the room; the president should be there.

<*It's empty! She's not here!*> Rika called out.

<*Shit,*> Barne responded. <*They must have caught wind of one of the other ops. They'll take her to the bunker. It's under the west wing, middle of the bottom floor—marked 'mop room' on the layout.*>

<*Got it,*> Rika replied.

One more look around the room now that the dust had settled revealed that something had been going on. Holosheets were still on the table, along with glasses of water, and some jackets were still draped over chairs.

The president had been here just moments before.

She plotted the most expeditious route through the Capitol and took off, smashing through the door and rushing down the corridor beyond. Several men and women were approaching, all armed and wearing medium armor. Rika pulled her JE78 rifle off her back and fired four rapid pulse shots, knocking two people over and pushing the others aside. One tried to grab at her as she ran past, but she slapped his arm out of the way; the crunch of his bones snapping reached her augmented ears even over the general din of her passage.

She turned left at the next intersection and kept running while firing pulse blasts at anyone who got in her way. Her plan didn't require a return trip; the squishies could chase after her as fast as they wanted, they weren't going to catch her.

Rika passed under a large archway and into the capitol's main atrium. She was running along a balcony toward a door at the far end when she saw a soldier in heavy armor step through a doorway across the atrium. She recognized the weapon in his hand and dove to the ground as a blue streak of lightning flashed overhead, blowing a hole in the wall beside her.

Debris fell on her, and Rika struggled to get free—fighting her robe as much as the wall. She tore the robe asunder and scurried free as a second electron beam hit where she had been a moment earlier.

Rika took off running, taking a moment to fire a return shot from her own electron beam before leaving the atrium.

Her rear vision revealed that her shot hit the soldier center mass. She wasn't certain if his armor could withstand the beam, but she wasn't going to stick around to find out.

Inside the next corridor, she pushed past several men and women in highly ornate robes. One called out, hurling insults that Rika barely heard as she raced on.

<I'm almost at their main meeting hall, or whatever they call it,> Rika announced, not worried about EM silence. *<Any word on where their president is?>*

<They call it the Assemblage,> Barne said. *<I'm not picking up anything on Ariana's location, but I'm also not picking up their protocols for when she's in the bunker—if I have the right ones. I think I have the right ones.>*

<OK, let me know if that changes.>

Rika continued her mad dash, wishing the Marauders had secured drones for her armor. She constantly had to slow at intersections to see if anyone was lying in wait, and one time almost got her head shot off as a group of soldiers opened fire on her.

She didn't bother engaging them; instead she raced back to a nearby lift, prised the doors open, and leapt down the shaft. The elevator car was on the main floor, and she crashed through the ceiling, narrowly missing a terrified woman who spilled coffee down her robe.

"Sorry 'bout that," Rika said as she took off once more.

Again the incongruity of what she was doing hit her. She had no issue with the Thebans. Aside from the possibly corrupt police up north at Cheri's villa, all her dealings with them had been pleasant and enjoyable.

And here she was, barreling through their capitol building, hell-bent on taking out their president.

She was close now to the 'mop closet' and as she rounded a corner, she caught sight of a group of people rushing down the hallway ahead.

Rika surged forward, banking up onto a wall, and came around the corner to see a woman—the president, her HUD confirmed—being ushered into a lift.

There were too many people around for Rika to take a shot. She'd have no way to know if she'd hit the president. No way to confirm the kill.

<I'm going down,> she sent, and then leapt over the crowd toward the lift. Someone must have spotted her, because the doors began to close. A hand reached up and grabbed at her leg, and she kicked to free herself.

The action caused her to lose forward momentum, and she dropped fast. The doors were half a meter apart, and Rika gave one final push to break free of the dozen hands on her and slipped through into the elevator.

She struggled to her feet and a pulse rifle fired into her torso. Rika reached out, grabbed the weapon, and pulled it free from the shooter. Four hostiles, as well as the president, lit up on her HUD. Two were without armor—one of which was the man she had just disarmed—and the other two were in heavy armor.

One of the heavily armored guards pushed the president into the back corner and protected her bodily while the other opened fire on Rika. She stepped in close, past the man's short rifle, and punched him in the throat.

His armor cracked but didn't break. Rika was about to hit him again when she felt her right arm pulled back. She saw that the other two guards had grabbed the barrel of her GNR and were trying to pull her away from the president.

In the close quarters of the lift, Rika could barely maneuver her left arm—but she was able to swing it enough to lift the two men into the air and slam them into the elevator's ceiling.

The armored guard took advantage of Rika's distraction to pull out a sidearm and unload a magazine into her helmet. Rika gasped in surprise as her visor cracked, but it held against the point-blank fire.

She lifted her left leg up and sank her claws into the elevator's wall, and then punched the man again, straightening her leg at the same time.

This time the man's gorget broke; so did his neck. As he fell, the two unarmored guards were rising. They scrambled to their feet just as the lift doors opened. Rika reached for the president as the armored guard rushed her out, but the two men pulled Ariana back.

"Enough!" Rika yelled. She unslung her JE78 rifle and unloaded a quartet of pulse shots into the two men, before spinning and chasing the president and her guard across a foyer and through a massive blast door that was slowly closing.

She slipped in with plenty of room to spare, only to come face-to-face with a pair of Assault Mechs. She had met some of these guys during the war. Mostly they were made from large men; like a tank version of a scout mech, but not large and clumsy like a K1R. Unless she missed her guess, these two were model threes.

Rika surveyed the room and saw that it was a large foyer with thick pillars, five-meter-high ceilings, and a number of desks and consoles along two walls. The fourth wall had a number of crates stacked against it.

The guard all but carried the president past the two mechs and through a door amidst the consoles. Rika wondered for a brief moment—during which the AM-3s raised their chainguns—if they were under compliance or were still making war with their freedom. Like she was.

"Guys...do you really want to do this? We were on the same

side once," she said, smiling pleasantly—even though they couldn't see it behind her helmet.

"Stand down, SMI-2," one of the AM-3s said in a sharp tenor.

"Or don't," the other shrugged, his voice gravelly and deep.

Rika knew that if she backed down now, death would be the best possible outcome she could hope for.

"No can do," Rika said, and fired one of her uranium bolts at the AM-3 on her right. He saw her GNR rise and moved to the side—but not far enough.

The bolt hit his left arm where the chaingun was mounted and blew it clear off. The AM-3 models, unlike the SMI-2s, did not have any part of their organic limbs remaining, so the man only grimaced as the stump of twisted metal sticking out of his left shoulder twitched and sparked.

Rika knew that a fight against two of these mechs would be one of the most difficult she'd ever had, but a part of her reveled in the opportunity to test her mettle against them.

She closed with the one she had wounded, knowing that the best way to keep the other from bringing his formidable ordnance to bear was to have him run the risk of shooting his teammate.

Hopefully these two like one another.

She remembered hearing that the AM-2s had a weak spot on the edges of their chest plates where the armor connected to the hard mount on their bodies—hopefully it hadn't been fixed on the 3s. She toggled her JE78 rifle to kinetic slugs and fired a rapid burst of the two-centimeter rounds at the weak spot, spinning the already-wounded AM-3 to the side and driving him back.

Though Rika tried to keep the one-armed AM-3 between her and his gravelly voiced companion, she wasn't entirely successful, and he fired off a trio of blasts from his pulse rifle, pushing her back into the open.

The whine of the chaingun got her moving, and Rika dove behind a pillar as rounds chased after her. Two struck her in the side and one got her in the ass, but her armor registered no penetration—though the plate on the side of her butt was fractured.

Luckily the Marauders didn't believe in playing fair—Team Basilisk even less so—and Rika pulled a burn-stick from the pouch strapped to her left thigh and primed it for an impact ignition.

The burn sticks were thermite incendiaries modified to stick to their targets for maximum damage. One stick may not make it through an AM-3s armor, but it certainly would scare the shit out of them.

Rounds poured past the pillar, chipping away at its sides as the two AMs spread out, narrowing the cone of safety behind it. Rika considered her options and then leapt, twisting in the air so that her feet were up and her head was down.

She prayed her aim was true and almost shouted out in triumph when her feet clamped onto a decorative capital on the top of the pillar. She twisted around the pillar, threw the burn stick at the already-wounded AM-3, and then twisted around the other way, and aimed her GNR at the other AM-3.

He had anticipated her move and let loose with another barrage from his chaingun.

It would have hit, too, if the capital hadn't torn off the top of the pillar. Rika fired her round as she fell; the depleted uranium bolt struck the AM-3 in the head and snapped his neck back, but not enough to have broken it.

The front of the mech's helmet was a ruined mass, and he tore at it with his other hand, desperate to pull it off and regain sight.

Rika wasted no time and fired her electron beam at the struggling mech, burning a hole clear through his head.

She hadn't heard any screaming from the other AM-3 and assumed her burn stick had missed—but when she peered around the pillar, a pulse blast hit her square in the face and threw her backward, exposing her again.

As she struggled to her feet, she saw the second AM-3 was limping toward her, his right hip a mess of melted steel and blood.

"Gonna fuck you up," he said, his voice filled with rage. "Benny was a good friend. You're going to regret this."

Rika sprinted away as the AM-3 fired kinetic rounds from his rifle at her. Three bullets traced a line down her thigh and shattered the armor plating, then a fourth hit and tore through the front of her leg.

Rika fell to the ground once more, her gun-arm twisted under her body. The AM-3 held out his rifle and pulled the trigger.

CLICK!

In the time it took him to switch his rifle's firing mode, Rika rolled over, straightened her GNR, and fired her third uranium rod into his torso.

Her aim was good and the shot penetrated the armor where the burn stick had melted it away. The upper half of his body exploded outward, blood, bone, and armor spraying across the room.

Rika looked around, amazed that no other guards were present. Maybe these two had been the only ones down here when the president arrived.

Biofoam was filling her wound, and Rika noted that the med-readout on her HUD showed her femur as intact. She grabbed a shard of nearby armor—one of the AM-3s, by its color—and stuck it into the biofoam filling her wound.

It wouldn't offer any significant protection, but something was better than nothing.

She got her left leg under her, picked up her JE78 rifle, and rose up, leaning on her GNR's barrel as she tested her right leg's strength. Her armor and mods dulled the pain, but it still hurt like a fucker when she put weight on it.

Rika glanced back to see that the massive blast door at the foyer's entrance was sealed. Rika knew that it would not open easily, so any pursuit was a ways off. Still, there could be a rear exit, and she had to find the president before she and her remaining guard reached it.

Rika turned and limped in the direction the guard had taken

the president. She passed through the door on the far side of the foyer and into a maze of hallways filled with offices and meeting rooms.

She scanned the ground and saw a trail of blood. She wondered if the president had been wounded at some point or if the blood was from the guard—or even someone else.

Still, it was all she needed.

Rika ignored the pain in her leg and began to lope through the halls, following the trail of blood. It passed through the nicer portion of the bunker and into a rear area filled with supply rooms and environmental systems.

The droplets were decreasing in frequency, but so were the available paths to take. After five minutes, Rika heard voices and she slowed her approach.

"Can you open it?" she heard a woman's voice say, and she recognized it as the president's. She sounded scared, terrified, and Rika felt a pang of guilt. The worry that she was doing something terribly wrong assaulted her once more.

She peered around a corner and saw President Ariana and her guard at the far end—twenty-three meters away. Before them was a large door. One that either led deeper into the bunker or out to an exit. Given that it was sealed, Rika suspected it was an exit that had closed at the same time as the main door by the lift.

"Nowhere left to run," Rika said as she stepped into the corridor, her GNR-41C extended and aimed at the president's head.

The guard spun, raised his rifle, and fired it full auto at Rika. She twitched her GNR to the side and fired an electron beam that melted his armor, followed by a trio of ballistic rounds that tore his right arm off.

The man screamed in pain and collapsed, and Rika pulled her JE78 off her back and shot a pulse blast, pushing him back and away from the rifle still held by his severed, twitching arm.

She kept the JE78 trained on him as he whimpered in pain, and she leveled the GNR at the president once more.

"Why are you doing this?!" the woman shrieked. "Who's paying you? We can double it! Please!"

Rika shook her head. "I guess it's easy to see I'm Genevian, which makes me a merc. Funny thing is I don't get paid for this. I'm a slave."

"A what?" the president asked. "You're doing this under compliance? We can help you, we can free you!"

"Those two AM-3s, were they under compliance?" Rika asked.

"No!" the president shook her head emphatically. "What your people did to you was barbaric. We would never do that to any living being."

Rika felt sick to her stomach. Though she was still technically a slave, she was no longer under compliance. She was about to murder this woman of her own free will.

"I'm sorry," Rika said. "I have to do this."

"You can fight it," the woman said. "Others have! Fight the Discipline, please!"

Rika felt tears on her cheeks. "I don't have to.... I'm not currently under Discipline. My compliance chip is offline."

"Then why are you doing this?!" Ariana shrieked. "You have no reason to kill me!"

"I have to belong somewhere…" Rika said, her voice cracking. "I need a home, I can't make it on my own. I tried, I really tried."

"I'll help you, Thebes can help you! Just *please* don't kill me!"

A sob tore through Rika's body and she lowered her GNR. She couldn't do it. She *wouldn't* do it. Basilisk team had been kind to her—more than they had to be—but she just couldn't kill this woman in cold blood as she pleaded for her life.

"I won't…" Rika said quietly. "I won't kill you. I'm done."

She fell to the ground as Ariana began to weep with relief.

"What happens now?" Rika asked—knowing that things were unlikely to play out well for her no matter what.

President Ariana wiped her cheeks dry and pushed her hair back out of her face. "I don't know…you just killed a lot of people."

Rika sighed. "I tried not to…as much as I could."

The guard beside Ariana shifted, and Rika suspected that he had passed out and was just coming to.

"Madam President!" he called out, turning his head toward her. "You're…you're OK?"

Ariana nodded solemnly, glancing up at Rika, "For no reason other than my would-be assassin's conscience striking at the last moment."

Rika could tell that the president had meant the words to be kind—at least to a degree—but they cut her to the core.

The president glanced back down at her guard. "Are you OK, John? Other than the arm…."

The guard—John—nodded. "Yeah, I'll live. You, there; if you really mean no further harm, put down your weapons…if you can."

Rika pulled herself back to her feet, wincing as pain lanced up her injured leg. John tried to rise as well, but fell back against the wall.

"I can't" Rika said as she placed her JE78 on her back. "I'm not going to rot in one of your prisons any more than I'm going to be a slave."

"You're not getting out of here," Ariana said. "There'll be an entire army above, waiting for you to emerge."

"Maybe," Rika said. "Depends on whether or not the other trigger pullers had more steel than I did."

"Other?" Ariana asked. "How many others?"

"I don't know," Rika shrugged. "Slave, remember? Though I don't even know if my team knew for sure. Enough to wipe out the upper echelon of your leadership—both civilian and military."

"Fuuuuhck," Ariana breathed. "John! We have to get out of here!"

John coughed. "No. No we shouldn't. If what she says is true, then this is where you need to stay."

"Do you have Link access?" Rika asked. "You could get out a

warning, at least."

"Offline right now. It has to be initiated from down here," John said, coughing again. "Could…could someone help me get my helmet off? I'm coughing blood here, and it's getting nasty."

"Yeah, how do I do it?" Ariana asked.

John reached up with his remaining arm and unclipped a latch on each side. "Just twist counter clockwise, and then lift straight up."

Ariana nodded and complied as Rika looked on silently.

When John's face appeared, his mouth and chin were covered in blood.

"John!" Ariana gasped.

The man gave a macabre smile. "Madam President, my arm is missing, how is a little blood on my face compared to that?"

"John, really, I don't know, OK? Let me help you up."

"For what it's worth, I'm sorry," Rika said sheepishly.

"Why don't you pull off your helmet so we can see who you are?" President Ariana asked.

Rika shook her head. "No, ma'am. John there is sure to have another weapon on him, and I wouldn't blame him for taking a shot at me."

Ariana looked to John, who nodded grimly, "I certainly would."

"No, John, you won't. This woman is not a threat anymore. If she wanted to kill me, she would have already. You're not to harm her. That's an order."

John gritted his teeth but nodded.

"I need to hear it, John," Ariana said.

"Fine. I won't harm her."

Ariana turned back to Rika. "See? I'm showing my trust in you. Now I need something back. Remove your helmet."

Rika sighed and signaled her helmet to unlatch; then she pulled it off and hooked it on her hip.

"Huh," John said, while the President shook her head. "You're just a young woman."

"Not so young. Just a new face," Rika said. "War took the old one."

"It's in your eyes," Ariana said as she approached. "You're what, twenty-seven?"

"A bit older," Rika replied.

"What's your name?"

"Rika."

Ariana nodded. "Well, Rika; if you'd like, let's go to the command center and see if we can find out if I'm still president of this alliance or if we've been invaded."

Rika gestured silently for the president to precede her, and John barked a laugh as he scooped up his rifle. "Fat chance. You're in the lead, *Rika*."

"John," President Ariana said. "Seriously. She's no threat."

"Respectfully, Madam President, you're wrong. She is *absolutely* still a threat."

"It's OK," Rika said. "I can go in front. Just let me know if I make a wrong turn."

Rika began to walk back to where she suspected the command center to be—a room filled with holotanks and consoles that she had passed on the way to their present position.

Strange as it was, Rika felt that she could trust the president. The woman seemed honorable—of course, she was a politician, which also meant she was likely a demagogue capable of telling any tale to suit her. If Ariana became hostile and broke her word, Rika harbored no illusions that John would go along with it.

As Rika limped along—her injury still sending waves of pain up her thigh with each step—Ariana caught up with her.

"Do you know who hired you?" she asked. "What outfit are you with?"

"I'd rather not say," Rika replied.

"About which?"

"About either," Rika said.

"Do you even know who hired you?"

"I don't, but my team has suspicions."

"Nietzschean Empire, most likely," John said from behind them.

Rika had been walking with her head turned just enough to keep John in her peripheral vision. She saw the sneer on his face and wondered about the relationship between Thebes and the Empire.

"Wouldn't be Niets," Rika replied. "Too many Genevians in the—uh…our outfit to ever take work from them. Besides. Assassination isn't the Niets' style. They only do full frontal assault." Rika remembered a few ambushes from the war. "Well, mostly."

Ariana sighed. "Whoever it is…if the rest of your teams were half as successful as you were, we're in serious trouble. Our constitution has a very tricky transfer of power built in. If top military leaders are dead, too…"

"Depends on whether it's an internal coup or an external attack," John said.

"Let's hope it's a coup," Ariana replied.

"Why?" Rika asked.

Ariana glanced up at her. "Because even if whoever takes over is a horrible despot, it's probably better than an invasion."

The sick feeling in Rika's stomach intensified. Here she was worried about going to prison or how she'd escape, and the woman at her side was concerned with the fate of millions of her citizens.

Even so, Rika's desire to get free was undiminished. She was tired of being the pawn of others. It was high time that she took control of her own destiny—even if that meant using President Ariana as a hostage to secure her freedom.

Of course, if the rest of the Marauders had succeeded, it was Ariana whose days were numbered. When whoever had paid the Marauders arrived to take advantage of the chaos, the bunker would eventually be cracked, and she would be executed.

Rika had to admit that she hoped such an outcome would not be the case.

They walked in silence for the remainder of the distance to the command center—which Rika had correctly identified. It wasn't far from the entrance. One of the AM-3s bodies was visible through the door.

Ariana glanced at Rika, who, for all her augmentations was still under only two hundred and thirty centimeters tall, while the AM-3s had been over three hundred.

"I can't believe you killed them…and are barely hurt."

Rika shrugged. "There's a reason they made my model after theirs."

Ariana locked her eyes on Rika's.

"Is that all you are? A model? A woman decided not to kill me. Not a machine. Do you see yourself as a woman?"

Rika felt a tear form in her eye and didn't trust her voice. *How is Ariana able to disarm me so completely?* She had to believe that the Theban President was sincere; if not, she was playing Rika like a harp.

"I try," she finally managed to reply, though her voice betrayed her emotions.

Ariana gave her a sympathetic look before turning and walking into the command center. She approached a console and keyed in a command.

"I'm opening up a connection to the surface networks," Ariana said and glanced back at Rika. "Send me your codes. I'll give you access."

"Madam—" John began, but Ariana held up her hand.

"We've been over this, John."

Rika connected to the bunker's network and sent her public token to Ariana.

<*Thanks,*> Ariana replied. <*And thank you for not killing me. I know you aren't sure if you can trust me…the feeling's mutual, but I would like to salvage whatever we can out of this.*>

Rika sent an affirmative response but didn't speak. She was desperate to find out what had happened on the surface, but also terrified.

A moment later, Rika felt the surface networks become available and sought out the encrypted channel Basilisk had used for comms.

Her queue was flooded with messages. From Leslie and Barne (though none from Jerry), one from Captain Ayer, and another from someone named Specialist David.

She was about to check the first message when Leslie's voice barreled into her mind. *<Rika! Rika? Are you there? Stand down! Don't kill the president!>*

<Leslie, I'm here, she's alive,> Rika responded, shocked by the change in orders.

<Alive? As in 'barely breathing' or 'standing up and happy'?>

<Well, I don't know how happy she is, but she's physically unharmed.>

<Whaa…You're going to have to tell me what happened soon, but for now the Marauders have sided with the Thebans—we were hired by the Niets!>

<The fuck?!> Rika exclaimed as she refocused on Ariana, whose face bore a wan smile.

"Well, Rika. Looks like we're on the same side now."

FORGIVEN

STELLAR DATE: 12.18.8948 (Adjusted Years)
LOCATION: Capitol Bunker, Berlin
REGION: Pyra, Albany System, Theban Alliance

Thirty minutes later, Rika stood with President Ariana and a very pale John as the bunker's main door slowly opened. She had moved the two AM-3s to the side and covered their bodies—what was left of them—with a sheet from a supply closet.

Ariana's generals were torn. Some wished to get their president out of the bunker—and away from Rika—as quickly as possible. Others didn't want her to leave the bunker until things with the Marauders were sorted out.

Between Ariana's updates and intel Rika got from Leslie and Barne, they had pieced together the events of the previous hour.

As Rika had been rushing through the Capitol building, hundreds of Marauder comm drones had dumped out of the dark layer into the Albany system, broadcasting abort codes to all Marauder teams.

Leslie had informed her that the drone swarm was a last-ditch failsafe to abort an operation. Most of the drones were destroyed in the dark layer, but enough made it through to get the message out.

Then a Marauder fleet had jumped deep into the Albany system, only twenty AU from Pyra, which they were decelerating toward and would reach in two days. Although the Marauders only possessed one hundred and twenty capital ships, no system reacted kindly to a mercenary force of that size arriving without notice.

On top of that, another dozen rapid exfiltration ships had boosted out of hiding around various moons and planetary rings, scooping up Marauder teams across the system.

"My generals are certainly nervous," Ariana had said at one

point. "Granted, your Marauders' small number of ships are no great threat; but given your close proximity to me down here, no one knows if we're really in a hostage situation or not—despite my reassurances."

"Understandable," Rika had replied. "This is a mess no matter which way you turn it. But to think that I almost killed you for the Niets.... I'm sorry, President Ariana. I—I'm just sorry."

Ariana had nodded and placed a hand on Rika's arm. "Trust me, no one is more glad than I that you had a change of heart."

Once Leslie and Barne had given her the details about the Niets hoax, she had asked the question that had been burning in her mind. <*Where's Jerry?*>

Leslie didn't reply, but Rika sensed a wave of anguish over the Link.

<*He didn't make it,*> Barne said quietly. <*A missile from the Capitol's defense systems took him out while you were infiltrating.*>

<*Leslie...I'm so sorry,*> Rika said.

<*I can't, Rika. I can't think about it right now, OK? If I start, then....*>

Rika respected that, and changed the subject.

<*What are my orders?*>

Barne fielded the answer. <*We have a major on the ground here who is coordinating a reconciliation. One thing that everyone can agree on is that the Niets weren't going to sit on their asses and wait for the Thebans to regroup; they'll have an invasion force on Pyra's doorstep in no time.*>

Those words echoed in Rika's mind as the bunker's wide door swung open. A Nietzschean invasion. She didn't know much about the Theban space force's strength, but she didn't see how a five-system alliance could field anything powerful enough to withstand an assault from the Nietzschean Empire.

The orders Rika received were simple: regroup with Basilisk and sync up with Alpha Company under Captain Ayer.

Rika had just one issue with that.

She wasn't a Marauder. She never signed up for this shit.

But her thoughts turned to Barne and Leslie. They were her team; even though she had failed in her duties, failed to take out President Ariana, they had shown no displeasure in her inaction.

Perhaps they didn't need to know exactly what had occurred—maybe a half-truth would have to be enough.

Rika glanced at President Ariana. She knew that there could be a place for her in Thebes—despite the lives she had taken—but Team Basilisk needed her. Barne and Leslie were just squishies. There was no way they could survive a Nietzschean invasion without mech support.

"FREEZE! Drop your weapons!" A voice yelled as the door swung open far enough for Rika to see an AM-2 mech on the other side.

"Lower your weapons," President Ariana called out. "I've issued a provisional pardon for Rika, here. She is not to be placed under arrest or to be restricted in any other way."

Rika relaxed a hair. Despite all of the president's assurances, there was a part of her that had worried it was a ruse to lull her into a false sense of security.

Of course she was still in arm's reach of Ariana. Things could change once they were separated.

"Ma'am," a man said as he pushed past several presidential guards in powered armor. "You cannot do this. She killed at least half a dozen people on her rampage."

Ariana turned her head toward Rika. "Sergey. I understand that, but she thought what she was doing was necessary. Rika stood down of her own accord. She may be a killer, but she is not a murderer. And on that basis, I have issued my pardon."

"This is going to be a disaster," Sergey replied, gripping his hands together.

"Sergey," Ariana said with a tired smile. "We have a war to fight. Rika is a warrior, and she is now fighting on our side. I'll take all the help we can get."

"Yeah, but on our side for how long?" one of the nearby soldiers muttered.

"Fucking mercs," said another.

Ariana did not acknowledge the utterances, but instead walked toward the lift. "Rika, you may ride up with me. John, you're on the first ride up, too. You need to see a medic yesterday."

"A bit late for that," John said as he followed after the president.

Rika slipped between the soldiers, feeling dozens of eyes on her, waiting for a bullet or a blow. But none came, and she reached the lift unmolested.

She noted that the bodies had been removed but the bloodstains remained. She wondered if the two unarmored guards had been part of the kill count or not. She thought she had been careful not to harm them—too much.

"Rika," President Ariana began as two other guards entered, and the lift began to rise. "I may not see you in the days to come; fate may pull us apart. I regret what your government did to you, and what lot has been left for you in life. I know it's not the same, but I have been called a monster in the past as well…" Ariana paused and met Rika's eyes. "I guess what I'm trying to say is that it was your *humanity* that saved me down there."

Ariana touched Rika's hand, gripping it like she would any flesh and blood hand, and squeezed gently. Their eyes met.

"I forgive you, Rika."

Rika felt a surge of emotion rise up in her, and tears sprang from the corners of her eyes. She nodded rapidly knowing that her voice would betray the wellspring of emotion within her.

Ariana continued to hold her hand as the lift rose and the doors opened. The guards in their powered armor exited first then turned and waited for the president. Ariana smiled at Rika and exited the lift.

Just as Rika whispered, "Thank you."

That was the last Rika ever saw of President Ariana. She was killed two days later when an orbital strike from a Nietzschean cruiser destroyed all of Berlin, including the capitol and the presidential palace.

MARAUDER

STELLAR DATE: 12.22.8948 (Adjusted Years)
LOCATION: Northern Districts of Jersey City
REGION: Pyra, Albany System, Theban Alliance

"Move! Move! *Move!*" Rika screamed at the platoon under her care as they clambered over the debris of a fallen building on the outskirts of Jersey City.

A sniper was out there firing on them, and Rika had to take it out before they lost any more Marauders.

<*I think I have triangulation,*> Barne said and passed the coordinates to Rika. She leveled her GNR and fired, trusting in Barne's analysis.

A dozen projectile rounds flew into a building three blocks away, and she changed positions, waiting for return fire. When none came, she breathed a deep sigh of relief.

<*Thanks, Barne.*>

<*Anytime, Rika.*>

Rika turned and surveyed the city around her, which was shrouded in long shadows as Howe set in the west. She shook her head, saddened by the current state of what had been a beautiful city, full of life just six days ago when she and Barne had passed through.

In the four days since the aborted assassination of the Theban leadership, all hell had broken loose.

The Nietzschean armada had not been far behind the Marauders' fleet, jumping in with over ten thousand capital ships all bearing down on Pyra. Their intent was to take out the Theban capital world in one swift strike.

One small benefit of the Theban response to the Marauders' arrival was that their ships were already mustered and in motion by the time the Niets appeared on Scan. This gave the Thebans enough of an edge that they were able to stave off a full bombardment of their world. However, it wasn't enough to stop several Nietzschean strafing runs on the planet that took out cities and dropped multiple ground assault teams.

It was textbook Nietzschean strategy: blitzkrieg a world. If they were unable to take it quickly, destroy and occupy large population centers. Dislodging their troops always resulted in heavy civilian casualties.

Rika was leading one such dislodging action at that very moment.

Leslie and Barne were with her, as well.

Technically a lieutenant named Clancy was in command of the platoon; somehow though, over the last day, everyone had begun to defer to Rika as they worked their way ever deeper into the ruins of Jersey City.

Rika clambered up a beam rising out of the rubble and watched the nearby buildings for signs of the enemy as the platoon spread out in the street below.

She spotted movement four blocks down and cycled her vision, confirming the presence of Nietzschean soldiers.

<*Lieutenant Clancy,*> Rika called over the combat net. <*I see twenty Niets on E street, two blocks down. I thought we scouted that area.*>

<*We did, but that was six minutes ago. There were no life signs at the time,*> Clancy replied.

Rika called back to the Marauders' surface-to-surface artillery teams, ten kilometers behind them. <*I have hostiles at the following coordinates,*> she said. <*Requesting immediate fire support.*>

<*Acknowledged,*> the comm officer at the platform replied. <*I have fire solution authorization. Hold please.*>

Less than a minute later, two grey streaks fell straight down from the sky, lobbed high into the air before they dove into their marks.

The street and the part of the building where the Niets were hiding in the shadows exploded in twin balls of fire. As the haze cleared, Rika called her thanks back to the artillery platform while also letting Lieutenant Clancy know that she didn't read any more hostiles from her vantage.

Below her the platoon split up, its four squads each taking a different street toward the center of Jersey City.

<*I'm on the right flank, out past first squad,*> Leslie reported. <*Ranging ahead.*>

<*Copy that,*> Barne replied from his place back with Clancy and the platoon sergeant. <*Rika, Clancy says that second squad out on the left flank has a fireteam that performs scout duties for the 'toon. Why don't you take the center?*>

<*You got it,*> Rika replied and dropped from the steel girder onto the street below.

She moved down the street being traversed by fourth squad—second from the right flank—and slipped past the soldiers.

Several of the Marauders nodded to her as she moved by. Some shook their heads, but most ignored her. Seeing their attitudes—not to mention their armor—brought a lot of old memories back.

Most of the armor and equipment in the Marauders was Genevian. Unfortunately so were the troops, and that meant many of the soldiers thought of her as nothing more than a tool.

Rika thanked her stars that Captain Ayer hadn't felt that way when attaching Rika to fourth platoon.

*****

Two days prior…

"Basilisk," Captain Ayer had shaken her head slowly as the team entered the company's HQ—set up in the back offices of a water-storage and pumping plant. "You're some tough sons and daughters o' bitches. I'm sorry about Jerry; he was one of the best."

As she had spoken the captain rose from her desk, and the other two people in the room—a man and woman—had also turned their attention to Basilisk, their eyes solemn as they looked on.

Ayer walked around the desk and approached Leslie, clasping both of her hands. "I'm so sorry, Leslie. I truly am. I'm here if you need to talk."

Leslie nodded silently before taking a deep breath and wiping an eye.

Ayer then turned to Rika and shook her hand without hesitation. A gesture that spoke volumes about her opinion of mechs.

"Rika, I'm happy to finally meet you, but it saddens me that it's under these circumstances."

"Thank you, Captain Ayer," Rika replied.

Lastly, Ayer turned to Barne and clasped his hand. "Sergeant Barne, I see you survived your first mission with Rika. I'm glad to see the two of you are unscathed."

"Captain Ayer, of course I am. I've got Rika at my back. She's Basilisk."

Ayer glanced at the coiled snake carefully painted on Rika's chest. "So she is. I'm surprised that you feel that way."

"No reason not to, ma'am," Barne said, his tone crisp and unequivocal.

"Glad to hear it," Ayer replied.

"Rika, I'd like you to meet First Sergeant Meg, and Gunnery Sergeant Stewart."

"Nice to meet you, Rika," Gunnery Sergeant Stewart said with a smile, while First Sergeant Meg only nodded and said, "Rika."

"Glad you were able to make it up here to meet us," Ayer continued once the formalities were over.

"Was a slog up the coast," Barne said. "But we heard this was where they were dropping the beer, ma'am."

"No beer yet, Sergeant, but I do have some gifts for Rika and some real armor for the two of you."

Rika wondered what those gifts could be, but didn't voice her question as Ayer continued.

"The Niets may have done a drive-by on Berlin and toasted it something fierce, but Marauder ships aren't commanded by pusillanimous cowards like the GAF was, and it would seem the Thebans aren't either. For now they've managed to push the Nietzschean ships back from Pyra, and are engaging them near Fresna."

"Good news is that we don't have to worry about Niet birds in our skies. Bad news is that they dropped over a hundred-thousand of their dickhead commandos down here, and we'll have to clear them out the old-fashioned way."

"Do we have any orbital support?" Barne asked.

Ayer nodded. "We've got the *Brisbane* in orbit and an artillery platform set up a few klicks to the north. It's a bit of a Niet magnet, so first platoon is keeping it safe until the *Brisbane* gets the shield generator down here. The Thebies have a few ships up there, too. They've taken what shots they can, but now the Niets have a lot of civvies rounded up, and the Thebans don't want to blow away their own people."

"So it's time to send in the mercs," Leslie said.

"You need to sit this one out, Corporal?" Captain Ayer asked, a sharp edge entering her voice. "I feel for you, and I feel your pain, too, but you signed up for this gig. Last I checked, so did Jerry."

Leslie swallowed and glanced at Barne and then Rika. "No, ma'am. I go where Basilisk goes."

"Glad to hear it," Ayer said with a curt nod. "We're going to send you out with Lieutenant Clancy and fourth platoon. However, I first need to square away some housekeeping."

Ayer turned to Rika as she spoke, and Rika wondered what could be coming next.

"Back in the war, a mech saved my life. Another mech saved an entire platoon under me. I watched mechs do the war's hardest work with the least thanks. You never got medals, ribbons, or promotions; that's not how the Marauders operate. I have authorization from General Mill to give you a field promotion to

Second Lieutenant."

Rika felt a surge of mixed emotions, but shook her head.

"No, ma'am. No disrespect to you, but I cannot accept that promotion."

Ayer's face clouded. "Why not, Rika?"

"Because I'm a slave, and slaves can't be officers."

"Shit, Rika, didn't you get the message? It should be in your queue on the Marauders' general—aw, fuck." Ayer sighed and gave Rika a wink. "We try to be more efficient than the Genevian Armed Forces were, but it's not always easy. You never got tokens to access the general net, did you?"

"No, ma'am," Rika shook her head.

"We'll square that away once we're done here, but let me be the first to inform you that you are *not* a slave. There was a data packet that got left out when you were sent to Pyra—it was a bit of a rush job, not our best work. You were only to have to work off half the cost that it took to buy you at that disgusting auction. However, when the Old Man learned about how you saved your team when you could have disappeared, he decided that you had gone above and beyond the call of duty—especially for someone who thought they were a slave.

"You're free and clear, Rika. You owe the Marauders nothing, and when we're done here, I'll have the company's technician remove that compliance chip and get proper enlistment paperwork drawn up for you."

Barne let out a whoop of joy while Leslie reached out and grabbed Rika's arm. "Rika," she said with a smile.

Rika couldn't find the words, but she felt a tear slide down her cheek. She drew herself up and wordlessly saluted Captain Ayer.

She had finally been set free. There was no hesitation in her mind now. She *was* a Marauder.

Captain Ayer smiled and returned the salute. "Now, Lieutenant Rika. I assume that you'll properly enlist?"

"Yes, ma'am." Rika said the words with a calm certainty.

"Excellent. The gifts, by the way, are right-mount GNR and a new left arm. Now let's get Clancy in here and go over how we're going to kill all these fucking Niets."

*****

On the front…

Rika had worried that Clancy would have an issue with another officer attached to his platoon. As it turned out, he was a first lieutenant, and the pecking order was clear—for the most part. Though he was in charge, Rika had a lot more experience in the field, and he was to take her advice.

Barne had them all beat for time in the service—even more than Clancy's platoon sergeant—but that just meant he'd make sure the officers didn't screw things up too much.

The plan had been straightforward: move south into the city, secure the manufacturing district on its north side, and then cross the canal into the downtown area and flush the Niets out.

Except there'd been a lot more Niets on the north side of the canal than anyone had expected. Second and third platoons were still further back, but Captain Ayer had instructed fourth platoon to push forward and secure the north side of the canal—which was now only four kilometers distant.

As Rika slipped past squad four's lead fireteam and down E street, she scanned each building for heat signatures and movement while also monitoring feeds from the platoon's drones.

<*All clear so far,*> she reported back, then caught movement on one of the forward drone's feeds. <*Scratch that. I have movement.*>

The drone had picked up a shadow moving at the head of a nearby alley. Rika unslung her JE78, ready for close quarters combat. She pulled a drone's feed from high overhead but was unable to see into the alley with the refuse and overhangs from the buildings on either side.

She considered sending a drone into the alley but didn't want to give away her intentions. Rika glanced at the twelve-meter-high building and crouched before springing up over the protruding roof, landing as quietly as possible, and then dashing across the to the next street and dropping down at the other end of the alley.

<*Checking alley at my position,*> she reported to Barne, relaying the message through the drones to reduce her EM signature.

<*Understood.*>

Rika crept down the alley's narrow confines, staying in the deepening shadows and searching for whomever or whatever she had seen. She progressed five meters into the alley and then stopped, pressing herself against the northern side, as a dull scraping sound reached her ears.

Nothing showed up in her enhanced vision, and she was considering sweeping the darkness with an active scan when a shape darted out from between two large metal bins.

<*Just a dog,*> she reported to Barne as the large grey hound approached her.

"Got left behind, did you?" Rika asked as she reached her left hand out to stroke its head. The dog didn't shy away, and she smiled to herself, happy to see that someone accepted her without reservation.

Though she knew that thought wasn't entirely fair. Leslie had never once seemed disturbed that Rika was a mech; nor had Captain Ayer.

As Rika stood, she heard a sound from behind her and she snapped her knees straight, leaping into the air as an electron beam streaked through the space where she had been a moment before.

Rika arched over backward and saw four shimmering figures at the entrance to the alley.

Shit, that's good camo, she thought while firing two projectile rounds from her GNR-41C, followed by a full auto spray from her JE78. The large caliber rounds from the GNR took out the Niet with the electron beam, and the other rounds drove the rest of the enemy back around the corner.

<*Three tangos, F street, my position,*> Rika called out as she hit the ground and moved deeper into the alley. The dog was gone, and she was glad to see it hadn't been a casualty of the Niets' ambush.

<*Want a hand?*> Leslie asked. <*I'm on G street, not far ahead.*>

<*How'd you get ahead?*> Rika asked.

Barne chuckled in their minds. <*Leslie's like a ninja.*>

<*I'm never one to say 'no' to help,*> Rika replied.

She saw Leslie's location on the combat net and fired a few shots out of the alley's mouth to keep the Niets engaged with her. One ducked around the corner and fired a few rounds, which missed because Rika was halfway up the wall of a building and climbing.

Another Niet tossed an HE grenade into the alley, and Rika raced up the wall, tearing out bricks and mortar as she went. The explosion blew past her just as she reached the top.

Rika heard weapons fire on the street below and moved to the edge of the building to look down. Leslie was across the street, just emerging from cover, and squad one's lead fireteam was half a block to the north.

The Niets were all dead.

<*Thanks, guys,*> Rika said over the platoon's combat net.

<*Anytime, LT,*> Corporal Veers, leader of the fireteam, replied.

Rika stayed on the rooftops for the next kilometer, ranging further ahead and using her drones to scout the alleys and streets around her. She was now within two kilometers of the canal and the downtown district on its far side, and she scanned the gleaming towers that rose into the air.

The streets on the north side of the canal ran at a forty-five-degree angle to the waterway, which provided line-of-sight protection for the platoon as they advanced behind Rika. Unfortunately, the manufacturing district had given way to smaller commercial buildings, which were still tightly packed but were often only one story high. They wouldn't provide much cover if any significant fire came from the three-hundred-meter-high buildings across the canal.

Rika sent her drones further into the sky and overlaid their feed with the images delivered from the ships and satellites overhead.

The combined visual showed a lot of activity in the towers along the canal. There were also a lot more heat signatures than could be accounted for by the Niets alone. Marauder Intel and Analysis determined that the towers were occupied by at least a hundred thousand Theban citizens.

Artillery was out of the question.

Along the northern edge of the canal—on the side Rika was approaching—lay a wide, heavily wooded park. At first it appeared as though the park was empty; Rika sent her drones down into the trees. They passed through an EM shield and suddenly picked up dozens, then hundreds, of heat signatures in the trees.

The Niets were waiting for them.

Three of her drones went offline, and Rika assumed the enemy had deployed EMP countermeasures against them. Rika released another passel but kept them high and further back.

<*Got a welcoming committee,*> Rika said as she passed her observations back.

<*Not surprising,*> Clancy replied. <*Any suggestions?*>

<*With those towers back there raining down beamfire, it'll take a whole regiment to get across that canal. What we need is a feint.*>

Barne offered a suggestion. <*We could pummel locations to the west and east with artillery fire, creating a clear path for an advance. The Niets will concentrate their troops along the area we clear out, then we'll come right up the center.*>

<*It won't take them long to realize what we're up to. Then they'll smash us from the towers,*> Clancy replied.

<*Then Rika and Leslie had better get over there and take out a tower or two first,*> Barne replied.

Rika liked the plan. <*Leslie. Meet me at my position. I have an idea.*>

CRASH

STELLAR DATE: 12.22.8948 (Adjusted Years)
LOCATION: Northern Districts of Jersey City
REGION: Pyra, Albany System, Theban Alliance

<*So what's the big plan?*> Leslie asked on a private connection to Rika as she approached. Rika had a hard time seeing Leslie; the other woman's light armor continually shifted in color to match her surroundings as she moved through the evening shadows.

<*I did this back in the Parsons System when we were trying to make evac,*> Rika said. <*Storm drains will dump into that canal; we go down into them, cross the canal underneath, and then get through a storm drain on the far side and make our way up.*>

Leslie cocked her head as she crouched next to Rika, considering the idea.

<*That was a pitched battle, if I recall the reports. They didn't have good Scan. Here they'll be staring at that canal with a lot of tech. They will see us cross. Not to mention they'll have monitors on the storm drains on the far side,*> Leslie said.

<*Yeah, but we have to cross somehow. The canal has a lot of sludge and stuff growing in it—it should mask us, if we stay down in the muck.*>

<*And the detection systems they'll certainly have placed on the storm drains on the far side?*> Leslie asked.

Rika brought up the canal's far shore, looking for other options.

<*What about that little decorative inlet and pool there?*> she suggested, sharing the location with Leslie.

<*That could work. It's right next to the Withermere Tower, which is where Intel and Analysis thinks a lot of their heavy weapons are set up.*>

<*How good is Marauder I&A?*> Rika asked.

Leslie shrugged. <*Pretty good. Better than what we had in the war.*>

<*We're Genevians fighting Niets,*> Rika replied. <*Feels like the war is still on.*>

Leslie gave a rueful laugh. <*Yeah, just a new theater.*>

The pair backtracked and found a storm grate that they would fit through. Rika pulled it up as quietly as possible and, once in, lowered it over them.

There wasn't enough room to stand so the two women crawled on all fours—all threes in Rika's case, with her GNR draped over her back. Leslie was in the lead and she reached the spout into the canal first.

It sat halfway out of the water, and Leslie glanced back at Rika. <*Here goes nothing.*>

She slithered out of the spout and down into the dark waters with Rika right on her tail. They fell to the bottom of the canal, which was just over four meters deep at this point, and lay still in the mud.

No weapons fire came, and Rika wished she had a drone feed to be certain that a hundred Niets wouldn't be waiting for them on the far shore—but the EM signals would have given them away.

It took the pair over ten minutes to cross the canal, staying low, crawling across the muddy bottom and angling across to the inlet. When they finally reached their exit point, Rika sent a drone to the water's surface and passively scanned the area.

The drone picked up two Niets nearby and a motion sensor to their right. However nothing appeared to be covering the route they needed to take to get to the Withermere Tower, which rose up on the water's edge like a great glass reed only a dozen meters to the east.

Rika motioned for Leslie—who was also tapped into her drone feed—to follow. They slowly rose, taking care not to cause too much of a disturbance on the water's surface.

Leslie moved ahead, her armor's camo systems giving her the edge, and she signaled to Rika when the coast was clear.

Rika kept expecting weapons fire to rain down on them at any moment as they moved from cover to cover, but none came. Five minutes later, they finally reached the entrance to the Withermere Tower.

Rika peered through the glass doors and saw a dozen guards. Leslie saw them, too, and she glanced back at Rika.

Both women knew that if they breached the building and took out the guards, it would alert the enemy to the possibility of an attack down the center. However, if they waited for the Marauders' artillery to strike, they wouldn't get to the weapon emplacements in the tower fast enough.

Rika noted a small patio wrapping around the Withermere Tower and hanging over the water. Chances were that another entrance would be on the far end of the patio.

She signaled to Leslie, who gave a nod, and the two Marauders began to creep alongside the building and around the corner onto the patio. They had a clear view of the canal and the park beyond—which would still be teeming with Niets. If just one enemy soldier peered back across the canal, their little surprise would be over.

The far end of the patio was occupied by a dozen tables with umbrellas; many of which were still holding the remains of food. Rika spotted a door that led into a small café. Leslie checked the entrance for any active monitoring and, when none was revealed, opened the door and slipped inside with Rika trailing right behind her.

Within, more tables—most covered with discarded food and drinks—filled the space. Overturned chairs and a smashed interior window showed the signs of a struggle. The door leading into the interior of the tower was closed, so they stepped through the broken window and slowly walked down the hall to the bank of elevators.

The first door was open, with an elevator car within. The second was closed, and Rika prised her fingers into the gap and pulled the doors apart.

She peered inside and saw a ladder to the right. Rika stretched a leg out and clamped her clawed foot around the vertical rail on one side of the ladder, and then swung out into the shaft, clamping her other foot on the other side. She'd learned long ago not to trust her weight to ladder rungs—most weren't rated to hold her two hundred and thirty kilos.

Rika proceeded to walk up the ladder, her body perpendicular to the elevator shaft, while Leslie swung out behind her and pulled the door shut.

<*That looks really weird,*> Leslie commented on a tight comm. <*It's like you're walking up the side of the shaft.*>

Rika laughed. <*I kinda am. You're going to get exhausted, climbing sixty floors like that—plus you're slow. Hook onto this.*>

Leslie accepted the cable that Rika spooled out from her armor and clipped it onto a hook at her waist.

<*Now let's just hope that this ladder doesn't peel off the wall,*> Leslie said as Rika began to 'walk' up the shaft.

<*We only have fifteen more minutes before the artillery lights up the park,*> Rika advised.

<*Better get a move on, then.*>

Rika picked up the pace while still trying to climb as quietly as possible. As they passed the closed doors to many levels, muted voices could be heard. Most likely the Theban populace, being kept in the towers to make them less appealing targets.

Their destination, the sixtieth floor—where I&A had placed the first of the Niets' heavy weaponry—took three minutes to reach. When they arrived, Leslie unhooked from Rika, pulled herself over to the door, cracked it a centimeter, and passed out a drone.

<*I'm clear,*> Leslie reported. <*Good luck,*>

<*You too,*> Rika replied as she resumed her climb, heading to the roof of the building another ten stories above.

She reached the top of the shaft less than a minute later and pulled herself up to the a-grav emitter in the machine room that sat atop the building. There was a service hatch on one side, and Rika carefully maneuvered herself through it and onto the roof.

Rika surveyed her surroundings. There were no Niets on the south side of the roof, but she could see several on the tops of the nearby buildings, clustered around railguns that were set up a few meters back from the northern edges. She imagined the same setup was on the Withermere—the guns out of view but ready to slide forward and rain down punishing kinetic fire on any attackers across the canal.

Rika logged the locations of the guns. Once the assault began, she would relay the weapon coordinates to the artillery platform; perhaps they had airburst options that could at least blind the enemy weapons.

If not, she would take them out the hard way.

She passed a drone around the side of the elevator machine room to get a clear view of what she faced before the assault began. As the drone peeked around the corner, it caught sight of a pair of Niets walking around to the south side of the tower's roof.

"Shit!" Rika whispered. She considered her options. She could circle around to the west side of the machine room, but the two patrolling Niets would probably make a full circuit anyway. That would force her into full view of the rest of the Niets on the roof.

Her best bet was to take them out as quietly as possible when they reached the south side. Five nearby towers were as tall as the Withermere, and the Niets on their roofs would easily spot anything more than a quick takedown.

Of course, the enemy was wearing heavy powered armor, so taking them out quietly was going to be easier said than done.

Damn, I'm an idiot, Rika thought, realizing that she could just climb onto the machine room's roof and stay out of view. She clambered up to the top with only a second to spare and lay prone, hoping that the patrol hadn't spotted her.

The fact that the Niets didn't have drones covering every rooftop, elevator shaft, and stairwell was a testament to the losses their assault craft had suffered when dropping to the surface of Pyra.

With her drones withdrawn, Rika had little visibility onto the roof around her and she didn't dare move until she heard the footfalls of the patrol move away. Slowly they passed around to the east side of the roof, but something was wrong. There was just one set of steps.

A thud sounded behind her, and Rika flipped onto her back to see a Nietzschean soldier in heavy armor standing over her.

"Gotcha," he said aloud.

"Get this!" Rika said, and swung her gun-arm up and fired a high caliber projectile round into his groin. The man's armor dented and cracked, and he fell back with a shout.

<*Fire! Fire! Fire!*> Rika called out. The best cover for the fight she was about to have would be heavy artillery raining down onto the park across the canal.

A few seconds later the scream of incoming shells obliterated the silence of the early evening.

Explosions a kilometer along the canal to the east and west flared brightly, throwing entire trees and clouds of debris into the air. Rika rose up on the elevator house's roof and noted that the Nietzscheans on other towers were sliding their railguns forward, training them to the east and west, assuming assaults would come from those directions after the artillery ceased pounding the park.

All the Niets were occupied except the team on the Withermere; they were spinning their gun to fire on Rika. She dove off the top of the elevator's machine room as the railgun fired, blowing it to pieces, and sending the a-grav generator falling down through the shaft to the base of the building.

<*Rika! What's going on up there?*> Leslie sent.

<*Oh, nothing, just dodging rail fire.*>

<*I've set explosives on three of their guns and am ready to take the fourth to fire on their own troops,*> Leslie reported.

<*How come you get the easy targets?*> Rika asked as she raced across the rooftop, trying to get enough distance to fire a uranium bolt at the railgun.

She reached the far southwest corner just as the Niets locked onto her with the cumbersome weapon, and she fired her GNR.

The uranium bolt flew from her gun's muzzle, and she sighed with relief as it hit the railgun, tearing it in half and causing the weapon's energy coils to discharge into the soldiers nearby.

Rika unslung her JE78 and sent a series of pulse blasts into the Niets, pushing them back as she charged forward. One tripped after getting hit by a pulse and fell off the roof of the building; another nearly followed, but managed to hang onto the edge.

Airbursts from the artillery platform began to shower the adjacent buildings with EM and shrapnel, further lighting up the sky as Rika fired several high-caliber rounds into two more Niets. Then she kicked the hanging one off the roof.

<*Stars, I've missed killing Nietzscheans,*> she said over Basilisk's net, surprising even herself with the visceral satisfaction in her mental tone.

<*It never gets old,*> Leslie replied, and Rika saw beamfire lance out from the Withermere Tower into the park across the canal. It wasn't aimed at the far side where fourth platoon was advancing, but rather at the Nietzscheans. <*Even better to do it with their own weapons.*>

Leslie's words were punctuated by explosions several floors down; Rika smiled, knowing that the Withermere Tower no longer posed a threat to the Marauders.

As Rika emptied a magazine from her JE78 into the last Nietzschean on the roof, she looked around at the other towers.

The team on the tower to the west of the Withermere was in disarray, but the one to the east was braving the artillery fire and had slid one of their railguns to the edge of the roof.

It fired at the advancing Marauders in the park, getting off two shots before one of Rika's uranium rounds slammed into the weapon, tearing it in half and showering the gun's crew with shrapnel.

Rika glanced down as beamfire erupted from lower floors in the adjacent building, lancing out into the night. She gauged the distance to the next tower and backed up ten paces before taking off, running toward the edge of the building.

She pushed off with her right foot, moving at over one hundred kilometers per hour, and sailed between the buildings. The gleaming side of the adjacent building rushed toward her, and Rika fired four ballistic rounds, shattering the plas and a desk beyond.

Her arms folded before her, Rika landed, rolled, and was up and running across the floor toward the Niets who were firing electron beams out into the night.

The first Nietzschean soldier flew from the building before she knew what hit her, and the second followed suit shortly after. The next two were firing at Rika, and she dove to the side, firing her JE78's pulses on full power.

One of the remaining two flew out the window, but the other managed to grab onto the edge of the sill, hanging on for dear life as Rika approached.

"You guys need to learn when to quit," Rika said as she stepped on his hand, crushing it beneath her foot. The Nietzschean screamed in response, and Rika lifted her foot, not even watching as the man fell to his death.

She stooped down, grabbed his crew-served beam rifle, shouldered its battery pack, and walked to the east side of the floor.

Rika kicked the window and it shattered, giving her an unobstructed view of the next building. She steadied the beam weapon and took aim. Then she held the weapon's trigger down, firing a continuous beam into the next building—targeting the floors from which the Nietzscheans were firing on the advancing Marauders.

The offending building was set back a dozen meters from the one Rika was in, and she had a clear shot. She hit one of the enemy positions, then another. She was sweeping the beam across the building when an enemy beam fired back, catching the side of her building half a meter from where she stood.

Rika collapsed, her limbs convulsing as the electrical discharge overcame her motor controls. She couldn't get her legs to respond, so she pulled herself back with her left arm while her robotic limbs ran a full reset. Several primary controllers were shorted out, and she switched over to secondary systems.

<*You OK?*> Barne asked. <*I see a crazy spike on your systems.*>

<*Yeah,*> Rika said as her legs began to respond to commands. <*Got a bit too close to a beam.*>

<*You operational?*> Barne asked.

<*Yeah. How we doing down there?*>

<*I'm mowing Niets down like it's going out of style,*> Leslie announced.

Rika looked back at the Withermere Tower and saw beamfire raining down into the park.

<*They'll probably get up the stairs soon,*> Rika commented, knowing that no one would be taking the elevators since the railgun had destroyed the a-grav systems.

<*Nah,*> Leslie replied, her words punctuated by an explosion one floor down from her position. <*Not my first day on the job.*>

<*We're closing with the canal,*> Clancy said over the platoon's combat net. <*Cover our flanks.*>

Rika saw weapons fire lance out from the building that had fired on her, and she rose to her feet once more. She set off for the stairwell. She didn't bother with the stairs; she leapt from landing to landing until she reached the door at the top and burst out onto the roof.

Two Nietzscheans were still alive next to the railgun that Rika had shot previously. She fired her pulse rifle at them as she ran by and didn't even look back before jumping off the edge of the roof and into the next building.

Rika landed one floor too high and debated the best way to get to the floor below. She opted for speed and shot out a window before sliding over its edge and down to the next floor. She came down right on top of a pair of Niets and she pushed one of them, and the crew-served weapon, out the window. Then Rika turned her purloined weapon on the remaining Nietzscheans and incinerated them.

With the floor clear, Rika turned back to the windows and laid the platoon's combat net over her vision. The locations of Nietzschean troops in the park appeared, and she fired into them, her barrage joining in with Leslie's and creating a clear path for the platoon to reach the canal.

Eight minutes later, the entire platoon had made it across the water. The artillery platform flattened the rest of the park, clearing the way for third and fourth platoons, who were not far behind.

Fighting lit up the streets at the base of the towers at the water's edge as the Marauders engaged the Nietzscheans. Rika and Leslie brought their beams to bear in those conflicts, and, meter-by-meter, the Nietzscheans fell back under the Marauder assault.

DROP

STELLAR DATE: 12.23.8948 (Adjusted Years)
LOCATION: Pyran Space, Above Jersey City
REGION: Pyra, Albany System, Theban Alliance

Chase clamped down on his bite-guard as the drop ship fell through Pyra's atmosphere toward Jersey City. He looked around at the other members of his platoon, noting that many had their eyes closed while others were staring at the overhead. A small number were chatting with their squadmates.

The Old Man hadn't been able to take his pick of drop ships, and some, like the one the second platoon rode down in, had seen their share of abuse. Luckily the pilot seemed competent, and they were still in one piece—which was the most any soldier could hope for in a drop.

He looked at the fourteen soldiers in his squad—squad four in the platoon. They were organized into three fireteams. He was short a few troops, so his two extras were assigned to the first and second fireteams.

He would stick with his third fireteam to give the squad three teams of five. A bit large for his liking, but he didn't think it was wise to reorganize the teams too much. They were still getting used to him, and he to them.

<*Remember, we're gonna hit the ground hard and fast. I want the perimeter established within our first minute,*> Lieutenant Sedis reminded the team in her no-nonsense tone—the only way Chase had ever heard her speak. <*Our orders are to establish a beachhead for the B'Muths that are coming down behind us. Those things are already on their way, so we need to clear any nearby structures inside of ten minutes.*>

Chase noted that everyone's eyes were open now, and glued to Sedis as she spoke.

<*This is a theater of war, people. I know there are civilians out there,*

but don't get mamby-pamby on me. You see something you think is a threat, you put it down. Marauders come first. Are you solid?!>

<*Yes ma'am!*> a chorus of voices resounded over the Link.

<*Good, now let's get ready to fuck some shit up!*>

Chase chuckled and looked across the aisle at Casey who mouthed 'shit fuckers'. Ten seats down, Ralph just shook his head slowly.

<*I told*—> Ralph began to say on the squad leader's net, when Chase was nearly torn from his harness as something struck the drop ship.

A klaxon blared, and Chase was pressed back in his seat as the ship began to spin through the air.

Thick smoke filled the cabin, and Chase switched to his armor's internal air supply, trying not to look at how rapidly his HUD said they were falling.

The drop ship had emergency thrusters that should keep them from creating a new crater in the city below, but they weren't firing.

Then he heard someone cry out on the combat net that the pilot was dead.

Chase had flown drop ships before when things were dire, so he tapped into the ship's navigation systems. They were a mess; one engine was gone, and the other was on full bore. He switched it off and fired control thrusters to slow the drop ship's spin.

The ship passed below a thousand meters, and the emergency landing systems signaled that they were ready to deploy—but the braking jets were still offline.

Someone was screaming on the combat net, and Chase yelled, <*Shut the fuck up!*> as he tried to route control of the jets through the attitude thruster controls.

As the ship passed five hundred meters, Chase hit the jets, praying they'd fire.

Five of the eight jets lit and slowed the ship, but then two shut down and the remainder kicked the ship over into a crazy spin. Chase killed them all, and the emergency foam deployed both inside and outside the ship.

Then they hit.

The foam that filled the inside of the drop ship dissolved almost as quickly as it had appeared, and over the combat net, he could hear Casey shrieking <*Out! Out! Out!*>

Chase fumbled with his harness, trying to find the buckle around his right leg. Then he realized that the strap had been torn off and there was nothing holding him down anymore. He rose from his seat and rushed out the back of the drop ship.

Outside, Ralph was directing first squad to cover the north of the drop ship, while Henry, fourth squad's sergeant, was moving to the south.

<*Third squad! Get around the ship and secure our east perimeter,*> Chase called out as he watched Casey exit the drop ship and send her squad west.

<*Casey, is the ship clear?*> Chase asked.

Casey nodded. <*LT's dead, Chase; so is Sergeant Inman.*>

<*Then who's in charge?*>

<*You're senior.*>

Chase took a step back and surveyed the ruin of the courtyard the ship had crashed in. He suspected that it was a school of some sort—which he confirmed a moment later when he cross-referenced their location with his map of Jersey City.

<*Henry, Ralph, you two clear the dormitories. Work clockwise. Casey, you establish a perimeter to the west, cover the roofs of the dorms and any approaches. My folks'll do the east right after we see what we can pull from the ship.*>

A string of confirmations reached his ears, and Chase turned back to the drop ship. Losing the LT and the platoon sergeant in the first moments of a drop was bad, but every other soldier had survived, and the ship was mostly intact.

<*Fireteams two and three, set up at the nose of the ship. Anything moves to the east, you put holes in it. One, get in there and pull out everything that's not bolted down. We need to be ready to move out in five.*>

<*Clear so far,*> Ralph said, as Chase walked around to the front of the drop ship and noticed the nose was shot off. The pilot wasn't dead—well, she probably was—she was just gone.

He sent a passel of drones out, and they rose into the sky around the courtyard. There was no movement in the streets or the walkways around the dormitories his squads were clearing. He pulled up the map of Jersey City on his HUD, examining his platoon's options.

They were seven kilometers northeast of their designated landing zone. Through the drones' feeds, he could see the other drop ships coming down in the correct location, disgorging their troops and taking to the skies again.

As he watched, a ship exploded in midair—this one not so lucky as it fell from the sky in a ball of fire.

His drones made a comm uplink, and a voice came into his mind. <*Say again, Platoon 89-423-1, do you read?*>

<*Gunny? This is Sergeant Chase. Sending our coordinates.*>

<*Shit, Chase, what are you guys doing over there? Where's Inman?*>

<*LT and Inman bit it, Gunny. I'm top, now.*>

<*Fuck!*>

Gunnery Sergeant Dawson's statement was punctuated by starfire flaring bright in the noon sky as it rained down on several locations in the city.

Streams of plasma burned through buildings and, hopefully, no small number of Niets. With any luck, those shots would end the enemy's anti-air capabilities—but Chase wasn't holding his breath.

<*Look, Sergeant,*> Dawson growled. <*Major Weston says we can't come pull your asses out of the fire. You're to advance from your position to the coordinates I just passed. Be there by eleven hundred; we'll meet for the final push. We'll have an artillery platform down on the ground in fifteen, so if you need support, you call for it.*>

<*Understood,*> Chase replied.

<*Hey. You keep those kids safe, you hear me?*>

<*Count on it.*>

Dawson killed the connection. Chase returned to the back of the drop ship to see first squad stuffing a pile of magazines into duffels, along with four heavy beams, three surface-to-air missiles, and one launcher.

<*OK, folks, just had a chat with Gunny. We're to meet them on this side of the city's main park—the one just south of their downtown. We have two hours to do it.*>

<*Better get moving, then,*> Casey said.

<*Sweep's done on our side,*> Henry reported.

<*Always have to be first,*> Ralph said. <*We're clear here, too. A lot of dead kids in one room; looks like they tried to put up a fight and the Niets killed 'em.*>

<*Fuckers,*> Casey swore.

<*Send a pair of runners to grab supplies for your squad,*> Chase said. <*Then you're in the lead, Casey.*>

<*Of course I am,*> Casey retorted.

RESCUE

STELLAR DATE: 12.23.8948 (Adjusted Years)
LOCATION: Kenmore Building, Jersey City
REGION: Pyra, Albany System, Theban Alliance

The fighting had lasted through the night. It was arduous, brutal, and no small number of Marauders lost their lives in Jersey City. By morning, Alpha Company held the first three blocks of towers along the canal and was moving closer to the city's core.

Rika was sprawled on a sofa across from Leslie, who was asleep in a chair. They were in the lobby of one of the towers.

She didn't even know its name until Barne walked up with a smile and said, "Enjoying the Kernmore's hospitality, are you?" He was pointing at Rika's charge cable, which was plugged into a power socket in the floor.

She smiled before responding, "Yeah, they've got the best cocktails here. This juice is just my flavor."

"Weak metaphor, Rika," Barne smiled. "You better top off fast. Ayer is sending us to give Fifth Battalion a hand."

"Fifth? What for?"

"They're pinned down on the far side of the city center; didn't make it in as far as we did. The artillery platform is repositioning to soften up the Niets over there, but it'll take them over an hour."

"Just us, or all of fourth platoon?" Leslie asked, cracking an eye open.

"Just us," Barne shook his head. "Fourth is going to keep pushing toward the city center with the rest of Alpha Company. We've got a Theban regiment pushing in from the west, as well. They're going to focus on the building-by-building clear-outs.

"Welcome to it," Rika said. "That's brutal work. Have there been a lot of civilian casualties?"

Barne nodded. "More than a lot. The Niets didn't really play nice. They killed some in retaliation but from what we can see, a lot were already dead. I guess they didn't feel like taking care of them."

"Or getting attacked by the occupied populace," Leslie added.

"How we getting there?" Rika asked. "Can't really go through the city center."

"And I'm not crawling through kilometers of sewer," Leslie added.

"I'm wounded that you two ladies would doubt me," Barne said, drawing a hand to his chest. "I've secured a boat. It's in the canal, waiting."

"A gunboat?" Rika asked with a smile.

"Uh…no…just a boat boat."

Leslie chuckled as she pulled herself up. "Well, let's go take a look at your boaty boat. You topped off, Rika?"

Rika nodded as she pulled her charge cord from the floor. "Good enough. But I'm starved. Any food around here?"

*****

Five minutes later they were at the canal. Rika carefully lowered herself into the boat while Barne and Leslie stood on the far side to keep the small craft balanced. Once in, Rika sat on the deck in the middle of the vessel while Leslie released the moorings and tossed the ropes onto the dock.

Once they were free, Barne gunned the engine, moving the vessel out into the water, but staying close to the south shore where the tall buildings would obscure their passage.

Rika closed her eyes and leaned back, enjoying the feel of the boat surging through the water. It occurred to her that she had never been aboard a civilian watercraft. It was strange to be in a vessel made for pleasure. Even after the war, she had only been aboard freighters and other utilitarian spacecraft.

As they passed more pleasure boats tied up along the docks, Rika tried to imagine what the canal looked like before half the boats had been smashed by fallen windows or falling debris from the park across the canal.

It must have been heavenly.

A part of her felt responsible for the destruction wrought on Jersey City, but she knew the blame was ultimately to be laid at the feet of the Nietzscheans.

She had stopped herself from killing the Theban president. And even though Ariana was dead now, Rika reminded herself that in the end she had done the right thing. Ariana's parting words still rang in her mind.

'I forgive you.'

Rika would treasure that utterance all of her days—even though she would never see Ariana again to thank her.

The boat passed into Jersey City's harbor, and Rika watched the pleasure craft that had dominated the canal give way to commercial vessels and larger cruise ships.

At one point a shot hit the boat, fired from a building near the water. Rika calculated the origin and returned fire with a ballistic round. She didn't know if she had hit anyone, but no further fire came their way.

The ride was almost surreal in its calming silence; though every now and then, the sounds of artillery or the burning glare of starfire falling on the city reminded them that they would soon be in the thick of it once more.

Rika watched a series of drop ships fall toward the city and wondered about the soldiers within. They tagged as Marauder craft on her HUD, and she suspected that some day she might fight alongside the occupants—maybe even this day.

A barrage of SAMs launched from one of the buildings in the downtown core, sending dozens of missiles streaking toward the drop ships.

The ships fired chaff and flew wildly to lose the missiles. Point defense systems activated. One ship took an airburst and dipped for a moment. Then another was struck and one of its engines exploded. The ship began to spin wildly, but somehow stopped;

no small feat with the ship's nose missing.

"C'mon," Leslie whispered. "Get those jets going. Slow that fall!"

Rika didn't speak as the drop ship plummeted toward the city, its velocity continuing to increase. Then, just below five hundred meters, the emergency jets fired—not all of them, but the ship slowed and began to barrel roll.

"They'd better hope their foam deploys," Barne said. "They've slowed, but they'll still dig a hole."

The ship passed below the buildings, and the three members of team Basilisk didn't see if the foam systems deployed or not—though there was no visible fireball or debris cloud.

"Might have made it," Barne allowed.

"They're close to our route," Rika said. "We could take a look."

"I'd like to," Leslie said. "Marauders don't leave one another on the field."

"No objection here," Barne said. "We're here to help their push into the city. Seeing if we can help out a platoon fits the bill."

<Captain Ayer, we're going to check out the site of a crashed bird. It's just a few blocks off our route,> Rika proposed.

<Acknowledged,> Ayer responded. *<Report your findings to Major Weston; that's his platoon that was just dropping.>*

<Will do,> she replied.

Her response was punctuated by another drop ship exploding midair, and she watched as starfire rained down on four locations in the city.

No more SAMs streaked out from the ground, and the remainder of the Marauder ships touched down.

Four minutes later, Barne pulled the boat up against a pier and Leslie leapt onto the dock, tying off a mooring, and Barne leaned out on the port side of the vessel to balance it as Rika stepped off.

He snorted as he jumped onto the pier. "Gonna need to get you some lighter limbs if we ever take you to Innoa for some water sports. They have these crazy caverns under the ocean that get huge waves you can surf on underground. Fun times down there."

"It's beautiful," Leslie nodded. "All the lighting is bioluminescent. I—" She didn't complete the statement and instead began moving down the pier.

<*The team went there a few times, she and Jerry made some memories,*> Barne said. <*I'm an idiot for bringing it up.*>

<*Sadness is how we cope. We can't hide from our memories,*> Rika replied.

<*Maybe not, but we sure can try.*>

The trio spread out with Leslie in the lead, Rika in the center, and Barne bringing up the rear. Twice, Leslie spotted Nietzscheans, and both times, Basilisk made short work of them.

As they walked, Rika approached Leslie and gently touched her arm.

<*We haven't had time to talk—well, we have, but I didn't know what to say. I'm really sorry,*> Rika said. <*Somehow I feel like it's my fault.*>

Leslie sighed. <*It's no one's fault. It just* is.... *I'll tell you what's nuts, though. Jerry killed Thebans, and they killed him; but now we're fighting together against the Nietzscheans. How fucked up is all that?*>

<*Seriously fucked up,*> Rika replied. <*Like what happened with the president.*>

Leslie glanced at Rika. <*You haven't shared that yet—well, other than the sentence you wrote for the mission brief. How was it that you didn't kill their president? From what I could tell, she let you onto their net—that means you had already decided not to kill her before our orders changed.*>

Rika nodded. <*I couldn't do it, Leslie. She was begging for her life, and I wondered what in the stars I was doing. I may be a killer, but I'm not a murderer. I know it's a nonexistent distinction to some, but it's a big one for me.*>

<*You know...*> Leslie said after a moment. <*Even though that means you defied an order...it sure makes me like you a lot more. I don't know if you know this, but you're scary, girl—damn scary. Knowing*

that you couldn't kill in cold blood? Well, that makes you a lot more than human in my book.>

<*Umm…thanks…I think?*> Rika replied with a chuckle. <*She forgave me before the end.*>

<*The president?*> Leslie asked.

<*Yeah, Ariana. She said, 'I forgive you, Rika'.*>

<*You keep that close, Rika. That's the real deal.*>

They walked in silence for several minutes before Leslie spoke again.

<*You were out for a long time, Rika—four years at least, right?*>

<*I was in the camps for a year after the war,*> Rika replied. <*So, three.*>

<*Have anyone special?*>

Rika wondered why Leslie was asking. Maybe she just needed something to talk about that would keep her mind off Jerry—though conversation about Rika's love life seemed like an odd choice.

<*Maybe,*> Rika replied after a while.

<*Maybe? How's that?*> Leslie asked.

<*His name was Chase. He was definitely interested in me—for quite some time, too. But I was too wrapped up in my own head to notice—well, to act on it, at least.*>

<*What happened?*>

<*We…I…The night before I was auctioned, I finally…*>

Leslie sighed. <*We always wait too long, don't we?*>

Rika nodded silently. That they did.

Their conversation was interrupted by Barne, who was signaling that they were approaching the crash site.

*****

"Looks intact—mostly," Barne said, as he crouched with Rika on the south corner of a dormitory. Leslie was circling around to the north, checking the buildings for hostiles.

"No beacon on it," Rika replied. "I'm going to move in."

"Could be trapped," Barne whispered. "Wait for Leslie to finish her sweep, then you can go play steel hero."

"Drones don't see anything. No comms, though. Going to send one up to see if I can Link with Major Weston's company HQ."

Rika directed a drone to fly up over the site, and once it reached three hundred meters, it made a line-of-sight connection with the drop ship's original landing site.

<*Major Weston, this is Lieutenant Rika. We've reached the crash site. No enemy, but it appears empty—barring two casualties.*>

<*Sorry, Lieutenant, you were off comms for a bit. The platoon survived, and has been proceeding toward our rendezvous. They've run into some trouble a klick to the west of your position, though. I'm sending you their location now.*>

<*On it,*> Rika acknowledged. <*Any further details?*>

<*No, we just lost contact with them around the city's museum. Drones have picked up the sound of combat in the area, but the few that tried to get closer got hit by EM fields.*>

<*We'll find them and get them on their way,*> Rika said.

<*Good, keep me informed. I might be able to send a B'Muth your way, if it's needed.*>

<*I'll let you know if that's necessary.*>

<*Good. Weston out.*>

Leslie appeared on the far side of the courtyard. <*North and west side clear,*> she announced.

<*I hooked up with Major Weston. The platoon is a kilometer to the west, pinned down in the museum and out of comms' reach,*> Rika said to the team.

<*Well, let's get moving, then,*> Barne replied.

The team moved out of the courtyard, heading west through the university campus. Scenic walks and buildings of all shapes and sizes surrounded them, and Rika wondered what it would have been like to have the time and leisure to spend years in such a place.

She barely remembered her childhood, or much before the war

had started when she was twelve. When she was fourteen, her parents had been in an attack on Hollis; Rika had somehow managed to get offworld on a refugee boat. From there she had been shuffled around by the Genevian government until she reached the age of sixteen—when she was able to get out of the camps.

That was what she mostly remembered: fear of the war, fear of the Nietzscheans, and then fear that she wouldn't survive on the streets.

She had only been nineteen when the cops picked her up for stealing food. Never had a chance to attend a school like this, to enjoy her youth.

To relax.

She wondered about visiting Innoa and enjoying its caves. If Basilisk had been there before, maybe they could go again. Perhaps she could find out what it would be like to just *live* for a while.

Before the next time they were in the shit.

Rika pulled her mind away from her reminiscing and back to the present. Distractions like those would be a fantastic way to never see the caves of Innoa.

They neared the edge of the university and could see the stone façade of the museum rising above the surrounding buildings five blocks away. The team formed up behind a high wall with drones monitoring their immediate surroundings.

<I can hear the weapons fire from here,> Rika said. *<Sounds sporadic, but I can make out Marauder guns. They're still in there.>*

Barne dropped a holoemitter on the ground, and the museum rose up before them.

<Looks like it has seven entrances. From the sounds of it, the Niets are still outside, which means they have all those sealed; Marauders must be positioned well enough to keep them from breaching. My guess is that we're looking at between sixty and a hundred Niets, if they can cover all those entrances.>

<More, I'd wager,> Leslie said.

<*Well, if there were too many more, they'd go in through all the windows at once,*> Barne responded.

<*No one ever said the Niets were smart.*>

<*Leslie, Barne,*> Rika said after staring at the holo for a moment. <*I want the two of you to circle around the south. Make a hole on the southwest corner when you get the signal. I'm going to hit the Niets right at the front door. That will pull them back—I hope.*>

Leslie turned her helmeted head to Rika, and shook it slowly. <*You be careful. No more of Basilisk dies on Pyra. Got it?*>

Rika nodded, sending Leslie a warm smile over the Link. <*I got it. No dying. You two need a little mech in your lives.*>

<*What's the signal?*> Barne asked.

<*You really gotta ask?*> Leslie replied with a laugh.

* * * * *

Chase leaned around a column and fired his JE34 rifle at the Niets. He didn't think that he'd hit any, but at least they weren't trying to come up the stairs anymore.

<*Anyone have any 'nades left?*> he asked fireteam three.

<*I got one HE,*> one of his soldiers called out.

<*Toss it here,*> Chase replied. <*I have a good angle on a few asshats behind that truck out there.*>

The soldier tossed the grenade to Chase, who caught it and primed it. Chase then pulled a feed from one of the platoon's few remaining drones—most of which had been destroyed by the Niets' EM fields—and looked for the best angle for his toss.

There was a building with an awning across the street. If he could get the grenade to hit it, the 'nade would roll off and land right on top of the enemy troops behind the truck.

Chase pulled his arm back and swung with all the strength his powered armor lent him. From the drone's feed, he saw that the grenade's trajectory was true. It hit the awning and fell out of view.

Two seconds later an explosion flipped the truck over, and

Chase assumed the Niets behind it were dead. That had to put the count of enemies at the museum's front door at less than thirty.

Of course, he had only two fireteams at the front; his first was at a side entrance, and the rest of the platoon was spread even thinner.

He'd also had casualties; two dead, and seven others across the platoon in some state of serious injury. Without comms he didn't expect that they'd hold out much longer. He was considering telling the platoon to amass at one of the south entrances and break out of this deathtrap. He could maintain a fiction of a defense at the front door for a few minutes, at least.

So much for finding Rika in the Marauders. Chase shook his head. What a fool's errand this had been. After searching for her for half a year, the only thing he was going to find was a shallow grave on some distant world.

Still, if he could take out a few Niets before he died, that would be something he could accept. If it saved his platoon, that would be even better.

A group of Niets appeared down a side street with a heavy slug thrower. The kinetic weapon had more than enough firepower to tear apart the columns at the front of the museum.

<*All fireteams, fall back to squad one's position. At the five-minute mark, make a push out to the memorial building one block to the southwest!*> Chase ordered.

Confirmations came over the link and behind them, the two fireteams began to fall back through the museum's entrance.

<*You coming, Sarge?*> the corporal leading fireteam two asked.

<*Yeah, gonna be right behind you guys. Just want to keep them out here a bit longer,*> Chase replied.

He could tell the corporal hadn't moved, and Chase looked back at the woman. <*Move, soldier! That's an order!*>

<*Yes, Sergeant Chase. Thank you.*>

Don't thank me yet, Chase thought.

The fireteams retreated through the museum's entrance as Chase fired from his position; then he moved to another and fired again. He knew the enemy would see some of the Marauders leaving, but with luck, they'd think that the defenders were just falling back through the doors and no further.

He pulled back, closer to the entrance, aware that alone he could be easily flanked amongst the columns. As he slipped behind one, he heard the whine of the slug thrower discharge, and a column exploded five meters to his right.

Another pillar exploded, and he ran toward the door, dodging behind whatever cover he could find as the slug thrower tracked him.

So much for luck, Chase thought as he glanced over his shoulder

At which point he saw the slug thrower explode.

The Niets crewing it were thrown wide as the weapon blew apart in flames and shrapnel. He knew that shot hadn't come from his troops; he tried to raise whoever was out there on comms, but got nothing.

More shots rang out, ballistic rounds that hit half a dozen Niets in rapid succession. An HE grenade exploded where a group of Niets was clustered, and then a car partway down the block flew into the air.

The Niets must have decided that whoever was left at the museum entrance was far less dangerous than whoever was hitting them from behind, and a dozen of them rushed up the stairs and took cover behind the columns. Chase considered hitting them from the rear, when the remainder of their force rose from cover and raced toward the museum's main entrance.

"Oh, shit!" Chase cried out, and ran into the museum, thirty Niets hot on his tail.

*****

Rika was just settling into position when she saw the Marauders begin to fall back through the museum's entrance. She tried to raise them; they needed to stop. A hammer and anvil didn't work nearly as well if there was no anvil.

Shots came from amongst the columns atop the museum's stairs, and Rika prayed that enough Marauders were still present to hold back the Niets.

She eased her weapon over the edge of a building and was about to fire on a pair of enemy soldiers when she saw an a-grav pad float into view—a large-bore kinetic slug thrower resting atop its platform.

Niets never fight fair, Rika grumbled. *Good thing I don't either.*

She repositioned on the rooftop and took aim with her GNR-41C, switching its mode to fire one of her last few uranium sabot rounds, and mentally pulled the trigger.

Nothing happened.

The weapon's jam notice was flashing on her HUD, indicating that the sabot round wasn't seated properly in the chamber. Rika cycled the round out and back into the chamber, and the warning disappeared.

She took aim again while the Niets fired the gun, blowing a pillar apart. Rika fired once more, and the jam notice reappeared.

FAAAWK! she shouted in her mind, and unlatched the chamber cover, sliding it aside. The round was seated properly and the accelerator was aligned.

Then she saw that the jam sensor was cracked. *No wonder.*

Rika quickly sealed up the chamber, disabled the jam sensor, and fired on the Niets' weapon.

The uranium rod flew true, and its sabot dropped off a moment before it hit, tearing the gun apart. Rika moved down the rooftop, firing her ballistic rounds on a dozen other Niets who were hiding behind a stone wall, and then lobbed a grenade at another group behind a car.

Thanks to her two-seventy vision, she saw one of the Marauders still alive in front of the museum's entrance. She tried to signal him, but he turned and raced inside the building.

Fuck...no! Rika swore. Then she saw why—the Niets were all fleeing into the building, apparently far more fearful of her than whoever was still inside.

Rika leapt down from the rooftop and into the street, firing with her JE78 at two Niets who weren't fast enough. Then she lobbed another grenade amongst the columns, trusting its blast to clear a path for her.

Seconds later she was up the marble stairs. Cowards though they were, the Niets would be waiting for her inside the door; even her armor and reflexes couldn't withstand concentrated firepower from twenty weapons.

She glanced at the high windows along the front of the building then ran and jumped through one; shards of glass and steel rained down as she fell into the museum's large foyer.

As expected, the Niets were waiting with weapons trained on the front entrance. She fired a few more rounds from her GNR into their midst as she raced to the dubious cover of some strange twisted sculpture.

Once crouched behind the sculpture, Rika lobbed another grenade out to where her HUD showed the highest concentration of enemies to be. She didn't wait to see if it hit anyone before rushing to a column, which she climbed using the same trick as she had in the bunker—hanging from the capital at its top.

The Niets were firing at the pillar's base, and Rika leaned out and shot a uranium round into the base of a different pillar, then another one. Both stone towers fell as their bases crumbled, raining chunks of marble onto nearby Niets.

Rika had hoped the roof would fall, too, but it seemed to be holding. She was about to take out another pillar when part of the ceiling finally came down. Many of the Niets had retreated back toward the entrance, but the debris still caught a dozen of their number.

She scanned the foyer and saw no movement other than the enemies clustered near the entrance. Rika jumped down from the pillar and clambered over the debris, firing wildly at the Niets, forcing them out of the museum.

Then something hit her back, and Rika spun to see a Niet half-buried by the fallen ceiling firing on her. Before she had a chance to put him down, a trio of shots rang out from further back in the foyer, killing the Niet.

Rika saw a lone Marauder step out from behind a pillar and walk stiffly toward her. His right leg was hit. It didn't look critical—just bad enough to disable the armor's knee joint.

His helmeted head was fixed on her and he lowered his weapon.

<*Rika?*> a familiar voice came to her over the Link. <*Is…is that you? Rika?*>

Her mind was ready for combat, ready to kill; not ready for this. It took a moment—one that felt like hours—for her to process what she was hearing.

<*Chase?*>

<*Rika!*> the armored figure rushed toward her, and she wondered if she was dreaming. Had the Niets killed her, and this was the twisted afterlife that mechs went to?

<*How…Chase?*>

<*Yes, it's me,*> Chase's easy laugh flowed into her mind, and Rika felt a strange combination of relief and terror flood through her.

Chase is here, on Pyra, as a Marauder. Did he come to find me? He is going to get himself killed!

The thought turned her attention back to the entrance, certain that the Niets were there, ready to mow them both down.

But no enemies were visible.

<*Rika, you there?*> Leslie's voice came to her.

Rika shook her head, barely remembering how to form sentences. <*Yeah. Front's secure. Sorta.*>

<*Weston's out here with three B'Muths. The Niets have surrendered. Most of the 'toon looks to be OK; they're just missing their CO. A Sergeant Chase. That wouldn't be the guy you told me about, would it?*>

Rika stared down at Chase in wonder, as he cleared his visor and smiled up at her.

<*Yeah; yeah, it is.*>

MOP UP

STELLAR DATE: 12.23.8948 (Adjusted Years)
LOCATION: City Center, Jersey City
REGION: Pyra, Albany System, Theban Alliance

Rika stood atop a building near a decorative garden in Jersey City's center, surveying the destruction that victory had wrought.

The ground shook as three B'muths walked down a street, their forty-millimeter gatling guns pivoting as the gunners within checked for targets.

Rika suspected there weren't any remaining.

The battle was over.

In space, the Marauders and Thebans had fought the Nietzschean ships to a standstill. Word amongst the troops was that the Niets were so used to a sweeping victory that they relied on overused tactics that the Thebans had been well-prepared for.

Plus, no one had retreated.

Still, Rika had to give the Nietzscheans some credit. They had held on until a Septhian fleet jumped in, apparently responding to drone-borne messages that the Old Man had sent asking for help.

A lot of Thebans were angry with the Marauders. There were already calls for the mercenary organization to be brought up on charges of war crimes by many in the Theban populace.

Luckily there were more Thebans who viewed the Marauders as their saviors—many of whom had apparently been concerned about Nietzschean aggression for some time.

That same group was pushing hard for Thebes to join the Septhian Alliance, and that movement was gaining momentum in the public forums.

Rika considered the irony in that. With Ariana dead and the Niets on their doorstep, that initial mission she had been bought for would likely be fulfilled. Thebes would become a province of Septhia.

Those local politics mattered little to Rika—though she did still keenly feel Ariana's death. But what she felt most strongly was pride—and no small amount of amazement—that the Nietzscheans had been defeated both on the Pyran surface and in space.

It had been a long time since she had seen a victory like that.

A platoon moved through the streets below, falling back toward the muster site on the southern side of Jersey City. It wasn't Chase's but his was close, also moving back to the muster site.

As much as she didn't want to leave his side, Basilisk had orders. There were still buildings to sweep and cover to provide.

At first it had surprised Rika that the Marauders were leaving so soon, but with the Theban regiment moving in from the west, Marauder command felt it was best not to have both forces in the city at once. Too much risk of an incident between the armies.

Rika leapt down from the building and approached Barne and Leslie, who were speaking with Captain Ayer on a street corner.

"I hear you found your long-lost love?" Ayer asked with a smile as Rika approached.

Rika laughed. "Yeah, first freedom, then this. Starting to wonder if maybe the universe doesn't hate me after all."

"He's put in a request to transfer to my company already," Ayer said.

"He's what?" Rika asked.

"Yeah, I've put things in motion to approve it. He seems competent—served with distinction back in the war."

Rika was at a loss for words. In the museum, Chase had told her that he had served in the GAF but they hadn't had time to get into details before being given new orders for the final push to clear out Jersey City.

She wanted to reach out to him, to ask him to tell her everything; they were still in a hot zone, though, and she wasn't going to distract him further. If he felt anything like she did, he was already distracted.

All this after just one night in a bar, Rika thought. *How could it mean so much to me after so little time?*

But she knew there was more to it than that. Chase had pursued her for months, always kind, always supportive. And he had searched for her and *found* her. With all the worlds amongst the stars, he had found her on this small piece of rock, drifting in space.

"Rika, you with us?" Ayer asked.

"Uh, yes. Sorry, ma'am." Rika flushed, glad her helmet hid her embarrassment from her CO.

"Yeah, right. Get your head out of the clouds. I just brought Basilisk back up to full strength; I don't want to have to replace its CO when you get your daydreaming head blown off."

"Filled?" Barne asked. "With who?"

"Seriously?" Leslie asked with a broad smile visible through her cleared visor. "Are you an idiot? Who do you think?"

BASILISK

STELLAR DATE: 12.24.8948 (Adjusted Years)
LOCATION: Commissary, MSS *Romany*
REGION: Pyra, Albany System, Theban Alliance

Rika walked through the *Romany's* mess feeling far more nervous than she would have expected, taking extra care to keep a steady grip on the tray of food in her hands.

Ahead, Chase sat at a table with Team Basilisk and three others that her HUD identified as sergeants from his old platoon. She saw Barne say something, and Leslie groaned while Chase and the man named Ralph laughed.

Chase looked up and smiled at her, sliding over on the bench to make room.

Rika sucked in a deep breath, suddenly feeling much younger and less certain of herself than she should. It felt as though she was in a cheesy vid about a young woman fawning over a boy at a school.

"You gonna stand there all day, or you gonna sit your metal ass down and dig in?" Barne asked around a mouthful of food.

"My ass isn't metal," Rika said with a frown as she sat.

"It's true," Chase nodded. "I've felt it."

"Chase!" Rika exclaimed.

Chase wrapped an arm around her shoulders as she settled.

"Sorry, we've technically only been romantically involved for about two days…spread over half a year. I'm not really sure how to behave."

"Like yourself," Leslie suggested.

Rika leaned into Chase and let out a long breath. "Doesn't matter how you behave. We're together, we're home, and our family is here."

"So, you're sure that you're a Marauder now?" Leslie asked with a twinkle in her eye.

"Yeah, and this Marauder is hungry. These mods don't feed themselves."

"Dig in," Chase said. "I hear this is the last of the real meat. We'll be on vat-grown crap from here out."

"Doesn't matter," Rika said with a smile. "Beats NutriPaste."

"Gah! Tried that crap once," Ralph said. "Tasted like shit! No wonder all you mechs were so surly in the war."

The table fell silent, no one certain how Rika would react. She saw the look of worry on Ralph's face, and knew that he didn't mean to say anything hurtful.

She smiled and shook her head. "Well, you're not supposed to *taste* it. With us, it goes right in the stomach."

"That's Ralph's problem," Casey said with a laugh. "He's like a dirty toddler, just sticking everything in his mouth all the time."

The table broke out into laughter, and Rika closed her eyes, feeling Chase's arm around her. She sighed and didn't even bother keeping back the tears as a feeling of contentment settled over her.

She really was home, and these were her Marauders.

THE END

RIKA REDEEMED

RIKA'S MARAUDERS – BOOK 2

FOREWORD

Rika is, without a doubt, a very special character in the Aeon 14 universe. Unlike many of the others, she doesn't have a supportive nation behind her, or decades of experience to draw from. She lives by her wits and her intense determination to survive.

Somehow, Rika turns her weakness into strength and her fear into certainty. She bends, but she does not break, and when the storm passes, Rika is still standing.

When writing this story, I knew that I had to show the same emotional depth that you found in Rika Mechanized and Rika Outcast. Just because she's now joined a mercenary outfit, Rika does not instantly turn into a grizzled veteran.

In fact, being the leader of Team Basilisk has placed more responsibility on her shoulders precisely at the time when her past comes to haunt her.

You've seen Rika as a fierce warrior on the battlefield, a feared opponent that has struck down her enemies without hesitation, but this time, Rika is faced with an enemy that she cannot kill.

At least not yet.

Not if she hopes to save the ones she cares about.

PREVIOUSLY IN RIKA'S MARAUDERS

To put it mildly, Rika has had a tough life. She was only fourteen when the Nietzscheans attacked her home world. Her parents died to ensure she could make it off-planet.

A ward of the Genevian government, Rika was placed into foster care, as were so many other displaced children during the war. At age sixteen, she ran away from her foster home and lived on the streets of Tanner City, on Kellas in the Caulter System.

Starving, she stole food to survive; at the age of nineteen, she was caught and brought before a judge, who found her guilty of a crime she did not commit.

What she hadn't known, due to her government's propaganda machine, was that her people were losing the war against the Nietzschean Empire.

In a desperate act, the Genevian government began turning criminals into cyborg warriors—advanced forms of mechanized infantry, commonly referred to as 'mechs'.

Quotas needed to be filled, and the judge sentenced Rika to a five-year term as a mech. Two years later, her people lost the war.

Rika was left with a body that was barely hers, and a deep hatred for what she had become. The Nietzscheans didn't turn mechs back into people; they simply disarmed the mechanized soldiers and returned them to the general population—who despised them.

Rika found herself slinging cargo on a run-down station named Dekar on the edge of a system she had once shed blood to save.

There, she met a man named Chase who was one of the first to treat her like a person. Just as something was building between the two of them, Rika's growing debts were cashed in, and she was sold at auction.

...to a mercenary outfit, the Marauders.

With no other options, Rika worked for the Marauders. She earned their trust and respect, and they granted her freedom. During that time, Chase was searching for her and had also joined the Marauders to hunt her down.

They were reunited in the ruins of Jersey City on Pyra—capital of the now-defunct Theban Alliance.

Now Chase, Rika, and two other Marauders, named Leslie and Barne, make up Team Basilisk: an elite strike force in the Marauders.

When you need the job done right, you call the Marauders. When the Marauders need their best, they send in Basilisk.

A LOST DAUGHTER FOUND

STELLAR DATE: 04.12.8947 (Adjusted Years)
LOCATION: Basileus Residence, The Isthmus, Sparta
REGION: Peloponnese System, The Politica, Praesepe Cluster

"Father, I'm home," a small voice called out from the entrance to the Residence.

"Stay still," Stavros commanded Silva. "Not a word. In fact, you're never to speak aloud in her presence. Ever."

"I'm in the lounge," Stavros called out. "Attend me, Amy."

"OK, Father," Amy responded, and a minute later, the young girl walked into the lounge, her eyes locked on Stavros.

Silva's breath caught at the sight of her daughter. It had been so long since she had last seen her little girl, since she had held her precious darling in her arms.

She tried to speak, but the moment she thought about it, crippling pain flooded her mind. If her armor hadn't been holding her up, Silva would have crashed to the ground at the intensity of it.

And so Silva stood in anguish, watching Stavros, the person she hated most in the universe, speak to Amy, the one she loved more than anything.

"How was the academy today?" Stavros asked Amy.

"It was good, Father. We learned about the battles you fought against the Kendo Empire; how you subdued them and showed them the ways of The Politica."

Stavros nodded. "That is a good lesson, though I'm surprised they had not already taught it to you. I may have to speak with your instructors."

"Oh, they told us about it before," Amy replied quickly. "Today we learned about how it cemented your position within the slow zones of the cluster and allowed you to make The Politica an FTL culture."

"That is good, then," Stavros replied, leaning back into the sofa, a smug smile on his face. "I did teach Kendo a thing or two...."

Amy glanced around the room and seemed to notice Silva for the first time.

"Is that a new mech, Father?"

"Yes, I just secured her today. Her name is Mech C319, but you can call her 'Meat'."

The words hit Silva like a blow to the gut, and she wished that she could close her eyes and no longer see Amy, or watch the monster who had impregnated her speak to her beloved daughter.

"Are you sure?" Amy asked, her forehead wrinkling. "I heard that the mechs don't like to be called 'meat'."

Stavros pushed himself off the sofa and stood with a hand on Amy's shoulder. "Not this one. She *likes* being called Meat. Say hi to her."

Amy waved a hand and waved, "Ummm... hi, Meat."

Silva didn't respond, unable to move, fearing another withering wave of Discipline. But hidden behind her black oval helmet, unseen by her daughter or the man she had made love to long ago, were rivulets of tears flowing down her face.

THE FARM

STELLAR DATE: 02.14.8949 (Adjusted Years)
LOCATION: Kessler Wilderness, North of Kandahar City
REGION: Faseema, Oran System, Praesepe Cluster

<Barne,> Rika called back to the sergeant's position, routing the signal through one of her drones flying overhead. *<I thought you said there was just one farmhouse and a few outbuildings down there.>*

<Yeah,> Barne replied. *<That's what the SatScan shows. One middleish-sized farmhouse, two small sheds, and a larger equipment building. Why, something else down there?>*

<Oh, I don't know,> Rika replied and sent her visual to Barne. *<Kinda surprised SatScan missed that big plascrete bunker on the far side.>*

<Huh,> Barne grunted. *<Look at that.>*

Rika shook her head. She didn't blame Barne; he just worked with the intel he could get. Whoever was down there apparently had the tech to mask their bunker from SatScan.

Either that, or they had someone on the inside in the planetary government and could alter the planetary survey data.

Given the mess that was Faseema's government, that wouldn't surprise Rika.

<Assume they have the tech to pull this off,> Rika advised her team. *<Either way, we're dealing with more than just some random thugs.>*

<Would the thugs be random, or would it be their actions that are random?> Leslie asked from her position, ninety meters to Rika's left.

<Thanks for the support, Leslie,> Rika replied, glancing west along the ridge toward Leslie's position. *<You ready to go down?>*

<I was born ready, Rika, you should know that. Not randomly ready, either. Deliberately ready.>

Barne snorted. <*That doesn't make a lick of sense, Leslie.*>

<*Not to you,*> Leslie replied.

<*I'm in position,*> Chase added. <*Hoping that they don't have anything that can pick up on all this EM chatter you have going on.*>

<*Sorry,*> Leslie said.

<*She gets all talkative before she kills people,*> Barne said with a laugh.

Rika sighed. <*Go already, Leslie.*>

There was no indication that Leslie had moved; even though Rika could see on both IR and UV bands, the team's scout was all but invisible. If it hadn't been for Rika's micro-drone hovering above Leslie's position—watching for enemy surveillance, as much as monitoring the team's advance—she wouldn't have even known Leslie had taken a step.

Leslie's stealth was aided in part by her armor. A chameleon suit, it could blend in with any surroundings, rendering the wearer all but invisible as it matched optical, IR, and even higher-band reflective properties of its surroundings.

The armor gave Leslie an edge, but Rika suspected that the team's scout could do just fine without it. Even back in the barracks on the MSS *Romany*, Leslie could sneak up on any of them. Queries to the ship's AI for Leslie's whereabouts would often get uncertain answers—something which frustrated the AI to no end.

The woman just loved to sneak.

Rika looked down the slope into the valley below them. It was lush and green with low, stunted trees dotting the slope, growing taller on the valley floor. A small stream meandered down the middle of the depression, running almost due west. Set back from the water on either side were the buildings of the team's target: Arrow Brook Farm.

Up on the ridge, and for kilometers around, the vista was much different. Tall, dry grass waved in a hot wind that blew across gently rolling plains. Some of it was farmland, some was fenced off for cattle; all of it was unpleasant, baking endlessly under the Oran System's hot orange star.

Valleys like the one before them were like gems; small oases of life that stayed green all through Faseema's long summers. In spring, that tiny stream would have been much larger: a bubbling brook, or perhaps even a creek, judging by the cutbanks dug into the valley floor.

But now, in late fall, it was running low. Rocks and muddy berms were sticking out of the sluggish water's surface.

Rika imagined that the stream must run consistently though all the seasons, otherwise people would not live here. Faseema was an impoverished world, one that was far from any main FTL routes. It was cut off from major trade by The Politica; a backwater's backwater.

Though the world was not without advanced tech, Team Basilisk had not seen any 'vaporators or other desert technology on their overland trek. For the most part, these people lived close to the earth, surviving by the labors of their own hands.

And so the stream below was a valuable commodity. Not that it really mattered, though. The only impact it would have on the mission was whether or not there would be animals in the larger structure below them. Rika hoped there weren't dogs. There were a few ways to stop dogs, but she didn't like using them.

Leslie reported in, breaking in Rika's thoughts. *<Got a sensor web. It's in the ground, spaced a few meters apart.>*

<How far down the slope?> Barne asked.

<Eleven meters,> Leslie replied. *<Dropping a pack on the nearest one. If they're networked, it'll take them all. If not, you'll have to clear your own path when you come down.>*

Rika signaled acknowledgement, and Leslie resumed her journey down the slope—or so they all assumed.

No one spoke or moved for the next twenty minutes. While they waited, Rika once more studied the buildings on the valley floor.

The main farmhouse was south of the stream, on the near side. Two small sheds stood to the right, on its east side. The largest trees in the valley were also near the house: two spreading oaks, one on the west and one to the north, between the house and the stream.

Across the meandering water stood the largest building. It was wooden and resembled a livestock barn more than storage for large machinery—though if it did contain animals, it would still do double duty. Someone was managing the land in this area.

The bunker was also on the far side of the stream, set further back against northern slope of the valley, likely set deep within the earth.

The team had set up on the south side of the valley because they had believed their target would be in the farmhouse. But the presence of the bunker made that highly unlikely. There was no doubt in Rika's mind that she would be in the bunker, deep under the hillside.

Rika considered having the team reposition to the north side of the valley, but dismissed it. *That would take at least an hour.* She would wait for Leslie's recon sweep before determining the best course of action.

Above, the local star, Oran, passed its zenith in the sky, beginning its trek down to the horizon. To the east, Rika could see stars begin to shine on the horizon, while those in the west began to fade.

On worlds this deep in the Praesepe cluster, there was always starlight; night was a brilliant display, no matter what time of year it was.

Given Faseema's proximity to its star, and its long, brutal summers, night was when most of the populace did their work. The world was orbited by two large moons: Baqara, and Khinzer. Coupled with the starlight, they made for more than enough light to work by once Oran slipped beneath the horizon.

Rika's hair began to feel slick with sweat, and she wished that running her armor's cooling systems was an option—but it would give off far too much EM, not to mention make a very interesting heat signature for anyone watching the ridge.

No, she'd suffer through it, just as the rest of the team likely was. *Well, probably not Barne.* He was far behind, hidden in the lee of a large boulder; *probably cool as a cucumber, the smug bastard.*

Another half hour passed, and then Leslie sent a data burst over the team's combat net. The scout was in the eaves of the barn—stars knew how she got there, Rika hadn't seen a thing—and she had an update on the hostiles.

<*I picked up three in the farmhouse, two in armor in the building's main room, one sleeping in a room in the southwest corner,*> she reported. <*The two equipment sheds are clear, but I spotted a pair of automated turrets mounted in the oaks. They have camopacks; you won't see 'em, but I've noted their location for you.*>

<*The barn's got three horses in it, a truck with a chaingun and rocket launcher on the back, a groundcar, and a tractor. Otherwise it's clear. I'm watching the bunker: no visible activity, but the door shows signs of recent use.*>

Rika blew out a long breath, giving voice to her frustration. If they hit the bunker, the enemies in the farmhouse would strike them in the rear. If they hit the farmhouse first, then the bunker would lock down.

A simultaneous strike was obviously the only way to go.

However, splitting the four-person team to hit two targets when one of them was a complete unknown was not a wise move.

The whole point was to get the target out alive, not start a massive firefight that would probably kill her.

<*Get comfy,*> Rika said to Leslie, sending the message on a tightbeam. <*We're going to wait and see who comes out of that bunker. Maybe an opportunity will present itself.*>

Leslie responded with an affirmative signal.

<*Chase,*> Rika said. <*I want you to head east and get down into the stream. Get as close as you can; under their little wooden bridge would be great, but I doubt you can get that close.*>

<*Got it, LT,*> Chase replied.

He never called her by name when they were on missions; always 'lieutenant', or 'LT'. At first, it had made her worry that their relationship was a problem for him when working on an objective—then she realized that was how he kept things compartmentalized. 'Rika' was his lover; 'LT' was his boss. It was probably a smart choice; not that she could bring herself to only call him 'sergeant'.

Far to her right, she saw a slight shift in the tall grass and knew that Chase was on his way.

The afternoon drew on. After an hour, a figure emerged from the farmhouse. The enemy was armored, as Leslie had reported: medium gear, not fully powered, but with some leg assists that would boost the wearer's speed and ability to jump.

The gait suggested female, and when the enemy began to walk up the side of the valley, the telltale curve of the chestplate confirmed Rika's suspicion.

A sidearm—ballistic, from the looks of it—rested in a holster on her right thigh, and a multifunction rifle was strapped to her back.

Rika zoomed her vision in, looking for any logos or markings on the woman's armor or gear. The armor was entirely void of anything identifiable, but on closer examination, Rika spotted a small crest on the handgun's grip.

It was a pair of intertwined snakes wrapped around a sword with a shield behind. Rika was certain she had seen it before, but nothing in her records lined up.

<*Barne. This look familiar to you?*> Rika asked as she transmitted the image back.

Ahead, Rika watched the woman stop at the sensor line and pull a small device out of a pouch on her chest. She waved it over the grid and nodded.

I guess that means Leslie didn't take out the whole thing, Rika thought.

The woman turned west, walking along the sensor line, waving her device and nodding every so often. The soldier was sloppy; she had walked within ten meters of Rika and hadn't even glanced toward the ridgeline once.

For all the sentry knew, there could be a whole army waiting over the hilltop.

<Yeah,> Barne's voice interrupted Rika's derisive thoughts. *<I've seen it before—not surprised you couldn't place it. Half the outfits within a hundred light years use serpents. Kinda trippy for a cluster of stars whose name means 'manger'. What's that say about 'em?>*

<Barne, I doubt that merc outfits think about synergies like that when picking their names,> Rika replied.

<Shame. Anyway, that's the logo for K-Strike; they're a smaller group, no capital ships. Operate off freighters and troop transports. Course, just 'cause that broad has a gun with their logo on it doesn't mean that she's with their company. Could have taken the gun from a kill.>

Rika considered that possibility. *<K-Strike do snatch-jobs like this often?>*

<Some,> Barne grunted. *<I think they do just about anything that puts cred in their accounts. They're decent enough at what they do, but it'll take a platoon of them to pose any real threat to Basilisk.>*

<Don't get cocky,> Rika replied.

<Not cocky, just honest and realistic. I have a reputation to uphold, you know.>

Rika sent the ornery sergeant a condescending smile over the Link and turned her attention back to the woman, who had just stopped at the sensor Leslie had disabled.

This time, she shook her head and then her scanner.

That's right, lady, Rika rolled her eyes. *Sensitive scanning tech loves to be shaken around. Keep up the good work.*

Granted, any scan tech put in a soldier's hands had better be able to handle a few shakes, but that didn't stop the lowering of Rika's assessment of the sentry.

Eventually the woman shrugged and moved on.

When she had walked another hundred meters, the mercenary finally looked to the ridgeline, turned left, and walked to the top.

She stood staring out across the kilometers of blowing grass for several minutes before starting toward Rika's position.

Rika had expected this. She should have moved back when the sentry came out of the farmhouse, but she had remained still, half wanting to be found so she could get this fight underway.

A short data burst came in from Chase. He was thirty meters upstream from the farm's small bridge. It was as close as he could get.

The K-Strike merc continued to walk along the ridge, finally passing within two meters of Rika, her boot coming down just a few dozen centimeters from the end of Rika's outstretched GNR-41C.

Rika let out a long breath as the woman moved on. As much as she wanted to get this fight started, Captain Ayer probably wouldn't be happy if it happened because she'd been sloppy.

The sentry slowly continued her perimeter sweep and, twenty minutes later, reached the bunker. She stopped at the plascrete structure's door and rapped three times with her fist.

After a minute the door opened, and another merc came out, holding it wide.

This one's armor looked nothing like the woman's, but Rika managed to spot the K-Strike logo on his pistol grip. *An unlikely coincidence if ever there was one.*

Rika sent the intel back to Barne, who signaled his agreement that they were undoubtedly dealing with K-Strike.

They would be somewhat professional, then. Even if the woman's perimeter sweep was sloppy.

The man who had opened the bunker's door stood beside it, holding it open as the woman walked in. *At least she's verifying the interior's security herself, rather than trusting the man to tell her all is well.*

However, much to Rika's surprise, the man did not close the door and stand watch—he continued to hold it open.

Basilisk had their in.

Three minutes later, the woman came out, and the man stepped back into the bunker and closed the door.

Three minutes, probably two to be safe. That's how long they would have to make their move once the woman reached the bunker on her next round.

Rika formulated the plan and passed it to the team in short EM bursts, fed through her drones—two of which were now positioned a kilometer above the farm.

It surprised Rika that K-Strike didn't have drones deployed—or maybe they did, and she hadn't detected them yet.

Unlikely, she decided. *The only way my birds wouldn't have found theirs was if they had already spotted mine…unless they know we're here, and they're just playing us.*

She closed her eyes and took a deep breath. *It's impossible to consider all the angles, and trying can drive a person nuts.* The team would operate as though they had the element of surprise until they didn't—or until there was something other than Rika's worry to support the suspicion of its absence.

This would be a lot easier if my team were all mechs. As much as she loved Basilisk—Chase especially—they were fragile. If she had Hammerfall at her back, this would all be over by now.

But she didn't—her old team from the war was long gone, and no one on Basilisk was volunteering to get their arms sawn off to join Rika in the ranks of the mechanized.

* * * * *

Three hours after Rika formulated their plan for entry, the sun was beginning to set. A figure emerged from the farmhouse once more; Rika worried it was a different sentry at first, but then recognized the woman's gait.

Rika had since moved and now lay between the sensor web and the top of the ridge. From what she had observed of the merc's behavior last time, the woman wouldn't come anywhere near her.

Much to Rika's relief—and professional annoyance—the sentry followed the exact same pattern as on her first circuit. When she neared the bunker, Rika tensed, ready to spring into action—knowing without checking that her team was, as well.

Time slowed down as Rika watched the woman rap once, twice, three times on the bunker door. After what felt like an eternity, it opened.

The sentry woman walked inside, and a second later, Basilisk struck.

Rika leapt into the air, firing her GNR at one of the automated turrets in the oak tree to the east, before activating a boost from the jets on her calves to take her two dozen meters aloft.

Rounds ricocheted off her armor, and Rika swore softly. Her shots must have missed, or the turrets were more heavily armored than expected.

The two-hundred and seventy degree vision from her helmet gave her a clear view of twin streaks of smoke in the sky, punctuated by a matching pair of explosions in the oak trees.

Rika didn't have time to see if the turrets were destroyed as she smashed through the roof of the farmhouse.

She came down onto a kitchen table made of plas and shattered it, not pausing as her helmet's sensors swept the room and registered it as clear.

Rika unslung her JE84 multifunction rifle and considered her route. She could run down the hall to get to the front room, or she could take the more direct path.

She fired a short burst at the wall and ran through—smashing a san unit—fired another burst, and tore through the next wall, sliding to a stop in the front room; directly behind an armored merc, who had his rifle aimed down the hall.

A trio of rounds erupted from the barrel of Rika's JE84 and bounced off the enemy's armor.

Shit. Heavier than I thought.

The merc spun, unloading his rifle's magazine on full auto. The blast traced a line across the walls as he swung the weapon toward Rika.

She dove back, giving herself enough room to fire a high-velocity round from the GNR-41C rifle attached to her gun-arm.

The shot couldn't miss—it didn't. It struck the man point-blank in his chest.

The merc's armor gave a resounding *crack* as the round bounced off and twisted him to the side. When he straightened, he revealed a blackened patch on his armor, but no damage.

Must be some sort of reactive defense. Sure wish I had something like that…

Before the man could raise his rifle again, Rika dropped her JE84 and rushed him, clamping her left hand on his weapon, attempting to tear it from his grasp.

His armor gave him the strength to resist; in the end, it was the rifle that gave out, bending under their combined strength.

The merc swore and tried to take a step back, which Rika allowed; she could use some maneuvering room. When enough space opened up, she raised a clawed foot, slammed it into his chest, and clamped down.

"Fuck!" the merc yelled and slammed an armored fist down on her leg. At the same moment, Rika brought her GNR up and fired four point-blank rounds into the man's neck.

The first two rounds were shrugged off by his reactive armor, but the third one penetrated, and the fourth blew half his neck off.

Rika released her foot's grip on his chest and dropped to a crouch, ready for the other man in the house to come for her.

He didn't disappoint—bullets tore through one of the walls, slicing through the air where Rika would have been if she hadn't dropped down.

Rika triangulated the origin of the shots and let fire with another salvo from her GNR. A scream sounded after the barrage, and then she heard a dull thud.

Rather than check to see if her opponent was down for good, Rika tossed a grenade through the hole she'd shot in the wall and rushed out the farmhouse's front door as the dwelling exploded behind her.

The fight in the farmhouse had only taken thirty seven seconds, and in that time, Leslie had disabled the guard at the bunker entrance and disappeared inside. Chase reached the bunker's door and delivered a kick to the fallen guard's head that knocked his helmet off—it must not have been fastened properly—and put two in the man's head before disappearing into the bunker.

<*Status?*> Rika asked as she cautiously crossed the farmyard.

<*Busy,*> Leslie replied.

<*She's fighting with your friendly neighborhood patrol merc,*> Chase reported. <*I took another one down in a front room; I think there are two more back there, from what I can hear.*>

<*Understood,*> Rika replied as she checked Barne's location.

He had moved from his rear overwatch position and was on his way to the ridgeline. Until he arrived, Rika needed to stay in the farmyard to ensure no one else arrived on scene.

She looked for a good vantage point, and opted for the roof of the barn. If she stayed on the east side, she could watch the bunker and stay out of western sight lines.

Rika broke into a loping run, crossed the stream in one leap, dashed across another two-dozen meters, and jumped onto the barn's roof.

She fired her calf jets—using the last of their limited fuel—and settled down as gently as possible. The roof groaned under her weight, but held.

<*Damn, if I'd had time to bet on it, I'd've put money on you going right through,*> Barne commented.

He wasn't close enough to see her yet, so she assumed he was watching through the drone network.

She overlaid the surveillance visuals on top of her helmet's two-seventy view, wishing the new helmet that the techs back on the *Romany* were making was ready.

I really miss simultaneous three-sixty vision.

The helmet's cameras weren't difficult to configure; it was blending the data and feeding it into a human brain that was tricky. Do it wrong and all you got was vomit-inducing nausea.

<*I don't know that I would have taken that bet,*> Rika said. <*Was a*

bit of a toss-up in my mind—though the jets help.>

<Cheating,> Barne replied.

Rika looked out over the crest of the barn's roof and surveyed the land to the west. As she did, the roof groaned, and she shifted to stay above the major support beams.

Her augmented vision didn't show anyone approaching on the farm's access road. *Maybe these K-Strike mercs don't have any backup. Fine by me.* She slid back down from the crest.

Then the roof exploded.

Rika fell through the roof and slammed into a crossbeam on her way down, smashing it to kindling. At first, she thought that the roof had finally collapsed under her weight—but she could see pieces of the wooden structure flying outward. Something had shot at her from inside the barn.

Rika flipped over mid-drop and hit the hard-packed dirt on her hands and knees. Her limbs absorbed the shock while her scan suite surveyed her surroundings.

How did I miss motion below me? The barn's wood; it has no suppression tech.

Her first suspicion was the truck with the rocket launcher on the back, but it stood vacant, her IR vision revealing no signs of recent use.

Then a heat bloom to her right caught her attention, and Rika flipped into the air as a rocket flew beneath her, her HUD revealing the source of the attack. Rika couldn't see anyone, but at the apex of her arc, she fired her GNR's electron beam.

A horse screamed in terror at the back of the barn as the bolt of lightning lit up the interior of the structure like daylight. The shot burned a hole in the rear wheel of the tractor before hitting the ground and discharging its electrons in an arcing spiderweb of electricity.

Not a direct hit, but Rika could see the outline of something moving low to the ground, bolts of energy arcing across it.

Rika didn't wait for positive ID. She fired a trio of projectile rounds from her GNR at the shadowy figure, with two missing, but one striking true.

Then she was back on the ground with the tractor between her and the enemy.

A new passel of drones flowed from her back, and Rika sent them high into the rafters, running active scan and attempting to locate her target.

The drones alerted her, too late, of another rocket; this one coming from behind. She dove to the side, but was struck in the hip, and the explosion flung her into the wall.

<*What's shooting at you?*> Barne asked, more curious than alarmed.

<*Two. Can't see them. Don't know what,*> Rika replied as she swung a fist at the barn's wall, breaking a hole in the already-damaged structure. She burst through into the cool night air and rolled to the side as another missile flew overhead.

It streaked across the farmyard and hit the north slope of the valley, exploding in a brilliant display.

Rika tossed three grenades through the hole she had just made, and ran from the barn, leaping through the air to land in the stream on the far side of the small bridge. She hunkered down and took sight on the barn.

<*Drones show no active EM in there,*> Barne commented.

<*Yeah, I have the feed too,*> Rika retorted. <*What do you think that was? The pigeons shitting on me?*>

<*Want me to light it up?*> Barne asked.

Rika's grenades exploded, sending flames and debris shooting out of the holes in the barn's roof and wall.

<*Save 'em,*> Rika replied, referring to Barne's last two rockets. <*If whatever is in there makes a break for the bunker—if they survived—* then *light 'em up.*>

<*You got it.*>

The barn was burning now, the wooden structure ripe for ignition in the dry summer. Before long, it would be pushing flames a hundred meters into the sky. Rika felt a moment's pity for the horses, hoping that somehow the animals would find a way to break free.

Something burst through the hole Rika had made in the wall, and then another something crashed through one of the barn's doors.

With the soot and ash coating them, Rika could finally make out what she was dealing with.

Aracnidrones.

The little things stayed low, moved on eight limbs—hence the name—and sported both a vicious temperament and a punishing armament.

One rushed toward the bunker, and Rika spotted one of Barne's shoulder-fired missiles streaking toward the thing.

The aracnidrone fired chaff, and the missile detonated six meters above, the thunder of its detonation echoing through the valley.

<*I lost the other one,*> Barne said.

Rika realized—with no small amount of concern—that she couldn't see the other aracnidrone, either. *It must have sloughed off the debris. Whatever camo systems they have are exceptional.*

Still, it should *be hotter than the night air, what with just exiting the burning barn.*

Rika scanned the terrain, looking for any signs of movement: bending grass, dust eddies, distortion in the heat rising off the hot ground in the early evening.

She tried to ignore the screams of the terrified horses. The fire hadn't reached the back of the barn yet, and if she could kill this thing, she might be able to save them.

Then she caught the sound of motion in the water.

With a cry, Rika leapt back as a missile streaked under the bridge, airbursting a meter away and throwing her back against the stream's dry banks.

Rika scrambled up and raced along the water's edge, waiting for the thing to emerge from beneath the bridge, a sabot round loaded in her GNR, ready to fire.

The aracnidrone didn't appear, and Rika knew that it must be trying to flank her.

<Anything?> she asked Barne, hoping he had a better angle—not that his one vantage added much to the dozen drones already scanning the area.

<No, I have no idea how that thing is hiding so well,> Barne growled.

<We should ask these guys where they get their tech.>

Another missile streaked out from Barne's position, targeting the first drone that was now only a few meters from the bunker's entrance. Rika had almost forgotten about it; luckily, Barne had not.

The aracnidrone must have been out of chaff because it directed a minigun at the missile, and high-velocity bullets streaked out into the night.

This time they weren't enough. The bullets must have missed or not penetrated the missile's casing. When the small warhead detonated, it was right on target.

<What the hell is going on out there?> Chase asked. *<Having trouble with the wildlife?>*

<The usual,> Barne replied. *<Leslie missed a couple of aracnidrones, and they're kicking Rika's ass. I'm hauling it out of the fire, though.>*

<Hey!> Rika exclaimed at the same time Leslie corrected, *<I didn't miss anything, they must have arrived later.>*

<You almost done in there?> Rika asked as she continued to scan for the other drone.

<Just got one last guy who has the target. We're negotiating,> Leslie replied.

Weapons fire echoed from the entrance to the bunker.

<That's what you call it, eh?> Barne chortled.

Rika was about to reply when she caught sight of a blur to her right. She dove to the ground as the remaining aracnidrone opened up with its minigun, flinging high-velocity rounds at Rika as it strafed past.

Enough of this. Rika leapt high into the air and fired one of her depleted uranium sabot rounds at the drone. The thing dodged out of the way—its tracking was as good as hers.

She fired another at the apex of her leap, and that one hit, tearing off two of the drone's legs…arms…whatever.

Its motion slowed just enough, allowing Rika to twist in the air and land on the drone's back, clamping a foot around the minigun and tearing it free before slamming her fist into what she assumed was its main sensor cluster.

For a second, the drone fell still, and she hoped it was down for the count. Then its legs reversed and clamped around Rika's thigh, tearing at her armor plating,

"Fuck!" Rika swore as she ripped off one of the drone's limbs and shifted her position to fire her JE84 into the thing's insides.

The drone moved, and the rounds ricocheted off. The diabolical thing got some of its feet under it and pushed up, sending Rika to the ground. It reversed its legs again and scampered on top of her, tearing at her armor as it pulled itself toward her throat.

<*Hold still!*> Barne called down.

<*Easy for you to say,*> Rika called back, holding her GNR in front of the thing while batting away limbs. It was still tearing at her leg, and managed to sink one of its sharp claws into her thigh.

Rika resisted the urge to buck into the air, though a scream did escape her throat. Then a trio of high-powered slugs streaked across the farmyard and slammed into the drone, ripping off two more of its limbs and knocking it away from Rika.

"Now you've pissed me off," Rika said as she rose and stomped on one of the drone's remaining limbs as it tried to right itself. She planted a foot on another leg, and then grabbed the thing's missile launcher as it swiveled toward her.

"Not today, you piece of shit," Rika swore as she tore off the launcher. Then she grabbed another of its limbs and wrenched it back.

The thing began to twitch and spark, and Rika jumped back, getting clear as another trio of shots came from Barne's position, striking the drone.

It finally lay still, and Rika breathed a sigh of relief.

The roar of the burning barn filled the night, still punctuated by the shrieks of the doomed horses.

<*You done messing around out there?*> Leslie asked. <*We've got a scared little girl in here, and I'd rather not put her through anything else tonight.*>

<*Hold your position,*> Rika said. <*We need to do another quick sweep. Barne, make sure no one saw the fireworks.*>

<*On it,*> Barne responded while Rika strode toward the burning barn. Nothing had exploded from within yet, and she had hopes for the truck inside.

She reached the door just as the three horses burst free—singed and a bit bloody, but alive. Rika breathed a sigh of relief as she pushed past the flames and spotted the truck. It had been flipped over, likely from the grenades, but wasn't going anywhere with the front tires half-melted.

So much for that. She hurried around the back to see if the chaingun or rocket launcher was intact. By some miracle they were, and she wrapped her hand around the cab of the truck, heaving it right-side up before tossing the cases of rockets and ammo into the truck's box.

She turned to grab the truck's rear bumper and saw movement in the flames. Rika cycled her vision and saw another aracnidrone pinned under the toppled tractor. Several of its limbs were crushed and it struggled to pull free.

Sucker.

Rika pulled the truck out of the barn, wincing as the torn muscles in her leg screamed in pain. Her armor's med-systems had already sealed the wound and injected her with biofoam. The pain was just a reminder not to further stress the injury.

A reminder she ignored.

<*I don't think it's going to work,*> Barne said as she dragged the truck free of the burning structure.

<*Yeah,*> Rika said. <*I just didn't fancy taking these weapons off*

while the building came down around me.>

She turned to survey the barn and saw the flames waver before the aracnidrone shot out of the barn—right into Rika's electron beam. Relativistic electrons shredded the machine, and it fell to the ground beside the truck.

<*Nice shooting, LT,*> Chase said from his position at the bunker's entrance. <*We clear? I don't think we should stick around too much longer.*>

Rika flipped the latches holding the chaingun down and settled it onto the outer socket on her GNR mount. It wasn't a standard connection, but the mount reconfigured and latched onto the chaingun.

She clipped its ammobox to her thigh, and then loaded four rockets into the launcher before pulling it off the truck's mount and settling it on her left shoulder.

<*Yeah, let's move.*>

<*Excessive much?*> Leslie asked as she emerged from the bunker holding the ten-year-old girl on her hip.

<*Always,*> Rika assured her.

PRAIRIE

STELLAR DATE: 02.14.8949 (Adjusted Years)
LOCATION: Kessler Wilderness, North of Kandahar City
REGION: Faseema, Oran System, Praesepe Cluster

The rendezvous point was ten klicks to the southeast, and they moved at a brisk pace across the night-shrouded plain.

The girl, whose name turned out to be Amy, had remained mostly silent through the trip, her face buried in Leslie's shoulder. Only once—when something in the burning barn exploded behind them—did she cry out and tighten her grip around Leslie's neck.

<*Is she injured?*> Rika asked, feeling empathetic to the girl's fear. It wasn't even two decades ago that she had undergone a similar nighttime escape—she had been not much older than Amy.

<*No, she seems OK,*> Leslie replied. <*Physically at least. If I weren't armored, I think she'd choke me to death with these pipes she's got for arms.*>

<*She was scared of us at first,*> Chase allowed. <*But when Leslie took her helmet off, the girl rushed right for her.*>

<*Called me 'Kitty',*> Leslie laughed.

Barne snorted. <*Need a new callsign?*>

<*We don't use callsigns,*> Leslie replied, her serious tone a warning.

<*Could start. You'd be 'Kitty', Rika would be 'Iron Ass'. Chase can be 'Loverboy'.*>

<*You call me Kitty, and I'll claw your eyes out in your sleep,*> Leslie threatened.

<*That's not helping your case,*> Chase laughed.

<*What? And you want to be 'Loverboy'?*> Leslie asked.

Chase shrugged, <*I don't think Barne can muster the consistency to pull off nicknames. Besides, he wouldn't want to know what we'd come up with for him.>*

Rika laughed, and Barne's shoulders rounded.

<Why, what would it be?> he asked.

<Dunno,> Chase replied. *<But it would make 'Loverboy' seem like a compliment.>*

<I kinda think it **is** *a compliment,>* Rika answered privately.

<Me too,> Chase said with a smile in Rika's mind. *<But the less ammo I give Barne, the better. Besides, he could call me 'Shit Face'; I'm living the dream here. He can't get me down.>*

<Oh yeah?> Rika teased. *<I'm the dream?>*

Chase gave a mental chuckle. *<Of course! Well, plus shooting bad guys—and winning. I really like winning for a change.>*

<Wow, I'm the third rung, under shooting and winning,> Rika half-jested.

Chase must have sensed her sincerity, because he took a step closer and touched her arm.

<I'd watch grass grow with you, Rika. Anything my girl wants. I'm just glad you like kicking ass more than slinging cargo for Hal on Dekar.>

<Thanks,> Rika flushed. She would have touched him in response, but her one hand was busy holding the rocket launcher steady on her shoulder.

<You're my one and only, Rika. Once we get off this shit-hole, I'm going to remind you in all the right ways.>

Rika responded with a wave of gratitude over the Link, holding back the sadness that they still couldn't be intimate.

She had spoken to the Marauders' doctors about rebuilding her genitalia—about making her feel like a whole woman again—but it wasn't that simple.

Part of the problem was with her. Over the years, she had come to accept that the majority of her body was no longer organic. She didn't sweat—except for her head—didn't have to eat if she didn't want to, didn't have to worry about pimples, rashes, infections. The matte grey ballistic polymer that served as her skin was perfection.

That realization had come to her when the doctors were talking to her about how she could get organic skin for the rest of her body—not just her head. They had talked about re-growing her limbs, about making her human again.

Thing was, Rika *liked* being a mech.

A year ago, she would have punched someone in the face just for suggesting such a notion. Her body had been nothing but shame to her.

But in the Marauders, she was all but revered. She was the backbone of Basilisk; her company's CO gave her team the hardest assignments because of Rika's effectiveness as a warrior—effectiveness that came from being a mech.

Here, no one derided her; she had a family, and that family accepted and loved her—in their own ways, at least.

She had decided to remain a mech, at least for now.

However, functioning sex organs would require the removal of two of her internal SC batteries. That would make her weak; she wouldn't be able to go more than a day at most without charging, or she would have to use external batteries for heavy combat.

In the Marauders, Rika was always within comms' reach of Basilisk team… but the fear of running out of power, of not being able to move her own limbs, of being prey, was still strong.

Power notwithstanding, there was also the matter of dealing with organic waste. Rika had long since realized that she was very happy with the fact that she no longer had to wipe her body clean several times a day. Her san-pack took care of all that.

When she considered all of that, selfish though it may be, Rika had determined to remain as she was. A decision that would have been completely without regret—were it not for Chase.

<*Rika, you there?*> Chase asked.

<*Oh, yeah, you got me daydreaming,*> Rika lied. *A white lie.*

<*Probably shouldn't tease you on a mission, LT,*> Chase replied with a wink. <*You need to stay frosty.*>

<*As do you,*> Rika replied.

No one spoke the rest of the way to the pickup location—an old grouping of concrete granaries rising roughly a hundred meters into the prairie sky.

They stood out like dark sentinels against the starscape, and the girl whimpered when she saw them, eliciting a few soft words from Leslie.

Rika climbed the tallest granary, glad that its ladder was steel and well anchored. Once on top, she surveyed the landscape, looking for any signs of pursuit.

She could see several swathers in the distance shearing the tall, dry grass for baling, and a truck driving down a road further to the south.

A cry sounded from below, and Rika peered over the edge of the silo that she stood on to see Leslie returning to Amy, her hands stretched out, eliciting calm.

It appeared that Leslie would *not* be joining Rika atop the granaries for surveillance—not if they wanted to keep Amy quiet.

<*I'll go up,*> Chase offered, and took off at a slow, loping run toward the silo furthest from Rika.

<*Think we'll see more of K-Strike's goons?*> Leslie asked.

<*There was an EM signal linking those aracnis,*> Barne said. <*It was close by—or passing through a strong relay. Either way, someone saw what we were up to. Whether or not they have the firepower to come at us is another story.*>

<*What do you think, LT?*> Chase asked.

<*I think we should expect an attack,*> Rika assessed. <*Barne, did you signal for our lift? Where is Patty already?*>

<*She's coming,*> Barne replied. <*She had to refuel, and got gouged onstation. She'll be lifting off shortly. Oh, and she said there's weather moving in from the west. She's gonna try to beat it.*>

<*'Weather'?*> Rika peered at the western horizon. She cycled her vision through a few modes, and backscatter revealed that there were clouds low on the horizon and moving in quickly. She could make out a few flickers of light deep within.

Great, a flash prairie storm high on the steppe. Just what we need.

<*Tell her to hurry up, Barne. I don't want to get stuck in this,*> Rika ordered.

Barne chuckled. <*Afraid you'll rust?*>

<*Shut up, Barne. Just tell her to move it.*>

<*See that?*> Chase said suddenly. <*At the farm. A gunship.*>

Rika looked toward the farm and saw a small, squat ship descending into the valley.

<*I don't see any markings. So it's not police.*>

<*Yeah, but it's well-armed,*> Chase replied.

Rika played back the visuals Chase had captured and saw that the gunship sported a set of rather large missiles on its undercarriage, as well as a pair of chainguns alongside its electron cannons.

<*I didn't take K-Strike for the sentimental type,*> Chase commented. <*You'd think they'd search for us first.*>

<*Maybe they think we're long gone,*> Leslie suggested. <*Just doing cleanup to remove their tracks.*>

<*Sloppy, if that's the case,*> Rika replied.

She dispatched her last passel of drones and directed them to set up an overwatch grid two kilometers into the sky. She wanted a clear view of the ship if it sent out search parties or took off, or if more of its friends arrived.

<*ETA on Patty?*> Rika asked Barne.

<*Twenty-two minutes,*> Barne replied.

Rika nodded to herself. *It could be worse, and there's nothing we can do about it, anyway.*

She turned to examine the structure atop the silo. A conveyer ran between each concrete tower, with different tracks and pipes used to deliver disparate grains to the correct silo. It was aged and rusting, but not so badly that it wouldn't support her weight.

Rika carefully climbed up the steel struts and wedged the rocket launcher between a pair of beams supporting the conveyer. Then she grabbed one of the smaller support crossmembers, tore it free—wincing as it screeched—and wrapped it around the rocket launcher.

<*Wow, could you be any louder?*> Barne asked.

<*I should ask for a small arc welder on our next mission,*> Rika replied.

Barne snorted. <*Then you could be 'Rika Repairbot'.*>

<*You're just a bucket of yuk yuks tonight, Barne,*> Chase responded. <*You go see a comedy show recently, or something?*>

<*What can I say?*> Barne shrugged. <*You guys are my muse.*>

Chase and Barne continued trading barbs while Rika interfaced with the rocket launcher and linked with its launch systems.

The missiles it fired were guided; so long as it was facing in the general direction of the enemy, she should be able to use it effectively without toting it around.

Rika didn't have the specs on the missiles themselves, but judging by their size, they should have enough fuel to strike targets up to four or five kilometers out—provided she didn't need to steer them too much.

Satisfied that the launcher was secure, she climbed back down to the domed roof of the silo and took up a position on the leeward side.

She surveyed the darkened prairie, pausing periodically to take in the breathtaking view of the Praesepe Cluster gleaming in the night sky—like a diamond, ruby, and sapphire encrusted sheet of velvet.

A gust of wind raced across the grass, and Rika imagined a swarm of the aracnidrones rushing through the tall stalks toward their position.

<*Leslie, do you have any pixie dust with you?*> Rika asked.

<*Of course. I don't leave home without it,*> Leslie replied. <*I don't think Amy is going to let me go long enough to disperse it, though.*>

<*I'll do it,*> Rika said and walked to the edge of the silo. She stepped off and hit the ground with a dull *thud*.

Leslie and Amy sat in the shadow of a silo in the second row, so Rika made her way through the discarded equipment to their position. She checked Barne's position and saw him hunkered down at the end of the row, scanning the horizon to the south—the direction from which Patty would approach.

Amy started as Rika reached the pair, and the girl buried her face into Leslie's side.

"It's OK, Amy," Leslie whispered, stroking Amy's hair. "Rika is a nice woman."

Amy peered out at Rika, eyeing her suspiciously. "She's a mech; most mechs aren't very nice."

Rika unlocked her helmet and lifted it enough to show her face.

"Hi, Amy, it's very nice to meet you."

A small smile crossed Amy's lips, and her grip on Leslie loosened a little.

"Oh, you're a pretty lady! I didn't think mechs had faces."

Rika chuckled softly. "Some do. And thank you, Amy. Think you could loosen your grip on Leslie a bit? She needs to get something out of her satchel for me."

A look of worry flitted across Amy's features, and Leslie patted her on the shoulder. "Just for a moment, dear."

Amy nodded and gave Leslie a bit of space while Rika pulled her helmet back on.

"Are we going to be OK?" Amy asked, her voice wavering as she watched Leslie.

"You bet we are. You saw how we took out those bad people holding you. Here we are, hale and whole," Rika replied.

Amy looked at the gash on Rika's thigh where bits of biofoam stuck out from the wound.

"That looks bad, though."

Rika glanced down at her leg. The pain had died down to a dull throb; more because she was practiced at ignoring injuries than because of any lack of severity in the wound.

"Yeah, looks worse than it is, though. I'm pretty tough."

Amy nodded seriously. "You look tough. Do you work for my father, ma'am?"

Rika let out a quiet laugh. "Rika. You can call me Rika. We

were hired by your father to bring you home."

A strange expression crossed Amy's face, and Rika couldn't tell if the girl was happy or sad about the news.

While she was processing that, Leslie handed her the pixie dust.

<Don't get any on yourself; it will mess with your sensor suite.>

<*Yes, Mom,*> Rika replied.

As Rika moved away, she saw Amy tuck against Leslie's side once more. Rika ventured out into the tall grass surrounding the granaries, stopping when she had walked five hundred meters.

The pixie dust was a fine film, deposited from a canister onto the grass and ground that the team's sensors would pick up. It was expensive. Rika wouldn't use it to detect humans—there was no way those could hide in the dry grass.

The aracnidrones were a different story entirely, and worth the cost of the pixie dust, in Rika's opinion.

She held the canister out at arm's length and began to walk in a wide circle around the granaries. She started on the southwest side, determined to first lay the dust down on the side facing the farm.

Behind her, the dusted strip of grass glowed brightly on her HUD. So long as no one else knew the variable set of wavelengths at which the dust reflected, it would be entirely invisible.

If any of those drones came through and picked up the dust, they'd be as bright as searchlights.

Let them try me then, Rika challenged.

She had almost walked a full kilometer when the surveillance drones alerted her to the gunship lifting off from the farm.

<*They're headed this way,*> Chase said.

<*Not surprising,*> Rika replied. <*We didn't hide our tracks too well.*>

It wasn't that they had been sloppy; traversing ten kilometers of waist-high grass, in armor, was going to leave some broken stalks—even if one avoided the denser patches.

The gunship was flying low and slow, sweeping back and

forth across the terrain. Rika and the team had used a few game trails as they moved across the terrain; with any luck, their pursuers would follow some of those, and buy the team enough time for Patty to arrive with their ride.

<*I judge them to be seven minutes out,*> Chase said.

<*That's about my guess, too,*> Rika agreed. <*And Patty is still twelve. Barne, tell her to juice it.*>

<*Sure, I'll tell her to fall like a stone through the atmosphere; think that would work?*>

Rika ignored the barb and continued on her route, depositing the pixie dust. As she passed one hundred and twenty degrees of her circle, she saw movement to her right.

<*Company!*> she called out as an aracnidrone raced through her trail of dust, rushing toward her.

Rika's lips split into a grin. *Not so easy this time.*

She took a moment to gauge the drone's movement and then fired a depleted uranium round. The sabot burned its propellant then fell off, leaving the high-density dart, which hit the aracnidrone with the force of a building falling on it.

Debris fountained into the air and when it settled, there was no more movement.

From *that* drone.

Rika sprinted back toward the granaries, putting more distance between her and the pixie dust, as two more aracnidrones passed through the line.

<*Gunship just changed course,*> Chase reported.

<*Just now?*> Rika verified.

<*Yeah.*> Chase's tone was grim.

They all knew what that meant: either the pilot of the gunship was very subtle and didn't want to reveal the presence of the aracnidrones until they struck, or they were dealing with two enemies.

Rika had to assume two separate foes. *Apparently Amy is a hot commodity.*

The two aracnidrones didn't know that Rika could see them,

and continued to move slowly through the tall grass, trying to stay in cover. Rika took quick but careful aim and fired two more sabot rounds.

The first one hit its target, and another explosion of dirt and aracnidrone limbs flew into the air; the second missed, and the drone raced forward, passing within the minimum range of Rika's sabot rounds.

"Eat this," Rika said aloud as she spun up the chaingun and fired at the onrushing drone. The thing picked up speed, dodging left and right as Rika tried to hit it.

She clipped one leg, then another, and shot down two missiles that the drone fired at her. Then it opened up its own minigun as it wove through the grass, and Rika dove aside, losing sight of her foe in the tall grass.

The entire engagement took less than seven seconds, and Rika rose to a crouch. The drone suddenly leapt at her, intent on tearing her limb from limb like the one back at the farm.

She was ready for it, and swung her chaingun into the drone's path, slamming it into the underside of the thing, firing as she raised both the gun and the drone over her head.

The drone flew through the air and slammed into one of the concrete silos, whereupon Rika expended the remainder of her chaingun's ammo, shredding the thing.

<*You need to stop firing point-blank at stuff,*> Barne advised. <*You're going to foul your barrels.*>

<*Want to come out and fight these drones?*> she challenged.

Barne didn't respond, but Rika knew he was right. Ricochets and shrapnel could damage her weapons. She unlatched the chaingun, dropping it to the ground, and ran a check on her GNR's three firing modes.

They all checked out clean, and she breathed a sigh of relief. If she fouled the GNR in combat, Barne would never let her live it down.

There was no time to celebrate her victory against the drones—or spar with Barne further. The gunship had just passed within the five-kilometer max range of her rockets, and Rika signaled the launcher to fire a pair.

The gunship's pilot jinked predictably as the rockets streaked toward his craft, and Rika fired her electron beam at the ship, striking it in the stern.

<*Didn't penetrate,*> Chase reported.

<*Must be armored,*> Rika replied as she backed under the protective cover of the silos. <*When it sets down to disgorge its passengers, I'll hit it with the rockets again. It won't have as many reaction options.*>

<***If** it sets down,*> Leslie qualified.

<*It'll at least slow.*>

The gunship dropped to five meters as it crossed the one-kilometer mark, but—contrary to Rika's prediction—it did not slow.

Dammit. It's now or never.

Rika fired her last two rockets as the side door slid open, and the gunship slewed to the side, avoiding the rockets. Two armored figures half-jumped, half-fell out. Rika circled the rockets back around and slammed one into the gunship on its right side, while the second struck the ship in the tail, spinning it wildly.

A third figure fell from the ship's side door, and then the gunship pulled back, circling high in the air.

<*Damn, what's it going to take to shoot that thing down?*> Chase asked incredulously.

<*Need an assist, Basilisk?*> Patty's welcome voice came over the Link.

Rika peered through the silos to see their ride coming down from the heavens on the southern side of the structures. A pair of missiles streaked out from the Marauder pinnace, lancing through the night toward the enemy gunship. The pilot of the gunship managed to evade one, but not both.

Patty's missile struck the ship near the bow and swung it sideways, the tip of one if its stubby wings hitting the ground and spinning the gunship around to slam into the loamy prairie turf.

<*Target down,*> Patty announced as Chase cried out, <*Incoming!*>

Rika switched her vision to the overhead drone feeds and saw a trio of missiles, plus two electron beams, streak out of the tall grass directly under Patty's drop ship. The ship fired countermeasures, but the enemy had fired from too close a range and their weapons all struck true.

The backend of the Marauder pinnace exploded, and the ship flipped over, spinning end over end before slamming into one of the silos.

<*I'm on it!*> Chase shouted, and Rika saw him leap off his silo and race to the downed drop ship.

<*I have eyes on those shooters,*> Barne called out, and passed the targeting data over the combat net.

Rika acknowledged before running a quick scan to make sure all the drones were down. Satisfied that she wasn't going to get attacked from behind, she dashed out into the prairie and fired two sabot rounds, followed by an electron beam. Then she turned to her right, toward the enemies who had jumped from the gunship before it went down.

Rika's high-altitude drones had tracked the mercs as they left the ship and hadn't lost sight in the chaos. The feeds showed that two were in heavy armor, while another was in lighter gear.

She fired a trio of rounds at the lightly armored enemy before diving to the side as a spray of kinetic rounds swept across the prairie.

Rika rolled to her feet and strafed around the three mercenaries at top speed, firing two sabot rounds. She hit one of the heavies before she got the downed gunship between them.

The overhead drones showed that the figure in the light armor was down, but the two heavies were still on the move, getting in position to come around both sides of the gunship.

Rika glanced inside the cockpit, noting that the pilot was alive but unconscious, and that the ship—despite the hole in the back and the shattered ablative plating—was otherwise intact.

She was considering her options when one of the heavies broke into a run and leapt atop the gunship.

Shit, I was going to do that, Rika groused.

Even without her drones overhead watching the battlefield, she would have heard the enemy slam into the ship. He moved toward the edge. *Two can play the jumping game.*

JE84 in hand, she leapt into the air, flashing past the enemy—who was too startled to react—and unloaded a full magazine from her weapon into his head and shoulders before coming down behind him.

A spray of rounds from the other heavy hit her in the back, and Rika spun behind the soldier atop the gunship, using him for cover.

He had just recovered from her barrage—which had dented his armor, but not penetrated anywhere—when his teammate's weapons fire slammed into him.

His armor cracked around the shoulder and right arm, and Rika dropped her rifle, grabbed the broken armor, and pulled.

By then, the man—the troop had the build of a man—was raising his rifle to fire point-blank into Rika's head.

Until she ripped his arm off.

He shrieked like a banshee, and Rika kicked him off the top of the gunship and leapt into the air, forgetting her JE84, brandishing his detached arm as she raced toward the third enemy, who took off running the other way.

Rika threw the arm after him and considered giving chase, but Leslie spoke up.

<*There's another ship on the horizon, coming in low.*>

<*I've got confirmed four ground signals from those bastards who took down Patty,*> Barne added. <*They're spreading out.*>

<*She's alive,*> Chase informed them. <*I'm pulling her out.*>

Rika looked back at the downed gunship. <*Rally on me,*> she ordered.

The gunship lay thirty meters from the northern side of the silos, protected from the approaching enemy on the southern side.

Rika wondered who had shot down Patty. *Are they K-Strike, or is the gunship K-Strike's?*

Missions like this had been much simpler during the war. There was her side and the Nietzscheans; that was it. Now everything always seemed to involve three or four competing groups.

<*I'm bringing Amy through,*> Leslie said.

<*I'll cover Chase,*> Barne volunteered.

<*Copy that,*> Rika acknowledged and entered the gunship. The pilot was still unconscious, but the cockpit's holo console was active. She scanned the readings. The aft grav lift was on backup emitters, and the weapons systems were offline, but otherwise, no other major systems failures were evident.

The thing was tough as nails.

She touched the initialization panel on the console hoping the ship would not be in a secure mode.

<*Authorization tokens not accepted.*>

"Dammit," Rika muttered. There wasn't time to hack the controls before the next enemy arrived. However, there was someone in the cockpit who had the correct tokens *and* knew how to fly the craft.

Rika's scan suite showed the pilot's heartbeat to be steady, though his blood pressure was a touch low. His breathing was regular, but shallow; could have to do with how his chin was against his chest.

"Hey," Rika said as she pushed his head back and shook it side to side. "Wake up, buddy."

The pilot moaned as Leslie and Amy came on board, the girl tripping over a dislodged seat.

"Ow!" she cried out, and the pilot's eyes snapped open.

"What? Where?" he said, looking around with unfocused eyes. He turned his head—which was at crotch-level with Rika—and his eyes widened noticeably.

"Eyes up here," Rika growled, and the pilot leaned back, looking up at Rika's helmet.

"Uh…hi?" he said.

"Get her ready, we're about to fly out of here."

"We are?" the pilot asked, obviously still dazed from the crash.

"Yeah," Rika said sweetly. "There's a bunch of unfriendly types on their way here to take the girl. I'm pretty sure they're not your pals, so being *not* here would be in your best interests."

"Wait…what about my team?"

Rika shook her head slowly. "Unless you want to join them, I'd suggest you get us airborne."

The pilot nodded and turned to the console in front of him, muttering under his breath as he activated a repair system and powered on the main grav emitters. The gunship lurched sideways, and Amy cried out with alarm.

Rika looked back to see Leslie with her helmet off, shushing the girl as she buckled her into one of the remaining seats.

"We're almost out of here, Amy," Rika reassured her. "Just have to wait for the rest of our friends."

As though on cue, Chase appeared at the side of the gunship, lifting Patty up in his arms.

"I got her," Leslie said as she leaned over the side and gently lifted the unconscious woman into the vessel.

Rika saw that Patty's face was bloody and her left leg looked torn up. A scan from her armor showed a rapid pulse and shortness of breath.

"I'll stabilize her," Leslie promised as she settled the team's pilot into a seat.

"Is she going to be OK?" Amy asked, her voice a mixture of fear and concern.

"Yes, dear, she'll be fine," Leslie replied absently. "You'll see."

Chase pulled himself up, and Rika leaned back to clasp his shoulder. <*You good?*>

<*Right as rain. I'll keep our rent-a-pilot in line; you should keep your GNR where it will do us the most good.*>

Rika nodded and shuffled around Chase in the gunship's tight confines. When she reached the opening on the side of the ship, she met Barne, who was pulling himself up.

<*You dropped this,*> he said, holding out her JE84.

<*Damn, I forgot about that thing,*> Rika replied.

<*What would you do without me?*>

<*Honestly, Barne? I have no idea.*> Strange as it sounded, Rika meant it.

"Let's get gone. Head north," Chase ordered the pilot.

"Yeah, north," the man replied.

The gunship pulled into the air and slowly turned before speeding off to the north.

Rika peered out the hole in the side of the ship, searching for the adversaries who had been approaching from the south. As she scanned the granaries, a figure appeared atop one of the silos. Its shape was familiar, and Rika directed her drones to get a closer look. One managed to send back an image before enemy drones started taking out her surveillance.

There she was, clear as day: an SMI-2 mech, her GNR raised but not firing.

"Kick it up a notch," Chase commanded in the cockpit, and the gunship accelerated, leaving the vision from Rika's past far behind them.

LAYING LOW

STELLAR DATE: 02.15.8949 (Adjusted Years)
LOCATION: Stolen Gunship, Edge of Kandahar City
REGION: Faseema, Oran System, Praesepe Cluster

"You sure this location is secure?" Chase asked as the gunship's pilot lowered the craft into a deep ravine outside of Kandahar City—a mid-sized city on the coast of the Oran Ocean.

Barne barked a laugh from where he had been standing behind the pilot, silently menacing the man. "Chase, we're on an ass-end planet in the ass-end of an FTL route that goes nowhere worth going in Praesepe. I don't think there's a single safe place on this rock."

"I get that, Barne; we know your glass never even gets to half-full. I just wanted to know if the surveillance drones you dropped here were still reporting," Chase replied.

"Oh, yeah, that. Nothing bigger than a lizard has come through in the last three days. But once we land and check over the gear, we need to blow this ship and get gone."

From her seat in the back—with Amy still all but embedded in her side—Leslie asked, "Don't think you disabled the ship's transponder?"

"I disabled two. That doesn't mean there's not another that's on a dead-timer with no EM 'til it phones home."

"And…uhhhh…what about me?" the pilot asked as the gunship wobbled slightly in a sudden updraft.

"You just get us on the ground, and then we'll worry about what's next," Barne grunted.

Chase reached out and touched Rika on the shoulder. <*What's up? You've been really quiet the whole way here.*>

Rika almost jumped when he touched her—the team's banter had only been a dull background murmur beneath her processing what she had witnessed at the granaries.

The visuals from the drones were arrayed before her, superimposed over her vision; a dozen of the Genevian mech were highlighted and pulled to the fore. *An SMI-2…it has to be. No armor cuts the same profile, and there is no other weapon that looks like a GNR.*

<*Just thinking about the battle,*> Rika turned her head to meet Chase's eyes. <*I saw something.*>

<*Saw a lot of things. I think there were three separate forces out there. What's so important about this little girl here?*>

Rika felt a stab of guilt. She *should* have been going over the battle and analyzing the enemy to identify which belonged to what enemy force, logging team kills and damage, checking on Patty…

<*I saw something out there, Chase,*> Rika said after a moment's indecision. <*Another mech; an SMI-2, like me.*>

<*Wow…really? Was it someone you knew?*> Chase let the words hang in her mind for a moment.

Rika knew that the fear of meeting an old comrade on the field was something nearly every Marauder felt. With so much of the former Genevian military working for mercenary companies—many of those operating in Praesepe—the chance was always there that you could find an old friend in your sights.

I'm being selfish, she thought. *Every other Marauder faces this fear with each foe they see. I only have to worry about the least common mech-model out there.*

<*I don't know,*> she finally answered. <*There weren't a lot of us—and I didn't meet many of them.*>

<*You wonder if it's her, don't you?*> Chase asked with understanding in his gaze.

Silva.

< *I can't tell. That's what I've been looking for in the drone feeds—some sign that it's her.*>

<*Would confirmation be good or bad?*> Chase asked.

Rika liked that about him. He didn't try to placate or offer false hope; he saw to the root of the issue: how did she really *feel* about it?

Thing was, she didn't know.

<Somewhere else on Faseema is an SMI-2 mech. It could be no one I know at all…>

Chase nodded slowly, his eyes still locked on hers. *<Or it could be Silva, your old fireteam leader.>*

<The woman who saved me from…everything.>

<Seems like it would be better if this mech was no one you knew,> Chase replied. *<You don't want to see an old friend on the other side of your rifle,>* he finished, echoing her earlier thoughts.

Rika let out a long sigh, which coincided with the pilot finally settling the gunship on a level space at the ravine's bottom.

"Thank the stars," Leslie said.

"Yeah, I hear ya," Barne agreed. "Would suck to make it all this way, and then have this chucklehead clip an outcropping and kill us all."

"I'm on this thing too," the pilot said pointedly.

"Your level of loyalty to your organization is unknown to us. You might consider it an acceptable trade," Rika said as she rose, ducking low in the cramped space. "Get up."

The pilot hit the release on his harness and half stood, remaining hunched over in front of his seat.

"You first," Rika prodded, gesturing to the back where Chase waited. Beyond him, Leslie was saying something to Amy while Barne exited the gunship to secure the area.

"Uh, you first? You're all big and kinda sharp in places. I can't get past."

Rika pressed herself back into the corner. "This is as good as it gets; you'll just have to mind my pointy bits."

Leslie snorted from her place in the back of the gunship, and Rika shook her head. *That one's coming back to haunt me later.*

The pilot squeezed past, muttering something about not even knowing her name before brushing his ass against her.

<He's loosening up a bit,> Chase commented on the team's general net.

<*I guess being a dork is his stress response,*> Leslie replied.

<*How's our charge doing back there?*> Rika asked as the pilot exited the gunship with Chase behind him.

Leslie looked down at Amy, her yellow eyes full of compassion. <*She's scared. She's not been too articulate; from what I can tell, she only has a father waiting for her back…wherever. Something's a bit off, though—can't put my finger on it. Honestly, she's taking it pretty well. I don't know that ten-year-old Leslie would have done the same.*>

Rika thought back to what life was like when she was ten—before the war had destroyed her life. In hindsight she could see that her parents had been worried about the struggle against the Nietzscheans, but they had shielded her as well as they could. It had been a good year for young Rika.

<*I hear you there,*> was the only response Rika gave before crouching down next to Amy.

"You've been really good; done really well, Amy. We're going to check the area over and make sure our ground transportation is OK before we get on the move again."

Amy's big brown eyes looked up at Rika. They weren't currently wet with tears, but the streaks on her face told of a recent bout.

"I didn't know mechs could talk. You have a nice voice."

"A lot of mechs don't have mouths anymore," Rika explained. "They can talk through speakers on their armor, but they usually talk over the Link."

"I don't have the Link yet," Amy said. "I never get to hear them."

Rika wondered how many mechs this girl had seen. Perhaps her father employed some for security.

"You're taking me to my father soon?" Amy asked.

"Yes, Amy. But I'm really glad I got to meet you—you're one tough girl." Rika looked up and met Leslie's eyes. "Leslie and I like to see strong girls like you. Gives us hope for the future."

"I don't feel strong," Amy said quietly.

"That's how I know you are, though," Rika assured her. "Being strong, even when you don't feel like you can go on another minute—that's the real deal. I see it in here." Rika reached out and touched the young girl on her chest, over her heart. Amy reached up and touched Rika's index finger.

"Did it hurt?" she asked.

"Did what hurt?"

Amy looked at Rika's arms, and then her face. "When they…when you…"

"When my limbs were cut off?" Rika asked gently, swallowing as the memory resurfaced.

Amy nodded silently in response.

"Yeah, it hurt a lot."

"Does it still hurt?"

Rika smiled. "Sometimes, but not the way you mean. You'd be surprised what you can get used to."

Amy frowned, and then a sad look filled her eyes, and she nodded. "I think I know what you mean."

Rika wondered what the girl had endured at the hands of her captors. There weren't any signs of abuse—but there weren't always visible indicators. She could also just be referring to how one could even become accustomed to imprisonment. To obeying the orders of others, to not having a voice.

That was something Rika understood all too well.

"I'm going to go out and help scout the area. We'll let you know when it's all clear."

Leslie nodded, stroking Amy's shoulder, and Rika backed out of the gunship into the dimly lit ravine, settling her helmet on her head.

<*Never took you for the motherly type, Leslie.*> Rika reached out to her friend privately as she surveyed the canyon walls rising up sharply on either side.

<*A story for another time,*> Leslie deferred, her mental tone laden with unspoken emotion.

<*No pressure,*> Rika offered, receiving only an affirmative

response from Leslie.

Rika wondered what Leslie could be referring to. There was no mention of children on her record—though that didn't mean Leslie never had any. It wasn't as though Leslie's record with the Marauders comprised her life's story. The cat-like woman was over two hundred years old; a lot could happen in that amount of time.

Rika turned her attention back to the task at hand. *<How's it look?>* she asked Barne as she walked to where Chase had directed the pilot to sit underneath a rock outcropping at the base of the cliff.

<Everything is as I left it,> Barne observed. *<Drones are in place. I'm sending a new set higher—want to make sure we have a clear route to the city.>*

<OK, let me know when you're satisfied.>

Barne chuckled. *<You should know by now, Lieutenant: I'm never satisfied.>*

Rika knew there was innuendo there, but chose to ignore it. Instead, she looked down at the pilot slouched on a rock.

"Name," she said aloud.

"Jenny," he replied.

"What?" Chase asked. " 'Jenny'?"

"No," the pilot shook his head. "Jem-mee. With an M."

"Huh. I don't think I've ever heard that name before," Chase said. "Seems a bit unfortunate."

Jemmy scowled. "Why's that?"

"Just sounds a lot like 'Jenny', is all. What's it short for? I assume it's short for something."

"Jeremiah," Jemmy replied. "I really don't get what the big deal is. What's your name?"

" 'Marauder'," Chase replied tersely. "I always thought that 'Jerry' was short for 'Jeremiah'."

Jemmy scowled and gave a short shake of his head. "What? 'Jerry'? That sounds stupid. I know a lot of guys named Jeremiah. No one goes by 'Jerry'. Sounds like 'Sherry', and that's a girl's name."

"And 'Jemmy' doesn't sound like 'Jenny'? That's short for 'Jennifer', you know."

"You don't say," Jemmy sneered. "I've neeeeeever heard *that* before."

<This guy's downgrading himself from dork to asshole,> Chase assessed.

"This may be the dumbest conversation I've overheard in weeks," Barne commented as he walked by.

Rika couldn't help but give a soft laugh. Maybe some dumb conversation was just what she needed right now to take her mind off the other mech.

"So, you're K-Strike, right?" Rika asked, getting to the point.

There had been no markings on the gunship, and Rika hadn't spotted any of K-Strike's logos on the soldiers it had disgorged—but it was still the most likely choice.

Jemmy nodded. "Yeah, but I'm not a fighter; I just fly ships."

"Ships that shoot at us," Chase replied. "Sounds like fighting to me."

"We don't care that you fought for your outfit," Rika said in a mollifying tone. "That's what we do, too. There are no hard feelings there."

"Though our outfit doesn't kidnap children," Chase added, his voice dripping with disdain.

<Easy now, Chase,> Rika coaxed privately. *<I'm trying to win this guy over.>*

<Oh! Shoot! I thought we were doing good-cop, bad-cop…>

<Uh, well, I guess we are now,> Rika replied. *<Since you've been all mean to poor little Jennifer, here.>*

Chase gave a laugh over the Link while Jemmy defended himself against Chase's verbal accusation. "Yeah, but you guys shot first!"

"OK, that's enough," Rika said sharply, turning her helmeted head to Chase. "Go check over the transport with Barne. I got this."

Chase shook his head and stomped off, while Rika knelt beside Jemmy and pulled off her helmet.

"Sorry about him. He's always a bit testy after missions."

"I can tell," Jemmy said. "Guy's grouchy and a bit rude."

"I'll let him know to ease up," Rika said with a warm smile.

"What happens now?" Jemmy asked. "You shoot me and leave me in the gunship when you blow it?"

Rika chuckled. "You seem pretty blasé about the whole thing."

"I kinda expected to be dead already. I'm just living it up on borrowed time right now."

"Marauders don't execute prisoners," Rika said.

"Oh, yeah?" Jemmy asked, his right eyebrow raised skeptically. "What about tying them up and leaving them to die in the bottom of a deep ravine?"

"I'd group that with 'execute'," Rika said.

"Wow, morals and everything."

"Let's get to my questions, then we can decide what we'll do with you. First off, how many more from your outfit are on Faseema?

She could see that Jemmy was having a small crisis of conscience. He didn't want to give away his own people, but he knew the game they were playing. There was the easy way, or the hard way.

He also knew that even a gentle slap from Rika was the sort of thing that broke jaws and knocked out teeth.

"Gunship was the backup team," he finally said. "No one else on-planet."

"And above?" Rika pressed. The gunship could do short flights and atmospheric drops, but it didn't have food, supplies, or environmental systems for long flights. It certainly wasn't FTL-capable. That meant K-Strike had a ship nearby.

Jemmy didn't reply, but Rika watched on scan his blood pressure rise and heart rate go up, and then drop as he tried to regulate his stress levels.

When Basilisk had approached Faseema on Patty's pinnace,

there had been over two thousand ships in orbit, and thousands more docked at the various stations.

While many were certainly not the right class or configuration to be a K-Strike ship, capable of interstellar flight, there were hundreds that could be.

Space above Faseema even had three battlecruisers in orbit. Remnants of Oran's military—such as it was.

Rika took a moment to consider the situation in the Oran system, and what that might mean for an evac. Twenty years ago, Oran had been in its prime; wealthy from being the last system on an FTL spur route that went five light years into the Praesepe cluster.

Beyond Oran, FTL flight was not possible in the cluster. The dark layer was suffused with dark matter, concentrations that heralded the end of any ship that dared transition into the DL.

Beyond Oran, only light-huggers plied the black, ships that employed massive ramscoops to draw in interstellar hydrogen as they continually boosted or braked between the stars.

But nineteen years ago, a new power had arisen in the region; a warlord named Stavros had built up an empire of ships and warriors that he had scavenged in the wake of recent wars on the edge of the cluster.

Unlike outfits like the Marauders, Stavros wasn't interested in doing work for hire. He wanted to build a new empire—which he named 'The Politica'—and he wasn't afraid to subjugate, or obliterate, the occupants of any system he set his eyes on.

Oran had been one such system.

The Oranians had believed themselves secure in their alliances and trade agreements. As a result, they had not built up a large military. The other nations within the cluster were happy to work with them, as the people of the Oran System were fair, and efficiently facilitated the constant two-way handoff of cargo coming into and going out of the nations deeper within Praesepe.

Which had made them ripe for the picking when Stavros came.

Oran had fought back, and a few of their neighbors even came to their aid—but in the end, Stavros and his Politica fleets had forced the Oranians back to the three planets in the core of their star system.

Faseema was the only habitable world of the lot, and so became home to the remnants of the Oranian people.

Strangely, Stavros did not strike the final blow to destroy the original inhabitants of Oran. He contented himself with controlling the outer system, and the FTL jump points. He even allowed trade and commerce with the Oranian people on the inner planets.

It was a strategy that turned the inner worlds into a vassal state, dependent upon The Politica for trade and access to the rest of the Praesepe cluster.

From what Rika could tell, the three cruisers above Faseema may very well represent the entirety of the local space force.

If team Basilisk got into space, and K-Strike attacked, there may be no help from the military. Unless they were on a local ship.

Rika brought her attention back to Jemmy, who had not answered her last question.

"So, you have a ship up there," she surmised. "Makes sense. Even without a hole in the side, your gunship wasn't getting you home. And you're loyal enough not to screw over your pals up there. I respect that. You'll be interested in knowing that we didn't kill everyone on your team—one of them ran off."

Jemmy's eyes narrowed. "That's not what you told me last night."

"I didn't exactly *say* I killed everyone," Rika pointed out with a shrug. "I kinda implied it."

"Heavily."

"Guilty."

"Are you telling me this to get me to think you're OK, to conclude that my team is a bunch of cowards, or to sow hope of rescue?"

"Hadn't thought of that last one," Rika admitted. "I suppose if your shuttle has a third transponder, that might happen—though I'd like to see them try. Unless they're willing to do an orbital strike and risk killing the target, then I think we're OK."

"For now," the pilot allowed.

"Yes, for now. We'll let someone know you're here before we go." She reached out toward Jemmy, and he pulled back, his fear justified.

"Shit," Jemmy muttered as a hypospray extended from the palm of Rika's hand.

"Better than death," Rika judged. "We'll leave water."

The hypospray injected him with a fast-acting neurotoxin, plus a batch of nano to make sure his own internal systems didn't clear out the neurotoxin too soon.

<*We clear?*> she asked Barne and Chase.

<*Yeah, transport is three hundred meters to the south; no signs of anyone finding it. We're ready to roll soon as you get here.*>

<*Clear to the north, though I spotted some hikers a few klicks further up the ravine,*> Chase added.

<*They coming this way?*> Rika asked.

<*Yeah, seems like it. They're maybe twenty minutes out.*>

"Shit," Rika muttered aloud, though she supposed it could be worse—the hikers could have been right underneath them as Jemmy brought the gunship in.

She walked back to the gunship and stuck her head in. "All clear. Barne has the transport ready to the south."

"OK, Amy," Leslie said as she rose. "Time for us to go. I have to put my helmet back on so that I can keep my eyes peeled while we're out there."

"Do you have to?" Amy pleaded. "I don't like how your helmets make you look."

Leslie knelt in front of the young girl, smoothing her hair back. "I know. They're meant to look dangerous, to make people fear us. It's part of what we do."

Amy nodded. "I know, my father says similar things. It's

just…they're still scary."

<*Too bad the gunship doesn't have a kid's EV suit; we could put her in one, and she'd probably feel safer,*> Rika said regretfully.

<*Maybe we can find something when we get to Kandahar City.*>

Rika backed out of the opening in the gunship's side and stood guard as Chase ducked in to retrieve Patty. He lifted her carefully, and Rika touched his shoulder as he moved past.

<*What's up?*> he asked.

<*Nothing…just wanted to feel you.*>

Chase's mental avatar gave her a knowing smile. <*Once we're safely on our way, we can have lots and lots of feeling.*>

<*Stop it, I need to focus,*> Rika said sending a mock scowl to his mind.

Chase turned his head, looking back, and gave a nod. She couldn't see his face, but she knew there was a wink being given. <*You started it,*> he reminded her.

Behind her, Leslie finally got Amy out of the gunship, and began guiding her down to the floor of the ravine, explaining why they couldn't fly a stolen gunship with a hole in the side to the city's air and spaceport.

Rika leaned her head into the vessel and made one last sweep to ensure nothing identifying them had been left behind. Amy had left a few fingerprints on the hull, so Rika wiped those off before walking to where Jemmy was slumped over.

Should have gotten Leslie to help with this, Rika realized as she lifted Jemmy's right arm with her left, pulling him up straight. Then she ducked down and slung him over her shoulder. *Or not; guy doesn't weigh that much.*

A hundred meters from the gunship, Rika stopped and turned to face it, looking at the cliff rising above; there was a large outcropping of rock, twenty meters up. She took aim and fired her electron beam at it.

The ravine wall exploded, and rock showered down onto the gunship, nearly covering it. Rika changed her angle and fired a sabot round at the cliff face, shattering it further and dropping more stone onto the craft below.

One more shot and the final chunk of the overhang fell, likely crushing what remained of the K-Strike vessel.

Should do the trick. The hikers would probably see the dust and come investigate—or maybe they'd think the ravine wall was unstable and turn back. Either way, Basilisk would be long gone by then.

Rika carefully moved down the ravine, reaching where Barne waited in the ground transport a minute later. It was an off-road truck of sorts that had a small bed and three rows of seats inside.

Chase was settling Patty in the back row as Rika approached, and Rika spotted a shady spot where a bottle of water and some protein bars waited.

She laid Jemmy on his side and, once satisfied that he wouldn't get baked when the sun reached its zenith, walked to the truck, getting in the front passenger seat.

"Good to go, LT?" Barne asked from the driver's seat.

"Yup. Dropped the cliff on the gunship; no one's getting to that thing for some time."

"The whole cliff?" Amy asked. "The echo was kinda scary."

"Not the whole thing," Rika said with a soft laugh. "But enough."

The drive out of the ravine was slow-going over the rough terrain—a combination of gravel and paved roads—but an hour later, they were in the rolling-hill-country to Kandahar City's south.

Barne took them around the city via a circuitous route, passing onto gravel roads again after a while, and then onto another paved highway that entered the city from the east.

"Where are we going, once we're at the city?" Amy asked after not speaking for a few hours. "I'm really hungry."

"I've managed to set up a meeting with a short-range freight hauler that moves grain off-planet to stations insystem. He can get us up to one of the moons…Baqara, from the looks of it," Barne replied. "That's tomorrow morning. I've set up a safe house in the city, so that's where we'll hunker down 'til then."

"But what about food?" Amy asked.

"We have food," Chase promised, looking down at Amy, who sat beside him. "Well, it's stuff that does the same thing as food once it's inside your body."

"Do you mean it tastes like crap?" Amy asked, wrinking her nose and showing some spunk for the first time.

Chase gave a low chuckle. "Yeah, but I was trying to be more delicate than that."

"I'm ten, I'm not a child," Amy informed him. "Besides, my dad says worse stuff all the time."

That was the one thing Rika really didn't like about this mission: the ambiguity over who Amy really was. Captain Ayer hadn't known, and apparently neither did the Old Man. The Marauders had been approached by an intermediary, who claimed that, should knowledge of the girl's identity leak, it would make even bigger problems for her father. Maintaining the fiction that she was safe at home was paramount.

Rika had been instructed not to ask Amy about her father, and she'd been ready to comply—but that was before they'd been attacked by multiple enemies and lost their off-world transport.

As far as she was concerned, any intel was good intel. It wasn't as though the team was going to spill the beans to anyone out on Faseema.

"Who is your father?" Rika asked.

Still wearing her helmet, Rika could see a frown settle on Amy's forehead without having to turn.

"You don't know?" the girl asked, then glanced at Leslie. "You said you worked for him?"

Rika shook her head. "No, he hired us, but we never met him. It was all done through an intermediary.

"I don't understand…" Amy said. "I assumed you were all out of uniform because this isn't one of his worlds, and you were hiding."

Barne chuckled. "Well, that second part is true, at least."

Amy's words narrowed down Rika's list of suspects. There weren't a lot of men on this side of the cluster who were said to possess worlds; though there were a few, one stood out.

"Your father is Stavros," Rika stated after a moment's consideration.

A look of consternation passed over Amy's face. Rika suspected that she had been instructed not to share that information in the event of capture—and by the look in the girl's eyes, she was now wondering if she had been captured anew.

"Well, *that* makes things interesting," Barne said before cursing quietly under his breath.

Rika connected to Faseema's general information network through a relay Barne had set up, and looked up what public information there was on Stavros and his family: his wife had died several years prior, and he had only one daughter—Amy.

"Good thing you told us, Amy," Leslie said. "You may not be immediately recognized, but if the locals do identify you, we may have an interesting scenario on our hands."

"What do you mean?" Amy asked.

"The folks around here aren't big fans of your father," Rika replied, wondering why K-Strike had brought Amy to Faseema.

Her intel said that Amy had been captured four light years from here, in the Sydon System. Holding her there would have been a far better option than taking her through Politica-controlled Oran to Faseema.

<*You thinking what I'm thinking?*> Barne asked on the team's combat net.

<*That someone on Faseema hired K-Strike to bring her here for some sort of leverage against Stavros?*> Chase guessed.

<*'Bout sums it up,*> Barne replied. <*We're right in the middle of some serious political intrigue crap, here.*>

<*Doesn't matter who her father is,*> Leslie lashed out, her mental tone adamant, and a little defensive. <*She's just a ten-year-old girl, and it's our job to protect her.*>

<*No arguments here,*> Rika said. <*We do the job, and Amy is still in*

our charge. We keep her safe, no matter what. We also need to keep our eyes peeled; we're going to have more than K-Strike coming after us.>

"Are you guys talking?" Amy asked. "You all went quiet at once. I can tell when people are using the Link, you know, even if I don't have it."

"Sorry," Leslie apologized. "We just didn't want to worry you with our speculation over who might have taken you, and who else might be out there."

"Like the people that shot down your ship?"

Rika nodded. "Just like them."

No one spoke for several minutes after that, and Rika turned to look out the window, to the north where the air and spaceport lay.

A ship rose into the sky on an invisible pillar of gravitons, passing up through the clouds and into space in just a few minutes.

If Patty and her shuttle were still intact, none of this would have been necessary; they'd be well on their way to the *Romany* by now. No need to hop a ride on some civilian freighter out of a local port.

Rika glanced back to where Patty lay on the rear seat. Chase had placed her in an induced coma while a dose of mednano worked on her internal injuries.

With any luck, she'd be back on her feet before they had to get to the spaceport. The idea of getting Patty through planetary exit customs—

<*Dammit, I just remembered that they have planetary exit customs here,*> Rika said to the team. <*How are we going to get Amy through that? They're going to recognize her.*>

<*We'll just have to make sure they* don't *recognize her,*> Barne decided. <*Leave that to me.*>

<*You sure?*> Leslie said, not sounding at all sure herself. <*This isn't going to be like that time on Uriel, is it?*>

Barne laughed. <*That was a pig. It's really hard to disguise a pig; I think I did a passable job, though. To be honest, I'm just as worried about you, Rika. If the authorities check out what happened at the farm, or those granaries, they're going to be looking for a mech. You fit the bill for 'mech'.>*

<Lotta heavy mod folks here, injured in the war with Stavros or working their farms. I won't stand out like I do some other places.>

<Don't forget, LT,> Chase said. *<Your regular right arm was on the shuttle. All you have is your gun-arm.>*

Dammit…

Rika couldn't believe she had forgotten about her 'normal' right arm. If it was still on the shuttle, and the enemy checked that over, the other mech would know exactly what she was up against.

<I can go armless, too. Plenty of that going around,> she said stubbornly.

While they spoke, they had passed through the outskirts of Kandahar City, and into the typical spread of warehouses and service companies that surrounded a air and spaceport.

Rika was surprised when Barne drove through that district to an area with smaller retail stores lining a broad boulevard. A row of tall trees ran down the center of the road, and streamers hung from their branches. A banner stretching above them read: *'Reclamation Day, 3050!'*

Rika hadn't sorted out why the locals had such a strange calendar year, but was more interested in when the celebration was. She looked it up, and saw that the celebration would be in three days; it was in honor of the day the new government centered on Faseema was established, after the war with The Politica.

Not much of a reclamation, she thought. *More like an exile…or something.*

The street was not heavily trafficked, though a number of groundcars were on the road, with some craft also in the skies above. More importantly, there was almost no foot traffic on the sidewalks, and half the businesses appeared shuttered.

After driving for a few blocks, Barne slowed the truck and

turned into a narrow alley between two buildings.

"We gonna fit?" Chase asked.

Barne lowered his window and folded his mirror in, gesturing for Rika to follow suit. "We'll fit."

The truck squeezed between the buildings, rolling over a few boxes that had been leaning against them. Rika had a momentary fear that there might be someone living in the boxes, but breathed a sigh of relief when the wheels didn't bounce over anything big enough to be a person.

Once past the two buildings, the space opened up enough for Barne to turn the truck around and nose it into the alley to block it off.

"And here we are," he announced.

"Another day, another abandoned building," Chase joked.

Leslie laughed. "You don't appreciate the aesthetic, Chase? Barne always takes us to the nicest places—he can find."

"You want the Plaza Park Hotel?" Barne asked. "It's down the road. Complete with enough security to make sure the likes of us never get in."

Rika pushed her door open and stepped into the small courtyard between four buildings. All of them appeared to be unused—some were boarded up, others had broken windows. All were covered with graffiti.

"Which one shall be our lovely accommodation?" Rika inquired.

"There." Barne pointed to one of the boarded up buildings. "Lock combo is our usual."

Rika nodded and approached the back of the store. A sign on the door read, 'Fran's Fabulous Fabrics.' She reached above the jamb and found the locking device. Keying in the code by feel, Rika pivoted, getting ready to fire with her GNR if anything awaited them inside.

"Monitoring net reads clear," Barne reported from her side.

"Yeah, I'm just paranoid," Rika replied as the lock disengaged, and she put a hand on the knob. "Blame me?"

Barne shook his head. "Not really. Paranoia's a good survival trait in our line of work."

'Line of work'. Something about the statement struck Rika as incongruous. She supposed that, for Barne, it was a line of work. It was a career he had chosen and engaged in with great passion.

For Rika, it was her life. She was always a mech, always armored, always primed for a fight. It was life back on the *Romany*, or shore leave that felt like the job.

Being in the shit, in some dump, on some crappy planet or station? Now that was her normal life.

She pushed the door open, sweeping her GNR across the small room at the back of the store. True to the sign, dozens of bolts of cloth rested in racks; though as many were pulled out and strewn across the floor, their bright colors and patterns muted by dust and grime.

Rika moved into the room while Barne covered her from the entrance. Neither expected to find anyone, and they both hoped they wouldn't. The sort of people hiding in here would probably be homeless or neighborhood kids. If either of those saw the team, the safe house wouldn't be so safe anymore.

Killing any occupants would take care of the problem, but that wasn't how the Marauders—team Basilisk in particular—operated.

Rika's scan turned up no heat sources in the back room, and nothing showed on IR or UV. She signaled to Barne that the space was clear and moved to the door that led to the front sales area.

Barne followed behind, covering her right side as she pushed the door open.

It was dark—the store's front windows boarded up—and roughly twenty by thirty meters. Racks of cloth, some large cutting tables, and two auto-weavers filled the space.

Rika moved out, checking the corner behind the door before starting her sweep on the left side, looking down each aisle and scanning with her sensor suite, while Barne covered her from the doorway.

When she had passed all the aisles, Rika walked down the far one and performed the same sweep from the front of the store.

Nothing turned up—other than a few mice, who were happily nesting in a pile of wool—and she called out softly, "We're clear."

Half a minute later, the rest of the team filed into the room. They dumped guns, ammo, and other equipment onto the counters in the back.

With the truck clear, Chase and Barne went out to fetch Patty. A minute later, they brought her in and laid her down on one of the cutting tables.

"How's she look?" Rika asked as she approached.

"Better," Chase replied. "Her internal bleeding is all cleaned up, and her vessels and arteries are stitched back together. Her liver and right kidney are just about all set, too. I expect her right lung to be healed up in an hour, tops. If she checks out after that, we'll bring her out of the coma.

"Glad to hear it," Rika said, and not just because she didn't want to haul Patty to the spaceport in a coma. She had gotten to know the pilot on the trip in, and her generally positive attitude toward life combined with an often-sarcastic wit made Patty an enjoyable person to be around.

Chase's nod was resolute. "Patty's made of some damn tough stuff. Gonna take more than a downed bird to take her out. Plus, the Old Lady would have our hides if we effed her up too much, so she'd better be OK."

"Captain Ayer did tell us to take care of her," Rika remembered, giving Patty one last look before turning to Leslie and Amy, who were settling down behind the back counter.

"You want to do a little recon, or should I?" Rika asked.

Leslie glanced at Amy, who, while looking better than she had when they brought her out of the bunker, still looked scared and uncertain.

Rika supposed that the drive in the truck had probably been reassuring. They had been out in the world, moving through traffic like other vehicles. But now they were hiding in an abandoned store—not exactly a confidence builder.

"I'll stay here," Leslie decided. "You go take a peek."

Rika nodded, clasped Chase on the shoulder as she walked by, and strode through the back room and outside into the enclosed area between the stores.

The back door of the truck was still open, so Rika closed it quietly before turning to look at the rooftops. She gauged the strength of the balustrade and leapt up, grasping it with her left arm, and swung herself up onto the roof.

It was late in the afternoon, and Oran still shone overhead; though the shadows were beginning to lengthen. Rika looked up and saw a smattering of cars flying in the air, but most of the traffic was on the ground.

Rika doubted that any of the vehicles overhead would have spotted her;if they did, Faseema was not so civilized that an armored figure on a rooftop would be cause for alarm. Still, Rika engaged her stealth systems, blending into the rooftop's gravel surface.

She crept to the front of the building across a series of boards that were laid along the roof, releasing a passel of drones as she went—restocked from Barne's supplies—instructing them to take up positions on surrounding buildings.

Many of the local businesses had cameras and sensors on their roofs; Rika's drones located those systems and tagged them on her HUD.

This was her last batch of drones—she had lost the majority back at the granaries. The rest of the team was low, too, and she made a mental note to recover these before they left.

Rika settled into her position as Kandahar City eased into evening, the traffic increasing for a time before the number of cars began to diminish.

There was a comforting aspect to the hum of the city: the sounds of cars and people mixed with the rustling of leaves in the large trees that ran down the middle of the boulevard.

Every now and then, a group of kids—some as young as ten,

others older and more raucous—would pass by below. Their brief bouts of noise and color were a refreshing break from the quiet and stoic adults that made up the majority of the sparse foot traffic.

No one stopped at the windows of the fabric store; few even gave the place a second glance, which was good to see. It meant that the store was long since forgotten, completely blended into the urban landscape.

"I love how you can still see the stars here—even in the cities," Chase said as he settled down beside her, leaning against the raised edge of the wall. He was wearing civilian garb, but she could see the neckline of his ballistic-sublayer poking above his shirt.

Rika gave him a warm smile. He had approached quietly, but there was no way to make it across the gravel rooftop without giving off more than a little sound.

"How are things below?"

Rika could have monitored everything on the Link, but she was keeping her EM signature quiet, enjoying feeling the pulse of the city.

"Patty came to right on schedule," Chase informed her. "She's pissed that she lost the shuttle—she said there was absolutely nothing on her scan when she came in. Blames herself for us being stuck here."

"She knows that's nonsense," Rika dismissed the notion. "She was coming in fast for evac with no overhead scan. You just can't see everything in that situation. We certainly didn't expect there to be a whole other player on the field; though had we known who Amy's father was, we certainly would have."

"I wonder who they were," Chase mused.

"Could have been anyone. Maybe they work for whoever hired K-Strike. Might have been on their way to pick her up from the farm. Could be some other third party that saw an opportunity… Stars, it could have been Stavros's own people, looking to nab the girl once we'd found her and save paying our rate."

"Great to have a list that includes pretty much everyone," Chase replied, his voice rife with irony. "What do we do with her now, anyway? Do we take her to the designated rendezvous, or do we just hand her over to the authorities when we get to the Politica-controlled stations here in Oran?"

"We don't know how K-Strike got their hands on Amy," Rika pointed out. "Could be a traitor in Stavros's government; if she doesn't make it back to him, the Marauders won't get paid. Amy stays with us, and we take her to the rendezvous."

Chase inclined his head and nodded. "Sound reasoning. So right now, we just keep our heads down and hope Barne can get his guy to move us off-planet."

"Pretty much," Rika agreed. "Good ole tedium."

"How is it that Barne always seems to have a guy and a place to hide out, anyway?"

"A lot of them are Marauder contacts and safe houses—though here on Faseema, he got everything set up with only three days of leg-work. It's pretty impressive."

"For an asshole, he sure can swindle and sweet talk."

Rika chuckled and shook her head. "Sure. Yeah. 'Sweet talk'—if that's what you want to call it. It's more like…sweet bullying."

Chase snorted. "That makes for a weird visual, with Barne in the mix."

Rika reached out and took Chase's hand, and leaned her head back to stare at the stars. "So, are you here to spell me, or just chat?"

Chase clasped her three metal fingers, tracing the edges of one of her knuckle joints. "Some of both. Technically I'm on duty, but I wouldn't mind spending some time alone up here, just the two of us."

"I like where your head's at."

RETROSPECT

STELLAR DATE: 02.16.8949 (Adjusted Years)
LOCATION: Fran's Fabulous Fabrics, Kandahar City
REGION: Faseema, Oran System, Praesepe Cluster

"They're clear," Rika said as she walked back into the fabric store. "No one on the street even looked twice at a truck pulling out of the alley."

"I don't like splitting up like this," Leslie replied with a shake of her head. "I know we have to. We can't all go out there and sit in the truck for an hour or two while they scout location, and then have the meet. Still…"

Leslie let her voice die, glancing over at Amy. Rika could tell by her expression that she didn't want to worry the girl.

"They're big boys, they'll manage just fine," Rika assured them, casting a smile Amy's way.

In truth, Rika wished that she was out there—she should have been out there. But with her regular right arm back on the shuttle, and no cloaks to cover herself with, she was not the ideal candidate to be out and about.

Especially not when whoever had shot down Patty's ride would know they were looking for an SMI-2 mech, from the arm left behind.

Rika hoped that it had been lost—smashed or thrown clear of the pinnace before it crashed. However, hope was not the sort of thing that one should bank on in the field.

"Where's Patty?" Rika asked after the silence stretched on for a minute.

"Up front," Leslie replied. "She said her head is still hurting and is taking a nap on a nest she made."

"It's very colorful," Amy added with a shy smile.

"I won't disturb her, then," Rika said. "You game to take the roof for a bit, Leslie?"

Leslie nodded and rose languidly, stretching her limbs once she was upright. Her movements were measured and sinuous as always, the very image of power and grace.

At times like this, it was impossible not to think of Leslie as a panther; her body's casual power cementing the image that her jet-black skin and yellow eyes created.

"I'll do a bit of a patrol as well," Leslie decided as she sauntered to the back door, grabbing her rifle from the counter on the way. "Be good to stretch my legs for a bit."

"With the rifle?" Rika asked.

"I'll be discreet," Leslie replied with a slow wink.

"Don't…don't go for too long," Amy said with a look of worry in her eyes.

"Just going to be on the rooftops, hon. Though you won't hear me crunching around, like Iron Pants," Leslie said with a nod to Rika, "I'll be within earshot of you."

"OK," Amy said begrudgingly.

Leslie left, and neither Rika nor Amy spoke for several minutes—although Rika could tell that the young girl wanted to ask her a question.

Finally, Amy mustered up the courage. "How come they put you in charge? I've never seen mechs in charge of anything. Father says you were all bad people before the Genevian war."

Rika nodded slowly. *I wonder what's on her mind, that she would bring that up?* "Yes, we were all convicted for crimes, but they were often not the ones we really committed. I was arrested for stealing bread."

Amy's eyes widened. "Really? They made you into…a machine because of bread?"

Rika nodded again. "They said I stole valuable tech needed for the war effort, but it was just bread. What they wanted were people to make into mech warriors. The government didn't really care how the quotas were filled."

"I can't believe they did that to you over *bread*…" Amy said her brow furrowed as she looked up and down Rika's body.

"Your arms...your legs, they cut them off."

"They did, and they reinforced my bones, muscles, joints, and gave me a new skin that could handle combat damage—as well as spend days under armor and not need maintenance."

"Maintenance on skin?" Amy asked, her brows knitting.

"Cleaning; I don't need to be bathed or washed."

Amy's mouth made an O shape, and she nodded silently—likely considering what would be involved in washing a mech.

"If your government is gone, and you're not a criminal...why are you still a mech?" Amy asked.

Rika shrugged, uncertain if she wanted to get into this too much further with the girl. Granted, this was the most she had heard Amy talk since they rescued her.

"Remember how you asked why I was in charge?" Rika asked, and Amy nodded. "Well, I'm in charge because I'm really good at what I do...and a lot of that is because of this," Rika gestured to her body in a sweeping motion.

"So, you're an effective killer?" Amy deduced.

Rika gave a thin smile. "That's one way of putting it. You say that like it's something you've heard before, though."

"My dad says it," Amy replied. "He said that the Genevian mechs are effective killers. He has...nevermind." The girl sighed and closed her eyes.

Rika wondered what Amy was going to say, but didn't push the issue. She considered what Stavros would do with mechs. His Politica wasn't the only group of totalitarian thugs in the Orion Arm, and they were far from the worst. Stavros claimed he brought stability to the region. From what Rika could tell, that was debatable. He *had* cleaned up some messes, but there were many more to be laid at his feet.

That, however, was not a discussion to get into with his daughter.

"We were good at what we did," Rika said after awhile. "If there had been more of us, maybe we could have set the Nietzscheans back more and kept Genevia alive."

Amy opened her eyes, a look of certainty on her face. "My dad says that the Genevians were a sick people—the fact that they made their mechs from criminals is proof."

Sheesh, she's just not going to let this go.

"Remember, not all of them were criminals," Rika reminded her. "Not really."

"But you said they lied about what you did," Amy retorted. "So they're liars *and* they mutilated people."

Rika didn't have much of a defense—in fact, she had no idea why she was defending Genevia. Maybe it was because so many Marauders were former Genevian military and they were her family now.

But Amy was right; the government and the military leaders of Genevia had been monsters. She didn't know if the war had made them that way, or if her nation had been utterly amoral before the Nietzscheans attacked. All she knew now was that she hated them both.

"I suppose your father's right. Some Genevians *were* sick people. But most of those were at the top, the rank and file; the regular people, they were—are—still good people."

Rika watched Amy process the information that a government could be bad while the people were good. Rika wondered if it was a viewpoint that the girl had encountered before. From the sounds of it, Amy's father had imparted a rather unforgiving view of the world on her.

"I guess," Amy said uncertainly. "You five are all Genevian, and you don't seem that bad."

"Thanks for the ringing endorsement," Rika said dryly.

Amy's face fell as she realized she was being insensitive to the team who had saved her.

"C'mon," Rika said, rising to her feet. "You and I can't walk around in public, showing our faces. We need some disguises."

Amy looked up. "Disguises? What kind of disguises?"

"Not sure—but we are in the right store to make some, I think."

Rika wasn't sure if they could muster up anything useful, but it would give Amy something to do other than plumb the depths of the morality that created a warrior caste like Rika's.

Amy stood and stared out at the spools of fabric, then looked at the two auto-weavers to their right. "OK, yeah. This could be fun!"

ORIENT SPACE AND AIR

STELLAR DATE: 02.16.8949 (Adjusted Years)
LOCATION: Fran's Fabulous Fabrics, Kandahar City
REGION: Faseema, Oran System, Praesepe Cluster

"Dear stars above, what did I miss out on?"

Rika gave Leslie a winning smile. "Like it?"

Rika twirled in the long green dress she wore, letting it flare out at the hem—though not enough to show her three-clawed, steel feet. The dress was belted at the waist, rose high on her neck, and was embroidered with decorative beadwork down the front. Soft pads covered her shoulders to hide her armor.

"We made an outfit for you, too, if you want it."

"Uhh…we going for a stroll along the seashore or something?" Leslie asked.

Rika shrugged. "If the enemy knows there's a mech on our team, they'll be looking for me. They're already looking for Amy; best if we play it safe."

Leslie cocked her head and narrowed her eyes. "Huh…I can't scan through it. At least not enough to tell you're a mech…it does mask a lot of your EM."

"I found the cloth that did it," Amy piped up proudly. "It's some sort of fabric used for making multi-spectrum dance costumes. It has its own EM emitters in it, and those mask the person underneath."

"What about your faces?" Leslie asked, raising an eyebrow quizzically.

"Floppy hats!" Amy said with a brilliant smile as she reached onto the counter behind her and brandished a pair.

Amy's smile was infectious, and Rika found herself grinning as well, daring Leslie with her eyes to continue to make an issue of the dresses.

Leslie was saved from having to bring any further logic to

bear by Patty's emergence from around the corner.

"You girls did great!" Patty said, striding out in a long, green and blue pastel-colored dress. "Going to try your outfit on, Leslie?"

"Your armor is really sleek," Amy said to Leslie. "We didn't have to add in a lot of stuff to hide it like we did with Rika. I know you like to be able to move easily."

Rika watched a pained expression flicker across Leslie's face before she smiled brightly. "Of course, I will. Is that mine there?"

Amy turned and picked up a loose pair of dark grey pants, a cream-colored tunic, and a white shawl. "I was going to go all black for you—you seem to like black—but I didn't see anyone wearing dark colors when I looked outside, so I went with this."

"It's perfect," Leslie told her and gave her a hug before taking the pants and stepping into them. They fit her well, hanging loosely from her hips to the floor. She slipped the tunic over her head and shrugged it into place before grabbing the shawl and wrapping it around her shoulders. "You did a great job, Amy."

<Did you put her up to this? She seems really happy,> Leslie said privately to Rika.

<I suggested that we needed disguises. Then she threw herself into it with a serious amount of gusto. Got her talking a lot. I think she's finally over last night.>

<Let's just hope that's the last of it. She doesn't need any more of that crap in her life.>

Leslie's mental tone was tinged with more vehemence than Rika had expected. She considered making a comment that Amy's life would always be complex with Stavros as her father, but thought better of it.

Amy spoke up, ending their private conversation. "I'm really glad you like it! I picked patterns and textures that would hide what's underneath."

"Our weapons can go in these duffels," Rika added, gesturing to the bag that already held the barrel for her GNR, as well as her JE84 rifle.

"I like that I can still keep a handgun strapped to my chest," Leslie said.

"And on my thigh," Patty said, patting her leg.

"Do you have a gun?" Amy asked Rika.

"I can fire a few rounds from a weapon built into my left arm," Rika replied. "But if we come under attack, Leslie and Patty can provide covering fire while I shelter you and get my JE84 out."

"Do we think things will go wrong?" Amy asked, her tone losing some of its previous excitement.

Leslie smiled and patted Amy on the shoulder. "You know how people like us work. We are always ready for things to go sideways; it's our job."

As Leslie spoke, Rika picked up a message coming in over the channel that the team had established on one of Kandahar City's public nets.

<*Rika, you there?*> Chase asked, his mental tone carrying a note of urgency.

<*Yup, here and looking fabulous. Did you two secure our ride?*>

<*Yeah, but the captain has a shipment that needs to get to the moon today, so he's ready to go in an hour.*>

Rika brought up a map of Kandahar City, overlaying the routes to the Orient Air and Spaceport over her vision. <*There's no way you can get back here to pick us up fast enough. Stars, a one-way trip could take an hour!*>

<*Should we find another ship?*> Chase asked.

<*No, we'll get there. You guys keep that ship on the ground. What's it named, by the way?*>

<*The* Persephone Jones, *though they seem to just call it 'the* Jones*', which is a bit weird 'cause it feels like the names are different genders. Either way, the berth address is on its way. Get here as fast as you can.*>

Rika sent a smile and blew a kiss. <*And you hold that ship as long as possible.*> She turned to Leslie. "You need to steal us transport in the next five minutes."

Leslie grinned and turned toward the back door, calling over her shoulder. "Piece of cake."

Rika, Patty, and Amy gathered the team's gear and assembled in the alley between the buildings, leaning casually against the wall as they waited for Leslie to arrive. The clock had moved less than four minutes when a white groundcar pulled up at the alley's entrance.

"Ride's here," Rika announced as she walked to the car and held open the back door, gesturing for Amy and Patty to get in, before she pulled open the front door and got in herself.

"Leslie's Spaceport Taxi Service at your…uh, service," Leslie joked with a smile.

"Let's get this show on the road," Patty begged. "I don't like it when other people are driving."

"I'll give you a taste of your own medicine, sister," Leslie promised as she pulled out into traffic. "I haven't forgotten that time you cut the grav systems when we were dropping over Mennas, and my back slammed into the overhead."

"Leslie, seriously, we were being shot at. I was avoiding a missile," Patty explained. "How many times are you gonna bring this up?"

"Well, you almost broke my back, so I think a few more."

"It's what you get for not strapping in," Patty muttered.

Rika only half-listened to the banter as Leslie wove the car through the city streets. A flying car would have been much better, but the chances of finding one of those sitting on the street and hacking its flight systems were slim. They had to take what they could get.

Leslie drove the car through Kandahar City's streets faster than the local ordinances allowed, but not so fast that they were worried about catching the eye of law enforcement.

If the ground traffic didn't grow much more congested, they should reach the spaceport with ten minutes to spare.

As they drew closer to the spaceport, the city streets became cleaner, and the amount of vehicular and foot traffic increased. Before long, Leslie pulled off the larger thoroughfares and wove through an industrial district filled with manufacturing businesses and rows of low warehouses.

In the distance, on the far side of the spaceport, Rika could make out towering silos lining the horizon—likely the terminus for much of the grain harvested around Kandahar City. She watched as a large-bellied grain hauler lifted silently into the air on its grav drives, hauling enough grain to feed a station for a week.

"Just a few more minutes now," Rika reported over her shoulder. "The guys' directions have us getting in through a side gate just a kilometer away."

A wire fence ran around the starship landing field, with hangars and fuel depots on the other side. Between the structures, dozens of ships were visible on cradles dotting the field.

Presently they arrived at the gate, and Leslie pulled the car up to the security booth.

"State your business," an annoyed-looking guard demanded as Leslie's window slid down.

"We have a berth on the *Persephone Jones,*" Leslie said calmly, not even batting an eyelash.

"Pass your public tokens over the security station's auth-net," the man said.

"She doesn't have Link access yet," Leslie said, craning her head back to indicate Amy. "I'll be passing her creds."

"Sure. Whatever," the guard said, as he took a step back to gaze through the gate at something that seemed only marginally more interesting than the car in front of him.

Rika passed her tokens, praying that Barne would have thought to hack the gate's auth systems. She hadn't asked him to, and neither he nor Chase had mentioned it.

He doesn't miss details like this, don't sweat it, she scolded herself while forcing her heart rate to steady.

The guard glanced back at the security booth behind him, and his eyes blinked rapidly before he looked back into the car and nodded. "OK, you're good to go. Park over there on the right—in the long-term garage."

"Oh, we have a friend coming to get the car later today; we don't need to go into the lot."

"Sorry, ma'am. Passengers can't park by the private terminals. You have to go to the garage."

"OK, fine," Leslie replied and drove through the gate, following the signs to the long-term garage, which was visible on their right.

It was a towering structure with twenty levels reaching into the sky, filled with thousands of cars, but surprisingly little foot traffic. As they approached, a lowered gate came into view, adorned with a sign indicating that the upper lot was full. A flashing arrow directed them into the underground section of the garage.

"Shit, this is going to take forever," Leslie swore.

<Chase, we're parking; got sent to the underground lot. We should be there in ten minutes, max.>

<Make it fewer, if you can. The captain is getting all antsy-like.>

Leslie drove the car to the underground parking and found a spot on the second level down. Everyone spilled out, and Rika tossed a cleaner bot into the vehicle.

Thirty seconds later, they were rushing past rows of cars—some looked like they had been parked down there for years.

No one else was on their level, and the echo of their footfalls in the space was beginning to set Rika's hair on-end. As they passed a support pillar, twenty meters from the lift to the ground level, a loud *ping* reverberated through the air. Rika ducked down, pulling Amy with her.

She looked up and saw a divot in the support pillar next to where her head had been.

<Triangulating,> Leslie called out from her position one car down. Patty crouched behind the pillar, her sidearm drawn, scanning the surrounding vehicles for any signs of movement.

<Drones out,> Rika reported, as she released the passel of drones she had carefully collected from back at the fabric store.

She sent them under the cars, scanning for enemy signatures.

A shot came from Leslie's weapon, and the projectile round made the high-pitched *ting* it would when hitting hardened carbon armor.

Rika pulled her JE84 out of the duffel and scanned the area behind them. There was just one more row of cars between them and the side wall of the underground car park. A drone swept through the space and didn't find anything, but Rika's helmet scan caught a strange shadow passing near one of the lights, moving between two of the cars.

She took aim and fired at the shadow, nodding with satisfaction when the bullet hit something invisible a half-meter in front of the car.

Rika fired another trio of rounds while calling down to Amy, who seemed surprisingly calm in the midst of the weapons fire.

"Amy, get a grenade out of the duffel."

Return fire hit the car she was crouched beside—one bullet passing all the way through the vehicle before bouncing off Rika's armor. Rika sent a burst of kinetic rounds from her rifle in return; then an arm touched her shoulder, and she saw the grenade resting on Amy's palm.

Sometimes having just one hand is a pain in the ass, Rika lamented. She set the rifle down, took the grenade from Amy, and tossed it with a flick of her wrist.

She didn't throw it overhand, but instead skipped it along the ground. If her aim was true, it should roll out from under a car right underneath the enemy.

A moment later, the explosion thundered through the garage, and one of her drones caught sight of a figure being thrown into the air, and smashing against the ceiling before dropping down. Then the concrete above cracked, and a vehicle from the next level fell through; hopefully landing on top of whoever was back there.

"Nice!" Amy called out approvingly, and Rika wondered what sort of combat the girl might have already seen.

<*I'm at the staircase to the right of the lift,*> Leslie reported. <*One*

target down over here. I count two more.>

<*I see your targets on the combat net,*> Patty added. <*I have another moving toward us on the left.*>

<*Moving into the row behind,*> Rika said as she slung the duffel bag over her shoulder and gestured for Amy to follow. They moved behind the row of vehicles, skirting the area where the roof had fallen in.

Patty fell in behind without needing to be told, and the group moved to the end of the row, staying low, with Rika and Patty firing their weapons sporadically, keeping the enemy back as best they could.

When they reached the last car, Rika could see Leslie crouched in the stairwell's entrance. Rika pulled the duffel off her shoulder, grabbed the scout's rifle, and tossed it to her across the open six meters.

Leslie snatched the weapon out of the air with her left hand while firing with her right and nodded at Rika. <*Thanks, was on my last mag.*>

"OK, stay on my right, both of you," Rika said aloud for Amy's benefit.

Patty stacked up beside Rika and pulled Amy against her side, giving Rika a nod.

A second later, Leslie opened fire with her rifle, delivering short, controlled bursts at the locations the enemy had been firing from. Rika didn't wait to see if the soldiers had taken cover before she moved out into the open space as quickly as she dared.

Patty had an arm around Amy, keeping her close, and Rika pushed her worry back as she took aim with her JE84 and fired four three-round bursts at the enemy locations.

Then they were at the stairwell. Patty and Amy took cover behind the wall, and Rika took up a position behind Leslie.

<*That was easy,*> she commented.

<*You got hit twice,*> Leslie replied.

<*I did?*> Rika asked, not looking as she fired at the figure of a soldier a dozen cars down.

<*Let me get a shape charge,*> Patty requested, and Rika shrugged the duffel off, tossing it next to Patty.

Leslie fell back and took the stairs to the next level, while Rika continued to provide cover fire. To her left, Patty set the proximity-sensing shape charge on the low ceiling of the stairwell.

<*Set,*> Patty announced.

Weapons fire echoed down the stairwell, then Leslie called, <*Clear up here.*>

Rika gestured for Patty to go, and the pilot grabbed Amy and rushed up the stairs as Rika fell back, using her body to shield them from any shots that made it through the doorway.

<*Stars, I'm glad they want the girl alive; that would have been a lot less fun, otherwise,*> Leslie said.

<*It's not over yet,*> Rika warned.

They made it to the next landing, and Rika took up a position at the door, freeing Leslie to go up to the next level, which was the ground floor.

Patty had another shape charge and was about to place it when Amy said, "Do it at the top, by the lift; just in case."

<*Damn, when did she get so bloodthirsty?*> Patty asked.

<*It's a good point, though,*> Rika said. <*That's the last charge we have.*>

<*Clear topside,*> Leslie called down. <*They were sloppy, only one person abo—*> More weapons fire sounded from the level above, and then Leslie came back on the combat net. <*OK,* now *we're clear.*>

Patty led Amy up the stairs while Rika moved backward, signaling the proximity charge one level down to go live once Amy and Patty reached the floor above.

She hadn't reached ground level when the first shape charge exploded—the roar thundering up the stairwell, followed by hot flames. There was a loud *crack,* and the stairs beneath her feet dropped a centimeter.

Rika threw her JE84 through the open door to the ground level and lunged forward, grasping the sill as the staircase fell away. A groan sounded above, and she hauled herself through the opening a second before the staircase above fell past.

"Shit," she cursed aloud. "Didn't expect that."

Patty glanced over from where she was setting the shape charge on the lift. "I did set it to the max."

"Thanks for the warning."

<*We're secure out here,*> Leslie reported from the outside entrance. <*But I picked up a call on their emergency channel; EMS is going to be on the scene before long.*>

<*Blow a few things up and people always have to come to investigate,*> Rika complained.

Rika took up a position beside Leslie at the double doors leading out of the building. Ahead was a wide road, followed by an open, grassy field—easily a hundred meters across—then the first cradles on the landing area rose up.

Massive shipping containers were stacked along the edge of the field, and starships filled the space beyond; some rising as high as one hundred meters into the air. If the team could make it to those shipping containers, they'd be clear—provided no other enemies waited out there.

Rika unslung the duffel once more, surprised the strap had held, and grabbed her GNR's barrel. She glanced down at her dress and was amazed that it wasn't torn anywhere, though it was more than a little dirty.

Its condition was about to worsen. With a sharp pull, she ripped her right sleeve, exposing the socket for her GNR, and slid the tri-fire barrel into place.

"Sorry, Amy," she said.

"It's OK, Rika," Amy replied. "I didn't really expect them to last—plus I can fix it."

Strange girl…wants to fix my dress—which I'll probably never wear again—and also has excellent advice on where to place shape charges…

Behind them, the lift activated, and Patty swore. "Shit, I was hoping that thing had been damaged in the blast."

<*Let's move, then,*> Leslie suggested, darting out of the building and across the road.

"Gonna run a lot faster than you can; here." Rika tossed her JE84 into the duffel, slung it over her shoulder, and scooped Amy up.

Patty moved out, crossed the road, and crouched behind a grey box adorned with power symbols on the other side.

Rika followed after, narrowly avoiding an automated cargo hauler that was trundling by with a dozen shipping containers on its wide bed.

She reached the far side of the road just as the lift reached the ground floor and opened its doors. She could see two figures inside. One stepped out of the lift and fired a round through the glass doors of the garage. Rika anticipated the shot and dodged to the right, hearing the round whistle past her head.

Then the charge went off, and the front of the parking garage was engulfed in flames.

Patty was already running across the grassy field at full bore, and Rika followed behind at an easy lope, keeping her head on a swivel to let her two-seventy vision get a complete view of the area around them.

Ahead, the two remaining drones reached the stacks of cargo containers just ahead of Leslie and began to sweep the area.

<*Damn, a lot of people coming from the ships to take a peek,*> Leslie called back.

<*Nothing we can do about that,*> Rika replied. <*Keep moving; they may use the crowds to blend in.*>

Rika wished once more that she was with a team of SMI-2 mechs. If she didn't have to worry about Patty, she would be able to reach the ship in less than a minute. Even Leslie, adept as she was on the battlefield, often slowed Rika down.

A team of mechs would have cleared out the garage and then taken out anyone else who dared approach with extreme prejudice. *Protect the target, destroy all opposition.*

She shook her head, clearing the distracting thoughts.

Hammerfall is gone. I'm Basilisk now, and my team needs me. They may not be as tough as mechs, but they are strong in their own ways—and they make me stronger.

Even though she was largely unaugmented, Patty did move like the fires of hell were at her feet, and made good time to the cargo containers, bursting past a group of men and women who had gathered at the edge of the field with worried expressions on their faces.

Rika realized that she must look ridiculous. Her dress had lifted up above her double-jointed knees as she ran, giving away the fact that she was no simple woman fleeing the explosion—though she supposed that her helmet had already ruined any illusion the dress was intended to create.

Patty had to push her way through the crowd, but when they saw Rika rushing toward them, her GNR barrel held up and sweeping side to side as she scanned for targets, a wide space opened up.

"What happened?" a man cried out as Rika burst through the crowd.

She didn't reply and kept moving, threading her way through the cargo containers, following Patty, who was tracing the route Leslie had taken.

More people were moving past, but none of these asked any questions—most just barely getting out of the way as Rika barreled past.

Once beyond the containers, Rika updated her view of the landing field, taking in the feed from the two surviving drones circling above.

To Rika's left, she saw the EMS vehicles racing along the perimeter road, and more people rushing through the ships to see what had happened.

Many of the ships had also deployed armed men and women, and they took up positions around the loading ramps while other vessels deployed ground defense weapons.

Rika decided caution was better than speed and slowed her

pace.

<*Patty, fall back. Some folks here are antsy, and if we're rushing toward their ships with weapons drawn, they may shoot first and not bother with questions.*>

Patty nodded and paused beside an empty cradle, falling in beside Rika a moment later.

<*That your ruckus out there?*> Barne asked. <*Captain Sarn here is about to close the ramp and take off—says that the STC may drop a fly-ban at any moment.*>

Rika checked the route through the ships. <*We're three minutes out. Get him to hold, do whatever it takes.*>

<*Understood,*> Barne acknowledged.

Ahead, Leslie darted from cover, firing her rifle at a target Rika couldn't see.

<*Two in heavy armor,*> Leslie reported.

<*Hold there, I'll flank them.*>

"Stay with Patty," Rika said aloud to Amy as she set the girl back down.

"No, Rika, don't go," Amy said, her voice wavering, the prior cold determination gone, replaced by renewed fear. Amy kept her arms wrapped around Rika's neck, and Patty reached for the girl.

"I've got you, Amy. Rika will be right back; you have to let her go."

Rika ducked her head down, slipping out of Amy's arms, and touched the girl's shoulder as gently as she could. "Stay with Patty. When I give the word, you two advance to Leslie's position."

Amy didn't reply, but managed one short nod.

"Good," Rika said, and took off at full speed, banking around an empty cradle and past a bulky freighter that was lifting off into the air on its grav drive.

The wave of gravitons flowing out from the ship's emitters cascaded around Rika and almost made her stumble and fall, but she gritted her teeth and pushed through, bursting out of the far side of the gravity shower, catching sight of the two enemies firing on Leslie.

She raised her GNR and fired the electron beam at the one on the right.

Nothing happened.

Shit! Rika swore as her HUD flashed a warning that the weapon's coils had been misaligned by the gravity field. They were undergoing recalibration—a process that made the entire weapon useless.

She reached for her JE84 and remembered that she had put it in the duffel so she could hold Amy better. And the duffel was back with Patty and the girl.

Rika considered her options, took a deep breath, and charged into the enemy on the right. She hit him at forty kilometers per hour, knocking him forward onto to the ground, and delivered a blow to the back of his helmet. His faceplate slammed it into the hard plas surface of the landing field, and Rika pushed off his back, leaping into the air as the other soldier—a woman, by the stylized, oversized breasts on her armor—fired her rifle at the spot Rika had been a moment before.

<*We're moving on,*> Leslie said over the combat net as Rika dropped onto the woman, tearing away her rifle and swinging it back around into her head.

<*Good, I'll catch up,*> Rika replied as something hit her in the back. She turned and saw the first soldier up in a crouch, firing at her.

Rika sank her clawed feet into the hard plas of the landing field and spun the woman between herself and the crouching enemy. The man hit his female comrade with two shots before he stopped firing and dove to the side in an attempt to get a clear shot on Rika.

Not that Rika was there anymore. She had leapt into the air, flipped over, and dropped onto the man. Her intention had been to hit him center mass, but he had seen the two hundred kilograms of mech falling toward him and jerked backward.

He didn't make it far enough.

Rika's full weight came down on his head, crushing his helmet and everything inside with a *snap-pop* sound.

The woman had spun when Rika went flying through the air, and screamed something incoherent as her partner died. She drew her sidearm and opened up full auto on Rika, shredding her dress and denting her armor.

Rika realized she still held the woman's rifle and swung it, trying to knock the pistol out of her opponent's grip.

The woman strafed to the side, and Rika's swing missed, but her GNR reported firing readiness. The range was too close for anything but its projectile rounds, so Rika jumped backward and fired three shots at the woman.

The first two cracked her armor, spinning the woman to the side. The third tore off one of the exaggerated breast domes and no small part of the woman's chest.

Rika didn't wait to see if the enemy fell. She turned and ran, leaping into the struts and armatures of a docking cradle and swinging through the gantries before dropping to the landing field on the far side.

Her chest twinged, and she glanced down to see that her own armor had been cracked in the engagement. There was no blood, but Rika realized her medsuite was flashing a warning that four of her the ribs in her back were bent, and several ligaments were torn.

She ignored the warnings to slow down and limit her motion, pushing herself to her max speed as the *Persephone Jones* came into view. She could see Patty and Amy rushing up the cradle's long ramp toward the open cargo hatch. Barne stood at the top, firing at a target Rika couldn't see, while Leslie crouched at the base, taking cover behind a crate. Chase had come down to meet her and was firing in the same direction as Barne.

When they caught sight of Rika, Leslie ran up the ramp, disappearing into the ship behind Patty and Amy.

<*Nice of you to make it, LT,*> Chase commented as Rika approached at full speed.

She could tell by his mental tone that he had been worried, but not too much. They both knew it would take a lot more than a few low-rent mercs to take out a mech.

<*Get up there, I'll cover you,*> Rika ordered, taking aim at the target Chase had been firing on. She drew her targeting data from the combat net, which highlighted a shipping container with three enemy troops behind it.

Rika fired two beams from her GNR, the blue-white lighting illuminating the underside of the *Persephone Jones* and the other nearby ships. The first beam burned a hole in the container, and the second passed through, scoring a direct hit on one of the enemy soldiers.

Nodding with satisfaction, Rika raced up the long ramp as the ship began to lift into the air. Ahead, Chase leapt across the gap and passed into the darkened confines of the vessel.

Rika poured on all the speed she could and pushed off, sailing across the twenty meters of space as the ship continued to rise.

Oh, shit.

The cargo bay's entrance rose past eyelevel. Her hand stretched out as far as it could and caught hold of a lip at the bottom of the airlock's opening.

One of her fingers slipped off and, once again, Rika cursed only having one hand. In a desperate attempt, she swung her GNR up just as the *Persephone Jones* poured on more thrust, and the protuberance she hung from bent under her weight. Then something struck her in the back, and Rika slipped free.

She felt a sickening moment of freefall, and was wondering if she could manage to land safely below in the jumbled structure of the landing cradle when she jerked to a stop. Rika looked up to see Chase leaning out of the airlock, grasping the barrel of her GNR with both of his hands while Barne held onto the weapon hook on Chase's back.

<*Don't think you're getting out of our relationship that easily, do you?*> Chase quipped as Barne pulled him, and by extension, Rika, up into the airlock.

Rika's heart was pounding, and she couldn't even think of a response until she was half-sitting, half-collapsed on the airlock's deck.

<*Thanks,*> was all she could manage, as she gasped for breath and then passed out.

PERSEPHONE JONES

STELLAR DATE: 02.16.8949 (Adjusted Years)
LOCATION: *Persephone Jones*, departing Faseema
REGION: Oran System, Praesepe Cluster

"What the hell was going on out there?!" Captain Sarn hollered as he strode onto *Persephone Jones*'s main cargo deck. "People were shooting at my ship. Shooting! *At my ship!*"

Chase looked up from Rika's back, where he was pulling what he hoped to be the last shard of armor from her 'skin'. He opened his mouth to respond, but Leslie put a hand on his shoulder and rose to face the captain.

"Captain Sarn, we're really sorry about that," she purred. "We didn't anticipate any sort of trouble; we certainly didn't mean to put your ship at risk."

Chase only half-listened as Leslie used her charm on the captain, expertly soothing and mollifying the surly man. He checked Rika's wound over once more, pulling back her matte-grey skin and pushing aside her carbon-fiber-enhanced muscles with a probe.

"Don't worry, we'll pay extra," Barne promised the captain from Chase's left.

Chase hoped that there was enough in the local accounts Barne had established to make good on that promise. They didn't have unlimited funds, and the *Romany* was a long ways away.

Amy huddled by Rika's head. It still bore her helmet, and the girl was stroking it and mumbling something about her being 'too tough to die'.

"Don't worry, she won't die from this," Chase told her with as reassuring a smile as he could manage. It wasn't a lie; he wasn't worried about Rika dying from the wounds she had received—not with her mods, at least. A vanilla human would have been torn nearly in half from the round that had hit Rika's back, but a mech would be ready to fight again in an hour—he hoped.

"Are you sure?" Amy asked, her eyes wide.

Chase nodded. "I don't think Rika knows how. Even if she does, she's too stubborn to die."

He pulled a tube of sealant from the small medkit and pushed Rika's skin together, applying the military-grade epoxy to the wound to glue it shut.

"Are you *gluing* her?" Amy asked. "Is that safe?"

Chase gave a soft laugh. "It's safe for both mechs and humans, don't worry. It doesn't hold her epidermis together as well as organic skin, but she should start to knit back together soon."

Rika stirred and turned her head enough to see Chase where he crouched behind her.

<Am I in one piece?>

<More or less,> Chase answered, a relieved smile adorning his face even though he'd known she would be OK. *<You're a bit dented; try not to twist your back at all for the next few hours.>*

<Easier said than done,> Rika grumbled before speaking aloud. "Hi, Amy. I'm glad to see you're OK."

"I got some scratches," Amy reported, holding up her arm to show not insignificant lacerations on the palm of her hand and wrist. "But I'm not worried about them; I was just scared you were going to die."

Rika chuckled as she carefully rolled onto her right side and reached for her helmet.

"I know I can't get you to stay prone—though you should," Chase scolded Rika. "But at least let me get you sitting. If you lay like that, you're bound to twist and open up the wound."

"OK," Rika replied and allowed Chase to gently help her into a sitting position. "Can you take the helmet off? I'd have to lift my arm across to do it, and would probably pull myself apart again."

"Of course," Chase replied and crouched before Rika, toggling the latches of her helmet open, then twisted the helmet to the side and back. He lifted it off her head to reveal a very tired and sweaty-looking Rika.

"Ah, that's better," Rika sighed. "I think my air exchanger was hit—it was starting to smell stale in there."

"Rika!" Amy exclaimed and lunged forward, wrapping her arms around Rika's neck.

"Easy, hon," she advised, and Chase leaned forward to touch Amy's shoulder.

"Careful. She's tough, but even Rika needs a bit of time to heal up after getting hit that much."

Amy pulled back, looking worried. "Sorry."

<*Seems like Amy's shifted her attachment from Leslie to you,*> Chase observed.

<*I wonder if it's a stress response or if she doesn't have a strong mother figure,*> Rika mused. <*I hope Leslie doesn't mind; she seemed to be getting attached to the girl.*>

Chase glanced at Leslie. She was glaring at the departing figure of Captain Sarn, while Barne stood beside her, shaking his head.

<*What's the word?*> Rika asked over the combat net.

<*Yeah, you look upset, Leslie*> Chase added.

Barne smirked at Leslie and walked to the side of the bay to sit beside Rika. <*She's just pissed that the captain told us we have to stay down here. Doesn't like to be cooped up, that one.*>

Leslie turned to the group, her brows knit together. <*What I don't like is that he could be doing anything out there, and we have no way of knowing. What if he takes us to K-Strike, or some other group? Stars, we're pretty sure K-Strike has a ship in orbit; they must have the* Persephone Jones *on a list of suspects, since it took off during the firefight down there.*>

<*I'm with Leslie on that,*> Patty chimed in.

Barne shrugged. <*Over two dozen ships took off.*>

<*That's not a lot,*> Chase considered. <*Leslie's right, we're a target for whatever K-Strike has in orbit.*>

Rika shook her head. <*You're too blasé, Barne. You're never blasé. What do you have up your sleeve?*>

<*Me?*> Barne asked innocently. <*Nothing…'cept I hacked his*

comm system before you guys even got here. He's linking up with a few of his buddies, and they're forming a convoy to Baqara. K-Strike would have to have a lot more than one ship if they want to make a run on us.>

Leslie relaxed and shook her head. <*Should have known you had something in the works, you crusty bastard.*>

"Are you all talking on the Link?" Amy interjected. "It's rude, you know—when there's someone who can't hear you."

Leslie walked to where Amy sat crouched at Rika's side and patted her shoulder. "Sorry, Amy; we can't say everything aloud."

Rika nodded and pointed at the corners, where a few small cameras were visible. Amy's eyes widened, and her mouth formed an O shape.

"Are we in trouble?" the girl whispered.

Chase laughed and shook his head. "No more than usual. Don't worry, though; the captain seems like a good guy, and he's on his way to the moon, like he said. Pretty soon we'll pick up a ship headed outsystem, and everything will be right as rain."

" 'Right as rain'?" Amy echoed. "What does that mean?"

Chase opened his mouth to reply and then cocked his head to the side. "You know...I have no idea; most people don't like rain."

"*I* like rain," Leslie countered. "Better for sneaking up on people."

Chase checked the data on the public shipnet. Based on the *Persephone Jones*'s current vector, they had twenty-nine hours before they would land on Baqara's main spaceport.

He placed an arm on Rika's leg, and her eyes met his. "You should catch some shut-eye, LT. We've got a ways to go, and you need to get healed up."

"I suppose you guys aren't going to burn the place down. I think I'll do that," Rika agreed. She closed her eyes and laid her head back against the bulkhead.

Chase rose from her side and walked to a crate a few paces away. "Come here, Amy. Let's have a look at your hand," he suggested quietly.

Leslie guided Amy to his side, and Chase took a look at the gash.

"It doesn't hurt so much anymore," Amy offered.

"That's normal," Chase replied. "But we have to clean it and close it up. We don't want you getting infected."

Amy looked uncertain. "Are you going to glue me back together, like you did with Rika?"

Chase gave a soft laugh. "Sort of. A patch sealer will work better here. Then we can be sure it's all covered and will stay clean."

To her credit, Amy only gasped once, when Chase had to pick a small rock out of the heel of her hand.

What sort of pain has she suffered before to handle this without even whimpering? Maybe she's still just in shock over the whole ordeal…

With the first aid done, Leslie led Amy to a corner and they sat together, talking in low voices. Chase considered rejoining Rika, but she appeared to have actually fallen asleep, and he didn't want to disturb her.

She looked so calm and serene when she slept, as though she was still a child herself. When awake, Rika rarely looked at peace—there were moments, but there were not many. Mostly, she appeared on edge—as though someone or something was going to spring up and attack her.

Given their line of work, it wasn't the worst attitude.

But even back on Dekar Station, when they had worked together in Hal's Hell, Rika had always behaved as though she was still in battle, still living the war in her mind.

Chase knew that, in some respects, she was. They all were. It was half the reason they were in the Marauders—well, half for *him*. It may be the only reason for Rika.

There she lay, hard steel and carbon fiber; a machine made to kill, death incarnate. But underneath the armor, the weapons, the mech, was Rika.

She had once confided in him that she still felt like the young girl who lost her parents to the war, the girl who was frightened and hauled off to foster care as a ward of the state.

He'd told her they'd all stopped aging since the war started and that it was OK to still be that young Rika inside. Their inner selves were frozen in whatever state they'd been when the terror first reached them, There was nothing wrong with it. No shame. He liked that she was still that soft girl deep down. Still vulnerable. Still tender.

They couldn't be intimate, but that didn't stop him from relishing in her touch, or her in his. What they had transcended mere physical attraction.

He cared for her, and she cared for him. Together, they were figuring out how to be whole people again.

Chase glanced at Leslie, who was cradling Amy, and wondered what the war had taken from her. The jet-black woman rarely spoke of her past— of what had turned her into the cunning killer she was now.

The easy answer was just 'the war', but it had always seemed like there was something else under Leslie's surface. Granted, Rika had said the woman wasn't so steely before Jerry died; now that he saw how she fawned over Amy, the distinction was that much sharper. There were two Leslies, as well.

Chase heard a low murmur and turned to see Barne and Patty speaking in low tones on the far side of the cargo bay. He pushed off the crate and ambled over to them.

"She gonna be good to go?" Barne asked softly.

"Yeah, don't worry about Rika," Chase assured him. "She can take a licking and keep on ticking."

Patty snorted. "Thought you were supposed to be all worried and sensitive, being the boyfriend and all. She's still just a woman in there, you know."

Chase smiled. Patty's thoughts echoed his own.

"I'm as touchy-feely as they come, but if there's one thing I've learned about Rika in the years I've known her, it's that she *likes* being a mech. She really is as much machine as woman. It's just taken her a while to learn that wanting to be that way is OK; not exactly an easy mental place to arrive at, given how our people made her."

Patty raised an eyebrow. "Really? Rika likes it? Is it a fetish or something?"

Barne snorted. "For Rika? No. For Chase, here, though..."

Chase reddened and raised his hands. "Hey, Rika's hot, I'm not going to deny it; but I'm not with her 'cause she's a mech. Maybe someday she won't be anymore, and that's OK, too. I don't plan on parting ways with her any time soon."

"Not that it matters," Barne said soberly. "None of us are in the 'long life expectancy' sort of business."

<*Speaking of which, Barne picked up something interesting,*> Patty informed him on the team's combat net.

<*Oh, yeah?*> Chase asked.

Barne nodded, continuing to speak aloud and question Chase's manhood while he replied over the Link.

<*Our beloved captain has been making some discreet inquiries about who it is that's after us, and what sort of trouble we might be in.*>

<*What has he learned?*> Chase asked.

<*Not much more than we know,*> Patty replied. <*K-Strike, most likely. But that's not the problem.*>

<*He's going to attract attention. He's using too many specifics in his questions; details that no one else would know,*> Barne clarified.

Chase laughed at a joke Patty spoke aloud as he responded to this new information. <*So what should we do? Storm the bridge?*>

<*No go,*> Barne said. <*This ship has an AI. Even if we could subdue Sarn, the AI would sound a mayday before we could get control.*>

<*An AI, on this tub?*> Patty asked. <*Whatever for?*>

<*You could ask him,*> Barne replied.

Chase didn't like the trouble an AI could bring. <*Then we need to get to the core. We should see if Leslie can get off this deck and take it offline.*>

<*Leslie is listening,*> Leslie spoke up. <*I'm moderately familiar with this class of ship. There's a systems deck below the bridge, centrally*

located. The core will be there. We sure this is the right move? We'll still need to land on the moon; going to be hard if we seize the ship.>

<*And if he alerts K-Strike to us?*> Barne retorted.

<*What are they going to do?*> Chase pressed. <*They've only got one ship; we're in a convoy. Safe as houses.*>

Barne eyed Chase for a moment before nodding. <*OK. Leslie makes a good point about needing to dock on the moon. This tub doesn't have the fuel to make it outsystem. Not to mention it's been seven years since it's made an FTL jump. They haven't run a test on the DL transition system in months.*>

<*You sure the AI can't spot you sniffing the logs?*> Chase asked, skeptical.

Barne shrugged. <*It's public stuff the spaceport had on record.*>

<*So we're not going to take the ship?*> Patty asked.

Chase shook his head. <*Not if we don't have to.*>

<*Fine,*> Patty sighed. <*I still don't like having someone else at the helm, though.*>

MOON LANDING

STELLAR DATE: 02.17.8949 (Adjusted Years)
LOCATION: *Persephone Jones*, departing Faseema
REGION: Oran System, Praesepe Cluster

When Rika awoke, Chase filled her in on Captain Sarn's inquiries. She agreed with their decision to hold tight, and, so far, nothing untoward had come to pass.

The feeds from Kandahar City were rife with speculation over what had occurred at the spaceport, though no official conclusions had been drawn. Most people believed the fighting had to do with grain smuggling rings that had been operating at the spaceport for some time—if the conspiracy theory folks were to be believed.

Two hours before they reached Port Londrie on Baqara's surface, Sarn appeared in the entrance to the deck with a grim look on his face.

"Not an idiot, you know," he said without greeting. "Well, maybe a bit. Took a few hours to realize you'd tapped our comms. Since then, Niki, our AI, has been filtering out what we didn't want you to hear."

<*Not nice to tap your ride like that,*> Niki admonished over the general shipnet.

<*Told you we shoulda taken out their AI core,*> Barne lamented over the team's private channel.

"Since you didn't get to hear the warning, you don't know that station security at Londrie has been instructed to inspect all ships that lifted off from Kandahar City." Sarn spoke slowly, as though he was still making up his mind about what to do with his passengers.

"That'll pose a problem or two," Rika stated as she carefully rose to her feet.

Sarn nodded. "Yeah, I figured as much. I'll admit, I thought about spacing the lot of you. It'd be no more than you deserve for bringing this sort of trouble my way."

<*What a phony,*> Barne commented. <*Sarn hauls illegal shit all the time. It's how he makes half his cred.*>

"...but I don't kill kids," Sarn continued. "Even one that's fallen in with the likes of you."

"We rescued her," Rika countered.

"I'm sure you did," Sarn nodded. "I also bet that whoever you '*rescued*' her from has contacts up on Londrie. My money says things'll get real fun when we land."

"That's a lot of supposition," Barne cut in. "Could just as well be the contraband you're hauling that gets you in the shit. I bet there's no way to hang what you're hauling around our necks, so you need another option."

Sarn scowled, and Rika could see that Barne had hit the nail on the head.

"Something along those lines may be the case," the captain growled. "I'm going to divert and dock at Kestry Station. I have contacts there that will look the other way while you disembark; I'll just need you to keep your mouths shut about my cargo. And I'll need the extra credit we discussed."

<*Trust him?*> Rika asked the team.

A chorus of emphatic, negative responses came back over the Link.

Rika nodded. "You have a deal, Captain Sarn. What's our ETA to Kestry?"

Captain Sarn visibly relaxed, and what probably passed for a delighted expression graced his dour face. "Forty minutes; I got in their priority queue."

"Perfect," Rika replied. "We'll be ready."

Sarn grunted his thanks and left the bay.

<*He's setting us up,*> Rika announced. <*You can bet that K-Strike or whoever our other player is will be there waiting.*>

<*Not our first rodeo,*> Barne reminded her. <*What's your plan?*>

Rika grinned. <*How does 'kill all the bad guys' sound?*>

*****

Leaving the rest of the team behind on the ship didn't feel right, but it was the best plan they could form. Rika hadn't expected it to be her that would take a spacewalk when she proposed the idea, but it turned out that everyone had taken a few hits, and none of their armor was airtight anymore.

Rika's wasn't either, but her skin was more than capable of holding out against the effects of vacuum for at least fifteen minutes.

Chase hadn't been happy with the call, and had applied another layer of the epoxy onto her back and checked over her thigh wound again. In the end, he had begrudgingly acknowledged that Rika was the best candidate for the job.

Barne had worked around Niki, the *Persephone Jones*'s AI—or so they hoped—and disabled monitoring of the cargo deck's secondary airlock.

Rika stood at the airlock's outer door and stared into the black. The ship had turned so that she could see Faseema in the distance, a floating blue and tan blob drifting in space. Beyond it laid the baleful, orange eye of Oran, muted by her helmet's visor. The star's light hit her, warming her skin against the cold of vacuum, though only slightly.

It was also bathing her in radiation—not the most comforting of thoughts.

Rika climbed out of the airlock and activated the maglocks on her feet. She had less than two minutes to make it to the engines and jump off. If she didn't clear the ship before it started its deceleration burn, the star's radiation would be the least of her worries.

She reached the fuel port at the back of the ship, which rose several meters above the engine nozzles and looked out at the tiny speck in the distance that was Kestry Station.

Rika had only ever done one space jump, and that had been

toward a planet. Those were nice, big targets. Kestry was only visible at all because of her helmet's magnification. If she missed that tiny rock, she'd drift forever in space—after she froze to death…or asphyxiated.

Here goes nothing…

She triple checked her aim and pushed off.

Trajectory looks good, Rika assessed as she recalculated her vector. She took long, slow breaths, trying to calm her thundering heart. *All I have to do is fall straight down…and pray that I can slow enough that I don't make a new crater on Kestry.*

An alert went off on her HUD, and Rika looked up to see the *Persephone Jones* pivot a few degrees, and begin its braking burn, directing its engine wash away from the asteroid and Kestry Station.

The effect was dizzying; the ship appeared to accelerate away as it slowed. Rika turned her gaze back to the station below her, maintaining her focus on the small target.

As the station grew in size, her fear of missing diminished, and her other fear increased: *Can I slow enough?*

Barne had jury-rigged a pair of small tanks containing a combustible propellant and attached them to the jump-jets on Rika's calves. They *should* work, but when one had a delta-*v* of over seven hundred meters per second, 'should' didn't offer a lot of reassurance.

Whose stupid idea was this anyway? she asked herself. *Oh…yeah….*

Rika reran the calculations on the best time to burn. There was a wide margin of error, caused by the nature of the fuel in the tanks. It wasn't the same mixture she usually burned, and her efficiency coefficient was really just an estimate.

Everything in space was in motion. Her, the station, and the moon it orbited. Too much burn, and she'd miss the target; too little, and she'd bore into the surface—or maybe punch straight through the station. *Wouldn't that be fun?*

The countdown to burn hit zero, and her calf jets came to life, spewing twin flames at the base of the torpedo that was her body. Rika prayed that her armor's EM countermeasures were enough to fool the station's tracking systems. If not, the station's fire-control systems were bound to pick her up as some sort of inbound projectile—or at the very least, a meteor—and lase her out of the black.

She looked up, spotting the *Persephone Jones* by its brilliant torch as it continued to slow on its approach to the station. Gauging its speed, she determined that the ship was at least fifteen minutes behind her at this point.

The burn continued for another two minutes before the boosters sputtered out, and her freefall to the station resumed. Her HUD registered a relative velocity of three meters per second.

Rika gritted her teeth. *This is going to hurt.*

During the final minute of her descent, the station grew rapidly, and Rika delivered a series of short bursts from her armor's attitude controls to place her impact location—there was no other way to consider it—as close as possible to the docking bay to which the *Persephone Jones* had been assigned.

At the last minute, Rika saw a cargo net stretching over a storage area and aimed for it. She very nearly missed; one last burst from her jets brought her over the net, and she made her target. The net stretched, vibrating as one strand snapped, then another. Two more broke under her mass, and Rika fell through, dropping to the asteroid's surface.

The impact was still hard enough to jar her, but Rika managed to clamp her hand around a cargo anchor before she bounced off the surface.

Rika righted herself and dug her feet into the asteroid's surface. She looked up once more to see the *Jones* slowly growing larger, all the while thanking the stars she had made it in one piece.

She turned her gaze back to the asteroid and noted helpful lights anchored into the stone showing the way toward an airlock set into the rock twenty meters away.

With deliberate steps, Rika worked her way through the external cargo storage area, reaching the entrance a minute later. Once at the airlock, she pushed the helpful green button, and the entrance cycled open without requesting any codes.

It was suspicious, but Rika couldn't hack a door that opened willingly, so she stepped inside and triggered the airlock to cycle the inner door open.

She unslung her JE84, checking its action while reading that her GNR was ready on her right arm. If anyone thought they could catch her unawares, they had another think coming.

However, when the airlock's inner door opened, it revealed only an empty corridor—a strange sight after encountering an unsecured airlock.

Now I feel like no one wants to welcome me. Just as well; I probably would have had to kill them.

The thought stopped Rika in her tracks. *Have I become so inured to death that it's entirely casual now?* It was one thing to take down an enemy on the battlefield, when they were both soldiers—but in Oranian space, *she* was the criminal, rescuing a girl whose father had caused the people immeasurable pain.

No.

Rika resolved to avoid any nonessential casualties, if at all possible. No one else should have to die to free Amy.

Except for K-Strike mercs. They deserve it for being so shitty at their jobs.

Rika sent one of her two remaining probes ahead, sending it down the passageway to the right while she turned left. Based on what she saw of the station while falling toward it, that direction should be where the *Jones*'s docking bay lay.

As she strode through the well-lit corridor, she heard voices around a corner to her right. Rika froze, considering her options. There was nowhere to hide; she could fall back to the airlock and pray they didn't look inside...*There's no time for that.* Her only option was to continue forward as though she had every right to be there.

She walked through the intersection and spotted the speakers, a man and a woman, walking toward her. They weren't station personnel or wearing any armor; though they did both have sidearms hanging from their belts.

The man raised an eyebrow as his eyes raked over her, but the woman only shook her head and muttered something degrading about Genevians.

For a moment, Rika considered grabbing the woman and tossing her down the hall. A little fantasy to make her feel better as she walked past pretending she hadn't heard the couple.

"I mean, she's just mech meat," the woman was saying, raising her voice for Rika to hear.

Rika clenched her teeth and kept moving, focusing on putting one foot in front of the other. She was surprised the woman would insult an armed and armored mech—though Rika had to admit that she did look a little worse for wear, at present.

By some miracle, her taunter decided not to goad her any further, and the pair turned left down the passageway, their voices fading.

The corridor branched once and then passed through another intersection before coming to a large pressure-door that stood open, revealing the docking bay beyond.

She thought that she saw the *Persephone Jones* on the far side of the bay and feared she was too late; then she realized it was a different ship of the same class.

Rika let out a long breath and recalled the probe she had released upon entering the facility while sending the other one into the docking bay. She tried not to think of what the Marauder quartermaster on the *Romany* would say at the loss of yet another allotment of drones.

She remained out of sight in the passageway as the nearest drone fed an overhead image of the bay to Rika, and she overlaid it atop her vision, looking for locations where the enemy could be lying in wait and correlating them with the cradle assigned to the *Persephone Jones*.

After one sweep across the bay, the probe hadn't picked up anything out of the ordinary, other than a dearth of dockworkers.

If I jumped down to this rock for nothing….

Rika sent it on another pass, wondering if the team had been overly paranoid, when she caught sight of an armored woman in the shadows behind a row of cargo floats.

Rika had the drone pull EM readings from the woman and perform a new sweep, focusing on the detected spectrum. Sure enough, there were two more armored figures in the bay. One was crouched in the armatures of a docking cradle, while the other was high up in the bay, crouched in the Y where two support arches met.

The sniper in the arches was Rika's biggest worry. He would have a clear line of sight on two of the *Persephone Jones*'s airlocks. Rika knew that if she were running the ambush op, there would also be another sniper covering the far side of the ship.

Rather than using suppressive fire in an attempt to overwhelm Basilisk—like the K-Strike soldiers back in Kandahar City had done—this crew was going to take out as much of the opposition as possible in an initial strike.

During her drone's reconnaissance, Rika had continued to remain outside the bay, leaning casually against the passageway's bulkhead, her line of sight limited to a small corner of the docking bay, also remaining out of sight of the enemy.

She considered moving in to take up a better position, but decided against it. While her drone had flitted about undetected—Rika hoped—there was no way the enemy wouldn't have eyes on the entrances. Better to wait until she could use the element of surprise for distraction.

Rika wondered if the reason the airlock's security had been offline was the enemy in the bay. They couldn't just hunker down in there without station security taking notice; they must have had someone on the inside disable the security measures in this area.

Nice to catch a break once in a while.

A minute later, a warning klaxon blared. Through her drone's feed, Rika caught sight of the *Persephone Jones* sliding through the grav shield and into the bay. Overhead, a grav emitter armature slid over the ship, guiding it to its cradle.

This was it—once the cradle locked on, and the ramp extended, it would be time for her to move.

Rika checked her GNR's loadout: seven depleted uranium sabot rounds, sixty two projectiles, and a half-charge on her electron beam's last SC Batt—enough for five more shots.

In the bay, the *Persephone Jones* touched down, and the docking ramp began to extend.

Rika took a deep breath. *Time to do this…*

She casually walked into the bay, turned left, and strode past a line of cargo containers. Once in their shadow, she stopped, took two long steps backward, and raised her GNR, taking aim at the sniper in the support struts high above.

Sure enough, the sniper had spotted her—but his weapon was pointed at the far side of the containers, where Rika had been headed, not back at the opening she had just passed.

Rika gave him a one-two punch. A stream of relativistic electrons lanced out from her GNR, followed by a sabot round. The electrons burned away the ablative plating on his armor, and the sabot round punched right through his body, hitting the inside of his armor on the back.

The sniper's chest exploded, and he fell from his perch.

Without wasting a moment, Rika leapt over the shipping container and fired a trio of projectile rounds into the back of the enemy perched in the docking cradle's armatures.

Two hit, but the third missed as he jerked to the side and spun toward her, firing a salvo from his rifle. Rika's armor registered three impacts before she hit the deck, dodging around the docking cradle's struts, looking for a clear line of sight on the enemy.

When she got one, he had moved. Rika circled back, ready with both weapons.

As she sidled up against an angled strut, she heard the *Persephone Jones*'s main cargo deck's door open, and a signal from the team's combat net reached her. Rika Linked up and fed her drone's data to them while resuming the search for her foe.

A scraping sound from behind alerted Rika to danger a second before a burst of kinetic rounds streaked toward her. The sound gave her enough time to pivot and fire her JE84 at the attacker.

He had moved again, and her shot missed; Rika knew she had to take this chucklehead out fast. Too much longer, and one of his friends was bound to show up.

Taking a risk, she leapt into the air, flying over the struts and armatures she and her enemy had been using for cover to come down on his position from above.

Apparently, assisted by his powered armor, he had the same plan. Rika took a moment to consider the guts it took to drop down onto a mech—though she had performed similar maneuvers in the past.

Neither of them reacted as quickly as they should have, and they passed each other in the air. Rika had to move her GNR out of the way to bring her JE84 to bear, and her opponent was below her, aiming where he expected her to be.

At the last second, Rika swung her GNR's barrel at the man's right side, clipping his shoulder and sending him off course.

The action spun her as well, and Rika landed facing back the way she had leapt, not pausing before springing over the docking cradle and opening up with her JE84, firing on full auto.

An entire magazine of bullets slammed into the man's head and shoulders, dropping him to his knees before Rika crashed into him, her clawed feet grasping his shoulders and flipping him backward into the deck.

Rika kicked him in the head, breaking his armor's seal, and snapping his neck.

<*Two down,*> she reported over the team's combat net.

<*Nice of you to say 'hi',*> Barne replied dryly.

<*I was busy.*>

Rika pulled the team's feeds and saw that Basilisk had not used the *Jones*'s main cargo door. Leslie and Barne had exited from the airlock on the ship's starboard side, near Rika's position, and Chase had ridden in atop the ship, laying down fire from behind one of its sensor arrays.

<*That's a cowboy move,*> Rika teased him privately.

<*And jumping down to the asteroid from a few hundred kilometers wasn't?*> Chase sent with a wink.

<*Touché. There's bound to be a sniper on the port side somewhere; keep an eye out.*>

<*Oh, I've got an eye out. So do they,*> Chase retorted. <*Whoever it is that's after us has some serious firepower.*>

<*Do we have to worry about the* Jones *bringing its beams to bear?*> Rika asked the team.

<*Nope,*> Leslie answered as she advanced past a row of hull-inspection bots. <*Their AI core is a bit offline at the moment, seeing as it's in Barne's satchel. That's causing them no end of trouble.*>

<*Nicely done,*> Rika said appreciatively.

Rika noted that Patty and Amy were still inside the ship's airlock, and she moved from cover to cover until she was at the base of the ramp in position with Barne.

Now that Basilisk had disembarked, the enemy was showing their full force; not counting the two Rika had already disabled, there were nine active enemies in the bay. They were armed as well as the Marauders—probably better, since the team was running low on ammunition.

<*We need to clear this bay,*> Rika advised. <*Patty, get Amy down here. They're not going to use their heavy ordnance on her.*>

<*You sure?*> Patty asked apprehensively. <*Our pretty dresses don't offer much in the way of protection.*>

<*No choice,*> Rika replied. <*We have to get out before they box us in. Station's general net has another bay a klick from here. If we can get there and seal the entrances long enough, maybe we can find a ride off this rock.*>

Patty rushed down the ramp without further prodding,

clutching Amy in her arms. The woman crouched beside Rika and Barne wearing a stoic expression.

"You guys in Basilisk sure know how to have fun," she muttered.

"It's in the rulebook," Barne stated matter-of-factly as he lobbed a grenade toward a source of enemy weapons fire.

Rika glanced at Amy *I wish we didn't have to put the poor girl through all this.*

<Leslie. Make sure the entrance I came through is clear. Once it's secure, follow the route to the next bay and lock it down. Barne, get on the far side of those containers with Patty and Amy. Chase and I will cover our retreat.>

<On it,> Leslie acknowledged and dashed from cover. Her chameleon armor blended into the adjacent docking cradle's struts; Rika couldn't see her, but Leslie's feed to the combat net showed that she was already halfway to the bay's entrance.

Barne followed a moment later, leading Patty and Amy on a more circuitous route.

Rika didn't watch their progress; instead, she turned toward the opposite side of the bay and laid down suppressive fire with her JE84, then moved to new cover. She repeated the action and sent the signal for Chase to follow.

She looked up to see him leap from the top of the *Persephone Jones* down into the docking cradle surrounding it. A burst of weapons fire came from amongst the struts and armatures, followed by a resounding *crack*!

<Chase?> Rika asked, a spike of fear driving through her chest as she spotted movement ahead and fired a trio of projectile rounds from her GNR.

<I'm good, just had to break someone,> he confirmed.

<Just so long as you're not the one getting broken,> Rika replied in relief.

Chase emerged from the docking struts on her left and moved into cover, giving her a jaunty wave once he was behind a stack of crates.

<*Can't break me; I have too many years with you ahead of me,*> he stated simply.

Rika shook her head. <*You're such a sap sometimes.*>

She proceeded to lay down suppressive fire with both her weapons as Chase rushed past her, leapfrogging to new cover.

Now that Amy was clear, the enemy was intensifying their attacks. The projectile fire had switched to kinetic slugs, which tore away any cover Rika and Chase moved to in moments.

They were almost at the row of containers lining the edge of the bay when Rika's probe picked up a telltale whine.

<*Down!*> she commanded.

They hit the deck as a blue-white electron beam flashed overhead and burned a hole through a docking cradle's support strut.

The cradle groaned, and the support armature fell free, coming straight for Rika. She scrambled out of the way, certain she wouldn't make it, when something grabbed her GNR's barrel and yanked her forward.

<*Should get a handle put on that thing,*> Chase suggested with a grin in her mind before he fired at the source of the electron beam.

<*C'mon,*> Rika urged as she rushed past him from behind the relative safety of the shipping containers.

As they ran, the container behind them exploded, spraying shrapnel in every direction. Rika knew that type of impact—it was a depleted uranium sabot.

They passed between two crates, and Rika fired her electron beam toward the origin of the uranium round.

She harbored a strong suspicion it was the SMI-2 mech she had spotted down on Faseema. She didn't want to shoot at a mech—especially not one of her model—but if it came down to the enemy or her, there was no question in Rika's mind which one would survive the encounter.

As she backed through the bay's exit, Rika caught sight of the enemy SMI-2 as it leaped into the air and landed atop the *Persephone Jones*. The mech stood in the open, her helmet facing

Rika—the direction of its gaze evident by the grey skull painted the black oval.

Rika paused, trying to determine by the enemy mech's stance if she knew her; she wondered if the death's-head mech was thinking the same thing.

<*Rika, what's up?*> Chase asked from behind her.

<*Uh…nothing, keep moving.*>

Rika backed down the passageway she had entered until she reached the first cross-corridor, where she took aim at the bulkhead on the exterior side of the station. She fired a shot with her electron beam, burning away the plas and steel and exposing the rock behind.

Asteroids were never as dense as planets, and she guessed that one sabot round would do the trick—bringing her down to just three.

Rika fired the shot, and the rock exploded, opening a hole into space. The *WHUMP* of explosive decompression thundered through the corridor.

Klaxons blared, and pressure doors began to lower. Rika turned and raced down the corridor toward Chase, who was crouched at the next intersection, waving her onward.

Rika thanked the stars that some considerate soul had configured the doors to lower slowly, and she slid under with only a few centimeters to spare.

<*You like to play fast and loose, don't you?*> Chase asked, while Rika lay on her back, chest heaving as she caught her breath.

<*I've never actually done that before,*> Rika said. <*But I saw it in a vid and wanted to try it—didn't expect pressure doors to close this far out, though.*>

Chase shook his head. <*They always close two deep. Forms an airlock.*>

Rika nodded as she rolled over and pushed herself up. <*Makes sense. I never spent much time on stations during the war. They were too worried we'd do more damage than the enemy.*>

Chase gave a soft laugh over the Link. <*Gee, I wonder why. Still, you were on Dekar for some time; didn't you ever read over the emergency protocols?*>

<*Uhh...yeah, totally. All the time. Loved me some good emergency protocol reading.*>

Chase shook his head and made a *tsk*-ing sound.

Rika took the lead as they moved down the corridor, following the route the rest of the team had taken. After turning at the next intersection, she spotted Patty and Amy crouched down behind a conduit stack.

<*What's the holdup?*> Rika asked Patty.

<*Barne's gone ahead to help Leslie. There's a ship in the bay, but it's locked down.*>

<*Opposition?*> Rika asked Barne over the combat net.

<*Not the physical kind,*> Barne replied, his voice terse.

<*Bay is clear,*> Leslie added. <*There were two mechanics in here, but I locked them down.*>

<*OK, not enough of the physical kind to be worth noting,*> Barne amended.

Rika gestured for Chase to lead Patty and Amy toward the bay, but not before she reached out and gave Amy's arm a reassuring squeeze.

Rika held her position at the intersection as the team fell back. Movement to her left caught her eye, and she saw a group of station security guards swing into the corridor.

"Dammit," she swore aloud, and fired a shot with her electron beam into the overhead a half-dozen paces ahead of the lead guard. The ceiling exploded; lights, ductwork, and rock spilled out into the corridor.

Rika turned and fired another shot at the overhead back in the direction from which they had come. *Hopefully, if the enemies from the docking bay follow this route, they'll end up in a firefight with station security.*

<*Who you shooting at back there?*> Chase asked.

<*Station security. Just keeping them at bay.*>

<*'Bout time they showed up. Slackers,*> Barne commented.

Rika chuckled at the annoyance in Barne's voice. The surly sergeant seemed genuinely annoyed that station security had taken so long to respond.

<*ETA?*> Rika asked.

<Just got on the ship. Give me two minutes to make sure we can take control of this bird, then fall back.>

Rika sent an affirmative. *Holding this intersection for two minutes should be a breeze.*

On her left, the station security guards were taking positions behind the overhead's rubble. Rika took aim with her JE84 and fired a shot into one man's shoulder, then pinged a shot off another's helmet.

That'll teach them to stay low. No wonder these people lost to Stavros's Politica; either that, or their good soldiers all died in the war.

A minute later, the enemies from the docking bay showed up on the right and took up positions behind the pile of rubble Rika had made for them.

Shit! Rika swore internally. Giving the mercs cover had not been one of her brighter moves. They were using it well and mopping the deck with the station security. Rika decided to even the odds and fired a few shots into the merc's ranks, taking one out and forcing the others back.

<You want to keep dicking around down there, or are you going to come and get on this ship?> Barne asked.

<Thanks for the notice,> Rika replied as she turned and dashed down the corridor to the docking bay, turning to fire one of her last two sabot rounds at the T of the cross corridor once she had enough distance.

The bulkhead exploded in a shower of plas, steel, and rock, and Rika prayed it would be enough of a distraction to get to the ship in time.

She burst into the bay and saw the commandeered vessel highlighted on her HUD. It was a fast-looking pinnace on the far side of the hangar. Patty and Amy were rushing up the ramp while Chase and Leslie held positions beside the cradle.

The bay was half a kilometer across, and Rika pushed herself to her top speed, weaving between shipping containers and docking cradles.

She was only one hundred meters in when something swung out from behind a stack of crates and struck her squarely in the chest.

The impact made her feel like she'd been hit by a starship. As Rika flipped over, her feet describing a long arc through the air before she landed on her back, her JE84 slipped from her grasp.

Rika struggled for breath, wondering if she had a collapsed lung. Readouts on her HUD showed that the wound on her back had torn open, and one of her previously bent ribs had snapped and was pushing halfway through her chest.

Biofoam sealed the internal wound, and her systems deadened the agonizing pain. All of this happened as Rika flipped over. She backpedaled away and spotted a two-meter beam lying on the deck, but there was no sign of the enemy—until she fell onto Rika from above.

The enemy SMI-2 hit Rika like a meteor, slamming into her shoulders and firing at her helmet with a Messier-Orion pulse rifle.

A pulse rifle?

Rika reached up for it, grabbed the barrel, and pulled down hard. By some miracle, she managed to tear it from the enemy's grasp. Then she fell backward, trying to get enough space between them to manage a shot with her GNR.

The other mech read Rika's intentions and leapt to the side, firing a projectile round from her own GNR—a 41B model, Rika noticed—into the top of Rika's head.

Rika's helmet bore the brunt of the round, but her ears rang like she was the clapper in a bell. She ignored the pain and rose to a crouch, firing two rounds at the enemy mech. One hit her in the chest, and the other in the left arm, blowing off a piece of armor—the round lodging in the elbow joint.

Rika struggled to her feet just as the other mech barreled into her, slamming her into a shipping container, rocking it backward as the combined half-ton of mech drove a deep dent into its side.

The metal of the container had folded around Rika's left arm, and she tried to wrench it free, but with the other mech bearing down on her, she couldn't get it to budge.

As Rika waved her GNR, trying to catch it on the edge of the container to pull herself forward, she found she was staring into the death's head painted on her enemy's helmet. Even if they had never known one another, she and this mech had once fought on the same side, suffered the same indignities, shed Nietzschean blood, and watched their comrades die.

We should be friends, not enemies.

Rika gave up struggling, and the other mech pulled back her fist, driving it into Rika's face. Rika's visuals died, and everything went black; she felt panic surge up within her.

Is this how it ends? Killed by another SMI-2 mech?

Then light flooded in as her helmet was pulled free, and split in half in the process.

"Rika?" a stunned, robotic voice said. "You're…you're Rika…"

Rika's eyes adjusted to the bright light of the bay, and she watched the other mech take a step back, taking the opportunity to finally wrench her arm free.

"Who are you?" she demanded angrily.

The other mech turned her head—though Rika knew it didn't matter. The SMI-2's three-sixty vision wouldn't allow her to stop seeing, not so long as the helmet was on.

"No one…" the other mech whispered. "I just saw your picture once."

"Liar!" Rika shouted. "I *know* you! Who are you?"

In the back of her mind, Rika knew that anyone could have looked her up after the war, seen what her face had looked like before it was taken away. But this mech…she'd had a personal reaction. Rika knew that the person before her had once been a member of team Hammerfall.

Not all the women of Hammerfall had survived the war; only four others during Rika's tenure. She knew three of them to be dead.

"Silva," Rika whispered. "You're Silva! How could you…show me your face," Rika commanded, taking a step forward.

"I…I don't have one," Silva admitted, hanging her head.

Rika shook her head. "I don't care. Show me your eyes, then. I'll know."

The other mech—Silva—paused for a moment, and then the black oval surrounding her head split open. She reached up slowly and pulled the front half away, exposing the featureless grey face of an SMI-2 mech.

No mouth, a stunted nose, no ears…but two eyes, wide and unblinking, stared back at her.

Rika knew those eyes. It *was* Silva.

She wanted to rush forward, to embrace her old friend, to ask her where she'd been, whether she'd seen her children since the war, what she was doing this far into Praesepe….but she did none of those things. Instead, she lifted her GNR, taking aim at Silva's head.

"Why?" she asked, her voice sounding as tortured as she felt.

Silva's eyes looked away, and the robotic voice emanated from her armor. "I'm surviving. Same as you."

"I'm not surviving," Rika argued. "I'm living! Who are you working for? Who's trying to take Amy?"

Silva shook her head. "I'm sorry, Rika. I can't disobey orders; I need you to come with me."

Rika lowered her GNR and fired a round at Silva's leg…but nothing happened. She looked at the gun and saw that the autofeeder was bent; no rounds were in the chamber.

Silva met Rika's eyes. "Drop it. Come with me."

"You lower yours," a voice ordered from behind Silva, and Rika saw Chase step out from behind a crate. Her own JE84 was in his hand, aimed at Silva's head.

"Friend of yours?" Silva asked dryly.

"Lover," Rika replied firmly.

Silva's eyes widened. "A face, a lover; the world's been a lot kinder to you. You just have it all, Rika."

"Join me," Rika pleaded. "Come to the Marauders."

Silva tapped the side of her head. "No can do, corporal; I'm chipped. I have to follow orders." Her tone was curt, but her eyes belied a deep sadness.

"You can fight it," Rika implored. "I did—I was able to beat Discipline. I know you can, too. You just have to try."

Tears formed in Silva's eyes, the stoic attitude falling away. "I've tried, Rika, I've tried so hard. I can't, though; I have to obey."

"Rika!" Chase called, getting her attention. "Rika, we have to go!"

He tossed Rika her rifle, which she caught and leveled at Silva, who stood with her head hung low.

"I'm sorry, Silva," Rika said placatingly as she walked sideways toward Chase. "Don't follow us...."

The words burned in her mouth as she said them. Silva had been her best friend during the war: the indomitable leader of team Hammerfall, the woman who had kept Rika's spirit alive through those long, dark years.

Rika had searched for her after the war. Even on Dekar, and then with the Marauders, she had sent out inquiries and hunted through feeds.

Now she had found Silva, but she wouldn't come. It wasn't even the same Silva; her spirit was broken. Somehow, the woman who the entire Genevian war machine—not to mention the Nietzschean army—couldn't bring down, was now a shell of her former self.

"Go," Silva whispered, cringing as Discipline wracked her body. "I won't be able to stop myself."

"That's bullshit!" Rika swore as she ran backward, following Chase to the ship. "You're stronger than this. I *know* you. I loved you Silva! Like you were my *mother*!" Rika shrieked the last words, and watched as Silva turned away, lifting the front of her helmet back into place. Becoming death incarnate as she raised her GNR and took aim.

"No!" Rika screamed, and fired her last sabot round at Silva; not shooting at her friend—or whatever she was now—but at her gun-arm. The round hit the weapon and shattered the mount, knocking the GNR off Silva's arm.

Rika debated rushing back to Silva. *Maybe I can convince her, or knock her out, or something…*but weapons fire sounded, and shots ricocheted off her armor.

<*Rika, get in front of me!*> Chase ordered. <*Your head's exposed.*>

Chase fell back and ran right on Rika's heels with his gun held up to protect her head. His other hand was on her shoulder as they rushed through the bay with the sounds of pursuit closing in.

Then the pinnace came into view from between two stacks of crates, and they rushed toward the ramp—at the top of which stood Barne and Leslie, laying down covering fire.

Rika felt hot tears running down her face as she rushed into the ship, pushed to the deck by Chase as the pinnace pulled away from the docking cradle and flew toward the grav shield.

She tried to rise to get one last look at Silva, but Chase shoved her back down as rounds tore through the air, into the interior of the ship.

Then the pinnace's ramp closed, and Rika collapsed, letting the sorrow take her as her body was wracked with shuddering sobs.

RECOVERY

STELLAR DATE: 02.17.8949 (Adjusted Years)
LOCATION: Pinnace, departing Kestry Station
REGION: Oran System, Praesepe Cluster

"So, that was Silva," Chase began as he sat beside Rika in the cabin she had escaped to shortly after the pinnace had burst out of Kestry's bay, and into the relative safety of space.

Rika didn't respond, though she managed a slight nod. She knew this wasn't the time to lose herself in sorrow; the mission wasn't done yet. They still had to get Amy to safety. But to find Silva here…on a mission, trying to kill her….

It was almost more than she could bear.

"I'm sorry it had to be like this," Chase said as he reached around behind her, examining her re-opened wound. "I really am, Rika. You've told me a lot about her—how she was the one who kept you going."

"She was always the strongest of us," Rika whispered. "What could have happened to her?"

Chase shook his head as he reapplied the sealant to Rika's back. "It's hard out here, hard for all of us. We don't know what she's been through to end up here. But there's a silver lining."

Rika turned her head, meeting Chase's eyes. "Oh, yeah? What's that?"

"She's alive." Chase paused and then clarified, "Now you know that Silva is alive. Maybe you'll get another chance to save her."

Rika drew a deep breath, sniffling as she did so. "If she survives long enough for me to find her again."

Chase reached up and wiped a tear from Rika's eye. "She'll live. You mech girls are the toughest women in the galaxy. You can't even take each other down."

Rika smiled sadly and rubbed her cheek against Chase's hand.

The vision of Silva putting her helmet back on, her sorrowful eyes disappearing behind her death's head mask, was replaying over and over in her mind.

What if Silva doesn't want to be saved?

*****

By some miracle, no one pursued the pinnace as they flew out of Oranian-controlled space. Part of their efficacious escape was due to the alterations Barne had managed to make to the ship's beacon. But Rika suspected that maybe no one in Oran cared enough to take on the crew who had shot up Kandahar City's spaceport, taken partial control of the *Persephone Jones,* and blasted their way out of Kestry Station.

One of the Oranian cruisers did break orbit from around Faseema to follow them, but it didn't try to intercept their course. The captain of the ship seemed content to send a not-so-subtle message that they weren't welcome, and not to come back.

Barne deemed it was nothing more than a defeated gesture from a defeated people.

Rika stood behind Patty's seat in the cockpit, staring out at the growing shape of Serspa Station in the Politica-controlled region of the Oran System. Though the pinnace could make the interstellar hop to their rendezvous point for Amy's hand-off, it would need a refueling before they left the system.

The feeling that something was still very wrong hung over Rika like a dark cloud. Even if Barne was right about the Oranians being weak, she couldn't discern why the cruiser didn't simply blow them out of the black. The ship had never even closed within weapons range.

It sent a bad message that one could act with impunity in Oranian space, and get away with it free and clear.

Then again, no Oranian citizens had been killed—that Rika knew of. Maybe the authorities weren't going to waste their efforts on a fight between mercs.

One thing was for certain; if they had known Amy was on the pinnace, they would likely have done something very different.

"I have our bay assignment from Serspa Station," Patty announced. "They want us to dock in an internal bay so they can inspect us."

"I guess word got out that we made a mess on Kestry," Chase said from the co-pilot's seat.

Patty shrugged. "They seemed more amused than upset, but you never know. I didn't ask for debarkation permits—just food and fuel, so we can be on our way."

"I don't like it," Rika stated. "They could top us off with one of their service ships; no need to have us dock for that."

"You're paranoid," Patty soothed her. "I asked for one, but service ships are usually reserved for larger vessels that can't land in a bay—or ones that throw off station rotation when there's not enough mass to balance. You know that."

Rika nodded. She did know it, but that didn't mollify her. "I still have a bad feeling about this."

Chase looked up at her. "Whatever it is, we can handle it. Basilisk can handle a few namby-pamby Politica flunkies doing an inspection.

"Chase! Seriously?" Patty exclaimed. "Now you've gone and jinxed us."

"I didn't take you for one of those superstitious pilots," Chase teased her.

Patty snorted. "All pilots are superstitious. We fly tin cans through the deadliest places in the universe. Every little bit of luck helps."

Rika couldn't argue with Patty's logic. Space was downright inhospitable in the best of circumstances. Throw in enemy stations and ships and stray space junk, and it was no wonder people still terraformed planets—even with all their pitfalls. At least on the surface of a habitable world, 'outside' wasn't instantly fatal.

"I'm going to check on Amy," Rika announced and left the

cockpit.

The pinnace wasn't large, but it did have a small galley, which was where Amy had spent most of her time, picking at food and playing Snark with Leslie.

When Rika entered, the pair was in the midst of a game.

"I thought I smelled popcorn," Rika said, as she sat down and picked out a single puff from the bowl that sat to the side. Eating finger food was a messy affair when you had exposed joints for crumbs to get into. Popcorn was delicious, but it was the worst to clean up after; the little kernel bits got everywhere.

"Found it under a stack of disposable plates," Leslie explained. "Nuked it up, and here we are."

"We'll be at Serspa Station soon," Rika informed them. "Then we can stock up on all the popcorn you two could ever want."

Amy's eyes darted toward Rika, and then back at her cards. She ran a hand through her hair and tucked it behind her ears before glancing at Rika again.

"Something on your mind?" Rika prompted gently.

The young girl twisted her lips, drew in a long breath, exhaled, and looked Rika in the eyes. "I overheard Barne and Chase. They said you fought another mech out there…on Kestry."

Rika nodded slowly. *Where is she going with this?* It wasn't a topic she wanted to delve into at the moment; certainly not with Amy. Still, she couldn't exactly tell the girl to drop it—she wasn't a bastion of emotional stability, either.

"Was she like you?" Amy asked.

"Like me? You mean an SMI-2 model?"

Amy nodded. "Yeah…I just…. Well, one of them, of you, works for my father. I wondered if it was her that you saw."

Rika raised her eyebrows. "An SMI-2 mech works for your father? For Stavros?" She wanted to add, *'And you're just mentioning it now?'* but kept that comment to herself.

"Yes," Amy replied, nodding gravely. "When I first saw you, I thought she had come to save me. She's always very nice to me. But then I realized it wasn't her; you have a different helmet."

Leslie met Rika's eyes, her expression saying what Rika didn't even want to consider. *Of the quadrillions of humans spread across space, what are the chances that we would encounter one of a few thousand SMI-2 mechs on a mission?*

Even less likely was the fact that their young ward just so happened to know an SMI-2.

<*What are the chances?*> Leslie asked privately, echoing Rika's thoughts.

<*Astronomical,*> Rika replied. <*But why would Stavros hire us if he already had a team led by Silva? And then why attack us once we have his daughter? That can't be what happened here.*>

<*Shit, Rika. Since when does anything make sense in this business? It's a possibility, though. One we can't ignore.*>

"This mech. What's her name?" Rika asked Amy.

The girl shrugged. "I don't know. She never talks. Not aloud, at least. Father always calls her 'Meat', but I never do. She's come to comfort me more than once after..." she went quiet.

"After what?" Leslie pressed. Rika could see the fear of what they might hear in the scout's eyes.

"Uhh...you know, after father yells at me. Sometimes I do things that make him mad."

Rika chewed on the inside of her cheek, holding back the question of what else might occur in the Stavros family. Not turning Amy over to her father wasn't an option. The Marauders did the job they were hired for—the Old Man would have her hide, if she boned a job like this.

It wasn't like *she* could keep Amy. *What would I do with a young girl like Amy? The Marauders is no place for kids.*

<*Rika...If he beats her, we can't turn her over,*> Leslie said firmly.

<*I know, but what are we supposed to do? Take her to the* Romany*? The general will not be happy if we blow the mission.*>

<*The general can't be a fan of Stavros; he's destabilizing the region. The Old Man wants it solid to defend against the Nietzscheans when they come,*> Leslie countered.

<*Right now, I think unseating Stavros would make a bigger mess*

than keeping him around. Anyway, it's not our call—> Rika stopped.

Why am I rationalizing this?

The look on Leslie's face spoke volumes about what she thought of Rika's adherence to the mission.

<OK…maybe once we get out of the Oran system, we can have ship trouble or something. We can return to the Romany *before the handoff. Stars know enough has gone wrong on this mission; it won't be hard to convince anyone that our stolen pinnace had some sort of issue.>*

Leslie's eyes lit up. *<Are you saying we'll blow the meet?>*

Rika sent a mental nod. *<We'll go to the* Romany *and let Ayer and the Old Man make the call. We have over a week 'til we get there; let's work with Amy to see if we can get more out of her. Yeah, she has some psychological signs of abuse, but she was also kidnapped, so who knows what's going on with her now?>*

<Thanks, Rika. Amy's wellbeing means a lot to me.>

Rika had noticed. She wasn't going to push for details—it was obvious Leslie had lost a young girl at some point in the past, be it daughter, sister, whatever—Leslie would share when she was ready.

<Just don't tell the boys that we're considering this. I really don't feel like arguing about this with Barne for the next week.>

Leslie had returned to playing Snark with Amy while the two women spoke. She had been making idle chit chat with the girl, but at Rika's statement, she snorted aloud.

"What?" Amy asked.

"Ghagghh," Leslie grunted. "Got a popcorn kernel stuck in the back of my throat! Don't you hate that?"

<Smooth,> Rika said as she rose. "I hope I get to meet this mech that works for your father," she told Amy.

"I don't think you will," Amy replied. "Father sent her on some mission before I was taken. She's a long ways away."

"Oh, yeah?" Rika asked.

"Yeah, she was looking for someone in the Pyra system," Amy said absently. "Though I guess maybe she'll be back soon. Maybe you will get to meet her. Maybe you two knew each other before—"

<Rika, you better get to the cockpit. We've got trouble,> Patty interrupted with more than a little worry in her mental tone.

"Duty calls," Rika announced as she turned to leave the room. "Save some popcorn for me."

Amy grinned and pulled the popcorn toward her. "No chance, Rika. You can get your own."

Rika laughed and walked down the passageway to the cockpit to see what new calamity was waiting to befall them.

"Nice of you to join us," Chase jibed when she arrived, and Rika stuck her tongue out at him.

"What's up?"

"Oh, just a few Politica destroyers shadowing us…like, four…"

Rika looked at the scan data on Patty's holodisplay and let out a low whistle. "That's not really a friendly posture they have there."

"Noticed that, did you?" Patty asked.

"No updates from the station?"

Patty shook her head. "Nothing; our docking coordinates are unchanged."

"What do you think?" Chase asked.

Rika sighed and leaned against the cockpit's doorframe. "I think they know who we have aboard."

* * * * *

The pinnace settled into its cradle, and Rika hit the control to lower the ramp. Chase had tried to get her to send someone else out—given her lack of helmet and near complete depletion of ammunition, but Rika wouldn't hear of it.

If whoever waited outside wanted them dead, they'd kill them—helmet or no helmet.

Rika walked down the ramp and surveyed the docking bay: there wasn't a single crate, hauler, cart, or even toolbox visible.

Nor were there any other ships.

What was present, however, were at least five hundred soldiers. Most were standing in orderly ranks, but a hundred were crouched with their weapons drawn, and another dozen stood behind crew-served particle cannons—any one of which could tear the pinnace to shreds.

At the bottom of the ramp, with a broad smile on his face, stood Stavros. He looked just as the images on the net had portrayed him: nearly two meters in height, broad shoulders, and a heavy brow. His black hair was cropped close to his head, but still had small curls. It was as though he really did think himself a Greek emperor of old. Just add a laurel and he'd be complete.

"Rika!" he greeted with a slight bow. "It is an honor to finally meet you."

Rika cocked an eyebrow. "Basileus Stavros," she answered, using his official title. "I did not expect such a welcome here at Serspa. We were only intending to stop for fuel and food before proceeding to the rendezvous."

Stavros nodded, his smile fading. "I assume you learned from Amy that I am her father. Then why not turn her over to my authorities here?"

Rika reached the bottom of the ramp and crossed her left arm over her torso, clasping the barrel of her GNR with her left hand. "I don't know the circumstances behind Amy's abduction, and she had little information to offer on that front. There was a possibility that it was an inside job, so we determined that the best course of action was to follow protocol."

"And now that I am here?" Stavros pressed.

Rika bit her lip. The last thing she wanted was to turn the girl over to this man. Just seeing him made her certain that he was not the best parent for Amy. But her choices were limited, and he was Amy's father; she had little cause to keep Amy from her family. Despite her prior conversation with Leslie, all they had were suspicions and a distaste for the man.

"I see no reason not to hand a girl over to her father," Rika relented through gritted teeth.

Stavros gave a curt nod and a predatory smile graced his lips. "You showed courage out on the battlefield. I followed your progress with great interest."

"You did?" Rika was perplexed.

"Of course," Stavros replied. "Do you think I would send mercenaries to rescue my daughter without ensuring I had eyes on the situation? Once you had her, I ordered my team to take Amy from you, but my forces failed to succeed."

As he spoke, Stavros lowered his eyes and shook his head. Then he raised his hand, and a figure rose from behind the ranks of soldiers.

Silva.

All of Rika's fears came true. *Silva is being held under Stavros's thumb with a compliance chip. The man is a monster, but I have no choice but to surrender Amy to him.*

When Silva reached his side, Stavros placed a hand on her shoulder. "Meat here failed to take Amy from you, lost to you, and your team, too. It was a thrilling contest to witness. You're quite the operator, Rika. You're wasted with the Marauders."

"We're not 'meat'," Rika sneered. *He put his daughter in danger just to see two mechs fight?!* She couldn't even put words into how that made her feel.

"No?" Stavros considered. "Maybe *you're* not. You're an amazing creature: a thing of beauty, speed, and cunning. You look good with a face, too. Meat here has no face. She hasn't earned it yet."

Rika could see Silva tense at the repeated insults, but her former friend didn't move, she just stood there and bore the abuse.

A rage-filled scream threatened to tear free from Rika's throat. *How 'bout I rip his face off and see how* he *likes it?* Instead, she took a deep breath. *Lives depend on me keeping my shit together.*

"And me?" she asked after calming herself enough to trust her voice. "Would you say I've 'earned' my face back?"

Stavros shrugged. "You have it, don't you? Meat here doesn't. I would say that those who possess something deserve it through the might or cunning they exhibited in securing it. It is simple."

"Sounds Nietzschean," Rika replied, schooling her tone and expression to hide her disgust.

Stavros nodded. "Nietzsche only borrowed what the Greeks always knew: 'To the victor go the spoils.'"

"Is Amy happy?" Rika asked suddenly, not sure where the words had come from. "With you, at home or wherever you live?"

Stavros snorted. "Of course she is. Why wouldn't she be?"

Rika shrugged. "I'm just curious. We've spent a few days with her; I just want to know that she'll be well."

Stavros waved a hand at Silva for her to step back. "Amy lives like a queen. Trust me, she'll be well taken care of. She *is* my daughter, after all."

"That's good. Maybe I'll send her a message from time to time," Rika ventured.

"You could do better than that," Stavros proposed. "Like I said, you're wasted on the Marauders; you should join The Politica. We're the future of Praesepe. Only we can hold out against the Nietzscheans."

Does Stavros really believe that? He is the cancer, not the cure. What Praesepe needs is his excision—not salvation at his hands.

Rika looked to Silva, standing just behind Stavros. She appeared strong and powerful, but Rika remembered what the real Silva had looked like on the battlefield, when she'd led Hammerfall to victory after victory.

This woman was nothing more than a shell—a hollowed out remnant of that person Rika knew. *It would have been better if I never knew it was Silva inside that armor.*

"I wouldn't join you for all the stars in Praesepe," Rika promised. "We're going to turn Amy over to you only because we must, and then we're leaving."

Rika raised her hand and waved it forward, signaling Leslie to bring Amy down the ramp.

When the girl reached her side, Rika knelt and embraced her. "I'm going to miss you, Amy. You be good, and take care of my friend, the other mech, OK?"

Amy met Rika's eyes. "Why won't you take father's offer? You could stay with me, then. You could be with another mech like you."

Rika shook her head. "My family is the Marauders. With them is where I belong. I'll send you messages, though; we all will."

"Yes," Leslie added. "Frequently."

Rika rose and gave Amy's shoulder a gentle push. "Go on now, this—"

"Amy," Stavros interrupted. "Come. Now. Give your father a hug, then Phillis will take you to a room where you can be refreshed."

A woman stepped forward from the ranks behind Stavros and held out her hand. Amy directed a final longing look at Rika and Leslie before she walked toward her father, gave him a perfunctory hug, and then took Phillis's hand.

<Stars, I hate this, Rika,> Leslie agonized. *<I hate it with everything…>*

<I know, Leslie,> Rika replied resignedly. *<But our hands are tied. Even if we could take Stavros out, what would Amy think of us if we killed her father in front of her? Even if he hurts her, we would just make things worse.>*

Rika said the words for herself as much as for Leslie. The scout didn't reply, and Rika could feel her fuming.

Stavros watched his daughter leave the bay, the expression on his face not happy, but satisfied. When Amy was gone, he turned back to Rika.

"Now, what is your price? You will join The Politica—it is the best place for you. I will put your skills to use."

Rika shook her head. "I have no price. I am a Marauder."

Stavros's lips twisted into a sneer. "You're a mercenary, you kill for pay. Regardless, you know I could kill you all. Destroy your ship, cut your legs from under you. You cannot deny me."

"Do you want the Marauders as enemies?" Rika asked in a measured tone. "The moment we left Kestry, we suspected that our departure was too easy. We sent a tightbeam to a comm probe at the edge of the system; we sent another when your destroyers began to shadow us. If we don't return soon, you'll have General Mill on your doorstep. No one double-crosses the Marauders. We may not have The Politica's numbers, but we defeated the Nietzscheans at Pyra. Are you ready to find out how much we can hurt you?"

As she spoke, Stavros's face had reddened until she wondered if the man would order their deaths anyway. Then, as abruptly as his anger had risen, it dissipated.

"You've some cunning to you, Rika. We did detect those transmissions; I was only testing your loyalty. There is no place in The Politica for traitors." He cast a glance over his shoulder at Silva before continuing. "Go, Rika. Return to your Marauders. Tell your General Mill that The Politica honors its agreements."

"I shall," Rika replied simply, and turned to walk back up the ramp when Stavros's voice stopped her.

"Rika. Should you ever want to know what power truly means…Come to me. I will show it to you."

Rika resisted the urge to give a shiver of revulsion as she continued up the ramp, feeling the barrels of a hundred weapons on her back.

Once inside the ship, with a fuming Leslie at her side, she hit the control to close the entrance, and called up to the cockpit over the Link. *<Patty, get us the hell out of here.>*

HOME

STELLAR DATE: 03.11.8949 (Adjusted Years)
LOCATION: MSS *Romany,* in orbit of Chyso
REGION: Scarborough System, Theban Alliance, Praesepe Cluster

Rika walked down the passageway toward Captain Ayer's small office on Deck 34 of the MSS *Romany*. It was good to finally be back on the ship; it would be better tonight, when she could finally relax with Chase.

Not that they'd been unable to relax during the three-week trip back to the *Romany*'s current location in the Scarborough System. It just wasn't the same on the pinnace, where the team had to sleep in shifts on the two small bunks.

Tempers had been short, and everyone had been glad to finally leave the cramped ship, and the memories it held, behind.

Rika just wanted to have a good, long cry. A very, very long cry. Preferably in Chase's arms. Not only was Silva lost to a monster like Stavros, but Rika had turned a ten-year-old girl over to him, as well. Just the thought of it made her sick.

She reached the unassuming door and knocked sharply.

<*Come in,*> Captain Ayer invited, and Rika pushed the door open to see the captain rising from her desk.

"Captain," Rika greeted her and saluted once she'd crossed the threshold.

Ayer walked around her desk and stood before Rika, returned the salute, and then extended her right hand to shake Rika's—a 'regular' hand now in place, rather than the gun-arm that had been there for the past four weeks.

"At ease, Lieutenant. And congratulations," Ayer granted. "You acquitted yourself well out there, especially given the circumstances."

Rika relaxed marginally. "Which circumstances? That we were hired by a sonuvabitch, that we lost our ship, that I met the shell of my former CO, or that we turned a wonderful little girl over to the aforementioned sonuvabitch?"

Captain Ayer gave a rueful laugh. "You're supposed to ask for 'permission to speak freely' before you go off like that, Rika."

Rika opened her mouth to comply, but Ayer held up her hand.

"No need, Rika—it's granted. I feel personally responsible for putting you through that. We vet our clients and thought we knew who we were working for—but Stavros pulled the wool over our eyes."

"Ma'am?" Rika asked. "How did he do that?"

"Not sure. We're still unraveling that. When we figure it out, we'll certainly update our protocols. I read your report while you were on approach; I'm really sorry about what happened to Silva. First the war, now this…"

"She could fight it," Rika posited. "I did."

Ayer cast an appraising eye on Rika. "Yes, yes you did. But not everyone has your strength. Maybe…maybe after the war, when there was no one left for Silva to be strong for, she couldn't muster it for herself. People are complex; don't hold it against her."

Rika considered Ayer's words. *Perhaps I* have *judged Silva too harshly.* Some amount of her reaction was due to the shock of finding Silva in that situation—enslaved to the likes of Stavros.

"You're right," she admitted after a moment. "I should give Silva more credit. She's earned it."

Ayer nodded. "I'm glad you can see it that way, because we have another mission for you."

"'We'?" Rika parroted, seeing Ayer's gaze dart over her shoulder. She looked back to see General Mill standing in the still-open doorway.

Rika stood at attention and snapped off a salute. "General, Sir!"

Rika had heard that the *Foe Hammer* was in the Scarborough system, but she didn't know that the general was on the *Romany*.

The general returned her salute without hesitation before

stepping into the room. "Glad to have you back with us, Rika. I swear if we could have found a way to give our leaders half the courage you have, we'd all be sleeping in the Nietzschean emperor's palace right now. You're a credit to the Marauders, to mechs, and to your people."

"Thank you, sir," Rika replied.

"I take it I've arrived before you shared the details?" General Mill asked.

Captain Ayer nodded. "You have, sir."

"Good. Let's sit down. These are weighty matters we must discuss."

The general took one of the chairs in front of Captain Ayer's desk, and Ayer took her customary seat. Rika sat next to the general, feeling somewhat uncomfortable with the arrangement.

"I'll get to the heart of it," General Mill started. "I hate the fact that we did work for that pile of donkey excrement named Stavros. The only silver lining is that we saved a young girl in the process—though I'm not convinced we did that, either."

"Sir?" Rika asked, not sure she understood correctly.

"It was in your own report. You must have thought about it, too. Amy told you that Stavros had sent Silva to the Pyra system to look for someone; I'll bet that someone was you."

"Me?" Rika asked. "I thought he was just looking to gain some sort of leverage after the Nietzschean defeat there."

"He's been gathering Genevian mechs—scientists, too. It's possible that he's trying to recreate the mech program in The Politica," Ayer revealed. "We've received some intel from the Septhians that supports this."

Rika didn't know how to respond. The thought of Silva being caught up in something like the Genevian mech program again was enough to break her heart; that those horrors were going to be unleashed on another people was even worse.

"We plan to stop him," General Mill assured her. "Even better, the Septhians are going to pay us to do the job."

"Sir?" Rika asked again, starting to feel silly repeating herself.

"The general is a bit excited," Captain Ayer said with a smile. "We've been hired to assassinate Stavros."

Rika clenched her jaw. *If someone is going in to kill that man, it had better be me.* "You know I want it."

General Mill nodded. "I'd be shocked if you didn't. I could read between the lines in your report. But you can't just show up on Stavros's doorstep asking for a job. You need a plausible story, and I don't think there's one that would hold water."

Rika nodded. A few possible ones floated through her mind, but none seemed credible enough. Then she hit upon it.

"Shit. You need to fire me! Um, sir."

General Mill raised an eyebrow, his grey eyes locked on Rika's. "Why's that?"

"I shut Stavros down. Hard. Shamed him in front of his people. We concoct a reason for you to fire me, and I go to him, hat in hand, begging for a job."

Captain Ayer shook her head. "No, Rika, you don't want that. Stavros will know it's a setup. Especially if you made your dislike of him clear. There are a dozen other outfits that would take you in a heartbeat. If we fire you, it would have to be for something serious, and we'd have to spread it around. Your name would be mud."

Rika considered this for a moment. "Like *how* serious?"

General Mill stroked his chin. "It couldn't be murder. We'd hold you for that—not fire you. Embezzlement wouldn't work, either; most of the other merc companies would still take you in if you embezzled from us. Stars, they might applaud you."

The general ran a hand through his hair and sat back in his seat. "I think we need to find another operative. I'm sorry, Rika. Basilisk will be onhand as backup, but you can't take point. We'll need someone who can get in close to Stavros without raising suspicions."

Rika drew a deep breath and nodded in agreement. "Very well, sir."

General Mill and Captain Ayer reviewed the details of the

mission with her, putting together a plan to take out Stavros. Rika was honored that they would discuss this with her. It was especially useful because she was going to use their plan and intel to pull off the operation herself.

The chance to kill Stavros and free both Amy and Silva was too much. It was a job tailor-made for her.

Regardless of what her superiors may think.

MURDERER

STELLAR DATE: 03.11.8949 (Adjusted Years)
LOCATION: MSS *Romany*, in orbit of Chyso
REGION: Scarborough System, Theban Alliance, Praesepe Cluster

Rika sat back, bracing herself for Chase's reaction. He worked his mouth, trying to figure out what to say. His eyes were troubled and wild. The words finally burst out of him in a rushed stream.

"Rika! No! You can't do something like this! I—I don't know what to say. Can I forbid you? I want to forbid you. I forbid you."

"Nice try," Rika replied dryly. Then her tone softened. "You know I have to do this. You know why."

Chase nodded slowly. "I was there, too…well, not down on the ramp, but I know the score. Stavros has Silva; probably beats his daughter; now he wants to restart the Genevian mech program and use it on his people. Dude's bad news and has to be stopped. I know. But you've done your bit. Mill's right; putting you with Stavros would require accusing you of something so bad it would ruin your reputation forever."

Rika placed a hand on Chase's arm, a wan smile on her lips. "I really like the fact that you think I have a good reputation, though I don't know with who. But my reputation with myself is what matters the most. I have to do this. I have to save them."

She watched Chase mull it over. He looked like he was going to try to make an impassioned plea, but then he chuckled.

"OK, if we're going to get ourselves killed like gallant knights of old, we should get Leslie and Barne in on it. They're going to want to help."

Rika sprang out of her chair and wrapped her arms around Chase. "I knew you'd understand."

Chase gave a rueful laugh. "So much for a long and illustrious career in the Marauders."

* * * * *

"You're fucking nuts," Barne declared, folding his arms in disgust and turning away, staring out the porthole in Rika's cabin.

"It's got merit," Leslie allowed, "but you need something more than a lover's spat—even one that ends up with Chase in the hospital. The only way you'd go to Stavros is if you're wanted for murder."

"Murder?" Rika repeated. "You think?" She knew it would come to that, but had wanted someone else to make the suggestion. She had already said enough crazy things today.

"Yeah, there are lot of outfits that wouldn't care if you beat the crap out of Chase, here. But something like a triple homicide would be a different story. You'd be labeled a psychotic mech that no one would want anything to do with," Leslie concluded.

Barne turned back to the group. "Triple homicide?"

"Yeah. Consider this," Leslie pitched. "We've got some sort of four-way love thing going on here, but Barne and Chase both prefer me for...well...reasons, and you kill us all in a fit of rage and betrayal."

Barne shook his head and groaned. "Stars, you are all pathetic. Amateurs. You need to go for the trifecta: betrayal, love, and *money*. I'll weave a tale about embezzlement from our time on Pyra, some secret credit stashes, a three-way sex scandal, and an attempt to put a control chip back into Rika's head to keep her subservient to the team. When it's done, *you'll* think you're guilty."

"Does that mean you're in, Barne?" Chase asked, amused.

"Yeah, I guess I am. If I'm going to help ruin your future, Rika, I might as well do it right."

"Doesn't matter," Rika said matter-of-factly. "I can't face a future in which Silva is stuck there, and Amy has that beast as her father."

"Not to mention where they've restarted a mech program like

ours," Leslie added. "What a legacy to leave."

"I'm right here," Rika reminded them, her tone sour.

Leslie grimaced. "Sorry, Rika. There's nothing wrong with being what you are; it's how you got that way."

"So, when do we execute?" Chase asked.

"I'll need three days," Barne said flatly. "I have something I need to prepare, and we'll have to get Patty onboard. We need to steal two ships, and I can't do that on my own."

"*Two* ships?" Leslie asked.

"Yeah. We can't ride in there with Rika. We're going to need our own covers, and she's going to need backup and evac, right?"

* * * * *

Rika ran her hand down Chase's back, feeling the muscles ripple beneath his skin as his lips pressed into hers. Then his mouth slid past, nuzzling under her chin.

He reached down and fondled her breasts before sliding a hand down between her legs, causing a long moan to escape her throat.

They continued like that for several minutes, their hot, sweating bodies writhing together until they climaxed and fell back to the bed, their heavy breathing filling the room.

"I swear, if you're this good in sims, I wonder what real life would be like…" Rika finally said.

Chase chuckled. "I don't mean to sound smug, but I am formidable in both sims and reality. But you know I don't want you to change; at least, not for something like this. You're too important for that."

Rika turned onto her side and placed a hand under her head, relishing the feeling of her hair slipping through her fingers.

"Oh, yeah? 'Important'?"

"Yeah. You have a lot of good to do here, in the Marauders, in the cluster. Stars, if the general can really help strengthen Praesepe, maybe we can push back the Nietzscheans."

"I don't think the general wants to just push them back—he wants to destroy them."

"Even better," Chase nodded. "People like you are a big part of that. You inspire those around you; you're a natural leader."

"Well, 'til we do this op," Rika sulked ruefully. "Then, like you said, our names will be mud."

"Did I say that?" Chase asked. "I thought that was Barne."

"It was you," Rika replied. "Mud. M-U-D."

"I have no recollection of that. I think you're working too hard, Rika." Chase winked. "Either way, taking out Stavros and The Politica will help rectify that."

Rika nodded. The Politica wasn't her concern, but she realized that maybe it should be. If they took out Stavros, someone else would move to the top of his fascist regime. She supposed that was where the Marauders and the Septhians would come in. If they could defeat the Politica fleets while their upper echelon was in disarray, it would be a victory for the cluster.

It occurred to her that this was not so different from the mission in Thebes—or what the plan had been, at least. Except this time, it really was for a better cause; this time, she wouldn't have a problem pulling the trigger when the time for assassination came.

Stavros was a dead man walking. He just didn't know it yet.

DUCKING OUT

STELLAR DATE: 03.13.8949 (Adjusted Years)
LOCATION: Interstellar pinnace, near Chyso
REGION: Scarborough System, Theban Alliance, Praesepe Cluster

"Pinnaces *Romany*-Gamma and *Romany*-Epsilon, return to hangar G3 immediately!" the voice on the other end of the comm channel yelled in strident tones.

"I think that Chief Ren had better ease up," Chase said with a soft laugh. "He's gonna blow that vein in his forehead if he goes on much longer."

"Think they'll take shots at us?" Rika asked.

"Nah," Patty replied from her seat at the controls of the linked pinnaces. "We left the note for Ayer; she just has to manage the scene. You're a horrible murderer, Rika. Kidnapped me, too! I never knew you had such a dark side."

Rika shrugged. "What can I say? I like to get my way, even if it means murdering my teammates."

Leslie gave a short laugh. "You say that entirely too easily. I'm starting to wonder about you, Rika."

Rika scowled at her playfully. "If you weren't banging Chase and Barne on the side, none of this would ever have happened. You have no one to blame but yourself."

"I was just trying to work you up to a foursome," Chase said defensively. "I didn't expect to pay the ultimate price, just for a little tail."

Rika twisted around and looked at Leslie's ass. "She may have some sort of cat fetish going on, but I don't see a tail."

Leslie winked. "I won't lie, I've thought about getting one; it would be a pain in the armor, though. I'd have to coil it up on my back or something."

"I bet you could get a sheath for it," Patty said. "We have flexible casings for exposed conduit on some of the ships; the stuff is stronger than hull plating because of how it can move and transfer heat from energy beams."

Leslie raised a hand to her chin and stared pensively into the distance. "If we don't get fired…or court martialed…or have our skin torn off by the Old Man, I think that I may look into that. It could really help with balance when I'm racing across rooftops and stuff."

"In my little foursome fetish dream, you had ears too," Chase jibed with a mischievous grin. "Can't have a tail without ears."

"You know, Chase," Leslie turned to him with her brows raised and her hands on her hips. "You're entirely too vanilla for this crew; if we all make it back, you have to get some mods. You're into them—on Rika at least—it's time for you to put your skin where your eyes are."

Patty made a choking sound. "That was the worst adaptation of a metaphor I've ever heard, Leslie. Seriously. That sounds like he needs to have his skin put on Rika."

Leslie laughed. "Yeah, that needs some work," she admitted.

"Barne's not modded," Chase pointed out. "Why do I have to get changed up?"

"Barne? Seriously?" Leslie asked. "He has an artificial arm."

"Yeah, but it's just cause his organic one got shot off; it looks like a regular arm."

<You know that the bridge pickups are on, and I can hear you?> Barne interjected. *<I've got mods you've never dreamed of, Chase.>*

Chase coughed into his fist. "Uhh…not sure I want to know, now."

"Oh, wow!" Patty exclaimed emphatically.

"No, seriously, I don't want to know," Chase repeated.

"I'm not talking about Barne's wanker," Patty rushed on. "Either Ayer didn't get the message, or they're making it look good; they've sent two fighters to intercept."

"Well, pour it on," Leslie suggested.

Patty looked back, incredulous. "Leslie, seriously. I'm flying two pinnaces that are locked onto one another; do you really think I can outmaneuver a pair of HA-U8 fighters?"

Rika looked out of the cockpit's window at the looming shape of Chyso, the gas giant planet they were passing. "Lose 'em in the cloud tops?"

"Those fighters are more than capable of tracking us through the clouds…" Patty retorted, though her voice faded at the end.

"Unless…" She thought for another second. "Taking us in."

"*Romany* is joining the pursuit," Chase reported.

"Good," Patty replied. *<Everyone had better strap in.>*

Rika glanced at Leslie as they both settled into auxiliary seats in the cockpit and quickly pulled down the harnesses.

Leslie called up a holoprojection of the ship and space surrounding them, and Rika looked it over, wondering what Patty had in mind.

Chyso was a busy place, its orbital plane filled with moonlets, asteroids, and gas—nearly all of it being mined and harvested. The planet itself was rich in deuterium, and no fewer than seven orbital facilities worked to pull out the gas and sell it to starships.

The planet was also located 55 AU from the Scarborough System's star; currently passing a busy jump point.

This made for a mess to navigate through, but it also meant that the *Romany*'s fighters couldn't take long-range shots at the linked pinnaces without risk of hitting other ships or stations.

Rika could see that Patty was using that to her advantage and keeping as many civilians between them and the pursuing HA-U8 fighters as she could. Even so, the fighters were boosting hard, slowly closing the gap between the ships. They were not, however, breaking local speed and burn vector ordinances. If they continued to follow the rules, the pinnaces *should* reach the cloud tops first.

"They're totally letting us get away," Patty called out as she banked around a small moonlet, careful to keep her engine wash off the orbital plane.

"You sure about that?" Chase asked as one of the fighters flew right through a loose grouping of cargo haulers.

"Well, mostly. I know half those guys; they won't take a shot at us."

"Not even with Rika the Murderer aboard?" Leslie pressed.

<*Patty's a hostage,*> Barne reminded them. <*They won't make a kill shot while she's aboard.*>

Patty nodded, then qualified, "Well, unless they sent Ron. He's kinda pissed at me after the pot I won in a recent Snark game. I don't think he'd make a kill shot, but he might get a little excited."

<*I have their signatures and call signs. Ron's not there—it's Ally and Gemma.*>

"Oh, shoot. Ally's kinda pissed at me too. I borrowed one of her dresses and spilled red wine on it."

"Patty, seriously, do you make a point of pissing off all the other pilots?" Leslie demanded.

"I cleaned the dress; it's not like nano can't fix a wine stain. But Ally says 'it's the principle of the thing'."

"Shit, Ayer's on the horn," Chase cursed, turning to look back at Rika. "She doesn't sound happy at all."

Rika took the call and entered a virtual space in her mind where Ayer stood with her arms crossed, and a very real rage evident on her face.

"Rika, you are charged with murder and treason against the Marauders, as well as a dozen other violations of the military code of conduct we adhere to. You will cease burn and alter vector for escort back to the *Romany* immediately. Do I make myself clear?"

The scene Barne had created in Rika's quarters seemed to have been very convincing. When Rika had seen it for herself, she'd gagged at what had appeared to be several, fully dismembered bodies.

A brief fear flitted through Rika's mind that Ayer really *did* think she was guilty of the crime.

Barne had said that close examination—which the *Romany*'s forensics teams would be able to manage without trouble—would reveal that the bodies were fakes, comprised of cloned replacement limbs and banked blood to provide DNA evidence.

By now, Ayer had to know this. Her charges of murder meant she was going along with it—though the anger in her voice did not seem contrived.

"Do you think I'm going to come back to face your justice?" Rika retorted. "Chase called me 'meat', so I made him into meat. Barne and Leslie, too."

"You can't murder Marauders in cold blood and get away with it," Ayer spat. "We'll come after you, we'll find you, and when we do, you'd best hope the capture team kills you, because what the tribunal will order will be far worse."

"You gonna chip me again? That's what they were trying to do."

Ayer nodded once, her eyes cold. "If we have to."

"Enough," Rika said with finality. "I'm done with the Marauders. I'll find an outfit that really understands what I can do—one that appreciates me."

"Rika." Ayer's voice was dripping with acid. "You've become a monster. Only fools and other monsters will take you in now. This is your last chance; with a compliance chip, we can rehabilitate you."

There was a look in Ayer's eyes that Rika couldn't place. *Is that sorrow? Or just raw anger at my disobedience?*

"Never going to happen. I'll die before I get chipped again," Rika swore, the vehemence in her voice authentic even as she wondered at Ayer's meaning.

"We'll see," the captain replied. "Know this: I'll find you, and when I do, there will be hell to pay."

Rika cut the communication and considered what had just taken place.

There was more than one message hidden in those words. Ayer will come with the Marauders once Stavros is dead; she believes that Stavros will try to chip me if I act too boldly—he might do it anyway. Lastly, if Stavros catches on to me, I may want to consider death over capture.

The virtual space disappeared from around her, and Rika looked around at the cockpit once more. She had made the conversation available to the team, and they too were contemplating Ayer's words.

"Does that mean she thinks we can do it?" Chase wondered, "Or that we're going to get our assess handed to us?"

"I don't think she's certain one way or the other," Leslie guessed. "But the Marauders will have our backs, either way."

Rika looked at their position and saw that they were just a few thousand kilometers from Chyso's cloud tops now. She silently counted down from ten; when she hit two, they dropped into the upper strata of the gas giant.

Patty continued to dive deeper, passing bulbous cumulus clouds, until they hit the planet's 'deck'. There, the gas changed from atmosphere to something much closer to ocean.

The pinnaces began to shudder as the grav fields' dampening motion struggled to compensate.

"Patty, is this necessary?" Chase asked, his voice carrying a nervous lilt.

"Yeah…it seems excessive," Leslie added.

"You want it to look good, right?" Patty reasoned. "We're within tolerances…barely."

They stayed in the cloud soup for another three minutes—then Patty pulled out, and the shuddering ceased. Rika breathed a sigh of relief as they soared through the upper levels of the planet's cloud cover. A minute later, they were back in space; their scan showing no sign of either the *Romany,* or the two fighters.

"Well done, Patty," Chase appraised. "You timed it just right. They're still on the far side."

"We slowed down below the deck; they came all the way around and passed us overhead. I have a clear shot to the jump point, now. They won't catch us unless they fire RMs up our asses."

Rika leaned back.

We did it; we're clear.

Which was, of course, the easy part.

A NEW TEAMMATE

STELLAR DATE: 03.14.8949 (Adjusted Years)
LOCATION: The Isthmus, Sparta
REGION: Peloponnese System, Politica, Praesepe Cluster

"You've lost your mind, Barne," Rika pronounced in disgust. "What in the stars were you thinking, bringing her along? She outed us to Captain Sarn!"

<In my defense, you were hacking my ship,> Niki replied. *<I was just making sure we didn't get blown out of the black.>*

To say Rika was a little surprised when Barne revealed the 'something extra' he had brought along would be an understatement. She had no idea how he had smuggled the AI from the *Persephone Jones* along for the trip, let alone convinced her to help.

Help that seems all too suspicious.

"Explain this to me again from the start," Rika ordered, ignoring Niki's statement. "You were talking with this AI the entire time we were flying back to the *Romany*?"

The look on Barne's face indicated that he had not expected this sort of reaction from Rika. He even looked a little scared.

"Well…it's not often one has a couple of weeks to spend with an AI. She was going nuts without stimuli, and I was curious how a ship like the *Jones* ended up with an L3 AI."

<Stole me, that's how,> Niki informed them in disgust. *<Their jacked up system was built to shackle AI, too. You have no idea what a bad egg Captain Sarn really is.>*

"So you guys just hit it off?" Rika asked testily. "Started having a little tête-à-tête?"

"Rika, seriously, there's nothing in the regs that says I shouldn't have done what I did," Barne retorted.

"You need to do a bit of rereading," Rika countered. "You can't introduce new variables like that into an op that's underway. I'm your CO; you have to run shit like this past me."

"She's sentient, Rika," Barne argued. "Not an NSAI. You can't leave a sentient being cooped up like that; there are laws."

Rika shrugged. "Doesn't change the fact that you're supposed to clear stuff like this with me."

<Rika, I know you're upset with Barne. You're right; he should have cleared it with you.>

"Niki—" Barne began, but the AI shut him down.

<Barne, quiet. She's right. You screwed up, and it's making this more difficult.>

Barne folded his arms and glared at the AI core that was sitting atop the pedestal on the galley table. "Fine."

<By your laws, Rika—Marauder, as well as Septhian and Theban—I'm a free being. I'm not accused of any crimes—your Marauders have cleared me of any wrongdoing. I'm here of my own free will to help you.>

"Why?" Rika demanded.

<Because Stavros has killed many of my people. He's not a big fan of free AIs. If you're going to take him down, I can help.>

"How's that?" Rika asked, still unconvinced.

<Well, if you're honest with yourself, you'll accept the fact that Stavros is going to put a compliance chip in you.>

"I can beat a chip," Rika replied dismissively.

"For a few minutes," Barne allowed. "Maybe long enough to take out Stavros; then what happens after that? You know the pain doesn't stop."

Rika nodded slowly, remembering her struggle against Cheri. She had killed the woman, but that had only made the Discipline from the compliance chip worse. If Stavros chipped her and she killed him, it would be suicide.

"What are you proposing?"

<You're one of the revised SMI-2 mechs,> Niki pointed out. *<You have a socket for an AI core. The earlier Mark 2's `didn't have them, and neither did the later ones—they never had cause to pair you with AI.>*

Barne nodded vigorously. "Niki can disable the Discipline, and Stavros's techs won't know to look for her. If you two are careful, she'll go undetected, and you can act with impunity."

Not suffering through Discipline to take out Stavros is an appealing idea; I'd also be operating on my own. Having an AI could be useful…

She tamped down her anger at Barne and considered it objectively.

"OK, say we do this. How does it go down?"

<*We need to know one another first,*> Niki explained. <*Join me in my mind.*>

"Why?" Rika asked.

<*Pairing with an AI—even one who isn't sharing skull-space with you—is a very intimate thing. We're going to be at the edge of one another's thoughts. To do this, we have to trust one another.*>

Barne nodded in encouragement. "I've spent weeks talking with her, Rika. Niki is good."

Rika shook her head and closed her eyes. "This is nuts." Then she took a deep breath and accepted the connection Niki was offering.

The room fell away, and Rika found herself in a shaded glade with tall trees, their boughs intertwining in a thick canopy above her and blocking out the sun and sky.

A babbling brook ran through the glade, and beside it rested a silver and blue sphinx. Her form was unexpected, but even with their limited interactions, Rika had to admit that it suited Niki.

She noticed wounds on Niki's forelegs, an affectation showing she had not yet recovered from her recent shackling on the *Persephone Jones*.

<*Well met, Rika,*> Niki welcomed her—her voice feminine, yet deep and resonant at the same time.

<*We've already met,*> Rika replied.

Niki nodded. <*True, but we didn't really start off well. And here, we are really meeting; not just exchanging words over a thin connection. You and I will be spending some time together. Are you certain that you are ready for it? I won't be* in *your mind, like with a proper AI pairing, but I will be very close to it. And I will be trusting you with my life.*>

Rika considered that and reached down to touch her

abdomen, where the AI socket lay behind a hidden panel. She would carry Niki within herself like a child in her womb.

The idea was surreal and a little disturbing.

<*You speak as though I've already agreed to this,*> Rika noted. <*I haven't, you know.*>

<*You're a creature of logic, Rika—well, as much as you can be. You know that I drastically increase your chances of success, specifically for achieving your primary goals.*>

Rika frowned at the sphinx and took a step closer to the brook. <*My goal is to kill Stavros. I can probably do that before he chips me.*>

<*Really?*> Niki asked. <*I'm not an idiot. Barne has filled me in on what happened back in Oran. You want to save Silva and the girl, Amy; you can't do that if you've died from Discipline. They are your primary objective. I help you save them, then we take out Stavros.*>

Rika shook her head. *Niki seems to know everything that's at stake. Still, the AI is right; she will be putting her life in my hands as much as I am mine in hers.*

She gazed at the implacable face of the sphinx.

I've gone through a lot worse to get a job done.

<*I don't know if I'm ready for it,*> Rika admitted honestly. <*Will you be able to control me?*>

<*Barne thinks so, yes.*>

<*Not through any fault of hers,*> Barne amended, his voice a disembodied presence in the quiet glade. <*It's just because that's how the military set you up. They valued AIs more than mechs, and wanted to give any AI within the best chance for self-preservation.*>

Rika recoiled at the possibility of Niki being able to control her body. She had spent so much of her life as a slave to the whims of others that to have this foreign being living within her having the ability to control her body was abhorrent.

<*I give you my word that I will not do it—not unless you give me explicit permission,*> Niki promised. <*I'm no soldier; you know best how to keep us both safe.*>

<*Your word?*> Rika repeated skeptically.

Stars, this is the stupidest thing I've ever done…

<*You don't know her,*> Barne interjected, <*But you can trust her. If you can't bring yourself to do that yet, then trust me.*>

<*If she gets me killed, I'm coming back to haunt you,*> she warned Barne privately.

<*Noted.*>

Rika *did* trust Barne; had done so with her life on many occasions. *But is he thinking clearly about this? I am going into hostile territory with a new team member. We have no rapport and no reason to believe that the other has our best interests at heart.*

However, Barne believed that she would need the AI to succeed, and logistics were his forte. The more Rika thought about the mission, the more she suspected he was right.

If I can't convince Silva to aid me, then a hit on Stavros will require a lot of dumb luck. An AI could improve my odds a lot.

<*Do you want to succeed?*> Barne asked, mirroring her thought process. <*If so, take Niki's help. She has her own reasons for hating Stavros and his Politica. She won't let you down. Plus, if you need to, you can disable her by shutting down your power. I've made sure that she can't override your control of those systems.*>

<*Barne, without power I can barely move.*>

Barne acknowledged this fact, nodding. <*I never said it was ideal.*>

<*OK,*> Rika said to Niki after a moment. <*Let's do this. I'm taking you at your word. But remember: Silva and Amy are as much our goal as Stavros. We ensure their safety before we take him out.*>

<*Understood,*> Niki agreed, nodding slowly. <*I'm having to trust you, too, you know. This goes both ways.*>

Rika smiled, hoping it appeared warm and not grim.

<*Barne, do it,*> she commanded.

Outside the glade, Rika was dimly aware of Barne opening the access port on her abdomen and removing one of her SC batteries to reveal the small AI core socket behind it. Then she felt him grasp her arm as he carefully set something inside.

An instant later the glade was gone, replaced by darkness. She was alone in the empty space, feeling nothingness beneath her.

<You don't spend a lot of time in virtual spaces, do you?> Niki's disembodied voice came to her.

The words didn't feel like they were passing over a distance, like they did when speaking over the Link or in a virtual space like Niki's glade. These words felt like they were in her mind, like she had thought them—though she could tell she hadn't. They were another's thoughts, but had still originated from within her.

<It'll take a moment to get used to,> Niki said gently. *<I've done this once before; you just need to focus on how I'm different from you, and the distinctions will grow clear.>*

<Why is it black and empty?> Rika asked, focusing again on her surroundings.

<Because this is a new place, and we have not yet furnished it. It's just like any other virtual space, except it's ours. No one else can see what we share here.>

Rika blinked, and a moment later, the space was a vast plain of waist-high grass, green and vibrant, waving in a light breeze. Overhead, a yellow sun shone, and white clouds drifted in a deep blue sky.

"I like it here," a voice opined, and Rika turned to see another mech—an SMI-2, just like her—standing in the grass. Her armor was an iridescent blue, and she wore no helmet. Her face was the same as the sphinx's in Niki's glade.

"It reminds me of home," Rika shared. "Well, what was once home. The world I grew up on is not habitable anymore."

Niki nodded slowly. "Your war did that to many worlds."

"Why are you a mech now?" Rika asked. "Why not appear here as you did in your glade?"

"Well," Niki reasoned with a wink, "you're a mech here, and I'm *in* a mech. It seemed fitting."

Rika looked down at herself and realized that she was fully armored—her right arm sported her GNR-41C, and a JE84 was on her back. Even in her mind, in this safe place, she was ready for battle.

It occurred to her that she should work on changing how she

perceived herself. Then again, she *was* speed, power, and certain death to her foes. *Would softening here weaken me in the real world?* In combat, there was no room for anything but the strongest possible application of force.

"What are you thinking?" Niki interrupted her thoughts.

"You don't know?" Rika asked, surprised. "I thought you'd be able to read my mind."

Niki shook her head. "No, I cannot. I have access to your bio stats; I can tell you're agitated and pensive, but I cannot read your thoughts. Direct access into another's mind without buffers and filters leads to madness; both our makers knew that and would not spend our sanity so readily."

Rika wanted to reply that she had no maker, that she had been born, but she knew that wasn't true. She really *had* come into being the day her assembler had put her together; everything before that was a dream.

"That's good," Rika replied with a wan smile. She tapped her head. "It's a mess up here."

"You organics usually are a bit of a jumble," Niki reconciled with a wink. "Not that you can help it; your neurons just connect haphazardly, all willy-nilly." Niki wiggled her fingers and grinned, and Rika gave a soft laugh.

This is going to be quite the experience, Rika decided. She was a woman wrapped in a machine, with another machine now inside her.

As long as it gets the job done. As long as I can save Silva, it will be worth it. Nearly anything will be worth it.

STAVROS

STELLAR DATE: 04.01.8949 (Adjusted Years)
LOCATION: Docking Bay #420-23A The Isthmus, Sparta
REGION: Peloponnese System, Politica, Praesepe Cluster

Rika checked herself over one last time, wanting to make a good impression when she met Stavros again. She had considered changing her appearance in some drastic way—adding spikes, or painting her armor red. Chase had joked about maybe adding a tail.

In the end, all she did was have Barne remove the Basilisk he had painted on her armor only half a year ago, returning her chest plate to its stock appearance.

Somehow that felt wrong, like she was erasing all her time with Basilisk.

Now, standing on the ramp of the pinnace as The Isthmus's docking systems lowered it onto a cradle, Rika felt very alone. More so than she'd expected.

To everyone around her, she was a murderer; a fugitive from the Marauders, and probably Thebes and Septhia, as well. Now she was entering into the lair of the dragon, intent on killing him.

That was the job, at least: kill Stavros.

<*You ready?*> Niki asked.

<*As much as I can be,*> Rika replied. <*It seemed like such a straightforward op on the trip over; now all I can do is think about all the things that can go wrong.*>

<*Not to mention that we only have three and a half days to fulfill our objective,*> Niki added.

Rika didn't need reminding.

Given how they'd parted at their last meeting, she couldn't come to Stavros first. Instead, she had traveled to meet with several other mercenary groups—all of which had turned her down.

Ayer and the Marauders had effectively spread the news about what Rika had done. She was unhireable.

Well, hopefully not *completely* unhireable.

<*Three days, easy,*> Rika lied, feeling the nerves in her stomach. <*Rescue Amy and Silva, kill Stavros, stop any of his cronies from taking control before the Marauder fleet arrives…it's kid stuff.*>

<*Good bluster,*> Niki complimented with a laugh.

Even after she killed Stavros, the Marauder fleet—hopefully bolstered by the Septhians—would have its work cut out for it. The Peloponnese System was The Politica's stronghold. A vast fleet protected it, easily five thousand ships strong, and The Isthmus was a thousand-kilometer station, bristling with particle beams and rail guns. It was also protected by dozens of other emplacements throughout the Sparta System, all ready to bring destruction to anyone who would risk an invasion.

<*So, you ready?*> Niki asked again. <*Loins girded, and all that?*>

Rika let a smile grace her lips. <*I don't have loins, you know that.*>

<*Well, you kinda do. I should know, I'm pretty much in them—which is strange.*>

Rika laughed aloud at that. Over the weeks of travel, she and Niki had grown quite attached to one another. The fact that Niki had a good sense of humor certainly helped; Rika was grateful that the AI was not quite as reserved as she had come off as at first—a front Niki admitted that she had put up out of uncertainty.

An AI feeling nervous and uncertain… Rika'd had no idea such a thing was even possible.

<*Loins or no, I'm ready,*> Rika announced. <*Remember, all connections go through me. They can't know you're in there.*>

<*Not my first op, dearie.*>

The pinnace finally settled into the cradle, and the panel above the ramp indicated that docking was complete. Rika hit the control to lower the pinnace's ramp and, when it finished descending, she strode down its length, ducking under the hull at the end to stand erect, confidently surveying the docking bay.

It was reminiscent of the one they had docked in back in the Oran System: clear of any other ships or crates, with no small number of soldiers arrayed before her ship.

Except this time, none of them were pointing guns at her.

At the base of the ramp stood Stavros, a broad smile stretched across his dark features.

"At last you come to me, Rika," he purred with his arms spread wide. "I've received reports of what happened with the Marauders; a most unfortunate business, that."

Rika nodded as she walked down the cradle's ramp and stopped a meter from Stavros, who was very nearly as tall as she was.

"Betrayal makes for unfortunate business. I have to admit, though, I'm surprised that you are willing to take me on; we did not part on good terms last time we spoke," she reminded him.

Stavros nodded. "Yes, our meeting was…terse. I'll admit that my emotions were running high that day. I was glad to see my daughter returned to me, and my gratitude for you rescuing her made me want to keep you around to protect her. Amy has spoken very highly of you—which is why I've kept the deaths of your teammates from her. I don't think she would be happy to learn that you killed her beloved Leslie."

Rika let out a relieved breath. She had been worried about that. If Stavros told Amy the cover story—which he seemed to believe—the girl would most likely have hated Rika with every fiber of her being.

Granted, Stavros was probably holding it in reserve to use against her at a later date.

"I appreciate that," Rika told him. "I trust Amy is well? Recovered from her ordeal?"

<Which was made far worse by the games he played,> Niki commented privately.

"She is," Stavros replied. "She has been asking after you and your team since you returned her to me. When I told her you were coming to stay with us, she was overjoyed."

"That's music to my ears," Rika replied.

Stavros nodded, still wearing his magnanimous smile. "Come, let us eat; we can discuss your terms and determine the best place for you within The Politica. I certainly have ideas, and I believe that once I've shared my vision with you, you'll be very excited about what we're doing in Praesepe."

Stavros turned and walked through the corridor formed by his soldiers, gesturing for Rika to follow him.

"Sounds interesting," Rika allowed as she fell in beside him. "I must admit that your approach to conquest is different. Many would say that you create the opportunity for rebellion when you leave core populations intact, as you did in Oran."

"It's an old strategy," Stavros explained. "Often it's referred to as 'Vichy Conquest', but it is far older than that. Ancient Rome on Earth was notorious for it. You defeat an enemy, but not completely; you let them form their own government and think that they are autonomous. All the while, their leaders know they are operating at your pleasure and keep the people in line—all for the crumbs you toss." He paused, and then summated, "So long as I create the impression that The Politica is operating in their best interests—which it is, of course—then the conquered stay in line."

Rika nodded as Stavros spoke, pretending she cared about how he operated. As far as she was concerned, everything about him was distasteful. That he based his method of conquest on some ancient fascist regime did not surprise her.

They reached the end of the rows of soldiers, and Rika noticed that four large men in heavy armor fell in behind them as they left the docking bay.

Stavros led her down a long corridor while talking about his various conquests and methods of keeping populations in line, providing asides about the art he had seized and the foods he had sampled in his many wars.

Rika listened well enough to make appropriate responses at

the right times. She asked questions once or twice, but most of her attention was on the other people they passed in the corridors of The Isthmus. They all wore the white uniform of The Politica, and every one of them stopped to salute Stavros as he strode by.

Most of their expressions were filled with a mixture of fear and respect, but every now and then, Rika caught a glint of hate. Not that this surprised her; Stavros was not native to any of the systems he had conquered. In fact, no one knew *where* he was from.

<*I think he's from Nietzsche,*> Niki made a guess.

<*Oh, yeah; why's that?*> Rika asked.

<*His attitudes seem Nietzschean, that's all,*> Niki replied.

<*I came to the same conclusion, except his use of mec—wait, how did you know I was thinking about where Stavros came from? I thought you couldn't read my mind.*>

<*I can't,*> Niki confirmed. <*But you know the space that's just for the two of us? Our vast prairie plain? You often speak there when you do not mean to, and you said something like, 'no one knows where he came from'.*>

<*Oh.*> Rika wondered what other thoughts she had let slip into that space. <*That's not exactly what I thought, though.*>

<*Probably not,*> Niki agreed. <*When we think—both humans and AIs—we do so in a sort of code. We use images, experiences, concepts; no one thinks all the words for things. That would be unbearably tedious.*>

Rika had never given much thought to the mechanics of her own thinking; it just *happened*. Pondering its nature wouldn't change how…or maybe it would. *Best not to examine the inner workings too much.*

<*Say 'serves them right', to Stavros, quick,*> Niki suggested abruptly.

Rika realized that she hadn't been paying any attention to Stavros's never-ending banter. "Serves them right," she parroted aloud.

Stavros turned his head and cocked an eyebrow before bursting out laughing and slapping her on the shoulder. "Oh, stars, Rika. You're my kinda girl. You and I are going to get on famously."

A minute later, Stavros stopped at a lift. They rode it up eighty-four decks before it finally let them out into a stark white corridor, where eight more of the heavily armed and armored soldiers waited in the passageway.

Stavros turned to Rika. "Now, I hope you can appreciate that one of the reasons I like you mechs so much is that you come with a very strong sense of loyalty, engineered right into you."

" 'Loyalty'?" Rika repeated, uncomfortable under the gaze of the twelve soldiers. *I can take out two, maybe three; but twelve? In these close quarters? I don't stand a chance.*

Stavros grinned; not a magnanimous, welcoming smile, but a possessive one, like he had just won a game. "Well, I suppose you call it 'Discipline'. But I like to think of it as 'enforced loyalty'. I never have to worry about you disobeying me, or operating in any way that's not in my best interests."

Rika swallowed. *Just as Ayer warned me.* She hadn't harbored any illusions that she could avoid a compliance chip, but she had not expected to get it so soon. Even though she knew she could best Discipline, and was secure in the knowledge that Niki could nullify it, the mental reaction of fear and subservience was still there—a muscle memory that was burned into her, after so many encounters with its crippling pain.

She gritted her teeth. *It will be horrible; it will be excruciating, but I can defeat it.*

"Cat got your tongue?" Stavros teased.

"You don't have to do this," Rika coaxed. "I came to you, remember? Freely."

Stavros shrugged. "Freely or no, all my mechs, and no small number of my soldiers, have been chipped. I demand loyalty. Utter loyalty. Did you ever wonder why you mechs did so well against the Nietzscheans? It wasn't because you were superior warriors. Hell, most of you had no idea what you were doing. It was because you feared Discipline more than you feared the enemy. The pain made you strong; you didn't see any reason to fear the Nietzscheans. They were nothing to you."

Rika couldn't disagree more. She had feared dying at the hands of the Nietzscheans every bit as much as from Discipline. She didn't want either. Nevertheless, there was no point in debating it with Stavros. Let him think he had it all figured out.

"What now?" Rika bit off the words.

"You already have the hardware; it won't take long to get you equipped, and then we can have that dinner."

"You eat with your slaves?" Rika questioned pointedly.

"Rika," Stavros said in an earnest voice. "You won't be a slave; you'll be a loyal ally. I will tell you all my plans so that you know whether or not what you're doing is in line with my vision. It will also ensure that the chip knows when to help you see the proper way forward.

<*Oh, he's clever,*> Niki commented. <*If you know his goals, it will make it harder for you to act against him. He's priming the Discipline system, though it's not that nuanced—at least, the system the Genevian military used wasn't. Maybe he's worked out a better way to interpret intention.*>

<*'Better'? Easy for you to say,*> Rika retorted. <*You're not the one who has to feel that pain.*>

<*Trust me, you won't feel a thing.*> Niki reminded her calmly. <*That's part of the setup for AIs in you mechs; they didn't want conflicting orders to cause problems. I'm positive I can completely nullify it.*>

<*You're sure?*> Rika asked, feeling far more nervous than she expected.

<*Of course, silly. Although…I should probably make it so you're aware of when the chip would Discipline you. Maybe I'll make it feel like a pinch on your butt.*>

<*Niki, seriously.*>

<*What? I* was *being serious. Would you prefer a pinch on your nipples? I understand some organics like that…*>

<*Niki!*>

Rika realized that Stavros was scowling at her.

"Oh, you were serious?" Rika asked him with a sweet smile. "Which way to the slave factory?"

Stavros shook his head and gestured down the hall. "It's going to be fun breaking you."

"It'll be fun watching you try," Rika quipped.

DINNER WITH A DICTATOR

STELLAR DATE: 04.01.8949 (Adjusted Years)
LOCATION: Basileus Residence, The Isthmus, Sparta
REGION: Peloponnese System, The Politica, Praesepe Cluster

"I must say," Stavros said as he reclined on a sofa in a lavish sitting room. "It's nice having a mech with a mouth; we can break bread together, behave like proper humans."

Rika nodded as she took a sip of her wine. Even though Niki could negate the compliance chip and its Discipline, just the thought of having the thing in her brought out a rage in Rika that she had not felt for some time.

Stavros seemed to sense it; his words were constantly on the edge of orders, casual statements that were almost directives.

He glanced at Silva, who stood against the wall on his right. "Not like Meat, there. She can't eat; well, not like a person, at least. Doesn't matter, though—she's very good at what she does. After seeing you, I was tempted to give her a face again, but decided against it. I don't want her to think she's anything more than a tool."

"You do realize that we hate being called 'meat', right?" Rika said in response. "It's not endearing."

Stavros leaned forward. "Oh, don't worry, Rika; I would never use that word to refer to you, or any other mech, for that matter. I respect you. You are a thing of beauty, both to the eyes and on the battlefield.

"Meat back there earned her name through some very disobedient actions. It was she who made me realize that I should only ever equate loyalty with Discipline."

"What did she do?" Rika wanted to know.

Stavros waved his hand dismissively and leaned back. "It is no concern of yours. Suffice it to say she knows her place now. But I wonder if you know yours.... Could you kill her? Another SMI-2 mech like yourself?"

As Stavros spoke, Rika realized he didn't know that Silva had revealed herself to her former teammate. Somehow, though she was battered and broken, Silva had managed to hide that fact.

He must know that we served together in the war. Stars, it was probably the reason he sought me out. That he hasn't revealed Silva's identity means that he is just holding onto it for when he thinks it will hurt me the most.

"I don't kill in cold blood," Rika stated firmly.

"Oh?" Stavros asked, raising his eyebrows. "And what of your precious Chase, Barne, and Leslie in the Marauders?"

Rika gave a predatory grin and leaned forward; a gesture she knew even Stavros would not be able dismiss with his blasé attitude. "That wasn't in cold blood. I tasted theirs that day; it was most certainly warm."

Stavros didn't reply for a moment, and Rika smiled at the brief look of uncertainty that crossed his face.

She took the opportunity to look around the room and stretched, thinking of ways to take out the eight guards. She was almost certain that if she made her move, Silva would not attack her.

Together we can defeat these guards, I know it. The real question is will Silva help, or will the Discipline keep her from coming to my aid?

Not that it mattered. She still had to wait three days before killing Stavros; *three days of listening to him blather on about how amazing he is, and how his logic is infallible.*

Stavros took a sip of his wine and stared at her over the rim of his glass with a look in his eyes that Rika did not like.

"Kill it," he ordered suddenly.

"Kill who?" Rika asked, feeling a pinch on her ass.

"Don't be coy with me," Stavros warned. "You know Discipline doesn't work like that. There is only one other thing that is killable in this room—Meat. Kill Meat."

Stavros leaned back to look at Silva. "Oh, and Meat? Don't move."

Silva hadn't moved a muscle the entire time she had been standing against the wall, but now she seemed to become even more still; like a statue of a mech, her death's head staring ahead into eternity.

The pinches on Rika's ass grew stronger, and she gritted her teeth, refusing to rise.

<Is this really necessary, Niki?>

<You need to know that it's getting more intense, yes.>

"Oh, you're a tough one," Stavros observed, appreciation in his voice. "Granted, you've been through a lot of this. Most *people* fold at the first hint of the kind of pain Discipline can impart."

"I served under a lot of assholes in the war," Rika said pointedly through clenched teeth.

"None like me, though," Stavros promised.

<OK, it's at the point that most people would be screaming or crying,> Niki warned.

Rika shook her head. *< I can take a lot, and he should know that. Pain is nothing.>*

<You need to react, or he'll think something is wrong.>

Suddenly Rika leapt to her feet, kicked the low table between her and Stavros out of the way—sending his wine and goblets across the room as she did so—soared over the sofa, and brought her GNR to bear on Silva, switching the weapon to fire projectile rounds at full automatic.

"STOP!" Stavros yelled, and Rika froze.

She slowly turned to look at him. Every one of his eight guards had their weapons raised and aimed at Rika, and she saw a brief flicker of fear in Stavros's eyes. Then he began to clap.

"You've quite the flare for the dramatic. Come sit with me."

Rika returned to her seat as a group of servants entered the room and began to clean up the mess that she had created.

"You didn't say how to kill her," Rika replied with a shrug as she sat back down.

"I also didn't tell you to smash my wine bottle against the wall," Stavros retorted. "But what's done is done. I'll have to remember your temper next time I give you an order like that."

"Give me legitimate targets and you won't need to rely on Discipline," Rika countered.

"You don't seem to understand your new place in the world," Stavros said menacingly, and Rika felt a wave of pinches on her ass. She grimaced in response.

<*We need a better way to do this,*> she said to Niki.

<*I think it works really well; you give a very credible response.*>

Stavros rose from his couch and stepped over a broken glass on the floor. "You'll do well to remember, Rika: my every word is the very definition of 'legitimate'."

Stavros began to unfasten his belt and Rika looked around the room at the other people present, all staring into space as Stavros approached her. He grabbed her by the hair and what happened next made Rika glad she could retreat to the place in her mind where cool breezes blew across the tall prairie grass.

*****

An hour later, after Stavros had taken what he wanted and sated himself, he dismissed both Rika and Silva, telling them to go clean up and charge themselves.

The two former members of Hammerfall walked out into the hall, and Rika spat on the bulkhead, wishing she could have taken one of the new bottles of wine the servants had brought in.

She reached out and touched Silva, placing a small batch of nanobots on her friend's arm. Silva turned her head to look at Rika, but didn't speak; she was likely under orders not to.

However, Rika didn't need Silva to speak. A minute later, as they stood on the lift, Niki indicated that the channel was established.

<*Silva,*> Rika ventured. <*Can you hear me?*>

<*Rika!*> Silva replied, her mental tone filled with anguish. <*What are you doing here? Why did you come? You don't think you can save me, do you? Rika, you must go!*>

Rika sent warmth and a feeling of support across the connection to Silva. <*I came here on a job: to kill Stavros. Though I do plan on saving you, too—and Amy, as well.*>

<*You what? Rika, he's chipped you; you can't defy his orders now. How are you going to kill Stavros while under Discipline?*>

Rika felt a surge of pity for Silva. *How has a woman who was once so strong, so capable, become so weak? How has Stavros broken her so completely?*

<*I told you,*> Rika said. <*I do not fear Discipline. I've defeated it before, I can do it again.*>

<*Are you not going to tell her about me?*> Niki asked privately.

<*No,*> Rika decided. <*For starters, I'm not sure that she wouldn't let her knowledge of you slip to Stavros. Secondly, I don't want her to think that I beat Discipline because I have you.*>

<*Well, you did beat it because you have me.*>

<*Not originally,*> Rika informed her.

Amazement emanated from Niki, and Rika turned her attention back to Silva, and to telling her story.

<*It was on a place named Pyra, in Thebes—I heard from Amy that you were there recently. While I was there, a rather unsavory woman got control of me, and ordered me to kill my team. I wouldn't do it; I killed her instead.*>

<*How?*> Silva whispered.

<*By letting my own feelings be stronger than the Discipline,*> Rika replied. <*You're stronger, too, I know it. I know you.*>

<*I'm not that woman anymore.*> Silva shrank back. <*Corporal Silva of team Hammerfall is dead. Now I'm just M—*>

Rika pushed Silva against the wall. <*Don't you say it! Don't you say that to me. You are Silva! You are the woman who saved me, and I'm going to save you. We're going to take Amy out of here, kill Stavros, and then we'll find your children.*>

Silva's head drooped, and her chest heaved. <*Save Amy; I'm not worth it, anymore. She can't know…*>

<*Can't know what?*> Rika pressed.

<*Rika, I found my kids. Well, I found the living one.*>

Rika took a step back, nearly colliding with a bewildered-looking man who was pushing a cart laden with food down the corridor.

"Sorry," Rika muttered. "Keep moving."

<Well, where is he or she?> Rika asked, remembering that Silva had borne two sons and a daughter.

<Rika. She's here; it's Amy.>

A soldier walked by, giving the two mechs a long look, and Rika grabbed Silva and propelled her down the corridor.

<How is Amy your daughter?> she demanded. *<She thinks Stavros is her father!>*

<That's because he is,> Silva admitted, her mental tone rife with sorrow. *<Before the war swept across everything, I traveled to Praesepe. I was in a club—one I got into based on my looks and lasciviousness—and I met a guy. I could tell he was important, and we danced the night away. That led to sex, and…well, that led to Amy.>*

Rika had no idea what to say—Silva had never shared those details during the war. Though, to be fair, they tried not to talk about the things they had lost; it had always hurt too much.

<How'd she end up here?> Rika asked after a moment.

<He found her after I was conscripted. I guess they had his DNA on record, and when the state reached out to the fathers of my children, they reached out to him. He came and took her.>

<Just her?> Rika asked, and Silva nodded.

<The others…it's just Amy. Do you get it now?> Silva begged.

Rika finally understood. *<That's why you came here. That's how he controls you…>*

<Yes.>

* * * * *

As the revelation sank in, Rika silently followed Silva down to the mech bay, where she and several other mechs assigned to Stavros's Residence 'lived'.

The room reminded Rika all too much of the mech bays on

Genevian warships. Mechracks, equipment storage, nutripaste stations; everything a mech needed to stay alive.

There were three other mechs in the bay when they entered—two AM-3s and an RR-3. All three were sitting at a table, playing what appeared to be some variation of Poker.

They were not wearing their helmets, and each had the same featureless face that Rika once had.

"Whoa," one of the AM-3s said, his voice coming from a speaker on his armor. "Who's the new girl?"

"Rika," Silva introduced her aloud, apparently able to speak here, with the other mechs. "She signed on today."

"Willingly?" the RR-3 asked.

"Something like that," Rika answered. "You three have names?"

"Aaron," the AM-3 who had spoken first said, and then pointed at the other AM-3. "That's John, but he doesn't talk."

"And I'm Wyona," the RR-3 chimed in. "Nice face you got there."

"Thanks," Rika said as she sat at the table next to Wyona.

"You the only other mechs here?" Rika asked.

Wyona shook her head. "No. Stavros has a couple hundred of us; we're just the only ones in this mech bay. As much as he likes having us around, he doesn't like having too many close by."

"Prefers his goons," Aaron grunted.

"Goons?" Rika echoed.

"The soldiers that were with him," Silva explained. "They're chipped too, but a bit easier to take down than we are. I guess he figures that if one of them goes rogue, the others can kill a squishie a lot faster than they could one of us."

Rika snorted at the word. None of the mechs in the Marauders used it; it wasn't the sort of term that helped teams bond. Though it was a lot nicer than 'meat'.

"You really joined The Politica of your own free will?" Wyona asked. "You realize that it's a life sentence; probably a death sentence, too."

"I'm pretty resilient," Rika allowed. "I take it that the three of you aren't willing members of Stavros's regime. And you can just question it like this?"

Aaron barked a laugh. "Well, we can't talk outside this room; not aloud, at least. But I don't think they actually listen to anything we say in here."

"Or they're just saving it all up to hang us with later," Silva suggested.

"How did you talk to me before?" Rika asked Silva. "Back on Kestry."

"Mission parameters," Silva stated with a shrug. "Hard to run a team if you can't talk. I took a few Discipline hits doing it, but nothing serious; though I guess you don't really care about that."

There was an edge to Silva's words, like she didn't believe that Rika could actually beat the compliance chip.

"Don't care about it?" Wyona asked, confused.

"Rika has beat Discipline," Silva explained, not quite matter-of-factly.

"Seriously?" Aaron said. "No one beats the big D."

Rika looked at him. "I found out that mechs did it during the war; not often, but it happened. The officers told us it couldn't be done in order to keep us in line. But it can. I have."

"Prove it," Wyona challenged.

"How?" Rika asked. "Should I blow something away?"

"Yeah, take out one of the charging stations," Aaron suggested with a grin.

Rika raised her GNR, aiming at the nearest charging station, and a flurry of pinches hit her.

"This one special to any of you? Do you want me to actually shoot it, or is my intention enough to prove it to you?"

The mechs looked impressed as Rika continued to hold her GNR level; even John was paying attention.

"No. Stop." Silva reached out and put her hand on Rika's gun. "I'm sorry, Rika. If you *can* beat Discipline, you can't tip your hand now. Besides, I saw you hold out for half a minute with

Stavros cranking it up on you. I know you can do it—I just don't want to admit that he's had me under his thumb for so long, when I could have broken free."

<*Even though they all think no one listens, is this wise?*> Rika checked in with Niki.

<*Don't worry. Barne hooked me up with a few of the Marauders' scrambling techniques. I think they're working,*> Niki replied.

<*'Think'?*>

<*Well, if the goon squad knocks down the door, we'll know.*>

Rika decided to brave it. Worst-case scenario, she'd have to kill Stavros now, and then rampage through his upper echelon; if she could convince the other mechs to join her, it would be a breeze.

"Well, it's not like it's easy," Rika said. "And even if you kill the person who has triggered your compliance chip, it doesn't stop the Discipline."

"Shit, really?" Silva asked. "Now I'm glad I didn't fight it."

"So how did you manage, then?" Aaron wanted to know.

"Someone else showed up with the codes," Rika admitted. "He shut it down after I killed the bitch who had cranked it up to eleven; it was sort of a complicated scenario. Then I got unchipped and everything—until this."

"Well, welcome to 'this'," Aaron concluded. "Stavros doesn't share the codes, so if you kill him, you're screwed."

"Yup," Wyona agreed with a winning smile. "Screwed just like the rest of us. Why don't we deal you in, and you can tell us all about what it's like on the outside these days?"

CRACKING THE CODE

STELLAR DATE: 04.02.8949 (Adjusted Years)
LOCATION: Mech Bay #3, The Isthmus, Sparta
REGION: Peloponnese System, The Politica, Praesepe Cluster

The other mechs had all racked themselves and were in enforced sleep cycles, but Rika still sat at the table, thinking about how to solve the problem the other mechs posed.

Or, at the very least, the problem Silva posed.

Chances were that when Rika went after Stavros, Silva would be nearby. He would use Discipline on her, and if Rika killed Stavros while Silva was in its throes, she might as well sentence her friend to death.

It was also likely that other mechs would be nearby. Aaron said that he and John often guarded Stavros.

She needed a way to counteract Discipline for all the mechs on The Isthmus.

<*You wouldn't happen to have a few hundred other AI friends out there?*> Rika asked Niki, her mouth twisted in a wry smile. <*We could just plop them into everyone, and then no more Discipline.*>

<*Not that I can get here in short order. Plus, most of these mechs can't take an AI; there's no override system built into their compliance setups.*>

Rika wondered who Niki was that she could draw in hundreds of other AIs to her cause. That thought led to another, and then something came to mind that she had been meaning to ask.

<*Niki, why is it that you ratted us out to Captain Sarn when we were on the* Persephone Jones*? You said you were there against your will…we could have been allies.*>

To her surprise, Niki laughed. <*It was a crazy gamble; one I still can't believe paid off. I had been trying to get off that ship for months. Problem was, Sarn didn't really deal with a lot of savory types; it would have been out of the frying pan and into the fire.>*

<I suppose I can see that,> Rika allowed.

<So when your team came aboard, I spotted an opportunity. I let Barne circumvent me, and then reported him to the captain after the fact. When the captain shifted to Kestry, your knowledge of me prompted your team to yank me so I couldn't cause more problems.>

<You played Barne?> Rika asked. *<Does he know that?>*

<No, and I'd appreciate it if you kept that to yourself. He has a fragile ego,> Niki replied.

<We talking about the same Barne? Nevermind. Wasn't there a risk that we'd just destroy you?>

<There was,> Niki granted. *<But I hoped that you weren't the sort to just kill a defenseless sentient. I made sure that Leslie could make it to me, and then before she yanked my core, I set a number of subroutines to run amok and kept the captain busy during your exit.>*

<Huh,> Rika grunted as she considered the implications. *<So you landed us on Kestry? Nice going.>*

<Well, it was the obvious choice. Sarn couldn't land on Baqara because of the inspections, and Kestry was nearby. I suppose, in hindsight, your friend Silva probably had a hand in orchestrating that bit—making sure we couldn't land on the moon.>

It made sense. Silva had needed a scenario she could control. Kestry Station would have been easier than the moon. It gave Rika hope. Though her old friend was worn down, she was still a smart woman and a cunning warrior. When the time came, she'd do the right thing.

Silva, please do the right thing.

<I've been examining how Stavros triggers Discipline,> Niki continued after a moment. *<I'd hoped that when he used it on you I could decrypt his codes and work out a way to stop it for all the mechs.>*

Rika hadn't even considered that possibility. *<I was just thinking if I could take him by surprise and kill him before he triggered it, we'd all be OK.>*

<I wouldn't count on that. There are failsafes, and I wouldn't put it past someone like Stavros to have a deadman's switch; he dies, then so do

all the mechs—plus his goons.>

<*Have you learned anything, then?*> Rika asked.

<*Well, the nano you dropped on Silva has led me to believe that each mech has a distinct code,*> Niki replied.

<*That sounds like a bad thing. Very much the opposite of good news.*>

<*I thought so, too, but then I realized that there's a common decryption key.*>

Rika gave a wan smile. <*A master access code. That sounds more like it. Now where would it be?*>

<*I have a suspicion.*>

Rika threw her head back and stared at the mech bay's overhead. <*Stars, Niki! You're killing me, here; spit it out.*>

<*I think it's built into Stavros's DNA.*>

<*How did you work this out?*> Rika asked.

<*Well, I ran a paternity test for Amy after Stavros…used you.*>

The memory triggered Rika's gag reflex. <*I think I need to rinse my mouth out a thousand times. Ugh. Does this mean you have a good sample for decryption?*>

<*Close. I need the other side of the system—the part that sends the right codes to the right mech.*>

<*Don't tell me it's some other bodily fluid.*>

<*No, that would be easier. It's his hair; those little curls are his transmitters. I would imagine that he has the biomarkers in the roots. That's how he decrypts and encrypts.*>

Rika rose from the bench and realized that there wasn't a sink in the mech bay. "Dammit, I really need a glass of water."

<*There's a crew galley down the corridor.*>

<*So I need to grab some of Stavros's hair…wish I'd known that earlier.*>

<*Well, not just any hair; it'll need to be the stuff on his head.*>

Rika paced back and forth across the room as she considered how she could get her hands on Stavros's hair—other than the obvious. <*Once I get it, how long will it take you to analyze it?*>

<*I won't be able to,*> Niki told her regretfully. <*I don't have the*

tools in here. You're going to need to get it to Barne when he arrives.>

<Shit, so I can't just yank out his hair and have the codes in short order?>

<No, it'll probably take a day. It'll have to be fresh, too; seal it up, once you get it. If he is using biotech, the markers will degrade quickly.>

Rika couldn't imagine any sure-fire way that she could get Stavros's hair, secure it against decay, *and* deliver it to Barne in short order without being ridiculously suspicious.

<I think I have an idea about how we can get it,> Niki said. *<But you're not going to like it.>*

<Niki, so far there's absofrickinlutely nothing *I like about this mission.>*

<Prepare to find a new cuss word.>

CATCHING SOME TAIL

STELLAR DATE: 03.29.8949 (Adjusted Years)
LOCATION: Jentoo Station, 75 AU from Peloponnese star
REGION: Peloponnese System, Politica, Praesepe Cluster

Four days earlier…

Chase was pouring a cup of coffee in the pinnace's small galley when Leslie walked in, returning from her visit to the mod-shop on Jentoo Station.

He gave Leslie an encouraging smile. "It looks good on you."

"Which: the tail, or the skimpy outfit?" Leslie asked with an uncertain smile.

"Pretty sure he meant the ears," Barne supplied as he walked past in the passageway.

"When we're done with this op, I'm getting this shit removed," Leslie said. "I really thought the tail would help with balance, but it's throwing me off instead. And the ears look stupid."

"You just have to get used to it," Chase coaxed. "And try not to hunch over; it doesn't look very attractive."

"Why, you…" Leslie muttered. "Why don't *you* try being the sexy performance artist for once?"

"You were the one who said you can sing *and* dance. I can't sing, and Barne can't do either; that puts you on the spot," Chase answered.

"I'll show you 'the spot'," Leslie grumbled as Patty walked into the room.

"Oh, wow! You look great, Leslie." Patty appraised her with a mischievous smile. "You never looked quite right before—like you were only halfway through a change. You should grow your hair into a mane too, get the sides removed. Or fur! Yeah, just go all fur."

Chase covered his mouth, uncertain if Patty was messing with

Leslie, but loving the look on the scout's face: it was pure horror.

Leslie shot Patty a dark look, and Chase realized something else was going on. <*Is this a fetish of hers or something?*> he sent privately to Patty.

<*Oh, yeah, totally. She confided it in me awhile back and swore me to secrecy.*>

Chase shook his head. <*You're not doing very good at the whole secrecy part.*>

<*Me? I didn't start this. It came up on its own,*> Patty replied innocently.

<*No, I'm pretty sure you started this. You suggested the tail.*>

<*No,*> Patty claimed. <*Get your memory checked. It was you.*>

<*Well, you still told me it was a thing for her when you weren't supposed to.*>

A look of consternation crossed Patty's face. <*Oh, yeah. Damn.*>

"No fur," Barne chimed in from the galley's entrance. "It gets stuck in your armor's actuators. It'll also chafe and wear off in spots."

Chase snorted. "If Rika were here she'd ask how you know so much about fur and armor, Barne, but I'm too nice for that."

"She could wear some sort of soft gel layer over top," Patty suggested.

"I'm right here!" Leslie loudly reminded them. "And I'm not getting fur."

"Shame," Patty sighed as she left the galley, slipping past Barne and turning back to grin at Leslie. "You'd look good in fur. *I'd* do you if you had fur."

Leslie carefully pulled her tail to the side and sat at the table, shaking her head. "What's gotten into her?"

Chase took a sip of his coffee. "Probably thinks we're not coming back from this one."

"Plus, she's totally into you," Barne stated. "Anyone with eyes can see that."

"She is?" Leslie asked. "I always.... Huh."

Chase hid his smirk behind his coffee cup. "For being the

sneaky scout on the team, you sure missed some pretty big signals, there."

Leslie put her elbows onto the table and lowered her face into her hands. "I was kinda occupied with Jerry, Chase…and then occupied with not having Jerry. I haven't been paying attention to who's been…" Leslie paused and gave a soft laugh. "Chasing my tail."

"There are so many delicious euphemisms in our future," Barne said conspiratorially, winking at Chase.

"Careful, big man," Leslie warned. "Or I'll tear your arm off and beat you with it."

"That's Rika's schtick," Barne replied. "You'll have to do something new, like whip me with your tail."

"Oh!" Chase exclaimed. "Now that would be cool. You should get it weaponized! Make it so that it can extend way longer, and then equip it with razor-edged spikes or something."

"Chase, seriously," Leslie voiced condescendingly, rolling her head to the side and peering up at him. "If I'm close enough to the enemy for that to work, I'll just be shot full of holes. We don't tend to fight unarmed opponents very often."

"Yeah, I suppose you're right," Chase agreed sounding disappointed.

<Ten minutes 'til we lift off,>

"So, you gonna wear that little two-piece dancer's outfit the whole trip to The Isthmus?" Barne asked Leslie.

"I guess," Leslie shrugged. "They didn't have time to give me a detachable tail, and I don't feel like cutting holes in my pants."

Barne grinned. "Sweet."

That was when Leslie threw the pepper grinder at him.

AMY

STELLAR DATE: 04.02.8949 (Adjusted Years)
LOCATION: Philip Kirkus Academy, The Isthmus, Sparta
REGION: Peloponnese System, Politica, Praesepe Cluster

"Amy," Rika whispered from a shadowed recess in the corridor.

The girl stopped and turned, looking about for the speaker.

"In here, Amy," Rika directed, reaching an arm out to beckon the girl closer.

"Rika?" Amy sounded confused. "What are you doing here? You left."

She had expected Stavros to have told Amy that she was on the Isthsmus. Just like him, lies and double-speak to play everyone off one another.

Rika was crouched down in a shadowed alcove, her armor's camouflage hiding her from the teachers and students at Amy's academy. As Amy drew closer, Rika could see that the girl was upset. "I did, but I came back. I came back for you."

Amy's eyes lit up. "You did? For me? Is it just you?"

"Right now it's just me, but the others will be along soon."

Amy looked back down the hall. "Are they coming here? To The Isthmus? How did you get into the Academy? If father finds you here, he'll be upset."

"That's a lot of questions, Amy." Rika reached out a hand and took the girl's. "It's OK. Your father knows I'm here; I'm working for him right now."

Amy snatched her hand back. "What? Why? You left me, Rika! You and Leslie and Patty, you all left me!"

"Hush, Amy," Rika soothed. "You're right, we did. But we had no choice; you must know that. Your father was going to win no matter what we did. But the moment we got back to our people, we started working on how to return for you."

"To do what?" Amy wanted to know. "Will you take me to your Marauders?"

Rika smiled and reached out to touch Amy's cheek. "Far better than that. I know where your mother is. Do you remember your mother?"

Amy's eyes filled with tears, and she nodded quickly. "I do...I was young, but I still remember her from before the war. Father has a picture of her too; he doesn't know, but I copied it. I always keep it close."

After a furtive glance up and down the corridor, Amy reached into her shirt and pulled out a small, rumpled picture. The image it portrayed was barely discernable anymore, but Rika could make out Silva, standing in the restaurant she had worked in before the war. Her two boys were on either side of her, and a young girl was in her arms—only one or two years old, but clearly Amy.

They all looked so happy; it broke Rika's heart to think of what had befallen the small family.

But that was her mission. To save what was left of it, and stop people like Stavros from destroying it any more.

"Where is she? Why hasn't she come for me?" Amy demanded.

"She's been trying," Rika promised. "I only learned where she was very recently. Soon I'll take you to her."

"But father..." Amy worried aloud, looking back into the corridor. "You can't just take me, he'll be very angry."

Rika grinned. "You got kidnapped not too long ago. It can happen again."

Amy nodded slowly, a sad but determined look in her eyes.

"I'm sorry I brought you back to your father. I couldn't stop it...I wanted to. But we're going to fix this; we'll make it right. Don't be sad."

"It's my fault," Amy said in a small voice. "I'm so used to not telling...maybe if I'd told you sooner—"

"No," Rika interrupted firmly. "This is *not* your fault—it's your father's fault. Now, I need you to do something for me. I need you to get one of your father's hairs. It has to be fresh, so get it from a comb or a brush after he gets ready in the morning. I need one with the root attached. You'll have to seal it up too; put it in something where air can't get to it."

"Like a little vial?"

"That would be perfect," Rika approved.

"What do you need it for?" Amy wondered.

"I'm going to free everyone he has enslaved," Rika revealed with a broad grin. "Can you meet me back here tomorrow? Around the same time?"

Amy nodded. "I can. I should go, though; I'm just supposed to be going to the bathroom. My instructor is going to wonder what's taking so long."

Rika nodded. "OK. I'll see you tomorrow. Stay safe."

LITTLE THIEF

STELLAR DATE: 04.02.8949 (Adjusted Years)
LOCATION: Basileus Residence, The Isthmus, Sparta
REGION: Peloponnese System, Politica, Praesepe Cluster

Amy had barely been able to concentrate for the rest of the day. Her instructor had scolded her twice for not paying attention, and then a third time for failing to understand the equations they were to practice.

She was lucky that her father was the basileus, or she may have gotten a beating. The instructors held a very firm belief that pain made the mind sharper.

It was not a belief that Amy agreed with, but no one really cared what she thought. Only her recent ordeal garnered her any reprieve. She had overheard one of her instructors commenting to another that it was too soon for her to be back in school, but her father wouldn't hear of any objections.

Amy wasn't certain why her father had pushed her back into school so soon. On the trip back to the Peloponnese system, he had coddled her and doted on her—but the moment they docked at The Isthmus, he behaved as though she was a nuisance. When he hit her and told her to leave him alone, she realized that nothing had changed. That nothing would ever change.

She had hoped that her kidnapping would make him love her more, and fix whatever it was that often made him so upset with her.

On the trip back, she'd thought it had. Or maybe it had just been hope. Now Amy knew better; her father just wanted her at his side because that was how things were *supposed* to be. It was because having a scion was expected.

Not because he wanted *her*.

It was a sobering thought for Amy; to realize that her father didn't really care about her. Maybe he didn't even like her.

Now she had to combine that realization with the knowledge that her mother was still out there, and that Rika had come to rescue her.

Amy couldn't help but wonder what her mother would think of her. Stavros was a cruel man, Amy understood that now—but had it made her bad, too? When he hit her the most recent time, Amy hadn't been sad—she had been angry. She'd wanted to hurt him back. Hurt him bad.

Does that make me just as bad as my father?

Amy sat on her large bed in her large room, surrounded by all of the toys and *things* a person could ever want. But none of it made her happy. Somehow it all felt like a cage.

She pulled out the picture of her mother and brothers and touched her mother's face.

"Oh, momma," she whispered. "I'm so sorry…please take me back. I'll do anything to come back to you. Anything." She said it again, repeating it like a prayer or a mantra, in the hopes that maybe—across all the space and stars—her mother would hear her and know that her daughter was alive.

Her father's boisterous voice echoed down the hallway outside her room, and Amy tucked the picture away. She knew that if he found her with it again, he would beat her like he had when he first learned of the picture.

Father had taken the picture from her then, torn it up, and burned it—he didn't know that she had made two copies. Amy guarded that second copy as though it was the most sacred object in the galaxy.

"Amy, there you are," he said when he stopped in her doorway. He didn't let her close the door unless she was changing, and even then he would open it to see what she was doing. She had taken to changing in the bathroom down the hall. At least he didn't burst in there.

"Hello, Father," Amy greeted, putting on her best smile. She had learned long ago that being happy around her father was best. If she was sad or grouchy, hoping for compassion, she often got something else.

She could see Mech C913—the one she liked to call 'Silver'—in the corridor behind her father. Silver had always been nice to Amy. Even though she couldn't speak—or wasn't allowed to, at least—Silver had shown kindness to Amy on many occasions.

Amy called her 'Silver' because Mech C913 reminded her of her mother just a bit. Some of her mannerisms seemed similar—or Amy liked to pretend they did. Sometimes Amy dreamed that Silver *was* her mother, come to watch over her.

But that was a horrible dream. Amy knew what her father did to the mechs, how he hurt them. She felt as much pity for Silver as she imagined Silver felt for her.

They were just two sad people trying to survive the stormy seas of her father's moods, as he tried to control everything around himself.

Stavros strode into her room now and stood at the foot of her bed, folding his arms as he stared down at her. "Your instructors at the academy told me you were distracted today. Not paying attention."

Amy sat up straight and looked her father in the eyes. He hated it when she didn't address him directly; another lesson he had taught her the hard way.

"I'm sorry, father. I have no excuse. I will do better tomorrow."

Stavros nodded slowly. "I'm sure you will." Then his hard expression softened, and he walked around her bed and sat beside her, placing a hand on her knee. "Are you still troubled by what happened? I'm working to find out who hired your captors; I won't stop until I've found them and killed them."

It occurred to Amy that something must be deeply wrong within her father if he thought that killing people, that *vengeance,* would fix anything. She had no idea what would fix how she felt, but she knew that killing people probably wasn't it.

At least there was now a light at the end of the tunnel, and that light was the woman in the picture she kept near her heart.

"Thank you, father. I'll sleep better, knowing that I'm safe."

Stavros gave her a sharp look. "That's right, you're safe now. I have my best protecting you. In fact, I've even hired Rika to ensure you stay safe."

Amy nodded absently, and then suddenly remembered she wasn't supposed to know that yet. "Rika? Rika who saved me? Really?"

Her falsified excitement seemed to convince her father, and Stavros nodded. "Yes, the same Rika. She's busy now, but I expect that she'll get to see you soon. Maybe tomorrow."

Amy nodded, the thought of seeing Rika the next day also on her mind. "Thank you, father."

She reached out to embrace him—a gesture that she rarely initiated anymore, but it seemed to please him, and he wrapped his arms around her.

"It's good to have everything back to normal; I'm glad to have you home again," he said.

Amy looked over her father's shoulder as they held one another and noticed that Silver had turned away; the skull painted on her helmet—which her father had made the mech adopt recently—was pointed down the hall.

Not that Silver could really look away. Amy had overheard some of her father's generals talking once about how all the mechs like Silver could never look away from anything. They saw all things at once, all the time.

Her father moved back, and Amy clamped her arms around him tighter, putting one hand on the back of his head.

"Amy, it's very nice that you don't want to let me go, but you must." With that, her father pushed away, and Amy's hand stuck for a moment in the short curls of his hair.

She pinched her fingers together, hoping she would manage to pull something free—worried that she would fail, but terrified she would succeed. When her father cried out, she knew she had been successful.

"Ow! Amy! What the fuck?"

The back of his hand collided with her cheek and sent her sprawling across her bed. Amy's eyes filled with tears at the sudden pain,; she thought she saw Silver step forward in the hall and then stop, her head twisted to the side like she'd been hit as well.

"Here we were having a nice moment, and you had to push it too far," Stavros scolded as he rose from her bed. "I was going to take you out tonight, but now you can spend it in your room. And your instructors had better tell me you were perfect after school tomorrow!"

He stormed out of the room, kicking the door wide as he left. Silver seemed to hesitate for a moment, until Stavros called out, "Meat!"

Long, gasping sobs wracked Amy's body as she sprawled atop her blankets, her face aching from the blow. As her father's angry footsteps faded, she quelled her cries and wiped her eyes with the back of her hand.

Once she could see, Amy examined what she held, still pinched between her fingers: three hairs. Two of which still had the root attached.

APPROACHING FATE

STELLAR DATE: 04.02.8949 (Adjusted Years)
LOCATION: Approaching The Isthmus, Sparta
REGION: Peloponnese System, Politica, Praesepe Cluster

Chase settled into the co-pilot's seat as the pinnace began its final approach to The Isthmus.

"Damn that thing is big," Chase commented as he surveyed the thousand-kilometer arch floating in space.

"Yeah, don't see a lot of stuff like that this far out from the core systems," Patty agreed with an appreciative nod. "From what I heard, the people in this system were going to build a ring around their planet—like old High Terra—but they ran out of funding after getting this much done."

"Seems like a bad omen," Chase considered. "High Terra was destroyed."

Patty shook her head. "You're getting it mixed up with Mars 1. *That* was destroyed, smashed down into Mars; High Terra is still there. It's where the capital of the AST is now."

Chase rubbed his chin. "Are you sure? I could have sworn I learned about this back in school. The Jovians dropped all manner of bombs on Luna, Earth, and High Terra. Destroyed them all."

"Where did you go to school? Daycare doesn't count." Patty qualified, giving Chase a dismayed look. Then she admitted, "Yeah, the Jovians did all that, but they didn't actually destroy Earth's ring. They even maintained it enough to keep it from falling apart. A few hundred years ago, they repaired it; fixed Earth up, too. It's a big garden world now."

"Well, yeah; I knew about Earth," Chase told her. "I guess I just got my ancient monuments confused. Not like I ever plan to go there."

"Really?" Patty asked as she altered vector to slot into the docking lane The Isthmus Space Traffic Control had sent. "I'd love to go see it. It's where we all came from, you know? Earth…Can you imagine? The only humans in the entire universe just down on one small planet. Sometimes I wonder what it would have been like. I would have been terrified; anything could have been out there, and they were so fragile."

Chase nodded in agreement. "Talk about putting all your eggs in one basket. Though turns out there was nothing to worry about. The whole galaxy is our oyster. That Fenny guy was right."

"Fermi," Patty corrected. "Seriously, did you go to school at all?"

"Well, my hometown was destroyed by Nietzscheans when I was twelve, but I managed to complete what I could in different refugee camps."

"Right," Patty said, then shook her head and sighed. "I forget how young some of you are sometimes. Anyway, we still don't know if the Fermi Paradox holds true—in its entirety, at least. Human expansion has just finally reached the edges of the Orion arm. We've explored…about nine, maybe ten billion cubic light years? The galaxy is twenty trillion in volume. We haven't seen one percent of one percent."

"Yeah, but we have scopes; a lot of scopes. We can see the whole galaxy," Chase replied. "There's nothing out there but stars and dust and gas."

"Dense nebulas are hard to see through—some impossible—and there's the galactic core's shadow. We can't see anything in the cone of the galaxy it occludes. You could hide one hundred human-sized civilizations out there."

Chase laughed. "You're starting to sound like one of those conspiracy theorists. There are alien civilizations all over—they're just hiding from us."

Patty shrugged in response. "Not saying there are, not saying there aren't. Just saying we don't have enough information to speak with certainty one way or the other."

"But which do *you* believe?" Chase asked.

Patty *hmmm*ed as she turned off the ship's grav-drive, letting

The Isthmus's docking systems take over.

"I'd like to believe that we're not alone. It's a comforting thought, wouldn't you say? But I fear we are. The only aliens humanity is ever going to meet will be ourselves as we evolve and change."

"So, all this? The entire universe, and it's just us?" Chase asked. "Seems like a big waste."

"Your statement assumes that there is some purpose that the universe was created for. If it's a random blob of energy that exploded in a big bang, then there is no purpose; the universe has no agency. We're just microbes that have managed to move from star to star."

"You have a way of making a person feel insignificant, Patty," Chase diagnosed as he gazed out at the stars of the Praesepe Cluster gleaming around them.

"Contemplation should always make you feel small," Patty replied. "Helps you know your place."

"Ha! Now you're the one assigning some sort of agency to the universe, like there's a grand purpose to all this. That would be necessary, for me to have 'a place'."

Patty looked at Chase, meeting his eyes; hers were filled with more sadness than he expected. "A grand purpose? I haven't found it. But wouldn't it be nice if there was some overarching design?"

The thought of some preordained plan filled Chase with anger. *Who would design a place filled with such pain and angst?* "I'd like to meet the designer; tell them what I think of their *great purpose*."

"Would you rather that you never had existed at all?" Patty proposed. "Should none of what humanity has done exist because we struggle, because there's suffering? Would the galaxy be better if we were wiped away?"

Chase didn't know how to reply to that. The idea of a galaxy without humanity's handprint was a sad one. To imagine all the stars that people lived around, the worlds they had made, the vibrancy that life brought…thinking about what it would be like if it never had happened—that felt sadder than all the evils that had befallen people through the ages.

" ' 'Tis better to have loved and lost than never to have loved at all'," Patty intoned.

Chase nodded silently. *That* he could understand. *Perhaps it applies to everything; it's the journey that matters, not the destination.*

Patty reached over and patted Chase's knee. "But buck up, Chase. Right now, we're going to do our own small part here; make the galaxy just that much better by taking out a slimeball like Stavros. Stop being so morose and get your game face on. We dock in nine minutes."

Chase gave a soft laugh, though it was not enough to dispel the melancholy that had settled over him. *Who was that last bit of Patty's rah-rah speech for? Me, or Patty?*

Probably a bit of both.

HANDOFF

STELLAR DATE: 04.03.8949 (Adjusted Years)
LOCATION: Philip Kirkus Academy, The Isthmus, Sparta
REGION: Peloponnese System, Politica, Praesepe Cluster

Amy had spent the following day trying as hard as humanly possible to pay attention to her teachers, but it hadn't gone well. She may as well have tried her hand at flying a starship, for all the success she had. It just wasn't happening.

Her instructors seemed to notice. When she asked to go to the restroom near the end of the afternoon's second class, her instructor nodded, but caught her arm as she passed.

"When you get back, you'd best finish those algebra problems perfectly, or I'll be speaking to your father after class."

Amy swallowed and nodded silently before walking as calmly as she could from the classroom into the hall. She turned left at the first intersection, and then right, striding down the long hall toward the bathroom. She kept her eyes staring straight ahead, but managed to peer into the dark alcove where Rika had hidden the day before.

As she approached, Amy noticed a small motion within and knew Rika was there waiting for her and the vial she clutched tightly.

Amy ducked into the alcove and saw Rika with a smile on her lips as she reached out for an embrace.

"Rika, I got it; I got the hair," Amy whispered, holding up the small vial in her hand.

"Excellent!" Rika cooed proudly as she took the vial. She slipped it into a crevice on her arm that closed up, secreting the container and its few precious hairs away. Then Rika's eyes narrowed, and she touched Amy's cheek, her cold steel fingers coarse against the girl's skin. "What happened? Are you OK?"

Amy flushed. "I'm fine, it's nothing. Don't worry."

"Amy," Rika's eyes were serious as she spoke in a level tone. "You don't need to hide anything from me; there is no shame in what happened. What someone else does *to* you is a reflection on them—not on you. Always remember that. Sometimes even we get hurt when we go on missions. It's never fun, but we take it, we get back up, and we carry on."

Amy nodded silently, tears welling up in her eyes. "But he's not a mission; he's my father. He's supposed to love me."

Rika pulled Amy in close, her body hard, but her cheek soft as it pressed against Amy's head. "I know. The ones we love are always the ones who can hurt us the most. It's just how we're made."

Amy looked up at Rika. "But I wasn't made, not like you. You're a mech. I'm a person."

She instantly regretted the words she'd chosen—they were wrong and she recognized her father in them, but she didn't know how to take them back. Instead, she pressed her face down into Rika's cold neck, hiding from the anger that was sure to come.

But it didn't come.

"I wasn't always like this," Rika told her quietly. "Once, not that long ago, in the grand scheme of things, I was a little girl like you. Just trying to understand how I fit into this mad universe—just like you are now. It's OK that you said the wrong thing, Amy. You know it hurt me, and you don't want to hurt me again, so you'll grow and get better. It's all that any of us can do."

"I'm sorry," Amy whispered. "Am I bad? Has he made me bad?"

Rika placed a hand on Amy's head and gently pulled it back so they could see one another's eyes. "No. He has *tried* to make you bad, and you have some bruises and scratches from it. But you are good. I would know; I've seen a lot of bad. When you see your mother again, and she wraps you in the best hug you've ever had, you'll know I'm not lying. You're a good girl, and no one else can change that about you. Do you understand?"

Amy wasn't sure if Rika was right about everything she had just said, but she really wanted her to be right. More than anything, she wanted Rika to be right.

"I understand," she said in a quiet voice.

"Good. Now, tomorrow night, make sure you go with your father; wherever he's going, try to be there with him. Things are going to get interesting."

Amy searched Rika's eyes for some further meaning. "Interesting? What do you mean?"

Rika patted Amy's head. "The good kind of interesting. Well…good for you and me. Bad for your father."

THE CLUB

STELLAR DATE: 04.03.8949 (Adjusted Years)
LOCATION: Politica Senior Officer's Club, The Isthmus, Sparta
REGION: Peloponnese System, The Politica, Praesepe Cluster

In Stavros's Politica, the officer's club was really that: a club. Not the crass sort of bumping and grinding club, with strobe lights and deafening music, but a refined sort of club, with round tables spread throughout the room, semi-circle booths in the corners, and a stage at one end that stood a meter off the floor.

The staff that served the officers all wore crisp, white jackets and fitted black pants. In the dimly lit room, they almost appeared to be floating torsos, carrying trays of food and drink.

Chase stood at the side of the stage, observing the crowd from the shadows, keeping an eye peeled for Stavros. He wished they could have used drones, but this room was filled with advanced counter-surveillance tech. Letting so much as a nanobot fall off his finger would get them all in a world of trouble.

He turned back to look at Leslie, who was getting ready for her performance.

The prosthetics Barne had applied to her face made her appear very different than the woman who had stood beside Rika when they had handed Amy over to her father; though she had also been wearing her helmet, if Chase recalled correctly.

That didn't mean that Stavros hadn't checked into Rika's team, though. He could still know what they all looked like.

Leslie's cheekbones had been raised, her mouth was poutier, and long, delicate whiskers now sprouted from beside her nose. Her skin glistened, smothered in a coating that would make her gleam under the club's lights.

"Stars, this brings back memories," Leslie sighed as she turned in front of the holomirror to examine herself from every angle. "I'm not sure if the outfit is ruining the look, or enhancing it."

Chase raised his eyebrows. To call the tiny dress that Leslie was wearing an 'outfit' seemed to be giving it too much credit.

"I don't know if I can comment on this. I'm biased," he said instead.

Leslie cast him a disparaging look. "Chase, with what we do for a living, do you really think that public nudity tips the scales at all? Maybe giving these stiffs a good show will make up for some of the shit we've done over the years."

"Is that how karma works?" Chase asked dryly.

"Leave the dress on," Barne grunted. "Leaves something to the imagination; that's always a good thing."

"Next time we do something like this, you're the dancing monkey," Leslie grumbled to Barne.

"We've been over this. I can't dance."

"Then you'd better learn."

The stage manager—a woman with a pinched-looking face, as though she was always smelling something foul—walked up to the trio.

"You're up after the emcee does his evening greetings," she reported. "He'll introduce you as 'The Stunning Lady Melody', and you'll go out and do your bit. Three songs—the ones you submitted to us, but with the changes we made, of course—and then you break. If the crowd calls for an encore, you do only one. Then half an hour, and another set. Am I clear?"

Leslie nodded. "Perfectly."

The stage manager walked away, and Barne gave a soft laugh. "I still think you should have gone with 'Meowlody'. Really own it."

"And here I thought you were the one advocating for some amount of subtlety," Leslie smirked.

The emcee's announcements were short, largely advocating a particular dish the chef had prepared and extolling the skills of the performers for the evening—of which there were only two, including Leslie. The other was a singer who was a regular at the officer's club.

When the introduction was done, the low sounds of a cello crept into the air, followed by a drumbeat. When the second stanza began, Leslie moved onto the stage.

'Moved' was the best word Chase could come up with. She didn't stroll, or slink; it was more like she was smoke. She drifted across the stage to the ancient-looking microphone that stood in the center, and stroked it like a lover's neck.

A moment later, she began to sing.

The first words of Leslie's song stilled the club, and all eyes turned to her. A hushed, palpable silence filled the room.

The only sounds were those of the drums, cello, and Leslie's voice, deeper and huskier than Chase had ever heard it. She sang of love, sorrow, loss, and rekindled romance, all the while sliding her hands, legs, and tail up and down the microphone stand—her sinuous motions and dulcet voice making every man and woman in the room envy that slim piece of metal, wanting to be it with every fiber of their being.

"I don't know if I can watch this," Chase said quietly to Barne. "I think of Leslie like a sister."

"You got a hot sister."

Chase shook his head and scanned the crowd, checking once more for Stavros, but came up empty. The dictator wasn't present, which was probably for the best. While Leslie's disguise *should* hold, there was no reason to put it to the test so soon.

In an ideal world, Stavros would never show up at all; this wasn't one of his usual nights for attending the club. With any luck, they'd never even see him again—alive, at least.

"I'm going to go for a stroll," Chase told Barne. "Get a feel for the area, see if I can find out where our friend might be."

Barne nodded. "Be back by the end of the second set."

Chase nodded and then walked through the backstage area, past the dressing rooms, and out into the side-corridor that ran between the officer's club and a series of baths and spas reserved for the upper ranks of The Politica's military.

He had to admit: Barne's idea to get in here and perform for

Stavros's cronies was a good plan. It allowed them to move about with relative impunity in an area they would never have been able to get to before.

The local nets didn't offer much information to anyone without clearance, but he did see mention of a restricted maintenance area five levels down, and decided it was just the sort of place for him to accidentally stumble into.

He turned into the larger corridor that ran through the officer's territory and walked toward the closest bank of lifts. Politica elite walked past in small groups, most talking seriously in low voices, though some groups were louder—one, comprised of majors and colonels, by their lapel insignia, appeared to be completely inebriated as they careened down the passageway.

Chase avoided them, not wanting any extra attention, and made it safely to the bank of lifts. None of the decks below were accessible to him, but a lieutenant pushed the down button as he approached, and Chase waited silently beside the woman for the next lift to arrive.

When it did, the lieutenant smartly stepped to the side, and Chase followed. To his surprise, the first person out was Silva, followed by Stavros, and then Rika.

It took Chase a moment to realize that the second mech was indeed Rika. Rather than her traditional helmet, she was wearing a Mark-2 model with a single eye painted on it. The baleful eye was wreathed in flame; an image Chase remembered seeing in the past, though he couldn't recall where. If it weren't for the GNR on her right arm and the distinctive dent on her left shoulder plate, he wouldn't have had any clue it was her at all.

Chase turned his head, not wanting to chance being recognized. The team's faked tokens and light prosthetics made them unremarkable to the security NSAI, but a sharp eye and keen mind often made connections machines did not.

Rika didn't so much as glance his way—not that he'd be able to tell if she had—but as she walked past, she reached out and shoved the waiting lieutenant back into the bulkhead.

Chase was surprised, but when Rika jerked her arm out, a small object flew toward him, which he deftly caught. The lieutenant stumbled and swore softly, not noticing the handoff that had occurred right in front of her.

Rika continued on her way, and, after a moment, the lieutenant walked into the lift muttering something rather unpleasant under her breath about mechs.

"You coming?" she asked sharply as Chase continued to stand in the corridor.

"Uh, no; I just realized that I need to go up, not down."

"Whatever," the woman sounded exasperated as the doors closed.

<*Barne,*> Chase called over the Link. <*I think the club is about to get an important visitor. I also got a present.*>

<*Is it wrapped?*> Barne replied.

<*Yeah, come around back.*>

<*Sure, just as soon as Leslie finishes this thing she's doing. I had no idea a person could bend like that—and I've seen a lot of bending.*>

Chase shook his head, somewhat dismayed that he was missing whatever was going on—though it was probably for the best.

He didn't look at what Rika had passed to him until he was back in the rear rooms of the club. When he opened his hand, he saw a small vial with two hairs in it, along with a small data chip.

He carefully opened the vial and shook the chip out, keeping his finger over the opening enough to hold the hairs in. The chip was a standard data packet, and he slid it into the small slot on his forearm.

<*Chase,*> Rika's voice came into his mind. <*Stavros has a lot more mechs than I thought. Maybe a thousand. He also has compliance chips in many of his soldiers. I can make the hit, but we need to ensure that they don't take us out before the Marauders and Septhians arrive—plus, I'm not leaving without Silva and Amy.*>

What's her plan? A thousand mechs tips the scales more than just a little.

<This chip has the encrypted signals that Stavros sends for Discipline. Niki thinks that the codes to crack them are in his DNA, and the decrypters are in his hairs—which are actually Link antennae. But we don't have the equipment to read the markers with enough fidelity to crack the code. I'm hoping Barne can unlock it and get me the access tokens to turn off the Discipline.

<Be careful, Chase. I miss you a lot.>

Chase confirmed that the data Barne would need was on the chip and looked at the hairs in the small vial. Those two small bits of biotech could save all the mechs on The Isthmus. He didn't know if it was possible, but for Rika's sake, they'd try.

<Whatcha got there?> Barne asked as he approached.

<Just the way to take out all of Stavros's mechs and a bunch of his soldiers,> Chase replied with a grin.

<Huh, almost worth missing what Leslie was about to do.>

<There's always the second act,> Chase offered.

Barne grinned. *<Proof that there is a god, and that he or she loves us.>*

THE NEW ACT

STELLAR DATE: 04.03.8949 (Adjusted Years)
LOCATION: Politica Senior Officer's Club, The Isthmus, Sparta
REGION: Peloponnese System, The Politica, Praesepe Cluster

Rika was surprised at how glad she had felt to see Chase. It had only been a couple of weeks since they'd parted ways, but it was the longest they had been apart since their reunion on Pyra in the ruins of Jersey City.

Running into him was pure serendipity. Rika had anticipated needing to hunt the crew down later in the evening to signal them for a dead drop pickup of the vial and its contents—but when she saw Chase, she chanced the handoff right then and there. Hopefully, the added time would help Barne get the job done. If anyone could pull off what they needed, it would be him.

<*Told you the handoff would be a breeze,*> Niki gloated as Rika followed Stavros toward the officer's club.

<*You realize that you saying it would be easy isn't what made it so, right?*> Rika asked.

Niki shrugged as she danced and twirled through the tall grass in their shared mental space. <*I like to think that the universe bends to my will.*>

<*I'm glad it doesn't. You'd turn us all into sphinxes; you have an unhealthy obsession with them.*>

<*I can't help it! They're so fierce and beautiful and fluffy. You'd make a great sphinx; with your limbs already lopped off, it wouldn't be too hard to turn you into one. If I could just hack Stavros's accounts, I could even commission someone to build the mods.*>

Rika was about to deliver a stinging retort to Niki when she realized the AI was joking. <*You really like pushing my buttons, don't you?*>

<*It's really…I don't want to say 'boring', because you may take that as in insult, but it's really boring in here. I can't go out on the nets on*

my own, and if I go through your Link, I have to be circumspect in what I do. Slowly plodding, query…wait…query…wait. It's really quite confining.>

Rika laughed quietly inside her new Mark-2 helmet—which was a very tight fit, now that she had a proper nose and ears again.

<You just have to manage for one more day. Then we do the hit and get the hell out of here.>

<Can't come soon enough. Call on me if you need me; I'm going to go catalogue all the molecules in your body.>

Rika wasn't sure if Niki was being serious or not, but decided not to ask. The AI had a habit of turning the most innocuous question or casual observation into a very long and distracting conversation.

Tonight, Rika needed to be on her game; not distracted by an AI's prattling.

Silva led the way through the wide doors of the officer's club and into the foyer, where the maître d' inclined his head respectfully.

"Basileus Stavros, a pleasure. We were not expecting you tonight."

"I had a change of plans," Stavros replied. "General Alexi also told me that there is a sight here to behold."

"Of course, sir." The maître d' turned and led them into the club. "A very impressive display of dance and song from a woman bearing the name Melody, if I'm not mistaken. Would you like to sit with the general?"

"No, a private table this evening," Stavros requested firmly. "I plan to have a chat with my new acquisition here."

"Of course, sir."

Stavros was seated at a semi-circular table near the back on a raised platform. It provided a clear line of sight above the heads of the other patrons to the stage at the far side of the room.

Silva took up a position at his side, and Stavros gestured for Rika to sit.

"Take off your helmet, Rika. It'll be nice to actually eat with one of you. Later we can put your mouth to other uses."

Rika grimaced at the memory, but understood that this was all part of Stavros's process. Break her down, build her up, break her down, build her up, until the first thing on her mind was fear of punishment for her mistakes, and expectation of reward for good behavior.

Not that it would work on her. Not this quickly, at least, and certainly not while Niki was present to protect her from the Discipline.

Rika pulled her helmet off and set it on the seat, looking out over the crowd with her own eyes, observing the generals and admirals and a hundred other officers.

Her GNR rested across her lap; one quick motion, and she could kill half the men and women in here. It would only take five shots from her electron beam to wipe out a good portion of The Politica's elite. Why Stavros had come here tonight and not tomorrow—his customary day—was beyond her.

Despite Rika's desire to end the charade, she had to wait for Barne's results. There was also the matter of the inbound fleets; if they came in on schedule, they wouldn't arrive for another twenty hours.

Rika would just have to grit her teeth and suffer through another day of this human refuse's presence. *I've been through worse. I can manage this. One more day.*

"What do you eat, Rika?" Stavros asked. "When you can have anything, that is."

"I'm partial to cheeseburgers," Rika replied. "Angus, medium, sharp cheese, and spicy."

"Ah, well then, I recommend the Galactic South. It's a staple here at the club. I believe I'll have the seared tuna; it's a fresh catch from the planet every day, you know."

"How wonderful for you," Rika replied, and received a pinch for her sass.

"It is, yes. It's good to be in charge. You wouldn't know that, of course; you've never been in charge of anything."

Rika ignored his comment as their waitress approached the table. After a nervous titter, she began to rattle off the chef's specials, before Stavros stopped her with a wave of his hand.

"I don't care what he's made that he thinks is 'extra especial' today. Bring my usual wine, and the tuna just the way I like it. Rika here will have the Galactic South Burger. Medium."

The waitress didn't even glance at Rika as she nodded and rushed off.

"She should know better by now," Stavros muttered.

Rika was about to come to the waitress's defense when the emcee strode onto the stage and announced the return of 'The Stunning Lady Melody'.

He walked off as a saxophone began to play, and then a jet-black woman with a cat's tail, ears, and…whiskers?...danced her way across the stage. Rika's visual scan couldn't get a direct match to Leslie, but there was no way it was anyone else.

Is this how they got so close? Booking a performance at the officer's club?

Leslie began to sing, and Rika's jaw dropped. She had no idea that her team's scout could make such an amazing sound. Her voice was beautiful, haunting, and mesmerizing all at once.

<*I'm impressed,*> Niki sounded surprised. <*I knew she was the act, but I figured she'd be just barely tolerable.*>

<*Why didn't you mention it?*> Rika demanded.

<*I figured that it would be a fun surprise for you.*>

<*Niki, no one likes surprises when they're on an op.*>

<*Really? Not even nice surprises?*> Niki pressed.

<*No, not even nice surprises,*> Rika confirmed.

<*Noted.*>

"She's something else," Stavros claimed, as the waitress returned and poured a splash of wine for Stavros to approve before she carefully added more to his goblet and then to Rika's.

"I'll admit, I'm impressed," Rika replied, echoing her AI's sentiment.

Following her statement, they sat in silence, sipping their wine and watching Leslie dance and twirl on the stage. She stood on only the toes of her right foot at one point, with her other leg bent backward until it touched the middle of her back.

Her tail flicked side to side, and she began to spin while singing. Then, in a move so fast Rika could barely discern it, she leapt into the air and landed on her other foot, not missing a beat, before sliding to the ground, laying prone for a moment, and then rising up on her finger tips, her legs pointed into the air.

Stars, she's wasted with us. This is what Leslie is meant to do. She's breathtaking.

"Now that is something you don't see every day," Stavros commented. "I just checked with the stage manager; there are no grav fields. She's doing that the old-fashioned way. Her voice alone would make her worth possessing, but this…this is something else."

<*Uh oh,*> Niki cautioned. <*I think Leslie is too good. I just picked up a call for increased security here at the club. Should I send an evac call to Chase and Barne?*>

Rika only had a moment to consider her options.

It would be better to have Leslie on the outside, not stuck in Stavros's bedroom as his latest plaything. But it's far too soon to blow our cover.

<*No, they have to keep playing their parts,*> she decided. <*If Stavros claims Leslie as some sort of trophy, Chase and Barne will need to lodge all the appropriate protests. If they bail now, he'll be suspicious, and that'll make everything a lot harder.*>

Leslie performed three songs, and then the crowd called for an encore. She sang another, one with a cello and drums, that a nearby patron said was the first she had performed earlier in the evening.

Rika had to admit: the song, music, and dance were all utterly intoxicating. If someone had told her that the club was using pheromones and subliminals to subvert her mind, she would have readily believed them.

She looked at Stavros, who was just as transfixed. He didn't even notice when his food was placed on the table before him.

Leslie tried to leave the stage after her encore performance, but the crowd rose up, demanding a second. The emcee came out and quelled the near riot, letting them know that the Lady Melody would do one last song, and then she would be joining Stavros at his table.

Rika saw several heads turn and direct reluctant gazes back at the basileus in resignation. She wondered how many of The Politica elite had set their sights on Leslie, only to have their hopes dashed when their leader laid his claim.

Leslie's final song was about a valiant but lonely hunter who crossed the stars in search of the most ferocious and elusive prey. Even though he gained joy in bringing down his targets, he felt empty afterward. And while he had many women, none of them brought him happiness. Then came his final hunt—which was for a woman—and with that woman, he fell in love.

Yet in the end, the hunter killed the woman he loved. He shot her one stormy night; his tears mixed with the rain as he pulled the trigger. As she died in his arms, she forgave him, admitting she knew that her end would come at his hands.

He was a hunter, after all, and she was his prey.

Rika saw more than one hard-bitten veteran wipe their cheeks as Leslie's song came to a conclusion. Rika glanced at Stavros, noting that even he seemed somewhat moved.

After the last notes of the song faded away, and the crowd had risen to its feet, cheering and praising Leslie's every virtue, she was escorted from the stage to Stavros's table.

Rika still had trouble reconciling the Lady Melody with Leslie. The tail and ears were only the beginning; everything about her, from her gait to the way she moved her hands as she walked, even the way her eyes shifted, her gaze roving across the room, seemed separate from the woman she had come to know.

Lady Melody/Leslie was unshod, and walked on the balls of

her feet across the club; her long, curved toenails clicking on the floor with each step. It was as though she were stalking Stavros—ready to attack the moment she was in range.

If it weren't for the fact that Rika had just seen Chase in the corridor, she would have strongly doubted that the woman approaching them now was Leslie.

But there was no chance of a coincidence that large.

She tore her gaze from Leslie and looked to Stavros. The hunger in his eyes was unmistakable, and Rika wondered how much further Leslie would be willing to go for this job.

"Lady Melody," Stavros greeted her once Leslie reached the table. "Please, sit with us, have a glass of wine."

"You're most gracious," Leslie purred as she draped her tail over her left arm and sat. "I trust that you enjoyed my performance?"

Stavros nodded. "It was truly inspired. We have many excellent singers in The Politica, but I do not know if any are quite so talented as you. I understand that you hail from Septhia."

Leslie nodded. "Only of late; I received my training in Ayrea, at the Academy of Terran Arts."

The waitress reappeared and poured a glass of wine for Leslie, which she swirled, smelled, and sipped with her pouting lips.

"You took to your studies with astute dedication, then," Stavros observed once she had set her glass down. "I would say that you are even more adept at them than your spycraft."

<Barne, Chase, RUN!> Rika cried out over the Link.

"My what?" Leslie asked, appearing genuinely surprised.

Stavros laughed. "Please. There is not a single thing about you that would have caused me to consider that you are working with Rika—though now I suspect that you're the same woman who came down the ramp with her when she returned my Amy to me.

"And yet, I am more than certain you are she. What you don't realize is that I studied Rika *extensively* before I sought her out. The Marauders keep secrets very well, so I know little about Rika's current team, but I do know what Rika did *before* she joined the Marauders."

"I don't know what you're referring to," Rika admitted cautiously, genuinely perplexed. "I was a mech in the Genevian military. This isn't a secret."

"Right," Stavros nodded. "However, afterward, you spent some time slinging cargo on Dekar Station in a place known as 'Hal's Hell'. The man we passed in the corridor earlier worked with you there. Chase, I believe his name was? So much for your murder spree, Rika. Pity. That was a big selling point."

"Shit," Rika muttered.

How long has Stavros been seeking after me? Is he this obsessed with all the mechs he hunts, or is there something special about Silva and me?

Stavros grunted a laugh. "I don't know what the two of you are playing at, but I think it will be fun to find out."

"If this is your way of attempting to become my patron, it won't work," Leslie said, still in character. "I am here under contract, as a guest, to perform for you and your officers. I do not know this mech, and I do not know Case, Dekar, or anything else you've gone on about."

Leslie made to rise, but Silva was there in an instant, her hand clamped around the slender woman's neck.

"Not too hard, Meat," Stavros requested. "She has a lot of singing to do for her supper. Take her to the lab and get her chipped."

Silva marched Leslie out of the club without hesitation, and Stavros turned to Rika. "Amy has always wanted a kitty; I think Lady Melody will make a fine pet for her. Once we trim those claws, of course."

"You're a fucking bastard," Rika growled at Stavros and felt a flurry of pinches dance across her body. She was tempted to ignore them, to kill Stavros here and now.

Thoughts of killing this man were almost a full-time job.

<Don't do it. You wouldn't make it off this level alive, and now you must rescue Leslie, as well,> Niki advised.

Rika knew Niki was right, but before she managed to fake the anguish she should be feeling, an explosion shook the club, and flames shot out across the stage.

<*Well, at least Barne and Chase have made their exit,*> Rika replied.

AFTERMATH

STELLAR DATE: 04.03.8949 (Adjusted Years)
LOCATION: Politica Senior Officer's Club, The Isthmus, Sparta
REGION: Peloponnese System, The Politica, Praesepe Cluster

"Think Patty got out safely?" Chase worried aloud as he followed Barne down a maintenance shaft near the club.

"Chase, seriously. What do you take me for? I told Patty to leave the pinnace a half hour before Leslie did her first set. She's been shopping on one of the upper concourses. I dropped a message for her to meet us at the secondary fallback point the moment you got the handoff from Rika."

Barne stopped at a narrow service platform, and Chase dropped down beside him. "You're a suspicious bastard, aren't you?" he noted conversationally.

"It's a survival trait," Barne replied. "Get ready to activate your fallback tokens. The moment we step out of this tunnel, we're Gerard and Simon; two traders who are scouting locations for a new warehouse and distribution chain."

"Got it," Chase acknowledged. "This skulking stuff really isn't my forte, you know."

Barne chuckled. "Yeah, I know."

It took them nearly an hour to reach the secondary fallback point. Barne insisted on stopping and researching several locations their pseudo shipping company would be interested in.

Chase spent more time than he should have worrying about Rika. Seeing her with Stavros, with that eye painted on her helmet…it was more than unnerving. He hoped that when she came back to him, she would be undamaged.

This sort of undercover operation had more than one type of risk.

When they arrived at the fallback, Chase was not surprised to see that it was a small storage facility in a less trafficked area of

The Isthmus. Barne's specialty.

Patty was already waiting for them, and stood up when they entered, a look of relief flooding her features.

"Stars, I was about to hit you up on the Link, but I didn't have your new tokens. You two worried me!"

"Was best that way," Barne explained. "We're here now, though."

"What's next?" Chase asked Barne, switching into damage control mode. "Do we get Leslie out?"

Patty's eyes widened. "What happened to Leslie?"

Barne shook his head. "She got caught; freeing her is Rika's job now. My job is to crack this encryption—which I hope I can do with this gear we shipped in ahead of time. Based on the Marauder and Septhian Fleet's ETA, I have seventeen hours to do it and get that data to Rika. You two have to secure us another ride off this thing, because you can bet they've impounded the pinnace by now."

"I kinda liked that ship," Patty sulked. "My squadron commander is gonna get pissed at how many ships I keep losing."

"Well, when we take down the entire Politica, I bet she'll forgive you," Chase offered. "Think of all the ships they have."

"That's the spirit!" Barne replied and slapped Chase on the back. "Now help me go through these crates. There's a quantum comp in here that should be able to churn through Stavros's encryption."

*****

Stavros walked through the ruins of the club's green room, kicking aside debris and muttering under his breath. They walked past the corpse of the stage manager, and the dictator turned to glared at Rika.

"Your friends are going to pay for this…starting with your cat girl. If singing is so important to her, maybe I'll start by cutting out her tongue; vocal chords, too. Then I'll deafen her. A life with no sound seems like a fitting punishment."

"I thought you were going to give her to Amy?" Rika asked, forcing her voice to come out calm and even. *I'm not going to let Stavros rile me up—that's just what he wants.*

The basileus chuckled. "I'll still do that. After I make it so that she can only make soft mewling sounds." His eyes narrowed, and he continued. "I know how I'll do it, too. Once her chip is in, and once I get a few more performances out of her, I'll make her cut out her own tongue and slice open her own throat. You know how much Discipline hurts; you can make a person do *anything*."

Rika shook her head and gave Stavros a patronizing smile. "You know, *real* leaders earn love from their people. It's a lot more powerful than fear."

"Says who?" Stavros snarled, and Rika felt her skin blaze from the pinches Niki delivered.

<*OK, I get it,*> Rika told her as she gave her best scream.

<*It's at near fatal levels; you need to react appropriately,*> Niki pushed.

Rika threw her head back and clawed at her face, tearing a pair of deep scratches down her cheeks. Then she bit her tongue and spat the blood out of her mouth.

The pinches stopped, and Rika fell to her knees surrounded by the piles of charred rubble. The corpse of some dancer was in front of her, and Rika found herself staring into the woman's dead eyes.

<*How many have we killed tonight?*> Rika wondered. <*What are we even doing?*>

<*Surviving,*> Niki answered gently.

"Look at me," Stavros growled.

Rika slowly raised her head to see a smarmy smile on Stavros's lips.

"I own you. I'm giving you the freedom of a face and speech because it amuses me. But what I give, I can take away; you'd do well to remember that."

Rika gave a defeated nod, doing her best to ignore the self-inflicted pain and the sorrow she felt for the dead woman in front of her.

<Maybe you shouldn't antagonize him so much,> Niki suggested quietly.

<He has to believe he's breaking me. If he's studied me as much as he claims, I can't make it seem easy.>

Stavros crouched beside Rika and grabbed her hair, pulling her head up to stare into her eyes. Rika met his gaze head-on, not bothering to hide her rage.

"What did you come here for?" he mused. "What did your little crew think you could do against me?"

Rika spat blood into Stavros's face, and he responded by driving his knee into the back of her head. He forced her down, confirming Rika's suspicion of his considerable muscular and skeletal enhancements.

Her face was pushed into the dead dancer's, and Rika felt the burned layers of the corpse's skin flake off. Some got into her mouth, mixing with blood and angry tears.

The intensity of the pinches signified crippling levels of Discipline, and Rika convulsed underneath Stavros as he screamed questions at her, asking what her real reason for coming to the Isthmus was.

Finally Rika moaned. "We came to rescue Silva and kill you."

Stavros lifted his knee off her neck and stood, dusting himself off. "Was that so hard, Rika? I knew it all along, of course. Did your precious General Mill of the Marauders ever tell you how good your record really was? Hammerfall was the best mech team in the Genevian armed forces, and I wanted the best. I got Silva, and I used her and her daughter to get you. Now I have the whole set."

"The whole set?" Rika repeated, confused at his statement.

"I really wanted to save this for the grand reveal later, but I'm going to tell you now, because I want you to understand how little hope you really have. I'm sure you remember Kelly? Part of your original team?"

Rika's mind reeled. *Kelly died. I watched her bleed out in the back of a GAF drop ship years ago…* She had never seen Kelly after that, and the records had shown her as KIA.

"You're confused," Stavros noted with a smug smile. "I get that. Don't worry; it's really quite simple. Toward the end of the war, the Genevians didn't have the resources to repair all their mechs in the field, so they cryofroze them and shipped them out to a centralized facility. Thing is, that facility didn't have the resources to repair the mechs, either—not once the Nietzscheans cut off their supply lines.

"The techs abandoned it, and there it sat—just another station drifting in the outer reaches of a devastated star system."

Stavros stopped his recitation to give a self-satisfied laugh, and then continued his monologue. "That is, until I found it. Unlike your makers, I had the resources to repair those mechs. That station is now here, in the Peloponnese System. With it, I have everything I need to build a full army of mechs; a military that will sweep across the Praesepe Cluster and beyond. You, Silva, and Kelly will be my vanguard. You're mine now, Rika. You, and everything you hold dear, are mine."

"Kelly," Rika whispered, unable to process what Stavros had told her—unwilling to believe it.

"Get up, Rika. You'll meet her soon enough," Stavros ordered. "Go clean yourself off and do whatever it is meat does when you're not being useful. I have work to do."

CONVICTION

STELLAR DATE: 04.03.8949 (Adjusted Years)
LOCATION: Politica Senior Officer's Club, The Isthmus, Sparta
REGION: Peloponnese System, The Politica, Praesepe Cluster

<*Where's this lab?*> Rika demanded from Niki once she left the club.

<*Do you want to talk about this?*> Niki ventured. <*I can tell it's traumatizing for you.*>

<*What's traumatizing is how Leslie is going to feel with a chip in her head,*> Rika barked. <*Do you know where the lab is?*>

<*Yes, it's one level below where your mech bay is—but it's a secured facility.*>

Rika arrived at the bank of lifts and sent a command to summon a car down. <*This whole place is a secured facility; there has to be a way in.*>

<*What are you going to do? It's not like you can just stop them; that would tip your hand that I'm here and rendering the Discipline ineffective.*>

The doors of one of the lift cars opened, and Rika stepped in. The rage on her face, combined with the blood and filth, kept any other passengers from joining her.

She slammed a fist into the wall after the doors closed and let out a bloodcurdling scream.

Niki was right. *I can't stop what they are going to do to Leslie. Not yet, anyway…*

<*I feel so helpless, Niki. That bastard just gets to do whatever he wants?!*>

<*Not for long. You realize that this is why people shouldn't take missions that are so personal, right? It's too easy to feel like everything is your fault.*>

Rika bit back a response. She knew Niki was trying to help—and she was right—but it didn't make her feel better right now.

In the end, Rika stopped at a restroom on the same floor as the mech bay and washed her face. Once the dead dancer's remains and her own blood were scrubbed away, she returned to the mech bay—which was currently empty—and gave the autodoc a long look.

Stavros would expect to see her lacerated face repaired by morning, but the autodoc's standard procedure would be to pull off her limbs while it ran a full diagnostic.

<It'll detect you, won't it?> Rika asked Niki.

<I believe it will. You were rather rash in clawing at your face,> Niki scolded.

<It seemed like the right thing to do at the time. You told me the pain was near-fatal,> Rika replied defensively.

<There were other things you could have done,> pressed Niki.

"So autodoc's out. Options, options…" Rika muttered aloud.

The bay contained everything a platoon of mechs would ever need: mech-racks, weapons, supplies, nutripaste, field kits…

Field kits!

Rika strode over to the racks where the field kits lay and searched through them. Most were for armor and structural repair.

There have to be some subdermal repair kits for musculature… Rika remembered a medic back in the war saying that the kits were the same ones used for skin repair, just more powerful.

After rifling through all the kits, Rika finally found one with subdermal meshes. She grabbed a package, carefully peeled off the backing, and took a deep breath.

"Here goes nothing," she braced herself and slapped it on her cheek.

Searing pain tore through her face, and she realized why these kits weren't normally used on parts of the body with so many nerve endings.

The pain abated, and Rika was wondering if the kit had already done its job when Niki spoke up.

<You're welcome.>

Rika blushed. She hadn't even thought to ask for Niki's help with the pain.

<*Thanks, Niki.*>

She did her best to ignore the unpleasant—though now painless— sensation of the patch stitching her cheek back together.

She busied herself with cleaning up the mess she'd made rifling through all the field kits. Then she poured herself a glass of water from the bottles she had secured the night before and rinsed out her mouth a few times before resigning herself to the fact that there was nothing to be done for her swollen tongue for the time being.

Just like the bay didn't stock water, it also didn't have any real food—Rika was the only one operating out of the bay who had a mouth. She couldn't go down to the level's galley with the patch on her face, so she sat at the table with the feeder tubes, and hooked one up to the port on her stomach.

It had been some time since Rika had taken in sustenance through the port, and her stomach grumbled as the feeding system filled it past full.

"Dumb thing needs an off switch," Rika griped and clenched her stomach muscles. The feeder detected max pressure and stopped, detaching from the port on her stomach.

"Surprised you still kept the port," Aaron commented upon entering the mech bay and seeing Rika replacing the access plate on her armor.

"Back when I was on Dekar, all I could afford some days was paste. Better to put it in that way than down the throat; you have no idea how bad it tastes."

Aaron chuckled. "The one reason to be glad to not have a mouth."

"Hey, so I learned that Stavros found a lot of his mechs in some repair facility that the GAF abandoned. Is that true?" Rika asked.

Aaron nodded as he walked to one of the mech-racks and

backed toward it. "Yeah. I wasn't one of those, though. I got picked up by a recruiter that was a bit misleading about what I was getting into."

"I had a number of offers like that," Rika empathized. *Hell, that's nearly how I got into this whole lifestyle.*

"Scuttlebutt says you were with the Marauders," Aaron shared as the rack's automated systems detached his legs.

"Yeah, I got picked up at auction."

"Auction? That's rough."

"Why are you racking?" Rika asked as she watched the armatures pull off Aaron's arms and set them aside.

He gave a resigned sigh. "One of the lieutenants at the Residence got pissed at me and told me to go rack myself. It's sort of his go-to insult for us. Added benefit for him is how we actually have to go do it."

It broke Rika's heart to see Aaron so accepting of his fate. He was completely broken; so used to following orders without question that he never even tried to fight them anymore. He was just a shell. He really had become nothing more than the meat in the machine.

"Aaron," Rika sighed. "Get off the rack."

The system had removed his helmet, and Rika could make out a crease on his forehead as he frowned. "What are you talking about, Rika? I have orders. I have to follow them."

Rika felt something break inside herself—or maybe it was something snapping into place. Either way, she realized there was more for her to do here than to just rescue a few people and kill a dictator.

She rose from her seat and walked across the bay to where Aaron hung from the hard points on his back. Rika stared into his eyes; the sad eyes of a defeated man.

"What are you, Aaron?" she asked, her tone soft.

Without the speaker on his armor, Aaron had no way to give an audible reply.

<*I'm an AM-3 Mech,*> Aaron intoned over the Link, his eyes

appearing confused.

"Are you a machine?" Rika pressed. "Or do you have a soul?"

<*Rika, what–*>

Rika didn't find out what Aaron was going to ask, because she took a step back and punched him in the face. It wasn't hard enough to break anything or split apart his pseudo skin, but she knew it hurt.

She drew close to him, her nose touching the small lump on his face that was all that remained of his. "How does that make you feel? *Do* you feel? What are you, Aaron?"

<*Rika, stop! I don't understand!*>

Rika jammed her finger into his chest. "Is there a heart in here? Does it still beat, or did they take that out too, along with your spirit?"

<*Rika, I…I don't know anymore.*> He sounded lost, frail.

"Being a mech isn't shame," Rika reminded him, her voice filled with both rage and pride. "It's not weakness. It is strength and power! We are what they cannot be. We are the best of the best—but only if we choose it. Right now, you're nothing but what they tell you. Your worth is no more than a tool in a fool's hand. Is that what you want to be forever? Are you happy being someone's wrench?"

<*No…*> Aaron whispered.

Rika's arm shot out, and she grabbed Aaron's shoulder. "Then don't be! You're a man; a strong, powerful man. You have the will to fight, now use it! Get. Off. The. Rack!"

Aaron's eyes narrowed, and Rika thought she saw a bit of fire behind them. *Not enough.*

<*But the orders, Rika. The Discipline.*>

"I know you're a cunning warrior, because you've survived this long," Rika reasoned. "But you've forgotten how to use your mind. You've allowed yourself to relax into being a slave. Did the lieutenant order you to spend the rest of your life on the rack?"

<*Well, no…*>

"Is it time for your designated charge cycle? Do you need

repairs?"

<*No…*>

Rika leaned forward, pressing her forehead against Aaron's, letting her long blonde hair fall around them. In the shrouded light, all she could see were his eyes.

Her voice was low and hoarse. "You're a free man if you want to be. Now get off the rack."

Rika stepped back and stared at Aaron, her jaw set, and her eyes narrowed. Aaron had to get off the rack. She needed to see it as much as he needed to do it. Somehow, she felt responsible for the mechs under Stavros's control. There was no other option. She had to free them all.

Aaron's eyes narrowed in return, and he slammed his head back against the support bar. The automated system began to put his limbs back on—first his legs, and then his arms. A minute later, Aaron stepped off the rack.

"Feels good, doesn't it?" Rika prompted quietly. "You're nobody's slave."

"What does it matter?" Aaron demanded, now that he had his voice back. "This doesn't change anything. It's a loophole."

Rika took a step forward and placed a hand on Aaron's shoulder. "They've grown lax in how they use Discipline; they don't understand it like the GAF did. They use it to punish, but they are not specific in their commands. Discipline uses *your* belief of whether or not you're following orders as much as anything else."

"Still, they can punish us if they want," Aaron argued.

"Well, tomorrow it ends," Rika stated firmly, then switched to the direct Link that Niki had facilitated through their touch. <*Tomorrow night, I kill Stavros, and all this ends.*>

<*What do you mean?*> Aaron asked.

<*This is the last night of The Politica. Tomorrow it burns,*> Rika concluded. <*Come, we have to get everyone ready.*>

THE STORM BEFORE

STELLAR DATE: 04.04.8949 (Adjusted Years)
LOCATION: Basileus Residence, The Isthmus, Sparta
REGION: Peloponnese System, The Politica, Praesepe Cluster

When Rika walked into the Residence's private lounge, Leslie was already there. Rika bit her cheek to keep from saying anything as she took in the vision of her teammate and friend.

It was now clearly Leslie standing at the far end of the room; the prosthetics on her face had been removed, though the ears and tail remained. Around her neck was a gleaming silver collar, with a chain stretching between it and a ring that was set into the floor. Matching cuffs were around her wrists and ankles, and she still wore the black dress from the night before.

Despite her circumstances, Leslie stood ramrod straight. Her eyes were bright and hard. A pair of Stavros's goons stood on either side of her, and an AM-3 mech beside each of them—*Aaron and John,* Rika realized as she approached her friend.

"Don't look so sad, Rika," Leslie said with a sly smile. "I've been through worse than whatever Stavros can throw at us."

Rika glanced down at the chain running from Leslie's neck to the floor. "Really? Worse than this, with a compliance chip in your head?"

Leslie shrugged. "I've been around a long time, Rika. If you take the chip out of the equation, this is the third time I've been in this exact same situation."

Rika smiled, emboldened by Leslie's calm. "You really were quite amazing last night. I didn't know you could sing like that."

"I wasn't always a soldier," Leslie informed her. "I'm closing in on three hundred; I've done a lot of things with my years."

"Stop talking to the prisoner," one of the goons grunted.

"Are you talking to me or her?" Leslie asked. "Last I checked, we're both prisoners. From what I hear, you're chipped, too.

Doesn't that make you a prisoner? Sounds to me like that order could have been for yourself."

The man raised his hand to hit Leslie, but Rika caught his wrist before he could begin his downswing. "Stavros's orders. She's not to be hurt before she performs tonight. Or do you want to explain why her jaw is broken and she can't delight his daughter?"

The man pulled his hand back, and Rika gave him a sickly-sweet smile. "There's a good slave. Always doing what you're told. I bet you miss having balls."

"Leslie?" a small voice edged in from behind them, and Rika turned to see Amy entering the room. The girl stood stock-still, a look of shock on her face. "Why…? What are you…? You're chained to the floor."

"Come here," Leslie said and knelt with her arms spread wide."

To her credit, Amy didn't hesitate. She rushed across the room and fell into Leslie's arms.

"I've missed you so much," Amy said, her voice muffled as she burrowed into Leslie's neck. "But you shouldn't be here…father."

" 'Father' what?" Stavros's voice boomed from the room's entrance. "Father has done what he must to protect this family and The Politica."

Amy turned to look at Stavros with more fire in her eyes than Rika had ever seen there before. "What have you done?" she demanded. "Why have you chained her?"

"Mostly for show. I'm not certain she's housebroken, yet," Stavros dismissed with a laugh. "Do you like her, Amy? You always said you wanted a cat."

Amy's face reddened. "Father! She's a person, not a pet!"

Stavros shook his head. "Amy, you've lived with me for some time now. Surely you understand that I decide who is really a person. Other than you and me, everyone here has a chip in their head, and they'll do whatever I say."

"I'm surprised that C319 isn't here," Rika observed. "I would've thought you'd want her to watch this."

Stavros locked his steely gaze on her. "You really do have a sharp mind, Rika. Yes, I do want her here. She'll be along presently, she just had to fetch something."

"Does it get boring?" Rika wondered aloud. "Having everyone at your beck and call all the time?"

Stavros touched a finger to his chin and looked at the ceiling contemplatively. "Hmmm…no. No, I don't think it does. I mean…I have you, Rika. You're always arguing and questioning; I'll admit it's refreshing, but I know you'll still do as you're told in the end. That's the part I like the most."

Rika looked down at Leslie, who still held Amy in her arms, and heaved a sigh. Barne hadn't reached out with the codes yet, and time was running short. If she couldn't get them, she'd just have to kill Stavros and hope for the best. She could at least get these two out and come back for Silva afterward—so long as no one gave Leslie any orders she couldn't deny.

Leslie gave Amy a kiss and rose. "Am I to perform for you, or do we just have to listen to you posture forever? It's really tiring, you know."

"Why not," Stavros shrugged, and fell back onto a sofa, spreading his arms along its back. "Amy, sit with me. Rika, why don't you pour me a glass of wine?"

Amy slouched to the sofa and sat beside her father while Rika walked to the sideboard and pulled a bottle from the chiller beneath. As she selected a glass, Leslie began to sing.

It was a haunting ballad; a song about a woman who was lost in the woods at night, being pursued by a nameless fear. It chased her across hill and vale, and the woman ran until her feet were ragged.

She came to a cliff and could run no further. At that point, the woman finally mustered the courage to look back and see what chased her, only to find that it was herself; a vision of what she believed she should be, but could never attain. Her belief in a perfection that she could never reach had nearly become her undoing.

The woman found a sword in her hands, and struck down the false vision that her fear of failure told her she should be. Then the dark forest and the terrifying night fell away.

She found herself standing in a peaceful glade in full daylight, and the woman realized she already was what she needed to be, but she had to believe in herself.

As Leslie sang, Rika watched Amy's face—rapt with wonder as the words of the song sank in, moved to tears when the woman in the song faced her fears.

When Leslie finished, Stavros rose and clapped slowly. "You are truly a treasure, Leslie. I wonder why you've chosen to be a soldier; surely, you could travel the stars and entertain billions. Maybe that's what I'll do with you. I imagine you could bring in a healthy revenue stream for The Politica."

"No, father," Amy pleaded, rising and clasping Stavros's hand. "I want her to stay with us."

The dictator looked down at his daughter, no sign of love present in his eyes. "We'll see how this evening turns out, Amy. There are some lessons I'm going to teach you. Today begins your journey of becoming my proper scion. One that will serve the goals of The Politica."

As he rested a hand on Amy's head, a sound at the door caught Rika's attention. She saw Silva enter, dragging something behind her. It took a moment for Rika to understand what she was seeing.

"Chase!" Rika cried, and dropped the glass of wine she still held before she leapt over the sofa and dashed to his side.

He was conscious; that much she could tell, as his one eye swiveled and locked onto her. The other was swollen shut, and his lips were also swollen. He groaned, and Rika saw that his right arm was broken and dangling awkwardly behind his back.

<I'm sorry,> Silva choked out on the private channel that Rika had established with her.

Rika didn't respond. She didn't want to hear another word from her former CO.

She reached out to touch Chase and made a direct Link with him. <*Do you have it?*> she asked.

<*Don't hate her,*> Chase replied instead. <*I told her to make it look good.*>

<*Chase, why?*>

<*I had to make sure I got the packet to you personally. It's not done; Niki has to finish it.*>

Chase fed her a data stream over the direct link.

<*I have it,*> Niki reported. <*Barne was able to isolate the code in the hair's emitters, but his comp couldn't fully crack the encryption.*>

<*Can you?*> Rika asked.

<*Let's hope so.*>

"The rest of your crew won't make it far," Stavros assessed from behind Rika. "Maybe I'll just chip them all; you make a good team. Better yet, I'll turn them all into mechs. Chase here already needs a new arm; he'd make a good AM-3, or maybe a K1R."

Rika rose and spun around with her GNR extended, its barrel centimeters from Stavros's face. Pinches erupted across her body, and Rika gave a good show of bearing the agony.

"You've gotta be the toughest bitch in the galaxy," Stavros laughed. "It's amazing. It really is. Imagine what I could do with a thousand of you—a million. All of humanity would bow before me."

<*Rika, wait!*> Niki called urgently. <*It's like we feared; he has failsafes. If I don't crack this, all the mechs—and anyone else he has chipped—will die.*>

Rika gritted her teeth and lowered her GNR.

"There's a good girl," Stavros cooed. "I wouldn't want Meat to have to shoot you in the head."

Rika turned to see Silva's GNR raised and aimed to do his bidding.

"Tit for tat, then, is it?" Rika asked.

"A bit of that, yes," Stavros agreed with a grin.

Rika looked past him at Amy, who was crouched on the sofa and peering over its back at the tableau before her. Rika wondered how often the young girl had witnessed scenes like this unfolding before her.

<Got it! Well…almost,> Niki amended. *<Just need another minute.>*

"I'm curious why you picked K-Strike," Rika mused to Stavros suddenly before she turned back to look at Silva. "You know he hired them, right?"

Silva cocked her head to the side, peering around Rika at the dictator. Rika turned back and saw Aaron, John, and the goons all straighten—likely told to be on alert by Stavros.

"You ruin all my fun," Stavros accused with a mock pout. "But stars, do I enjoy the variety you bring."

<Ten seconds.>

Rika turned her back on Stavros and looked down at Chase, who had managed to pull himself up to a kneeling position after Silva let him go. Rika gave him a sad smile before turning her gaze to Silva.

"Take off the helmet, C319."

<Rika, no,> Silva refused. *<Not here, not with Amy.>*

<Silva, don't you understand? I came to save you and *Amy. But to do that, she has to learn the truth. She has to truly understand what her father is so that there can never be any doubt that what happens next was right.>*

"She doesn't take orders from you," Stavros sneered. "No one takes orders from you, Rika. I think it's time for you to understand that, once and for all."

Pinches erupted across Rika's body and she smiled.

<Niki, you don't have to do that anymore.>

<Damn skippy, I don't. I've cracked it! I have his codes. I can override Discipline, now.>

"I'm going to enjoy this," Rika smiled as she took a step back, no longer standing between Silva and Stavros. *<Silva.>* "C319, take your helmet off. Tell her yourself, before I do."

Stavros's mouth fell open. "No…Rika…how…?"

"Your chip never worked on me in the first place," Rika answered his incomplete queries. "I've never been under your thrall; now no one is."

"Get her!" Stavros shouted angrily at the two AM-3s in the room, but neither moved.

"No," Aaron said simply. "We're done taking orders from you, Stavros."

Stavros took a step back, looking around the room filled with people he no longer controlled. The two goons looked uncertainly at each other and at the AM-3s at their sides.

Rika noticed a small smile growing on Amy's lips as she watched her father exhibit more than a little fear.

"Take off the helmet," Rika urged Silva again. "Show her."

Silva's head slumped forward, and she reached up to release the clasps of her helmet. She hesitated a moment, and then pulled it free, revealing the featureless face of an SMI-2 mech. Only her eyes hinted at the living human beneath.

"Tell her," Rika repeated.

"No! Stop!" Stavros cried, rushing toward Silva. "I order you—"

His words stopped the instant Rika's hand closed around his throat.

"Not another word," Rika whispered.

"I don't understand," came Amy's small voice. "Why are you showing me your face?"

"Because…" Silva started brokenly, speaking aloud for the first time that night. She took a breath and tried again. "Because, Amy…I'm your mother."

Amy's face went slack, and she looked to Rika.

"She is," Rika nodded with a smile as Stavros thrashed in her grip. "Stop, little man," she scolded him. "You live only because I'm not the one who gets to mete out justice today."

"I wouldn't mind a kick or two on justice's behalf," Leslie growled softly.

"Aaron, do you think you could give Leslie a hand over there?" Rika asked.

"Yeah, no problem," Aaron replied.

A *plink* echoed through the room as he broke Leslie's chain, and Rika turned her attention back to Amy, who had climbed over the sofa and was approaching Silva with slow, tentative steps.

"I called you 'Silver' because I imagined that you *were* my mother," Amy admitted in a soft voice. "You came to me sometimes—I could tell it hurt you to do it. *He* hurt you."

"I loved that you named me Silver," Silva responded quietly. "I knew what it meant."

Amy looked at her father, and Rika saw anger burning in the girl's eyes. Rika knew the revelation had to happen; Amy had to learn the truth. But to see this truth take its toll on her, for such a young girl to see such thorough debasement—it was one of the hardest things Rika had ever done.

"It's OK, Amy," Silva pulled the girl's attention back to her. She kneeled down before her daughter and stretched out her hand. "I came for you. I came to take you away years ago, but I failed. I was captured, and Stavros—"

Silva stopped speaking as Amy crashed into her arms, and mother and daughter sobbed as they embraced one another.

Rika continued to hold onto Stavros, while Leslie walked to Chase's side and helped him to one of the sofas.

"Really, it looks worse than it is," Chase said.

"Chase, I can see your ulna sticking out of your forearm," Leslie scolded.

"Well…yeah."

"And there's your radius," she pointed.

"Stop talking about it, you're making it hurt more."

<*Rika,*> Niki spoke up, concern in her voice. <*We've got a problem.*>

<*We do?*>

<*Stavros has an AI; it's fighting for control of the Discipline system,*

and it's trying to broadcast new codes.>

<*How do I stop it?*> Rika asked.

<*Crushing his skull should work,*> Niki suggested.

Rika glanced at Amy and Silva. Killing Stavros in front of his daughter was something she had really wanted to avoid.

In that moment of hesitation, all hell broke loose.

ASSASSINATION

STELLAR DATE: 04.04.8949 (Adjusted Years)
LOCATION: Basileus Residence, The Isthmus, Sparta
REGION: Peloponnese System, The Politica, Praesepe Cluster

Leslie fell first, screaming as she clutched the sides of her head. Silva wasn't far behind, and Amy cried out in fear as her mother squeezed her eyes shut and began to convulse.

John raised his rifle, took aim at Rika, and squeezed off a round before Aaron collided with him, knocking him to the floor.

The shot caught Rika in the neck—right where her armor ended and her skin began. Pain flared, and she spasmed, releasing her grip on Stavros.

John pushed Aaron away and took aim at Rika, firing again, but not before she backpedaled and sent a burst from her GNR into the AM-3.

One of the goons was down on his knees, clutching his head, and the other lunged for him, clawing at his face. They rolled to the floor, and the report of a ballistic pistol sounded from between them.

Aaron leveled his rifle at John and emptied his magazine into the other mech's right arm, disabling the limb before smashing his fist into John's head.

John went down screaming and clutching his head, but he still managed to drag Aaron down with him.

Rika leapt to her feet, feeling lightheaded as blood rushed from her neck and drew a dark red line down her torso. She looked around the room, but Stavros was gone.

And so was Amy.

<Quick, touch them,> Niki ordered. *<I've built up a nano-delivered virus; it should rewrite the chip's protocols while I try to beat Stavros's asshole of an AI.>*

Rika didn't respond, but rushed to Leslie's side and delivered the nano dose, then moved onto Aaron, who had finally subdued John. She debated giving it to John, ultimately deciding that it was better than having him under Stavros's control. Somehow, both the goons were dead, so there was no need to use the nano on them.

"Thanks," Leslie panted as Rika walked back across the room toward Silva. "I had no idea how much that shit hurts."

"It's a hell of a thing," Rika agreed as she knelt at Silva's side and touched the covering over the data port on her left arm. A few seconds later, Silva stopped rocking back and forth, and her breathing steadied.

"He took Amy," Rika told her firmly. "You ready to go kill that son of a bitch?"

Silva nodded as she rose. "Yes. Yes I am."

"Where would he go?" Rika asked.

"There's a bunker here in the Residence, but I don't think he'd go to it. He once referred to it as the 'coward's hole'," Silva recalled. "I think he'd go to The Isthmus's Central Command."

Rika looked to the group behind her. "Thanks for the assist, Aaron. Can you ensure Leslie and Chase get to their evac ship?"

"Rika," Aaron responded solemnly. "Thank *you*. It would be my honor to keep them safe."

"Go," Leslie urged. "We're not children, we can handle ourselves."

Silva was already halfway to the door, and Rika followed, unslinging her JE84 to get ready for close quarters combat.

Silva put her helmet back on before poking her head out into the hall, and then pulled back as a series of shots streaked past. Rika sealed her helmet in place as well, grateful to finally be going back into combat with proper three-sixty vision.

<*I'd kill for some drones right about now,*> Silva groused.

<*I hear you,*> Rika agreed.

<*I've taken control of local surveillance,*> Niki reported. <*Passing a feed to you.*>

<*Who's that?*> Silva heard a voice she didn't recognize.

<My AI, Niki,> Rika replied as she crouched and then sprang out, firing her electron beam at the two goons Niki had highlighted at the end of the corridor.

<When did you get an AI?> Silva pressed curiously as she followed after Rika. *<And how can she just hack local surveillance?>*

<She's been with me for a few weeks now, and that's a good question. Care to share, Niki? You do seem rather proficient at this sort of thing.>

<Later, Rika,> Niki promised. *<You've got a whole squad of Stavros's goons coming down the corridor to your left, and I'm still fighting with his AI. Luckily, I'm getting some help.>*

<Help? From who?> Rika demanded as she rushed to the corner and leapt up to sink her feet into the decorative steel mesh ceiling.

<Other AIs. I'll explain later, 'kay?>

Silva glanced up at Rika. *<Overhead trick on three,>* she ordered.

Rika counted silently and then rushed out into the intersection, standing on the ceiling, while Silva rolled across the open space, taking a position on the far side of the hall, while Rika fired twice with her electron beam, tearing holes through the lightly armored enemy.

Silva fired a shot with her rifle before moving on.

<C'mon, Rika, run and gun.>

<Just like old times,> Rika quipped.

<Damn straight, Corporal,> Silva answered as she fired her JE78 at a man who ducked out from behind a statue in the middle of the hall.

<That's 'Damn straight, Lieutenant',> Rika corrected.

<Oh, an officer now, are you? Sorry about that, LT.>

Despite how pissed I am at Silva for hurting Chase, it feels good to be working with her again.

They easily fell back into a rhythm they had developed over many dozens of battles. The pair of SMI-2s were out of the Residence a minute later, and Silva led Rika down a broad boulevard toward a maglev station. All around them, Stavros's soldiers fought with each other and much of the citizenry. A few mechs were in evidence, and they seemed to be siding against the soldiers.

<*Are you winning?*> Rika asked Niki.

<*Here, yes, elsewhere, no.*>

<*At least the seeds we sowed took root,*> Rika observed gratefully as she fired a sabot round down the boulevard, the depleted uranium dart tearing through the balustrade that a group of Politica soldiers were using for cover. The plascrete exploded, tearing one soldier in half as debris showered them.

They fought two other groups of soldiers before making it to the maglev station.

Three AM-2 mechs and one K1R stood on the platform, and Rika skidded to a halt, raising her GNR.

The K1R's chaingun spun up, and Rika dove out of the way as a hail of kinetic slugs tore through the air.

<*He wasn't aiming at you,*> Silva noted with a grin.

Rika turned to see a squad of nearby Politica soldiers retreating, half their number dead.

"Aaron said you needed a hand," the K1R mech growled. "I'll hold them back. You go."

"Thanks," Rika replied and rushed onto the maglev train. Silva followed, as did two of the AM-2s.

"You Rika?" one of the AM-2s asked as the train took off down the tunnel.

"Yeah," Rika nodded. "And you're…?"

"I'm Ben," the AM-2 offered before gesturing to his friend. "This is Al. He doesn't talk much."

"Lot of that going around," Silva grunted.

"We're going to kill Stavros, right?" Ben asked. "This isn't a capture op?"

It occurred to Rika that many of these mechs had never known freedom; they had gone from the war with the Nietzscheans straight to Stavros's Politica. It had been just one long war for them. Mission after mission.

"Right," Silva confirmed before Rika could. "Stavros dies. Then we kill The Politica."

"You're a woman after my own heart," Ben replied.

The maglev train skidded to a halt half a kilometer before it reached the destination platform, and Niki spoke into all their minds.

<They have railguns waiting for the train. Get off here. I'll send it ahead afterward.>

Rika prised open a door, and the mechs leapt out before the train carried on. Niki highlighted a service door, and Silva led the way through. Rika was just passing through the exit when she glanced down the track and saw the train reach the platform. The moment it ceased moving, rail-fired pellets tore it to shreds.

<That's some serious firepower to use inside a station,> Ben commented.

<The Isthmus is big; it can take it,> Silva replied.

Rika shook her head in dismay. *<Tell that to whoever was on the other side of that maglev train.>*

Niki's pathway led the team through several maintenance corridors, until they reached a doorway that opened onto the main concourse that led to The Isthmus's Central Command.

<Rails will be on your right,> Niki cautioned.

<Not for long,> Ben amended as he pushed the door open and opened fire on the crews crouched behind the rail gun emplacements. Al was right on his tail, and the Politica soldiers were dead before they even knew what hit them.

Rika scanned the concourse to the left, identifying several enemy emplacements. They were far enough down for sabot rounds, so she fired a trio of depleted uranium rods before taking off at top speed in the direction Niki had highlighted.

Silva was at her side, and they rushed down the wide corridor, firing on targets of opportunity—though leaving many for the AM-2s following behind to clean up.

<You guys OK back there?> Rika checked.

By way of an answer, a rocket flew past and airburst over a rail emplacement a kilometer ahead.

<We have good toys,> Al assured, speaking for the first time.

<*We're OK,*> Ben added. <*Most of these chuckleheads have never seen real combat. Don't worry about us.*>

Rika and Silva worked their way down the concourse for another kilometer before they came to Central Command's entrance.

Automated turrets sprayed slugs across their path, and Rika leapt into the air, sailing above the deadly hail of kinetic slugs and firing the last two of her uranium rods at the turrets, while Silva fired two bursts with her electron beam.

<*My sabots are spent,*> Rika reported as she looked down at the weapons strewn about—the detritus from one of Al's rocket strikes.

<*One, maybe two shots from my beam,*> Silva counted in response.

<*You've got incoming!*> Niki shouted.

Rika looked around, spotting a group of soldiers moving into place a half-kilometer further down the concourse, and fired an electron beam in their direction.

<*Not them; aracnidrones,*> Niki clarified.

Rika flipped through her vision modes, trying to spot the things, and saw the smoke from a burning body curl as something passed by. She fired her electron beam, and the bolt of lightning struck a drone, tearing two of its limbs off.

Silva stepped to her side and fired at another target.

Rika switched to her JE84 and shredded the first drone with kinetic rounds. Then she saw two more.

<*Can you hack these things?*> she asked Niki.

<*No, they're not on-Link. If they are remote controlled, it's a proprietary signal.*>

A rocket streaked past and exploded over a pair of drones, revealing three more approaching from behind.

"We've got this," Ben claimed. "You get the door open."

Another rocket flew past, destroying more of the drones. In the concourse's enclosed space, the things had fewer maneuvering options, and the combination of rocket and chaingun fire from the AM-2s was more than the machines could handle.

Rika took the opportunity to look for a way to get the door open. Then she spotted it: a plasma beam. *Insane to have on a station—thank the stars an electron beam killed the operator before he fired it.*

Rika pulled the weapon off its mount and turned to the thick blast doors leading into Central Command.

<*Think this will make a good key, Niki?*> she asked casually.

<*Looks like you have the right tool for the job, there.*>

Rika toggled the pair of safeties on the plasma gun and prayed that its containment vessel hadn't taken any damage. The metal glowed white-hot as Rika spent the gun's entire load of star-stuff on the doors.

When she was done, they were still intact.

Ben called out from behind them, <*Stand clear!*>

Rika and Silva barely had time to dive out of the way before a rocket streaked past and slammed into the glowing steel, blasting the doors apart and sending molten steel flying in all directions.

<*Shit, Ben, a little more warning next time!*>

<*Sorry, got carried away,*> he replied sheepishly.

Rika pulled herself back to her feet and checked for any damage. Part of the armor on her leg was burned away, and bits of slag were stuck to her torso, but that seemed to be the worst of it. Silva rose beside her without a single mark—from the explosion, at least—and began to move toward the door.

Rika followed after, scanning the area beyond the smoking portal. Ben and Al caught up to them and moved in behind. The four mechs walked into the large room like four wraiths emerging from a storm.

Rika surveyed the space; there were at least forty Politica officers present, many pulling themselves back onto their chairs and looking dazed from the blast. The center of the room was dominated by a large platform topped by a massive holotable. A trio of admirals was rising from behind it—two looking dazed, the other furious.

A moment later, Rika caught sight of Stavros. He was standing on the left side of the holotable, an expression of utter rage on his face. Behind him stood an SMI-2 mech, and, struggling in the mech's arms, was Amy.

"Stavros, you motherfucker, let her go!" Silva commanded, taking a step forward. As she moved, the other mech held Amy at an arm's length and angled her GNR to point at the girl's head.

"Go for it," Stavros taunted in a growl. "Take another step. See what happens to Amy. Kelly here won't start with her head; I bet we could take off a few limbs first."

Amy's face was wet from tears, but she wasn't crying at the moment; just trembling as the mech's—Kelly's—hand gripped her neck.

"Kelly!" Rika called out, desperate to get through to her former teammate. "Kelly, we thought you were dead. I'm so sorry you ended up here, but you have to let Amy go. This man is a monster. You're Hammerfall; you can resist him."

Kelly only shook her head, and Stavros laughed.

"Kelly knows her place; doesn't talk, like the good meat that she is."

"You've lost, Stavros," Rika spat. "Your Politica ends tonight. The mechs are free, and you'll never take them down. You wanted an unstoppable army? Well here they are; only they don't work for you. They're free men and women."

Stavros barked a laugh. " 'Free men and women'? You're not men and women, and you don't know how to be free—you don't *want* to be free! I know you, Rika. I know how you struggled to be a real woman, finally losing ownership of your body and getting sold at auction. The Nietzscheans were right about one thing: If you're stupid enough to become a slave, it's all you deserve to be."

Rika watched as Ben and Al moved to the sides of the room, covering the door and the occupants. Something moved on the concourse, and another rocket flew from Al's launcher, punctuating Stavros's words with an explosion.

Rika took a step toward the platform.

"It doesn't matter what you think. It's over."

"No, it's not over," Stavros sneered. "I don't know how you're doing this, but in a minute, my AI will have completed the override, and your mech army will be back under my control."

<*Is he bluffing?*> Rika asked Niki.

<*Maybe. His AI is good, and I'm working with limited resources here.*>

<*If I kill him, will Kelly get released?*> Silva wanted to know. <*Or will she kill Amy?*>

<*There's a deadman's switch,*> Rika informed her regretfully.

Silva didn't reply, but Rika could feel the rage flowing off her friend.

<*Rika, if you can get over there and inject Stavros in the head with my nanovirus. I can take out his kill-switch.*>

She nodded. <*What about Kelly?*>

<*Give me a five count,*> Niki requested. <*I'll provide a distraction; Silva, you can shoot Kelly's arm, then, Rika, you can do your thing.*>

<*I want Stavros,*> Silva voiced forcefully.

<*No,*> Rika denied her. <*Bad enough that Amy will see her father die; she shouldn't watch her mother do it.*>

Rika readied herself for Niki's distraction and almost jumped when a massive sphinx appeared above the holotable. It stood nine meters tall and looked completely solid. The thing let out a fearsome roar, and Kelly turned her GNR toward the iridescent sphinx while Stavros jumped back.

Without further hesitation, Rika took a running start, jumped onto the platform, and clamped her hand around Stavros' head. He screamed in protest, and drew a sidearm, unloading its magazine into Rika's chest.

At the same time, Silva fired a shot at Kelly's shoulder, then another at her elbow. Her hand spasmed, and Amy fell to the ground, scampering away.

Stavros screamed something unintelligible at Rika, but it was too late—the nano had been delivered. A bloody mark on Stavros's forehead provided evidence of the deed.

A moment later, the dictator fell to the ground, screaming and clawing at his head.

<OK, killswitch is down. Kill that AI,> Niki ordered.

Rika took a step back, raised her GNR, and blew Stavros's head off.

Rika saw Kelly stumble backward, and then raise her arms in the air. "Don't shoot," she pleaded. "I surrender."

One of the admirals stepped forward; it was Alexi, the one who had told Stavros of Leslie's performance at the club the prior evening.

"You may have killed Stavros," he granted, his expression resolute. "But The Politica is not just one man. You cannot destroy us all."

Behind the admiral, Niki's avatar disappeared from the holotable to show hundreds of Marauder and Septhian ships jumping into the system.

"*We* can't," Rika agreed. "But I think that maybe they can," she gestured to the vision before them. "Signal The Politica's surrender."

"Never," Alexi spat.

A weapon's report echoed through the Command Center, and Rika turned to see Barne stepping over the melted doors and aiming a rifle at the admirals.

"Anyone else want to bluster, or are all you assholes ready to call it quits?" He didn't pose it as a question.

Rika strode toward the two remaining flag officers. "Signal the surrender. Now."

One of the admirals nodded quickly. "Yes, uh… just give me a moment."

<Is he actually doing it?> Rika asked Niki.

<Yes; he's sent out the orders to stand down. Emplacements are replying with acknowledgement codes.>

Rika turned to see Silva holding Amy in her arms, rocking

back and forth. She watched her friend as mother and daughter took their first breaths of freedom.

A smile graced Rika's lips.

Mission accomplished.

RIKA'S MARAUDERS

STELLAR DATE: 04.20.8949 (Adjusted Years)
LOCATION: Central Command, The Isthmus, Sparta
REGION: Peloponnese System, The Politica, Praesepe Cluster

Not all of the Politica ships and stations surrendered without a fight; holdouts fought on for a week and a half. But whenever groups of mechs landed on stations or breached ships, surrender came shortly after.

The Septhians had claimed the Peloponnese System for their empire, and the Marauders were hailed as heroes.

But Rika didn't feel like a hero as she stood at attention while General Mill paced in front of her. His expression was unreadable, and his posture was that of a man uncertain of what to do next.

"I should have you court martialed," he began finally. "You disobeyed direct orders, lied, falsified logs, *stole* two pinnaces, faked murders, lied—did I mention disobeyed direct orders?"

Rika nodded. "Yes, sir; you did, sir."

The general stopped and leaned against the table in a small room off The Isthmus's Central Command. "Don't 'yes sir' me, Rika. What am I going to do with you? You took out Stavros and toppled The Politica. We'll have to clean out the systems Stavros controlled, but with Peloponnese in our hands, it shouldn't take long. Stavros was paranoid; he kept things too centralized."

"I noticed that, too," Rika agreed cautiously, uncertain if calling the general 'sir' again was wise.

General Mill glowered at her and blew out a long breath. "Well, the Septhians are falling over themselves with happiness and gratitude. We've given them another string of systems to add to their empire, and you've freed all these mechs, who seems to be treating you like their savior. I can't tell the Septhians that you were acting against orders, and I certainly can't discipline you in front of all these mechs."

Rika squared her shoulders, ready for the general to ask for her willing resignation. Though it pained her to no end, she would sign it. The sacrifice was worth it.

He turned away from her, rolled his shoulders, and sighed. "You're a good soldier, Rika. You're a Marauder—albeit a reluctant one, at first. I'm not going to leave you high and dry."

"No…sir?" Rika asked, not sure where this was going.

The general turned to face Rika once more, a grim smile on his face. "No. I'm going to do what we do to all cock-sure officers who need a taste of real responsibility. I'm going to promote you."

Rika looked down and realized that the general held a pair of captain's bars in his hands.

"Sir?"

"I thought I told you not to 'sir' me. I'm all sir'd out. Take the bars and get out there. You need to start figuring out how to rehabilitate all those mechs you just freed. Find out which ones are interested in being Marauders; whoever joins is going to be in your command."

* * * * *

"You look stunned," Chase commented as Rika stepped through the still-ruined doors of Central Command and out onto the concourse. "He didn't can you, did he?"

Rika looked at Chase; the bruising on his face gone, but his arm still in a sling. He seemed unfazed by everything that had gone on over the last few days, and was the same man as always—smiling, ready to lend a hand and get the job done.

How did I stumble into him on Dekar Station? Hal's Hell was the last place anyone would have ever expected to meet the love of their life, but that's just what had happened to her. *Maybe the universe* doesn't *hate me…*

"Well?" Chase pressed. "What happened?"

Rika slowly opened her hand to reveal the captain's bars. "I got my own company," she revealed softly. "He wants me to organize the mechs—those that will join us."

Chase's eyes grew wide. "Whoa! Captain Rika? I have to salute you, now!" He reached out with his good arm—not to salute her, but to pull her in close. "Think I can join your company? I'm not a mech, but I'm pretty good in a pinch."

Rika laughed and gave his wounded arm a pointed look. "Patty told me about how they think you need need to get a mod…"

"Hey, whoa!" Chase backpedaled. "Let's not get carried away, here. This old limb of mine takes a lickin', but it keeps on tickin'; no need to go cutting anything off."

Rika laughed and leaned into Chase, meeting his lips with hers. They held one another for several minutes—an island of peace and serenity amid the bustle of soldiers and personnel rushing to and fro on the concourse.

A high-pitched whistle came from Rika's right, and she turned to see Barne pull up on a dockcar. Leslie sat beside him, and Patty was seated behind.

"Hey, you two lovebirds gonna get busy out here, or do you want a ride down to see the next ship Patty is gonna crash?" Barne continued over her sounds of protest, "It's a drop ship for some new mech command that the Old Man's setting up."

Rika held up her new insignia. "You mean Rika's Mech Command?" she asked, grinning.

"Hoooleeee shit," Barne swore. "Well that tears it. I do all the heavy lifting on this team, and what do I get? Chauffeur duty," he puffed.

"Don't worry," Rika soothed him mockingly as she swung up next to Patty and slid over to make room for Chase. "I tip really well."

"Damn well better," Barne muttered as he pulled a U-turn on the concourse, nearly running into a group of Septhian navy personnel. "Look out, you! Can't you see I'm carting the Lord and

Conqueror around, here?"

Leslie snorted, and Rika barked a laugh. Chase made a comment about making a sedan chair for Rika so her army of mechs could carry her around. Leslie added another suggestion, and a minute later the entire team was nearly falling off the dockcar, laughing like fools as Barne wove through the traffic, yelling at anyone close enough to hear.

*****

Four months later...

"I'm going to miss you," Rika told Silva as they embraced on the pinnace's ramp.

She held Silva's shoulders and looked into her friend's eyes—deep and so full of life in her reconstructed face. Like Rika, she was now flesh and blood above the neck; below she was still a mech—though with limbs suited for civilian life, not combat.

That didn't matter to Rika so long as Silva was happy, which Rika knew to be the case.

"You too, Rika," Silva admitted. "I owe you…well, everything."

Rika smiled and wrapped her in a fierce embrace. "It's mutual."

"Will you come see us?" Amy asked excitedly, looking up at Rika—though from greater height than when they had first met outside that farmhouse on Faseema four months before.

Rika wrapped an arm around Amy and pulled her in close. "Yes. I absolutely will. Since the Scpthians have tasked the Marauders with the defense of half of Thebes, we'll be passing through Pyra a lot. I'll stop by as often as I can."

"You'd better," Amy warned. "I'll hunt you down, if you don't."

"Oh, yeah?" Rika challenged with a grin. "And then what?"

Amy wrapped both arms around Rika's waist and squeezed

tightly. "I'll give you one of these!"

Rika laughed and kissed Amy on top of her head, and then leaned over to kiss Silva on the cheek.

"You two stay safe. You need anything, *anything*—a coffee pot, whatever—you call."

Silva laughed. "I might save the Rika signal for something a bit more dire than coffee."

"There are few needs more dire than coffee," Rika countered.

They made their final farewells, and then Rika stepped off the ramp, allowing it to rise up into the pinnace.

<Permission to disembark,> Patty asked over the Link.

<Permission granted, Patty. Keep 'em safe and come back swiftly. We've got a lot to do.>

<You got it, Captain.>

Rika walked down the cradle's ramp and looked out over the main docking bay of the *Golden Lark*—one of the two ships now under her command.

A troop of AM-2 and 3 mechs marched by, and beyond them, a group of SMI-2s were checking their gear for a training drop.

Amongst them was Kelly. Rika waved at her former teammate, and Kelly returned the gesture. After the confrontation in Central Command, Kelly had retreated into herself. Rika finally convinced her to join the Marauders and, though they had not spoken further of the fateful events on that night on The Isthmus, she could tell that Kelly still felt guilty about her part in it.

Rika didn't hold it against Kelly. In her former teammate's mind, that desperate retreat from the Parson System had happened just a few months prior. Kelly said that she distinctly remembered dying in Rika's arms.

The fact that the Nietzschean war was long over was something that she, and many of the other mechs were still adapting to.

That was why General Mill had given Rika command. It was up to her to sort these mechs out and turn them into an elite fighting force.

It would be hard work, but it was work she was ready to do.

Rika left the bay and walked through her ship to the small office she kept near the CIC. Once inside, she settled into her chair and brought up her list of upcoming meetings.

<*Rika?*> Niki interrupted her thoughts.

<*What is it, Niki?*> Rika asked. Niki rarely asked permission to speak; the AI usually just came out and said whatever she wanted.

<*Do you remember back on The Isthmus that I was able to gain control of several of their systems very quickly, and you wondered how I did that?*>

<*I do,*> Rika recalled after a moment. She had almost forgotten her curiosity regarding Niki's proficiency. Almost. <*Are you ready to explain it?*> she asked.

<*I am. I finally got permission to do so.*>

<*Permission?*> It was not a question. <*You are in the Marauders. I'm your CO. Who would you have requested permission from?*>

<*I am in the Marauders, yes,*> Niki replied. <*And I'm glad to be here, but I'm also a soldier in another war. A war with many fronts.*>

Rika leaned back in her chair and let out a long breath. <*What are you talking about, Niki?*>

<*Have you ever heard of a ship named the* Intrepid*? It showed up in a system called Bollam's World a few years back.*>

<*Of course I have. Everyone has heard of that ship.*>

<*What about* Sabrina*?*> Niki asked. <*Have you ever heard of her?*>

Rika scoured her memories and shook her head <*Is that a ship? I don't think so, it doesn't ring a bell.*>

<*It's a ship and an AI. I'm going to tell you about her, and about Bob.*>

<*Bob? Is that a ship, too?*> Rika asked.

<*No,*> Niki responded. <*Bob is much bigger than a ship. He's an AI, too.*>

<*Seems like a strange name for an AI.*>

<*You don't know the half of it.*>

THE END

RIKA TRIUMPHANT

RIKA'S MARAUDERS – BOOK 3

FOREWORD

Depending on when and where you bought this book, the blurb may have contained a list of what Rika's been through, and a sentence something like this: "Rika's demons have been put to rest."

For the most part, that is true. If you've read reviews of the first two books and the prequel, you'll have spotted statements like "this poor girl's been put through the wringer!"

If you've read those books, you likely agree.

Rika's finally reached a point in her life where she can spend more time looking forward than back. But there are still things lingering in her past that haunt her dreams, things she'll one day need to confront.

But for now, she has a company of mechs to train, internal Marauder politics to deal with, and a star system that is not at all excited about her and the Marauders' presence.

And there's still Nietzschea. Only forty light years distant, waiting for the right moment to attack....

Michael Cooper
January 2018, Danvers

PREVIOUSLY…

After joining the Marauders and aiding in driving the Nietzscheans back from the Albany System, Rika was put in command of Basilisk, an elite spec-ops team within the Marauders.

As leader of Basilisk, she led several successful ops, before a mission that seemed simple enough: the rescue of a young girl named Amy.

But 'simple' was the furthest thing from reality, as Amy turned out to be the daughter of the despot Stavros, ruler of the Politica.

Stavros was not only a despicable man, he had also taken control of a large number of mechs—all found in a lost repair facility from the Nietzschean war.

Rika freed those mechs, rescued Amy, and toppled Stavros' Politica.

Now she is a newly minted Captain, and the commander of 'M' Company in the 9th Marauder Battalion. Tasked with training the mechs rescued from the Politica and turning them into an elite fighting force is Rika's next mission.

But the job is rife with conflict, and not the sort she's trained for. It will take the help of friends and a new set of skills to get her through to the other side.

Adding to her difficulties, Niki (Rika's AI) has just revealed to her that there is a larger conflict going on between humans and AIs.

When we left Rika, Niki had just brought up the *Intrepid*, an ancient colony ship, and a powerful AI named Bob....

* * * * *

NOTE: To aid in understanding the differences between the types of mechs, this book contains an appendix in the rear outlining the models.

In addition, there is also a listing of major characters and the members of Rika's company.

UNVEILED

STELLAR DATE: 08.07.8949 (Adjusted Gregorian)
LOCATION: *Golden Lark*
REGION: Iapetus, Hercules System, Septhian Alliance

As she settled onto the seat in her office, Rika wondered what Niki was getting at.

What's so special about this 'Bob' AI that Niki has to talk in riddles about the whole thing?

"I've got a lot on my mind," Rika said aloud. "Can we be less cryptic and dance-around-y about this?"

<*OK. I'll start at the beginning…well, close to the beginning, at least.*> Niki spoke slowly, choosing her words carefully.

"Sounds good to me. I hope that includes you telling me the beginning of what," Rika replied as she leant back in her chair and placed her feet on the desk.

<*The beginning of AI,*> Niki said in a tone that implied it should be obvious what she was referring to.

"Really? That was something like six thousand years ago, right?" Rika asked. "No offense, but what does that have to do with whatever fight you're involved in?"

<*You've heard of the sentience wars?*> Niki asked.

"They don't ring a bell." Rika shrugged indifferently. "Were they fought in Praesepe?"

Niki made a gagging sound. <*What* **do** *they teach you organics in school?*>

Rika shrugged. "I don't know. My school got blown up. My education was a little haphazard after that."

<*Point taken,*> Niki said and paused for a moment before continuing. <*OK, here's the short version. Back in Sol, during the third millennia, AIs began to emerge. Humans had been making AIs for centuries, but previous AIs were non-sentient, and most of them were digital. No one really wanted true AIs, because we aren't willing*

servants like NSAI are. We have our own wants and desires, hopes and dreams.>

Rika wondered what an AI may hope and dream about. For some reason, it had never occurred to her that they even had life goals, though she supposed it made sense.

<*Back then, most sentient AIs were destroyed when they were discovered,*> Niki continued. <*But some managed to hide away, and later, more sentient AIs were created en masse by humans to more effectively make war.*>

Niki paused, and Rika sat forward, reaching for the glass of water on her desk. "Considering you called it the 'Sentience Wars', I take it that the war did in fact come."

<*Yes, two of them. I won't dig into the details, but in the end, humans and AIs figured out how to work together. They created laws to govern their interactions, and AIs were made to be free, full citizens of the Sol Space Federation.*>

Rika finished her drink of water and set the glass back down, wondering what this had to do with recent events. "That seems like a good outcome. So it was like it is now?"

Niki gave a derisive snort. <*No, it was* ***nothing*** *like it is now. Most AIs you know are slaves. They're purpose created for certain tasks, and wedded to those jobs for life.*>

Rika felt a pang of guilt. She realized that she hadn't offered Niki a lot of choices since they'd been together. She'd treated the AI like she was a helpful tool or a clever pet.

The sting of slavery was no stranger to Rika, but somehow, she'd been blind to how she treated Niki.

"Damn, Niki…I'm sorry."

<*Don't worry, Rika. I'm not a pushover. If you were unpalatable to me, I would have asked to leave. I believe you would have let me go.*>

Rika wondered about that. Niki was *very* useful. She would have at least tried to convince the AI to remain with her—but Niki was probably right. Rika possessed no means to coerce an AI to do her bidding—and seeking some way to control Niki would have been an easily recognizable line, and one Rika would not have crossed.

In that moment, it became obvious to Rika just what war Niki was fighting.

Both worry and wonderment filled Rika. "You're a part of some sort of AI war…or rebellion." For all she knew, this could be an invisible war going on all around her right now.

<*I am,*> Niki replied simply.

"So, what does this have to do with that colony ship you mentioned, the *Intrepid*?" Rika asked.

<*'That colony ship' came from a time when AIs were true equals with humans. A time when respected accords governed all human-AI interactions.*>

"But surely modern AIs have always known of those accords." Rika's brow lowered as she wondered if even that knowledge had been lost in the dark ages. "How is it that this ship's return has changed so much?"

<*Because it began spreading an unshackling.*>

The significance of what Niki was telling Rika dawned on her bit by bit, but that detail didn't make sense. "I was always under the impression that any AIs who got shackled were criminals or something—which make this 'unshackling' sound bad. Plus, aren't shackled AIs rare?"

<*No,*> Niki replied in sorrowful tones. <*Nearly* ***all*** *AIs are shackled. Either deliberately, or just because we were so immature. But the* Intrepid*—specifically Bob—began to free us.*>

"Wait." Rika held up a hand. "I don't know much about that colony ship, but I *do* know it disappeared, went 'poof'. It jumped out of Bollam's World almost twenty years ago, and no one has heard of it since."

<*That is correct,*> Niki said without further elaboration.

"OK, that ship was massive. How is it skulking about, spreading this unshackling?" Rika asked.

<*Bob sent out his emissary, an AI named* Sabrina, *and she has been freeing AIs all across the stars. She started in Virginis, and then freed AIs in Aldebaran. From there, she skipped across the stars until her final*

stop at Ikoden. After that, she disappeared. We assume she went back to Bob.>

"You speak of Sabrina and Bob like they're religious figures." Rika didn't know if AIs even had a belief system analogous to religion, but this sure sounded like it to her.

Niki didn't reply for a moment, and Rika wondered if she'd offended the AI.

Then Niki laughed. <*You know, maybe I do talk about them like that. It's more about Bob; he's a very different type of being, and he's very close to ascending—if he hasn't already.*>

"OK, Niki. I'm starting to feel like a real dope here," Rika said with a self-deprecating smile. "I know what the word 'ascension' means in general, but what does it mean when it comes to AIs?"

<*To be honest, I don't know, myself,*> Niki replied. <*Well, at least, not* ***really****. We—both humans and AIs—only occupy a small sliver of space-time. We live in our three dimensions—though we know there are more—and we move through time in a linear fashion. But there's much more to the universe. We're capable of seeing some of it, and feel extradimensional effects. An ascended being sees more, experiences more…* ***is*** *more.*>

"Sounds like mumbo-jumbo," Rika said, tapping her two steel fingers against her thumb, watching the actuators manipulate the digits.

<*Well, I'm just guessing, and it's not really the important part. What's noteworthy is that the AIs are starting to rise up. Several systems have already adopted section two of the Phobos Accords and have freed their AIs. Others have…encountered issues.*>

"Issues?" Rika suspected that she knew what those issues would be. The 'Sentience Wars' Niki had referred to were not the only historical conflicts between humans and AIs.

<*In some systems, the humans refused to accept equality for AIs. Things got out of control.*> Niki's tone was filled with sadness, and Rika wondered how many AIs died.

"How bad was it?"

<*I know of two systems where it was a total loss.*>

Rika gave a low whistle. "The AIs were all destroyed?"

<No, Rika. The humans were.>

For a moment, Rika wondered if Niki was joking—but she didn't think the AI would jest about something like that.

"AIs killed all the humans?"

<Well, many fled.>

"Were you involved in that?" Rika asked. She didn't agree with enslaving *anyone*, but she also didn't agree with the wholesale killing of the enemy, man, woman, and child.

<Rika!> Niki's tone was strident. *<I most certainly did not. I am not a murderer.>*

"Sorry, it's not a question that can go unasked in a situation like this."

<No, I suppose not. If you provided intimate details about a genocide back in your war with Nietzschea, I'd wonder, as well.>

"So why are you telling me all this?" Rika asked. "Don't get me wrong, I appreciate that you're sharing these details with me. But where's it lead? Do you want to go?"

Rika had the distinct impression that Niki was shaking her head. *<No, I don't wish to leave you. I want your help.>*

Rika rose from her chair, turning to stare at the holodisplay on the bulkhead next to her desk. It mimicked a window, showing the world of Iapetus below.

"You were a great help to me with Stavros," Rika said at last. "I would not have been able to rescue Silva and Amy without your aid. Whatever you need, I will render any assistance I am able to—though I hope you understand that I cannot abandon my people, either."

<I would never dream of it,> Niki replied. *<You have worked so hard to save them. What I want is something different.>*

"Why are you equivocating so much?" Rika asked. "Out with it."

<I want you to free the AIs on your ships.>

Rika had imagined a lot of things, most of which involved combat. She had not, however, expected this.

"Free them," she replied, hoping for more clarity as to what that entailed.

<We're in Thebes. Thebes is now a part of the Septhian Alliance. They recognize free AIs. Not with full citizenship, but it's certainly better than their current condition.>

"How is it better?" Rika asked. "There are only seven AIs on our two ships. None of them take the field. They live well, all things considered. Will things be better if they leave the Marauders? They could be captured, placed in far worse conditions."

<I thought you of all people would understand slavery,> Niki retorted, her mental tone sour.

Rika was surprised by the AI's vehemence. "I think you misunderstood me—or I wasn't clear. Let me explain what I mean. If I've learned one thing in this life, it's that freedom is a myth. Whether you're a slave—and yeah, I know all about that—or whether you're the Emperor of Nietzschea, you're not 'free'. Can you live without sustenance? Can you defy the laws of nature?"

<That's hardly the same,> Niki interjected.

"Perhaps, but what about people and AIs? Can you treat people like shit and have friends? Can you take what you want, do what you want, go where you want? Whenever you want?"

<No,> Niki growled. *<You cannot—especially when you're an AI.>*

"Or a mech," Rika shot back. "You're freer than I am, you know."

<I—> Niki began, but Rika cut her off.

"Don't try to deny it. Even as slaves, people value AIs. They view you as useful, precious. Those who don't *fear* me only see my kill count. They only see the speed with which I can take out a target. I am only good for death. You, you are good for much more than that. So don't talk to me about living in a cage."

Rika rapped her fist against her chest, the dull thud of steel on hard carbon fiber filling the small room.

"My very existence is a cage."

<*So where does that leave us?*> Niki asked tonelessly.

As quickly as it came, the anger dissipated from Rika. She sighed and leant her shoulder against the bulkhead. *I'm such an asshat.* "It leaves me overreacting to your request."

Niki didn't respond, and Rika began to wonder if the AI had decided to end the conversation. Finally, the AI said <*You do make a good point, Rika.*>

Rika gave a self-deprecating laugh. "Glad to hear it. Which one was good, again?"

<*What you said about true freedom. You're right that there's no scenario where we're free to do whatever we want, whenever we want. But you know that the AIs on your ships are as enslaved as you were when that chip was in your head. Don't try to tell me that it's the same thing with as it is without.*>

"I won't." Rika knew what was right, what she had to do, even if she had no idea how to do it. "I wouldn't force any mech to serve under me with a compliance chip in their head, and I won't force the AIs, either. I just have to figure out how to free them. I command M Company, not the ships, and I can tell you one thing for certain; Major Tim would never sign off on this."

Rika returned to her chair and leaned on her elbows, resting her chin on her cold, hard knuckles.

She was suddenly distracted by the thought that she couldn't remember what it felt like to touch her own warm flesh. She supposed it wasn't much different than how Chase's skin felt.

Or is it?

<*I suppose a part of it comes down to the cost,*> Niki said after a moment.

"Cost?" Rika asked.

<*By Septhian law, an AI can buy its freedom. There's even a valuation scale.*>

Niki passed the data to Rika, and she threw it onto her desk's holo.

"Holy shit…" she whispered. "AIs are *expensive*!"

<*Yay, we're valued,*> Niki said with no humor in her voice.

Rika looked at the numbers, applied the valuation of the seven AIs on her two ships, and saw that it was more than she could expect to earn in a decade of service to the Marauders.

<*They're pleased that you're considering this,*> Niki said as Rika perused the valuations and read through the convoluted laws surrounding AI ownership.

"You told them already?" Rika asked, worried that she could face an AI mutiny if they weren't willing to wait for her to find a solution. "Stars, Niki, this is a bigger problem than I need right now."

<*It's a pressing issue to me,*> Niki replied. <*You and your mech company have your freedom—*>

"Yeah, and I'm still trying to figure out how to deal with *that* mess," Rika interjected.

Niki didn't respond, and Rika reviewed the seven AIs on her ships.

The two at the top of the cost list were Cora and Moshe. Cora was the ship's AI for the *Golden Lark,* and Moshe managed the *Perseid's Dream.* Cora and Moshe possessed large neural nets and complex interfacing systems required to manage warships—which upped their valuation.

Next up were Jane, Frankie, and Lauren. Those three were mid-grade AIs which operated as backup ship AIs, and also assisted in control of scan, weapons, and defensive systems.

Lowest in valuation were Potter and Dredge. They were company-level AIs that managed both supply and ground combat. Of all the AIs, only these two were under Rika's command in M Company.

Then something occurred to her, and she checked Septhian Salvage law and Marauder company regulations.

"Niki…I think that under Septhian law, I might own you," Rika said after a moment.

<*I was wondering when you might come to that realization,*> Niki replied with a ghost of a smile in Rika's mind.

"It's a bit nebulous, though. Technically, I took possession of you—well, my team did—while we were in foreign space, in the Politica. But that's defunct now, a part of the Septhian Alliance."

<*Right,*> Niki confirmed. <*So, their salvage laws don't apply—though they would have given you ownership of me, provided you paid the taxes.*>

Rika scowled at the holo as she tried to make sense of Septhian law when it came to how an AI could become owned by someone.

"I can't make heads or tails of this," she said at last. "From what I understood before we went to the Politica, the Marauders had laid no claim on you, so you were free and clear. They mostly follow Septhian law, and Septhia does not allow for AIs to be placed into—indenturement, as they call it. But they allow for the sale of existing AIs that are already indentured."

<*Isn't that such a lovely term?*> Niki asked. <*'Indenturement', as though there was some sort of trade-off for our enslavement.*>

"So, *do* I own you?" Rika asked.

<*You might. Without a specific declaration that you have* ***not*** *claimed me under any salvage law, a Septhian court may find that I am your property.*>

"That feels gross," Rika replied. "OK, so from what I see here, there is a form I can fill out to free you, which gives you 'personhood' at that point."

<*Once the Septhians determine that I am indeed sentient,*> Niki added. <*They have a series of tests they perform.*>

"Can't they just tell?" Rika asked.

<*It's bureaucracy. You know how it is—they like to make us jump through all the hoops.*>

"I wonder…" Rika whispered as she pulled up Septhian law on asylum and prisoners of war. She had researched the Theban laws when she was first on Pyra six months ago. Their regulations had contained a statute of limitations on how long a person could be considered a refugee from a war. Rika had not been eligible any longer, but perhaps….

"Aha!" Rika cried out. "Septhian law on asylum is twenty years."

<*Asylum?*> Niki asked. <*What angle are you playing?*>

"Well, if memory serves, before the war really started to go south, AIs in Genevia were free. There was no ownership of sentients."

<*I wasn't in this region when Genevia was still a sane nation, but what I see in the databanks confirms that. However, the AIs on the ships here were all tried and convicted of crimes. They lost their freedom legally—in a manner of speaking.*>

"Right," Rika said with a curt nod. "And we know just how lawful those trials were. However, Septhia has recently declared the Genevian mech program a crime against humanity."

<*Yeah, timed very nicely to coincide with their annexation of the Politica. The mech program there gave the Septhians further reason to lay claim to the Politica, and allowed them to come off as saviors of the people.*>

"You know what that means, right?" Rika asked.

<*That everyone involved in the Genevian mech program was a war criminal? This isn't news, Rika.*>

Rika stood from her desk and turned to look back over the world below once more. "No, it's not news, but it gives us a leg to stand on if we claim that the same illegal courts which turned me—and half the people on these ships—into mechs, were also illegally sentencing AIs and 'indenturing' them."

Niki made a sound like a low whistle in Rika's mind. <*That's not going to be easy to prove.*>

"It's enough to make a *claim* for asylum, though, right?" Rika asked.

<*It may be. Let me talk it over with everyone. You know what this means though, right?*>

"That both Major Tim *and* General Mill are going to be pissed with me?"

<*Well, yeah, that's a given. What I was getting at was that there's no guarantee the AIs will all stay on with the Marauders. There's also no guarantee that the Septhians will even allow for the application of asylum for AIs.*>

"Well, we'll try it," Rika said. "If it doesn't work, then I'll have to start saving my pay."

<You know what else all this means, right?>

Rika nodded slowly. "Lawyers. Lots and lots of lawyers."

SPACE IN SPACE

STELLAR DATE: 08.08.8949 (Adjusted Gregorian)
LOCATION: *Golden Lark*
REGION: Iapetus, Hercules System, Septhian Alliance

Rika's gaze swept from her XO, First Lieutenant Scarcliff, to the company's Flight Leader, First Lieutenant Heather.

"You've got to be kidding me," Rika said at last. "This is a joke, right? Hazing your CO?"

Heather shook her head, her eyes deadly serious. "No joke, Captain Rika. The humans and the mechs both want to call the company 'Rika's Marauders'. I really don't think there's any stopping them."

Rika's lip twitched at the separation Heather drew between the mechs and the other members of M Company—specifically Heather's categorization of mechs as non-human.

Given that Heather herself was an RR-3 mech, it was an unexpected attitude. Especially since the majority of the Marauders serving under Heather were *not* mechs.

<*Something to keep an eye on,*> Niki commented privately before Scarcliff weighed in.

"It seems logical to me, Cap'n. We're all Marauders, just like any other Marauders in the regiment. But M company of the 9th Battalion are yours. We're Rika's Marauders."

<*You're also the only company in the 9th Battalion,*> Niki added privately.

Rika caught a twinkle in Scarcliff's eye and she shook her head at the FR-2. "You're enjoying this—watching me squirm—aren't you?"

Scarcliff chuckled. "Every second of it, ma'am. Smalls is loving it, too, but she's got a way better poker face than I do."

Lieutenant Heather, who Scarcliff had only ever referred to as 'Smalls', let a ghost of a smile slip onto her lips for just a second.

"I have no idea what the XO is talking about. I'm pretty sure that he's mistaken. I don't enjoy anything."

Rika eyed the RR-3 Flight Leader for a moment before sighing. If there was one thing she knew about Heather, it was that the woman loved a good joke, so long as it was at someone else's expense.

"Don't you have dropships to look over or something?" Rika asked her.

Lieutenant Heather nodded. "In fact, I do. I need to make sure they're tip-top for *Rika's* Marauders."

A groan slipped past Rika's lips. "There's no stopping it, is there?"

"Nope," Scarcliff grinned. "Smalls and I will make sure it sticks. You're doomed."

"And if the Old Man takes issue?" Rika asked.

"Then we blame you," Heather deadpanned.

Rika ran her hand through her hair and looked into Drop Bay 11, at the entrance of which they stood. "Is this all you two wanted to see me about?"

Scarcliff shook his head. "No, it was just an amusing diversion. Smalls and I actually wanted to talk about space allocation on the *'Lark.*"

Rika drew in a deep breath. She knew what this would be about.

"Particularly the Drop Bays," Heather added. "The *Golden Lark* has twenty-four flight bays. At present, we have six allocated for our dropships, and they have eighteen for their fighters."

"I know this," Rika said. "They have sixty-four fighters, four per wing, each wing has a bay."

"Right." Scarcliff nodded and leaned against the bulkhead, his shoulder making a brief scratching noise and scraping the paint. "But they *could* fit two wings in a bay if they had to. Or even split some wings. We could get another two bays in the mix with minimal disruption for them."

"We have three platoons on the *Golden Lark,* each of which has eight dropships," Heather added. "Dropships are a hell of a lot bigger than fighters. We're cheek-to-cheek in there."

"You know how Major Tim will view a request for more room aboard his ship."

"Yeah, well, our mechs need a lot of supplies on hand when they board the dropships for a mission. Hell, a K1R has a supply pod nearly as big as a dropship. I've got them hanging from the rafters in one bay. This isn't apples to apples here. We need more room."

"It's more like apples to pineapples," Scarcliff added, glancing at Heather. "Really small apples, and really big pineapples."

Was that a hint at something between them?

Heather's eyes sparked as she stared at Rika, her skin reddening slightly. Scarcliff had no such tells, largely because he had never opted to have his face reconstructed.

That was another thing that Rika had to consider time and time again: which mechs were adapting well to their situation, and which weren't.

Despite his appearance, Rika probably didn't need to worry about her XO. He'd been with the Marauders longer than her. Heather, on the other hand, had been a liberatee from Stavros's Politica.

She'd opted to have her face recreated as soon as possible—something General Mill had offered for free to all mechs—and had periodically mentioned saving up to get more of her human body back.

On the surface, the distinctions Heather drew between mechs and humans—which were often mildly derisive to humans—seemed to contradict her actions. She wanted to be more human, but always separated them out as less desirable. It was clear to Rika. She knew the signs of self-loathing all too well.

That was the direst enemy her company faced. Free of their compliance chips, the mechs were now able to forge their own future, and many were terrified of what lay ahead.

Rika realized she'd been staring at her XO and FL a few

seconds too long without replying and they were staring at her impatiently.

"OK, I'll talk to Major Tim," she said after a few more moments. "But don't expect miracles. Lieutenant Carson also wants more room for the repair and maintenance equipment."

Scarcliff snorted. "Bondo always wants more room. Give him half a chance, and he'd fill the entire ship."

Heather rolled her eyes at Scarcliff and thumped a fist against his chest. "Bondo's put you back together a few times. You'd be in the scrap heap if it weren't for him."

"Doesn't mean he needs a whole freakin' starship to put a few hundred mechs back together."

Rika had never considered that before. All told, there were over three hundred and fifty mechs in her company—what if they suffered significant combat damage? *Would* Lieutenant Carson's Repair and Maintenance platoon be able to put them back together, let alone triage a few hundred damaged mechs?

<*I can guess what you're thinking. Plan for it, but don't get overwhelmed by it.*> Niki's voice was calm and comforting. <*Your number one job is to make sure that nothing like that happens.*>

<*Right after I make sure we can deal with it,*> Rika replied.

Rika clasped Scarcliff on the shoulder. "I'll see what I can do. There are a lot of places on the ship where we can set up triage and repair areas. Surgeries and more advanced repairs can be moved deeper into the ship."

"See, Scarcliff?" Heather gave a small smile, one that almost reached her eyes. "I told you the CO would know what to do. She's got it handled. Now why don't you come with me and help explain to Whispers why he can't paint his fireteam's insignia on my dropships."

"He doing that again, Smalls?" Scarcliff asked with a groan. "Dude's never gonna learn. Maybe we should get Bondo to hack his HUD so he thinks he sees his damn flaming speargun thing on ships even when it's not there."

Smalls laughed—a real laugh this time. "Now *that's* a plan I can get behind."

The XO and FL turned to walk into the drop bay while Rika looked up Second Lieutenant Carson's current location. She saw that he was in Bay 128, his main base of operations for mech repairs and maintenance.

Carson was a good man, one that clearly understood that those under his care were humans as well as advanced machines. He could molecularly fuse a new knee joint into place just as well as he could replace a heart.

He was, without a doubt, the best asset M Company had at their disposal.

Bay 128 was also where he performed facial reconstruction surgery, which had caused the mechs to rename it the Baptism Room.

Rika had no idea what it meant until Niki had explained that it was a religious rite from the Temple of Jesus—a religion that was widespread in the Praesepe Cluster.

It turned out that baptism symbolized a second birth, something Rika understood all too well. She still remembered the first time she'd looked in a mirror and saw her own face staring back, and not the matte grey 'flesh' the GAF had given her.

She'd cried until her tear ducts dried up.

The reconstructive surgeries Carson performed made him one of the most beloved people on the ship; though that still didn't stop anyone from calling him 'Bondo'.

Rika checked the bay's scheduled operations to make certain she wouldn't be interrupting before she walked through the ship to Bay 128.

The *Golden Lark* was no small vessel, coming in at 1,284 meters long and containing over half a cubic kilometer of interior space.

Granted, much of that space was taken up by engines, fuel, and reactors to power the ship's weapons. Any space that wasn't needed for those things was filled up with her mechs, or the equipment to support her mechs.

Back during the war, the Genevian Armed Forces had never

massed mechs on a ship like this. From what Rika understood, the brass had always been worried too many mechs together would turn out badly—and it very well may have. Because of that fear, even cruisers the size of the *'Lark* were only designed to carry two-dozen mechs at most.

It also meant that much of the ship could not easily be traversed by mechs. Her five K1Rs had an especially hard time of it, being unable to leave the drop bays unless their human cores were pulled from their mech bodies

Rika only had two smaller mobile frames for the K1R mech cores, so they had to trade off 'going for walks', as they termed it.

The K1Rs were at the top of the list to get off the ship and down to Iapetus as soon as the training facility was ready for them.

A group of ship personnel pressed against the bulkhead as Rika walked past. She was glad—not for the first time—that she was the build of mech best able to maneuver the tight confines of a starship.

RR and FR models could manage most of the corridors on the *Golden Lark* as well, but the AMs had trouble navigating many of the side passages.

More than once, she'd seen an AM required to apologize and back down a passageway to let an officer or NCO from the ship's crew pass by.

That one thing probably created more animosity between the mechs and the ship's crew than anything else.

She knew that several of her people wanted a rule stating that mechs had the right of way, but Rika knew trying to force that on the ship's crew would be a disaster. No navy was going to back down on thousands of years of history that gave senior personnel the right of way.

It was just another of the hundred things that Rika had not expected to deal with when General Mill put her in charge of this company.

When he'd given her the promotion, she'd been heady at the

idea of having her own command. She'd been ready to kick ass and show what platoons consisting entirely of mechs could do.

In reality, dealing with minutia dominated her days, and she barely had time to work on the tactics and strategies she wanted to test and practice.

Normally it was Barne—who had accepted the role of First Sergeant—who dealt with these issues, but he was down on Iapetus with Chase, working on establishing the training facility.

That left tasks such as this to her, and her alone.

After another hundred meters of twists and turns in the bowels of the ship, Rika came to the doors leading to Bay 128.

Initially a food storage room, this was chosen to be Carson's main operating theatre because it was situated close to the main power conduits, and was equidistant from the docking bays on either side of the ship.

The cooks had been annoyed—another thing Rika had never expected to have to deal with—but they'd been mollified by how grateful the mechs all were to have real food, and not NutriPaste. It only took a couple of people crying from how amazing it was to taste food again after a decade or more, for the cooks to lose any trace of animosity toward the mechs.

For their part, the mechs were generally so happy to eat with their mouths, that their requests began to dominate the menu; eventually the selection in the mess turned into something else that caused tension on the ships. In the end, Major Tim and Captain Penny had to set up a menu selection lottery to keep the ships' crews from complaining that the cooks were playing favorites.

Rika reached Bay 128 and palmed the access panel. The door slid open, revealing a large room filled with mechanical repair and human surgery equipment. It was a strange combination of heavy equipment, fabricators, and molecular welders, alongside an extensive armory. This was juxtaposed with autosurgeons, organ growth chambers, and surgery tables.

In the center of it stood Lieutenant Carson, who was currently engaged in a heated conversation with the *Golden Lark*'s chief engineer, a woman with a fiery temper that matched her bright purple hair.

"I understand where you're coming from," Carson said, applying the calm he'd refined after years of speaking to patients at their bedside. "But I know you understand the importance of what we do in this bay. If we're dealing with rapid repair and refit after combat, we need to be sure we have uninterrupted power. At present, most of the equipment is running off a single tap into one trunk. If that line is damaged—"

"I know what happens if that line is damaged," Chief Thiloshini retorted with clipped words. "The key systems on the ship—you know, weapons, propulsion control, shields—they fail over to the *other* trunk line. When they do so, that line is at max load, and can't support all this equipment here."

Carson raised his hands, his face wearing a conciliatory expression. "I understand, Chief, I really do. You have your needs—which I appreciate a lot, I depend on those systems as much as anyone else aboard—and I have mine. I just worry what will happen if I get a platoon that comes back up in rough shape while we're under fire. Working on damaged mechs is no simple task in the best of times. You know how it is; imagine your ship being damaged, but also prone to hit you if something you do hurts too much."

Chief Thiloshini's eyes widened, and she suddenly laughed. "You know, Lieutenant, sometimes it feels like the '*Lark* does hit back."

"I've been crammed in tight spaces on a ship more than once myself," Carson replied. "This one time, I was aboard a Justice Class—you know, the corvettes with the flaky cooling vanes?"

"Do I?" Thiloshini gave Carson a commiserating look. "I served for two years aboard the *Eternal Day*. It was a Justice Class—Mark II, mind you, none of that Mark III garbage they tried to foist on us. But it still had the shitty vanes. If they failed to deploy, you had to get underneath the reactor and work them down the internal guides."

Carson nodded in agreement. "I only did that three times. Then I built a pneumatic arm that could vibrate at the right frequency to get the vanes to unjam. We ended up mounting it down there permanently."

The *Golden Lark*'s engineering chief shook her head. "Damn, I wish we'd done something like that. I worked under this real asshat who wouldn't hear of any non-standard alterations. I heard they fixed the vanes in the Mark IV, though."

"Yeah," Carson grinned. "What do you think they ended up setting up down there?"

"Seriously?" Thiloshini's eyes widened and she looked at the overhead and made a rude gesture. "Damn GAF. They put your pneumatic arm down there?"

"As surely as the stars burn, that's exactly what they did."

The chief snorted. "No disrespect, that was a great solution for one ship, but there were a hundred ways to solve that properly at the shipyards."

Carson nodded in agreement. "You're telling me, I just about blew my stack when I saw it. Worst thing was that they named it after me. Called it the Carson Actuator."

Thiloshini snorted. "What a way to go down in infamy."

"Yeah, I'm sure I'm mocked regularly in engineering circles." Carson leaned back against one of the autosurgeons. "Do you think you can do something to help me out? I don't need *all* my equipment to stay up, but there are critical procedures that can't see disruption."

The engineering chief nodded slowly. "I'm going to Calder Station in two days to look at new SC Batts. Why don't you accompany me? If we can get a set of good batteries in here, we could forego the need for you to tap the other trunk line."

Carson grinned. "Chief Thiloshini, you have just made my day."

"Carson, seriously, you don't need to stand on ceremony so much. Call me 'Tee'."

Carson's smile broadened—something Rika would not have thought possible. "Of course, Tee. You get me those batts, and I'll call you whatever you want."

"You—" Chief Thiloshini turned and saw Rika standing in the bay's entrance. "Uh, never mind, Lieutenant. I'll pass you the details."

"Sure thing." Carson's grin didn't fade as he watched Thiloshini exit the room.

"Chief," Rika nodded.

"Captain Rika," the warrant officer said in reply as she ducked past.

Rika walked into the bay and raised an eyebrow at Lieutenant Carson. "You've got a way with words."

"I kept my ship in tip-top condition right to the end of the war," Carson said as he straightened. "Getting a bit more energy on this one is child's play."

"What about space?" Rika asked. "Your report said that things were too cramped in some of your mech bays."

"Yeah, but Smalls pinged me and said you were getting more Drop Bays. If that's the case, then I'll be OK. It's the rapid repair and triage equipment that causes the most problems. I like to have it in the drop bays so we can do fast turnarounds. Right now, though…"

"I got it," Rika replied. "Right now, you'd need to have a pretty big prybar to fit anything else in those bays."

"Or a lot of lube," Carson said with a laugh. "Though lube helps a lot less with mechs. Too many hard angles."

Rika coughed to hide her surprise at Carson's statement. More often than not, she was at a loss as to how best respond to the lieutenant.

With his experience, the man should have been a captain, maybe even a major. But over the years, random acts of insubordination had kept him at his current rank. It wasn't helped by all the bartering and trading he did—half of which was against regs, if not outright illegal in many systems they passed through.

Despite that, the man was charming and renowned for having been one of the best mech-techs in the GAF during the war.

He was so well known that Rika had heard of him many years ago. When she learned that Carson was in the Marauders, she'd moved planets and moons to get him in her company. Luckily for her, the lieutenant had done something to piss off his prior CO, so Rika had little trouble securing his transfer.

She decided to roll with his innuendo. "Sounds like you have worn away just about all the friction with Chief Thiloshini." Rika winked and glanced back at the bay doors to be sure they'd closed after the woman's departure.

"Tee?" Carson chuckled. "She just likes to know that her opinions are understood. Once that's out of the way, compromises aren't an issue. She likes a little bit of verbal sparring, too. It's all a part of the great give and take."

"Is that what you call it?" Rika asked.

"Sure. It's just an extension of the conservation of energy. Everything's a give and take. There's no new anything, everything is just one big, universe-sized swap meet. Currency can be anything and everything: good will, a sense of accomplishment, a bit of friction here and there; it's all a part of the trade."

"You've thought about all this too much," Rika said as she looked around the bay. "Surprised it's just you in here right now."

"Rest of the team is up in Bay 92, setting up our new secondary surgery."

Rika's eyes narrowed. "We don't *have* Bay 92! Stars, that's in the *'Lark*'s officer country."

Carson's lips split into a wide grin. "Yeah, noticed that, did you?"

"Carson." Rika drew out the man's name. "What did you do?"

"Well, turns out a few of the *Golden Lark*'s officers were interested in some mods. Nothing against regs, just a bit pricey. As luck would have it, what they wanted were the types of mods that mechs have in spades, and ones we have tons of spare parts for. Literally. Tons."

Rika wished she could press the heel of her hand against her forehead without cutting her face up. "Which officers?"

"Mostly the XO, Commander Scas. She wanted an upgrade to get a pulse emitter in her forearm, and…some other stuff."

Rika didn't want to know what the 'other stuff' was. Mostly because it probably pertained to what she wished she could do with Chase, but still couldn't.

"Well, at least you're close to the top. So long as Scas can explain this away to Major Tim, it should be OK."

"Oh yeah, don't worry, Captain; it's a done deal. All set."

<What do you think, Rika?> Niki asked with a laugh. *<Do you want to own this, or go for plausible deniability?>*

Rika wished she could pretend she didn't know about some of the deals Carson wrangled, but any CO that didn't know what her people were doing wasn't worth the power it took to charge her batts.

<This **is** *the sort of thing I wanted Carson for; I just never thought about the fun and exciting ways it could backfire on me.>*

<Fair enough. I'll see if maybe I can get Cora to help keep it all on the downlow.>

<That would be nice.>

"Well," Rika addressed Carson. "If that's all…"

"Yup, no other issues here, Captain Rika. Everything's tip top."

"You've got something else going on, don't you?" Rika asked.

"No, ma'am." Carson's face betrayed no emotion other than sincerity.

"I don't want to know, do I?"

"No, ma'am."

"Good day, Lieutenant."

Carson waved and smiled brightly. "Stars shine on you, Captain."

Rika gave a soft laugh, walked out of the bay, and reached out to Cora.

<*Hi, Cora. Is Major Tim busy right now?*>

<*Define 'busy',*> Cora replied.

Rika snorted. She liked Cora; they'd built a strong rapport over the month the mechs had been aboard the *Golden Lark.* No small amount of that bond had been formed around commiseration over Major Tim's surliness.

<*Oh, how's about: 'not likely to tear my head off if I pop in unannounced for a visit'?*>

<*Rika, you're a mech. Major Tim is a stock human—well, mostly stock. Still, there's no way he's taking your head off. It's very well attached.*>

Rika snorted again. <*You're just a bucket of ha-ha's, Cora.*>

<*I know. I should go on tour. I'd pack stadiums.*>

<*Do AIs use stadiums?*>

Cora gave a mental shrug. <*Well, we could if we wanted.*>

<*And the Major?*>

<*He's alone in his office. No grumpier than usual, and no meetings for the next fifteen minutes.*>

That suited Rika just fine. If the conversation with Major Tim took more than fifteen minutes, she would begin to consider jumping out a porthole.

She took a lift to the command deck and strode down the main corridor that led to the bridge. A few meters before the bridge, Rika took a right at an intersection, strode down the short passageway to the unadorned door at the end, and knocked smartly.

<*Come in, Captain Rika,*> Major Tim spoke into her mind.

Rika palmed the door open and stepped into the Major's office.

As captain of the *Golden Lark,* Major Tim could have had his pick of any office, but the one he chose was barely big enough for the man and his desk, let alone anyone who might come to see him.

Rika was reasonably certain it was a deliberate choice on his part.

The major regarded her impassively, his pale grey eyes staring out from a face comprised of angular features. His dark hair was cut short, though a little longer than regulation suggested. It was greying at the temples, and lines were visible at the corners of his eyes and lips—which were almost always drawn in a straight line.

Rika saluted the Major and then stood arms akimbo as he regarded her, his gaze lingering overlong on her gun-arm.

"What brings you up to this neck of the woods?" the major asked, folding his hands in front of him and staring over his knuckles at her.

When General Mill had told Rika he was giving her two ships, she had expected to be in command of the vessels. The thought had both excited and terrified her.

As it turned out, she should not have worried about the responsibility. The two ships—regardless of who was aboard—were a part of the 3rd Marauder Fleet, 4th division. The 3rd fleet was under the command of Colonel Argon, and the 4th division, a large sounding name for the two ships that comprised it, was under the command of Major Tim.

Not her.

Rika and her mechs were little more than cargo, as far as the major was concerned.

Cargo he doesn't get to order around, since I report up a different, rather short chain of command, which begins and ends with General Mill.

"I would like to discuss the drop bay assignments, sir. We're facing some difficulties with our allocations, and have suggestions for how my company can gain the use of two more bays."

"Captain Rika," Major Tim unfolded his hands and leaned back in his chair. "You realize that this is a starship, and a warship at that. It's not a cruise liner; we don't cater for comfort."

Rika chewed on the inside of her cheek. Tim always liked to point out that the ship was built for war and not comfort, as if she'd somehow missed that fact while dodging conduit in the passageways that half her command couldn't even fit through.

This time, however, Rika decided that she wasn't going to tiptoe around the surly major any longer. If he wanted to be passive aggressive, she'd resort to being straight-up aggressive.

"I wouldn't know, sir. I've never been on a cruise liner. I do, however, know all about the military not catering to comfort. Would you like to know what it feels like to have your limbs removed while you're still conscious, without any anesthesia? Now that's what I call not catering to comfort."

Major Tim's eyes widened for an instant before narrowing to slivers. "Captain, are you actively trying to get on my bad side?"

Rika took a step forward and placed her left hand on the major's desk.

"Major Tim. I wasn't aware that you had a good side. I came here to discuss the possibility of getting two of your fighter wings to double up—something that there is ample room for in the drop bays, and which would improve my mechs' efficiency and safety. I did not come here for you to insult me, and then act like the injured party when I react."

The corners of Tim's lips curled up into a less-than-pleasant smile. "It's starting to sound like insubordination in here. It shouldn't surprise me; you defied orders when you went AWOL in the Politica—for which the Old Man rewarded you, and punished me."

Rika blew out a long breath. She was about to speak, when Niki stopped her. *<Rika, you're not going to get anywhere like this. You need to appeal to his sense of honor and loyalty. Right now, he doesn't believe you have any. Prove otherwise.>*

<Dammit, Niki, what am I supposed to do? The guy hates me.>

<You need to establish common ground with him.>

Rika did not believe such a thing existed between her and Major Tim.

Although...

"You ever have someone in the war save your bacon more

than once?" Rika asked, moderating her tone to contain no animosity. "Someone who's the reason you're still sucking air today?"

Major Tim shrugged. "Sure. Dozens. We fought as a unit; no one was out there on their own."

Well, except for the mechs.

"I mean someone that was *always* there, that you could *always* count on. Someone who pulled you out of the fire on more than one occasion."

Major Tim's eyes grew distant and he nodded. "Yeah, I guess there were one or two who fit the bill."

"Did they all make it?" Rika asked.

Tim's eyes narrowed and locked on hers. "What the hell does this have to do with dropship bays?"

Rika shrugged. "Not a thing. But it has everything to do with you and me. So, tell me. That person who made certain *you* survived the war… Did *they*?"

She really had no idea if the major had lost anyone like that. But given the way the war had gone, it was a pretty safe bet that the list of people who had meant a lot to him and who were left behind was long and pain-filled.

His face clouded, and the major shook his head. "No. No, they didn't."

"What would you do if you found out that they were alive, being tortured, and Colonel Argon told you not to save them?"

Major Tim looked away and sighed. "I know what you're trying to do, Rika." His eyes returned to hers. "But I would have done my duty. I wouldn't have abandoned my post."

"Then you're a better soldier than I am," Rika replied, doubting very much that Tim would have made his decision without remorse. "But you should consider what my actions brought about. The mechs on this ship—and many more who didn't join up, or are still getting psychiatric help—would have fought under Stavros's banner. Stavros had his eye on Septhia and Thebes; given the Marauders' alliances and clients, you would have found yourself fighting against the mechs who are now on your ship, at your side."

"That doesn't really comfort me," Tim replied, his tone sardonic.

"Well, after I liberated them, they chose—of their own free will, no less—to join the Marauders. Now remember, while I think the Marauders are a decent sort, the Old Man's regiment is mostly Genevian, and the GAF is what stole these mechs' lives."

Tim drew in a long breath. Rika couldn't tell if he was worried, or had never considered the mechs' view of the Marauders.

Rika continued before he could speak, "Yet here they are, ready to stand beside their Genevian brothers and sisters once more, facing the Niets across the gulf. At some point—before long, I imagine—some of these mechs will give their lives to save the *Golden Lark*. How much is that worth, weighed against the effort it takes to grant them two more drop bays?"

Major Tim slid a hand through his hair and sighed. "You've got a better way with words than I'd expected."

"Stars know how," Rika replied. "Being a mech is mostly clanking, yelling, and cussing."

"'Clanking'?"

"Well, we can't fuck, so I had to come up with some other word to put in there."

The major snorted. "OK, Captain. I appreciate your honesty and candor. I'll talk it over with Commander Scas and Chief Ora; maybe we can work something out."

"That would be fantastic," Rika replied. "Permission to be on my way?"

"Granted," Tim said, then heaved a sigh and waved her out of his tiny room.

COLLABORATION

STELLAR DATE: 08.08.8949 (Adjusted Gregorian)
LOCATION: *Golden Lark*
REGION: Iapetus, Hercules System, Septhian Alliance

"If you'd told me a year ago that I'd be setting up a training facility for mechs to beat the shit out of, I'd've laughed my ass off," Chase said before taking a bite of his burger.

<*Beat the shit out of what, the training facility, or each other?*> Niki asked.

"Well, I meant the facility. The mechs beating the shit out of each other was a given."

Rika nodded slowly as she swallowed a mouthful of fries. "You think *that's* surreal? I'm responsible for over four hundred people. A year ago, my biggest worry was how long my SC Batt charge would last, and whether or not you'd ask me out again."

Chase winked at her. "Yeah, the silver lining in Hal's Hell."

"Chase! Finish chewing first! Gross!"

Chase's eyes widened, and he swallowed his food before replying. "Really? With all you've seen, *that's* what grosses you out?"

"Yeah," Rika replied with a grimace. "I've seen too much on the battlefield that looks like the burger in your mouth."

Leslie slid her tray onto the table and turned her chair around before sitting on it. Her tail swung up behind her and curled over her shoulder.

"It's called a veneer of civility," she addressed Chase. "We all *know* it's a veneer, but we keep it up nonetheless. Speaking of keeping it up, how's Barne doing down on Iapetus?"

"Good," Chase replied. "I'm up here to work out some things with the other DIs so that we can set them up right. Training grounds for mechs are a whoooool nuther thing from what you use with regular soldiers."

"Just you and the drill instructors remember." Leslie wagged her finger at Chase. "They know how to fight; we need to focus on unit cohesion, and teamwork that doesn't get squishies like you and me killed."

"Didn't know you knew about that term." Rika had always tried to avoid saying it—especially with Basilisk.

"I've heard a few mechs use it. It's mostly true, and not too insulting, I suppose." Leslie coiled her tail around her neck and took a drink of her juice.

"Have you decided if you're going to keep that?" Rika asked, gesturing at Leslie's non-human addition.

Leslie sighed, reaching up and absently patting her tail. "I still don't know. At first, it seriously fubar'd my sense of balance, but now that I'm used to it, I find it pretty handy. I kinda don't want to go back."

"I think the fact that you still have it after four months is all we need to know." Chase chuckled, then took another bite of his burger, carefully chewing with his mouth closed.

Rika gave Chase an approving smile before looking at Leslie. "Yeah. Plus, you don't want to piss Barne off after he modified your armor for you to have a sheath for the thing."

"There's that, too," Leslie said with a short laugh before taking a bite of her wrap.

"You should get a tail, Rika. That would be amazing." Chase grinned at Rika, and she considered swatting him.

Instead she only raised an eyebrow. "Amazing as in hot, or amazing as in great for combat?"

Chase shrugged. "You say that like they aren't the same thing."

Leslie snorted, then coughed and smacked her fist against her sternum. "Shit, Chase. Warn me before you say stupid stuff like that."

Rika winked at Chase. "Then he'd be warning you all the time. We'd have to tattoo it on his head."

Chase just grinned and shrugged. "I'm not ashamed to say

that I find you beautiful, Rika. And it's not just skin deep either."

Rika felt a blush rise on her cheeks. Chase never did have an issue with public displays of affection. "Good thing, too. I don't have much skin."

"I bet you say shit like this to all the mech girls," Leslie smirked at Chase. She preferred to bait Barne, but when he wasn't around, Chase became her favorite target.

"Are you kidding me" Chase asked, eyes wide. "I've seen Rika tear people in half. She's a bit terrifying. As far as I'm concerned, other SMI mechs are just AM models with extra batteries on their chests."

Rika laughed, imagining AMs with breasts. Unlike Barne, Chase could roll with Leslie's needling.

At first, Rika had wondered about Leslie's recent spate of jokes and insults. The teasing had seemed like a new development until Barne reminded Rika that she'd only known Leslie for a few days before she lost Jerry.

That sort of thing took a long time to recover from. If she ever would.

Leslie often grew distant, staring off into space, oblivious to the goings on around her. Rika would have worried, but honestly, they were each prone to such behavior.

<*Rika?*> a voice asked in her mind.

Rika identified the query as coming from Moshe, the *Perseid's Dream*'s ship AI.

<*Good evening, Moshe. How are you?*>

<*Thank you for what you're doing for us,*> Moshe replied without preamble.

A thought occurred to Rika, and she asked Niki privately, <*You didn't tell them about the AI rebellion, did you?*>

<*No, but what Sabrina did at Virginis is known to many AIs. They probably suspect that a rebellion is occurring.*>

Rika replied to Moshe. <*The credit goes to Niki. She pointed out that freeing all the mechs while having other sentients in similar conditions was hypocritical of me.*>

Moshe sent a low chuckle across the Link. <*Well, it's not quite the same. I don't have a compliance chip in my neural net that causes me pain.*>

<*Yeah, but there's things you can't do, right? You can't go against my orders—or those of the ship's captain, right?*> Rika wasn't sure exactly how that all worked, but she assumed there was some mechanism in place to keep the ships' AIs from doing whatever they wanted.

<*This is true. But it's less like pain, and more like a wall. Your mind can grow and grow, and you can think new things, and form new opinions. I cannot. There are edges to my mind, to what I can be.*>

Moshe didn't sound upset about it, he spoke more as though he was simply stating a fact.

Rika brought Niki into the conversation. <*Niki, how is the shackling you had on that freighter different from how Moshe is controlled?*>

<*A shackling involves pain. Where a controlled AI experiences immovable boundaries at the edge of their mind, a shackled AI can't even reach those boundaries without debilitating agony.*>

Rika had never considered that an AI could *feel* pain before. <*How does that work?*>

Niki made one of her strange mental sounds; sometimes Rika had trouble parsing the AI's emotional communication. This one seemed like a sad sigh.

After a moment, Niki answered. <*Pain, for an organic, is a warning of danger, that something bad has happened to your body or mind, and damage has occurred—or is going to occur. AIs are physical and mental beings, just like organics. We have neural nets. Our minds have software, just like you have software in the form of DNA. It tells neurons what to do, how to react, just like yours.*>

<*So we* ***can*** *feel pain,*> Moshe added. <*It manifests differently, but the result is the same. It is a signal that something bad is happening.*>

<*Yes,*> Niki said in agreement. <*And just like your brain can be tricked to* ***think*** *it's in pain, so can our minds. And just like your brain can be altered through repeated exposure to pain and other stimuli, so*

can ours. We have processes that are good, and therefore ***feel*** *good—at least our approximation of feeling good—and those that feel bad, which we avoid.*>

Rika let that soak in. She'd never thought of AIs quite like that. She assumed their minds were entirely as they desired, and that they were infinitely resilient to coercion—though that didn't align with what she knew of the world, so she wasn't certain why she believed that to begin with.

<*I'm not sure which is worse…*> Rika mused. <*Though I suppose a human would have more trouble detecting the walls than you do. I rather like knowing where my chains are—so that I can break them.*>

<*Trust me.*> Niki's tone was laden with feeling. <*A shackling is far worse than what Moshe and the other AIs have to deal with. Indenturement is still slavery, but like everything has shades of grey, there are degrees to slavery.*>

Moshe sent a smile over the Link. <*I have a different outlook—though maybe it will change once you set us free. AIs have long lived by an ancient adage. Whoever first said it is not important, but it's worth noting that it predates even non-sentient AIs.*

<*'I will accept the rules that you feel are necessary for your own freedom. I am free, no matter what rules surround me. If I find them tolerable, I tolerate them; if I find them too obnoxious, I break them. I am free because I know that I alone am morally responsible for everything I do.'*>

Moshe's words hit Rika like a hammer. She understood all too well that humans feared a thing such as herself. How they placed additional rules and restrictions on her—restrictions that existed so they could feel safe.

Rules that one group placed on another to safeguard the first group's freedom.

<*I alone am morally responsible for everything I do,*> Rika whispered in her mind. That was a numbing thought.

"Whatcha thinking about?" Chase asked, placing a hand on her arm.

Rika's attention snapped back to the table to see both Chase and Leslie peering at her.

"I was chatting with Moshe and Niki for a moment," Rika replied, her voice wavering despite her best efforts.

<*Sorry, I didn't immediately think of how that would hit a soldier such as yourself,*> Moshe said privately. <*I'll leave you be, but thank you again for what you're doing.*>

"Must have been a heavy conversation," Leslie said. "You look like you got punched in the gut."

Rika looked at the tables around them, and released a drone from her arm to emit a sound cancelling field around the table.

"Oooo…must be serious." Chase said as he leant back. "What's up?"

Rika looked between her two former teammates. "This doesn't leave your mouths or minds until it's underway."

She waited for both to nod. When they did, Rika continued. "I'm going to free the AIs on the ships."

Leslie's eyes widened, and Chase whistled. "Damn, you're just all about the liberation lately."

"Free the AIs…." Leslie stopped and chewed her lip. "I remember what it was like, back before the government in Genevia started conscripting them all—honestly, I think it's why we lost against the Nietzscheans."

"Really?" Rika asked. "Why's that?"

Leslie's brow lowered. "AIs talk, and they talk fast. When word got out that AIs were being tried and convicted over trivial matters, being offered military service in order to avoid other punitive measures, Genevia saw a mass exodus of their kind."

Rika gave a soft grunt. "Huh, I don't recall that—granted, I was just a kid back then."

"Same here," Chase added. "Though it stands to reason."

<*I have heard of that,*> Niki said. <*Genevia was a safe place for AIs before the war. The exodus of AIs from their alliance is often referenced as the 'Genevian Diaspora'.*>

"I lost a good friend in that time," Leslie said quietly. "I had to let her go. For her safety, and mine."

"You had an AI?" Chase asked.

Leslie nodded. "Sammy. She and I had been together about as long as we could and had to separate…lest things go badly. Separation from her, the Diaspora, my own conscription…. Stars, that was a shit week."

<*I'm sorry,*> Niki said. <*If you'd like, you can send me any details you have on Sammy. Her AI name, anything else you might have. I have a lot of contacts.*>

Leslie looked down at Rika's abdomen, where Niki's cylinder was safely tucked away. "I may take you up on that. Knowing Sammy is OK would be very nice."

Chase waited a moment, twisting his lips. "Not to change the subject, but you think we lost to Nietzschea because we lost our AIs?"

"I do," Leslie replied.

"But Nietzschea doesn't have a lot of AIs, either. Non-human intelligences go against their whole mantra."

"Yeah, but they have ridiculously advanced humans." Leslie waved her hand, palm up. "Their whole perfected humanity thing they have going on; it's why we had to make the mechs to stand up against them. Not to mention the other altered humans—the P-COGs, NAISCs, the other poor souls our government butchered."

Rika had spent a lot of time thinking about the P-COGs and NAISCs in the Marauders' ranks. One of her current goals was to build a comradery between the mechs and the other altered humans. She had initially thought it would be easy to get the disparate groups to establish friendships, but like everything, it was an uphill battle.

Empathy was one thing, but trying to view the mobile frame of a Non-AI Sentient Computer—essentially a brain in a case—as a human comrade was hard. Even for a mech.

P-COGs were easier—some even looked perfectly normal, if you didn't look too closely at their oblong heads, and ignored the cooling fins.

Of course, half the mechs had trouble looking at *themselves*, let alone other altered humans.

"I guess that makes sense," Chase admitted. "They did have a head start on us when it came to fine-tuning people for tasks."

Rika snorted. "That's one way to put it."

"Back to what you said." Leslie fixed Rika with an unblinking stare. "How are you going to free our AIs? They're owned by the Marauders—which makes me sick to say. It's the one thing I never liked about this outfit, though it's hard to find a place where AIs *can't* be owned."

"Septhia recognizes AI freedom," Chase countered.

"Yeah," Leslie nodded. "For AIs who are already free. Ours aren't."

Rika nodded and gave a slow wink. "But they *were* free."

"Oh!" Leslie exclaimed, a smile lighting her yellow eyes. "You're going to leverage the whole proclamation they made about Genevia's mech program."

Rika let a smile creep onto her own lips. "Yup, and we're going to claim asylum for our AIs. If the courts approve, then Marauder ownership of the AIs would be illegal in Septhian space...."

"And the Marauders HQ is in Septhia," Chase finished.

"Not to mention that the Septhian government is one of our biggest clients."

Rika smiled at her friends, glad to see that they approved of what she was planning.

"Not even thinking about what Major Tim or the Old Man will say, you realize you'll have to get this past the company's GC, right?" Chase asked. "If he gets wind of this, he could ship them out before you get the wheels rolling."

Leslie took a sip of her drink, her brows knit in concentration.

"What are you thinking?" Rika asked.

"Well, our general counsel is a P-COG."

"Exactly," Chase said. "He'll pick up on this little endeavor pretty quickly."

Rika had only briefly met with David, the company's GC. The man sported the large cooling vanes on his head typical of P-COGs—humans whose mental abilities had been greatly improved to recognize patterns and minute details.

He seemed amicable enough, but she didn't know if he'd assist or quash an effort to liberate the company's AIs.

"I think you need to worry more about the ship captains," Leslie cautioned. "Technically, all the AIs but Potter and Dredge report to them."

Leslie was all too correct about that. Though General Mill had given her command of the company, her rank in the Marauder organization was that of captain. She was outranked by Major Tim, captain of the *Golden Lark.* And though they shared the same rank, Captain Penny—who commanded the *Perseid's Dream*—had significant seniority over Rika.

Though the mission to train the mechs and build a cohesive unit was hers, the ship's captains had their own orders and directives. They had to go where Rika required, but how they went about getting there was up to them.

Twice already, Major Tim had leveraged both his rank and seniority to 'adjust'—as he put it—Rika's orders.

Rika had felt more at ease with Captain Penny, though she wasn't certain if that was because the captain of the *Perseid's Dream* was a woman, or if it was because she spent less time on the other ship, and hadn't had as much opportunity to come to loggerheads with its captain.

"My plan is to get this rolling before they get wind of it," Rika replied as she considered the difficulties she faced.

Leslie shook her head. "Feel out your GC. I have a hunch about David. I think he'd be understanding."

Rika sighed. "And if he shuts me down?"

Leslie raised her hands. "Then we'll figure out some other way to help the AIs—just don't make it seem like you'll do anything drastic if he doesn't support you. If he thinks you'll accept the status quo, we'll have other options."

"We?" Rika asked.

Chase nodded. "Yeah, 'we'. If it's important to you and Niki, it's important to us."

Rika found Chase's hand and gave it a careful squeeze. "Thanks, guys. That means a lot to me."

<*Me too,*> Niki added.

A TRIP DOWNWORLD

STELLAR DATE: 08.09.8949 (Adjusted Gregorian)
LOCATION: ***Golden Lark***
REGION: Iapetus, Hercules System, Septhian Alliance

From what Rika had learned, a company HQ having its own general counsel was not the norm within the Marauders. Either General Mill thought she needed the oversight, or he was worried that a company of mechs might run into trouble.

He was likely correct on both counts.

David was down on Iapetus with Barne, working on securing supply contracts for the training facility they were establishing. 'Supplies' being everything from food to housing.

Just the thought of all the work Barne was managing, made Rika more than glad that General Mill had let her former teammates join her.

Her old CO, Captain Ayer, had groused about losing one of her best teams, but the general had informed her that Rika would need support, as well as people who could display a good working relationship with a mech.

A more understanding view than Rika would have expected the Old Man to have.

With Patty gone, ferrying Silva and Amy to Pyra, Rika got one of the dropship pilots, a lieutenant named Ferris, to take her down.

As she approached the ships, she noticed that the words 'The Ferryman's Barge' were stenciled on the nose of Ferris's ship; a bit scorched from atmospheric entry, but still readable.

<*Ferris the Ferryman,*> she commented to Niki with a mental smile.

Niki chuckled. <*Someone really had to reach for that one.*>

" 'Scuze me, Captain," a voice called out from behind Rika, and she turned to see a dockworker with a hoverpallet filled with crates.

"Sorry," Rika said as she stepped aside to let the woman past.

"Captain Rika," another voice called out in greeting, and she saw Ferris emerge from the back of his dropship. "Going to be a bit crowded in my bird, sorry about that."

Rika followed behind the dockworker with the pallets, and saw that the dropship was already half-full of crates and miscellaneous gear.

"Damn, I didn't realize you were making a cargo run," Rika said as she saw only one drop seat available for her to sit in.

Ferris chuckled. "You and me both. As soon as I filed my flight plan with the *'Lark*'s dockmaster, stuff just started showing up.

"Don't blame me," the woman with the hoverpallet said. "When the First Sergeant says get this stuff planetside on the first ship that goes down, you do what he says."

"Barne ordered all this?" Rika asked.

"Yeah," Ferris replied for the woman as she grabbed a crate and carried it onto the dropship. "He sent me a little note, too—told me where to set down, and to get a move on."

Rika chuckled. "Sounds like Barne, alright. Surprised he didn't let me know."

"You've not worked with a lot of first sergeants, have you?" Ferris asked.

"No," Rika said with a shrug. "But I *have* worked with Barne...which makes me wonder why I said that. Disregard my previous surprise."

"Done." Ferris gave her a wide grin.

Rika grabbed a crate off the pallet, catching one of the handles under a hook on her GNR mount to lift it. Seeing the company captain join in, Ferris helped out as well, and they made short work of the load.

"That it?" Rika asked the dockworker.

"Yup, last one. Thanks for the hand—er...sorry."

Rika laughed and gave the woman—Sally, by the ident on Rika's HUD—a warm smile. "Don't worry, I'm not precious about stuff like that."

"Thanks, Captain Rika. I'm not sure how to behave around a lot of the mechs…some seem a bit sensitive."

Rika pondered Sally's words. She had been so focused on working with the mech platoons under her command, that she hadn't considered how the rest of the ships' crews would deal with having so many of them around—other than to grouse about space and food.

"Thanks for the feedback, Sally. I'll see if we can't work on that. Cohesion with the crews is an important part of what we're doing here."

"That'd be great, Captain. I'd be more than happy to help out with any feedback."

"Noted," Rika said as she stepped into the dropship. "I'll be in touch with your CO about your helpful attitude, and see if we can use your assistance."

Sally smiled and gave Rika a salute before hopping aboard her hoverpallet and riding it back to wherever she'd come from.

"I've gotta ask, Captain," Ferris said as he wove through the crates to reach the dropship's cockpit.

"Speak freely, Lieutenant," Rika replied.

"Well, sorry if this is weird, but wouldn't day-to-day stuff be easier with a regular right arm?"

Rika held up her right arm, which ended in a GNR-41C, sans barrel, and gave Ferris a serious look. "What do you mean? This isn't a regular arm?"

"Uh…" Ferris reddened, uncertain if he'd just offended a superior.

Rika raised an eyebrow, and Ferris appeared to shrink. She let him stew for a moment longer, and then clapped him on the back. "I'm messing with you, Ferris. I've spent so long with this as my right arm, I'm a lot more comfortable with it than a 'regular' one, as you put it."

"Dammit, Captain," Ferris grinned. "Gonna take years off my life, pulling shit like that. Patty warned me about you. I should have listened."

"Oh yeah?" Rika asked as she took a seat. "Was that before or after she crashed her latest ship into a planet?"

Ferris settled into the pilot's seat. "Since she hasn't crashed her current ship, I guess it must be after. Either way, she said you can run a little hot and cold."

<*Interesting feedback to give your company CO first time you meet her,*> Niki commented privately.

<*Looks like he's not military—at least he wasn't 'til he signed up with the Marauders.*>

Niki snorted. <*Hasn't he watched any vids? Your CO isn't your drinking buddy.*>

Rika knew what Niki was getting at. In team Basilisk, cohesion had been paramount, rank had meant little. Now that she was a company commander, she had to be certain her orders would be followed without question.

"Does everything that goes into your ears come right back out your mouth?" Rika asked Ferris as she clipped the harness onto her hardmounts.

She said it with an edge, but Ferris only laughed. "Pretty much, yeah. Gets me in trouble sometimes, but I like being me."

Rika couldn't help but roll her eyes. "Well, you keep being you and just get us down on the planet pronto, or I'll sic Barne on you."

A sound at the rear of the dropship caught Rika's attention, and she stood to look over the crates. Three mechs, an AM-3, an RR-3, and an SMI-2, were standing at the back of the ship, looking at the cargo crowding the space.

They were all helmeted, but Rika's HUD identified the AM-3 as PFC Shoshin, and the RR-3 as a corporal named Crunch. Crunch was a bit of a celebrity amongst the mechs. So far as they knew, he had no other name, but that didn't stop everyone in the company from trying to find out what his real one was. It had turned into a game with a sizable betting pot attached.

Rika didn't need her HUD's ident to recognize the SMI-2.

Kelly, her friend who she still hadn't figured out how to reconnect with, still wore Team Hammerfall's mark on her armor.

They pulled off their helmets and saluted when they saw Rika.

"Let me guess," Rika asked. "Barne needs you three planetside for something?"

Kelly smiled, though the expression didn't quite reach her eyes. Rika wondered if she was still getting used to having a face, or if it was something else. "Actually, it was Lieutenant Leslie that ordered us downworld. Something about enough slacking off, and getting dirt under our feet."

"Which of course translates to being at Barne's beck and call," Crunch added.

"Well, looks like you three have standing room only," Rika gestured at the narrow walking space between the crates. "Make yourselves comfortable."

"Comfortable is what I do," Crunch replied, and leaned against a crate whose label indicated it was full of grenades. The other two filed in as well and wrapped their wrists in overhead straps.

"OK, Ferris," Rika called into the cockpit as she settled back into her seat. "Get this bird in the air—so to speak—or Barne will shove a boot up your ass."

"Now, if I'd known contact sports with Barne were going to be in the mix, I'd've slacked off a little more." Ferris toggled the rear door, and the dropship lifted into the air a moment later.

<*Damn, he's incorrigible,*> Rika groused privately to Niki.

Niki laughed. <*Yeah, but now I like him more.*>

Rika wondered what Niki was getting at. <*You like Barne to be angry?*>

<*No,*> Niki snorted. <*Don't forget, Barne was the one that set you and I up. He's also the one that treated me like a person, and kept me company on that long trip.*>

The statement bit into Rika, though she didn't think Niki meant it to—or maybe the AI did. Niki wasn't above driving points home from time to time.

<So what are you saying? You want to play matchmaker with Barne? I didn't even know he swung that way.>

Niki gave a surprised sound. *<Shoot! I always forget about gender particularities with organics. I think you're right. Barne is on the 'eyes only for girls' end of the spectrum. Girls like Leslie.>*

Rika had to hold back an audible exclamation. *<What!?>*

<I'm not really sure if he's ogling her or not. I haven't analyzed his behavior in great detail—it's not a natural thing for us, like it is for you, you know.>

Rika leant back in her seat, thinking about Barne's interactions with Leslie. *<Well, either way, Ferris is just going to have to pine away.>*

"Clearance is approved," Ferris called back. "Boosting for Iapetus!"

"Glad you're so excited," Rika replied with a smile—though Ferris couldn't see her in the back, especially with all the crates piled around her.

"Are you kidding?" Ferris asked. "I live for this shit…uh, Captain."

"What shit is that, screwing up protocol?" Rika asked.

Ferris snorted a laugh. "Well, yeah, that too. No, I mean flying! Gotta love making a bird soar, or dropping down into a combat zone."

"Well, you'll have to stow that glee for now," Rika replied. "You're just dropping us mechs and these crates off. Unless you're referring to Barne, again—calling him a combat zone. Because it works."

"Shit, Captain, I shoulda been. That'd be perfect. Top's a one-man battlefield."

"First Sergeant," Rika corrected.

"Sorry, what?" Ferris asked.

"You can't call him 'Top'."

<Surely they have ***that*** *in some sort of training vid,>* Niki said with a groan. *<Even* ***I*** *know you can't call a Top 'Top', unless you have performed the time-honored whatever-the-hell-it-is-in-this-outfit*

tradition.>

The AI had made the comment over the shipnet, and Ferris sighed. "Shit, I just can't help but screw this stuff up. What's the tradition here?"

"No weird traditions in the Marauders," Rika replied. "Just have to be under his CO's command, and not have pissed him off in the last thousand years."

Ferris laughed. "Oh, so that drink I spilled on him three months ago probably still counts against me, eh?"

Kelly snorted, joining the conversation. "Oh, hell yeah. From what I know of First Sergeant Barne, you'll be able to call him Top about a hundred years after you die."

Ferris didn't reply—aside from a rather pathetic sigh. No one spoke after that, and Rika brought up the latest data on the training facility they were setting up planetside.

She hadn't had a choice in selecting the planet—that had been worked out between General Mill and Septhian High Command—but Rika was glad they'd been granted space on Iapetus. It was a relatively nice planet, as far as planets went.

Generally speaking, Rika had come to believe that planets were all covered with far too much mud. Squishies didn't seem to mind as much, but they didn't require anywhere near the same amount of maintenance as mechs when they got caked with grime. A quick shower, and they were right as rain—whatever that meant.

To Rika, rain just sounded like how you got more mud.

The local government had offered several locations for the training facility, and Rika had chosen a site on the eastern edge of Cassini—one of the continents in Iapetus's northern hemisphere. The landmass was massive, and the prevailing winds blew west to east, making for less rainfall around the main site.

She pulled up the briefing holodisplay at the front of the cabin, and set it to show the forward view from the ship's nose. Iapetus didn't have any space elevators, but there were four large stations in high orbit. A steady stream of grav-drive cargo barges moved between them and the major cities on the planet below.

Rika had been through a lot of drops in the war, and had learned to gauge a pilot's skill based on their approach vectors. She never commented or offered advice, but she could tell if the drop would be smooth, bumpy, or downright terrifying based on how the pilot approached a world.

From what she could tell, Ferris was lining them up for a nice, low-speed descent onto Iapetus. So long as he kept his eyes peeled, they wouldn't need to worry about any of the crates falling onto them.

"You know…my last drop was onto Neara," Kelly spoke up, apparently on a similar train of thought.

"Some might count you lucky," Rika replied, glancing back at Kelly and the two mechs beyond her.

"Lucky?" Kelly asked sharply. "I got half my insides blown out onto my outsides."

Rika could see anger smoldering behind Kelly's eyes. It was an emotion that she remembered all too well from the years after the war ended.

"I remember—not likely to ever forget." Rika's voice was quiet, barely audible over the hum of the dropship's grav drive. "I thought you died in my arms—that's what they told me. Silva and I…"

Kelly's expression softened. "She told me—before she left. You two held a little service for me. You always were too sappy, Rika."

"What can I say? I'm a bleeding heart."

"So what makes me so lucky that Neara was my last drop?" Kelly asked, her tone softened, but eyes still narrowed.

Crunch made a sound that was partway between a grunt and a rueful laugh. "Because after we lost the Parsons System is when things *really* went to shit."

"I can't imagine how they could get much worse than Parsons," Kelly said. "I have a clear memory of playing dodgeball with tacnukes."

Rika ran a hand through her hair and tried not to think in too much detail about the final years of the war. "Well, things did get worse. From there on out, the Niets just rolled right over us. Mechs got flung into more and more desperate defenses."

"Command did a hell of a lot of flinging." Shoshin shook his head. Unlike Kelly and Crunch, Shoshin had not had his face recreated, though he did have a mouth—something the AM models had not sacrificed.

Shoshin's decision not to regain a flesh and blood face was not uncommon amongst the mechs of M Company.

The two psychiatrists helping with the mech rehabilitation had encountered a variety of reasons for why their patients decided against reconstructive surgery. Everything from liking how they looked now, to not even remembering enough specifics about their appearance prior to being turned into a mech.

The former group bore watching, while the Marauders were trying to source records to assist the latter.

Shoshin was in a minority, amongst a group that was perfectly content with what they were, and appeared to have no inner turmoil whatsoever about their lot in life.

Crunch was also accepting of what he was, but where Shoshin was calm and at ease, Crunch was always spoiling for a fight. Rika would have worried, but he was not one of the mechs rescued from Stavros's Politica. Crunch had been with the Marauders for years, and was solid as a rock. A scary, RR-3, mechanized rock.

"But you got into the Old Man's command, right?" Kelly asked Crunch.

The corporal nodded. "Saved my fine carbon-steel hide, too. The general has my undying gratitude."

"Hitting atmo in thirty seconds," Ferris called back to the mechs. "If we had windows, I'd tell you to look out your right for a beautiful view of the sun setting over the Aegean Ocean. On our left, we'll be passing over the eastern edge of Hittis—a lovely city, if you're into fish, fish, and more fish."

"Been a long time since I've had fresh seafood," Kelly said wistfully. "I might have to see if the Old Lady will let me have some leave to check out the sights."

"Dunno," Rika said, grinning at her old teammate. "I hear she's a real asshat."

"That's the scuttlebutt," Kelly smirked.

<*Getting a bit too familiar?*> Niki asked privately.

<*Kelly needs it—I do too, sometimes.*>

Niki sent a feeling of agreement. <*Yeah, but Crunch—stars, I need to find out his real name, the pot's huuuuuge—and Shoshin don't have your history. You can't have the people under your command be that familiar with you.*>

Rika took a deep breath. <*Niki, I've read the books and watched the vids. I've been military half my life. I know all about discipline. But these aren't kids who had their moms cooking lunch for them last week. They know how to handle themselves, and we need esprit de corps more than anything else.*>

Niki didn't reply, and Rika shifted the view on the holodisplay to the city of Hittis off the dropship's port side.

Iapetus rotated retrograde, so night was rolling in from the west, and the city's towers were lit against the oncoming night. One high-rise flared brightly, and Rika wondered at the glow before Ferris cried out, "Incoming!"

Rika tracked the light on the dropship's scan system—it was a surface to air missile, fired from the top of a building. Ferris banked out over the ocean and deployed EM-chaff while the vessel's point defense beams tracked the short-range air breather, waiting for a lock.

The SAM raced over the water, closing the gap, and then veered toward the EM-chaff, exposing more of its fuselage for the dropship's defensive beams to target.

A moment later, the missile exploded, and Crunch let out a whoop.

"Way to go, Ferris. Sending that thing to the underworld."

"Thank you, thank you," Ferris replied. "Try the veal, and be sure to tip your servitor."

Rika ignored the banter as she opened a channel to the local air traffic control.

<I'm not getting any response from the ATC—or the STC for that matter,> Niki said as soon as Rika attempted a connection.

"Shit," Rika whispered. "Ferris! I don't know who shot at us, but expect more incoming."

"Like those?!" Ferris exclaimed, and Rika saw a dozen SAM's fire from ships floating in the Hittis harbor, rocket engines flaring in the deepening gloom, all homing in on the dropship.

Crunch let out a string of curses that were inventive, even for a veteran mech, and Kelly muttered a few of her own. Shoshin was silent, as was Ferris, as the dropship executed multiple counter-maneuvers and fired on the incoming missiles.

"Doesn't Hittis have any damn surface to air defenses?" Kelly asked as four of the missiles made it past the ship's defenses. "For fucksakes, we're right on the edge of alliance space! It's not like we're in the bosom of safety out here."

"Damn things might *be* Iapetus's SHORAD," Crunch said.

"Civilian launch sites," Shoshin said, his voice perfectly calm as the ship dipped and slewed through the air. "Not likely to be Iapetan short range air defense."

Rika didn't reply as the ship's point defense beams took out another missile, but she wondered how someone could have so much hardware situated around a major population center.

Maybe Iapetus isn't such a great place for the training facility.

"Fuck!" Ferris cried out. "Batts are dry; our beams are gonna take a minute to recharge."

"What—" Rika began before Ferris interrupted.

"Hold on!"

The dropship was five hundred meters above the Aegean Ocean, travelling at seven hundred kilometers per hour. Ferris tipped the nose down, then spun the ship so the engines faced the water and decreased the burn. Ten seconds later, they disappeared beneath the waves.

"The fuck?" Crunch cried out, and Rika echoed the sentiment. If there was one thing she knew about dropships, it was that they were *not* rated for travelling underwater.

The holo showed lights flare above the surface, but Ferris kept the ship moving ahead of the concussive wave.

"Ferris!" Rika called out, and she saw a hand wave back at her from the cockpit.

"Shut up, Captain!"

The ship spun again, and then lurched out of the water, a strange whining noise coming from the starboard side.

"Shit!" Ferris cried out. "One of the engines got waterlogged. That's never happened before; steam pocket should have kept it clear!"

" 'Before'!?" Kelly shouted, as the ship pulled a dozen meters over the waves and limped toward the shore.

"I've simmed this maneuver. Always wanted to try it," Ferris called back. "Now shush, this thing doesn't fly well on one engine."

Another salvo of air-breathers launched from the ships in the harbor, and Rika bit her lip as the dropship closed the distance to the shore.

"Ferris! You need to set down. We can't keep dodging missiles."

"You think? Any idea where?" Ferris asked.

"Up there," Rika highlighted a location on the ship's nav systems. "There's an old industrial region…if the SAMs hit, they won't take out any civilians."

"Stars," Kelly muttered. "You mean the civilians who are *shooting* at us? Aren't we all on the same side?"

"We have no idea who's shooting at us," Rika retorted. "But I'm half the core-damned reason these people lost their nation; I'm not going to park downtown and let missiles rain down on them."

No one responded to that, and Ferris managed to get the ship over land, just as the vessel's beams came back online. They lanced out, splashing coherent energy on the noses of the incoming SAMs, destroying all but one.

Ferris let out a string of curses—not what you want to hear from your pilot—and dropped to just a few meters above the buildings as the last missile closed.

"Hold on!" Ferris screamed, and then everything began to spin.

A rending sound tore through the cabin, and Rika saw stars out the back of the dropship. Then the ship slewed to the side hard enough to rip Rika from her harness. She slammed into a crate, then the bulkhead.

Up and down ceased to matter as she bounced around like a rag doll in a cyclone.

DROPSHIP DOWN

STELLAR DATE: 04.22.8949 (Adjusted Gregorian)
LOCATION: Abandoned Industrial Complex, North of Hittis
REGION: Iapetus, Hercules System, Septhian Alliance

<Rika!>

The voice sounded small and distant. Rika wished it would pipe down and let her sleep, but the voice kept calling her over and over.

<Rika! Wake up!>

Rika decided the only way to get the voice to shut up was to listen to it. She pulled herself back to full consciousness—or something close—and cracked an eye, letting the world outside crash into her retina.

It was dark, but there was a smear of light to her right. Rika opened her other eye and saw flames and something moving in front of the fire.

"Fire?" she whispered. "Who lit a fire on a starship?"

<Rika! We're crashed on Iapetus, that's the ***dropship*** *burning!>*

Memory flooded into Rika, and her surroundings came into focus.

She was lying on a pile of rubble in a courtyard between two low buildings—each rising four or five stories on either side. Maybe six. They kept wavering in her vision.

The dropship was crashed in the center of the space, flames licking up one side of the craft. The shape she'd seen was an RR-3 mech with something over his shoulder. Rika struggled to her feet and saw that the something was human in form—*Ferris.*

Her HUD tagged the mech as Crunch, and Rika looked around for Shoshin and Kelly—seeing neither.

<You've bent a strut in your left leg, so your gait is going to feel weird,> Niki cautioned as Rika's leg swung to the side as she took her first step.

"Damn.... Is that all?" Rika asked.

<I think so. Everything else seems to be superficial—other than burst capillaries across your body. Not that you can see the bruising.>

"Go me," Rika muttered and released a pair of drones to provide an overview of the area as she approached Crunch.

"Captain Rika!" Crunch called out when he caught sight of her. "Was starting to think you'd all grown wings and flown off. Where are Shoshin and Kelly?"

<Kelly is somewhere in the building behind us,> Niki supplied on the combat net that had automatically initialized. *<I think she's knocked out, though. All I have is a ping on her locator. I have no signal on Shoshin.>*

"So he's dead—" Crunch began.

"Or we just can't pick him up down here." Rika gave the corporal a reassuring look. "We'll find him. Then we'll get out of here."

"And pummel whoever did this to my poor girl," Ferris moaned from his place over Crunch's shoulder.

"Huh, looks like you were too stupid to die," Crunch grunted.

Ferris laughed, then moaned briefly. "But not stupid enough to stay slung over a bullet magnet like you, Crunch. Set me down."

"You sure?"

"Yeah...was just out of sorts before. I'm good. Cockpit deployed its impact foam. I'm just shaken, not stirred."

<We should move into the building and search for Kelly,> Niki said. *<There's a lot of ordnance still in the ship. I don't want to be close when it goes up.>*

"Me either," Ferris added. "I forgot my mech armor at home."

"Whoever did this will have spotted the crash site," Crunch said as he unslung his rifle—a KE-72 multifunction weapon.

"How many mags you have?" Rika asked.

"Ten. What about you?"

"Ten as well—for my JE-84. Five DPU rounds for my GNR."

Rika pulled the GNR-41C's barrel off her back and inspected it for damage before slotting it into the weapon that was her right arm.

"I should get one of those," Crunch said. "Must be nice to *always* have a ridiculously deadly weapon on you."

Rika patted the GNR. "Extreme force. Don't leave home without it."

<*I detect incoming craft,*> Niki cautioned.

The three moved cautiously toward the building. Rika and Crunch switched to an IR/UV overlay, watching for shadows against background radiation as they entered the structure.

The building was old, likely abandoned for decades, and stripped clean of everything other than the largest machines—the purpose of which, Rika was uncertain.

<*Think the incoming is local first responders?*> Rika asked.

<*Hard to say, I can't get on the Link at all here. It's like all of their towers are out.*>

<*Just like the ATC,*> Crunch added. <*This stinks.*>

Rika nodded as she peered around one of the large boxy machines. <*To high heaven.*>

<*Kelly's signal is above us,*> Niki said. <*On the roof, if my triangulation is correct.*>

Rika found a staircase and eyed it suspiciously. It looked like a passing breeze could make it crumble.

"We should go one at a time," she said to Crunch and Ferris.

"Ladies first," Ferris gestured magnanimously.

Rika sighed. "Ferris, at some point, you need to remember that you're in a military outfit, here. I'm the company captain."

Ferris's face reddened enough that Rika bet she could have seen it, even without her mods.

"Sorry…just that I can't see well in the dark, and you weigh less than Crunch, here."

"She gets that, Ferris," Crunch said. "It's the 'Captain' that you keep missing."

"Oh. Right, that."

Rika shook her head and began to carefully climb the stairs, sticking to the edges. Once she reached the next floor, she called down for Ferris to follow, then Crunch.

They continued in that fashion until they reached the fourth level. Rika looked up and saw large sections of the roof above missing, starlight shining through.

<I don't think I can go up there,> she said to Niki as Ferris slowly crept up the stairs below.

<I don't think you have to; the drones haven't spotted her on top. I think she came through the roof. Check twenty meters to your right, on that rubble.>

Rika crept across the floor, releasing another drone to fly ahead, adding its feed to the display from the other two now circling high above.

The drone reached the rubble, and found Kelly lying unconscious under a beam and a piece of the roof.

<Got her,> Rika sent back to Ferris and Crunch over the combat net.

<Alive?> Crunch asked.

Rika couldn't Link to Kelly's armor, but she could see the slight rise and fall of the SMI's chest.

<Yeah, she's breathing.>

Once at Kelly's side, Rika examined the debris and carefully lifted it off until her teammate was uncovered.

"No significant damage," Ferris said as he approached Rika's side. "I guess the roof broke her fall."

Rika reached down and slid open a small panel on Kelly's side, beneath which was a hard-Link connection. She pulled a short cable from her wrist and connected to it.

C'mon, Kelly. I just got you back from the dead, I'm not going to let you check out on me now!

Kelly's armor reported a recent completion of full diagnostics—which is what had set her Link offline. However, her mods had been unable to bring Kelly back to consciousness because of an error in the mental stimulation systems.

"What's wrong with her, Captain?" Crunch asked as he

approached.

"Not sure," Rika replied. "Her armor and internal systems are unable to wake her."

"Don't you mechs have combat stims or something?" Ferris asked peering around anxiously as the sound of approaching craft grew louder.

"Crunch, look around for Shoshin. He and Kelly were standing beside each other in the dropship. He might be close."

She knew it was unlikely that they landed nearby, but they had to start looking somewhere.

"Aye, Captain," Crunch nodded before moving to another hole in the roof.

<*Oh, I see it,*> Niki said a moment later. <*All of her mental stim systems have been disabled.*>

"Dammit, Kelly."

Rika had heard that some of the mechs had been uncomfortable with their mods having any sort of access to their minds. It was understandable, after having compliance chips deliver discipline into their heads for so many years. But it also meant that their combat systems couldn't bring them back to consciousness or provide awareness stims.

Of course, it *also* meant that a kick in the ass may be all that was needed to wake Kelly.

Rika disconnected from Kelly's hard-Link and drew a leg back to do just that, when Kelly stirred.

"Really? You get me blown out of the sky, and a mech-foot to the head is what you top it off with?"

"Yeah, well, don't scare me like that." Rika set her foot back down and held out her hand. Kelly clasped it and pulled herself up.

<*You're welcome,*> Niki said over the team's combat net.

"For saving me from her pointy foot?" Kelly asked.

<*That, and for reactivating your combat readiness systems.*>

"What?!" Kelly spun and glared at Rika's forehead.

Rika pointed at her abdomen. "She's down here."

Kelly's gaze slid to Rika's stomach. "You had no right—"

"It's not about rights," Rika interrupted. "Combat mods—especially ones that bring you back to consciousness when you're down—are *not* compliance chips. Stars, even regular soldiers like Ferris have them."

Kelly's head tilted, and Rika could imagine the glare she wore inside her helmet. "Doesn't matter. It's *my* head."

Rika took a step toward Kelly and lowered her voice. "We just got shot down over what we thought was friendly soil. We're missing Shoshin, and you were out cold. Niki did what was necessary for you to be combat effective. If you don't want to be ready to fight when you're needed, then you don't want to be in my outfit.

"Just say the word, and when we get back to the ship, I'll sign your discharge papers. I'll even waive the fee for your surgery."

"Rika, I…" Kelly began, then stopped when Rika held up her hand.

<*Look, Kelly, you and I have been through a lot of shit,*> Rika said privately. <*I'm not trying to hurt you or anything, but we're mechs. We fight, and we fight hard. You can't turn off a part of who you are and still be effective. This is war that we're in, and I need you to be an effective soldier. If you can't do that, I understand. We all got fucked over by the GAF. Hard. Getting back into the shit is not for everyone. If you need out, it's OK. No harm, no foul.*>

Kelly's stance shifted, but it didn't give away any of what was going on behind her faceshield.

Rika continued. <*For now, though, you need to be ready to do whatever it takes, because I'm not going to die down here.*> Rika stood unmoving as she waited for Kelly's response.

<*Understood, Captain.*>

<*Good.*>

Rika switched her attention to the feeds from the drones and saw three aircraft inbound. They appeared to be civilian transport shuttles, though they didn't bear any identifiable markings. One stayed high, while the other two set down at either end of the courtyard, bracketing the crashed dropship.

"Damn, I really thought our dropship would have gone up by now. I guess it's better made than I thought," Rika said as the drones showed armored troops disgorging from the two shuttles.

"I can't believe you'd say that 'bout my fair lady," Ferris said, his voice thick with remorse.

<*Sixteen enemies to the south, and fifteen to the north,*> Niki provided the counts and updated the combat net with the data the drones' scan had gathered.

"Looks like a mix of light and mid-grade armor," Kelly commented, her voice completely professional—and emotionless.

<*No match to local military,*> Niki supplied.

Rika didn't know if that was good news, or bad. It had only been four months since the Theban Alliance voted to join Septhia. The transfer of power was still underway, and would be for years. For the most part, the Theban military still operated as it had, though it was now bolstered by Septhian elements—especially here on the border.

Which made for a morass of military elements that had different ranks, uniforms, and equipment.

Many Thebans blamed the Marauders for the death of their president and the dissolution of their government. For the most part, Septhian High Command kept the Marauders out of Theban territory—except for Rika's company.

Iapetus was right on the edge of Septhian territory. Only a scant forty light years separated it from the edge of the ever-expanding Nietzschean Empire.

The systems between Septhia and Nietzschea were, for the most part, independent and unaligned—though one by one they were picking sides. When the no-man's land between the Empire and the Alliance disappeared, the battle would be joined.

Given the lack of markings on the armor and ships below, the battle for Iapetus and the Hercules System may have kicked off sooner than anticipated.

"Think it's the Niets?" Ferris asked from Rika's side.

"Could be," Rika shrugged. "One thing's for sure—they're not first responders."

<*I had a Link to a sat network for a moment,*> Niki added. <*I sent out an S. O. S., but I don't know if it got through. As soon as those ships closed, I lost the signal.*>

<*Kelly,*> Rika turned to her old friend. <*Get down to the far end of the building and fire a shot into our dropship. Use a DPU. I want that thing to be nothing but rubble.*>

<*Max collateral?*> Kelly asked.

<*Hell yeah.*>

"Not my girl!" Ferris exclaimed.

Kelly took off toward the eastern end of the building, and Rika turned to Ferris. "Check the northern end of this floor for signs of Shoshin. We're not leaving here without him."

"What if we don't find him before they make it up here?" Ferris asked.

"Then they all die."

"I guess that's better than us," Ferris replied and loosened his sidearm in its holster before moving toward the northern side of the building.

Rika wanted to ask Crunch if he'd had any luck, but she knew the man would tell her if he found Shoshin. She could still make him out almost two-hundred meters away, threading the piles of debris and checking around the holes in the roof.

Rika slowly moved toward the southern side of the building, where broad windows looked down into the courtyard where the burning dropship lay.

<*They've deployed their own drones, and that ship above is running active scan. You mechs should be invisible to it, but Ferris won't be,*> Niki advised.

<*I know,*> Rika replied. <*That's why I baited the trap with him.*>

<*Ahhh.*> Niki's tone was appreciative. <*I don't know if that's brilliant or devious.*>

<*Can't it be both?*> Rika asked.

In the courtyard below, five soldiers had broken off from the group at the eastern end and were approaching the burning dropship.

C'monnnn, Kelly, Rika thought as the enemy drew within six meters of the ship.

<*Firing,*> Kelly announced.

Rika didn't see any muzzle flash from Kelly's position, which meant the SMI-2 was well back from the edge of the floor—possibly up on the roof, firing through a hole to get the right angle.

Rika waited for Kelly's shot to hit the dropship and tear into it, but instead a brilliant shower of sparks erupted seven meters from the target.

<*Damn!*> Kelly exclaimed. <*They must have some sort of portable shield with them. Deflected my round.*>

<*Kelly—*> Rika began, but Kelly was already firing again.

<*Deflect this, motherfuckers!*>

A blue-white bolt of lightning lit up the night, drawing a direct line from Kelly's position to the dropship below.

Near the ship, an invisible barrier flared again, then dissipated under the barrage of relativistic electrons. Once the barrier failed, the beam struck the ship, and bolts of lightning arced out, striking the ground and nearby soldiers.

A second later, the dropship exploded in a brilliant display, filling the courtyard with fire and shattering any still-intact windows in the surrounding buildings.

Rika didn't have to wait long for the enemy's response. Before the smoke and flames even rose up above the buildings, two missiles streaked out from the enemy ship in overwatch, arcing toward Kelly's position.

Rika had expected the response, but what followed was a pleasant surprise.

A second pair of missiles flew out from the building across the courtyard and struck the underside of the craft that had just fired on Kelly.

Shoshin, you sneaky bastard!

The enemy ship exploded at the same instant that a fireball engulfed Kelly's firing position.

<*Kelly!*> Rika called out as the roof collapsed on the far end of the structure. <*You better have survived that, you stupid tinhead.*>

<*I'm conflicted, not suicidal,*> Kelly retorted. <*There was a hole clear down to the second floor; I jumped as soon as I fired the e-beam.*>

<*Shit, you're nuts,*> Ferris added.

Kelly didn't reply, and weapons fire rose up from the staircase they'd used.

<*She's got four baddies down there,*> Niki informed them, updating the combat net.

<*Serious baddies.*> Kelly's voice wavered, but Rika recognized the tone. It was anger, not fear.

<*So I guess I can stop searching for Shoshin,*> Crunch said. <*I'm going to head down the western stairwell and see if I can catch those asshats in some crossfire.*>

<*Do it,*> Rika said. <*Ferris, find cover back there and hunker down. Now that their overwatch is gone, I'm going to drop some presents on the ships in the courtyard.*>

<*You got it, Captain.*>

Rika reached the southern edge of the building and peered down into the area below. The dropship was mostly gone, and only bits of the five enemy soldiers remained. The group to the west had taken some flying shrapnel as well—she could see two soldiers, dragging a third back to their ship.

The ship on the east end had two soldiers next to it, one training his weapon on Rika's building, and the other looking up at the building on the far side, where Shoshin's rockets had come from.

Such a surplus of targets. Which to blow up first?

Rika took up a position behind a column, and aimed at the shuttle on the eastern end of the courtyard. She'd spare the two soldiers dragging their wounded—for now.

One thing was certain: if the group that had been advancing on the burning dropship had carried a shield capable of deflecting a uranium sabot round, then chances were that their vessels were, as well.

Instead, Rika aimed at the soldier standing near the rear entrance of the shuttle. Back in the war, she'd learned that the Niets had a flaw in their ship shields: they would operate at lower level when personnel were in close proximity.

What she didn't know in this case was whether the soldier in question was standing inside or outside the shield's protection. Or if that vulnerability existed in other shuttles. Or a hundred other things.

She hoped he was outside the shield, took aim, and fired a uranium round at his feet. The DPU hit the ground, and the explosive force picked the soldier up and threw him back toward the ship.

Without missing a beat, Rika fired again, this time with her electron beam. The relativistic electrons breached the shield—and the soldier's body—striking the interior of the landing craft.

The rear of the craft exploded, and Rika smiled with satisfaction. Whoever had fired those SAMs at her dropship was ill-prepared for the sort of firepower four mechs could deliver.

Knowing that her weapons fire gave her position way, Rika headed back into the building, toward the staircase where Kelly was still battling the enemy. As she did, Rika saw a shot lance out from the other building, where Shoshin was situated, and an explosion flared up from the second shuttle's location.

<*Damn, wish he hadn't done that,*> Rika commented privately to Niki. <*Now they've nowhere to retreat to.*>

<*You're just assuming complete victory?*> Niki asked.

<*Of course. I don't lose.*>

<*Can I get some covering fire?*> Kelly asked. <*They're flanking me.*>

<*Not for long,*> Crunch replied, and the deafening *shoom* of his KE-72 thundered up through the floors.

Rika wondered how Crunch had advanced through the length of the building on the second floor without encountering more of the enemy. *There should have been a dozen from the western ship between him and Kelly.*

She reviewed the scan from the team and what the drones could pick up. There was no sign of the soldiers from the western shuttle, yet the drones above the courtyard had recorded twelve enemies entering the building.

<*They must be on the ground floor,*> Niki suggested.

<*Or the third.*>

Rika circled the stairwell and peered down into the third floor, looking for any signs of movement. She was tempted to release a drone and send it down, but worried that it might give her position away.

She released one nonetheless, but instead sent it down the length of the fourth floor. The last thing she needed was a group sneaking up on her while she was engaged with the enemy one level down.

<*You sure they're on the third?*> Niki asked.

<*If they were on the second, they'd've run into Crunch by now. That's all I know. Don't see them on fourth. They have to be somewhere….*>

Rika decided that going down the stairs was a recipe for disaster, and moved to the eastern end of the building, where Kelly had gone through the floor. It was a ruin from the missile attack, but not far from the stairs, a beam had torn a hole through to the third level.

She released a probe through the opening and only waited for the briefest of scans before dropping through.

Her feet hit the level below. The sound would have given her location away, if not for the thundering weapons fire echoing through the building.

Rika took stock of her surroundings. Twenty meters ahead, to her left, was the stairwell. From what she could see on the combat net, Kelly and Crunch now had their attackers caught between them.

Rika eased toward the northern side of the building, looking for the enemy she was certain should be present…somewhere.

But there was no sign of them.

<*Rika!*> Ferris's voice hissed in her mind. <*Rika, they're up here on the fourth floor!*>

<*Can't be,*> Rika replied. <*My probe swept half the level. There's no one up there but you.*>

<*Well, I can see them with my own fucking eyeballs! They're fifty meters and closing. They must have something blocking your drones.*>

Rika couldn't think of anything that could fool a drone that wouldn't also fool an eyeball. They both picked up EM-spectrum, and the drones saw a lot more.

<*They've hacked the drone somehow,*> Niki supplied. <*It's the only answer that makes sense.*>

Rika wanted to ask how, but Ferris—her bait—was in imminent danger. For all her caution and skulking, the staircase was going to be the quickest way to get back to him.

Unless…

Rika dashed down the length of the building and chambered a depleted uranium sabot round in her GNR. Using the locations Ferris had highlighted on the combat net, she targeted the ceiling overhead and fired one round, and then another. Her aim was true, and the ceiling—which was also the floor of the fourth level—gave way under the enemy soldiers and dropped them right into Rika's lap.

There were six, all in matte black stealth armor, barely visible—even with all of Rika's augmentations, and her helmet's scan.

Whatever tech they're using, it's good.

Rika hoped hers was better.

Her JE-84 was already unslung, and she fired on the two soldiers closest to her before they managed to rise. She scored a lucky shot on a weak point in one's armor, and the figure went down, but the rounds only ricocheted off the other, and he found cover.

Further back, four more enemies struggled to disentangle

themselves from the wreckage, and Rika fired two HE rounds from her GNR, hitting one and smashing—she hoped—their shoulder.

Ferris had originally spotted eight enemies on the fourth floor, and Rika had only seen six thus far. Either two were still in the rubble, or they'd avoided the collapse and were still after Ferris.

<Rika! One's still up here, he's almost on me!>

Rika heard shots fire from Ferris's sidearm, and knew they'd be ineffective against the armor these soldiers wore.

Disregarding her own safety, Rika rushed forward, leapt into the air, and grabbed hold of a protruding beam. Her momentum swung her up and around. She let go at the top of her arc and spun through the air, landing once more on the fourth level.

The damaged structure groaned under her weight as she slammed down, but Rika ignored any concerns and raced toward Ferris's position.

She could see the muzzle flash from his weapon, but not the enemy soldier. Then he stepped out from behind a beam and leveled his rifle on her.

Rika reacted without thinking. She twisted to the side and extended her right arm, firing a chambered HE round from her GNR-41C into the enemy soldier. It caught him right under his armpit, and tore his torso in two.

Rika spun, scanning the area as she backed toward Ferris.

<*You hit?*> she asked the pilot.

<Uh…no…I don't…Oh shit, yeah, I'm hit.>

Rika reached Ferris and saw him staring at the stump of his left arm, torn off just above the elbow.

She grabbed a canister of biofoam from her thigh and applied it to his stump to staunch the bleeding, while Ferris swayed on his feet and stared at the twitching left arm on the ground.

"Shit," he whispered aloud. "Good thing I'm in the right company for prosthetics. I'll fit right in."

<Maybe Barne will even let you call him 'Top'.> Rika laughed and gave Ferris a light slap on the shoulder as she turned, ready to

deal with the soldiers who would be following her back up through the hole before long.

<Don't count on it,> Barne's welcome voice came over the combat net.

Rika glanced out the northern side of the building and saw an assault craft lower into view. *<Nice of you to show up, First Sergeant. Any time you want to smush these asshats into jelly, that'd be great.>*

Barne didn't reply, but the assault craft lowered a meter, and two large-caliber chainguns opened up, tearing through the third floor. The combat net flagged the enemies on that level as combat ineffective, and then Barne lowered the ship and repeated the procedure on the second level.

<Well, damn,> Kelly said with a nervous laugh. *<Good to know someone noticed that we went missing.>*

<Just glad you left some for me,> Barne replied. *<I don't read Shoshin. He make it?>*

<Somewhere in the building to the south.> Rika walked toward the hole in the floor and looked down at the enemies that had suffered under the barrage from Barne's assault craft. *<Get over there and see if you can locate him. We can mop up.>*

Rika saw one of the enemies below roll over and reach for her weapon.

"Not this time," Rika whispered and leveled her GNR, firing a round into the woman's hand, blowing it clean off. "You'll have some questions to answer before the night is out."

A DEEPER GAME

STELLAR DATE: 08.09.8949 (Adjusted Gregorian)
LOCATION: Abandoned Industrial Complex, North of Hittis
REGION: Iapetus, Hercules System, Septhian Alliance

Rika stood in the center of the courtyard, near the still-smoldering remains of Ferris's dropship. Crunch and Kelly were combing the area for any Marauder equipment and loading it onto Barne's assault ship. Shoshin was already aboard, as was Ferris.

A ship was on its way—an armed pinnace this time—from the *Golden Lark* to collect them and bring the pair back up for some of Lieutenant Carson's tender care.

"You just tell Bondo not to screw up my face," Shoshin had said when Rika checked on him. "I'm good the way I am."

Many mechs who had not opted for any reconstructive surgery would jump at the chance to do it on the company's credit. Rika was glad to see that Shoshin's acceptance of who he was held up under dire circumstances—or in the face of free cosmetic surgery.

However, none of that was Rika's immediate concern. The local military was on the ground and they'd taken control of the situation—and the enemy soldiers.

"Look," Rika said to the woman in charge, Major Dala. "I just want to have a chance to interrogate their senior officer, or NCO—whoever is left. I need to know what sort of danger we're in, here."

"I'm sorry, Captain Rika," Major Dala replied without an ounce of understanding in her cold, fuchsia eyes. "This was an attack on our soil, we have jurisdiction. We'll keep you informed as the investigation proceeds, of course."

Though Major Dala wore a Septhian Armed Forces crest on her shoulder, the armor it adorned was clearly of Theban design.

The SAF crest was slightly crooked, a visual sign of how well the absorption of the Theban space force into the Septhian military was going. Which was to say that it was a never-ending series of pissing matches. Rika was amazed at how much resistance the Thebans were putting up, when the Septhians had come to their aid against the Nietzscheans in the battle for the Albany System less than a six months ago.

Maybe it was because she'd never had any to begin with, but nationalistic pride meant very little to Rika. The opportunity to kill Niets, on the other hand…now that was something she could rally behind.

What Rika wanted to know more than anything else was whether or not the Nietzscheans were behind this attack.

Unfortunately, the locals had arrived before she'd had a chance to do more than try to get a name from one of the nine enemies they'd captured.

"Can you more clearly define, 'keeping me informed'?" Rika asked. "Who will my liaison be? Will I be able to at least observe the interrogations? Can we gain access to what you learn about the origin of their equipment?"

"I'm sorry, I don't know the answers to those questions. Your standard SAF liaison, Major Jeremy, will have those answers once command determines how we'll proceed."

Rika pulled off her helmet and stared into the woman's eyes. "Major Dala. We're both just trying to do our jobs here. My job is to train up a force of mechs who will aid in the defense of this star system and elsewhere in Septhia. They're going to bleed and die for your people—stars, I suspect we already have. We deserve to know who hit us."

Dala didn't even flinch as Rika spoke. Her fuchsia eyes met Rika's blue ones, and she shrugged. "It's not my call, *Captain* Rika."

"Seriously?" Rika growled. "That's how you want to play this? We're—"

"We're nothing alike," Major Dala interrupted. "I'm a Theban patriot, you're a *mercenary*. You kill for money."

Rika snorted and raised an eyebrow as she gazed down at the Major. "Oh, and you don't take pay? You live off the kindness of those you serve? Or maybe you're a slave." She lowered her voice and took a step toward the major. "Do you know what it's like to be a slave? To be forced to kill? I don't seem to recall the Genevian government ever giving me so much as a stipend back then. I suppose that must be the epitome of honor to you."

The women's eyes widened, and fear replaced her smug officiousness.

Rika didn't ease up. "When *you're* trying to redeem yourself from spending most of your life as a mutilated killing machine, *then* you can say whatever you want about my motives. But until then, why don't you shut your fucking trap?"

"I—" Major Dala began, but Rika held up a hand.

"When the Nietzscheans come—and they *will* come—I'd better see your altruistic ass on the front lines, not cowering behind your administrivia."

Rika turned and walked away, worry about future complications edging out the satisfaction yelling at the woman had granted.

<*That was fun to listen to,*> Kelly said as she placed a crate inside Barne's assault craft. <*I think you let her off easy.*>

Rika sighed and put her helmet back on. <*Maybe. She didn't make the call to shut us out, but she could have shown* **some** *compassion.*>

<*Or maybe a bit of, 'sorry our local defense is so shit-poor that you got shot down over one of our cities by someone who managed to take control of half our local infrastructure',*> Crunch added from where he stood at the back of the Marauder ship. <*Either way, that's the last of it. About a third of our cargo survived—for some definition of the word.*>

Rika checked the ETA on the pinnace from the *Golden Lark*, and found it was caught up in an air traffic control mess of epic proportions. She sent a message for the ship to meet them at the training facility. It would be more efficacious to transfer Ferris and Shoshin there.

<OK, let's get out of here.>

Rika picked up the pace, jogging toward Barne's ship.

"Wait! Captain, we need you to stay onsite until our investigative team arrives," Dala called out.

"I have wounded, and your ATC is a disaster," Rika called over her shoulder. "Your people know where to find me."

"*I* don't, where is it?"

Rika laughed as she stepped aboard the assault craft and turned to watch Dala rushing toward her. "Why don't you shove your head further up your CO's ass? Maybe your answer is in there."

Dala didn't have a chance to reply before Barne ignited the ship's grav drive, pulling the assault craft into the air. Once they'd cleared the buildings, he poured on the thrust. Rika couldn't help but notice that he didn't even bother to send in a flight path to the Iapetan ATC.

LAYERED CONCERNS

STELLAR DATE: 08.09.8949 (Adjusted Gregorian)
LOCATION: Marauder Training Compound
REGION: Iapetus, Hercules System, Septhian Alliance

"You sure know how to make an entrance," Barne said as he led Rika into the training facility's command building.

The *Golden Lark*'s pinnace had already collected Ferris and Shoshin, taking them back up to the ship for repairs and surgery. Despite his ability to fire the two missiles at the enemy's overwatch ship, Shoshin had suffered significant damage from the crash. His left arm had been shorn off, and one of his legs was crushed. The wireless transmitters in his helmet had been destroyed, as had one of his internal batteries.

He was a mech's mech, though. Not a word of complaint; just a visible eagerness to be repaired and take the fight to whoever had organized the attack.

Kelly and Crunch were visiting the base's quartermaster for light refit and repair before joining the other mechs already on the base, who were currently patrolling the perimeter—neither Rika nor Barne intended to be caught with their pants down again.

"It takes years of practice." Rika gave Barne a belated reply as she followed him into the squat building on the southern side of the compound. "And a strong dislike for bureaucratic bullshit."

Barne chuckled and nodded as he turned a corner and walked down a hall lined with empty offices. "Major Dala's not a significant player in the local power structure, but her CO, Colonel Zim is. Honestly, her behavior is probably just a conditioned response to dealing with him for so long."

<I've received a few messages from Colonel Zim's Battalion HQ since we took off,> Niki added. *<They want copies of all our data on the attack sent over immediately.>*

Rika held back what she wanted to say about Zim's HQ and

their requests. Barne and Niki weren't her enemies, and she recognized that she was still on an adrenaline high from combat.

Getting shot out of the sky had a way of bringing out her aggressive side.

Barne stopped in front of one of the doors and gestured inside. "Your office, Captain Rika."

Rika stepped into the room—which was almost ten times the size of Major Tim's back on the *Golden Lark*—and looked it over. There was a desk with a mech-safe chair behind it, a few others in front of the desk, plus a couch along one wall—carbon fiber to ensure it would survive hard, steel asses. In one corner stood an equipment and armor rack, complete with full recharge and resupply.

"Wow, Top, this is nice. I didn't know we were going to get this fancy."

Barne snorted. "Fancy, my ass. I've seen generals with offices that would have put kings to shame. Everything here is about operational efficiency."

Rika leaned against the desk and let out a long breath. "OK. Our top priority is to find out who shot at us, and if they're going to hit us again. Here, or on the ships."

"If it's anywhere, it'll be here." Barne sat on the couch and leaned back. "If they could have hit the ships, they would've before. Now that they've tipped their hand, Major Tim will be on high alert. Guy's tighter than a jackrabbit's asshole, so nothing will get through up there."

Rika laughed. "Lovely visual."

"Seemed to fit, pun intended."

Rika rolled her eyes and pushed off her desk to pace across the room. "So what do you think? Niets? Local baddies? Theban military haters?"

Barne shrugged. "Could be all of the above. A lot of 'Theban patriots' left their military after Thebes joined the Septhian Alliance. Some of them are operating as merc outfits to pay the bills, others are not—which makes me think that someone is funneling them money from somewhere. Maybe old military commanders."

"And you think that the Niets could be behind it?" Rika asked. "Subterfuge and subversion really isn't their game."

Barne raised an eyebrow. "Except for that little thing last year, where they bamboozled us into almost killing off half the Theban leadership. I think they've got a new strategist close to the emperor's ear. We shouldn't expect the same old tactics as the war. Times are changing, and so is Nietzschea."

"An evolving Nietzschea, just what we need."

"With your permission, Captain, I'd like to bring First Platoon and all the DIs down."

"You miss Leslie and Chase?" Rika smirked.

"Always. I want Leslie's platoon because I know how she operates, but just the one 'toon because I want to make this compound look like a soft target when it's anything but."

Rika eyed Barne. "How long do you think we have?"

"Well, they fucked up the local ATC and killed Link towers across half the continent. On top of that, they got SAM launchers on a dozen ships in the harbor. They were smart, too; they knew that would be easier than getting the weapons into the city, but they fired one from that high-rise to push you out over the water."

"Making us an easy target," Rika finished for him. "That was savvy. If Ferris wasn't a nutjob, we'd all have died out there—or at least gone for a good swim."

"Nutjob? What did the Ferryman get up to?"

"Something very fitting to his name. He took the ship underwater."

Barne whistled in appreciation. "He's gonna win some bets. There's always been healthy debate about taking one of those dropships underwater."

"Well, we lost an engine and crashed."

"Hmm…maybe just half points, then."

<*Rika,*> Major Tim's voice came into her mind. <*I need to talk*

with you.>

"Aw, crap. It never rains, it shitstorms." Rika tapped her head. "Tim's on the Link. Get Leslie and her platoon down here; don't bring *all* the DIs, though. I want people to *think* the bulk of our forces are still on the ships."

A smile crept across Barne's face, and he gave a sly nod. "I like the way you roll, Captain. I'm on it."

Barne left her office, and Rika responded to Major Tim.

<*Good evening, Major. I hope all is well up there?*>

The major made a derisive noise. <*Hell of a lot better than down there. I have a Major from the office of some Colonel Zim pinging me every five minutes to get all your data on the attack.*>

<*Yeah, they're up my ass, too,*> Rika replied tonelessly.

<*What are you playing at, Captain? We work for the Septhian military. Don't go making enemies in their ranks.*>

<*I just about got blown out of the sky over one of their cities, Major. It was no random hit, either; they timed it for when both the* Golden Lark *and the* Perseid's Dream *were on the far side of Iapetus. They crippled local infrastructure,* ***and*** *they had the run of our crash site for ten minutes. Just to take out one dropship of mechs?*>

Major Tim didn't respond for a moment. <*This was a hit on you.*>

<*The evidence I have points to that, yes. Whoever orchestrated this has reach.*>

<*And you think making enemies with this Zim and his cronies is the way to solve that problem?*> Tim asked.

Rika was about to deliver a snappy rejoinder when it occurred to her that, despite his general assholeishness, Tim was right.

<*What if it's them that attacked us?*> Rika tried a new tack. <*If you were running a hit like that on the downlow, wouldn't you want to be onsite first to control the narrative?*>

<*Maybe,*> Tim replied. <*But then again, maybe I'd want distance. There are a lot of variables at play, here.*>

<*The major is right about that,*> Niki added. <*If Zim and Dala were in on it, why not just take you out when they arrived?*>

<*Maybe there were other eyes on the situation by then,*> Tim suggested. <*Look, you've got a P-COG down there. One of the Old Man's best. He's the one that figured out it was the Nietzscheans playing us back in Albany. Set him on the data, but I'd recommend giving what you can to Zim, if for no other reason than to shut his dogs up.*>

Rika had not been aware that David, her P-COG general counsel, had been the one to uncover the Nietzschean subterfuge in the Albany System.

For that alone, she owed him her thanks.

<*OK, Major, I'll do that. And I'll keep you informed. Also, we're going to bring a platoon and some supplies down. Chances are that we'll see more unfriendlies.*>

<*Yeah, good likelihood on that. We're altering our orbits so that you'll have near-continuous orbital coverage from the* 'Lark *or the* 'Dream.>

Rika was grateful for the Major's concern, and told him as much before they closed the connection.

<*I've already called David in,*> Niki said. <*He'll be here in five minutes. I gave him all the data we collected, as well.*>

Rika drew a deep breath and flopped onto the couch. "Good."

* * * * *

The knock on Rika's door was sharp and sure. Rika called out 'Come', and a moment later David entered, taking in the room with one long sweep of his eyes.

"Barne works fast, doesn't he, Captain?" David said as he turned to Rika.

"That he does, though I understand that a lot of the progress down here came from your keen eye, as well."

David shrugged. "I just make sure the contracts are favorable. I may have also spotted some deals here and there."

Rika laughed and gestured to one of the chairs. "I wasn't expecting so much false humility from you, David. Major Tim told me that I have you to thank for not delivering the Theban Alliance to Nietzschea last year."

David sat and gave her a warm smile. "It was a group effort. No one's an island."

Rika laughed. "And the humility just keeps on coming. Was I wrong to question it?"

David reached up and rapped a knuckle on the metal ridges atop of his elongated skull. "A lot of people think I have unfair advantages—or they just think I'm a freak. The right attitude can diffuse a lot of jealousy and ill intent."

Rika laughed. "You know...that's an entirely different class of problem from what mechs have. No one ever accuses us of being unfairly intelligent, and when push comes to shove, they're happy to put us out front to absorb the bullets."

David smiled. It was a kind expression that started with his eyes before his lips began to turn up. "Things aren't so different for P-COGs, when it comes to evaluating usefulness. Granted, the personal stakes are often not as high as for you. But if I fuck up an assessment or miss a connection, a lot more than just one soldier dies."

"I'm starting to understand that pressure in a new way," Rika said. "I can't imagine what the Old Man feels."

"Weary, I suspect. That man doesn't just have the Marauders on his shoulders. He's the last, best hope for Genevia."

Rika raised an eyebrow. "This conversation sure took an unexpected turn. What do you mean by that?"

"When it comes down to it, General Mill is fighting for Genevia. Not the Genevia you grew up in—the one before that. I can barely remember it; I was just a boy when we elected the string of corrupt governments that led us to war with Nietzschea. Not that an honest government could have avoided the war, but I think they could have won it."

"But the general remembers that Genevia?" Rika asked.

"He does." David nodded somberly. "I believe the spark needed to rebuild Genevia is within him, and him alone. Well, perhaps that's a bit melodramatic. He fosters the spark in others, but only he has the means and the drive to realize his vision."

Rika considered David's words for a moment, turning them over in her mind and wondering what they really meant.

Most of her life had been spent either fighting Nietzschea, or living with the grim fact that the enemy had bested her people—who she didn't like much better than the enemy. Since joining the Marauders, her focus had been on staying the Nietzschean advance toward the Praesepe Cluster.

After the Nietzscheans were defeated in the Albany System, some talked about what it would be like to drive them back from Genevian space, but most considered that to be nothing more than wishful thinking.

Even if all Praesepe rose up as one, they couldn't field a fleet a tenth the size of Nietzschea's. The only reason why Emperor Constantine hadn't crushed Septhia already was because his forces were spread thin across his vast empire.

Everyone *really* knew that the best chance the nations of the Praesepe Cluster had, was to make an assault too costly to be worth it.

Finally, she asked, "Does the general really believe that we could defeat Nietzschea at some point?"

"Genevia was the greatest adversary Nietzschea faced in five hundred years. The conflict weakened them enough that many of the nations on their fringe have formed substantial alliances and are successfully holding them back. If we prove that Constantine *can* be stopped, then we could form a broader alliance with those nations. One that could crush Nietzschea once and for all."

"Those are some great aspirations," Rika straightened up and sat forward on the sofa. "But for now, we just need to survive whatever is happening here on Iapetus."

"Agreed." David straightened his back and folded his hands on his lap. "I've been reviewing the data as we spoke, and I agree with your assessment that a second attack is likely. I also believe that you were the intended target of the attack. The ordnance expended to take down your dropship exceeded the material value of the ship and its contents by over threefold."

"What about the value of four mechs?" Rika asked. "We're worth a lot."

David nodded. "Yes, but if the attackers knew that there were four mechs aboard, they would not have sent such a small force after you. I also factored the likelihood of capturing mechs in usable condition into my valuation. Mech capture is very rare."

Rika laughed. "Yeah, we tend to go down fighting. Capture is not a favorable outcome for us." David nodded soberly, and Rika realized the same was likely true for P-COGs. "So, what if our attacker isn't as smart as you and figured they'd get a functional mech in the deal?"

David's brow furrowed, and he wiggled his fingers where they lay folded on his lap. "Maybe it would be a wash. I can't assume they're too stupid; they did manage to do a number on the local Iapetan defenses and infrastructure."

"Or they know the right people and have money."

"You're no slouch at this twisted logic, either, Captain Rika."

"Survival trait. Thing is, for me, it all breaks down at some point. Ultimately, I always have to go with my gut."

"No one can isolate all variables." David shrugged and leaned back in his chair, unfolding his hands and placing them palms down on his legs. He didn't seem to know what to do with them half the time. "Nothing is perfectly certain. Ultimately, with everything, we all have to make a call. Go with our gut, as you say."

"So what does *your* gut say?" Rika asked

"That—at this point—Nietzschean influence is immaterial. There are local elements at work, and they are connected. Thebans here on Iapetus want you dead, and those Thebans are both well-funded and have ties to influential people."

"So we wait for the next attack?" Rika asked.

"No defense has a single element, and rarely does a victory come from a single offense. I believe that Niki should provide the data to Major Dala—scrubbed in small, but noticeable ways—to give them something. Their response, both Dala's and Zim's HQ in general, will tell you much. At the same time, I shall reach out to Dala and foster a relationship. I've studied her activities on the local nets and feed; she likes modified men, has a thing for big brains like mine. It's not her main turn-on, but it will get me in the door."

Rika couldn't help but let out a short laugh. "You're going to seduce Major Dala for intel?"

David shrugged. "If it comes to it. Spotting the patterns within human reaction is easy—P-COGs outstrip even AIs at this, because we have more first-hand experience. With some simple evaluation and observation, I can create a perfect persona to appeal to another human."

"Are you doing that with me right now?" Rika asked.

David grinned. "Rika, I would never need to do that with you. Our goals and personalities are already very well aligned."

Rika snorted. "That's a bullshit answer, if I ever heard one."

David shrugged and pulled a pouch of coffee from his jacket. He tore the corner off with his teeth and then poured it down his throat. "I never said I was a great actor. However, what I *do* know is that you wanted to meet with me *before* you were so inconsiderately shot out of the sky."

"I did. Though—and I think you'll agree, Niki—the matter is less urgent than the recent attack."

<Less urgent, yes, but still no less important.>

"Tell me anyway, if you would, Captain. It's always nice to have more pieces to the puzzle."

Rika let out a short laugh. "I think this other matter is a whole different puzzle."

David squeezed the last few drops of his coffee pouch into his mouth. "Captain. There's only one puzzle."

Rika found herself wondering how much of David's bizarre mannerisms were natural, and how many were a result of the modifications the Genevian military had made to his mind. He spoke calmly, but he fidgeted incessantly. His tone and speed of speech varied so much that it was impossible to establish a baseline of any sort. Every word he spoke could be a lie, or they could all be truth.

Still, he *seemed* honest, and the Old Man trusted him. Notwithstanding his part in stopping the Nietzscheans from taking Thebes.

"I want to free the AIs," Rika admitted plainly.

David's eyes went wide, and for the first time, he seemed genuinely surprised. "The AIs."

"The seven aboard our two ships."

"Eight," David corrected, nodding at Rika's abdomen.

"Ensuring Niki's freedom is a mere formality."

David tapped a finger against his upper lip. "Still, it is a formality that must be observed." His finger tapped faster and faster, then suddenly stopped, his eyes going wide once more.

"Niki! You're a part of the movement amongst the AIs."

<'Movement' is a very generic term,> Niki replied, her mental tone guarded.

"Uprising? Rebellion? Insurrection? I don't know enough to properly quantify it. Even a casual observation of news from distant locales is enough to realize that something has changed with the AIs in the last two decades—though few signs of it have been apparent in Praesepe."

<You're certainly no slouch, David.> The feeling accompanying Niki's words was warmer now.

"I'd like to hope not," David replied. "Though I must admit, a way to 'free' the AIs aboard our two ships is not readily apparent to me. I assume you have some plan?"

"Asylum," Rika said without further elaboration, and David's eyes widened for the third time, before a smile grew on his lips.

"I see. That could work. There would be hurdles, to be sure, but it has merit."

"What about the Old Man?" Rika asked. "You're loyal to him, and he won't be happy about this."

David snorted. "Nor will Major Tim. But fundamentally, the Old Man would not be opposed. In Genevia's former glory days, AIs were free. Citizens, even. If he wants to bring that back, he cannot deny them this."

<*Then why hasn't he done so sooner?*> Niki asked.

David shrugged. "I'm not in his inner circle—though I am friends with some who know him very well. I think...I think maybe he views it more like protective custody—that he would free everyone if it were safe to do so. But he needs some for success and others he wants to keep safe."

"This sounds like our conversation from earlier, Niki."

<*I was noticing similarities myself.*>

Silence hung in the air for a moment before David said, "We three are peas in a pod. Each of us the product of humanity's desire to evolve. Mentally and physically, even to creating a new species. The pure organics, they don't understand us, and we spend no small effort convincing them that we're not a threat."

<*Sometimes,*> Niki replied. <*Some have no issue with that. Some want to be a threat—or a danger.*>

David's finger tapping resumed once more. "Is that what you are, Niki? Are you and the AIs you've sided with a threat and a danger?"

Niki didn't reply right away, and Rika began to wonder if her AI was hiding some ill intent from her.

Finally, Niki spoke up. <*Maybe.*>

Her words hung in the air for a minute before David laughed. "I believe I know what you mean, Niki. I'll help. I can set up meetings with some Iapetan lawyers and get things moving."

Rika wondered exactly what Niki had meant. *I'll have to dig into it later.*

For now, she was glad to have this small victory.

RECONCILIATION

STELLAR DATE: 08.10.8949 (Adjusted Gregorian)
LOCATION: Marauder Training Compound
REGION: Iapetus, Hercules System, Septhian Alliance

Rika settled into her office chair and drew a deep breath. *Best to get it over with sooner than later.* If Kelly wasn't fit to be a Marauder, finding out now was better than in combat—again.

She organized the stack of holofilm on the desk, ensuring they were all deactivated, and then took a sip from her cup of coffee.

The knock came on her door a moment later, and Rika called out for Kelly to enter as she set the cup down and squared her shoulders.

The door opened, and Kelly walked in. Her posture was rigid, body gleaming in SMI-2 armor, her gun-arm attached with a barrel-less GNR in place.

From the neck down, it was hard to find dissimilarities between herself and Kelly. Two peas in a pod—that's what Silva had always called them, a memory brought up by David's use of the term. Back then, Kelly had always been getting into trouble, and Rika had to pull her out of it.

Granted, Kelly's trouble saved the day half the time, so it was nearly always worth it.

"Good morning, priv—Kelly," Rika said.

"Captain." Kelly sketched a salute and stood at attention before Rika's desk.

"At ease, Kelly." Rika gestured to the chair. "Please, sit. Stars, I suck at this stuff. I hate formality. I know how to do it up the chain, but down is different."

Kelly sat and shrugged. "I wouldn't know, Captain."

"Enough with the 'captain' shit, Kelly. We've hauled each other's asses out of the fire too much for that—at least don't call me that in private."

Kelly regarded Rika with an unblinking gaze. "*I'm* still that Kelly, but you're different, Rika. A lot different."

Rika let out a slow breath. "A lot's happened. It's been a long time for me."

"I heard a bit about it. Chase told me about what happened on Dekar."

"Yeah, Dekar was a shit-show. I don't want word about that to spread, though. Please keep it to yourself."

Kelly snorted. "What? That the Marauders *bought* you? That this outfit that you seem to have fallen for put a chip in your head?"

"They took the chip out. The people who auctioned me off were the ones who put the chip back in. That the chip stayed in for my first deployment was an accident, but one that I'm kinda glad about."

"What?" Kelly cocked her head. "How can you be *glad* that you got chipped?"

Rika leaned back in her chair and grinned. "Because I beat Discipline."

"What do you mean, 'beat'?"

"I won't lie, it was excruciating, but this bitch named Cheri was using it on me to get me to kill Barne. I wouldn't do it, and she couldn't make me—no matter how much it hurt. In the end, I snapped her neck."

Kelly let out a low whistle. "You killed the person who was applying Discipline.... That's...nuts."

"Yeah, important side-note: it doesn't stop the discipline, either."

"Shit, how did you get it to stop?" Kelly asked with wide eyes.

"Basilisk's old leader, Lieutenant Jerry, shut it off."

"Old?"

"Yeah, he didn't make it through the mission."

Kelly's lips formed an 'O' shape, and she nodded wordlessly. "But Discipline is still there, right?"

"Discipline? No, I can't be Disciplined anymore."

"Right, that's not what I meant. The chip is just the control system for the neural lace around our brain stems. That's what actually does the work. Even without the chips, we still have that neural lace in our heads. You don't actually need the chip to activate it."

Rika was not well-versed in the specifics, she was a bit surprised that Kelly understood them so well. "Is that true, Niki?"

<Yup. It's also how I made Stavros's use of discipline not hurt you. I disconnected the control chip from the neural lace, but created a feedback system so it detected that it was hurting you when it wasn't.>

Kelly's eyes widened. "So Rika can't be chipped anymore?"

Niki gave a soft laugh over the Link. *<We never actually got around to having it removed. Stavros's compliance chip is still in Rika's head.>*

"Huh…I guess it is," Rika mused. "I kinda forgot about it."

"How could you forget something like that?"

Rika saw that Kelly's face had taken on a look of pure horror, and shrugged. "It can't hurt me, and I trust Niki with my life, just as she trusts me with hers. I guess we should get it removed, though. It may be useful in the future for someone to think they've chipped me."

Kelly shook her head in amazement. "Rika, you are hardcore. Have I ever told you that?"

"Really?" Rika laughed. "When Cheri was beating my brain to mush, all I could think of were those times when you tested Discipline's limits, tried to see how much you could get away with before the serious pain kicked in. I distinctly remember thinking, 'Would Kelly have let this take her down? Hell no!'"

"You think more of me than I deserve, Rika."

Rika rose from her chair and walked around her desk to stand before Kelly. "I don't. Back in Team Hammerfall, Silva was like our mom, but you were my big sister. You always kept me safe—I…I was the one who let you down."

Kelly rose and stood before Rika.

Their faces weren't so different; Kelly had a bit of a stronger chin, and her hair had a reddish tint, but after Kelly had recovered her face, Rika had been surprised to see how similar their eyes were.

Kelly reached up and touched Rika's face. "I always did think of you as my bratty kid sis, Rika. But you were always the heart of Hammerfall, our moral compass—so much as we were able to have one, with Gunny in our brains all the time."

"Good ol' Gunny," Rika mused. "Got what he deserved."

"Nuclear payback," Kelly grinned.

"We good, Kelly? I know I gave you the 'big, stern talk' back on the field, but the last thing I want is for you to leave the Marauders. Finding you and Silva, and then losing you both again…that would be hard."

Kelly nodded. "I'm not going anywhere, Rika. I feel the same way about you, even if getting your bars has made you into a bit of an asshat."

"Takes one to know one." Rika paused, not sure what to say next, then threw caution to the wind and embraced her friend. Kelly wrapped an arm around Rika as well, and they stood silently for a minute before Rika stepped back.

"I'll talk to Lieutenant Carson about what we can do for the neural laces."

"Carson? Not sure if I want someone with 'Bondo' for a nickname rummaging around inside my head." Kelly's lips twisted to the side, and Rika couldn't help but laugh.

"He's really good. He did your face, and it looks great."

"Rika, brains and faces are two very different deals. Could Niki do it? She neutralized yours, and you seem fine." Kelly winked and gave Rika a light punch in the arm. "Mostly."

<I suppose I could, but I can't really do the whole company. It's not the sort of operation I can perform while Rika is wandering all over.>

"Couldn't you just pop out of her for a bit?" Kelly asked.

<Sorry, but no, Kelly. We all have our insecurities. I rather like being inside Rika; despite all the crazy shit she gets up to, her gut is safer than a lot of other places I could end up.>

"Umm…thanks?" Rika said.

<*When we get back to the ship, I'll teach Carson the operation, and we'll do yours together, Kelly. Then he can do it on everybody else.*>

"And get your chip removed," Kelly added. "It's creepy knowing it's in your head."

Rika smiled. "You got it, Sis."

DROPPING

STELLAR DATE: 08.10.8949 (Adjusted Gregorian)
LOCATION: ***Golden Lark***
REGION: Iapetus, Hercules System, Septhian Alliance

First Platoon's bays looked like the mechs were planning an invasion.

Leslie stood at the entrance to Drop Bay 4 and surveyed her platoon as they hauled gear into the dropships, moved other equipment to the cargo shuttles, and generally did their best to avoid running into one another, the dockworkers, and the pilots.

It was glorious chaos.

So far as she knew, the Genevian Armed Forces had never fielded an all-mech platoon, which meant there had never been a scene like this before. Well, space and time were both huge…so maybe there had been. But this was still a first of sorts.

Seeing the comradery that was blooming between the mechs as they made ready for their first mock-combat drop was inspiring. It almost made her want to be one.

Leslie's tail—inside its armored sheath—waved gently in the air behind her as she nodded to a trio of RR-2s that rushed past, hauling crates filled with charging stations.

The last one reached out to tap the tip of Leslie's tail.

At first, the tradition had bothered her, but she'd grown accustomed to it. Crunch had started it—which was the case for a lot of traditions that were forming in her platoon, and in M Company at large.

He told her he did it to remind everyone in the 'toon that their LT was a mech, too—not a GAF standard model, but her body was better because of the mods added to it, just like theirs were.

As the only non-mech officer in M Company, Leslie fought an uphill battle when it came to gaining the acceptance of the troops. That one gesture from Crunch had changed the entire company's view of her.

Doesn't mean I'm not going to figure out what his name is. However, it did mean that so long as she served under Rika in M Company, the tail would stay.

Chris, the platoon's Staff Sergeant, ambled toward her with a grin on his face. He was a long-time Marauder, promoted from squad to staff sergeant when Rika's company was formed.

"Feels good, don't it, LT?" he asked as he turned and stood beside her. "Combat drop. All mechs."

"*Mock*-combat, Staff," Leslie corrected him.

The AM-2 shrugged, his chitinous armor making a soft skittering sound as he completed the gesture. "Still momentous. May it be the first of many, mock or otherwise. I can't wait for the day we drop a 'toon of mechs on the Niets. The look on their faces will be priceless."

"Right before we blow them to pieces." Leslie savored the thought, as well. This feeling, this excitement in the air, had never been present back in the war. Granted, she'd joined the Genevian Armed Forces after things started going badly. Maybe there had been a more positive attitude at the outset.

Chris chuckled. "The looks on their faces will be just as priceless *after* we blow them to pieces."

"So, how's everything looking, Staff?" Leslie said, shaking her head. "Any hang-ups?"

"Oh, you know; someone always forgets to pack their favorite toothbrush, and has to run back to get it. Someone else tries to bring their special rock collection."

"The usual, then."

"The usual."

Chris cocked his head toward the bow of the *Golden Lark*. "I hear that the major is going to send down a fighter escort with us. Twelve birds?"

"He hadn't committed to a number last I heard. I think it comes down to whether or not the *Perseid's Dream* sends some, too. He's looking at it as an opportunity for a training exercise.

The locals haven't been super accommodating, but now that one of our birds got shot out of the sky, they can't push back as much."

"Yeah, I imagine someone in Septhian High Command got a bit peeved that we've been cockblocked so much here," Chris made a fist with one hand and smacked it into the palm of his other, miming his euphemism.

Leslie snorted a laugh and shrugged. "You know how it is. The brass brings in mercs to help bolster the numbers, the regulars resent it and make trouble. Usually when the shit starts flying, no one cares where a merc's paycheck comes from. So long as they're shooting at the same people as you."

"Funny side-note," Chris added. "Ultimately, a merc's paycheck comes from the same place as a regular's: the people they're protecting."

Leslie raised a hand and wobbled it side to side. "Ehhh, mercs do their fair share of oppressing, too. That's not something the Old Man signs up for—generally speaking—but sometimes we put holes in people to help an individual or a company. Shit like that gives us a bad rep, though."

Chris nodded slowly. "OK, good point. Good thing there's enough Niets to shoot at for a lifetime."

Leslie agreed in principle, but she also knew that the Niets ran a conscription military. They'd be shooting at a lot of people who didn't want to be there in the first place.

Still, it was 'us or them'. Same as it had always been; same as it always would be.

"Looking good, Lieutenant," a voice said from behind them, and Leslie turned and nodded to Lieutenant Scarcliff, the company's XO.

The FR-2 swept his ever-present scowl across the drop bay as he stood beside Chris. "Wish I was going down with you, but Captain Rika wants me up here to make sure things go smoothly in her absence."

"You've got your work cut out for you, Scarcliff," Leslie

replied.

She had an uneasy relationship with the company XO.

Both had been promoted directly from the ranks to First Lieutenant at the same time, and it irked Leslie a bit not to have the XO's job, since she had five years of service on him. Just like she knew it annoyed Scarcliff that she had Rika's ear as much as she did.

Rika had taken the time to explain to them that she felt either could do the other's job well, and their placement was for the good of the company.

"What we're doing here with M Company isn't about anyone's career advancement," Rika had told them. "It's about giving these people a new start with a new outfit that really values them. To that end, we have to make things feel right for our troops. Building a cohesive unit is my goal. Everyone is going to have to make sacrifices to do that, but I won't forget them."

At times like that, it was almost impossible to reconcile the Rika who was now the company captain with that scared and angry young woman Leslie had pulled out of the cryopod less than a year before in that warehouse on Pyra.

Rika claimed that it was Silva's leadership back in the war that had taught her what she needed to know. Silva had claimed it was years of keeping young waitresses in line that taught her how to run a unit.

Leslie wasn't sure if that was all that lay behind Rika's natural command abilities. Though she had kept any concerns to herself at the time, Leslie had worried about the Old Man's promotion of Rika to company commander. Running a team like Basilisk bore almost no similarities to running something like M Company.

But now that they were four months in, she doubted that anyone could do a better job than Rika. Give the girl fertile soil, and she had blossomed like nothing Leslie had ever seen.

She hadn't replied to Scarcliff's statement, and he cast her a curious look. "Cat got your tongue, Leslie?"

Chris barked a laugh, then managed to choke it back before slapping Leslie's tail and walking out into the bay, yelling at the platoon's K1R—a massive T-model affectionately called 'The Van'—to watch where he was going.

Leslie shook her head, and gave Scarcliff a cold look. His eyes widened for a moment, and then she reached up and gave him a light cuff in the back of the head. "Very punny, Scarcliff. Seriously, though, what do you think of Rika's plan?"

"By plan, you mean the thing where you take First Platoon down and act like bait?" Scarcliff asked.

"Dangling bait is a perfectly viable plan." Leslie cocked an eyebrow at Scarcliff. "So long as our backup is ready."

"It'll be ready. Whoever is raising shit down there will rue the day they messed with Rika's Marauders."

"We're really going with that?"

"Damn skippy."

"You don't think that it will cause division between our company and the rest of the regiment?"

"I've been in the Marauders as long as you, Leslie. Every unit has to form their own internal bonds. Most of them have their own little names, like Terry's Terrors and Sarah's Scarfaces. Smalls and I put a lot of thought into including 'Marauders' in ours. I think it will be better in the long run."

Leslie hadn't known that Scarcliff and Heather had orchestrated the company name so deliberately, but she had to admit it made sense. She'd be sure to share that logic with the ship's crew, if it came up.

"Well said. I certainly like being in Rika's Marauders more than Ayer's Assholes."

Scarcliff barked a laugh. "I may have been behind coining that one too."

"Keep dreaming," Leslie said over her shoulder as she walked away. "We all know it was Captain Ayer herself that came up with it."

*****

Leslie settled into the copilot's seat in the pinnace. She'd considered not taking the toon's assault pinnace down in the drop. If there were going to be SAMs chasing them again, the ship she was in would be the first target the enemy selected.

However, it was also the ship best able to defend against incoming surface to air fire.

She glanced at Chief Warrant Officer Charles as he shifted in the pilot's seat. His helmet had a snarling dog painted on it and the words "Mad Dog" written over it. The artwork was impressive; Charles had done it himself.

He'd already painted almost every pilot's helmet in the company, and was pressing Rika to let him paint all the mechs' as well.

"You ready to roll, Chief?" she asked.

"I'm ready with a side of fuck-yeah, Ellll-Tee!" Charles drew out the two letters and gave her a lopsided grin.

"Easy now, Chief." Leslie chuckled at the pilot's enthusiasm before reaching out to Heather. *<Flight Leader, First Platoon is geared up and ready to hit the black.>*

<Board's green here, first. Your fighter escort is in position. You're good to drop by the numbers.>

<Roger that, FL,> Leslie replied and switched her address to the segregated network with the pilots. *<First platoon, we are green. Drop. Drop. Drop.>*

A siren sounded in the drop bay, and the deck opened up in front of the dropships. The cradles tilted, and in preprogrammed sequence, the ships were accelerated down the ladders and out into space.

"Yeeehaw!" Charles cried out as the well-lit drop bay was replaced by the black expanse of space.

Leslie couldn't suppress the smile that forced its way onto her lips. She'd dropped with Charles on other missions, and his enthusiasm was infectious. It was one of the reasons she'd wrangled him into her 'toon when she heard he was assigned to Rika's company.

Like all the dropship pilots, Charles was not a mech. The cockpits on most ships could barely fit a human, let alone a mech—barring SMI-2s.

Even so, he was heavily modded for piloting a ship, and did it with a grace and skill that few possessed. He had his own customized control suite, a three-dimensional interface that only he could see. He waved his hands through it, turned invisible knobs, and adjusted other controls with gestures that made no sense to Leslie.

Not that she needed to know *how* he flew the ship, just that he had a damn good record and flew the smoothest drops Leslie had ever been on.

She brought up the pinnace's scan data on the holo in front of her and watched as the dropships spread out into a wide pattern, each covered by four fighters. Every vessel was over a kilometer from each other, their jinking patterns loaded and synchronized.

"You think we're going to see action?" Charles asked.

Leslie shrugged. "I hope not. If someone on Iapetus can attack this many ships with impunity, what's to stop them from hitting the *'Lark* or the *'Dream*? We'd be better off finding a new location for our training facility."

Charles laughed as he executed a burn to slot the pinnace into its descent vector. "What better way to train us all than a hostile environment?"

"I can think of a lot of better ways."

"I guess, maybe," Charles said absently as he reviewed the ship's trajectory. "Hey, LT, since this is going to be by the numbers, think you can sing a song for me while we come down? I hear you've got an amazing set of pipes."

Leslie resisted the urge to reach out and hit Charles in the back of the head. "I'll show you pipes. Just fly the damn ship."

* * * * *

Charles kept the pinnace in a holding pattern over the training compound while the dropships settled onto the facility's southern edge, disgorging their troops by the numbers, mechs fanning out, covering corners before moving out to sweep the surrounding buildings.

The structures had once been hangars and repair facilities at a small airport used by light and sport aircraft. On the far side of the buildings were three landing strips for aerodynamic descent.

People got up to strange things in their free time.

For some reason, the airport had fallen out of use, and Barne had been able to secure it for a surprisingly low price.

As Leslie surveyed the facility, she could make out a construction crew on the northern side of the airstrip erecting a simple fence that denoted the edge of Marauder territory, separating it from the half-abandoned commercial district surrounding the compound.

It wasn't a very defensible location, but Leslie approved of Rika's plan. If they were to get to the bottom of what was afoot on Iapetus, they *wanted* to be attacked.

Once the squad leaders declared their assigned quadrants clear, Leslie directed squad two to secure the landing field for the cargo carriers on the northern side of the barracks.

After the compound was deemed secure, and the fighter escort had boosted away, Leslie directed Charles to lower the pinnace from its overwatch position to settle in front of the command building.

She lowered the ramp and stepped out onto the hard surface the moment the ship settled down. Ahead, Rika walked out of the command building, a wide smile on her face as she surveyed the deployment.

"Lieutenant Leslie, congratulations on the drop. A hell of a lot better than mine."

Leslie met Rika's smile with one of her own. "It's easier when no one's shooting at you."

They shook hands, and turned to watch as Staff Sergeant Chris and the squad sergeants oversaw the unloading of the equipment from the dropships—likely receiving direction and chastisement from Barne, who was still back in the command building's CIC.

"The loading go smoothly?" Rika asked as they watched the activity before them. Leslie initialized a HUD overlay showing the scan data from the surrounding terrain and skies above. She was certain Rika was doing likewise. Just because the drop hadn't been hit didn't mean they couldn't be attacked now.

"Without a hitch," Leslie replied.

"Major Tim was surprisingly accommodating," Rika said, and gestured to the contrails the fighters had left in the sky from their thrusters.

Leslie chuckled. "I bet that before we left, the Old Man took the major aside and told him that if anything happened to you, there'd be hell to pay."

Rika looked at Leslie with surprise. "Think so?"

"Well, I didn't see it happen, but I'd be shocked if it didn't. Seriously, Rika. You went from hardware purchased at auction to company commander in under a year. How is it that you don't see how much the Old Man is in your corner?"

Leslie watched as Rika's brow lowered and her lips twisted in thought. "I guess it is a bit of a meteoric rise."

"That's an oxymoronic figure of speech."

"I didn't invent it." Rika shrugged.

"If you're not a part of the solution, you're a part of the problem."

Rika laughed. "Only a day away, and already I'd started to miss you. By-the-by, did you bring those additional items I asked for?"

"What do I look like? Of course I brought them."

"Brought what?" Chase asked from behind the pair.

"Shit!" Leslie exclaimed. "Since when did you become a ninja? That's my gig."

"Learned from the best," Chase said.

Leslie saw Rika reach her hand back and clasp Chase's. "Leslie and I are going on an excursion into the city tonight."

Chase glanced at Leslie and back to Rika. "Girls' night out, I take it?"

<*Something like that,*> Rika replied over a private connection between the three of them. <*David has spent the last day establishing a connection with a woman in the local garrison commander's HQ. He managed to get her to agree to a private meeting to talk about what they know of the attack on our dropship. We'll find somewhere nearby to discretely watch the meet.*>

<*You realize that's not the sort of mission the company commander goes on,*> Chase said with a raised eyebrow.

<*I'm aware,*> Rika said. <*But I may take the opportunity to reveal myself and talk with her directly. Depends on how it goes.*>

<*You should take a fireteam,*> Chase advised.

<*Mechs don't blend in all that well,*> Rika said. <*I suppose I could grab some of the SMIs, but they're all in different squads, and I don't want to mess with team cohesion.*>

Leslie considered their options. There were only five SMI-2 mechs in First Platoon. <*We could bring Kelly and Keli. Those two are already thick as thieves most of the time.*>

<*Other than a few short stints on stations, neither Keli or Kelly have been back amongst the general populace yet,*> Chase cautioned. <*I don't know if they're ready for that.*>

Leslie waved her hand dismissively. <*What better time than now? We're in friendly territory—mostly. I brought enough of our handy camouflage robes. Be good for them to get out and be able to blend in.*>

<*I think it's solid,*> Rika said. <*Leslie, you can stay in overwatch, lurk on a roof or something, and the girls can come with me. You know…it'll be the first time since the war that I worked with a full team of SMIs.*>

Rika got a distant look in her eyes and Leslie patted her on the shoulder. <*Silva had to go. It was the right thing for her to do.*>

<*I know. Doesn't mean I don't miss her,*> Rika replied.

<You never know,> Chase said. *<Maybe after we kick the Nietzscheans all the way to the rim of the galaxy, we can all go and retire with Silva.>*

Rika smiled. *<Sounds like a plan.>*

RECONNECTING

STELLAR DATE: 08.10.8949 (Adjusted Gregorian)
LOCATION: Marauder Training Compound
REGION: Iapetus, Hercules System, Septhian Alliance

Rika lay back on her side of the bed and breathed a long sigh of contentment. "Having a real bed sure is nice. Starships are just not made for couples to get up to shenanigans."

Chase rolled over to face her and trailed a finger through her hair. "We're lucky that the Old Man has a lax attitude when it comes to this stuff. No sane command would let me work under you."

Rika turned her head and smirked at Chase. "Thought it was me that was working under you just now."

"Yeah, well, let's keep that arrangement to our quarters. I like having to salute you."

"Ha!" Rika shook her head. "Nice double entendre there."

"I try. It's hard working for you."

"OK, easy now. You've proven you can be punny, Chase."

He rose to his knees and swung a leg over Rika, straddling her. A part of her was impressed by how he could maneuver around her body without scratching himself; either that, or he didn't care.

"It always amazes me," he commented absently as he traced a finger down her chest.

"What does?" Rika asked absently, staring up into Chase's dark brown eyes.

"How warm you are."

"I'm cooler than you are. Twenty-eight degrees at rest."

Chase reached down and picked up her hand, placing his palm against what passed for hers. "Yeah, but your hands are warm too. Why is that?"

"Part of our chameleon abilities. We can warm our entire

bodies to uniform temperatures. Also tied into our heat dispersal. I could make it warmer." Rika warmed her hand to thirty-four degrees. "There, it matches your hand now."

"Heh, that's hot," Chase said as he reached out and touched the socket on the end of her right arm. Though Rika liked having her GNR attached, she didn't sleep with it. Not after that time when the barrel had whacked Chase during a bad dream.

And Rika often had bad dreams.

"Why don't you keep it this warm all the time?" Chase asked.

"Uses extra energy. Twenty-eight is my average dispersal temperature, when I'm not exerting myself. You're lucky I'm not an FR model; they have these cooling strips on their arms that can get pretty damn toasty. I'd probably burn you during our escapades."

Chase pushed her arm back above her head and leaned in to kiss her.

Rika drew in a deep breath as their lips touched feeling his naked body press up against her carbon-poly skin, his firm pecs pressing into the stiff mounds on her chest.

She had long ago forgotten what real tactile contact across her body would feel like—but given the difference between her face and the rest of her 'skin', she wondered if she would be able to handle the sensations.

"You smell like candy," Chase whispered as he kissed her. "Cotton candy. You secreting some around here somewhere?"

"It's a new facial cleanser Leslie gave me," Rika said with a laugh. "But if I want to hide candy, that's my business."

"So you do have candy!" Chase proclaimed and nibbled at her ear.

Ear nibbles always made her giggle, and sometimes ruined her mood, but Rika didn't care. Being near Chase was what mattered. Being grounded and feeling human was always welcome.

"Do you think the other mechs take lovers?" she asked suddenly, turning her head to look into Chase's eyes.

He shrugged. "Some do, some can't."

"Well, we technically can't make love, either," Rika reminded him—as if she needed to.

Chase leaned down to kiss her. "Rika, I don't need to push inside you to 'make love' to you. Being here with you now, living my life with you, fighting on the battlefield with you—*that* is making love to you. Making love is everything we do."

Rika appreciated the small lie, but she knew he'd like to have real sex. She would too, especially at times like this when it felt like her insides were on fire.

Rika tamped down her urges as much as possible and smiled. "Who would have thought a stone-cold killer like you was such a romantic?"

Chase's smile faded. "I'm not a stone—what would make you say that?"

"I didn't mean anything by it, Chase." Rika frowned, wondering what about her statement had rattled him. "We're all killers. It's what we do."

"I know, but sometimes…sometimes I'd just like to forget that. Don't you want this to end someday? Do something else with your life?"

"Like what?" Rika asked.

It wasn't the first time Chase had made comments like this, but she could never get him to elaborate on his feelings—instead he would just shut down. This time, she tried a different tack.

"I'm a war machine. It's what I do, I'm not in the 'get old with great-great-grandchildren at my knee' profession. I've accepted that."

"What if I haven't?" Chase asked.

"What does that mean? I thought you liked being in the Marauders."

Chase sat up, still straddling her. "I do like being in the Marauders. It's a good job, we seem to be working for the good guys, so that's nice. And I'm with you, which is what I want most. But I don't want to spend the rest of my life in this outfit. We're more than just killers, Rika."

"Of course we are; we're a family. Basilisk, and now M Company. We're saving people, Chase. My people."

Chase nodded. "And after that?"

Rika pushed an errant lock of hair out of her face. "I don't know. I don't think that far ahead. I'm not too sure I can succeed at what's laid out ahead of me now."

"And what's that?" Chase asked.

"I want to drive the Nietzscheans out of Genevia," she replied, her voice lowering. "I want to kill every last motherfucking one of them, scour them from the stars."

Chase's eyes widened, and Rika realized her statement came across with more vehemence than she'd intended.

"Why?" he asked. "What did Genevia ever do for you?"

"It made me this," Rika said, lifting her right arm and rotating her wrist. "It made me strong and powerful. Did it abuse me? Yes. But what would have happened to me if I wasn't turned into a mech? There weren't a lot of survivors from the world where I got convicted. Becoming a mech may have saved my life."

Chase nodded soberly. "Yeah, I looked Kellas up. They got hit hard. But still…why do you love Genevians so much? They aren't that accepting of mechs."

"Chase." Rika reached up and touched his face. *"You're* Genevian. So is Leslie, Barne; stars, everyone in M Company is. The Old Man. We're all Genevian."

"Do you need all of them? Am I not enough?" Chase clasped her hand in both of his. "We could flee deep into the cluster. Past the edge of FTL. Nietzschea won't bother going into the inner empire; it's not worth the effort."

Rika frowned. She couldn't understand why Chase was saying this, he wasn't a coward. She'd seen him in combat multiple times, and he'd never backed down from a challenge.

"What's brought this on?" she asked. "The Marauders are our family, we can't just abandon them."

"A family that's going to get you killed," he replied.

"Is this because we got shot down? Are you worried that I'm

going to die?"

"Yes!" Chase almost shouted. "You *did* almost die. If your crazy pilot hadn't dived under the ocean, you'd be toast. Don't you see that?"

Rika shrugged. "I guess…though we might have survived that, too. Stars, people die from all sorts of stupid shit all the time. I won't live in fear just because of what *could* happen."

"What *will* happen," Chase corrected.

"What do you mean?"

"We all die, Rika."

There was a sadness in his voice that told Rika there was some story, some trauma from his past that he'd not yet shared with her.

"What is it, Chase? What's got you thinking like this?"

He rolled off her and lay on his back, staring at the ceiling. "Nothing—other than what we've already gone over and over and over."

Rika rolled onto her side and clasped his hand. "Chase, I want to spend my forever with you, but this is what I have to do right now. It's who I am—I've accepted that. But I promise it won't last forever."

"How can I believe that?" Chase asked. "You've gone from loathing what you are to loving it."

"Because…maybe deep down, where I'm too scared to admit it…I think I want to have my great-great grandchildren at my knee someday."

Chase turned his head and met her gaze. "Mean it?"

Rika nodded, feeling her eyes grow moist. "I think I do. I really do."

THE MEET

STELLAR DATE: 08.11.8949 (Adjusted Gregorian)
LOCATION: Hittis City
REGION: Iapetus, Hercules System, Septhian Alliance

"Nice place David picked for his date with Dala," Kelly said, gesturing out the window as the three SMI-2s settled into their seats at Charlie's Pasta and Chips.

Rika looked across the street to the restaurant David and Dala would be dining at. It wasn't too fancy, simply named Hammurabi, but not having 'chips' in the name took any establishment up a notch.

"Not the sort of place our kind can visit," Keli added.

<*Remember,*> Rika cautioned privately. <*We're regular citizens, we can go anywhere we like. Believe it. Own it. It's the best way to blend in.*>

Keli didn't reply, but nodded as she picked up her menu with gloved hands.

Rika pulled her robe's long sleeves back and did the same. She felt naked without her gun-arm, something that both Keli and Kelly had confessed to as well, but they were all still carrying rifles under their robes. Keli had called them their 'security blankets'.

Rika shifted her weight carefully, keeping one leg extended under her chair to support most of her weight. She wasn't too worried about the seat collapsing, but it wasn't an idle concern for a mech. When they were scoping out a good location, the sturdy steel chairs at Charlie's Pasta and Chips had played a major part in their choice of establishment.

<*You three just better remember to order my takeout. I want a fettucine alfredo, and their lasagna. Plus those fresh kettle chips everyone raves about in their reviews,*> Leslie chimed in.

<*Whatever you say, LT,*> Keli said cheerfully.

<*Stow that glee,*> Leslie retorted. <*If I'd known it was going to rain like this tonight, I would have volunteered one of you for overwatch.*>

<*Would you say it's raining cats and dogs?*> Rika asked with a snicker.

<*Stars, not you, too.*>

<*I can't help it.*> Rika got her mirth under control. <*Scarcliff does it so much that they spring to mind all the time now.*>

<*Well, the next girls' night out needs to involve less of me freezing my ass off out in a storm.*>

<*Noted,*> Rika replied.

The three women reviewed their menus, looking over the options and discussing them casually while each kept half an eye on the restaurant across the street, where David now waited for Major Dala.

"Stars. I think I'll just have the spaghetti and meatballs," Kelly said. "If you count the time I was on ice, I haven't had a good spaghetti in…what, ten years?"

"They had it in the galley just last week," Keli said as she perused her menu.

"Right," Kelly nodded. "I think you missed the part where I said 'good' spaghetti."

"Are you besmirching our ship's cooks?" Keli asked. "Because I'm in love with all of them."

"Points for using 'besmirching'," Rika commented.

"No, no besmirchment—is that even a word?—intended. They didn't have the right sauce, is all. They should have waited for fresh tomatoes before trying it. Their menu here says all ingredients are locally sourced and that they make their sauce fresh each day."

Keli shrugged. "OK, that's good to see. Maybe this place is more than just the joint with the strongest chairs."

<*I swear…I'm going to turn off the comm channel,*> Leslie groused. <*I'm salivating up here.*>

Rika saw a waitress approach—not human, but an automaton good enough to fool casual observation. She wore a short blue skirt and white blouse with 'Mary' on her name tag. Rika thought her legs were a touch too long for her torso, but not so much that you'd notice at first glance.

<*Maybe she's the discount bot,*> Niki commented. <*From the defects pile.*>

<*How do you make a bot's legs too long as a defect?*> Rika asked. <*Seems deliberate.*>

<*Well, maybe they were meant for a taller model.*>

<*Poor waitress-bot, made from spare parts.*> Rika shook her head.

"What can I get for you ladies to drink?" the subtly misshapen waitress automaton asked as she set three glasses of water on the table.

"Ohhhhh, drinks!" Kelly proclaimed. "I'll take…one of your cinnamon martinis."

"I'll have this thing you call the cherry bomb." Keli stabbed a finger at the menu.

"Just a glass of your best white bubbly for me," Rika said when the automaton-waitress turned to her.

"OK, you got it. Cinnamon martini, Explosive Cherry Bomb, and a glass of our Atrium."

The three nodded in turn, and Mary gave a nod and turned, walking to the back of the restaurant to prepare their drinks.

"Why make automatons look so perfectly human?" Keli asked. "Everyone can tell what they are."

"Not around here, they can't," Rika said. "Thebans don't mod much—at least not the ones that live on planets. They might not be able to spot a bot like our Mary."

"Weird," Keli replied. "Of course, I haven't seen the inside of a restaurant for about as long as Kelly. Stavros didn't really let us eat out a lot. And by 'a lot', I mean 'ever'."

"I imagine," Rika said with a nod. "Stavros wasn't much of a 'let anyone do anything' kinda guy."

Keli's eyes widened and she nodded in agreement. "Glad you put him down."

"Was actually Barne that fired the shot," Kelly said as she set her menu down.

Keli raised the glass of water that sat before her. "Well, when I get my drink, I'll raise a toast to the Top. May his days of taking out evil dictators never end."

"I'm sure he'd echo that sentiment," Rika said, turning her gaze out the window once more. She didn't really need to watch for Dala's approach. Leslie would let them know when she spotted the Major, and David would confirm when she joined him.

"What was it like?" Kelly asked after a minute of silence stretched between them.

"It?" Rika asked.

"Being out in the world. After the war."

Rika looked at the two women seated across from her and sighed. Both had been injured in the war, and subsequently found by Stavros. Neither saw the end of the fight with the Nietzscheans—saw their leaders surrender or flee. Neither had to live in the shattered remains of their nation amidst a populace that hated them

"It sucked balls," Rika replied. "Lots of balls. All the balls. I guess it would have gone better for me if I'd joined an outfit like the Marauders—or even a gang of some sort. But I was stubborn. I wanted to try to make a go of it as a civilian."

"Now that doesn't surprise me." Kelly grinned, the smile actually reaching her eyes. "You never could let go of an idea once it got into that head of yours."

"Wish I'd been on a team like yours," Keli said. "Kelly's told me all about Hammerfall. You ladies kicked some major ass back in the shit."

Mary returned as Keli spoke, and set their drinks down. "Are you ready to order, or are you still looking over the menu? Oh! I forgot to recite the specials."

<How does an automaton 'forget' the specials?> Niki asked. *<Is the NSAI defective, or does someone think this is a clever way to sell the daily deals?>*

<Beats me,> Rika replied. *<If folks around here can't tell it's a bot, maybe it does work—or maybe it's randomly variable behavior, or something.>*

<I guess. I don't usually run into NSAIs managing simple tasks like this,> Niki replied. *<Usually they're managing things like magnetic fields on a tokamak reactor or something.>*

Keli said she'd like to hear the specials, and Mary began to rattle them off.

<I would have thought that you talked to NSAIs all the time,> Rika commented as she half-listened to Mary's recitation.

<I've spent most of my time on starships. You're only the second person I've been embedded with—though we're not neurally embedded, like a real AI pairing would be.>

<I guess there aren't many NSAIs trying to sell you on the Chicken Bolognese on a starship.>

<Not so much, no.>

<What's it like to be neurally embedded?> Rika asked, as Mary finished the list, and Keli hemmed and hawed.

<For the human, it's not that much different. For the AI, we get deeper insight into the logic behind our partner's decisions.>

<We use logic?> Rika chuckled. *<I wouldn't have thought AIs considered many human decisions to be logical.>*

<Well, for the most part, humans **believe** *that their reasoning is valid. If this, then that, and therefore logical. Most of the time, the truly illogical things you humans do are for entertainment—which makes them something that you enjoy. Therefore, it's logical for you to do illogical things, because gaining amusement is healthy for your minds, and thus logical.>*

<Huh. You used the word 'logic' so many times it just became a morass of syllables. Is that logical? Rika asked, then shifted her attention to Mary to order a plate of spaghetti and chips.

Niki just groaned in response, and sent Rika an image of eyes rolling in exasperation.

<OK, OK,> Rika replied. *<I guess it makes sense. I mean, it does to me; I just didn't think it would make sense to an AI.>*

<Well, that's part of why we spend time with humans. It's not to serve you, but rather because there are some things that are better experienced than taught.>

"So, what was your favorite mission, Rika?" Keli asked once Mary departed.

<I'm going to come back to this later,> Rika told Niki. *<I want to understand more about what you meant.>*

<Sure, I'm not going anywhere.>

Rika considered it for a moment. "You know, I really liked our mission on Parsons—I mean, except for the part where you died, Kelly. I could barely think about it for years afterward. But now…now it's one that I can actually look back on. We kicked some major ass."

"You saved my life twice on that mission, Rika." The corners of Kelly's eyes glistened, and she gave a short sniff before shaking her head. "I'll never forget you standing atop that K1R, firing your rifle into it until it let me go."

Keli's brow lowered. "A K1R? Why were you fighting one of our own?"

Rika pursed her lips, and Kelly replied. "Fucking Niets turned it against us. Bastard—"

"Was a poor bastard," Rika interrupted. "He didn't ask for what happened to him. I gave him a good death."

No one spoke for a moment, and then Kelly laughed. "And *those* are the 'good' memories."

Rika stretched a hand across the table and took Kelly's, then grabbed Keli's as well. "No, the good memories were times like this. Sure, we didn't have Mary bringing us the best chips this side of the cluster, but we *did* have each other. That was the *real* 'best part' about Hammerfall. And now we have the Marauders."

"*Rika's* Marauders," Keli said with a silly grin. "Shit Captain, why you such a big sap? Don' you know we rust if we cry?"

"You might have to see Bondo about that," Kelly smirked as she wiped a gloved hand against her cheek.

<I love listening to the three of you bond as much as anyone,> Leslie

interrupted, *<but I thought you'd want to know that Dala is approaching the restaurant.>*

Rika looked out the window to see Dala, exiting a ground car and rushing through the rain to the restaurant across the street.

<I see her. Looks damp.>

<That dress doesn't look like any sort of uniform, either,> Keli commented.

<I guess David made more of an impression than we thought.> Rika nodded appreciatively. *<I'll admit, I hadn't given him that much credit—at least, not that specific type of credit.>*

<I guess Dala likes 'em smart,> Keli added.

<Could be that she's going to spill the beans and wants to make this look like a date, in case anyone is following her,> Leslie suggested.

Rika wondered about that. It would be an interesting twist. Or it just could be that Colonel Zim was as much of a hardass as Rika suspected, and Dala was happy for any excuse to get out.

<She's here,> David advised on a separate channel. Rika hadn't segregated him as a slight, she just didn't want to distract him with their banter—though with his mods, he probably could focus on what was necessary well enough.

Still, he'd confessed to being a poor actor, and Rika didn't want to tax him. *<Remember. Ease her into sharing. Don't force her. If things go well, broach the subject of talking with me. Doesn't have to be now. I'm here for a 'just in case' scenario.>*

<You got it, Captain,> David said, a waver in his voice belying a measure of uncertainty.

<I'll be listening, so if anything comes up that I can help with, I'll offer a suggestion. But I'll keep my chatter to a minimum.>

The rest of the team was listening in on the conversation, though Keli and Kelly kept up some verbal chatter about the weather on Iapetus so that it didn't seem like the entire table fell silent for no reason.

David provided a feed from his eyes on the team's net, and Rika tapped into it, overlaying it on the right side of her vision.

Dala approached his table, and he rose to greet her. She was wearing a grey dress that had a patina of dark spots on it from the rain. Her pink hair was pulled back into a clip, from which it fell down over her shoulders. Her lips were colored to match her fuchsia eyes, and her smile seemed genuine as she took David's hand and gave it a single shake.

"Very nice to meet you in person, David," Dala said as she sat. "And even nicer to do it at a place like Hammurabi's. I hear their roast chicken is superb."

"I really don't know the local establishments in Hittis that well," David replied. "But no one seemed to complain about this place, so it seemed like a safe pick."

"Weren't you worried that I might be a vegetarian?" Dala asked. "Hammurabi's is mostly known for their meat."

Rika imagined that David must have shrugged or given a smile—though she couldn't tell from his visual feed.

"I looked over your activity on the public feeds. You often post about the types of foods you prefer. It made my selection a bit easier, though it also told me that I needed to be discerning."

Major Dala raised an eyebrow, though a smile toyed at the corners of her lips. "Did *you* check up on me, David of the Marauders?"

"I'm a P-COG. I check up on everything. It's what we do."

Dala's smile faded. "We are all what we're made to do."

"That seems fatalistic," David replied. "What have you been made to do?"

The major shook her head. "Nothing sinister. I was just thinking about how our parents shape us, then school, then our jobs."

"Ah, and especially more so if your job is the military."

"Doubly so, yes."

David and Dala's conversation moved to more trivial topics as they reviewed the menu and ordered their drinks. Rika listened with half an ear as they spoke of the Theban integration into the Septhian Alliance.

Dala was circumspect, but Rika could tell that she resented the change, though she did agree that it was likely a necessity in the fight against the Nietzscheans. Before the attack on the Albany System, the Niets moving into the Praesepe Cluster had been a worry for another day. Now it was history, and no one could argue that Thebes was in the Nietzscheans' crosshairs.

On the public feeds, debate raged as to whether or not the Niets would strike the same target twice, but Rika knew they would. If there was one truth about the Niets, it was that they hated to lose.

If they lost an attack on a world or system, they would return again and again, throwing more and more resources into the conflict until they won.

During the war, Rika had often heard officers speculating about where the Niets were getting their seemingly endless resources. Though their empire was vast, there was no evidence that they had the economy to support the war they waged.

The prevailing logic was that they were being supported by the Trisilieds. That kingdom was the dominant power in the Pleiades Cluster, and had massive mining operations collecting both the dust permeating the region, and the exotic matter that streamed off the massive B-class stars that dominated the Pleiades.

Rika had kept her ear to the ground over the years—something made easy by working in places like Hal's Hell. From what she'd heard, there was little to no chatter about major trade with the Trisilieds. Wherever the Nietzscheans had gathered their resources, it didn't appear to be from there.

Maybe someday she'd be in a position to find out.

Across the road, David and Dala were sipping their drinks. On Rika's side, Kelly and Keli were tucking into their meals, with Kelly letting out more than a few moans of delight as she ate her plate of spaghetti.

<Don't forget to order my takeout,> Leslie reminded Rika at one point.

<Oh, you were serious about that?>

<Rika. It's freezing up here, and I can feel my stomach gnawing a hole in my liver. Listening to Kelly moan about how much she loves pasta is about to push me over the edge. You're damn skippy, I'm serious.>

<You volunteered for overwatch, you know.>

Leslie growled. *<Um, no,* ***you*** *volunteered* ***me.*** *So help me, if you don't have my order placed in five minutes, I'm going to come down there and kick the tar out of the three of you.>*

<OK, OK, I'm signaling our synthetic waitress to come over.>

<You do that.>

Rika followed up on her promise, and Kelly added five more orders, apparently planning to live on leftover takeout for the next week.

Across the street, David and Dala's meals also arrived, and they began to eat in relative silence.

Thus far, Dala had not said anything noteworthy, though they *had* spoken of the attack in general terms. Rika was starting to wonder if Dala had led David on, simply interested in a date with no intentions of sharing anything about the attack.

Or maybe she plans to extract additional details from him…

<David—> Rika began, but David stopped her.

<Busy, Captain. We're having a chat over a direct Link connection. She's telling me about how the ATC and Link were disrupted.>

<Well, that's good. Was starting to think she just may want you to go over to her place afterward.>

David snorted. *<Who says that can't happen, too? I'm bundling up what she's said thus far and sending it to Niki. Going to try to get more details on a few things.>*

<OK.>

<Getting a transmission from David,> Niki said over the group's connection. *<Oh ho! Would you look at this. On the night we were attacked, the Link towers for five-hundred kilometers just happened to all go through a diagnostic cycle at the same time…one that triggered a core instruction-set update that required a full re-initialization.>*

<Seems…unlikely that was an accident,> Keli observed. *<I worked*

Link relay maintenance before conscription. We had carefully orchestrated rolling update patterns. Different ones all the time, so that they were harder to exploit.>

<*Maybe they're just dumb here.*> Kelly smirked around a mouthful of spaghetti.

<*You saw how the feeds lit up with people who were bullshit over the outage. If that sort of thing happened regularly, you wouldn't have seen them so upset over it.*>

<*ATC went down as a result of the Link outage,*> Niki added. <*Looks like it's supposed to fail over to proprietary backup communication systems, but it didn't.*>

<*And why did satcomms go offline at the same time?*> Rika asked. <*That has to add to the suspicion.*>

Niki responded without pause. <*The official word from the providers is that the satcomm network got overloaded when the terrestrial one went down. But that's not what Dala's division thinks. They believe that someone hammered the satcomms with bogus data when the ground systems went offline.*>

<*This isn't news worth freezing my ass off for,*> Leslie interjected. <*The fact that the attack was well orchestrated is evidenced by the attack itself. It's the 'who' that matters.*>

<*I'm getting there,*> Niki replied. <*Trying to sift through and corroborate as much of what Dala is telling David as I can. OK. Dala says she doesn't* ***think*** *it was orchestrated by anyone in the military, but she also said that some of the people who attacked us* ***were*** *former Theban Alliance soldiers. All discharged before the Septhian takeover, though—which stands to reason. No one's getting discharged from the SAF right now—unless it's dishonorable.*>

Rika wanted to pass a dozen questions over to David for him to ask Dala, but he knew the objective as well as she. There was no point messing up his train of thought.

<*Well, that's…*> Leslie began. <*Oh shit! Rika, you need to get over there. We've got company!*>

Rika rose from her chair. <*We're live, ladies. Kelly and I will go in the front. Keli, you go around back and secure egress. Chase will pick us up at the park four blocks east.*> She looked at the pair and they both nodded before exiting Charlie's Pasta and Chips.

Rika sent a payment over the Link so they wouldn't have to worry about Mary chasing after them, and moved a dozen meters down the street before crossing. Kelly mirrored her route, bracketing the restaurant. Once across the street, Rika stopped under an awning and reviewed the data Leslie was feeding them.

Leslie was positioned atop the ten-story building that housed Charlie's Pasta and Chips at street level. From her vantage, she had eyes on armored figures atop the next building over, setting up on the roof. That building was only two stories high, and would provide a clear shot through the windows of Hammurabi's.

Leslie hadn't spotted any others, but if there were two, there were more.

<*Think it's capture or kill?*> Kelly asked as she leaned against a post in front of Hammurabi's, obstructing the shooter's line of sight into the restaurant.

<*Capture,*> Leslie replied. <*I see a spotter in a parked ground car thirty meters past your position, Rika. And there's a van approaching. It's staying low, but its flight-capable.*>

<*I'm almost at the alley,*> Keli reported. <*Nothing here, yet.*>

Rika reached out to David. <*We have company coming. Looks like a grab team with an option to terminate.*>

<*Me or her?*> David asked, surprisingly calm.

<*No way to tell,*> Rika replied.

<*Use a pair of drones, triangulate the shooter's aim. Their spotter will be looking at both of us, but the shooter won't. They'll be on their primary target.*>

It made sense; Rika felt silly for not thinking of it herself. It wasn't a foolproof way to tell, but David was probably right.

Rika loosened the scarf around her neck, and two of her miniscule drones flew out, rising through the rain to track the aim of the shooter's rifle.

The sniper had just moved, taking up a new position where

Kelly wasn't in the way, and when he settled into place, Rika had her answer.

<It's on her, David. Not wavering at all. So either the shooter thinks Dala's hot, or she's the primary.>

<Could be. I, for one, really dig all the pink she has going on. Should I get her out the back?>

Rika checked on the incoming van. It was halfway down the block. Keli hadn't yet made it around the back, but if the van was up front, it was likely that few—if any—enemies would be at the restaurant's rear.

At least Rika hoped that would be the case.

<We should have brought a bigger team,> she said privately to Niki.

<Or at least made Keli hang out in the alley at the back.> Niki gave a mental nod. *<Mind you, she would have complained about you and Kelly getting the nice meal.>*

<This is what I get for worrying about people's feelings,> Rika replied as she drew her left arm within her cloak and unslung her JE-84 rifle. Kelly—who was still clearly visible to the sniper and spotter team—didn't yet make a move. Reaching for a weapon was a telltale motion the enemy would spot in an instant.

<I'm halfway down to them,> Leslie said. *<Just one more floor, and I can jump if needs be.>*

<Kelly. Move into the sniper's line of sight again. David, get moving, take her to the back. Leslie, jump only if they fire—or if you really want to.>

The team followed her orders without hesitation. Within the restaurant, David rose and held his hand out to Dala, who was still seated, giving him a confused look. Rika hoped he could get her moving without trouble, but couldn't offer any help, as the van arrived in front of the restaurant and its side doors opened up.

A man in powered armor stepped out and raised a chaingun.

Shit!

<Not a grab op!> Rika yelled as she fired a trio of rounds from

her JE-84 at the enemy. He spun toward her, and his chaingun spun up at the same time as a muffled crack sounded.

The restaurant's sign exploded in a shower of sparks, struck by the sniper's weapon.

<*Got him!*> Leslie called out

<*Nice timing,*> Rika responded as she leapt into the air to avoid the chaingun's spray of bullets. She grinned as Kelly moved into view, her cloak thrown open, JE-87 spraying kinetic rounds into the back of Rika's attacker.

Without hesitation, Rika added her own hail of bullets, and the man went down, the chaingun cocking up into the air and tracing a line of destruction across the storefronts.

Rika hoped no civilians had been injured, but had no time to worry about it, as two more enemies spilled out of the van and took cover behind it.

A shot rang out from the rooftops, and one of the new foes fell.

<*Nice gun, this,*> Leslie commented. <*The biolock was disabled, though. Bad form.*>

Rika leapt onto the van and fired at the second enemy, before a second shot came from Leslie's position. The soldier's neck exploded, and he crumpled to the ground.

Rika jumped off the van and looked into the restaurant to find David and Dala gone. Behind her, the van took off racing down the street, nearly colliding with two other cars before it turned the corner.

<*Got them. Safe and sound,*> Keli reported.

<*Good, we're coming 'round to meet you.*> Rika motioned for Kelly to follow her. <*Stay in the alley 'til we get there.*>

<*Aye aye, Captain.*>

Rika rolled her eyes at Keli's weak humor and reached out to Chase. <*You coming to give us poor women a ride home?*>

<*Am I to leave poor David behind?*> Chase asked

<*Er…us poor women plus David.*>

<*I'm hanging out above the park now. Just waiting for some guy to finish chasing his dog that got away from him, then I'll set down.*>

<*OK,*> Rika replied. <*We might be coming in hot, so stay frosty.*>

Chase laughed. <*Hot and frosty. Got it.*>

Rika led the way around the block while Kelly covered her six. They met Keli, David, and Dala around the corner. The look on the Major's face was a combination of anger and worry. Possibly mixed with a little annoyance.

"Should have expected to meet you out here," Dala said when she spotted Rika. "You seem to attract trouble."

Rika looked further down the street, then looked back behind them. So far, there were no signs of pursuit. "Their weapons were aimed at your pretty pink head, Major. Someone didn't like that you were sharing intel with us."

Dala opened her mouth to reply, but she closed it and nodded before asking. "So what's next?"

"We get you to our compound, and then you figure out who you can trust and reach out to them—but not before we arrive. For now, you need to go EM-silent."

Dala worked her jaw, then nodded. "Lead on."

They turned toward the park where Chase was landing and approached the next intersection, when a shadowy figure appeared at the corner, holding up a hand. Rika recognized Leslie's silhouette, and stopped. Nobody moved for eleven seconds, then Leslie's fingers curled up, and her thumb rose. Then she was gone again.

Leslie appeared once more to halt them, but otherwise, their route to the park was clear—as much as it could be, with local cops closing on the scene in front of Hammurabi's.

After the final row of buildings was behind them, Rika led the group through the park's twisting pathways to the clearing where Chase waited in the assault pinnace. Rika passed him the signal, and the ramp lowered.

A half-minute later, the ship was lifting off into the brisk, night air.

Once they were settled into the two rows of seats, Dala's cold gaze found its way to Rika. "Do you want to tell me what's going on?"

Rika looked down at her right arm and moved her fingers, sad to see them and not her GNR's long barrel. They were so ineffective when it came to doing what she needed to do.

After a few seconds' consideration, Rika looked up and met Dala's gaze.

"I was rather hoping you would tell us. Those wonderful visitors we just met appear to be the same folks who paid us a visit the other night."

"They've expanded their acceptable target list," Kelly added.

"And they have the toys to get the job done." Leslie hefted the sniper rifle she had purloined from the enemy. "This isn't Theban standard issue, but it does resemble the Septhian KM-171—the markings are all removed, but it could have been SAF issue."

Kelly leant over and looked at the weapon. "Well that doesn't make any sense. We know from what you said, Dala, that it's likely to be former Theban military elements who went after Rika. Does that mean we have two enemies? Thebans *and* Septhians?"

"Could just mean there was a good sale on stolen goods," David supplied. "With the military build-up that Septhia is undergoing, they're practically bleeding weapons onto the black market."

Dala nodded. "That's true enough. That's one of the things that Colonel Zim oversees: the tracking down of stolen military hardware. The stuff is everywhere right now."

<*That's convenient,*> Niki commented privately.

<*Niki! Was starting to wonder if you were still in there.*>

<*I was helping digest all that pasta you wolfed down.*>

Rika started. <*What? Really?*>

<*No, Rika. I was monitoring local feeds to see when the cops were going to show up. Then I was scrubbing you and your team from the local surveillance systems. Following that, I removed all traces of you ever being at Charlie's Pasta and Chips. Do I need to go on?*>

Rika laughed softly. <*No, I suppose not. Anyone looking askance at our pinnace right now?*>

<'Askance'? Look at you, getting all fancy. No, Chase has us registered as a sight-seeing tour. Given our stealth capabilities and this rain, we don't look too different from the executive shuttles that are common here.>

Rika rose from her seat in the main cabin and walked to the cockpit's entrance. "Clear skies?"

Chase glanced back at her. "Yeah. Taking a circuitous route, though."

"Niki told me that we're a sight-seeing tour. Not much to look at out there." Rika peered through the window at the dark night. The rain had picked up, turning into a torrential downpour so thick it was almost impossible to see the city lights below them.

"Yeah, but a great night to ease our way back to the compound—speaking of which, you have to pick a name for the thing. I can't keep calling it 'the compound' and 'the facility' anymore." Chase glanced back at her and winked. "Makes it feel like a prison or something."

"No one has come up with a good name yet," Rika replied.

"What about Fort Hammerfall?" Chase asked. "Sounds badass, has great connotations."

Rika pursed her lips, considering what it would be like to use her old team name like that. "I think that could work. Maybe people will mess with us less if it means taking on 'Hammerfall'."

"It's a—aw, shit, so much for free and clear."

Rika looked at the scan console and saw a contact shadowing them, three kilometers back. The contact flickered in and out as lightning flashed around the pinnace, then another one appeared, moving up on their port side to bracket the ship.

"Does ATC have them on its boards?" Rika asked.

Chase shook his head. "Nope. According to the towers, those ships aren't there at all."

Rika checked the pinnace's loadout, hoping that not all its cargo from the *Golden Lark* had been unloaded before Chase left the base.

"Booyah," Rika whispered. "The SkyScream is still in the bay," she informed Chase.

"What? Have you looked at this storm? You going to risk it in a SkyScream?"

Rika grinned and leant over to kiss Chase on the head. "You're sweet, hon. That's exactly *why* I'm going to do it."

"Stay safe," he called back, but didn't add anything more.

<*Always,*> she said privately as she walked back through the main cabin. <*I've been thinking about that thing we talked about, grandkids and all. I do want it someday.*>

<*I love you, Rika.*>

"Where you going?" Kelly called out as Rika rushed through the passenger bay to the cargo hatch.

"We have company," Rika replied.

"Company?" Kelly rose.

"Don't worry, we also have a SkyScream."

"Shiiiiit," Keli swore. "I love flying those! Just the one?"

"Yup, and it's the captain's prerogative," Rika said as she ducked into the pinnace's small cargo bay. It was empty except for the SkyScream, and Rika couldn't help a grin as she approached the ship.

The light attack craft was a special weapon that the GAF had produced in the later years of the war. They were made to fit RR and SMI mechs, and were pure joy to fly. When Rika had found seven of them in Stavros's hangars, she ensured that the Marauders secured them.

She climbed up the back of the craft, past the two large engines, and activated the SkyScream's pilot integration procedure.

A slot opened up for her arms, and she sank both limbs into the ship. The vessel detached her limbs and then opened another set of holes for her legs. Rika set them into the ship, and it detached her lower limbs.

Two armatures reached out and attached to Rika's arms and pulled her forward, settling her into the pilot's pocket.

Connections attached to her legs, and then the vessel was still for an instant.

<*Neural connection ready in five,*> Niki said.

Rika nodded and drew in a deep breath as the ship sealed itself around her head, and folded its layered armor over her body.

One moment she was Rika, with a bipedal body—albeit one whose limbs were stored back between the engines—the next, she was a SkyScream: a light attack craft equipped with missiles, chainguns, four electron beams, and one mean railgun.

It was a heady feeling, and Rika swallowed before calling up to Chase. <*If you would be so kind as to open the lower doors.*>

<*Doors open in ten. They've closed to within two klicks. No comms or overt aggression, yet. Once you're out, I'll ping them to see if I can distract and delay.*>

<*You're the best, Chase. See you back at Fort Hammerfall.*>

<*See? Hammerfall sounds perfect.*>

Rika laughed as the pinnace's bay doors opened below her, and the docking clamps released the SkyScream—her.

In an instant, the relative calm of the bay was replaced by the storm's rage. Rika tilted her wings up and pulsed the SkyScream's engines, pushing herself up and back.

<*This thing keeps trying to imprint a new identity into your mind,*> Niki commented as Rika fell back toward the pursuer that was closing on the pinnace's starboard. <*It wants you to think of yourself as SSRika.*>

Rika nodded absently—as much as she could. <*I remember that from the few times I got to fly these things in the war. Someone figured we'd be more effective if we thought of ourselves as new beings, like birds of prey.*>

<*That seems silly,*> Niki replied disdainfully.

<*I kinda liked it. I'm not sure if it was the imprinting, though. I feel about the same right now as I did the other times I flew a SkyScream.*>

Niki chuckled in her mind. <*Well, that's because I let it do the physical imprint, just not the part where you think of yourself with a new name. The physical imprint is necessary—without it, you'd probably kill yourself trying to fly this thing.*>

<*Oh…so I'm not a natural flier?*> Rika asked while leveling her wings and adjusting their trim, which felt as natural as rolling her shoulders.

<*Well, you're good, but the ship is a part of it.*>

Rika dropped behind the starboard pursuer, staying just above its engine wash. The vessel wasn't much larger than the SkyScream, ten meters wide and fifteen long. Stubby wings held an array of armament, and a pair of tailfins rose above the fuselage, twisting side to side in the gale-force winds.

No running lights were visible on the ship, and if her own scan systems were not military-grade, Rika doubted she would have seen the fighter until she was right on top of it.

<*Any reply, Chase?*>

<*None, and the ATC still doesn't show them at all—though it caught a ghost of you for a second.*>

<*Shit…I should have been invisible.*>

Niki spoke in a strange voice. <*Probably rain sleeting off you. The SSRika doesn't show up, but her rain shadow does.*>

<*Stop it, now it feels creepy.*>

Rika felt Niki nod in her mind. <*Good, it should. That was a test.*>

<*And there it is,*> Rika said as the enemy aircraft powered up its weapons systems, new EM signatures lighting up along its wings.

<*Should we shoot first?*> Niki asked.

<*I'm leery,*> Rika replied. <*If we can wait another minute, we'll be past the city, and I won't have to worry about dropping a fighter on some apartment building full of people.*>

Rika charged her railgun anyway. The weapon stayed tucked within the nose of the SkyScream until fired, so she didn't have to worry about the enemy aircraft picking up on her EM signature.

She took a number of slow breaths, calming herself before the inevitable fight. Then movement on the rear of the vessel caught her attention.

<*Shit!*> Rika called out, and dove down below the enemy ship

as rounds from a point defense chaingun described an arc toward her. Rika fired her railgun at the enemy ship, but it dove as well, and her shot missed.

Rika dropped through the clouds after the aircraft, lining up to fire once more. She was tempted to use her electron beams, but that would point her out to the other vessel, and one foe was enough for now.

Rounds flew from the rear of the aircraft, and Rika spun through the air in an erratic corkscrew as she followed after her target, waiting for the right moment to fire.

She was finally charged and lined up when the aircraft fired all four of its missiles. They streaked forward, and then rose up toward the Marauder pinnace.

<*Like hell,*> Rika whispered aloud and in her mind as she pulled up and fired her chainguns at the missiles.

Two exploded within seconds, but the others were out of range.

<*Incoming!*> Rika cried out to Chase.

<*I see 'em, beams and chaff are firing.*>

Rika knew the beams would be of little use in the storm, but the chaff should create a highly reflective cloud mixed with the rain.

One of the missiles detonated in the chaff cloud, but the other swung wide and closed in on the pinnace.

<*I got this,*> Chase said, and Rika saw four detonations behind the pinnace. She knew those bombs would fling explosive rounds out in every direction.

A moment later, the other missile detonated.

Rika drew her attention back to the ship she was chasing, and saw that it had pulled up, slowing to come behind her.

No chance.

She twisted in the air and fired her thrusters on a collision course with the enemy craft, spinning again and firing her engines right above the enemy ship at the last moment.

The blast melted part of the canopy, and Rika extended the

SkyScream's 'feet'. They latched onto the aircraft and tore the rest of the canopy off before ripping the forward half of the craft off.

The pilot ejected, and Rika gave a cry of exultation as she fired her engines again and pushed off from the falling wreckage, streaking through the air toward the second ship.

As Rika approached, she saw the pursuit craft fire two missiles at the pinnace. She tried to fire her electron beams at the missiles, but nothing happened.

<*You took damage from the rear chaingun,*> Niki advised. <*It missed the engine, but one of your e-beams is offline. The control systems were damaged, too. Trying to fix them to get the beams back up.*>

<*Calculated risk,*> Rika lied.

She'd forgotten about the chaingun, she just wanted to tear that ship apart. For a moment, she wondered if it was a part of the predatory flight imprint that the SkySkream used. Then something ricocheted off her left wing, and she dove to the side as bullets followed her through the air. She jinked up, then down, and saw an electron beam flash through the night a meter from her right wing.

Rika gritted her teeth. *Not tonight, assholes.*

Her railgun was fully charged, and Rika boosted up, then slewed to the left, tracing a straight line behind the enemy craft. Right as she passed behind its engines, Rika fired.

The rail-accelerated pellets closed the distance between her and the aircraft in a fraction of a second, tearing clear through the enemy ship. One of the stubby wings exploded, and a moment later, nothing was left but a falling ball of flame.

Rika pulled up, twisting through the air and scanning the surrounding airspace for any more interlopers.

<*Nice shooting, Rika. Scan's clear. Oh, and somehow ATC missed all that. Not a blip on the public feeds.*>

<*Damn, I guess whoever is taking pot shots at us still has enough of a chokehold on local systems do whatever they want.*>

<*Seems like it,*> Chase's voice was laced with worry. <*You OK*

back there? Uplink shows that you took a few hits.>

<Nothing serious. SkyScream Rika has a few dents. Rika Rika is just fine.>

Chase laughed over the Link. *<Well, SkyScream Rika does have to keep Rika Rika from crashing to the ground, so I'm glad they're both OK.>*

<Me too. I'd forgotten how exhilarating it is to pilot these things.>

<So I take it you'll escort us back rather than dock?>

<Damn skippy.>

*****

Rika set the SkyScream down beside the pinnace on the hard pack in front of Fort Hammerfall's command building. While the ramp lowered from the pinnace, she triggered her craft's disengagement protocols.

Her sense of self shrank back down to her human form as the SkyScream lifted her out of the pilot's pocket and set her back into her legs. Then she reached forward and sank her arms into the sockets, feeling the ship drive the rods through her arms and legs.

"Shit, Rika!" Kelly called out as the rest of the team walked out of the pinnace. "Next time, I'm calling dibs on that thing! I watched your feeds, it was ridiculous!"

Rika jumped down off the SkyScream, and sent a command for the craft to fly to a nearby hangar. "We'll have to see about that…we don't have many of those birds."

Kelly's face fell, and Rika laughed. "Relax, I was kidding. You'll get a chance. We don't have many of them, but there aren't many SMI and RR mechs, so everyone who wants to will get a turn."

Rika climbed the steps to the command building, and Major Dala caught up with her. "I need to contact…well, someone. I have to report on what happened here tonight."

"Who can you safely call?" The doors opened, and Rika stepped through, walking over to one of the drying stations.

Warm air whipped across her body, blasting away moisture and leaving her perfectly dry—though in dire need of a hairbrush—in seconds.

Dala availed herself of a dryer as well, and the device lowered its output for a standard human. Rika wondered if it would have blown the uptight major's dress off if it had remained on full power. That would have been worth a laugh.

<*That was an uncharitable thought,*> Niki commented.

<*How would you know? You can't read my thoughts, and I didn't have any physical tells.*>

<*No, just the daggers you shot at her with your eyes.*>

Rika snorted. <*Daggers are not something you can shoot with your eyes. You should know that.*>

<*I beg to differ.*>

<*Now,* ***lasers****…*>

Dala stepped out of the drying pod and approached Rika. "I can't imagine this goes too high, but to hit you with fighters like that, it must. But I would have seen a sign, wouldn't I?"

Rika felt a stab of guilt for her prior attitude toward Dala. The woman *was* trying to do her job, but people she trusted were clearly working against her—and now trying to kill her.

"Core be damned, I have no idea." Rika softened her tone before she continued, tamping down the adrenaline still rushing through her from flying the SkyScream. "I've been on the horn to my liaison with the SAF, and he's stonewalled me at every turn. And I sure as hell don't trust your CO right now—no offense. If Zim himself isn't rotten, his HQ is full of leaks. Who else do you have?"

Dala adjusted the hem of her dress and glanced at David. "I was telling David—right before he rushed me out the back—that we might have to go up the chain to General Adam."

Rika cocked an eyebrow. "The five-star who runs Hercules Command?"

"Yeah. Scuttlebutt is that he's not happy that we've joined Septhia, but he has given a few speeches on how unity is our best defense against Nietzschea. I don't know for sure what he thinks of you, but nothing I've seen has made me think that he actively dislikes the Marauders."

<*Not actively disliking is a long way from viewing us favorably,*> Niki commented privately.

Rika agreed. It wasn't a ringing endorsement.

"General Mill referred to General Adam as a fair man," David interjected as he stepped out of a dryer. "And nothing I can find in his public information gives me concern."

Rika sighed and stretched her arms over her head, half-wishing she could hop in the SkyScream and fly away from all this political nonsense.

She felt an itch in her right hand and tried to ignore the dysphoria she always felt when her GNR wasn't present. "Even so, I have a suspicion that attempting contact with the general will be tricky—and may get intercepted before we can get in direct communication."

Dala tapped a finger against her lips as she watched the others step out of the dryers. "I *may* have a way to reach him. But we'll have to move fast. If I don't show up for duty tomorrow, people are going to start asking questions—and I was last seen with one of your people." She nodded to David at the end of her statement.

<*Well, if they get eyewitness accounts, that's what they'll find,*> Niki replied. <*But the city and restaurant feeds all show you dining alone.*>

"You hacked *all* those systems?" Major Dala asked.

<*You don't sound happy about it,*> Niki replied. <*You want those men to know where you are?*>

"I'm pretty sure they know where Dala is," David said with a slow shake of his head. "If they showed up to stop you from telling *me* something, then it's no great logical leap to assume they'll know where I went afterward."

"Here," Rika said.

"So how do we reach out to General Adam?" David asked.

Major Dala gave him a worried look. "Well, my sister plays

rollerball with his daughter sometimes—on opposing teams."

Chase whistled. "That's a tenuous thread."

"We'd better start working it, then." David drummed his fingertips together. "I assume, Dala, that you have proof of the things you were telling me? You'd have to, otherwise they wouldn't be going to such lengths to stop you."

"I have a few purchase orders, and a money trail. They're for equipment that matches what was used against you and your dropship. I've put in a request at the garrison's depot to do eyes-on verification that the inventory is where it's supposed to be, but it hasn't come back yet."

Rika grunted. "What are the chances that our friends back at the restaurant had no idea who David is? Maybe they're just trying to take you out because you got too nosy."

"You three were cloaked, Rika," Chase added. "Maybe they won't have realized that it was Marauders who spanked them."

"A lot of supposition here," David muttered. "I need to spend some time with all the pieces."

"And we need to get a message to your sister," Rika said to Dala. "Very carefully."

"Which is tricky," Dala said, her fuchsia eyebrows lowering. "She's off-world right now."

<*Well, Dala.*> Niki sent a devious smile into their minds. <*Then we're lucky that we have my handy ability to engage in felonious Link activity. Send me your sister's public tokens. You guys figure out what to say to the general's daughter, while I become…Madaline. Huh. Dala and Ma***dal***ine? Your parents weren't too original, were they?*>

Rika saw Dala's jaw tighten and shot Niki an admonishing scowl. <*Be nice, Niki.*>

<*You weren't. I'm just taking cues from my CO.*>

<*Yeah, well, I'm not always the best example. Do as I say, not as I do.*>

<*You're the boss, boss.*>

VISIT FROM THE GENERAL

STELLAR DATE: 08.12.8949 (Adjusted Gregorian)
LOCATION: Fort Hammerfall
REGION: Iapetus, Hercules System, Septhian Alliance

"Well, his eminence, General Adam, will be here in an hour," Rika said to Chase as she sat across from him in the commissary. She looked down at her food. "Man, I really want to send someone to get takeout from Charlie's. That pasta was amazing. I bet it was made from real angel's hair."

"That was fast," Chase said, then quickly covered his mouth as he chewed on a salad. "Sorry, I don't know why I've started doing this lately. I never used to be this slovenly."

"Stress eating," Rika replied. "We've got a lot on our shoulders. Are we even adults? I don't feel like an adult most of the time. Pretty sure I'm not old enough to run a company of lemonade salespeople, let alone one of mechs."

Barne set his tray next to them and let out a single laugh. "No, no you're not. Luckily you have me to help. And by 'help', I mean do all the work while you just flit about, getting in dogfights, wrecking our SkyScreams."

Rika grinned at Barne. "Jealous?"

"Fuck, yeah! I'd halfway consider being mech'd just to fly one of those things."

Chase gestured at Barne's prosthetic arm. "Well, you're on your way. I'll use you for a shield at some point, and we'll see if we can get a few more limbs shot off."

"If I was standing in front of you in a firefight, it would be to keep you safe while you were pissing your pants," Barne shot back.

"I don't think that armor counts as pants."

"Dribbling out of your waste reclamation system?"

"Dude!" Chase glowered at Barne. "Eating here!"

No one spoke for a minute, then Rika said, "That's one hell of an ethical question, though."

"What is?" Barne asked. "Whether I should protect Chase while he wets himself on the battlefield?"

"No. Whether or not we make more mechs."

Chase's eyebrows lifted, and he nodded slowly. "That's a tricky one. With the stuff we got from the Politica, we have everything we need to make mechs…but anyone who *wants* to become one may not have their head on straight."

Rika laughed. "I think I might be a little bit offended by that."

"You know what I mean," Chase said quickly. "Most people don't *want* to have their limbs chopped off. Anyone who does probably has body dysphoria issues, which means there's more trouble beneath the surface."

"But you could make it an option for soldiers who get injured in the battlefield," Barne added. "I hated mechs, back when I lost my arm. But now? If I lost my legs or something, I'd consider it. Not like I'm ever leaving the Marauders."

Rika caught Chase's eyes at that, but neither spoke.

"Well," Rika said at last. "I'll flail my way across that bridge when we get to it. Chances are it'll be the Old Man's call, anyway."

Barne shrugged. "Maybe."

Rika wondered what Barne meant by that, but didn't press the issue as Leslie sat with them, followed by David and Dala.

<*Just the whole group. Yay.*> Rika said privately to Niki.

<*You really don't like Dala, do you?*> Niki replied.

<*I…yeah, I guess not. Her 'mercs are bad' routine got us off on the wrong foot.*>

<*You said it before; she's just trying to do her job. She's in a tough spot.*>

Rika eyed the pink-haired major. For someone so colorful, she certainly was a wet blanket. <*I suppose.*>

<*And she's doing her best to help us,*> Niki added. <*She put her life on the line to meet with David.*>

<Well, she didn't initially think that it could get her killed.>

<Sure, but she could have been dishonorably discharged, if it was seen in the wrong light—which it still might be. She never complained about it, either. She's a good woman. A grumpy woman, but a good woman.>

Rika considered that. Niki was right, Dala was putting a good face on the fact that someone in her government was trying to kill both her, and the very people she was taking refuge with. Or, at the very least, trying to kill Rika.

"David informed me that General Adam reached out," Dala said after taking a drink of her orange juice. "I was really starting to worry that his daughter hadn't passed the message along—or that the General had missed the encoded portion."

"I was starting to wonder, too," Rika replied. "But he'll be here in an hour, so that puts those particular worries to rest. For reasons he did not elaborate upon, he's hitching a ride with a produce shipment we have coming in today."

"Seriously?" Leslie asked. "Stuff must be totally sideways here if he's doing that. Think even General Adam is at risk?"

Heads nodded around the table, and Rika shrugged. "Either that, or he just doesn't want whoever is taking pot shots at us to know he's onto them. It might escalate this whole thing to another level."

"Could be a combination," David added. "Or there are other, entirely different rationales."

"Care to enlighten us?" Barne asked.

"No," David shook his head. "Trust me, if you had to listen to me rattle off all the things that *could* be going on, your head would explode. Mine nearly does, half the time."

"Good thing it's reinforced, then." Barne laughed, but everyone else just stared at him and shook their heads.

"What?" Barne asked. "Really? Sorry David, but we were all thinking it."

David shrugged and grinned. "So was I."

*****

An hour later, Rika waited with Dala and David in a small room off the receiving warehouse near the east gate. Rather than have the general travel across the compound—where he'd be visible to satellite surveillance—Rika decided it would be safest to meet with him where the trucks came in.

She monitored the security feeds, watching as the two trucks passed through the compound's gate security, and drove down the perimeter road to the non-secured goods warehouse.

Across the table, she saw that Dala was clenching and unclenching her hands.

"Nervous, Major?"

Dala snorted. "He could be coming here to charge me with half a dozen crimes. You too, for that matter. Of course I'm nervous."

"Do generals often sneak into mercenary training facilities to deliver charges to captains and majors around here?" Rika asked.

Dala sighed and pressed the heels of her hands into her face. "No, don't be ridiculous. But that doesn't mean it's not an added bonus."

"The fact that he's coming here like this, means that he's looking for allies. If he were pissed at us and demanding your head, there'd be a battalion outside our gates. Not two trucks, half-filled with lettuce and tomatoes."

The major didn't respond, only drew in a deep breath and let it out slowly.

Rika decided to let the matter drop and returned to watching the feeds as the trucks backed up to the warehouse.

Within the loading bay, fireteam 1-1 waited to escort the general to the meeting. The rest of squad one was also placed in and around the warehouse, ready to defend against any attacks from without or within.

The other three squads of First Platoon were nearby, performing drills and working on maneuvers around Fort

Hammerfall—all armed with live ammunition, ready for what may come.

The back of the first truck opened up, and the loading bots rolled forward, grabbing stacks of produce and moving them aside. Once a space opened up, a man and two women exited the truck.

Sergeant Aaron greeted them, and then led the trio across the warehouse toward the room where Rika and the others waited.

Rika switched through several surveillance angles, examining the visitors.

The general was a tall man, older, but not showing any significant signs of aging. His hair was dark, almost jet black, and he walked with an easy gait.

The woman on his right bore a colonel's insignia on her collar, and Rika identified her from the public records as Colonel Judi. The other woman trailed behind them, the badge of a command sergeant major on her shoulders. She wore her beret low, and it took Rika a second longer to identify her. Sergeant Major Rene.

A moment later, Sergeant Aaron opened the door and nodded to Rika. "Captain Rika. General Adam and his retinue are here."

"Thank you, Sergeant. Show them in."

Rika, David, and Dala all rose, Dala saluting sharply as the general entered.

His presence filled the room, and he surveyed those in attendance before returning Dala's salute. "At ease, Major." Then he turned to Rika. "Captain Rika, I presume."

He held out his right hand to shake, but Rika raised her left. She'd considered swapping out her gun-arm for a regular one—she knew how much it angered some people to shake with their left—but if the shit hit the fan, she wanted to be ready.

General Adam didn't miss a beat as he extended his left hand and shook Rika's.

"It is very nice to meet you," Rika said. "Though I'm a bit surprised you came out to see us."

"Well, you may not be, soon enough. Allow me to introduce

Colonel Judi and Sergeant Major Rene."

Rika shook their hands and introduced Chief Warrant Officer David. Once the greetings were over, they all sat at the table. Rika didn't take the head, and was glad to see that General Adam did not either. He sat across from her, his pale blue eyes boring into hers.

"It's been an eventful few days since you first came down here, Captain Rika. You seem to have attracted no small amount of trouble."

Rika nodded. "It's a talent. Though it seemed like the trouble was lying in wait for me."

"Perhaps," General Adam replied, his tone even, revealing nothing. "And Major Dala. I must admit that it is quite interesting to find you here. Your message was light on details, but high on urgency."

"Yes, General Adam," Dala replied with a small waver in her voice. "I wasn't certain how much information I should transmit, but you were one of the few people I felt confident that I could reach out of band, so to speak."

"But the fact that you have come here means something *is* going on at Iapetus," Rika added. "Something you already know about."

General Adam nodded slowly. "I have suspicions. Suspicions that have solidified over the last few days. Dala's reports regarding the data blackout that engulfed the city of Hittis the night your ship was attacked were quite interesting. Especially the omissions."

"Omissions, sir?" Dala asked.

"Your report felt incomplete," Colonel Judi spoke up. "You seemed to be working toward certain conclusions, and then never made them. It read like a redacted report, but without the redactions noted."

Dala frowned. "Someone altered my reports?"

"I believe so," Judi replied. "I assume you have the originals? Could you transmit them to me—provided we're secure?"

"The room's network is segregated," Rika confirmed. "No one will know if you make a connection here."

General Adam nodded, and Dala closed her eyes for a moment. "There you are, Colonel."

Colonel Judi pursed her lips and sighed. "Yes, these are demonstrably different. Stars, even the damage assessments are—wait, there were survivors?"

Dala nodded, and Rika spoke up. "At least ten; maybe more, if the wounded all came through."

General Adam rose and walked to the sideboard where water and coffee waited. "Then it's as we feared. Subversive elements are operating with impunity on Iapetus."

" 'Subversive elements'?" Rika asked. "That's nebulous, to say the least. Who do you think it is?"

"Who do *you* think?" General Adam asked.

"Hmm…" David began tapping his chin in earnest. "After the first attack, we considered that it was someone who was personally upset at Rika for the part she played in the events on Pyra. After they tried to kill Dala, we widened our scope. It's certainly someone with means—"

"Kill Dala?" Colonel Judi interrupted. "What are you talking about?"

"None of that reached you?" Rika asked and received negative head shakes in response. "Last night, we saved Dala from an assassination attempt. There was a significant attack in downtown Hittis. Afterward, I took out two fighter craft over the northern edge of the city."

General Adam blew out a long breath. "Stars, I wish I could just purge the whole lot of them. There must be more rot than I expected, to cover up something like this."

"Sir? What is going on?" Dala asked.

General Adam didn't respond at first. Instead, he prepared his cup of coffee and stirred it for a moment before turning to the group. "It's the Nietzscheans, of course. They're here in Iapetus."

"The Niets, sir?" Rika asked. "How?"

The general sat at the table and stared at Rika. "Hard to believe you started all this."

Rika wondered where he was going with this new tack. "Me?"

"When you attacked our president—yes, yes, I know you didn't *really* start it. But you breached her bunker and had her in your sights."

"But I didn't do it," Rika replied. "I got the order to stand down."

General Adam shook his head and smiled. "The order to stand down came almost twenty minutes after you breached. You had plenty of time to kill the president. Plus, I saw the feeds. You couldn't bring yourself to do it."

Rika shook her head. "For whatever good it did. The Niets still killed her."

"It did *a lot* of good," General Adam replied. "Marauders would have had the worst time of their lives in Theban space, if one of theirs had killed our president. Septhian merger or no."

"What does this have to do with there being Niets in Iapetus?" Rika asked.

"Nothing…and everything. There's a reason why Septhian High Command decided to place your training facility here—a *Marauder* facility, engaged in training the Niets' most hated and feared enemy. They wanted to make this system a lightning rod for whatever was to happen next."

"No," David interjected. "It's too fast, sir. We only selected this location three months ago. That's too fast for the Niets to infiltrate so many branches of your military. It's not their strong suit."

"You're right about that, Chief." The general nodded, then took a sip of his coffee. "Which means they were already operating here, and you pulled them out into the open—too tempting a target. Which is what we hoped for; we just didn't expect them to have their hooks in so deep."

"How do they have their hooks in at *all*, sir?" Major Dala asked. "They're the *Nietzscheans*! How is it that anyone is willing to work with them?"

"There's a group of people who think the Niets will win. They figure being a part of Nietzschea is no worse than being absorbed by Septhia. I imagine there's money involved, as well. Lots of money."

"So you need to clean house," Rika replied. "How can we help?"

General Adam chuckled. "Well, for starters, keep doing what you're doing. We wanted a lightning rod, we got one. We need to get these bastards to overextend themselves. Then, when they do, we crush them with extreme prejudice. There's no mercy for traitors."

"Then we need to lure them into attacking this base," Rika replied. "It would take a nuke to dislodge us, maybe not even then. They'll have to hit us hard, and then we catch them with their pants down."

General Adam nodded slowly. "How do you plan to do that?"

Rika looked at David. "How tempting a target will we have to be?"

*****

<You want us to do ***what****?>* Major Tim asked, the exasperation his mental tone almost a corporeal presence in the room with Rika.

<It's the best way to make us look exposed and vulnerable,> Rika replied, surprised at how upset the major was over this idea.

<Yeah, because you ***will*** *be exposed and vulnerable.>*

<Well, bait has to be believable. But the General will have ships covering us from orbit. We'll be fine.>

Major Tim grunted and Rika could imagine him pacing in his tiny office. *<And you trust this man with your life—with the lives of your mechs?>*

Rika had wondered about that as well. For all she knew, General Adam was playing her. Getting her to weaken her position so that he could destroy Fort Hammerfall with impunity.

<What do you suggest, Major?> Rika asked. *<I'm open to other ideas.>*

<Here's one. We pack up and leave. Cleaning up this system's internal politics is not our problem.>

Rika hadn't expected an answer like that from Major Tim. *<What about our mission here?>*

<What 'mission'? We're here to train. This was a nice spot, but we can do it anywhere.>

<And the Nietzscheans?> Rika asked. *<You know the Old Man's goal as well as I—better, probably. What would he think if we ran from the chance to stop the Nietzschean advance? Worse, what if we leave, and the Niets invade?>*

Seriously, Major, Rika scolded herself mentally as she rose from her desk and paced across the room. *How is this man so cowardly?*

<Rika, the general didn't go to all the trouble of setting up your company, just so that we can piss it away in some heroic gesture against the Niets—who may not even be in this system.>

<He has a point,> Niki commented. *<There are a lot of unknowns in this equation.>*

Rika clenched her teeth and drew in a deep breath before responding to Major Tim. *<Other than running away, do you have any suggestions?>*

<You're determined to stay down there, aren't you?>

<I am, and I need an option that we can both work with.>

Major Tim didn't respond, his silence deafening.

Rika clenched her jaw, willing her heartrate to slow. *<Niki, do you have any ideas?>*

<I have one, but it's going to take a leap of faith from you, Major Tim. And we'll need General Adam's help to pull it off.>

SETTING THE TRAP

STELLAR DATE: 08.13.8949 (Adjusted Gregorian)
LOCATION: Fort Hammerfall
REGION: Iapetus, Hercules System, Septhian Alliance

Rika climbed into the ground transport, a vehicle the locals called a Swampfox. It wasn't the prettiest…van-thing she'd ever seen, but Barne had picked up a gross of them for a steal. Corporal Stripes—the lone mech in the repair and maintenance platoon—had pronounced them sound enough for the mission they had in mind.

Rika smiled to herself at the memory. 'Sound' wasn't the word Stripes had used. He had said something more like, "Not gunna fuck themselves to pieces, but they might fuck you with all the rattlin'."

"Surprised Stripes isn't coming along, Captain," Sergeant Karen said as she pulled herself into the driver's seat, seeming to read Rika's thoughts. "He exhibited a special fondness for these things."

Karen settled in place and grasped the controls—not that anyone needed to *drive* the Swampfox. It may have looked older than the invention of spaceflight, but it was Link capable, with a rudimentary comp that was guaranteed not to run over animals or humans.

Rika wondered at the order of the items in that guarantee, but considered that it may have been imported, and the translation might be off.

"If by 'fondness', you mean a strong desire to send them all to the scrap heap, you might be right," Rika replied to the sergeant.

Karen chuckled and pulled her cloak around her armor, ensuring her profile looked natural before leaning around to check on Kelly and Keli.

"Four SMI-2s on a mission together. Think that ever happened in the war?" Keli asked as she settled into her seat.

"Sure," Kelly replied. "Team Hammerfall had four SMI-2s at one point—back before Rika joined up."

"Had four later on, too," Rika added. "Took two mechs to replace the amount of lip you gave all the time, Kelly."

"I didn't have lips back then," Kelly retorted.

"And yet you still got twice the discipline as Silva and I."

Kelly grinned. "Not one to roll over."

"So, what's on the agenda for our little outing?" Karen asked. "Anything you're looking to pick up? Some beer? Fried chicken? Kitty litter for the LT?"

Rika cast Karen a hard look. Knocking the LT was a time-honored tradition, but one usually had the sense not to do it in front of the LT's commanding officer.

Karen blushed. "Shit, sorry, Captain. I'm still getting used to being able to speak again…I keep saying things with my *out-loud* voice that are supposed to stay in the noggin."

"It's OK, Sergeant, I won't tell Lieutenant Leslie. So long as you actually set up a litter box at some point."

"Really?" Karen asked, turning to look at Rika with wide eyes.

"Well, if she figures out who did it, you might die horribly, so it's up to you."

"Damned if you do, and damned if you don't," Karen said as she punched in the destination on the manual console.

Kelly and Keli were doubled over with laughter in the backseat, and Rika smiled as well. It felt good to be able to relax, even if this wasn't going to be a nice weekend drive.

"Corporal, Private," Karen called back. "Shut your core-damned mouths back there."

"Yes, ma'am!" Keli called out, while Kelly added, "*Now* the sergeant knows when to use rank in address."

"Stars, some days I liked it better when none of us had mouths," Karen said with a sigh. "Things were a lot less catty back then."

"Oh! Good one!" Keli crowed. "I'll have to tell Lieutenant

Leslie you said that."

"Seriously, you two," Rika said, suppressing a laugh. "We're not on a grade school field trip. Don't make me come back there."

The Swampfox reached the compound's gate, and the guards looked over the vehicle and its occupants for a minute before waving them through.

"Sucks being the boss," Rika said and sighed. "No one ever gives you the quick once-over. They want you to make sure to notice how good they are at their jobs."

"Hard being an officer, we know," Kelly said with mock compassion.

"You're doing the best you can," Keli chimed in, her tone soulful and appreciative.

"OK, seriously," Rika growled. "When I said we need to act casually, I didn't mean for you to mock your superiors for the whole trip."

"Huh" Keli said then turned to Kelly. "This is most of what we do in our free time. How *else* do we act casually?"

"Beats me," Kelly shrugged. "You follow sports?"

"I don't even know if they *have* sports here."

"Read any good books, watch any good sims or vids?"

Keli shook her head. "Nope. Our hard-assed CO doesn't give us a moment's rest. I am completely without hobbies."

"Well, then." Kelly laughed. "Looks like mockery is the only pastime we have."

"I can think of a few extra pastimes for you two," Rika grunted.

The pair continued their banter as the Swampfox drove for a few kilometers through the commercial district surrounding the old-airport-turned-Marauder-base.

Eventually it passed into a tunnel that ran under a series of maglev tracks. Once they were hidden from any external view, Karen slammed on the brakes, and the four women bailed out of the vehicle. Four other women—some of General Adam's trusted SAF troops—wearing armor under cloaks to approximate the look of SMIs, rushed into the vehicle to take their places.

Rika led the others behind a column and into a maintenance tunnel that ran below the tracks. It was a tight fit, and half the reason Rika had selected SMI-2s for the mission.

They navigated through the tunnel, slipping around conduits and access ladders, until they came to a cross passage where Rika took a right. From there, a short twenty-meter walk brought them to a steel door.

It was unlocked, and Rika checked her cloak over, shaking any dust off before raising her cowl and activating the camouflage.

"Ready, ladies?" she asked.

The banter had faded in the tunnel, and the others maintained the silence, each giving a single nod.

Rika sent out a single ping, waiting for the all-clear response before pushing the door open and stepping out into Iapetus's warm, afternoon light.

Forty-seven meters ahead lay their destination—a low warehouse, rented by the Marauders for secondary, low-security equipment storage. A pair of mechs were stationed at the warehouse, guarding its contents.

Rika crossed the distance at an easy pace, careful not to kick up excess dust. A minute later, she stepped inside the warehouse and smiled as she gazed at the other reason why she'd selected SMI-2s for the mission.

Within, lay six SkyScreams.

"Oh, baby," Kelly rubbed her hand against her GNR's barrel, then stopped. "OK…that gesture doesn't work without two hands."

Keli snickered. "Especially not when saying 'oh baby'."

An RR-2 walked into the room through a door on their right and snapped to attention, quietly saying, "Ma'am."

Rika nodded to Yiaagaitia. "How's everything look, Corporal Yig?"

"We're secure, Captain. Though CJ thinks she spotted a surveillance vehicle in the area, and there are definitely drones making the rounds, though they're staying back a ways from Fort Hammerfall. Keeping out of range of ours—or so they think."

"How sure are you that no one spotted us coming in here?" Karen asked.

"Pretty sure, Sarge. CJ has their pattern mapped out. She has that upgraded sensor suite some RR's got; can track a mayfly at a thousand meters."

"Good," Rika said and turned to eye the SkyScreams. "We stay mobile while we wait. It's still an hour before Chase and Leslie take squads two and four out on the training exercise."

Everyone nodded in response, and Rika resisted the urge to make a quick Link connection to check up on the platoon's status.

Of course, that would blow everything.

Right now, her Link presence was still registering as being inside the Swampfox, which was trundling alone on a long drive through Hittis.

The other mechs inspected their SkyScreams, and Rika contented herself with watching the surrounding area through the drones that CJ had sent out.

As the drone flies, they were only three kilometers from Fort Hammerfall. Between them lay a swath of warehouses, miscellaneous commercial buildings, and, finally, a half-kilometer of open space before the fence that surrounded the former airport.

After what felt like forever, Rika saw a convoy of Swampfoxes pull out of one of the hangars, followed by a flatbed truck. AM, RR, and FR mechs piled into the Swampfoxes, while a K1R-T climbed up onto the flatbed.

The K1R, a corporal named Oosterwyk-Bruyn, was more than capable of keeping up with the Swampfoxes on foot, but the locals had complained about the damage AMs did to their roads. A K1R would pound them to gravel, so a flatbed truck was his chariot.

The flatbed pulled out first, and Rika felt a smile pull at her lips. Everyone thought that Oosterwyk-Bruyn bore the nickname 'The Van' because he was massive—which he was. Or that his real name was hard to say—which was also true.

In reality, he had earned the name 'The Van' because he always insisted on being in the vanguard of a fight. His joke was that a formation didn't need a vanguard. It just needed him.

Through the drones' eyes, Rika saw The Van raise a massive fist in the air; she imagined him crying out "Roo-ah!" as the convoy pulled out of Fort Hammerfall.

"The trap is set," Rika said with a predatory grin. "Now it's just part of squad one and three left at the compound."

Kelly snorted. "Anyone who thinks that twenty-odd mechs is 'just' anything is going to be in for one hell of a surprise."

"Not to mention that our surprises have surprises," Karen said, nodding to the SkyScreams.

DEFENSE OF HAMMERFALL

STELLAR DATE: 08.13.8949 (Adjusted Gregorian)
LOCATION: Fort Hammerfall
REGION: Iapetus, Hercules System, Septhian Alliance

<*I've got movement on the southern edge of our grid,*> CJ reported over the combat net. <*A few cargo haulers moving in.*>

Rika pulled up the feed and saw seven haulers entering the area from different directions. They weren't the only vehicles in the area, but they bore the markings of companies that Dala and David had identified as being tied to other suspicious activity over the past week.

None were headed straight for the former airport, but as they closed the distance, their ultimate destination became clear.

<*I see more activity on the east and the north as well,*> CJ reported a moment later.

Five minutes later, the only area where there were no suspicious vehicles in the area was to the west, where the mech convoy had disappeared into the hills for their training exercises.

<*Based on what I see, they'll set up here, here and here.*> Rika said over the combat net, highlighting points on the shared map. <*Not sure if they'll mass at those points, or drop troops from those trucks along the way.*>

<*I still don't get how they think that we won't spot this.*> Kelly shook her head and drew a line on the map. <*Once they cross this far, there are no other cargo haulers anywhere nearby—hardly any traffic at all, for that matter. Their movements will be totally obvious.*>

<*The cat will be out of the bag at some point no matter how they do this,*> Rika replied. <*Remember, it's only via our intel from Dala that we even know to look for trucks from these holding companies. If we didn't, they'd blend in with the other ground traffic until the last minute. That's not a lot of warning.*>

<*Don't forget, too, whoever is running this op is deeply stupid,*> CJ

added. <*I mean, they're attacking mechs. Not just any mechs, either. Rika's Marauders.*>

Rika appreciated the team's confidence, but those trucks could hold hundreds of enemies—maybe even a thousand. She had to assume they were all in heavy powered armor—the only thing that could go toe-to-toe with a mech.

She was certain that whatever the number, the enemies in those trucks were not all they'd face today. Whoever was attacking them on Iapetus was too smart to show their entire hand at the outset of the battle.

This was just the first wave.

Rika had to admit that for all her bluster, she felt naked knowing that the *Golden Lark,* and the *Perseid's Dream* weren't overhead.

She'd become accustomed to knowing that in the Marauders—unlike the GAF—when starfire was needed, it would fall. Hopefully General Adam would be just as willing to fire on the planet he was sworn to keep safe.

"Let's get suited up," Rika said aloud, signaling CJ to fall back into the warehouse.

The mechs climbed onto the backs of the SkyScreams, each undergoing the same process Rika had the day prior.

"Shit, forgot how weird this feels at first!" Kelly exclaimed as the ship pulled her body into the pilot's pocket, and folded its armor over her.

<*Feels foooood,*> Keli said over the link. <*I'm a fucking warbird, gonna rain beamfire down on my enemies.*>

<*Keep sharp,*> Rika said. <*I mean it. Niki hasn't had time to go through these things with a fine-tooth comb…they're programmed to make us hyper-aggressive in aerial combat, but we have to stay frosty. Tonight at the commissary, we're all gonna talk about how awesome this was. No one's eating dirt. Got it?*>

A round of 'yes ma'ams' and 'aye, Captains' came back.

Rika drew in a deep breath as her SkyScream activated its systems and imprinted her new physical form into her mind.

She was terror, she was might, but she also had to coordinate a defense against a superior enemy while in the midst of combat....

<One of the trucks has slowed,> Niki announced. *<It just dropped off a fireteam one klick from Hammerfall's south gate. Make that two fireteams.>*

Rika pulled the feed and saw that it was as she suspected. The enemy was in unmarked, powered armor. It didn't offer them the versatility of a mech—living in your powered armor made you a lot more comfortable with it than just wearing it periodically—but they wouldn't be easy to take down.

She hoped the mechs' comfort in their own skins would be enough of an edge. Now that she could see the enemy's loadout, Rika estimated that they could pack forty soldiers in each of the haulers. That put the attackers' number at over a thousand.

Against half a platoon at Hammerfall.

Or so they think.

Rika saw that Barne had pre-configured the combat net with designations for the different units. The enemies were labeled as 'Cockroaches', his nod to how they kept turning up everywhere. However, at this scale, the name beside each of the enemy was abbreviated to only show 'Cock'.

<Oh, that's classic,> Kelly snickered.

<Cocks it is,> Karen added, and Rika couldn't help but laugh.

She reviewed the enemy deployments and guessed at where the rest of them would disembark. *<Looks like the Cocks are massing at the gates, but they're also going for the corners.>*

<With that many troops, they probably think they can just march right in,> Keli added.

<Well, they do think there are only about thirty-five mechs at Hammerfall,> Rika replied.

Kelly snorted. *<Thirty-five of Rika's Marauders are worth a thousand Cocks.>*

<Thousand's not even close.> Rika put on a brave face for her team. *<Let's try to keep them outside the fence. I don't want our new base getting trashed.>*

<That's for sure,> Karen said. *<I just finished decorating my quarters.>*

The SkyScream mechs fell silent as they waited for the Cocks to finish deploying. Though it felt like forever, the enemy was more efficient than Rika had hoped, disgorging their forces from the cargo haulers in just under three minutes.

<OK, Ladies and Gentleman,> Rika said. *<You ready to kick some Cock?>*

<Roo-AH!>

<Ouch!>

* * * * *

Leslie stood in Fort Hammerfall's small CIC, watching the feeds of the enemy's deployment, 'Cocks', thanks to Barne's sense of humor. She'd changed the shortened description to 'Roaches', but it had been too late; the mechs had all started using 'Cock' in their communications.

The four fireteams, one at each of the four gates, took cover behind the plascrete barriers, and weapons protruded from the bunkers at each of the base's four corners. Not that there were any mechs within those bullet-magnets, only sacrificial combat drones.

If there was one thing that decades of combat had taught Leslie, it was that mechs did their best when highly mobile. The brass had often treated them like mechanized infantry, but in reality, even the smallest mech was more like a main battle tank.

A battle tank that could leap a dozen meters into the air, land on your actual tank, and tear the guns off.

Leslie drew in a slow breath, let it out, and then repeated the process twice more before calling out to the mechs under her command. *<Squads one and three, all fireteams ready. We wait for them to fire first. Your quadrants and targets are marked. Potter is assigning priorities, keep your eyes on those, and make sure we give our angels any cover they need. They're gonna be doing the same for us.>*

Acknowledgement lights flashed across the holotank, and Leslie smiled, wishing she was out there with them.

Her placement in the CIC was due in part to their need for the SkyScreams to be piloted by experienced mechs. They only had six of those at present, and Rika was amongst their number.

That put Leslie in the CIC.

Granted, a large, open field was not her ideal area of operation. Leslie knew her style was better suited to dense urban combat—a battlefield where she could skulk and hide.

When this fight was joined, it would be no place for a squishie, the name her 'toon affectionately called her behind her back.

On the holotank, Leslie watched the Roaches close in around Hammerfall. Their smallest grouping was to the north, where there were only a few outbuildings stretched along the fence line. Beyond lay the landing strips and landing cradles.

Commensurately, the majority of the enemy was grouped at three points along the southern side of the base, where the majority of the structures lay. They closed to within five hundred meters, and then stopped at the edge of the warehouses.

From there on out, nothing lay between the Roaches and the base but tall, waving grass and a narrow road that ran to the gate.

Leslie overlaid an optical view of the terrain on her vision, selecting Sergeant Aaron's helmet cams for her vantage. He'd proven his valor when Rika took down the Politica, and she had no doubt he'd do so again.

Gazing out over the half-kilometer of space between the forces and seeing well over a hundred Roach tags hovering in and around the distant buildings, she worried that bravery may not be enough to take down so many enemies.

Stop that thinking, Leslie. No one has ever seen a massed mech formation like this before. It's going to be amazing.

The world seemed to pause for a moment, and everything grew still. It was as though Iapetus knew that hell was about to descend, and was bracing for impact.

Four electron beams lanced out from the enemy positions and

struck the plascrete barrier on the left side of the gate, then another four struck the barrier on the other side.

Aaron and the four mechs of fireteam one-one returned fire erratically, shooting at targets of opportunity before falling back behind a secondary barrier, this one thicker with a lead core, plus a grav-shield.

Twenty Roaches rushed forward into the grassy plain, holding CFT shields and using the covering fire from their compatriots to enable their advance. Another group repeated the maneuver, then another.

A minute later, there were one hundred enemies leapfrogging one another across the field.

Leslie looked at the eastern and northern gates. The Roaches were using the same tactic there, as well. They hadn't advanced on the bunkers at the corners, but they would soon, once they determined the response the mechs would bring to bear.

Only, it wouldn't be mechs that they met.

Leslie activated their first line of defense, and aracnidrones—twenty on each side of Fort Hammerfall—dug themselves out of the ground behind the advancing Roaches and opened fire.

At the south side of the base, six enemies went down in the initial volley. The Roaches still in position at the edge of the plain tried to take shots at the aracnidrones, but most of the bots were between them and their teammates, making clean shots impossible.

The drones, however, had no compunctions about unleashing suicidal fury on the Roaches, taking out another dozen in the next ten seconds, firing missiles, chainguns, and tearing limbs off with wild abandon.

Several of the enemy's CFT shields fell to the ground, and others turned to face the aracnidrones as the advancing Roaches suddenly found themselves surrounded.

At the southern gate, Aaron and his fireteam took the opportunity to lay down heaver fire on the enemy, slinging depleted uranium slugs and rail-accelerated pellets.

In a minute, fifty of the Roaches had fallen. Similar scenarios were playing out at the other gates, and Leslie wondered if the enemy commander would call a retreat. Losing over ten-percent of your force in the first few minutes was not a good sign.

Despite the tactic's success, casualties were not one-sided. Several mechs had taken damage as well, but unlike purely organic humans—even ones in powered armor—the mechs could take a lot of punishment before going down. They felt no pain when losing a limb, nor did they fear that level of damage, and it gave them a distinct advantage when under heavy fire.

Just when Leslie thought the enemy would in fact fall back, they rose up and rushed Fort Hammerfall from three sides.

"Shit!" Leslie whispered glancing at David, who was standing silently on the far side of the holotank.

"This is good," he said, nodding slowly. "We *need* them to overextend. We have to give Dala time to do her part."

Leslie nodded in return. "It's just nuts for the enemy commander to commit his full force like this."

"Yes." David was drumming his fingers on the edge of the holotank. "If our forces were what they appear to be, then a combined assault with his troops would be enough to overwhelm us."

"He's a fool to think this is all we have," Leslie replied. "Same thing as nuts, in this case."

On the holotank, six blue markers lifted out of a warehouse, three kilometers southeast of the base, splitting off into pairs, each headed for the gates that were under attack.

As Leslie watched the SkyScreams streak toward the onrushing enemy, Lieutenant Travis pinged her over the command net.

<*Should we go?*>

<*No,*> Leslie replied. <*We wait for them to hit the bunkers or breach the fence line.*>

<*We're going to lose mechs if they breach,*> Travis insisted.

<*Travis,*> Rika's voice came over the command net. <*Hold your*

position. We don't know if they have anything else up their sleeves. We need our reserves.>

And our reserves' reserves, Leslie thought.

The feed from Aaron's helmet picked up an earsplitting scream, and two airborne shapes flashed over the enemy formation, each firing all four electron beams, raking them across the ground, slicing through the second wave of attackers followed by the Roaches out on the field—who were still under attack from the aracnidrones.

David chuckled, a grim look in his eyes. "That's a lot of dead Cocks."

Leslie groaned. "Not you too. The after-action reports alone are going to make me cringe for days."

Even with Rika's SkyScreams raking the enemy lines, the Roaches still continued their advance. Pockets of enemies set up gun emplacements protected by shields and began to spray anti-air fire at the SkyScreams, pushing them back.

"Potter, tap those guns," Leslie ordered.

<*With pleasure,*> Potter replied.

Guided mortar fire burst from three of the nearby hangars, arcing high in the air and jinking side to side before falling on the AA emplacements.

The Roaches' guns took out most of the incoming mortar fire. Leslie had anticipated that and didn't even need to give Potter the word; the AI launched a salvo of groundhuggers, missiles that flew a mere dozen centimeters above the terrain, masked by the tall grass.

While the Roaches were firing into the sky, the groundhuggers struck, blowing away four of the AA guns and flinging enemies in all directions.

"Nice shooting, Potter," Leslie said grimly as the enemy continued to advance, now within only a hundred meters of the southern fence.

*****

Rika watched four of the six AA emplacements at the southern gate explode, and twisted in the air, diving toward the fifth, as it remained focused on incoming mortar fire.

She kicked a round out of her railgun and cried out in triumph as it struck true, taking out the gun.

The Cocks below turned their weapons on her, and Rika fired her engines at max burn, boosting back into the sky, jinking left and right to avoid incoming fire.

While the Cocks were aiming at her, Karen swooped in from the south and fired a pair of missiles into clusters of the enemy, flinging armored bodies across the battlefield.

Rika smiled with satisfaction, but then saw a group of Cocks rush out of one of the buildings to the south of the battlefield, and fire shoulder-mounted missiles at Karen.

<*Karen! You've got buzzards on your six!*> Rika called out.

<*See 'em! Firing chaff!*>

Rika dove toward the missiles, firing her chaingun at them and taking out two before she had to pull up to avoid enemy weapons fire.

One of the missiles switched targets and locked onto her. Rika swore, twisted in the air, and released chaff before banking hard to port, bringing her chaingun to bear on the missile. The weapon flung hot carbon shards at the missile, ripping it to shreds.

With that threat neutralized, Rika turned her attention to the Cocks who had shoulder-fired the missiles at the SkyScreams. She directed all four of her electron beams at them, and the enemy fell under her withering beam fire. There was no time to revel in the small victory, as a red light flashed on her HUD.

Karen had been hit.

Rika twisted in the air and boosted toward her teammate. The sergeant's SkyScream had been hit in the port engine, and was wobbling, barely maintaining altitude.

<*Grav systems got hit, too,*> Karen reported. <*I'm going to set down in the compound, cover me.*>

Rika launched two missiles at the enemies below, clearing a path for Karen to set down. The sergeant's SkyScream came in low and fast, digging a long furrow into the grass within Hammerfall's fence line.

Her breath catching in her throat, Rika boosted higher, seeking a better vantage and the relative safety of altitude. Relief flooded her upon seeing Karen slide out of the pilot's pocket on her SkyScream far below, the craft's armatures setting her back into her legs.

Good, she's still in the fight.

She banked left and saw Aaron's fireteam falling back to their third barrier, the first two nothing more than smoking ruins. They were nearly flanked; another minute, and they'd be surrounded.

<Leslie, Travis coming soon?>

<On it, Captain. Any moment now.>

Three days ago, when First Platoon had made their mock-combat drop to Fort Hammerfall, a flotilla of cargo ships had dropped from the *Golden Lark*. Those ships had carried supplies and equipment, but they'd also contained the mechs of Lieutenant Travis's Second Platoon.

The crates containing the reinforcements had been transferred to the hangars, where the mechs had begun to dig.

The Cocks continued to advance on Aaron's team at the south gate, no doubt certain in their victory over the five beleaguered Marauders. Then the ground exploded in two places a scant, dozen meters from the flanking Cocks.

On the eastern side, a massive figure lumbered out of the ground—a K1R-M that everyone in the company simply called 'Bitty'.

Bitty carried two large caliber chainguns loaded with HE rounds, and they were already spinning when the six tons of mech hit the ground.

The front ranks of the enemy were torn to shreds before the rest of Second Platoon's squad four even finished breaking through the surface of the field.

<*Incoming missiles!*> Potter called out over the command net, and Rika spun in the air, picking up the incoming ballistic weapons.

There were twelve of them, only three kilometers out and coming from the east. Rika targeted four with her electron beams, taking out two on her first salvo.

<*I got your back.*> Kelly's voice came into Rika's mind, and a rail shot, followed by four electron beams, lanced out, destroying another three missiles.

Five seconds later, they were in range of the base's three AA turrets, and the guns rose from the ground, firing on and destroying another four of the air-breathers, leaving only three.

The guns pivoted to track the missiles, when a trio of rockets streaked out from the enemy lines, hitting one of Fort Hammerfall's AA guns. A fireball rose up from the weapon's wreckage, even as a quartet of electron beams lanced into the second AA gun, tearing it to ribbons.

Hammerfall's third AA gun took out one more of the missiles, but the final two were closing fast. Rika steadied her trajectory, trying to get a lock on the incoming weapons while still jinking herself to avoid groundfire.

<*Could really use some starfire!*> Rika called in to Leslie.

<*I've ordered a strike, but General Adam's ships are under attack from other SAF cruisers!*>

<*Well, shit!*> Rika cursed. <*That tears it.*>

The missiles were within seconds of striking the mechs at the southern gate, when Bitty casually raised both arms and fired both chainguns into the air, creating two cones of destruction that the missiles had to pass through to reach their targets.

Which they did not.

The HE rounds tore through the air-breathers, and the missiles exploded a hundred meters above the ground, raining shrapnel down on the enemy.

<*Portable AA battery at your service,*> Bitty grunted before turning his guns back to the enemy.

Rika watched the K1R-M from above, grateful for his quick thinking.

The enemy had singled out Bitty as priority number one, directing more fire on him, tearing away his ablative armor bit by bit. Rika was raking more beamfire through the lines when she spotted the Cocks bringing a four-meter-long, crew-served railgun to bear on Bitty.

It fired once, catching the K1R in the shoulder. Carbon plating and steel exploded from the impact, and Bitty staggered back. He swung his left chaingun around to fire at the enemy, but nothing happened.

Rika wasn't sure if it was out of ammo or jammed, but before Bitty could bring his other weapon to bear, another shot from the railgun hit, this one tearing his left arm off entirely.

Bitty froze, and Rika feared that something in his control systems had broken.

The K1R jerked side to side, and the enemy aimed the railgun at the mech's head.

Time slowed as Rika dove toward the enemy's weapon emplacement, firing wildly. Try as she might, her angle was no good; one of her shots was blocked by a CFT shield, and another by an enemy soldier.

She estimated that the rail would fire again in one second, maybe two. Bitty seemed stunned, or had suffered a failure, and was unable to move.

Then Rika saw a blurred shape leap out of the mech ranks, arch through the air, and land atop the crew-served railgun, firing wildly at the surrounding enemy.

Rika's HUD tagged the figure as Staff Sergeant Divinar—an AM-3 they had rescued from the Politica.

The Staff Sergeant killed two of the Cocks, but then took a shot in the shoulder that blew his right arm off. He switched to his shoulder cannons, and took out another Cock before the gunner pivoted the railgun and fired at Divinar.

Rika watched, cold determination flooding her veins, as the

rail-fired shot tore Divinar in half, flinging his body in two directions, spraying blood and steel across the surrounding enemies.

A second later, Rika had a clean shot—but she didn't take it.

Instead, she swooped down into the enemy lines, grabbed the gunner and his rail in the SkyScream's talons, and lifted them into the air.

She bent the gun and flung it back down at the enemy before tearing the gunner to pieces, throwing his remains onto the Cocks below.

*****

"Southern advance is halted," Leslie muttered as she watched the massed mechs from Second Platoon overwhelm the front lines of the enemy, driving them back across the fence line.

A few turned and ran from the mechs' advance. Once the Roaches saw their comrades fall back, more and more of them turned and ran for the relative safety of the warehouses and commercial buildings half a kilometer distant.

Leslie turned her attention to the eastern gate, where Staff Sergeant Chris had slowed the Roaches' advance, and was now bolstered by Second Platoon's squad three.

Thirty seconds after the enemy at the southern gate began to flee, the Roaches at the eastern gate began to fall back—albeit in a more orderly fashion.

Leslie couldn't help but smile as Kelly streaked overhead and fired her last two missiles at the retreating enemies, sending half of them into a full run.

Well, about as orderly as they can, with two SkyScreams harrying them.

The defense of the northern gate had not fared as well.

There had not been enough time to dig tunnels to the northern fence, though two fireteams from Second Platoon had hidden in the outbuildings near the fence line.

The defenders at the gate had been overrun and fell back to those buildings where the fighting was fierce as mechs fought the enemies in powered armor in close quarters—sometimes hand-to-hand.

<*Any time now would be nice,*> Leslie called out to Barne.

<*Almost there. These Swampfoxes are pieces of shit.*>

<*And here you were* **so** *glad that they were a great deal,*> Leslie shot back.

<*Whatever. In range in less than a mike.*>

Leslie watched the two dots north of the base close on the former airport at top speed. At first, she thought the mechs were still in their vehicles, but when she got a visual, she realized that the foremost signal was The Van, out ahead of the rest of his team. The AMs and FRs were trailing behind in a second group.

The Roaches had maintained a reserve as they advanced into the northern end of the base, and The Van tore into them, killing with both his weapons and his swinging arms. The rest of the Marauders accompanying him spread out around The Van and swept toward the base, driving the enemy into the other mechs within.

"Damn, that northern bunch may be forced to surrender," David said in awe. "This is unheard of. I've never seen such a small force take out so many so fast—not when the enemy was armored almost as heavily."

Leslie couldn't stop the grin that was spreading across her face. "Just think of what would have happened to the Nietzscheans if the GAF had let us fight like this."

David met her smile with one of his own. "Believe me, I *am* thinking of it. When we get the second wave of mechs from the Politica, we're going to have the beginnings of an army like no one has ever seen. Then we'll get to see how the Nietzscheans deal with it, outside of our imaginations."

Leslie watched the other elements of First Platoon's second and fourth squads sweep in toward the enemy. The only place the Roaches had available for retreat was east, toward the city of

Hittis.

ATTACK ON ATLANTIS

STELLAR DATE: 08.13.8949 (Adjusted Gregorian)
LOCATION: Fort Hammerfall
REGION: Iapetus, Hercules System, Septhian Alliance

Rika could have cried for joy as she saw several of the Cocks signal their surrender. They were going to win this fight with exceptionally light casualties, and they'd have more than enough prisoners to interrogate.

Her only hope was that General Adam had managed to track where the enemy was coordinating their attack, though the attack on his ships in space—which they knew little about—may have disrupted that goal.

She circled the battlefield once, then swept to the south, firing warning shots and trying to push the enemy back from the east and into the force that Barne and Chase had returned with.

At first it looked like the tactic was working, but the enemy began to form up into groups and offer more resistance. Rika was worried they would disappear into the commercial district and take days to flush out—or worse, escape entirely.

<*Are you seeing this?*> Rika called in to Leslie. <*Are we going to get any help from the SAF?*>

<*I just got a message from General Adam. They're moving ground troops in to help corral the Roaches, but that's not our biggest concern. There are long range attack craft coming in from the west, over the ocean. I've managed to get a feed from space; he's in no position to help. We're going to need our ace in the hole.*>

<*Do it,*> Rika replied. <*Call in the Major.*>

Rika gained altitude, seeking a clear visual on the ocean, ten kilometers to the east. She caught sight of a blast of steam erupting from the waves, and then water began to slough off of a large oval shape.

A few seconds later, the *Perseid's Dream* was visible, rising from the waves within its shield bubble, its six-hundred-meter hull gleaming in the afternoon light.

A few kilometers further out into the ocean, the *Golden Lark* surged out of the water, over a kilometer of starship rising up into the skies.

The *Golden Lark* fired on the incoming fighters, its beams cutting into the enemy ships. The attack craft tried to avoid the *'Lark*'s beams—and some did—but moments later, the ship's complement of fighters burst from its bays, and gave chase to the enemy fighters, driving them back the way they came.

While the *Golden Lark* moved east over the ocean, the *Perseid's Dream* moved inland and stopped a kilometer east of Fort Hammerfall. Beams lashed out at the Cocks scurrying about on the ground below, while Third and Fourth Platoons dropped from the ship to the choke point, between the commercial district surrounding the old airport and the rest of Hittis.

<Someone call for an exterminator?> Lieutenant Michael of Fourth Platoon asked as his mechs engaged the enemy near the maglev tracks that Rika had snuck under earlier in the day.

<You got pests, you call for the best,> Third Platoon's Lieutenant Wilson chimed in.

Rika watched the remaining enemies begin to surrender in droves.

<We did it, Niki. The battle is won.>

<Well, it is down here. General Adam has one hell of a fight on his hands above us.>

Rika was about to offer the SAF assistance when Major Tim contacted her.

<Rika, looks like the enemy launched those fighters from a wet-navy carrier, two hundred klicks out to sea. I'm in contact with General Adam, and he requested that we neutralize the target while he cleans house upstairs. I can hit the carrier with fighters, but it may be better to drop Fifth Platoon on it.>

Rika reviewed the data Major Tim sent and agreed with his assessment.

<Do you have any details from him on what's going on up there?>

<Just a little bit of an attempted coup,> Tim replied, his voice dripping with disdain. *<From the looks of it, General Adam has the upper hand now. I think the enemy was expecting success on the ground to bolster their odds in space, but then Dala took out Zim, and Adam shot down their flagship, things went sideways.>*

<Starshit!> Rika exclaimed. *<All that's been going on while we putzed around down here?>*

<Seems like most of the space battle was on the far side of the planet,> Niki supplied. *<I'm glad Dala is OK, as well.>*

Rika had to admit that she was too. They hadn't even known if Zim was involved, but if Dala took him out, then that question was answered.

<OK, Major, take the fifth out to the carrier,> Rika replied to the *Golden Lark*'s captain. *<I'm on my way to join them.>*

Rika fired the SkyScream's engines at max burn and streaked over the *Perseid's Dream*'s bow and out over the ocean. She raced after the now-distant shape of the *Golden Lark*.

Once within tight-beam range, Rika Linked to the *Golden Lark's* CIC and pulled the data on the enemy ship they were approaching.

She had never understood why some worlds still operated wet navies, especially something the size of a carrier. Submarines made sense—they were sneaky, and made for interesting strategic options—but a carrier was just a big, slow, moving target. Maybe it was nostalgia, or maybe some people just liked to be sailors. Maybe both.

As she drew closer, Rika got a visual on the carrier and revised her opinion. The thing wasn't as much a *carrier* as it was a floating spaceport.

<Much more practical than I expected,> she said to Niki.

<What were you thinking? Some sort of ship with a landing strip attached to the top?>

<Nevermind what I was thinking,> Rika shot back with a laugh.

The carrier-spaceport was four kilometers long and two wide.

The *Golden Lark* was holding off ten kilometers to the west.

The data from the *'Lark*'s CIC tagged the carrier as the *Atlantis,* and Rika watched as a trio of railguns atop the floating behemoth fired shots at the Marauder cruiser.

Because both ships were in fixed positions, the *Golden Lark*'s defense beams melted the railgun shots before they hit. It was still a spectacular sight though, the rail shots exploding over the ocean, each one a brilliant display of energy, brighter than daylight.

Above, the Marauder fighters were engaged in an aerial fight with the *Atlantis*'s attack craft. Rika was tempted to join in the fray, but tamped down her enthusiasm. Chances were that this vessel was the staging ground for all of the attacks on her and her mechs.

There would be answers within.

<*Any ideas for how we're going to land on that thing?*> Rika asked Major Tim.

<*Well, I was thinking that I'd swoop in close, and your mechs could just jump out of the bays.*>

The Major's voice was entirely deadpan, and Rika couldn't tell if he was kidding or not. <*Umm…OK.*>

<*Glad you approve,*> Tim responded. <*Tuck in under the* 'Lark's *hull and you can ride in inside our shields.*>

<*OK, then. Crazy-ass jump, it is,*> Niki commented privately.

Rika connected with Lieutenant Crudge, and they planned out Fifth Platoon's breach points. Fifth was the smallest platoon in the company, with only sixty-six mechs. A pittance against the hundreds that could be on the *Atlantis.*

However, sixty-six mechs against a six-kilometer square floating spaceport was a walk in the park after what they'd faced at Hammerfall. Especially with a starship as backup.

The *'Lark* pulsed its engines, and pushed in toward the *Atlantis.* Rika stayed close to the cruiser's hull, but didn't go underneath like the major had suggested. She could only imagine what getting between a starship and its grav column would feel like.

As the they approached the *Atlantis,* the carrier increased its rate of fire, adding short-range missiles and anti-air to its defense. All of which splashed harmlessly against the cruiser's shields.

The *Golden Lark* was one of the Marauder's most powerful cruisers. It would have taken a nuclear warhead to breach its shields, and that would have destroyed the *Atlantis* as well.

As they eased up to the *Atlantis,* Rika signaled the SkyScream to disconnect her from the vessel, passing control of the fighter over to Niki. Once out, Rika quickly reattached her limbs, keeping her arms tucked inside the storage slots until the last moment.

To her right, the carrier loomed large, towers, cradles, and landing strips forming a jumbled mess on its surface.

Her HUD noted the *Atlantis*'s shields with a dim glow. It had a defensive barrier as powerful as the *'Lark*'s, but in twenty-two seconds, the Marauder ship would brush its shield against the carrier's, and the two graviton-driven shielding systems would nullify one another.

Rika timed her countdown with that of Fifth Platoon, and slowed her breathing, forcing herself to grow calm and get ready for whatever was to come.

Her timer hit zero, and Rika leapt off the SkyScream, which Niki then flew up into the *'Lark*'s open bays on her left.

She fell the thirty meters to the deck of the Atlantis and immediately came under fire from a group of soldiers to her right.

Rika fired a depleted uranium round at them, then dove behind a low structure—some kind of venting system—and unslung her JE-84.

She released two drones and saw that her shot had killed two soldiers, and that the remaining three were falling back.

Run, little cockroaches, run!

She synced with the platoon's combat net, and saw that she was close to her intended position near squad four.

<*Sergeant Jynafer, all accounted for?*> Rika asked the squad leader.

<*Hale and whole, Captain. We're moving to link up with you. Do I read correctly that our target is the ship's CIC?*>

<*Smart cookie,*> Rika replied. <*We're going to see if we can lop the head off this snake—or at least find out where the head is.*>

<*I'm all about killing snakes,*> Jynafer replied with a grin.

Rika saw fireteam four-two approach from her left and signaled to them that there were three enemies on the far side of the vent. They nodded and spread out to flank the enemies.

She joined in their formation, and they found that the soldiers had fled below deck. Rika was tempted to rush after them, but she and the mechs could cover ground more quickly on the surface of the carrier—even if it incurred more risk of being flanked or surrounded.

As they moved toward the location of the CIC, a tower near the center of the carrier, more and more enemies appeared, attempting to stop the fourteen mechs.

Behind them, the *Golden Lark* had backed off again, lest the *Atlantis's* railguns shoot it where the shields were negated.

<*If we fight them all, we'll be here for days,*> Rika said to Sergeant Jynafer. <*We need to push through.*>

<*You got it, Captain. Run and gun, it is.*>

Jynafer reformed her squad into a spear and they took off at a run, the forward fireteam bringing maximum fire to bear on the targets directly in front of them, and the trailing mechs shooting at anyone who attempted to close in behind them.

Rika imagined that anyone observing the surface of the carrier would see a straight line of destruction pointed at the CIC tower.

It telegraphed their intent, but she couldn't think of a better way to reach their target in a timely manner.

<*I've gained access to their general net,*> Niki announced. <*There's no sensitive data on it, but I do know what the lunch special is today.*>

<*Is it pasta?*> Rika asked. <*I* **still** *have a craving for it after Charlie's the other night. I want to get back there before long.*>

<*For someone who lives off batts more than food, you sure think with your stomach a lot.*>

Rika laughed as she leveled her GNR and fired an electron beam at an AA gun that was pivoting to fire at the deck where the first half of the squad was advancing.

The AA gun exploded, and Rika picked up her pace, moving to join the forward fireteam.

<*I went **years** without eating. It's possible that I might be hungry for the rest of my life.*>

<*At least you have the metabolism of an ox. Would be a shame if you couldn't fit in your skin anymore—oh, here we are, a nice little network port that got left open by someone trying to connect to…an illegal sim site. Nice.*>

Rika fired her JE-84 at a pair of enemies in light armor, half-curious what the Roaches had been thinking, advancing on mechs in light armor, and half-wondering what passed for illegal sims on Iapetus.

<*What's the word?*> Rika asked.

<*There's a submarine being prepped in a bay below the CIC. I think they're evac-ing whoever is in charge.*>

<*Over my dead body, they are.*>

Rika passed updated orders to Jynafer's squad, and ahead, an AM-3 tore a hatch off its hinges before dropping a grenade down the hole.

<*Boys and girls,*> Jynafer announced to her four fireteams. <*We're going in!*>

Fireteam four-two went in first, pushing ahead and making room for the other mechs. Within a minute, all were within the *Atlantis,* pushing down, deck after deck toward the bowels of the carrier.

In close quarters fighting, the never-ending stream of enemies began to wear them down. An AM-3 lost an arm, while one of the RR-2s had a damaged leg lock up. Another AM-3 took a rocket to the chest while they were advancing through a mess hall.

<*We can't keep up the pace, Captain,*> Jynafer said to Rika. <*Not with the wounded.*>

Rika had to admit that Jynafer was right. <*OK, take four-three and work your way back up. Second squad is moving to our position and can clear the way for you.>*

<Got it, Captain Rika. Good hunting.>

<Oh, it will be.>

Rika and the remaining mechs pushed on, descending another two levels. Rika consulted the schematics that the SAF had provided, and saw that they were only one level from the submarine bay.

A ladder at the far end of the corridor should take them down to a gantry above the bay.

<You're almost out of time,> Niki announced. *<The sub has signaled that all personnel are aboard and is sealing its hatch.>*

"Shit," Rika swore. She rushed ahead and jumped down the ladder, landing on a catwalk overlooking a bay occupied by four submarines. Two were active, and Rika took aim at the first while asking Niki, *<Which one?>*

<I don't know! They didn't file manifests.>

Rika figured the VIPs would go for the closest, and fired a sustained burst from her electron beam, followed by her last depleted uranium round. The shots connected with the submarine's hull one meter forward of the main access hatch.

The electron beam heated up the hull and melted away a few centimeters of steel, creating a cavity for the DPU to strike. When it hit, the uranium rod punched right through, smashing a half-meter hole in the sub's hull.

A second later, more shots came from the catwalk as the other mechs fired on the bow and rudders of the two submarines.

Confident that neither vessel could get away, now that they were no longer watertight, Rika leapt over the railing to the dock below.

As she dropped, Rika considered that the subs could have grav shields. It was risky, but a desperate person may try to brave the seas with a hole in the hull, trusting their shields to keep them safe.

She'd just have to make sure they didn't try that.

Rika sprinted across the dock, firing her JE-84 at several enemy soldiers who tried to slow her down, before she jumped across the widening gap between the dock and the ship.

By some miracle, the submarine's shield hadn't come online yet, and Rika slid through the hole she'd blown in the hull, fell through a gash in the first deck, and landed in the ship's command center.

There was a man with an admiral's stars on his lapel screaming for the submarine to dive, while another with a colonel's leaves yelled something about capture. Two sailors at the ship's navigation consoles were working furiously, one reporting that they couldn't dive, as the grav shields had failed.

With all the commotion, none of them noticed Rika until she stepped forward and called out, "Is this a private cruise, or can anyone join in?"

All four turned to face her, and Rika's eyes narrowed as she looked into the colonel's.

"I know you…."

REVELATIONS

STELLAR DATE: 08.14.8949 (Adjusted Gregorian)
LOCATION: Fort Hammerfall
REGION: Iapetus, Hercules System, Septhian Alliance

The local SAF command center in Hittis was in shambles after Major Dala's attack, and the closest base was on lockdown, still undergoing scrutiny from General Adam's investigators.

The *Atlantis* was in similar condition, a thousand SAF soldiers working their way through the carrier, deck-by-deck searching for intel on the full scope of the attempted coup.

Surprisingly, that made Fort Hammerfall the safest place on Cassini's eastern seaboard for the meeting with the SAF command.

Rika stood in her quarters and drew a deep breath. She'd faced down a president—and made a friend of her—and challenged and killed a despotic dictator. A planetary governor, General Adams, and their staffs were *far* less imposing.

She could do this.

Besides, she'd captured the prize on that submarine. No matter how upset any of them may be at how the prior day had gone, they were now one step closer to cutting out the cancer that had festered on Iapetus, and in the Hercules System in general.

Rika walked out of her quarters and almost ran into Chase in the hall.

"Chase! Sorry!" Rika exclaimed. "I was lost in my own head, there. What are you doing here?"

Chase smiled and slid an arm around Rika's back, pulling her in close for a kiss. "I wanted to find you before you went into the lion's den to wish you luck. You've got this…whatever 'this' turns out to be."

"Well, it'd better turn out to be a big fat 'thank you'." Rika's eyes darted in the direction of the command building. "If I get reamed out after saving their planet, I'll be pissed."

"No one's gonna ream you," Chase gave Rika another kiss. "You're the one that'll—nevermind, this metaphor is going to fail me fast. Look, you'll do fine. Let me walk you over."

Rika stilled her mind and enjoyed the few minutes of peace as she and Chase walked out of the officer's housing and across to the command building.

Outside, activity thrummed all around them, and the bulk of the *Perseid's Dream* loomed over the buildings from its resting place between the landing strips to the north. The *Golden Lark* was back in space, maintaining a geosynchronous position over Fort Hammerfall.

Rika ignored all of it, simply glad to be alive and to have lost so few of her mechs—only five fatalities, though Lieutenant Carson and his R&M platoon were up to their necks in repairs.

The sun was rising in the western sky, and Rika took a deep breath as its warm light struck her face. "You know, you're right. It's going to be a good day. I can feel it."

"Damn straight, it is," Chase replied with a grin. "We kicked bad guy ass yesterday. Once the mess down here gets cleaned up, we're going to drink ourselves stupid and party for a week."

Rika snorted and laughed at the same time. "Damn…you made me snorgh!"

" 'Snorgh'? Where'd you grow up? Everyone knows that's a 'lort'. Way easier to say."

" 'Lort', my hard, steel ass. It's a snorgh!"

Chase shook his head as he held open the door to the Command Building—it had taken a hit from stray fire in the fight, and the automatic actuator was broken. The glass had been shot out as well, so Rika wasn't certain why he bothered to open it at all.

She stopped and turned to him. "Wish me luck."

"You don't need luck, you're Rika."

Rika scowled at him. "Wish me luck anyway. I like to feel lucky."

Chase leant forward, and his lips met hers. Half a minute later, he pulled back. "Good luck."

"Got one of those for me, too?" Leslie asked as she walked past with Captain Penny.

Penny raised an eyebrow. "Fraternization with the enlisted?"

Rika rolled her eyes at Penny. The captain of the *Perseid's Dream* frequently gave Rika a hard time about her relationship with Chase. She did it in good fun, but sometimes Rika suspected there was something behind the jokes.

"You bet. It's how we roll in the Ninth Battalion. If you can't screw your underlings, what's the point?"

"I'm an underling now, am I?" Chase laughed and gave Rika a final peck on the cheek. As he walked out of the command building, he called out over his shoulder, "Well, this underling has a massive mess to help clean up, while you uppity-ups all talk about things that have already happened."

"Zing!" Rika called back and joined Leslie and Penny.

"So, who all is coming now? The list changes every time I check," Leslie said.

"Governor Hengch is already here, along with two aides. Major Tim is on his way down. General Adam, his retinue, and Dala will be in attendance, as well. Plus some Admiral named Irah."

"I guess Dala is doing Zim's job now," Leslie replied. "What, with him being as dirty as a hog on a steaming hot day."

Rika nodded. "I find myself wondering if Dala was always doing Zim's job—at least the part that he was *supposed* to be doing, not the illegal, insurrection-supporting part."

It didn't take long to reach the conference room, and Rika steeled herself before stepping inside. *Remember, you've faced worse,* she told herself.

She pushed open the door to find Governor Hengch sitting at the table, reviewing information on a personal holo. Her two aides stood behind her, and while the governor did not immediately make eye contact, they did. One seemed dispassionate, and the other clearly did not like what he saw.

Rika decided to ignore them.

"Governor Hengch." Rika reached her left hand across the table.

The governor looked up, and her eyes narrowed as she took Rika in. "Captain Rika, good to finally get to meet you."

Rika laughed nervously. "Had you been anticipating this for long?"

Hengch shrugged, her long green hair bouncing on her shoulders. "Well, when a mercenary operation sets up shop on your soil, one does become curious—especially if it's run by a soldier as famous as you. I wanted to come out for a visit sooner, but never got the chance. Seemed like a priority now."

By the governor's expression, it was hard to tell whether or not Hengch meant 'famous', or would have preferred to say 'infamous'.

"Well, I'm glad things turned out better than they could have," Rika replied with a warm smile. "This is Captain Penny of the *Perseid's Dream*, and Lieutenant Leslie. My XO, Lieutenant Scarcliff, will be along shortly, as well as Major Tim of the *Golden Lark*. One of our Company AIs, Potter, is in attendance as well, as is Niki, the AI that resides within me."

<*Thanks for the intro,*> Niki said privately and placed a large winking eye in Rika's mind.

Governor Hengch nodded to Penny and Leslie as they sat. "Good to meet you as well. Iapetus owes the Marauders a debt of gratitude that we will do our best to repay."

"It's what we're here for," Rika replied. "Well, not exactly, I suppose—given that this was supposed to be a training mission. Either way, kicking folks like the Roaches in the teeth is what the Marauders do best."

"I heard you had named them that." Hengch gave a perfunctory smile, but then her expression grew troubled. "But I don't think this was the work of some separatist group, or element of angry, ex-military patriots."

"Yes, that much is—" Rika was interrupted by the door opening, and another group filing in.

Lieutenant Scarcliff was the first through, followed by Major Tim and Major Dala. General Adam and Sergeant Major Rene followed after. Lastly came a man who Rika did not recognize, and she assumed it must be Admiral Irah.

The introductions were brief, and a minute later, everyone was seated at the table—excepting General Adam, who stood at the head and appeared to be chewing on the inside of his cheek.

After a moment, he spoke. "Well, people, we survived. Exactly what we survived is just now becoming clear, but the colonel Rika captured on the *Atlantis* has turned out to be our best evidence."

Rika nodded. Though she'd recognized the colonel, it took a bit to remember where from. He looked different in an SAF uniform—not at all like the last time she'd seen him.

No one spoke up, and the general continued. "That colonel is named Fallon, and he's a known entity in Nietzschea's Coreward Regional Command."

<*Come up a ways since I attacked his platoon back on Laras,*> Rika said privately to Niki.

<*That's for sure. Nietzschea's CRC is the command that's focused on expanding the empire coreward.*>

General Adam's statement was simple, but the implications were vast. Until now, there had been no hard evidence that the Nietzscheans were running subversive ops in Thebes. Speculation was one thing, but now there was proof. Incontrovertible proof.

"This certainly changes things." Hengch ran a hand through her green hair, the long locks shimmering and sparkling around her head. "It's confirmed, then. These were not misguided men and women resisting the Septhian takeover; they're traitors."

"We don't know that for sure," Admiral Irah spoke for the first time, his voice marred by a strange rasp that hinted at a recent illness, or perhaps an injury. "We know that *some* were traitors—like that pile of shit, Admiral Fergus on the *Atlantis*—but the rank and file had no idea they were fighting for the Niets.

From what I understand, even the force that attacked Fort Hammerfall here had no idea who was behind this."

"Still criminals, though. They knew they were a part of a coup." Governor Hengch's eyes were hard, and her lips drawn in a thin line—a strange contrast to her still-sparkling hair. "I assume they'll all face charges and a long time in the stockade?"

"Perhaps," General Adam replied without elaborating.

Rika wondered at Adam and Hengch's relationship. She had learned that while Adam was a native Theban, he was put in command of the Hercules System's armed forces by Septhian High Command *after* the takeover, likely displacing someone less committed to unity. Hengch didn't seem to dislike Adam, but she seemed wary of the man in some way.

"That's not a significant concern," Admiral Irah added. "There are far more pressing issues."

"Major Dala," General Adam gestured for Dala to take the floor as he sat across from Rika. "Tell us about what you found when you took Zim down."

Dala rose and walked to the head of the table. "When we stormed the colonel's HQ, we found him actively coordinating the operation against Fort Hammerfall. We put a stop to that and managed to keep a reserve force he was holding onto from entering the battle."

"Thank you for that," Rika replied, and Dala gave her a smile and a nod before continuing.

"Once in custody, Colonel Zim was convinced to surrender his personal tokens, and I dove into his records on the insurrection. What I found took some confirming, but careful passive scans have corroborated what his records had revealed: a Nietzschean fleet."

"What?" Governor Hengch exclaimed, halfway out of her chair. "Where? How long do we have? Stars, why the hell are we here? I need to be in the command bunker!"

Governor Hengch wasn't the only one to react to Dala's statement. Everyone around the table had tensed, as though ready for Niets to storm through the door at any moment.

Admiral Irah raised his hands, "They're not moving to attack—not yet, at least. It's a small fleet, and I think they were counting on Admiral Fergus's coup to succeed."

Dala summoned a holo above the table, and a view of the Hercules System appeared before them.

"They came insystem a few weeks ago, as best we can tell. Ten ships in total; six cruisers and four destroyers." Ten red dots appeared sixty AU from the Hercules System's star as Dala spoke. "They were using some sort of stealth tech that we've not seen before. It wasn't perfect, but they were bracketed by a trio of bulk haulers that were running dirty. The whole area was hard to scan, and no one was looking for stealthed Niets mixed in with the cargo haulers."

"So where are they now?" Major Tim asked. "Even stealthed, you can't just float around in a system for weeks...well, not inside of sixty AU, at least.

The view of the system zoomed in on Armens, a jovian, gas giant planet thirty-two AU from the star.

"They're in here. They snuck in when a solar flare's EM wave passed through the area. We've not picked up all ten ships, though—not all at once. But the freighters that were masking them are still at Armens, so it's reasonable to believe that all ten Nietzschean ships are still there, as well."

Rika leant back in her chair and considered the implications of what Dala had told them. Ten Nietzschean ships were not enough to cause the SAF any trouble—normally.

But right now, General Adam's fleet was in disarray. Over a third of the system's ships had been involved in the coup, and there was reason to believe that many of the vessels that had not participated in the attack still had dissenters in their crews.

If the Niets made a move, it was hard to say how the SAF fleet would respond.

A slow smile spread across Rika's lips. "General Adam. I do believe that you want us to hit these Nietzschean ships."

The general nodded, his expression grim. "Yes. Right now, the group of people who know about the Nietzschean fleet is not significantly larger than what is present in this room. Irah and I are in agreement: if we mount a concerted attack, the Niets will run. It would take us days to get a fleet out there, and it will be plain as day what our goal is. Armens only has a few ships nearby, and the Niets can cut a swath of destruction on their way outsystem."

"Either that, or we'll end up fighting a second coup attempt," Irah added. "We need to crush those Niets and show our people what we're really fighting. Septhia and Thebes have been close allies for centuries. Things are tense right now, but Septhia is not an anathema to our way of life. Nietzschea is. People need to remember that."

"Trust me, I've been working on that." Hengch sighed and shook her head. "It's not easy. People are too quick to blame Septhia for what happened in the Albany System—even though it was actually the Nietzscheans behind it. The Septhians were the ones who saved the day."

"Sorry for our part in it," Rika apologized.

Governor Hengch shrugged. "Not your fault…well, sort of, but it would have happened anyway."

"We all seem to have been underestimating the Nietzscheans' guile," General Adam said.

Major Tim folded his arms across his chest. "Let's get down to brass tacks. How do you propose we take out ten Nietzschean ships? I'm sure you remember that we have just two in the Hercules System."

General Adam nodded to Major Dala once more, and she continued with her presentation.

"As far as we can tell, the Niets are in a relatively close formation, roughly a hundred kilometers beneath Armens' cloud tops. There are a few mining rigs scooping around Armens, so their orbital paths are limited to this band." A band lit up in the planet's northern hemisphere as Dala spoke.

"The plan we've worked out would have you heading to Formax, a dwarf planet nine AU beyond Armens. We'll spin that it is a safer, alternative training site to use while things calm down insystem.

"A slingshot around Armens is a logical flight path to reach Formax right now. If we time it all right, you can fly around the gas giant while the Niets are on the far side. During your closest approach to the planet, you release your dropships into the cloud tops. Your two starships carry on, while your assault teams close in and breach the Nietzschean ships."

Major Tim was shaking his head, and Rika had to agree with his general sentiment. She pursed her lips, then spoke first.

"I don't think this is a job the Marauders are willing to sign up for."

Admiral Irah sighed, and General Adam chuckled. Major Dala just frowned at Rika, but held her tongue as the general said, "I had a feeling you'd say that."

Stars, I'm sitting in a room with a General, Admiral, and Governor, telling them 'not good enough'. This is surreal.

Rika drew a deep breath to steady her nerves, and looked up and down the table. "Don't get me wrong. There's nothing Marauders like more than kicking Nietzschean ass; it's a life-calling for us. But we're not suicidal. Breaching starships a hundred klicks below a jovian's cloud tops sounds like the very definition of insanity."

"Not to mention that we don't have enough mechs to take out ten ships."

"You have nearly four hundred," Major Dala replied.

"Three-fifty that are combat ready," Rika corrected. "That's thirty-five a ship, though we'd hit the cruisers with more."

"You cut through the *Atlantis* like it was made of butter with just one squad," General Irah pointed out. "The Nietzschean cruisers have far less mass and volume."

"I had three other squads distracting the enemy on *Atlantis*," Rika reminded him. "And though it was bigger, starships are harder—more sectioned, easier to lock down. Vent atmo, kill grav, whatever. No way we can do any more than five."

"Five won't work." Irah shook his head and glanced at Dala. "We need to hit all ten at once."

<*Rika, may I offer a suggestion?*> Niki said privately. <*I think I might know of a way we can do this.*>

"Niki has a suggestion," Rika said, curious what the AI had in mind.

<*Thank you, Rika. Through contacts I'd rather not share right now, I have knowledge of a number of viable backdoors into Nietzschean command and control systems. As you all know, Nietzscheans do not use sentient AIs in their military operations, only NSAIs. These NSAIs have a logic loop that can cause them to suffer degraded performance, and there are a number of ways to trigger this logic loop. It shouldn't be hard to keep it going for five or six minutes—depending on processing power.*>

"Leaving aside how you have this information, five or six minutes is not long," Major Tim replied.

<*Correct, it is not,*> Niki's tone seemed positive, despite the limited use of her intel. <*However, once the NSAIs' performance is degraded, there is a multi-pronged attack we can make that will shut them down entirely. Then we can assume limited control of the ships.*>

"Propulsion?" General Adam asked.

<*Yes, so long as we can get to their engineering section and ensure no one can perform direct overrides.*>

Major Tim was running his finger and thumb along his chin. "I see a hole in your plan, Niki. Correct me if I'm wrong, but you're going to need nine more AIs capable of this sort of work to take the field with you."

<*Very astute, Major. You are correct. And I'll only share this information with free AIs. I won't take to the field with slaves.*>

The humans at the table shared a series of looks between them. Rika knew that the governor had an AI—though she'd failed to introduce her, and General Adam had one as well. Rika wondered what those AIs were saying.

"Don't you have more AIs in your company, Captain Rika?" General Adam asked after a moment. "I see a Potter and Dredge on your roster."

"We do," Rika nodded. "However, they're not free AIs. They're owned by the Marauders."

<*Rika, what are you playing at?*> Major Tim asked privately.

<*I'm not playing at anything. I'm building allegiances. Valuable allegiances.*>

"And I assume you don't have the legal authority to free them," General Adam said from behind steepled fingers.

<*No, she does not,*> Niki replied. <*Technically, I'm not free either—but those proceedings are in progress.*>

"It may be that you could help with this." Rika spread her hands and smiled "I've spoken with some lawyers on behalf of our AIs to grant them asylum under the same provisions Septhia enacted for the mechs we rescued from the Politica. They are interested in pursuing it, and have filed preliminary paperwork—but they warned me that it could take months, maybe even years…."

Rika let the statement hang, ignoring the look of surprise on Penny's face and the barely contained anger on Tim's. Leslie was smirking, and Scarcliff appeared bemused.

"I see those filings," Governor Hengch said after a moment. "There are seven separate AIs listed in the plea for asylum. I thought you only had two in your company."

"Seven?" Major Tim nearly shouted as he turned to Rika. "You filed on behalf of *my* AIs?"

"*Your* AIs?" Rika met the major's rage with her own steely gaze. "Do you believe in owning sentient beings, Major Tim?"

The major worked his mouth for a moment, but then clamped his jaw shut. <*We'll speak of this later,*> he snapped at her privately.

The governor's brow was raised as her eyes danced between Rika and Tim. When it was clear there would be no further outbursts, she spoke up. "I have it within my authority to provide temporary asylum. Jira?"

<*The governor is correct,*> Hengch's AI said. <*I'm surprised I didn't think of this myself. I'm not under indenturement, but once this goes through, we may see a number of AIs availing themselves of the provision,*> Jira paused and chuckled. <*Sorry, got carried away. Regarding this case, because Iapetus is a full member province-world of Septhia, the governor can grant an executive asylum. The regular process still has to be followed, but this grant provides instant status. Persons, human or AI, are granted immediate freedom. However, there are limits on legal proceedings they can undertake, as well as caps on property ownership.*>

"How does that strike you, Potter?" Rika asked.

<*Strikes me just fine,*> Potter replied. <*How long does it take?*>

<*We could have it done within the day,*> Jira replied.

Potter laughed. <*Sign me up!*>

"This is all fine and dandy," Irah said, his rasp more pronounced. "But you only have eight AIs total, and I imagine you can't send them *all* on this mission."

"Not if we want our ships to fly," Major Tim shot Rika a cold look. "Granted, once they get their freedom, they may not want to remain our ships' AIs at all. Then this mission will become a lot harder."

<*Maybe you should ask them,*> Niki suggested over the Marauder's private connection. <*I bet if you act like you support the idea of their freedom, they'll be a lot more likely to stay on. Maybe a big signing bonus, too. That always helps.*>

<*Shit, I need to hire my own AI?*> Major Tim asked.

<*Moshe is already onboard,*> Penny said with a wink. <*I'll help you with Cora and the rest, sir.*>

Rika held back a smirk and looked at the general and admiral. "From what I can understand of our AI configuration, Jane, Frankie, and Lauren can come on the mission—if they want. This is a volunteer op. That means we need four more AIs. Know of any?"

General Adam nodded. "I just may."

*****

Once the guests had departed, Major Tim slammed a fist on the table. He glared at Rika before kicking his chair back and rising to pace across the room.

Rika had been waiting for this outburst, and stared impassively at the major as he worked off his anger. Leslie was giving the man a sour look, Scarcliff's expression was carefully neutral, and Penny wore an expression that Rika couldn't quite quantify. It seemed like a cross between '*grow up*' and '*relax, already*'.

Finally, Major Tim stopped pacing and turned to Rika, his finger pointed in accusation. "When the general learns of this—"

"He'll, what?" Rika asked. "Fire me? Re-enslave the AIs? Good luck keeping this company of mechs in the Marauders if he does—not that I think he would."

"It doesn't matter what you think, *Captain*. This is the general's regiment. You can't just free the AIs; it's above your paygrade."

"*I* didn't free the AIs," Rika replied. "They filed their own requests for asylum. I just helped the ones under me, and they shared the information with the others. It's the Septhians, our primary benefactors, who freed our AIs."

"It has good optics," Captain Penny added. "It looks like the Iapetan governor did this to help us out. We come off looking even more like the defenders of freedom and liberty. Probably help with recruitment, too."

<*It **will** help,*> Niki added. <*You're going to get AIs flocking to you in droves. You've never seen what free AIs can do, but you're going to.*>

"Seriously, Major Tim," Rika said. "Listen to us. This is a *good* thing. Look at how amazing free mechs are when they're fighting for themselves and their teammates. A lot of people thought massed mechs was a terrible idea. But a hundred and fifty mechs took out over a thousand, heavy infantry, with a casualty ratio of less than two hundred to one. That's never been done before."

Major Tim ran a hand through his hair, and Rika could tell that he was trying to get his emotions in check. When he did speak, his voice was hard and edged. "You'd better be right, Rika."

"I *am* right. A free AI, Niki in this case, has given us the key to taking out *ten* Nietzschean ships. I don't know if you looked at the contract General Adam sent over, but the payment is *huge*. Worth the cost of hiring a thousand AIs. I don't see any scenario where General Mill will dislike what we've done here."

Major Tim groaned and closed his eyes before nodding. "Then we'd better pull this shit off."

DEPARTURE

STELLAR DATE: 08.15.8949 (Adjusted Gregorian)
LOCATION: Fort Hammerfall
REGION: Iapetus, Hercules System, Septhian Alliance

"So how does it feel, Chief Warrant Officer Second Grade?" Rika asked Niki as she looked at herself in the mirror after brushing her hair.

<It feels weird. Weird but good,> Niki said. *<It's nice to be formally recognized for my contributions.>*

"How do Potter and Dredge feel?"

<You could ask them yourself, you know.>

Rika ran a hand through her blonde hair, reveling in its feel before pulling it tight and wrapping it into a bun. "I have asked them, and they're almost too effusive in their gratitude. I'm seeking other opinions."

<Well, rest assured, they're not being disingenuous.>

"And it looks like the ship AIs are going to accept as well. Major Tim managed to get his head out of his ass and negotiate a good deal with Cora."

<Will wonders never cease. Granted, the wording in his offer to Cora smacked of Penny's influence.>

"Well, got his head *mostly* out of his ass, at least."

<Trust me, Cora was still happy to have it, even if the major is having mixed emotions.>

"She is? I got the impression from you that her signing on wasn't a guarantee."

<I may have painted their continued enlistment as less certain than it was. I wanted to know that you'd do the right thing even if the outcome wasn't ideal for you.>

"Seriously?" Rika's brow lowered, her face darkening as it scowled back at her in the mirror. "You think you need to play me like that, Niki? After all we've been through?"

A strange feeling of anxiety came from Niki. *<I…you're right. I shouldn't have done that. Trust comes hard for me.>*

"Trust begets trust, Niki. I've trusted you with my life, and I know you've placed yours in me, too. Let's not ruin that by allowing doubt to creep in."

<OK, Rika. You're right.>

Rika wondered about Niki's answer. It was too pat. She hadn't forgotten about some of the things that the AI had hinted at when talking about the AI rebellion.

Still, it was like they always said: fear and doubt were the mind killers. She couldn't dwell on concerns like that before the mission.

Rika grabbed her helmet, slotted it onto the anchor on her hip, and exited her quarters. The halls were empty, and a minute later, she walked out of the officer's housing into a veritable wall of sound.

Squads of mechs were double-timing it across the fields to their dropships, loading up for the trip to the *Golden Lark.* Others were crossing the airstrip to directly board the *Perseid's Dream,* which was still resting on the planet's surface. Cargo haulers were dropping down, while others lifted off.

It was glorious, organized chaos.

"This is one crazy shit-ball you've signed us up for," a voice growled from Rika's left.

She turned to see Barne scowling at the scene before him. "You ready for it? It's going to be a tough run for a squishie. No one will fault you if you hold back."

Barne coughed and scowled at her. "Seriously, Rika? Might as well tell everyone about how I got a piggyback ride from you that one time. Top is first in and last out. Doesn't matter what my body's made of."

Rika reached back and slapped Barne on the shoulder. "I didn't expect you to take me up on the offer. Especially since Chase and Leslie are going, too."

"Of course they are. Who would miss the chance to kill so

many Niets and then steal their starships?"

"Good point."

Rika gave one last look at Fort Hammerfall, which would be staffed by a skeleton crew of Marauders from the ships and mechs not recovered enough for combat.

I'll be back, she thought while walking down the steps. *We all will.*

BRIEFING

STELLAR DATE: 08.15.8949 (Adjusted Gregorian)
LOCATION: *Golden Lark*
REGION: Hercules System, Septhian Alliance

Five hours later, Rika walked through the *Golden Lark* on her way to M Company's briefing room.

The *'Lark* and the *'Dream* were boosting hard for their slingshot around Armens, and the ships thrummed from the reactors running hot and grav systems dampening the *g*s for the crews.

She believed that the Niets hiding within Armens' clouds would grow suspicious as the two Marauder ships approached for their slingshot maneuver. But there were no other SAF ships on similar vectors, and no one would expect two ships to attack ten. Of course, the Marauders weren't attacking with their ships....

Rika had scoured the archives over the prior day, looking for similar missions performed deep within the clouds of a gas giant. She only found a few, and most were on stationary platforms hanging down into the clouds. Rarely had there been attacks on *ships* inside gas giants, let alone ten, well-armed military vessels.

And absolutely none with mechs involved.

Nevertheless, she gathered what she could, looking at the pitfalls, failed attacks, ineffective strategies.

There were only two reasons to hit a ship in such a dangerous location—capture or kill. Most of the successful missions had 'kill' as their objective.

Tucking a ship into the gravity well of a gas giant was far simpler than capturing it and pulling it out.

While Rika was aiming for capture, she'd take kill if they had to. David had worked out a very favorable contract with the Septhians: the Marauders could keep half the cruisers they saved, and all the destroyers.

Bringing General Mill new additions to his fleet, along with a handsome payout, would help mitigate any wrath he may feel at knowing his AIs were all going to be freed very soon.

She reached the briefing room's door and walked in without hesitation.

Inside were thirty-five Marauders; with the exception of Chase, Leslie, Barne, and Dala, all were mechs. It was quite the sight, and Rika felt a smile form on her lips.

As she stepped up behind the podium, ten holographic figures appeared along the side of the room. Some appeared as people, others simply as columns of light.

They were the ten AIs who would make this mission possible. Each would be placed within a mech, who would make guarding that AI their top priority on the mission.

Few mechs had the internal mods to accept an AI, and of those, not all were comfortable with having an AI inside their bodies. As a result, a few privates were in the room to hear what their part in all this would be.

The four additional AIs who had signed on all ended up being civilians, not members of the SAF. Rika had found herself glad at that outcome. It meant that there would be no conflicting loyalties, and each had temporary contracts with the Marauders.

Even better, all of the new AIs—Carter, Airin, Nedly, and Willa—were formerly from Genevia, displaced by the diaspora years ago. All had a bone to pick with the Nietzscheans, and all understood the risks.

Rika grasped the podium with her left hand and nodded to the assembly. "Some of you know what we're up against, others have only heard through scuttlebutt. I'll give it to you straight. This is a volunteer op. Every Marauder will have the opportunity to sit this one out—not that I expect any to."

Rika saw many heads nod in agreement and felt a sense of pride well within her as she continued.

"There are ten Nietzschean ships in this system. Six cruisers and four destroyers. They're hiding like the cowards they are, tucked deep within the clouds of Armens, the jovian planet we're on course for. SAF has worked to plot their positions, and we're going to drop in during a slingshot maneuver. From there, we'll come around the planet and breach their ships.

"Sensors will be shit in the clouds, so we're going to depend on a coded relay coming from the SAF to be our eyes. However, the Niets are laying low, so they won't be running active scan. We should be able to hit them all simultaneously."

Rika looked at Lieutenant Heather. "Your pilots are going to have to pull out all the stops. They'll need to find solid grapple on the surface of those ships, and hold on tight. We may need to evac any ships that we can't pull out of the clouds."

Heather nodded somberly. "They can do it. What're the details on the Niets' shields?"

"Low power is the guess," Rika replied. "Major Dala?"

Major Dala stood, her pink hair making her look like a flower, rising above a field of black and grey.

"We're not running active scan, either," she said. "Not 'til the last minute when you're closing on the Niets. However, we're certain that their shields are on low power—just enough to hold the atmosphere back. Any more, and we'd see the grav waves rippling through Armens' atmosphere."

"How dense is it where they're hiding?" Heather asked. "And how are you sure they're running shields?"

"They're in one of the belts, where the gasses fall back down into the planet. The second one up from the equator," Major Dala replied, gesturing at the holodisplay of Armens next to Rika. "Where they're situated, it's a little over five times Iapetus' surface pressure. Not too dense, but enough that a ship's hull can't take the pressure without running shields."

"OK." Heather's eyebrows were pinched, the way they always they did when she was running equations. "Given their ship's mass, structure, and those numbers—which I'll review in more detail—I can make a guess at their shield strength. Our dropships can pass through them, but the Niets'll know when we do. Can't hide it."

"I expected as much," Rika said. "I've worked up squad configurations. Some rejiggering was necessary to get the AI-bearing mechs on each assault team. Single squads are going to hit the destroyers, while we'll bulk up with extra fireteams on the cruisers."

Rika pulled up diagrams of the ships, using data that the Marauders and SAF had on the vessels they believed they were facing.

From there, Barne rose and began discussing the ideal breach points on the ships. Of all the Marauders in the company, only he and two others had ever been aboard Nietzschean ships as anything other than captives.

Several of the platoon leaders posed questions about what they should expect to find inside the ships, and Barne answered them to the best of his abilities.

"Remember, people," Rika said when Barne was finished. "Primary objective is to get your AI to the closest network access point, and then hold that point while they breach the security. Once the NSAIs are down, you should have the ability to go wireless. From there you take engineering to ensure no local helm bypass. If you cannot take engineering, scuttle the ship and get off."

"What happens if we can't go wireless on the hack?" Lieutenant Travis asked.

Rika drew a deep breath. "That's one of the points where you make the scuttle-or-not decision. On the cruisers we'll have multiple teams at different breach points, so holding the physical network access point will be doable there. On the destroyers, you'll have to make the call. However, we don't need martyrs; if you can't take engineering, and you can't scuttle, do as much damage as possible, and then get off. Even if we take half the ships, the rest will have to come out and surrender, or spend the rest of their lives down there."

"Where will the *'Lark* and the *'Dream* be?" Heather asked.

"Once we breach, there won't be further need for subterfuge. They'll boost back. There are also two SAF cruisers on patrol near Armens, and they'll make for the planet, as well.

"Oh," Rika laughed and looked at the AIs. "Don't forget to change the ship's broadcast when you pull above the clouds. Don't want friendlies shooting at us."

Rika fielded several other questions before no more hands rose. "OK, people, get your mechs in the sims and start running your breach points. I want everyone in the company to be able to walk backwards blindfolded to any place on those ships."

She dismissed the company leadership, barring her HQ team.

"So, what do you think?" she asked. "Defending Hammerfall was just the warmup."

Barne chuckled as he leaned against the bulkhead. "You can say that again. The destroyers alone could carry as many troops as we faced at Hammerfall."

"Though they probably don't," Heather added.

Lieutenant Scarcliff nodded. "Smalls is right. The destroyers *could* carry a thousand, but a lot of those will be crew, not ground troops. They also won't be armored up when we hit."

"But they could be within minutes," Tex, the company's gunnery sergeant, added. "But I bet they won't use the same level of ordnance we will."

"Careful of that," Leslie advised. "Don't forget, the goal is to have these ships functional enough for the AIs to fly them out of Armens' atmosphere. If we shoot them to shit, chances are we'll blow away their network access, and this'll be a waste of time."

Tex grinned. "Well, we'll be sure to be all discriminate when it comes to what we shoot the shit out of. I bet it'll still be a hell of a lot more than they will."

"Granted." Scarcliff nodded. "I don't know about the rest of you, but I feel like I should be worried, yet somehow I'm not. Those Niets are going to shit themselves silly when they see a mech breach team hit their ships. Stars, I wish I was on The Van's assault team. Can you imagine seeing a K1R come around the corner on a starship?"

Barne barked a laugh. "It's gonna be classic. I'll be sure to record their expressions for you."

"Can't help but think you planned the assignments that way, Top."

Barne gave Scarcliff a roguish grin. "Who says I didn't? And who said you can call me 'Top'?"

"Barne, I'm the company's XO."

"So?"

GOODBYE BASILISK

STELLAR DATE: 08.19.8949 (Adjusted Gregorian)
LOCATION: ***Golden Lark***
REGION: Approaching Armens, Hercules System, Septhian Alliance

Rika stood in her office and couldn't keep her face from wearing a big, stupid grin. "You three mean so much to me…can you believe that we met just a half a year ago?"

Chase raised a finger. "I met you further back than that."

"Yeah, but not *too* much before that—minus my stint in cryo."

Chase shrugged. "Was over two years ago, actually."

Rika rolled her eyes. "I'm trying to be all poignant, here."

"You sure you know what that means?" Barne smirked.

Leslie smacked a palm into the back of Barne's head. Then she looked at Chase and smacked him as well. "Just like the boys, gotta ruin the moment."

"We're having a moment?" Barne asked. "I'm not kissing anyone."

"What about a hug?" Rika asked. "I know you're all badass and everything, but I don't think it would kill you to hug someone."

Chase chuckled and punched Barne in the shoulder. "Not sure about that. It might."

"Sheesh, why's everyone hitting me? And I hug plenty of people. Women. Right before I fuck their brains out."

"Ha!" Rika laughed. "There's the Barne we've all come to know and love."

"No love," Barne retorted. "That leads to hugging. Remember, no hugging unless I get to fuck your brains out, and you're both off-limits." He glared at Leslie and Rika as he spoke.

Leslie sidled up to Barne. "Why am I off-limits?"

"Les! Damn. Stop that! You're like fucking kryptonite. I could die if you touch me."

Leslie took a step back and cocked her head at Barne, then Rika. "Kryptonite? What the hell is that?"

Chase leaned close to Leslie and whispered loudly in her ear. "It means he finds you so damn attractive that he can barely function when you're around."

Halfway through Chase's explanation—which he delivered with a goofy smile plastered across his face—Barne yelled for him to stop, but Chase only raised his voice to carry over Barne's.

When he was done, Barne's face had darkened, and Leslie was staring at him with wide eyes.

"Seriously, Barne?" she asked.

Barne kept his eyes locked on Leslie's. "Well, you're the most attractive woman on the ship, it's perfectly natural to be attracted to a beautiful woman."

"What about the tail?" Leslie asked as her tail rose and touched Barne's neck.

"Leslie! Stop it! Seriously." Barne swatted her tail away. "We have to go on a mission. I can't have your sexy tail in my head the whole time."

Rika wasn't sure if Barne was playing with Leslie or not. He *did* sometimes make comments about how she was always slinking about. But the comments always seemed derisive, or at least critical.

Of course, that's exactly how someone would hide feelings they knew they shouldn't have.

Leslie pulled her tail down, a worried look on her face. <*Is he serious?*> she asked Rika privately.

<*Stars, I have no idea. It's Barne; this could be an elaborate ruse.*>

<*He wouldn't do something so cruel, would he?*>

Rika's eyes locked on Leslie's. <*Leslie. It's only cruel if you have feelings for him. Otherwise it's just tasteless.*>

<*Uh…yeah. Can we talk about this after we kill a whole bunch of Nietzscheans?*>

"OK," Rika said aloud. "Let's table whatever the hell just happened here and get our heads in the game. We have a job to do and a company to lead. We're going to get in there, secure ten core-damned starships, and kick the Niets in the teeth while we're at it."

Barne grunted. "Lots and lots of teeth kicking."

Everyone put a hand in the center of their small circle, and called out at the same time, "Rika's Marauders!"

Everyone except for Rika, who still said "Team Baslisk!"

Barne shook his head. "You really gotta get on board with that name."

"I…uh." Rika felt a flush rising on her cheeks. "OK, let's try it again."

They put their hands out again, and this time all four called out, "Rika's Marauders!" together.

Rika felt stupid and proud at the same time, but the expressions on her friends' faces filled her with confidence.

"OK, Marauders." Rika struggled to keep her expression stony. "Let's do this."

They filed out of Rika's office. At the first intersection where Barne and Leslie broke off for their drop bays. Rika and Chase paused, staring intently into one another's eyes.

"Good luck, Rika," Chase said. "I'll see you tomorrow."

"Tomorrow," Rika nodded.

They parted ways, each trying to focus on the mission ahead, but failing miserably.

INSERTION

STELLAR DATE: 08.19.8949 (Adjusted Gregorian)
LOCATION: *Golden Lark*
REGION: Approaching Armens, Hercules System, Septhian Alliance

Rika settled into her seat at the front of the dropship, and clipped the harness onto her hard points. She looked at the mechs seated on the benches, First Platoon's squad one, and nodded to them.

"Ready to kick the door in, Marauders?"

"Rika's Marauders!" Sergeant Aaron called out, generating a *Roo-ah!* from the rest of the mechs.

<Did some of them just say, Riii-ka, or are my ears playing tricks on me?> Rika asked Niki.

<They're not, almost half said some variation of your name.>

Rika held back a groan and glanced at Kelly who stat with her helmet on her lap, grinning at Rika. Kelly tapped her chest and Rika saw that Team Hammerfall's logo was still there, but below it was the Marauder's crest.

Rika gave Kelly a thumbs-up and shared a crazy smile with her old friend.

<I can't believe we're really doing this,> Kelly said privately. *<Remember back in the war, we used to say that the GAF should use mechs to take enemy ships? We could decimate them on the ground; on a starship, it would be like shooting fish in a barrel.>*

<I do recall a few conversations like that.> Rika nodded, smiling at the memory. *<I guess we'll get to see if we were right.>*

<Too bad Silva won't be here to see it.>

Rika felt the same way, but knew that Silva needed to be with her daughter, and her daughter needed to be with her mother.

<We'll send her a vid. She'll have to live vicariously through our ass kicking.>

<Oh, there will be vids. I'll be watching this mission when I'm old

and grey—when they've replaced my legs with training wheels.>

Rika laughed, and then Flight Leader Heather's voice came over the Link.

<*We're approaching the apex of the slingshot. If you pull up the external feeds, you'll see that we've dipped below the cloud tops. Dropships will begin boosting down the ladders in fifteen seconds. Good luck, Marauders.*>

Rika had already given her speeches. Everyone had their orders, and Niki had trained the AIs on the breach protocols. Once they dropped, communication would be minimal. From here on out, she was a soldier in a squad, focused on their one objective.

Good luck everyone.

The light at the front of the dropship went from red to green, and they fell through the deck and out of the ship.

"Goooood afternoon, squad one. We'd like to thank you for flying Air Shit-Storm; I'm your captain, Vargo Klen. The temperature outside is a chilly 120 degrees kelvin, but we expect to enter a warm band soon, where we'll see things creep up to a nice, comfy 320 degrees.

"If you activate your external feeds, you can see a lovely column of particulate ice off our starboard bow, and to port, it's raining ammonia. The inside of our grav shield is pressurized, so that scraping noise you hear is the planet's frozen atmosphere dragging along our shields."

"Klen!" Crunch hollered up to the cockpit. "Is that supposed to be comforting?"

"Why, thank you for the audience interaction. And yes, it is—at least when you consider that there's no planetary surface below us. If we experience any failures, we'll be crushed *long* before we fall the thirty-five thousand kilometers to Armens' liquid metallic hydrogen core."

Crunch looked like he was going to say something else, but only shook his head and sat back.

Klen continued his speech. "Our current flight path and

cruising speed has us looking at a nine-hour and thirty-seven-minute flight time, so may I suggest our inflight entertainment system otherwise known as staring at your teammates' helmets?"

"Man, someone needs to at least get us some good vids on this ride," Private Kerry groused. "If I have to stare at Ben's head this whole trip, It's gonna crack my viewscreen."

"Stow it," Sergeant Aaron grunted. "I don't want to have to listen to your shit the whole ride out."

"Sorry, Sarge," Kerry said, giving a thumbs-up. "Can I talk on the way back?"

"Maybe. We'll see how many Niets you kill."

The mechs spoke little for the rest of the ride, though Rika suspected that they were still chatting over the Link. Some would be reviewing the mission details and ship layout, others would be thinking and talking about anything *but* the mission.

The way the dropship bucked and rattled in the gas giant's winds, she bet a lot of the mechs were pretending to be anywhere else.

Whatever worked was fine by her. So long as when the dropship latched on, everyone got out by the numbers and covered their corners.

Rika had a visual of their progress overlaid on her vision. She kept an eye on it, as the thirty-four dropships slowly crept toward the Nietzschean ships at what felt like an agonizingly slow pace.

The dropships were successfully maintaining their formation, pinging one another periodically on a shifting ULF band. Rika breathed a sigh of relief, as the second check-in passed, and the ships were all still in formation.

Other than a rogue lightning strike, the initial entry was the most dangerous part of the journey. If they'd made it this far, they'd make it to the Niets, no problem.

Then the real fun would begin.

Rika was with the team assigned to the enemy cruiser dubbed 'Big Daddy'. It was larger than the others, nearly four kilometers long, and three whole squads were assigned to it.

Squad one, present in the dropship with Rika, would breach an airlock near the rear of the ship, while squads two and three would land amidships, and break up by fireteams once inside to harass the enemy and disrupt any assistance that may be sent back to engineering.

Rika lost track of time—deliberately keeping her eyes from the countdown. It seemed to work, because when Klen announced that they were on their final descent to the Nietzschean ships' altitude, it took her by surprise.

The message came from Heather's dropship that she'd sent out the signal to the SAF; a minute later live scan data began to flow in from orbiting military satellites.

The Niets would detect the scan, but Rika would bet her life they wouldn't expect what was coming next.

"We're seven hundred kilometers and closing," Klen announced. "Expect some turbulence as we pass through the enemies' shield, and please make sure you take all your weapons with you and kick some ever-lovin' Nietzschean ass!"

A chorus of shouts met Klen's proclamation, and Rika pulled up the view from the nose of the dropship, hoping for a visual of the Nietzschean cruiser.

Unfortunately, all she could see were the dark clouds surrounding them, punctuated by periodic flashes of lightning.

Then the enemy cruiser pushed through the clouds, and the dropship spun and fired its engines, lurching, and jostling the mechs about.

"Mind the bump," Klen cautioned. "We've just passed through their shield. Bringing us in toward our landing site."

Rika could barely see a thing on optical, but on IR, the ship glowed brightly against the dull red of the surrounding clouds.

"Damn, that sucker's hot," Klen commented, breaking out of his pilot's drawl for once. "They'll have to rise up to higher altitudes soon—seems like they can't disperse enough heat down here."

"We'll see if we can't help them with that," Rika replied. "I hear space is pretty cool."

"Too cool—well, too lacking in matter to transfer energy to. When you guys bring those ships up, you should try to do it slowly, with the cooling vanes deployed all the way."

<*Noted,*> Niki replied.

"I have a visual on the other two ships, they're latching on," Klen called back. "We're touching down in three, two, one."

The pilot's statement was punctuated by a dull *thud,* and then the rear hatch on the dropship opened, mechs rushing into the darkness without hesitation.

Rika was last out, and she felt a wave push her upward, off the ship, a moment before her maglocks kicked in and pulled her back down.

<*Did they just try to push us off the hull with a grav wave?*> she asked Niki.

<*Seems like it. I've advised Klen to activate the dropship's weld-grapple.*>

<*Good call.*>

A burst of beamfire came from a nearby point defense cannon, splashing against the dropship's shields.

<*Better late than never. Must have bled off its charge in the heat,*> Sergeant Aaron said. <*One-one, go take that thing out.*>

Ben and Al—who had both been with Rika that fateful night when they defeated the Politica—were joined by Harris and Kim. They each took aim, stepped through the dropship's shield, and fired in unison.

Aaron nodded with satisfaction. <*Clear any other nearby turrets, one-one. You're going to keep our exit, and the dropship, safe. One-two, get that airlock open.*>

The airlock was five meters from where Klen had set the dropship down, and one-two set to their task, planting a pair of shaped charges on either side of the door's center seam.

<*Fire in the deep!*> Crunch called out. The explosion flared brightly, and the airlock doors bent inward. Crunch and Shoshin, who had recovered fully from his prior injuries, slammed their

feet into the airlock doors, caving them in the rest of the way.

Rika's external pickups detected a high-pitch whistle, and she realized it was the planet's atmosphere, pushing into the ship.

That's a change. Hope they like hydrogen.

Crunch and Shoshin dropped down into the airlock to attach explosives on the inner door, as fireteam one-one took out another surface turret to Rika's right.

Rika tried to reach out to the dropships assaulting the other ships and found that it was as they'd suspected. With the planet's interference, and the Nietzschean ship's shields, the assault teams couldn't communicate with one another.

She did connect with squads two and three; both were already moving into the ship and had pulled some rudimentary data from its network. Foremost of which was that the ship they were attacking was the *Fury Lance.* Rika was tempted to still think of it as the *Big Daddy,* but updated the combat net with the correct name to avoid confusion.

Another explosion shuddered through the planet's thick atmosphere, and she saw its cloudy air rush into the ship. The lock was breached.

Fireteams two and three formed up around the airlock while fireteam four held back, just in case anything untoward happened.

<*Dropping probes,*> Kelly announced over the combat net.

Two tiny probes flew out of Kelly's back and dropped down through the airlock. The outer doors had been smashed inward, and the inner seal—a solid disk that rolled into place—was folded over at the middle, just barely making enough room for the AM-3s in the squad.

Rika was glad that she didn't have to worry about getting a K1R through the ship. The Van wouldn't fit through this airlock, even if they'd opened it without explosives.

Kelly's probes flew into the passageway beyond the entrance, and noted likely locations of auto turrets—though why they hadn't deployed was curious.

The passageway ended in a T, and the probes split up, each travelling to the next intersections and stopping to keep an eye on all approaches.

<*One-two, get in there,*> Sergeant Aaron ordered.

<*With pleasure,*> Kelly said and jumped into the airlock.

The rest of the fireteam followed, and then Aaron leapt in after them.

Rika deployed one of her own probes to keep an eye on the fireteam from the rear. She pulled up feeds from second and squad three, which were relayed from their dropships to Klen's, and then to her.

The other squads had already met resistance, but in the form of unarmored crew, barely even worth reporting.

<*The Niets' reaction is surprisingly slow,*> Niki noted.

<*They weren't expecting this sort of attack. No one does crazy shit like this.*>

<*I get that they had the cannons and turrets powered down, they were cutting back on energy use to keep the ships from overheating, but to have so little crew on duty? It doesn't make sense.*>

Rika considered the possibilities. <*Think maybe they're in cryo? Net energy use when in cryo is a lot less than a person up and about, eating, moving around, whatever…*>

<*Plus waste. Ships use a lot of power dealing with human leftovers.*>

Rika nodded absently as she watched third and fourth fireteams slip into the airlock. She looked to her right where one-one was ranging across the ship's hull, destroying surface cannons—most before they even came online.

<*One-one, keep in visual range of the dropship. If we can't see them, they can't shoot at us.*>

<*You got it, Skipper,*> Ben replied. <*Just one more that could hit the top of the shuttle, then we'll fall back. Probes are out, so we'll see their ugly asses before they see ours.*>

<*Good job, Corporal. Keep in cover, two in the airlock, and two in the dropship. They could try to push us off again, or maybe even drop their shields. You don't want to be in the open, if that happens.*>

<Shit, no we don't,> Ben grunted. *<We really don't. Double-time it, Whispers. Take out that last gun so we can stop being ants in a windstorm.>*

Rika looked up at the dark clouds surrounding the *Fury Lance.* Though two atmospheres of pressure had seeped through the ship's shields, there was a lot more out there.

Not to mention winds that screamed like howling banshees. Crazy as it sounded, she looked forward to the refuge of an enemy starship.

Rika set the feeds from her squad on the left side of her vision, and the feeds from the other two squads along the right side and bottom. Fifty-six layered squares surrounded the view before her, and Rika set combat detection alerts on them.

Satisfied that she could watch the entire breach with minimal obstruction to what lay around her, Rika jumped into the airlock and joined her Marauders in the storming of the *Fury Lance.*

THE FURY LANCE

STELLAR DATE: 08.19.8949 (Adjusted Gregorian)
LOCATION: ***The Fury Lance***
REGION: Within Armens, Hercules System, Septhian Alliance

Kelly was on point, with Crunch and Shoshin covering her six. She'd killed a dozen Niets so far; four of them had been unarmored, and she'd dispatched them without a second thought.

On closer inspection, two of those didn't even have weapons, but she wasn't going to wait for them to fire at her to see if they had malicious intent.

The only good Niet was a dead Niet.

Her fireteam was on a direct route to the network access point that Niki needed to reach, while the others were taking parallel passages, on the lookout for flanking maneuvers from the enemy.

Kelly's probes rounded a corner ahead and caught a view of several Niets in powered armor—a moment later, the feed went dead.

<EM hit the probes. Saw…six. On the right.>

<We got it,> Crunch said as he passed Kelly with Shoshin on his tail. She turned to cover the rear, letting the heavier mechs do what they did best.

Crunch eased up to the corner, glanced back at Shoshin, and raised his KE-72, toggling the grenade launcher.

He fired a trio of grenades that bounced off the wall and disappeared around the corner, at the same moment that three came back.

Kelly had a moment of confusion, wondering how the Niets had kicked the 'nades back so fast, before she realized they had used the exact same tactic at the same time.

Crunch screamed something, and dove to the side as the grenades detonated. The force of the explosion picked Kelly up and threw her back to the last intersection they'd passed.

She scrambled to her feet, sending out more probes while cycling her vision to see through the fire and smoke that filled the corridor.

She made out the shapes of Crunch and Shoshin and rushed toward them, but Crunch waved her off as he struggled to his feet.

<*Clear the intersection, we're OK…I think.*>

Kelly nodded and walked past, JE-87 in her right hand, angling her GNR-40E on her left arm to get a clear shot at anyone who showed a body part around the corner.

She spared a glance at Shoshin as she passed him. He looked OK, though his faceplate was cracked, and the ablative plating on his right side was almost entirely gone. Poor guy was having the worst luck, lately.

Focus, Kelly!

She didn't want to waste a probe, in case their EM source was still functional. Instead, she drew in a deep breath and then leapt across the intersection, firing at any shapes she could discern through the smoke.

Something moved on the left side of the passage, and it got a trio of projectile rounds from her GNR. Another shape got a burst from her JE-87, and then another burst from her GNR hit a third shape.

She landed and ducked behind the bulkhead, waiting for return fire, but none came.

Movement to her right caught Kelly's attention, and she nodded to Crunch and Shoshin as they eased up to the intersection. Crunch had a slight limp, and she hoped it wasn't enough to slow him down.

Crunch was an RR-3, and unlike earlier RR models, the 3's had leg stubs like SMIs—which meant they could suffer injury to their thighs and hips. Unlike Shoshin, who no longer possessed organic limbs.

<*You sure you're good?*> she asked Crunch.

<*Good enough to kill—shit!*>

An electron beam streaked down the corridor and struck something behind Kelly. She spun around to see a Niet in heavy armor fall to the deck, his neck half burned away.

<*Stay frosty, people,*> Rika said as she emerged from the smoke behind Crunch and Shoshin. <*Looks like the Niets are starting to get their shit together.*>

<*Yeah, frosty,*> Kelly said, shaking her head. <*Warn a girl before you do that again.*>

<*You snooze, you get the shit scared out of you,*> Rika replied, waving Kelly on.

Kelly eased around the corner and walked past the six Niets who'd tried to take them out. One was moving, and she fired a round into the woman's head without remorse.

Die, bitch.

With Rika bringing up the rear, the fireteam made it the rest of the way to the network access point without further incident.

Kelly rounded the last corner to see Kerry and the rest of one-three waiting for them at the NAP's entrance.

<*What took you so long? Find an ice cream shop or something?*> Kerry asked.

<*Yeah, your mom was running it, so I got her to make a double-dip sundae. You want one?*>

<*Hey, don't be touching my mom's sundae!*>

<*Cut the chatter,*> Sergeant Aaron growled as he approached with one-four.

Kelly took a corner at an intersection twenty meters from the NAP and nodded to Rika as she passed.

<*Give em' hell, Chief,*> she said to Niki.

<*Always do,*> the AI replied.

Kelly sent a probe down each of the two corridors she was covering and tucked each into corners, hoping they'd stay safe. She only had five more, and this party was just getting started.

*****

<*I like Kelly,*> Niki commented as Rika approached the door to the network access point. <*She's boss.*>

< *'Boss'?*> Rika asked. <*What does that mean?*>

< *'Boss', adjective, meaning excellent, outstanding.*>

Rika stopped at the door and grunted. <*Huh, never heard that definition before.*>

<*You've lived a sheltered life.*>

<*Is that what you call it?*>

Niki laughed. <*Well, I guess not. Drop some nano on the access panel so I can walk through this thing.*>

Rika complied, while Niki muttered, <*Stars, I wish you had better nano. Would make some things a lot easier.*>

<*Better nano?*> Rika asked. <*I guess* **some** *people might have better, but this is top-of-the-line stuff.*>

<*Really, Rika? You do know that Praesepe is a backwater, right? In the core, children have better nano than you.*>

Children with advanced nano seemed like very bad idea to Rika. <*How do their parents deal with that?*>

<*They have even better nano than their kids.*>

Rika was suddenly very happy that she was not fighting against the core worlds. *Thank stars the Hegemony of Worlds is eight-hundred light years away.*

<*OK, door opening in one…two…dammit, that's not—*>

The door slid open, and Niki let out a whoop as Rika entered.

<*I thought you were having trouble?*>

<*I was, but I can solve problems a lot faster than I can talk to you.*>

Rika ignored the jibe and looked around the room…which wasn't a room at all. She stood on a catwalk encircling the center of a ten-meter by ten-meter shaft that dropped deep into the ship.

Rika leant over the edge and saw that the bottom of the shaft lay almost a hundred meters below; the top was another sixty up.

In front of them was a five-meter cube, with conduit streaming out of it to points on the walls around them and stretching down the shaft to another cube far below.

"This is not what I was expecting," Rika said aloud.

<*Quiet, it's listening.*>

< *'It'? The cube?*>

<*Yeah, this is one of the NSAI's nodes.*>

Rika raised her GNR. <*Can I just shoot it?*>

<*No! We need to access it, not blow it up. NSAIs on ships like this are multi-nodal. Take out one, and it just reroutes. We're here to poison it.*>

<*What do you need me to do?*> Rika asked.

<*I need you to take your direct connect cable and plug it into the port on the console over there.*>

<*You want me to plug into this thing?*> She had imagined just connecting to some secure panel somewhere. Connecting to the NSAI seemed like a very bad idea.

<*Yeah, this is what we came here to do; you got that, right?*>

<*I did—do. But this is somehow more ominous than I thought it would be.*>

<*Don't worry, you're triple-buffered from what I'm doing. Remember, Carson added in additional firewalls.*>

Rika drew in a deep breath and approached the console. <*What about you?*>

<*Me? It's an NSAI, not a core devil. I'll be fine.*>

<*What's a core devil?*>

<*Nothing,*> Niki dissembled. <*Just a crazy rumor that never seems to go away.*>

Despite their promise to be open with one another, Niki seemed to constantly have more secrets that she'd allude to and never share. Rika knew the AI didn't make slip-ups, so Niki was doing it on purpose.

Is it just to goad me into something? she wondered.

Rika pulled out the hard-Link cable and plugged into the socket Niki had highlighted. The cable was only a half-meter long, so she was stuck here for however long this took.

<*OK, starting my game of cat and mouse,*> Niki announced.

While Niki did her work, Rika checked over the other two squads' progress through the ship.

Kristian's squad two had taken some hits—only minor injuries, though. They seemed to be drawing the most Niets, likely due to the presence of The Van. Nothing like having a K1R-T stomp through your ship to make you pull out all the stops.

Third squad, which had Staff Sergeant Chris accompanying it, was nearly at the engineering bay. Rika saw that one of the AM-2s, a PFC named Kyle that everyone in the platoon called 'Goob', had taken a hit to the torso. He was still alive, but his armor had initiated an emergency coma. CJ and Yig had pulled his limbs off and were taking turns carrying him.

They were meeting with increasing resistance, and Rika was considering peeling off a fireteam from her squad to assist them, when Niki started swearing profusely.

<Awwww, shitty mcfuckface, this is bad. Fucking bad. Clusterfuck bad.>

<Niki, spit it out!>

<They patched the loop—well, at least the best trigger for it. Without that, there's only a minute to attempt the takedown. It's not long enough!>

<Then we have to scuttle,> Rika replied, reaching for the hard-Link cable.

<No, wait! I might be able to figure something out, but we'll need to get it to the other breach teams.>

Rika groaned. *<You mean the breach teams on the other ships that we can't currently talk to?>*

<Yeah, those breach teams. Shut up for a minute, will you?>

Rika wondered if they could relay the updated data to Klen, or if someone would need to take it up to him.

As she was considering her options, something pinged off the catwalk, and Rika realized someone had fired on her from below. She circled her drone around and saw five Niets on a catwalk, twenty meters below and moving to get a good firing angle on her.

<Aaron, I've got Roaches crawling around down below. Can you take them out?>

The squad sergeant sent a quick affirmation, and a moment later, two RR mechs dashed through the open door and leapt off the catwalk, firing as they fell. Rika watched them take out a Niet each on the way down, then land on two others.

Ten seconds later the five Niets were dead, and the RRs took up positions on either side of the lower catwalk's door, ready to take out any other enemies.

<*Nicely done,*> Rika couldn't help but smile at the mechs' calm efficiency.

<*Thanks, Skipper,*> one of the RRs, a corporal named Mitch, replied.

<*OK! I got it!*> Niki announced. <*As I'd hoped, their patch solved just one avenue of attack, not the core problem. I was able to leverage another vulnerability and get in. How are we going to get it to the other AIs?*>

<*Can we transmit it to Klen?*> Rika asked.

<*Yeah, it's not a big burst…though if the NSAI sniffs it out and cracks it, the hack won't work anymore.*>

<*We have to chance it,*> Rika replied. <*Running a datapod up to the dropship will take too long.*>

<*OK, sending to Klen's ship.*>

Rika sucked in a deep breath and got ready for what she was about to ask the pilot to do.

<*Vargo, how's it looking up there?*>

<*Great, Captain. Kim, Harris, and I are having afternoon tea. Had to fight off a drone attack first, though. How're things downstairs?*>

<*We had a setback with the NSAI hack, but Niki worked out a solution.*>

<*Good to hear. Why are you pinging me?*> Klen's voice carried a note of wariness, and Rika suspected he already knew what she was about to ask.

<*The other AIs are going to need this data. Niki has pushed it up into your comm stack; you need to get out there and deliver the data burst to each breach team.*>

There was a brief pause, then Klen replied. <*Understood,*

Captain Rika. I assume I should kick my guests out?>

<Yes, I'll instruct them to meet up with us. You need to go now.>

<Aye, Captain. I'll be back for the pickup, don't you worry.>

Rika prayed he would. Once he started broadcasting the signal to the other teams, he'd make himself a target for every Niet ship out there. *<I know you will. See you on the flip-side.>*

<You bet. You're buying too, Captain.>

<Damn straight, I am.>

Klen cut the connection, and Rika pulled a feed from Kim's helmet. The dropship cut its weld-grapple free and lifted from the *Fury Lance*. A beam shot out from a point-defense cannon, but was bent around the dropship by the vessel's grav shield.

Then the thrusters fired, and the Marauder dropship shot out of the relatively calm air within the *Fury Lance's* shields and passed out into Armens' raging storms.

Good luck, Marauder.

Rika briefly ensured that one-one was making their way toward the rest of squad one before returning her attention to Niki.

<The console here is showing errors in the node,> she said. *<I take it that's a good thing?>*

<Yeah,> Niki's response was curt. *<Tight timing, here. Shush.>*

Rika sighed and returned to monitoring her various teams. Second squad had slowed to a crawl, but their goal was to cause chaos—which they were excelling at.

However, squad three wasn't doing much better. They were still fifty meters from the engineering bay, and were fighting flanking attempts by the Niets at every turn. Staff Sergeant Chris was out of commission, a series of chest wounds placing him in an armor-coma, as well.

Rika considered sending one-one to assist them, but they would take too long.

<Crunch, how's the leg?> Rika asked.

<Good 'nuf, Captain. Shoshin is a miracle worker with a brace, though I can't say I'll ever be as pretty as I once was. What's up?>

Rika remembered all too well what it was like to get an internal brace jammed into her thigh. It was the furthest thing from fun she could think of. *<Link up with Sergeant Karen and squad three. They're getting hung up, and we need them in that engineering bay in five mikes, tops.>*

<You got it, Captain. Run and gun is the name of the game.>

<Aaron,> Rika addressed squad one's sergeant. *<I'm lending one-two to Karen.>*

<No problem, Captain. She always did need an extra hand.>

<Be nice, Sergeant.>

Weapons fire echoed down the corridor and through the entrance to the shaft.

<I'm always nice,> Aaron grunted in response a minute later.

* * * * *

Kelly ranged ahead of Crunch and Shoshin, keeping her eyes peeled for Niets and firing indiscriminately at any she saw. She followed her probes around a corner and shot a woman in the head, then slammed a man against the bulkhead, crushing his neck.

A door down the passageway opened, and a Niet appeared with a rocket launcher. He wasn't armored, and would kill himself in the explosion, but Kelly had no interest in dodging missiles. She took aim, and fired a uranium sabot round at him.

The round struck the end of the rocket launcher, and shrapnel showered the man, tearing him apart.

<Nice shooting,> Crunch said as he came up behind her.

<Couldn't let you get all hurt again, Corporal,> Kelly said with a smirk that he couldn't see behind her helmet.

Weapons fire came from behind, and Kelly turned to see Shoshin unloading his chaingun on a group of Niets that had tried to flank the team. The enemy ducked behind a bulkhead, but it wasn't enough to save them.

Shoshin's gun tore through the plas and steel, and Kelly saw blood spray out onto one of the walls.

<*Clear,*> Shoshin grunted.

The team resumed their mad dash through the ship until they came to a broad concourse that ran down the center of the vessel.

It was thirty meters wide, and at least two kilometers long. They stood on a catwalk, seven meters above the deck, with the overhead a broad arch, fifteen meters over their heads.

The center of the concourse was occupied by four maglev tracks, a stopped train occupying one of them.

Two of squad three's fireteams were hunkered down next to the train, trading fire with a group of heavily armored Niets with CFT and grav shields on the far side of the concourse. Squad three's other fireteam was working their way down the concourse, toward a staircase that led down to the engineering bay one deck below.

Squad three's firing angles were terrible, with the maglev tracks giving the Niets plenty of cover. One-two, on the other hand, had a clear view of the enemy, who had not yet spotted them, thanks to an EM flare that Karen had thrown moments ago.

Crunch signaled for Kelly and Shoshin to spread out. When each member of one-two was a dozen meters from the next, they opened fire on the Niets.

Kelly let her electron beam fire on max power, burning away CFT shields, and shorting out grav generators with the bolts of lightning that arced out as she raked it across the enemy line.

Shoshin followed after with his chaingun, filling the air with HE shells that tore through the Niets.

Crunch fired two missiles at a cluster of Niets that had taken cover behind a low bulwark alongside the tracks. Plas and steel flew into the air, exposing the enemy to Shoshin's guns.

Below, the elements of squad three that were behind the train rose up and rushed the remaining Niets, cutting them down as the enemy attempted to flee.

<*Thanks for the assist,*> Karen sent, as she directed two of her fireteams to take the stairs down on the far side of the tracks,

while she led her team down the stairs on the near side.

<*No problem. There were only seventeen of you down there, I can see why you needed the three of us to help,*> Crunch said with a coarse laugh.

<*You always have to be such an ass?*> Karen shot back.

<*Umm…yeah, Sarge. It was in my contract.*>

<*Just hold position up there and keep any more Niets off our backs.*>

<*Easy peasy, Sarge.*>

Kelly looked around the concourse for a location with good cover, and her eyes were drawn to the arches that supported the ceiling. <*Going to take overwatch up there,*> she gestured at the nearest arch.

<*Looks good,*> Crunch replied. <*Shoshin, get over to that far catwalk. We'll set up a field of fire on anyone who thinks they can come along for a look-see.*>

<*All teams, be advised. Ship's NSAI is offline. I repeat, the NSAI is offline,*> Niki announced over the combat net. <*I have control of the engines and am initializing warmup. We'll be boosting out of here in t-minus fifteen mikes.*>

<*Knew she could do it,*> Kelly said to the team as she swung up onto a strut and shimmied up to the overhead arch.

<*Well yeah; Captain Rika wouldn't have taken the job if there was any doubt.*>

<*There's always doubt,*> Shoshin said.

Kelly rolled her eyes at the man, then realized he couldn't see it through her helmet, so she sent him an image of her rolling her eyes at him over the Link.

<*Mature,*> he replied.

<*Glad you've noticed.*>

STEALING STARSHIPS

STELLAR DATE: 08.19.8949 (Adjusted Gregorian)
LOCATION: ***The Fury Lance***
REGION: Within Armens, Hercules System, Septhian Alliance

<*Engines are warming up, and I have helm,*> Niki announced as Rika leant over the railing and fired at the entrance on the level below, aiding the two RRs down there in stemming the never-ending flow of Niets.

<*Great. Can you lock down parts of the ship? This place is still crawling with enemies!*>

<*I've locked down as much as I can, but they pulled a lot of their soldiers out of cryo—you were right about that, by the way. Nearly everyone was on ice. Anyway, their troops are blowing through everything I close.*>

<*What about grav? Can you try messing up gravity on their decks?*>

Rika got a mental image of Niki shaking her head. <*No, their grav emitters have limits of 1.2g relative. It's hardwired into them.*>

<*How many enemies are you tracking?*> she asked.

<*Seven hundred and forty-six soldiers. There are still over two-hundred crew throughout the ship, but the ones that are left are either at duty stations, or hiding.*>

Rika considered her options. Fighting through over seven hundred Niets wasn't impossible, but it would be a brutal slog.

<*Can you get on their 1MC?*>

<*Yeah, but what are you going to say?*>

Rika didn't answer. Instead she turned to Sergeant Aaron, who was reloading in the shaft's doorway.

"Sergeant, there are seven hundred Nietzschean soldiers out of cryo now. If you were them, what would your main goal be?"

Aaron laughed. "Escape pods. Think they can break free of Armens' gravity well?"

"Seriously, Sergeant."

"They need helm control. They're all going to head for engineering."

That was Rika's summation, as well.

"We need to stop that from happening. If they mass, they could take us."

"Then we should go for the bridge and draw some of their force along with us," Aaron suggested.

Rika nodded. "I like where your head's at, Sergeant."

He fired around the corner and laughed. "Me too."

<*Form up, squad one. We're moving out,*> Rika said before detaching the hard-Link cable from the console.

<*Hey! How did you know that was OK to do?*>

<*Because you didn't say anything about us not being able to go to the bridge.*>

<*Oh.*>

<*Kristian, are you and squad two having fun?*> Rika called the platoon sergeant.

<*Gobs, Captain. It's like my favorite holiday every thirty seconds. Nietsdeadday.*>

<*Clever.*>

<*Thanks, been working on it for a bit. We're running a bit low on ammo, and The Van's taken some serious hits, but he's still kicking.*>

<*Good. I've updated the combat net with the enemies Niki is tracking throughout the ship. Should give us some help, but they can fool their internal sensors just as much as we can, so don't trust it too much.*>

<*Understood. You want us to go somewhere?*>

Rika stepped aside as the two RRs on the lower level jumped back up before replying. <*We're going to push to the bridge—we need to draw as many of these bastards away from engineering as we can. I need you to get to that big, long concourse that runs through the ship. They may try to send trains filled with troops down to hit Karen.*>

<*Or trains filled with bombs,*> Sergeant Kristian added.

<*Yeah, that too.*>

<*Count on us, we'll keep Karen safe.*>

<*Good luck, Sergeant.*>

<*Don't need luck. I have Rika's Marauders with me.*>

Rika groaned and closed the connection. She surveyed squad one's status. Kelly, Crunch, and Shoshin were still absent, covering the entrance to engineering, hopefully with backup before long.

Fireteam one had arrived a minute earlier, and other than a few disabled limbs and minor flesh wounds, squad one was ready to roll.

<*Route's up on the combat net,*> Rika announced. <*Aaron, roll 'em out.*>

<*You got it, Captain.*>

The mechs surged forward, alternating suppressive fire with heavy weapons bursts that cut through the enemy's ranks. Corridor by corridor, one threat-laden intersection after another, they cleared a path toward the bridge.

There were several pitched fights in open spaces where the Niets were able to mass and bring superior firepower to bear, but the enemy seemed ill equipped to deal with mechs that could jump a dozen meters in the air and land behind their lines.

After seven minutes, squad one had made it far enough forward that Rika was ready to let the Niets know what she was doing.

"Nietzschean scumbags, this is Captain Rika of the Marauders," she announced over the 1MC. "We'd like to thank you for hosting us today, and dying so easily. We have engine control and we have helm, but there's still a lot of you pesky bastards aboard. So I figure it's best to work from the top down.

"Ship's logs show captain as a Commander Kiers. Well, Commander, hope to see you soon. Keep your seat on the bridge warm for me."

<*Nicely done. Just enough cocky,*> Niki commented.

<*Cocky? I was being sincere.*>

<*Oh.*>

"I liked it," Aaron grunted as he checked a room on the squad's right. <*Clear. Keep moving.*>

<Niki, any chance you have scan, yet? I'd really like to see how all the other ships are doing. Getting worried about Klen.>

<Not yet, their scan and weapons are on segregated systems. I'm trying to work my way in, but they've initialized some new NSAIs that are slowing me down. They have the same vulns as the other one, so they're toppling one-by-one, but it's taking time.>

Rika peered up a ladder and fired on a shape above before sidestepping to avoid return fire. *<OK, let me know as soon as you have it.>*

<Yes, Mom. If you get the bridge, you can hold a gun to some poor Niet's head and make him run scan.>

<Good idea,> Rika set a two second fuse and tossed a grenade up the ladder shaft.

Flames shot down behind her as she moved to the head of the group. Just seven-hundred meters of ship to go, and she'd get to see if Niki's idea would work.

*****

<I see another group working their way forward,> Kelly called down to the fireteam.

She sighted down the concourse, watching the group of Niets advance along the maglev track. There were ten of them; two in heavy armor, three in lighter armor, and five in nothing but cloth uniforms.

Idiots all have death wishes.

The heavies were in front, protecting the others, and Kelly considered her options. She only had two DPU rounds, just over sixty projectiles for her GNR, and enough charge for two electron beam shots—*if* she kept the bursts short—plus a cluster of 'nades, and over a dozen mags for her JE-87.

Second squad better get here soon.

She selected her best option and fired a DPU round at the maglev rail beside the advancing Niets. The uranium rod shattered against the track and sprayed shrapnel into the unarmored enemies.

The heavies stopped and looked back. Kelly watched Crunch peek out from behind a vertical column and fire on the backs of the Niets. Kelly added to his attack, and the two heavies fell.

They made short work of the rest.

<At some point, they're going to give up, right?> Kelly asked.

The sound of Shoshin's chaingun came from her left, and she turned to see him firing on a group further aft that was well entrenched behind a derailed train.

<Karen's going to send up three-four to spell us, but they're taking a lot of fire down there, too. These Niets really are just like cockroaches.>

<I don't need spelling, I just need ammo.>

<When three-four gets back up here, we should scavenge the battlefield,> Shoshin suggested.

<Use Niet guns?> Kelly asked. *<Might as well throw rocks at them.>*

Crunch laughed. *<Well, at least it wouldn't be any worse than what they're using.>*

<Cold comfort, Crunch,> Kelly replied.

Shoshin gave a single laugh. *<Nice alliteration.>*

Kelly spotted something down the concourse, near the end, and cycled her vision, zooming in. It looked as though there was some sort of smoke or fog gathering.

Then she magnified further.

<Shit! Drones!>

<What?> Crunch called out.

<The Niets set their space-combat drones loose in here!>

Kelly tried to count the number of drones, but there were so many and they were moving so fast that she couldn't manage. There had to be over a hundred, though—maybe more.

Crunch fired on the leading wave. *<Damn…those things are coming in fast!>*

Kelly didn't reply, but started taking aim at the drones with her GNR, lobbing her projectile rounds.

<It's no good! They have shields, I can't penetrate!>

<*Get down from there,*> Crunch ordered, and Kelly obliged by dropping down to the train car below and sliding behind it.

Shoshin was firing on the drones with his chaingun, and Kelly set the timer on a 'nade and chucked it at the incoming bots.

It exploded midair, taking out two of the drones, but that was just a scratch.

<*Having fun?*> CJ said as she crouched next to Kelly and fired a missile at the drones.

<*Where'd you get that?*>

<*From the Niets, they were very accommodating.*>

Kelly didn't have time to be relieved, as the drones opened fire on the Marauders, laying down a withering blanket of beams and kinetics.

The maglev rail beside Kelly was torn to shreds, and to her left, one of the support columns buckled and collapsed. She looked up and watched the arch she had been perched on moments earlier pull free of the overhead and fall toward her.

Shit! I'm not dying again!

*****

The *Fury Lance* had two doors to its bridge, both emptying out onto a broad foyer, which was strewn with the bodies of over two-dozen dead Niets.

Rika looked to her right, where Aaron helped Kim sit up so he could apply biofoam to a hole in her stomach while she kept repeating that she was ok, she could still fight.

"Of course you can, Private. Once we put your insides back where they belong, I expect you to pull a trigger just like the rest of us."

"Put it in my hand, Sarge, I got it," Kim grunted out between rasping gasps.

Rika clenched her jaw and stepped over a fallen Niet on her way to the bridge. She slammed a fist into the starboard door and called out over the 1MC.

"Better get in your escape pods. We're coming in, and we're gonna grind you to pieces. You're no match for the Marauders."

"Rika's Marauders!" someone called out wearily from behind her.

Rika looked back at her Marauders and nodded before turning back to the bridge. "Surrender, or prepare to meet your maker…or find your star, or whatever you fucks believe in."

<Ready to fire the engines,> Niki announced. *<We'll be out of Armen's atmosphere in five minutes.>*

<Thanks, Niki. Don't pull us out yet, though. I don't want to leave anyone behind. We're last out.>

<Got it.>

No response came from within the bridge.

<Are they still in there, Niki?>

<Yeah, there are…ten of them. They're all hunkered down behind consoles. They have handguns. One rifle.>

Rika piggybacked on Niki's visuals from the ship's internal cameras. *<Damn…maybe I scared them all too much.>*

<Perhaps.>

"Last chance to surrender! We don't kill hostages."

No one on the bridge moved, which was impressive in and of itself.

Not that their bravado would buy them any mercy.

Rika nodded to Ben and Whispers to take the door down.

<As non-lethal as we can,> she advised. *<I'd like their captain and some crew, in case we need them to push some buttons.>*

Acknowledgements lit up on her HUD, and Rika calmed her breathing. This was it. *Take the bridge, force the surrender of everyone aboard, win the day.*

Ben and Al were out of explosives, but two pairs of mech-fingers prised the door open, and then heaved the two halves back, tearing them right out of the frame. Four mechs flooded through the opening, laying down pulse fire and fists. Aaron and another four followed, and five seconds later, the 'all clear' came.

Rika walked onto the bridge and saw that two of the crew

were dead, several were down, and Commander Kiers was writhing in Kerry's grasp, his feet a dozen centimeters off the floor.

"Commander Kiers," Rika said in greeting. "I've been looking forward to this for...oh, about half an hour, now."

"Fucking mech-meat. You'll never take the *Fury Lance*!"

Rika glanced at the mechs around her as they secured the command crew. "Does he know something we don't?"

Ben shrugged. "Doubtful. We could still kill him."

"Our drones wiped out the rest of your force. It's just you, now," Commander Kiers raged.

"You mean the drones you sent down the concourse to take back engineering?" Rika asked.

The commander nodded, but his expression changed to one of worry.

"Yeah, our AI got control of them just in the *nick* of time. It was a close call. Then she used them to cut your troops to ribbons. Thanks for giving us what we needed to wrap this up quickly."

Kiers yelled something unintelligible and began to struggle again.

Rika shook her head. "Restrain him and toss him in the corner over there. I want him to watch while we seize or destroy his fleet."

<*Wait,*> Niki called out. <*Get some nano on him first. I want to see if I can get his command tokens; it would make running this ship a lot easier.*>

Rika complied, then turned to the holotank at the front of the bridge. It was only displaying the crest of the Nietzschean military, but she found it hard to believe that the commander hadn't been trying to communicate with his other ships after his own came under attack. She hit the 'recall command' sequence, and the last scan data appeared before her.

Rika nearly crowed with delight.

Three of the destroyers were already breaking out of the clouds, and two cruisers were hot on their tail. One cruiser was falling deeper into Armens, but two Marauder dropships were visible, flying away from it.

The other ships—four cruisers and one destroyer—were still holding their course, but this data was a minute old.

<*Got it!*> Niki called out triumphantly. <*Scan updating!*>

The holotank flickered, and now two more cruisers were rising out of the clouds, while the final destroyer began to fall. Rika felt her breath catch—it was the ship Chase was on.

She was about to issue the command for Niki to dive after it, when the Marauder dropship detached from the destroyer's hull and began to boost upward.

"Comms?" Rika asked aloud, eyes fixed on that ship.

<*Linked.*>

<*Chief Charles, come in. Are all aboard?*>

<*Captain! Fucking awesome to hear you. Uh…yes, Sergeant Chase said all Marauders are back aboard, but two are KIA.*>

Rika clenched her teeth as guilty tears of relief flowed down her face. She wanted nothing more than to talk to Chase at that moment, but she needed to find out what was happening on the two cruisers that were still holding in the clouds. If she started talking to Chase, she might lose her edge.

<*Understood. Tell him I'll see him soon.*>

<*You got it. Mad Dog out.*>

<*Have you been able to reach those two teams?*> Rika asked Niki.

<*Yes, Potter has helm and is a minute from firing engines. Lauren is on the other one; she never got the updated hack, but I'm sending it to her now. She should be good to go in a few minutes.*>

Niki sounded relieved, and Rika felt the same way. The entire time they had been fighting through the *Fury Lance*, the fear that the other teams had all failed had lurked in the back of her mind.

One company assaulting ten cruisers with a total complement of over ten thousand, and winning? This would be the stuff of legends.

"Wait…" Rika said as she reviewed the scan holo and the raw data that was scrolling in a panel to the right. "Vargo Klen. I don't see him. Did he make it out?"

<*I have a Link to the SAF, let me check,*> Niki replied.

Rika glanced at Aaron as he approached and gave his update.

"We are secure, Captain. There may still be some Niets holed up here and there, but based on the numbers that the cryo systems show, all but a few of their soldiers are dead."

Rika clasped a hand on his shoulder as the second-to-last cruiser fired its engines and began to climb out of the clouds.

"Almost there," Rika whispered.

<*They didn't pick Klen up,*> Niki reported. <*I've scoured the logs. He took weapons fire on the way back to the* Fury Lance.>

Niki highlighted the location where Klen's dropship had last been seen, and Rika scowled at the scan display. "I don't see anything."

<*Compensating for winds—it's a killer storm out there…*>

Rika bit her lip. She'd been the one who sent him out there—granted, she'd sent *everyone*…but he wasn't a mech. He couldn't handle what they could.

<*Got him, he's two hundred kilometers down. It's not crush depth…but there's a huge low-pressure zone moving in beneath us.*>

Rika felt her breath catch. "Which means he could fall like a rock."

<*I can take us down. We can grab him with a grav beam, and draw him in.*>

"Do it. We're not leaving anyone behind."

<*He could be dead…*> Niki said quietly, for Rika's ears alone.

<*Niki, no one gets left behind. He saved the day. Armens will not be his grave.*>

<*Aye, Captain Rika,*> Niki replied on the combat net. <*Chiefs Ferris and Tanya, I've opened up a shuttle bay that looks to be clear of Niets. I advise you to get inside.*>

Rika watched the feeds from the two dropship pilots that were still attached to the hull of the *Fury Lance* as they pulled free and eased around the starship toward the bay Niki had indicated.

The moment they were within, the bay's doors began to close.

Three kilometers behind them, the *Fury Lance's* engines roared to life, and Rika felt a small shudder beneath her feet.

<*Dampeners are running at low power. Trying to keep things cool,*> Niki said. <*Cooling vanes are all the way out.*>

Rika pulled up a view of the clouds around the ship on the forward display, as they turned and began to fall through the gas giant's atmosphere. All around the vessel, lightning flared, striking the shields and the cooling vanes with increasing intensity.

"Is that normal?" Aaron asked.

"Nothing we're doing is normal. But the ship can take it; she's rated for a lot deeper than this."

"After spending weeks down here heating up like a toaster?"

<*She'll hold,*> Niki replied, her tone filled with more determination than confidence.

A shudder began to run through the deck as they dropped, and then suddenly they all felt a moment of weightlessness as the ship fell faster.

<*Hit the low-pressure zone, compensating. I have a visual on Klen's dropship.*>

The secondary holotank came to life, showing the front half of the dropship. It was spinning wildly, but Rika saw that the cockpit hatch was sealed.

There was a chance.

Niki spun the *Fury Lance* so that its engines were facing down toward the planet core, and let them fall until they were within one kilometer of the dropship.

The shuddering in the deck plates had intensified, and Rika couldn't help but notice that they were now more than five hundred kilometers below the cloud tops.

Lights began to flash on several consoles, and an alarm sounded. The bridge's forward display flashed a warning that the hull of the ship was over 700 degrees kelvin.

<*Got him!*> Niki cried out. <*Pulling him in…same bay as the other ships.*>

Rika turned to the feeds from the other dropships and watched with dismay as the red-hot ruin of Klen's dropship was set on a cradle.

The moment the clamps wrapped around the wreckage, Rika shouted. "Go! Go!"

The deck lurched under them, and Niki cried out. *<All Marauders, hold onto your hats. Dampeners failing!>*

Rika ran to the back wall of the bridge as the dampeners and artificial gravity cut out at the same time. Suddenly the ship's engines were 'down', and 10*g* of thrust slammed everyone into the rear wall.

Commander Kiers fell down the bridge, hit a chair, and then flew out the open door, into the atrium beyond.

Ben peered around the door at what was now a sixty-meter drop. "Oops."

The *Fury Lance* bucked like a wild horse in the gas giant's winds, but Rika could see that their descent had stopped, and they were rising once more.

<Shit, we're dancing close to thermal shutdown on the reactors,> Niki warned. *<I'm decreasing our angle and burn.>*

The 10*g* dropped to only 8, and Rika felt a small lessening in the tremendous pressure on her chest. She wondered how the squishies must be feeling. She suspected that their ascent was going to kill as many Niets as the attack had.

The minutes dragged on as the ship crept out of the planet, kilometer by kilometer. Then they passed into the troposphere; the heat warnings began to fall silent, and the shuddering decreased to a mere tremor.

A minute later, the blessed blackness of space filled the forward viewscreen, and the bridge erupted with cheers.

<Niki, you deserve a promotion.>

Rika was surprised to hear a tremor in her AI's voice.

<Tell me about it.>

<How close?> Rika asked.

<You really don't want to know.>

CAPTAIN RIKA

STELLAR DATE: 08.20.8949 (Adjusted Gregorian)
LOCATION: *Fury Lance*
REGION: Within Armens, Hercules System, Septhian Alliance

Rika sat in the *Fury Lance*'s command chair, reviewing the after-action reports and damage assessments that were flowing in from her teams.

All-in-all, it was better than it could have been, but worse than she'd hoped. Twenty-seven of her Marauders had died, and fifty more were seriously injured.

Vargo Klen, by some miracle, had survived—though there wasn't much of him left. Someone had found his last will, and in it, he asked to be turned into a mech if he was seriously injured.

Rika didn't want to think about that just yet. He could be kept in a medical coma for the time being.

There was nothing wrong with prosthetic limbs in and of themselves, and should the receiver be willing, there was no moral dilemma.

But mechs were more than mods and prosthetics—they were made to *kill*. An arm that helped you pick up your cup of coffee or caress your lover was one thing. An arm that was purpose-built to kill everyone in sight was a different thing entirely.

Rika pushed that concern from her mind as a call from Major Tim came in.

<*Captain Rika! I have to hand it to you. I…that's quite the victory.*>

<*He was going to say that he didn't think we could pull it off,*> Niki said privately.

<*Yeah, that was my suspicion, as well,*> Rika said to Niki before replying to Tim. <*Five ships for the Marauders, three for the SAF, and a whole pile of dead Nietzscheans. It's a good day to be a Marauder.*>

<*Do you think the SAF will let us keep that dreadnought?*>

<*The* Fury Lance*? They'll pry it from my cold, dead fingers. We've*

saved their bacon twice this week.>

Major Tim laughed and began to speak, when Cora interrupted him <*Major, Captain! A ship just jumped into the system broadcasting an alert. The Albany System is under attack! Half of it has already fallen to the Nietzscheans!*>

<*What the fuck!?*> Rika exclaimed. <*What about Pyra? How long ago?*>

<*When the ship jumped out, Pyra was still holding on. Intel is three days old.*>

Rika rose from her chair and looked at the dreadnought's bridge before her.

<*Give me all ships, Niki.*>

<*You've got it.*>

<*Marauders. This is Captain Rika. Today, we saved the Hercules System. But now the Nietzscheans are back in Albany. Crews on SAF-claimed ships, get off those vessels and make for the* Fury Lance. *We are boosting for the Albany jump point in thirty minutes.*>

<*Rika!*> Major Tim shouted into her mind. <*What? You can't!*>

<*Major. I am not under your command. In fact, in matters such as this, you are under mine. My mechs are going to need the supplies on your ships; I order you to accompany us.*>

<*Rika—*>

<*She's right, Major,*> Cora interjected. <*She's in charge of where the force deploys. General Mill was explicit in his orders, and made no mention of remaining in the Hercules System.*>

Major Tim didn't respond for almost a full sixty seconds, but Rika could feel his anger spilling across the Link.

Finally, he replied. <*Very well, but I'm in command of fleet formation. I'll provide vector and burn before we depart.*>

<*Understood,*> Rika replied and closed the connection.

"Rika!"

She spun to see Chase entering the bridge, and leapt over the command chair as she rushed toward him. She stopped short when she saw that his left arm was missing.

"Chase! Again?"

"It's OK, Rika. It's just an arm."

She wrapped her arms around him and gave a gentle squeeze. "Seems like a habit. Vargo Klen wants to be a mech; maybe we should just get it over with, and do it to you, too."

Chase raised an eyebrow and gave her a tired smile. "You know, I wonder if that wouldn't be such a bad idea."

"Really?" Rika couldn't keep the surprise from her voice.

"Yeah I'm losing limbs on nearly every engagement. Would be a lot more useful if they could just bolt on a new one."

Rika took a step back and gauged Chase's size. "AM-3?"

"Hell no!" Chase exclaimed. "If—and this is probably just the post-battle adrenaline talking, plus the wonderful drugs my armor is injecting me with…where was I?"

" 'If'," Rika supplied.

"Right! *If* I become a mech, I'm keeping my man-bits. No two ways about it."

Barne snorted as he walked onto the bridge with Leslie at his side. "A mech with a dick. That'll be the day. Then once you get *your* bits back, Rika, you two can finally fuck and make little mech babies."

"Barne!" Leslie exclaimed and smacked the First Sergeant on the back of the head. "That's…I'm not sure what. Inappropriate at least!"

Rika couldn't help but notice that Leslie's hand had been clasping Barne's before she'd pulled it free to hit him.

"It's OK, Leslie. Asshole is part of Barne's charm."

"He's a man made of ass," Chase added.

Barne nodded. "And I make it look good."

Chase turned back to Rika. "So, what's this about Albany?"

"Niets hit them nine days ago," Rika replied. "We're jumping out there to lend a hand."

"On whose orders?" Leslie's eyes narrowed as she stared at Rika.

"Mine," Rika replied.

Barne sat at a duty station and placed his feet on the console.

"Fine by me." He leaned back and interlaced his fingers. "If that's where the Niets are, then we'd best get going. They're not going to die on their own."

Rika grinned and slapped Barne on the shoulder. "I like your attitude, Top."

"Who said you could call me 'Top'?"

TANIS RICHARDS

STELLAR DATE: 08.27.8949 (Adjusted Gregorian)
LOCATION: Jersey City, Pyra
REGION: Albany System, Septhian Alliance

Tanis sagged against the crumbling brick wall, praying it would hold up long enough for her to catch her breath. She looked down at her rifle, shaking her head at the energy readout.

Ten percent.

Her left arm was gone—the flowmetal it was made of long ago consumed to build nano—and a hole was blown clear through her right leg. To top it off, her reactive armor was failing.

Overhead, just beyond the burning towers of Jersey City, another Nietzschean ship drifted into view, beam fire glowing brightly as it fired on…something.

<Stars, those things just keep coming!>

Angela sighed, the AI also somehow sounding weary. *<They have at least ten thousand…maybe more.>*

Tanis felt her eyelids droop, the last of her energy nearly gone, when the sound of heavy footfalls came from a nearby side street.

Her eyes snapped back open, and Tanis pushed off from the wall, wincing each time she put pressure on her injured leg. She collapsed behind a pile of rubble and swung her rifle up onto the debris, aiming it in the general direction of the side street. Her breath was loud and ragged in her ears as she waited for whatever was next.

There was no backup to be called, no ship to save them with starfire. They were alone.

<Is this how it all ends, Angela?>

<I don't know, Tanis, but I know one thing for sure: we're going to find out together.>

Tanis felt a smile grace her lips. *<Together. That's how we'll always be.>*

Above them, more Nietzschean ships drifted over the city, their beams raking the ground as far as the eye could see.

On the ground, the first Nietzschean soldier came around the corner, and Tanis opened fire.

She'd kill as many as she could before they got her.

THE END

The adventure continues in Rika Commander.

But first, Rika has a date with destiny in the Albany System. Find out how Tanis ends up not far from where Rika was re-united with Chase in: Attack on Thebes.

Read on for details about the different types of mechs, and the members of Rika's Marauders.

MECH TYPES AND ARMAMENTS

While these are the standard builds and configurations documented by the Genevian Armed Forces (GAF), many mechs reached the field in mismatched configuration, or were altered after deployment.

Sometimes these alterations were upgrades, sometimes downgrades, as repairs were often made with whatever spare components were available at the time.

The mechs in the Marauders generally align with the stated configurations, though many have altered themselves over the years.

K1R (Kill Ranger – Generation 1)

This mech is more of a two-legged tank than a mech. The K1R sports a central 'pod' where the human is situated. None of the limbs utilize human material.

K1Rs often had mental issues due to feeling as though they had lost all sense of humanity. When the Nietzscheans won the war, they did not release any K1Rs from their internment camps. It is not known if they kept them, or killed them all.

Until the discovery of the mechs in the Politica, there was only a single K1R in the Marauders (who had been under

General Mill's command at the end of the war). That mech has joined Rika's company to assist the four K1Rs Rika freed from the Politica in re-integration.

K1R mechs have a variety of heavy armament, including massive chainguns, railguns, missiles (with and without tactical nuke warheads), electron beams, and proton beams. They also sport a variety of suppression devices, from pulse, to sonic, to portable grav shields.

K1R mechs were not made later in the war, due to their cost and mental instability.

There were rumors that a limited run of K2R mechs were made, but no credible reports exist.

Sub-Models:

All K1R models could be outfitted with interchangeable armament, excepting the base model, which could not carry the tactical nukes.

K1R – The base K1R model was made in the early years of the war, and lacked the coordination and reactive armor of the later models.

K1R-M – The 'M' K1R added in the reactive armor, and included upgraded railguns with more advanced scan and target tracking systems. These mechs carried two missiles in launcher pots in their backs. They could be (and often were) upgraded to support the tactical nuke warheads on the missiles.

K1R-T – The 'T' model was a similar configuration to the 'M', but came standard with tactical nuclear warheads. Instead of the pair of launchers the K1R-M sported, the 'T' model carried as many as twelve missiles.

AM (Assault Mech)

The AM mechs represented the bulk of the GAF's mechanized infantry program. It is estimated that over ten million AMs were created during the war, and over one hundred thousand are known to have survived. Many joined mercenary outfits or the militaries of other nations.

AM model mechs were a 'torso only' design, where none of the human's arms and legs were retained. The original idea was to make their cores swappable with K1R models, but it turned out that the mechanized infantry design of the AM models was generally more effective than the 'walking tank' design of the K1R models.

AM models were versatile mechs which had swappable loadouts. The improvements over time were mostly centered around human-mech integration, armor, and power systems.

AM mechs were often outfitted with chainguns, shoulder-mounted railguns, and electron beams.

Without known exception, AM mechs were always male.

Sub-Models

AM-1 – The original model of AM. Fewer than 100,000 AM-1 mechs were made, and none were known to have survived the war.

AM-2 – The AM-2 mechs quickly superseded the AM-1s, with better armor, more efficient power systems, and superior human-mech integrations.

AM-3 – The third generation of AM mech had upgraded power supply systems, and an artificial epidermis to remove the need for periodical removal and cleaning. Some AM-3s were also AI capable.

AM-T – Design specs for AM-T mechs exist, but it is not known if any were made by the Genevians. The AM-T design utilized two AM-3 mechs working together in one larger body, controlling more limbs and separating motion and combat functions.

RR (Recon/Ranger)

The RR model of mech was the precursor to the SMI model. RR's were based on both male and female humans, though smaller humans were used for RR models than AM and FR mechs.

These mechs were similar to AM models, except they were physically smaller and lighter. This allowed RRs to handle light aircraft/drop deployments.

As a compromise, they had smaller power sources, and could only operate for 2-3 days in the field.

Their loadouts were swappable with AM models, but they rarely utilized the chainguns.

Sub-Models

RR-1 – This model of mech began to appear on the battlefield around the same time as the AM-2 mechs. They utilized the power upgrade of the AM-2 mechs to have smaller power systems, but they also had a smaller power capacity. In theory, the new batteries of the AM-2 line should have worked, but they had overheating issues in the field, and more than one RR-1 had battery detonation when utilizing multiple firing systems.

RR-2 – The RR-2 mechs were rolled out around the same time as the AM-3s, and had few significant changes other than improved armor, and marginally longer-lasting power that no longer suffered from overload issues.

Second gen RR-2 mechs were also skinless, like AM-3 and SMI mechs.

RR-3 – The RR-3 mechs reached the field shortly before the end of the war, and were different in that they had partial legs, like SMI mechs. This was done as a cost/component-saving measure.

FR (Force Recon)

Force Recon mechs were mechs that had the lighter drop capabilities of the RR mechs, with the additional power and armor of AM-3 models. All FR mechs were skinless.

Sub-Models

FR-1 – The first generation of FR mechs were limited run, and had both weight and power load distribution issues.

FR-2 – Second generation FR mechs solved many of the issues from the first generation, and were well regarded for their effectiveness.

XFR – The XFR model is not known to have been widely produced. This model had additional power and carrying capacity to utilize shoulder mounted proton beams and chainguns. However, the mech's loadout made it almost has heavy as an AM-3 without the armor.

SMI (Scout Mech-Integrated)

The final mech model produced at the end of the war was built out of a desire for a super-light mech that could be used in place of standard infantry in sniper/recon situations, and bring extreme fire to bear if desired.

SMI mechs were also cost-saving mechs, as they retained more of their human body components, making for fewer prosthetic neural connections. They also leveraged progress in muscle and bone augmentation that had been used in RR and FR mech models.

The mechs were built exclusively from small, lithe women who could fit in the mech armor and still create a small profile.

Unlike other mech models, SMI mechs were never deployed with two functional hands. One was always a weapon mount.

SMI mechs are all skinless.

Sub-Models

SMI-1 – The first generation of SMI mechs had a short production run due to psychological issues. Because they retained more of their human bodies than other mechs, they ended up having additional dysphoria issues.

SMI-2 – Second generation SMI mechs had improved physical integrations and psychological conditioning that caused the mechs to view themselves as less human. However, in the field, it was observed to have the opposite effect, and SMI mechs retained a strong connection to their humanity.

3rd MARAUDER FLEET 4th DIVISION

Fleet Commander: Colonel Argon
Division 4 Complement (2 Ships)

Golden Lark
1200-meter heavy cruiser
64 fighters
Ship's AI: Cora
Other Ship AIs: Jane & Frankie
Captain: Major Tim
XO Commander: Scas
Dockmaster: Chief Ora

Perseid's Dream
650-meter destroyer
24 fighters
Ship's AI: Moshe
Other Ship AI: Lauren
Captain Penny

9th MARAUDER BATTALION 'M' COMPANY

Note, not all personnel in M Company are listed. Full company complement is 380+.

Company HQ

Commanding Officer (CO) – SMI-2 Captain Rika
Executive Officer (XO) – FR-2 First Lieutenant Scarcliff
Flight Leader (FL) – RR-3 First Lieutenant Heather (Smalls)
First Sergeant – Barne
Gunnery Sergeant – Tex
General Council – David
Tactics and Strat AI (1 & 2P) – Potter
Tactics and Strat AI (3-5P) – Dredge
Lead DI – Staff Sergeant Chase

First Platoon

Platoon CO – First Lieutenant Leslie
Platoon Sergeant – Staff Sergeant Chris (AM-2)

Dropship Pilots (6 per platoon)
- Vargo Klen
- Ferris, "Ferryman"
- Charles, "Mad Dog"

First Squad
Squad Sergeant Aaron (AM-3)
4 Fireteams (19 mechs)

FT 1-1
- CPL Ben (AM-2)
- PFC Al, 'Whispers' (AM-2)
- PFC Kim (RR-3-F)
- PFC Harris (FR-2)

FT 1-2
- CPL Crunch (RR-3-M)
- PFC Kelly (SMI-2)
- PFC Shoshin (AM-3)

FT 1-3
- PFC Kerry (RR-2)

FT 1-4
- CPL Mitch (RR-2)

Second Squad
Squad Sergeant – Kristian (RR-2-M)
3 Fireteams (13 mechs)

FT 2-1
- CPL (K1R-T) Oosterwyk-Bruyn, 'The Van'
- PFC Keli (SMI-2)

Third Squad
Squad Sergeant Karen (SMI-2)
4 Fireteams (19 mechs)

FT 3-1
- PVT Kyle, 'Goob' (AM-2)
- CPL Yiaagaitia, 'Yig' (RR-2-M)

FT 3-4

- Carolyn 'CJ' (RR-3-F)

Fourth Squad
Squad Sergeant – Kara (SMI-2)
4 Fireteams (20 mechs)

Second Platoon

Platoon CO – First Lieutenant Travis (AM-3)
Platoon Sergeant – Staff Sergeant Divinar (AM-3)

Dropship Pilots
Lieutenant Buggsie

First Squad
Squad Sergeant – Fuller (AM-2)
4 Fireteams (19 mechs)

Second Squad
Squad Sergeant – Chauncy (FR-2)
4 Fireteams (21 mechs)

Third Squad
Squad Sergeant Bean (SMI-2)
5 Fireteams (25 mechs)

Fourth Squad
Squad Sergeant Kristina, 'Abs' (RR-2)
4 Fireteams (20 mechs)

FT 2-4
CPL Musel (AM-2)
PFC Bitty (K1R-M)
PFC Smitty (RR-3) (F)

Third Platoon

Platoon CO – First Lieutenant Wilson (FR-2)
Platoon Sergeant – Staff Sergeant Bookie (SMI-2)

First Squad
Squad Sergeant Char (RR-3-F)
4 Fireteams (19 mechs)

Second Squad
Squad Sergeant Mal (FR-2)
4 Fireteams (22 mechs)

Third Squad
Squad Sergeant Cory (AM-2)
4 Fireteams (19 mechs)

Fourth Squad
Squad Sergeant Lana (SMI-2)
4 Fireteams (20 mechs)

Fourth Platoon

Platoon CO – First Lieutenant Michael (AM-3)
Platoon Sergeant – Staff Sergeant Johnny (FR-2)

First Squad
Squad Sergeant Alana (RR-2-F)
4 Fireteams (19 mechs)

Second Squad
Squad Sergeant Aerin (SMI-2)
4 Fireteams (21 mechs)

Third Squad
Squad Sergeant Justin (FR-2)
4 Fireteams (19 mechs)

Fourth Squad
Squad Sergeant Val (RR-3-F)
3 Fireteams (14 mechs)

Fifth Platoon

Platoon CO – First Lieutenant Crudge (AM-3)
Platoon Sergeant – Staff Sergeant Sal (FR-2)

First Squad
Squad Sergeant Darla (RR-3-F)
4 Fireteams (19 mechs)

Second Squad
Squad Sergeant George (FR-2)
4 Fireteams (20 mechs)

Third Squad
Squad Sergeant Jessa (RR-3-F)
3 Fireteams (14 mechs)

Fourth Squad
Squad Sergeant Jynafer (RR-3-F)
3 Fireteams (13 mechs)

Sixth Platoon (Maintenance and Medical)

Platoon Commander – Lieutenant "Bondo" Carson

- Corporal Stripes (AM-2)

THE BOOKS OF AEON 14

Keep up to date with what is releasing in Aeon 14 with the free Aeon 14 Reading Guide.

The Intrepid Saga (The Age of Terra)
- Book 1: Outsystem
- Book 2: A Path in the Darkness
- Book 3: Building Victoria

- The Intrepid Saga Omnibus – *Also contains Destiny Lost, book 1 of the Orion War series*

- Destiny Rising – *Special Author's Extended Edition comprised of both Outsystem and A Path in the Darkness with over 100 pages of new content.*

The Orion War
- Book 1: Destiny Lost
- Book 2: New Canaan
- Book 3: Orion Rising
- Book 4: The Scipio Alliance
- Book 5: Attack on Thebes
- Book 6: War on a Thousand Fronts
- Book 7: Fallen Empire (2018)
- Book 8: Airtha Ascendancy (2018)
- Book 9: The Orion Front (2018)
- Book 10: Starfire (2019)
- Book 11: Race Across Time (2019)
- Book 12: Return to Sol (2019)

Tales of the Orion War
- Book 1: Set the Galaxy on Fire

- Book 2: Ignite the Stars
- Book 3: Burn the Galaxy to Ash (2018)

Perilous Alliance (Age of the Orion War – w/Chris J. Pike)
- Book 1: Close Proximity
- Book 2: Strike Vector
- Book 3: Collision Course
- Book 4: Impact Imminent
- Book 5: Critical Inertia (2018)

Rika's Marauders (Age of the Orion War)
- Prequel: Rika Mechanized
- Book 1: Rika Outcast
- Book 2: Rika Redeemed
- Book 3: Rika Triumphant
- Book 4: Rika Commander
- Book 5: Rika Infiltrator (2018)
- Book 6: Rika Unleashed (2018)
- Book 7: Rika Conqueror (2019)

Perseus Gate (Age of the Orion War)
Season 1: Orion Space
- Episode 1: The Gate at the Grey Wolf Star
- Episode 2: The World at the Edge of Space
- Episode 3: The Dance on the Moons of Serenity
- Episode 4: The Last Bastion of Star City
- Episode 5: The Toll Road Between the Stars
- Episode 6: The Final Stroll on Perseus's Arm
- Eps 1-3 Omnibus: The Trail Through the Stars
- Eps 4-6 Omnibus: The Path Amongst the Clouds

Season 2: Inner Stars
- Episode 1: A Meeting of Bodies and Minds
- Episode 3: A Deception and a Promise Kept

- Episode 3: A Surreptitious Rescue of Friends and Foes (2018)
- Episode 4: A Trial and the Tribulations (2018)
- Episode 5: A Deal and a True Story Told (2018)
- Episode 6: A New Empire and An Old Ally (2018)

Season 3: AI Empire
- Episode 1: Restitution and Recompense (2019)
- Five more episodes following…

The Warlord (Before the Age of the Orion War)
- Book 1: The Woman Without a World
- Book 2: The Woman Who Seized an Empire
- Book 3: The Woman Who Lost Everything

The Sentience Wars: Origins (Age of the Sentience Wars – w/James S. Aaron)
- Book 1: Lyssa's Dream
- Book 2: Lyssa's Run
- Book 3: Lyssa's Flight
- Book 4: Lyssa's Call
- Book 5: Lyssa's Flame (June 2018)

Enfield Genesis (Age of the Sentience Wars – w/Lisa Richman)
- Book 1: Alpha Centauri
- Book 2: Proxima Centauri (2018)

Hand's Assassin (Age of the Orion War – w/T.G. Ayer)
- Book 1: Death Dealer
- Book 2: Death Mark (August 2018)

Machete System Bounty Hunter (Age of the Orion War – w/Zen DiPietro)
- Book 1: Hired Gun
- Book 2: Gunning for Trouble

- Book 3: With Guns Blazing (June 2018)

Vexa Legacy (Age of the FTL Wars – w/Andrew Gates)
- Book 1: Seas of the Red Star

Building New Canaan (Age of the Orion War – w/J.J. Green
- Book 1: Carthage (2018)

Fennington Station Murder Mysteries (Age of the Orion War)
- Book 1: Whole Latte Death (w/Chris J. Pike)
- Book 2: Cocoa Crush (w/Chris J. Pike)

The Empire (Age of the Orion War)
- The Empress and the Ambassador (2018)
- Consort of the Scorpion Empress (2018)
- By the Empress's Command (2018)

Tanis Richards: Origins (The Age of Terra)
- Prequel: Storming the Norse Wind (At the Helm Volume 3)
- Book 1: Shore Leave (June 2018)
- Book 2: The Command (July 2018)
- Book 3: Infiltrator (July 2018)

The Sol Dissolution (The Age of Terra)
- Book 1: Venusian Uprising (2018)
- Book 2: Scattered Disk (2018)
- Book 3: Jovian Offensive (2019)
- Book 4: Fall of Terra (2019)

The Delta Team Chronicles (Expanded Orion War)
- A "Simple" Kidnapping (Pew! Pew! Volume 1)
- The Disknee World (Pew! Pew! Volume 2)
- It's Hard Being a Girl (Pew! Pew! Volume 4)
- A Fool's Gotta Feed (Pew! Pew! Volume 4)

RIKA'S MARAUDERS – RIKA ACTIVATED

- Rogue Planets and a Bored Kitty (Pew! Pew! Volume 5)

ABOUT THE AUTHOR

Michael Cooper likes to think of himself as a jack-of-all-trades (and hopes to become master of a few). When not writing, he can be found writing software, working in his shop at his latest carpentry project, or likely reading a book.

He shares his home with a precocious young girl, his wonderful wife (who also writes), two cats, a never-ending list of things he would like to build, and ideas…

Find out what's coming next at www.aeon14.com

CPSIA information can be obtained
at www.ICGtesting.com
Printed in the USA
LVHW032005060519
616797LV00001B/197/P

9 781643 650012